The End of Judaism

An Ethical Tradition Betrayed

HAJO G. MEYER

For Chris

"That which is hateful to you, do not do to your neighbor. That is the whole Torah."

- Rabbi Hillel (1st century B.C.)

CONTENTS

ACKNOWLEDGMENTS

FEELINGS OF GRATITUDE of a general nature, not directed toward specific persons, are akin to religious feelings. If I were a believer, which I am not, I would perhaps be inclined at this point to recite the *Shehechyanu*, an admirable Jewish prayer that is used on special occasions to give thanks for having made it to the present in one's life, and for being able to consciously experience the moment.

My thanks first of all go to my original Dutch publisher, Oscar van Gelderen, who encouraged me to write this book on the basis of a single newspaper article. My wife, Christiane Tilanus, who after many years as head of an obstetrics ward at a major hospital knows everything about the birth of infants, proved to be the ideal helper in the birth of this undertaking. Without her diligent and unremitting critique, her inventiveness, and her creativity, this book would have looked very different, or might never have seen the light of day. My thanks also go to the art historian Loek Tilanus, who read the text critically and made many helpful suggestions in its early stages, including his recommendation that "writing means leaving out." I also wish to thank the historian Wiebe Brouwer for reading the first draft, and for his advice on structuring the book.

The reader may judge just how much I owe the BBC radio journalist Peter Day, who read and corrected the first draft of a chapter that I wrote in English. I also owe thanks to the radio journalist Job de Haan, who encouraged me to continue after reading an early draft. My editors, Adriaan Krabbendam and Maarten van der Werf, played an essential role in the publication of the Dutch edition of the book.

My son, Leo Meyer, also worked through a later draft of the text and offered numerous helpful suggestions.

I thank my German publisher, Abraham Melzer, for having the courage to publish such a controversial book exclusively on the basis of a telephone conversation and a few short articles in German. It quickly became clear that our attitudes toward the themes and problems raised in this book were remarkably similar. Thanks to the translators who rendered the Dutch text into German for their quick work, their ability to identify with my thought processes, and for our pleasurable collaboration. I thank my reader at Melzer Verlag for editing the last chapter, which I wrote in German.

In regard to the English edition, I wish to thank Ilse Andrews for her help in translating two key chapters and in reviewing previously existing translations of four others. Special thanks go to my nephew, Stefan G. Meyer, for overseeing the translation, editing, and publishing of this English edition, to his editor Carol Givner, for her thoughtful recommendations regarding the restructuring of the text, and to his proofreader, Cynthia Joan.

In arranging the material, I let myself be guided by Gustav Mahler, who in the handwritten score of his Third Symphony used subheadings similar to those I have employed in order to reflect what inspired his musical descriptions.

INTRODUCTION

Autobiographical Background-
What My Personal Experience Tells Me

My Own Conditioning

I once had a discussion on a radio program with the head of *Likud Nederland*, the Dutch branch of former Israeli Prime Minister Ariel Sharon's party. The subject of our talk was the significance of the Israelis' so-called "targeted killings" of certain Palestinians suspected of being terrorists or preparing terrorist attacks. Sharon's government was conducting such assassinations without informing the public of the facts on which their suspicions were based. There was no fairness about these operations, nor was the public apprised of any proof. I considered them to be profoundly counterproductive because they did little more than provoke fresh rounds of suicide attacks. When I stated as much, my interlocutor suddenly said, "Mr. Meyer, you've been brainwashed." To which I answered, "You're absolutely correct, and do you know by what? By the historical events that have conditioned me over the course of my life."

The events that occurred between 1933 and 1942, in particular, were extremely intense and affected me so much that, as a result, I evaluate and interpret everything through the lens fashioned from these experiences. I was subjected to humiliating interrogations, had to undergo all sorts of collective punishment, and for many years had no access to education. I was forced to watch my proud father be humiliated, viewed the progressive impoverishment of the Jewish community to which I belonged, and was made to feel like a social pariah. These experiences sensitized me to the discriminatory and humiliating treatment of any people who are forced to live as second-class citizens. This sensitivity has been heightened by the fact that the Jewish people are themselves currently harassing and humiliating another people—the Palestinians. Whenever I read or hear about these events or watch reports on television, memories from my formative years come bubbling to the surface. In order to make my views about the main themes of this book understandable, I must therefore say something about the key facts and experiences of my life—that is, how history conditioned me.

Family Background

There's no way around it, I am and remain what in Israel is called a *yekke*. This means that I am still conscious of being a Jew who was born in Germany. I was molded by the values that determined the course of German Jewry from about the second half of the 18th century, in the elaboration of which the philosopher of the Jewish Enlightenment, Moses Mendelssohn, played an important role. I will return to the significance of Mendelssohn, whose renown extended well beyond his Jewish coreligionists later on, but for the present I will limit myself to several observations about the social, religious, and family circumstances in which I grew up until I was fourteen.

It is important to note that there was no appreciable Jewish proletariat in Germany between the final decades of the 19th century and Hitler's seizure of power. German Jews exceeded the population as a whole in terms of income, education, and qualifications. In my hometown of Bielefeld, Westphalia, for instance, only 2% of the population between 1870 and 1933 was of Jewish extraction, whereas the number of Jewish students attending my *Gymnasium* (high school) during that same period was 10%. This statistic indicates that the percentage of German Jews with a higher education was larger than that of the German Gentiles among whom they lived.

My family can be traced back to the end of the 17th century. Both sides of my family had lived in Westphalia since that time. When my mother was nine years old—she was born in Dortmund—her father, Julius Melchior, moved to Berlin in order to be a member of the board of directors, and eventually the CEO, of the Patzenhofer Brewery, whose brand still exists. His residence, which he built in the most exclusive section of Berlin, is still standing. My mother's four brothers all finished their studies at the university. One of them became a professor of surgery at the University of Breslau; another, after concluding his course of study in mechanical engineering, became a department head at the *Allgemeine Elektrizitäts-Gesellschaft* (AEG), the big electricity corporation founded by the Jewish industrialist Emil Rathenau. Thanks to his technical knowledge, he became an officer in the engineering division of the German army during World War I. This was one of the reasons why he survived the war in Berlin in spite of the fact that he and his non-Jewish wife were childless. (A German Jew with a non-Jewish wife was much safer during the Nazi period if he had children.) In the end, he was named house air raid protection warden,[1] even though he wore a yellow star.

My mother would have liked to study medicine, but my extremely Victorian grandmother wouldn't hear of it. That was not a fit profession for a decent girl from a good home. The result was that my mother ran away from home at the age of 26, finished a short course in nursing, volunteered to work as a nurse in a field hospital on the Eastern front, and almost died of diphtheria, which she contracted there. Another result of her work on the Eastern front was that she met my father, who had been so severely wounded at the Battle of Tannenberg (1914) that he was unfit for front-line duty. He was made a sergeant, given responsibility for maintaining military order in the hospital, and married my mother at the end of 1916.

Her mother was not exactly thrilled. My father, a jurist, attorney, and notary, was, at least at first glance, from a lower class than my mother. His father had been a horse trader, which was not a particularly respected occupation. Today, used car salesmen are held in about the same esteem. This social 'blemish' was compensated for in a number of ways by his wife's personality and culture.

My paternal grandmother, Theodora, was the paradigm of a young Jewish woman of the type that emerged from the so-called court Jews and protected Jews—in her case, from the small principality of Lippe-Detmold. Such Jewish women were generally very well educated. They were versed in the literature of the classical German writers, as well as those of classical antiquity, and the most successful of them held salons in their homes in Berlin. My grandmother never did that, but she read her Greek and Latin authors in the original. In addition, in contrast to my maternal grandmother, she was a warm and sensitive woman who cared for her family of seven children with much love on a short budget. My father worshiped her his entire life, and this may have something to do with the love and attention with which he showered my mother. One of my grandmother's brothers, Dr. Max Meyer, was the village physician in Oerlinghausen, twelve kilometers from Bielefeld.

My father had four brothers and two sisters. In contrast to the custom in my mother's family, all of the children—including the girls—were encouraged to study, but with the proviso that they graduate from the *Gymnasium* without failing even once. In addition to my father, another brother and the youngest sister met these stringent requirements. Accordingly, that daughter was also a permitted to attend university. However, because the parents couldn't finance studies for three children, they had to scrape together the necessary money themselves. My father borrowed it from a well-to-do physician named Dr. Joseph, one of the pioneers of plastic surgery, who had married into the family.

Unfortunately, I never knew my father's mother. She died relatively young from worry and heartache over the fate of her five sons, who were all sent to the front during World War I. Her youngest (and favorite) son was killed during the first few weeks. But that did not mean that my father's family, like almost all German Jewish families, was not extremely patriotic.

Almost all German-Jewish families, and certainly mine, held *Bildung*, or general education, in particularly high regard. We were supposed to know about antiquity, German classicism, music, theater, and opera. "Don't you know that? That's a part of a general education!" was a comment we heard frequently at home. We were expected to know a lot, learn a lot, and care about two things in life: to get a good position so that we could contribute something valuable to society; and most importantly, to try to become and remain decent people with moral principles and an active conscience.

JUDAISM IN MY FAMILY

The way in which Judaism was practiced in my parents' house requires some explanation. Neither of my grandparents' families was still traditional let alone orthodox. True, we knew which foods were kosher or *treife* (non-kosher), but as a child I knew absolutely no one who observed the Jewish dietary laws. It should be noted that Westphalia was the cradle of German Reform Judaism, a liberal movement whose aim was to reform Jewish religious services. No one in the Bielefeld synagogue wore a *tallit*, or prayer shawl. Only the rabbi wore a rudimentary, stylized shawl that was as wide as a woolen scarf. If someone did come into the synagogue wearing a *tallit*, which happened now and again, we'd whisper to one other, "Hey look, he's from Eastern Europe." Every once in a while we actually went to synagogue, but mainly on high holy days. Going to synagogue primarily served a social function. My father, as a well-known lawyer in a mid-sized city, and a member of a very small Jewish community consisting of two- to three-hundred families, could not afford not to make such appearances with his family now and then.

Halacha, the Jewish religious law, meant nothing to our family. Ethics, achievement, and dedication—that was the important thing. In addition, we took pride in having survived as a people since antiquity, and in having achieved so much as German Jews, particularly since the time of Moses Mendelssohn, when Jews had still been primarily traders and moneylenders.

CONTENTED, SUCCESSFUL JEWISH CITIZENS

Both of my parents had intense feelings about World War I. One brother had been killed in action. They had experienced hunger, wounds, and disease. My father's mother had died of grief, poverty compounded by inflation, and last but not least, the shame and dishonor of being part of a nation of losers—and here I mean the German, not the Jewish nation. Still, as I recall, I grew up in a harmonious and happy family up until 1933. My mother was a warm, intelligent, and upright woman, the caring soul who managed our home.

My father was much more distant. He worked hard in his practice, and he had little tolerance for the noise that my two brothers and I made (I was probably the worst offender). He was successful, however, and the fact that he represented the Bielefeld city administration—a lucrative and respected client—was a source of great satisfaction to him. As a result, our family had nothing to complain about from a material perspective. Until Hitler's seizure of power, our parents kept two maidservants, who lived with us and helped my mother cook, keep house, and look after my two elder brothers and me. Our parents expected that in exchange for their loving parental care we would do our best in school, bring home good grades, and that our behavior would leave little to complain about. An atmosphere of warmth and security reigned in our home.

HITLER'S RISE TO POWER AND ITS EFFECTS ON MY FAMILY

Just how Hitler managed to become a member of government within a democratic society is the subject of innumerable books. The only thing I want to mention here is the fact that in the last democratic election for Parliament on November 6, 1932, Hitler's party, the NSDAP, won only about 33% of the votes. How he then managed with relative ease to seize absolute power after being named Chancellor is also a chapter for the history books. Similarly, it would require a more gifted writer than I to adequately portray the sense of shock that Hitler's seizure of power triggered in my family. To those interested in such a work, I recommend *The Oppermanns* by the German-Jewish writer Lion Feuchtwanger, originally published in 1933. [2]

My parents' basic position was that they felt they were good Germans, and rightly so. Germany was their homeland, and they had sacrificed everything they had for it, including their health and their lives. As a result, their attitude toward the ongoing political events was ambivalent. They were optimistic and hoped that this charlatan, Hitler, would soon be exposed. However, they also recalled the era before the Jews had been almost completely emancipated in the Weimar Republic, and this was cause for concern. A warning sign came as early as April 1, 1933, when Jewish lawyers were barred from entering courthouses. Although this measure was later suspended, it was a harbinger of things to come.

I also recall another far-reaching event that affected my parents, and particularly my father, who was a legal scholar through and through, and believed firmly in the rule of law. In 1934, one of his brothers was denounced to the Gestapo by a coworker who had designs on his managerial position in a department store. According to the informer, he had told a disparaging joke about Hitler in a bar. A trial took place in Leipzig, which my father was able to watch from the gallery. My uncle, a highly decorated war veteran who had been wounded four times on the Western front and been awarded the Silver Wound Badge and the Iron Cross, first class, was sentenced to several years in the concentration camp at Dachau. When my father returned home from this trial, which mocked any concept of justice, he was a broken man. He had lost all faith in Germany as a constitutional state, and for the first time the true nature of this regime became clear to him. Of course, he had no idea just how durable it would be.

There was every reason to prepare for the worst. And to my recollection, my parents did just that, and more often than not in exemplary fashion. The maidservants were let go, and we children did household chores from then on. They took special measures with my eldest brother, who was a somewhat shy boy, with few friends. He was a model student who always got good grades. He had just passed the intermediate school examination shortly after Hitler seized power. He was supposed to continue school until he passed the *Abitur*, or final school examination. He was also an outstanding flutist, who had just recently appeared on the radio as the soloist in a Mozart flute concert given by the school orchestra. My parents were so panicked about the ongoing political developments, however, that they pulled him out of school and got him an apprenticeship as a sewing machine technician.

The reason for my parents' behavior was that they, like many other German Jews, believed that the next generation had to distance itself from intellectual professions and take up manual ones. They thought that this would help counter the anti-Semitic stereotype that Jews were trying to take over Germany and the world. This decision had serious consequences for my brother's later life. He was a talented flutist, but not much of a technician, and suffered from this setback for the rest of his life.

A JEW IN SCHOOL WITH NAZIS

I was completely different from my brothers. I was small, agile, good at sports, and had lots of friends. At first, I didn't notice the changes that were taking place. I continued to play on my class's soccer team, and even after Hitler's seizure of power my non-Jewish classmates (with two or three exceptions) treated me as they always had. We continued to visit each other regularly. Up to the end of 1938, I had a friend with whom I built model gliders; I helped another friend (member of the nobility) work on his moped. The teachers, almost without exception, treated me fairly. Only two of them openly insulted Jews in class. I recall one teacher's disdainful reference to "the Jew Marx, who spread ruinous poison upon the German people." That was an unpleasant moment for me. Strangely, even this Nazi, who I feared would flunk me, gave me passing grades. Until November 1938, the other teachers were more interested in the welfare of their students, and any sympathies they might have had for the Nazis did not manifest itself in open anti-Semitism.

This impression was confirmed a few years ago when I visited my old school for the first time and saw my final report card. The last entry, dated November 9, 1938, simply read, "Withdrew from school." There was not one word about the reason, which was that after the *Kristallnacht* (Night of Breaking Glass), the November 9th pogrom that Hitler carried out against the Jews, Jewish students were forbidden to attend non-Jewish public schools. Nevertheless, this cowardly omission was more than made up for by the comments about me written several months earlier, when Hitler was glorying in his power: "Overall attitude good. He demonstrates sincere effort. His physical goals are in

line with his adequate physical talents. Citizenship good;
intellectual goals and overall performance satisfactory."
Only my grades in English left something to be desired.
Over time, however, harassment by students and teachers
under the sway of Nazi ideology increased to the point
where I no longer felt comfortable going to school.

Too Late... Out of Hope

The natural question to ask is why, under these circumstances,
our family remained in Germany. First, my parents simply
couldn't imagine how bad things would get. The greatest
tragedy of the *Kristallnacht* was not simply the fact that it
happened, but that it happened only five and a half years
after Hitler's seizure of power. As a result, the true face of
the regime became evident only after it was too late. Second,
the Western democracies were prepared only to accept a
limited number of German-Jewish refugees, if any at all.
The horrifying reports by those who had managed to flee
were characterized in Germany as "atrocity propaganda,"
but even outside Germany they were met with great
skepticism. Third, my father was simply no longer strong
enough to sell neckties door-to-door as an impoverished
refugee, and studying law in a foreign country presupposed
language skills that he did not have and which would have
taken years for him to acquire.

Thus, my parents invested their hope in their three
sons, who would be able to make a go of it wherever they
went. They intended to follow later, and allow themselves
to be initially supported by their children. In addition, due
to my father's service as a front soldier in World War I, he
had permission to defend Jews in court as a so-called legal
consultant, that is, without a robe and without admission

to the bar. Although this highly ambiguous position represented a considerable loss in prestige for him, it did afford him a certain amount of satisfaction. Sometimes he was actually able to help his Jewish clients. Regardless of how terrible and discriminatory the anti-Semitic laws were, the letter of the law still had to be followed. This was true even under the Nazis, at least up until the end of 1942. As a result, my father was able to make a modicum of a living.

The *Kristallnacht* threw a wrench in all my parents' plans. My eldest brother had to discontinue his engineering studies in Chemnitz, which he had begun after his apprenticeship examination as a sewing machine technician. My second brother had finished his *Abitur* and begun a course in typing and stenography at a private secretarial school. Both of my brothers had been making plans to emigrate for some time, and at the last minute they managed to get out of Germany. One of them went to England, the other to the United States. I, like my parents, however, was close to despair. The public schools were barred from admitting Jews, and the Jewish schools that I could have attended were filled to capacity. I couldn't even take up a manual trade because after November 1938, no company would hire a Jewish apprentice. This was a terrible position for someone indoctrinated in the value of education to be in. I had always been told to "make sure that you learn something, because what you've got in your head no one can take away from you." Thus, at the age of fourteen, I was convinced that my entire life would be ruined because I hadn't learned to do anything early on in life. As the saying went: What "Hans" fails to learn as a child, he can never make up as an adult. In many respects I still believe that.

Refugee in the Netherlands

While Jewish schools all over Germany turned me down, word began to spread toward the end of 1938 that the Netherlands would accept about 300 Jewish children, and England about 600. Even without further details, my parents and I decided (I was actually included in the deliberations) that we had to grasp at any opportunity for me to leave Germany. In hindsight, this was a somewhat naïve assumption. Given the experience of World War I, we should have known that Holland was not exactly the safest refuge. But this shows just how panicked we were. If we had only waited two weeks longer, I would have ended up in England, and my life would have been completely different.

So, on January 4, 1939, I was permitted to leave Germany for Holland with other German-Jewish children between the ages of six and eighteen. Although my parents and I knew a Dutch family that was prepared to take me in, the Dutch government strictly prohibited this. I had to stay in a refugee center. The children there were not permitted to go to school, and to make matters worse they were transferred from one place to another. Between January and November 1939, I lived in five different refugee centers. When I finally found a blacksmith in Driebergen, in the province of Utrecht who was prepared to take me on as an apprentice, the local police picked me up after a few days. Then it was back to doing nothing in the center again.

Just how bad things were is demonstrated by an event of which I have a complete written record because, thanks to the courage of a non-Jewish German, all of the letters that I sent to my parents in Germany were saved.

Several weeks after my arrival in Holland, I reported that, "a man from the refugee committee came to our center and said that it might be possible for some of us to attend an "Ambach school." At the time, I didn't know that *ambachtsschool* was Dutch for technical school. I only understood the word "*school*," and I wrote home, "Of course, I signed up immediately for training. By the way, what is an "Ambach school?" That I volunteered to join a school when I didn't even know what kind of a school it might be shows how desperate I was. As far as I know, no technical schools were ever set up for refugee children.

THANK GOODNESS FOR WERKDORP WIERINGEN

If you think nothing is accomplished by nagging or complaining you are wrong. Given certain circumstances, it may be the only way to get out of a difficult situation. At least, this was true in my case. Every time one of the officials from the refugee committee visited us (which was only every couple of weeks) I complained to them about how much time I was wasting. I wanted to learn something, I told them, and it didn't much matter what. My parents also wrote to the committee with the same request. As a result, I was eventually one of thirty lucky children permitted to go a model refugee camp in Wieringen. By now, the war had broken out and no children were permitted to leave Germany any more.

Those of us who were allowed to transfer to Wieringen were several years younger than the rest of the young refugees already there. I learned a great deal from these older people, most of them former students. Among other things, I had the opportunity to get training as a metal worker. At least as important was that at Wieringen we learned to do heavy physical labor. Sometimes, we metal workers were called on to help bring in the harvest or hack ice in the drainage canal in the middle of winter. We had to stand in high boots with water up to our waists in order to dredge the canal. Wieringen also had a collection of books and records, so I was able to read and listen to music to my heart's content. One of the former students, who had almost completed his studies in mathematics and physics, gave me lessons almost every evening, so that by the time we were forced to leave Wieringen in March of 1941, I was able to enter secondary school again and complete it almost on time.

Final Exams, and Life in Hiding

When the German troops marched into the Netherlands, most of the Wieringen refugees were taken to Amsterdam. Again threatened with idleness, I took to nagging again and managed to be accepted into the fourth class of the strictly Orthodox Jewish high school—even though I was totally non-religious and didn't understand a word of Hebrew. Thanks to the generosity of the school directors, who made allowances for my faulty Dutch and my even poorer knowledge of Jewish culture (with the exception of history), I managed to get through. As a result of two very lucky circumstances, I was able to take the final state school examination, even though my group and I were ordered deported.

The first stroke of luck was that a former Jewish colleague of my father from Bielefeld who also fled to Amsterdam, and to whom I wanted to say my goodbyes before my deportation, reacted in a manner typical of German-Jews at the time. "What, you only have one year to go to the exams?' he asked. He got me a position as a mailman in the internal postal service of the Jewish Council, which kept me from being deported for a year. His reasoning was that if I got deported after that, I'd at least have my school exam in my pocket. Because being a mail carrier took up the entire morning, I only had the afternoons free for school. Then there was a second stroke of luck. My future foster parents, the Emanuels, had received permission to open a private Jewish school. They managed to get the money that made it possible for me to complete my education there.

I went underground one day after successfully completing the final exam for students at private schools. My first attempt, however, failed miserably because I fell in with a notorious traitor. Luckily, I realized it in time. With the help of the Emanuels, I was able to stay out of sight for a year. They courageously hid me in their own weekend house not far from Amsterdam, which they made to look uninhabited. The house was a duplex, and their neighbor took me in. I spent a good part of the day with the Emanuels, reading and discussing subjects of mutual interest.

Except for a few scary moments when the Germans searched the house I was able to keep my head above water. The news that the Nazis were beginning to lose the war boosted my morale. In spite of the fact that we never went out onto the street and spent only a few moments in the garden behind the house, our little community, including the Emanuels, their neighbors, and occasional underground guests, got along surprisingly well.

THE NEAR-END OF THE ROAD: AUSCHWITZ

As it happened, this garden turned out to be my undoing. One afternoon, the neighbor who had taken me in asked me to fetch some wood for the oven from the shed. As soon as I emerged from the house, Germans from the Green Police with weapons drawn barred my way. I was arrested and brought in for interrogation by the Gestapo in The Hague several days later. I had a poorly forged ID, and the German security officer who was interrogating me realized immediately that my name was not Wim Engeltjes. It seemed pointless not to tell the truth, so I told him that my name was Hajo Meyer, and that I came from Bielefeld.

"What a coincidence," he responded. I'm from Oerlinghausen."

"My father's uncle lives there," I replied.

"Oh, who's that?" he inquired.

"Dr. Max Meyer," I answered.

"What, he's your father's uncle?" he responded. "Why, he's the best doctor in the world... He saved my wife's life!" he exclaimed.

"If he did that for you, perhaps you could do something for me," I suggested, in turn.

The security officer was SS Master-Sergeant Koch, a man described in detail in the autobiography of Friedrich Weinreb,[3] a Polish-Jewish econometrist and Talmudic scholar.[4] The result was that I was brought next morning to the Westerbork transit camp, which was the last station in Holland for people who were to be deported to Auschwitz. For most of my life, I viewed Koch has a horrible criminal. Only recently did I realize that he could not afford simply to let me go. But what he did do was to stop interrogating me about my contacts with the underground. No pressure was put on me, and I certainly wasn't tortured. As a result, I was never tempted to betray my illegal contacts. Perhaps that was his way of repaying my uncle. I was soon deported to Auschwitz from Westerbork.

Auschwitz was actually a complex of camps, the largest of its kind established by the Nazi regime. It included three main camps, Auschwitz I, Auschwitz II, also called Auschwitz-Birkenau, and Auschwitz III, also called Auschwitz-Monowitz, all of which deployed incarcerated prisoners at forced labor. The camps were located about 37 miles west of Krakow. Auschwitz inmates were employed on huge farms, or forced to work in coalmines, stone quarries, fisheries, and especially armaments industries. Between 1942 and 1944, the SS authorities at Auschwitz established 39 sub-camps. Some of them were established within the officially designated "development" zone. Others were located in Upper Silesia and Moravia.

In general, sub-camps that produced or processed agricultural goods were administratively subordinate to Auschwitz-Birkenau, while sub-camps whose prisoners were deployed at industrial and armaments production, mining, or quarry-work were administratively subordinate to Auschwitz-Monowitz. Periodically, prisoners underwent selection. If the SS judged them too weak or sick to continue working, they were transported to Auschwitz-Birkenau and killed. Prisoners selected for forced labor were registered and tattooed with identification numbers on their left arms. They were then assigned to forced labor at the main camp or elsewhere in the complex, including the sub-camps.

Like most other concentration camps, Auschwitz I had a gas chamber and crematorium. SS physicians carried out medical experiments in the hospital and pseudoscientific research on infants, twins, and dwarfs, and performed forced sterilizations, castrations, and hypothermia experiments on adults. Between the crematorium and the medical experiments barrack stood the "Black Wall," where SS guards executed thousands of prisoners. Auschwitz-Birkenau also contained facilities for a killing center that played a central role in the German plan to dispose of the Jews of Europe. It included four large crematorium buildings, each with a disrobing area, a large gas chamber, and crematorium ovens. Trains arrived at Auschwitz frequently with transports of Jews from virtually every country in Europe occupied by or allied to Germany. New arrivals underwent selection. The SS staff determined the majority to be unfit for forced labor and sent them immediately to the gas chambers, which were disguised as shower installations to mislead the victims.

A number was tattooed on my arm in Monowitz, which housed prisoners assigned to work at the Buna synthetic rubber works established in 1941 by the German conglomerate I. G. Farben. My training at Wieringen came in handy when I was identified as a skilled worker and immediately transferred to Gleiwitz. Although we first had to erect the camp itself under the most miserable conditions, here too, I benefited from the hard physical labor that I had learned to do at Wieringen. Nevertheless, I got weaker and weaker. It was fortunate that once the camp construction was well underway, I was transferred to the railroad repair shop of the *Reichsbahn Ausbesserungs Werk*, where I was able to spend the bitter cold months in a more or less warm place without having to do hard labor. This, and dumb luck, accounted for my survival, but just barely.

CHAPTER 1

LESSONS FROM AUSCHWITZ-
What the History of the Holocaust Can Tell Us

DOES AUSCHWITZ HAVE NOTHING TO TEACH?

I ASSUME THAT readers know something about the day-to-day business of Auschwitz, such as the mass gassing of living human beings and their cremation, usually immediately upon their arrival in the camp, and the deaths of many others from exhaustion, punishing labor, hunger, disease, and cold. I will not recount these here, since the facts are well known. Suffice it to say that the name "Auschwitz" carries an understandably personal significance for me. For the vast majority of people, however, it has a meaning similar to the word "Holocaust," which is used as shorthand in contemporary speech and journalism for the mass murder of millions of European Jews during World War II.

The consequences of this horrific event are still palpable today and will affect us for years to come. The direct psycho-traumatic effects on survivors, and its indirect effect on subsequent generations as a result of trans-generational traumatization can hardly be overstated. Although more than sixty years have passed since the actual event, the subject of Auschwitz comes up almost daily in one form or another. Suits for compensation are still brought, and either recognized or rejected. A book is published that claims that the memory of the Holocaust is a being milked for financial purposes, or that the entire German people yearned for Auschwitz from time immemorial, or, somewhat less extreme, that Hitler and his inner circle had planned the total physical annihilation of the Jewish people from the very beginning. Every once in a while, a criminal who was involved in the horrors of Auschwitz is still tracked down in some remote corner of the world.

I am aware that I am one of the few remaining Auschwitz survivors in the Netherlands. I consider it my duty, as long as I am able, to pass on to the next generation something of what I learned there. The direct impetus for my decision to write on this subject, however, came from a pointed comment made by the female Dutch writer Carl Friedman. When I remarked that, to my regret, many Jews had learned the wrong lessons from the crimes committed against our people, she made the following categorical statement in the Dutch daily *Trouw*: "The long and the short of it is that Jews learned nothing from Auschwitz because Auschwitz has nothing to teach."[5] This statement is one that I am prepared to dispute, but in order to understand what lessons can be learned from this catastrophe, some questions of great consequence first need to be asked, including how such a phenomenon could be occur in a highly culturally developed country like Germany.

XENOPHOBIA AND HATE

The Holocaust, as the systematic destruction of a particular ethnic group by another group that considered itself superior, is the most extreme variant of xenophobia, in which people of one ethnic or religious group do not want to share land with those of another. We only need to think of former Yugoslavia (Serbs against Croats and Albanians) or Ireland (Protestants against Catholics) to realize that this type of xenophobia can lead to ethnic cleansing. The roots of this particular crime lie primarily in the contempt of one group for another, or their own feelings of superiority. A sufficiently large proportion of the population—or in any case, more than a few—must share these feelings. The ingredients for this kind of hatred of one group for another to develop include prior collective humiliation, brought about by a group that may or may not have anything to do with the hated other, fear of renewed humiliation, and guilt feelings of some type projected onto the group targeted for discrimination, expulsion, or even annihilation.

Hate corrupts the soul in which it dwells long before it strikes out against the hated group. Such souls are condemned to live in an impoverished, or at least simplified, world, whose inhabitants are black or white ghosts without contour and without nuance. Individuals who live in such impoverishment know nothing of the fine distinctions that make the world so vivid and diverse. Black is black and white is white. Bad is bad, good is good. Everything is reduced to simple categories, and this lack of nuance leads to a seductively simple view of the world. "The Jews are our misfortune," was all a person needed to know during the Nazi dictatorship. It invoked and explained everything bad that the Germans had ever experienced—at least for some, and, thankfully, for only a limited time.

GERMANY AFTER WORLD WAR I

There was truly no lack of misfortune in the aftermath of World War I. It hit Germans all the harder because only half a century earlier it seemed that a Golden Age had dawned. During the second half of the 19th century and the beginning of the 20th, Germany had become one of the most powerful nations in Europe. The Germans invented entire new branches of industry, and the sciences and culture blossomed. Militarily, Germany seemed unbeatable. Its great archenemy, France, had been decisively defeated in the Franco-Prussian war. No wonder that Germans entered the war in 1914 with the firm belief that victory was around the corner.

They were, however, in for a rude awakening. After four long years of brutal battle, Germany and Austria had lost more than three million young men. All of the sacrifices had been in vain. The victorious Allies placed the entire blame for the war on Germany, which was forced to cede important regions to France and Poland. When it could no longer pay the enormous reparations that were assessed, France occupied the entire Rhineland. In short, Germany was brought to its knees. Then came the unprecedented inflation, which hit those hardest that had managed to accumulate only a few meager savings. Unemployment affected more workers in Germany than in other countries, and to an extent not seen before. After the intoxication of the so-called *Gründerjahre*, the period of rapid industrial growth in Germany between 1871 and 1873, this humiliation and impoverishment could hardly have been more dramatic. In this situation, Hitler stepped into the limelight and captured a large portion of the German population with his delusional ideas on the harmful worldwide influence of the Jews.

Anti-Semitism

Paradoxically, the French Revolution of 1789 was an important turning point in the development of modern anti-

Semitism. As a product of the Enlightenment, the equality of all human beings was inscribed on its banner. Jews, too, were human beings, and therefore had to be treated like all other citizens. This idea was spread by Napoleon over almost all of Europe, and if needed, was implemented by mild force. As a result, Jews were emancipated in most countries. They were given the same rights as other citizens and were able for the first time to choose their professions. Their traditions made them extremely studious and industrious. In a short time, in central Europe in particular, they began to be very successful in the law, medicine, journalism, business, and science—to name just a few in which they were significantly overrepresented in the population.

Naturally, the ideas introduced under Napoleon were not understood or internalized by everyone right away. The anti-Semitism that branded Jews as the murderers of Jesus Christ, which had been incited by the Catholic Church for centuries, could not be dismantled in one day. These archetypal anti-Semitic feelings and ways of thinking continued to proliferate and were stoked by envy and jealousy. History held two more surprises in store. Nationalism, which was an outgrowth of the Enlightenment and emphasized the differences between nations and peoples, began to grow. The Jews, at least in so far as they were viewed as a people, were viewed as markedly different from the others among whom they lived.

At the same time, scientific racism, which posited the inequality of human races—advanced in France by Ernest Renan and Arthur de Gobineau, among others—gained respectability. These ideas were further elaborated by people such as Houston Stewart Chamberlain, an Englishman living in Germany, and by the German court chaplain (*Hofprediger*) Adolf Stoecker. They attempted to prove that, as a result of inherited characteristics, Jews were inferior to the Nordic (Aryan) races. Chamberlain's 1,200-page magnum opus, *The Foundations of the Nineteenth Century*, a testimony to both his enormous erudition and colossal muddle-headedness, exerted a great influence on many citizens and pseudo-intellectuals, among them Adolf Hitler.

The influence of another extreme nationalist and racist, Heinrich von Treitschke, a highly respected professor of history in Berlin was as bad, if not worse. American historian Fritz Stern wrote:

> By 1879 it became clear that the atmosphere in the Reich had changed. In that year two dignitaries with impeccable credentials warned in decorous tones against the Jewish danger and thus legitimized the existence of a "Jewish question." One was Adolf Stoecker, court chaplain and hence regarded as representative of crown and church, and the other was Heinrich Treitschke, widely hailed as Prussia's greatest historian and as an ornament of the University of Berlin.[6]

Thus, Treitschke helped mold the future intellectual elite of Germany. As German historian Christian Graf von Krockow noted:

> The historian Heinrich von Treitschke was one of the intellectual spearheads of anti-Semitism. As a historian and demagogue of rank, he preached from the lectern, and his influence can hardly

be overstated. He educated an entire generation of Wilhelmine academics.[7]

Krockow also cited the reminiscences of Heinrich Clasz, who studied under Treitschke, about the very liberal milieu in which he had grown up, characterized by patriotism, tolerance, and humanity. Treitschke changed all that:

> We young men were advanced: we were nationalist to the core and wanted nothing to do with toleration if it protected the enemies of the people and the state.

This remark from an academically trained former liberal illustrates the disappointing passivity of German intellectuals and those in the free professions and universities in the face of the Hitler regime's discrimination against their Jewish colleagues.

HITLER'S SUCCESS

After all the inexplicable humiliations and difficulties the German people had to endure during the First World War and even more so afterwards, for many of them Hitler was a breath of fresh air. He had simple explanations for everything, and many, although by no means the majority, were unable to withstand his powers of persuasion. He told them that an international financial "World Jewry" intended to destroy Germany by the "Dictate of Versailles" and the ruinous inflation that engulfed the nation. The inferior Jewish people were bent upon nothing less than poisoning noble German blood by racial mixing. It was not hard for people to be convinced of the inferiority of the Jewish people. All they had to do was look at its impoverished representatives living in the Polish and Russian ghettos. This simplification, in combination with the promise to reestablish Germany's position of respect in the world, was enough to induce a part of the population to vote for Hitler.

In the *Reichstag* election of November 6, 1932, the last democratic election before Hitler's seizure of power, the National Socialists won only 196 of 608 seats in parliament, garnering only 33% of the vote.[8] Nonetheless, Hitler was named Chancellor by more or less democratic means on January 30, 1933. His ascent to power was largely made possible by his clever manipulation of the disunity among the other parties, which had made Germany practically ungovernable. By skillfully playing on weaknesses within the Weimar government and the disarray of his opponents, Hitler managed to gain absolute power for himself within a few short months.

Given the minority that actually voted for Hitler in the 1932 election, his later influence must be traced to reasons other than his anti-Semitic platform. Among these were his economic successes. In large measure, Hitler did for Germany what Roosevelt did for the U.S. during the New Deal. Apart from public works projects and the revitalization of industry, one of the most decisive factors was the impressive progress made by *Reich* Economics Minister Hjalmar Schacht in reducing unemployment within an extremely short period of time, as well as Hitler's equally impressive foreign policy successes. These included the reoccupation of the Rhineland, the reincorporation of the Saarland, and the "union" with Austria. Throughout all of these successes, which strengthened the self-confidence of the Germans, the anti-Semitic measures taken were a marginal phenomenon. Moreover, many people, including many Jews, believed that German anti-Semitism would die down after a time, particularly when, in 1936, many of the anti-Jewish measures were loosened, and Jews were released from concentration camps in anticipation of the Berlin Olympic Games.

DISCRIMINATION INCREASES IMPERCEPTIBLY

Although it may surprise those who are only familiar with the final solution epitomized by Auschwitz, a review of the press at the time indicates that, at least until November 1938, the anti-Jewish measures known as the Nuremberg Laws were largely invisible to the population at large. They primarily affected the ability of Jews to practice certain professions such as in law or the civil service, and placed limitations on education, particularly at the universities, although a few institutions of higher learning continued to accept Jews during that time. In addition, social contact with non-Jews was made difficult, not least because even the suspicion of a sexual relationship was enough to land a person in a concentration camp. What was visible, of course, were the "Jews unwanted" signs at the entrances to hotels, cafés, movie theaters, parks, swimming pools, and the like. Although the law did not mandate these, they gave anti-Semites license to attack Jews wherever they ran into them.

There was, however, no question as yet of a "final solution," in the sense of organized mass murder. In December 1938, Hitler sent Hjalmar Schacht, the architect of Germany's economic resurgence, to negotiations in London. The German government wanted to freeze Jewish assets, estimated at 1.5 billion Reich marks, as security for an international loan with which to finance the emigration of Jews.[9] Among possible destinations: Madagascar, Rhodesia, and British Guyana. In contradistinction to most other countries in Europe, Jews had lived in Germany without interruption at least from the 9th century on. Thus, among those targeted to be forced out of the country, many had been rooted there for hundreds of years. Hitler's attempts to persuade the Western powers to contribute to this plan by making some area in their colonies available for this purpose were, however, in vain.

The historian Gerald Reitlinger made an interesting remark in his important 1953 book, *The Final Solution*, in connection with the occupation of Czechoslovakia in the spring of 1939:

> An immense number of Jews were thus turned over to the Gestapo *without the benefit of that minimum of protection that the law in Germany still provided for the Jews* [emphasis mine].[10]

The point here is that there *was* still a modicum of protection for the Jews in Germany at this time. The Nazis were endeavoring to convince the world that Germany was a civilized country, albeit an anti-Semitic one, and the physical destruction of the Jews only began to take shape after the invasion of Poland in September of 1939.

HOW THE HOLOCAUST CAME ABOUT

Deep humiliation, poverty, and chaos after World War I, as well as perplexity and panic among large segments of the population at how low Germany had sunk, certainly paved the way for the Holocaust. Hitler's success was also based in part on latent anti-Semitism, which blamed Jews for all the Germans' misfortune, and on the promise of an economic upswing, which he initially achieved. Anti-Jewish measures were introduced step-by-step and without much protest. Given the obvious successes of his new government, the population more or less accepted whatever Hitler did, excusing excesses with empty catchphrases like, "As soon as Germany is strong again, all this will be reined in." Large-scale acts of violence did not really occur until the *Kristallnacht* on November 9, 1938, and the first mass murders after the invasion of Poland in September 1939. The Holocaust as a phenomenon—that is, the systematic annihilation of Jews—was first put into motion at the Wannsee Conference of January 20, 1942.

The lesson to be drawn from this is that the breakdown of only a few psychological barriers is required to make what we now call "ethnic cleansing" possible. First, a people in a social group must be branded as pariahs. To this, an ideology must be added that underscores the inferiority of this social group. Third, the members of this group must be denied access to important educational opportunities so that they stand out negatively in relation to the other people in the society. Finally, their access to earning a living must be ever more restricted so that rapid impoverishment follows.

Thus, any form of discrimination on the basis of ethnic origin or religion is evil and can be the beginning of much more fatal oppression. This bitter lesson has led many citizens in various European countries to fight against discrimination and racism under the banner "Never again Auschwitz." The fact that this battle has not yet ended—as demonstrated by events all over the world—and that it was used during the Cold War to promote less pure objectives, takes nothing away from the honest conviction of these people.

LEARNING FROM AUSCHWITZ

Auschwitz stands as a symbol for the systematic murder of millions of human beings on the basis of their ethnic origin. This was done on an unprecedented scale, using the most modern forms of organization and methods of industrial production. In other words, it was an efficient mass-production factory for killing human beings. The number of deaths produced per square meter and per month was higher than had ever been achieved before. Hegel's dictum that an increase in quantity above a certain limit entails a change in quality is an apt description of this crime. This philosophical formulation recognizes that a raindrop and an ocean are qualitatively two completely different things, despite their common substance. The quantitative difference brings about a new quality.

Applied to the phenomenon of Auschwitz, this meant that the purely quantitative accumulation of human beings fighting for survival in the barracks led to a complete alteration in the quality of life. Seldom before in history had so many people been condemned to live in such a close space. Life in a submarine is not comparable, because such service is voluntary, and crewmembers are subjected to stringent psychological tests. The experience of captives on a 17th or 18th century slave ship might be more apt, although our understanding of the actual psychological experience of those human beings is limited.

Each individual concentration camp inmate saw approximately the same things and experienced more or less the same treatment. However, it is my firm conviction that each of the witnesses still living carries around different memories. Because we were under such stress, our minds were literally turned inside out, and as a result, this horrific collective experience was borne by each inmate in solitude. Thus, paradoxically, nowhere was one lonelier than in Auschwitz. One of the consequences of this intense individualization caused by extreme overcrowding is that only the most limited and general statements can be made about how any particular individual experienced the situation. Another is the recognition that what we suffered there cannot really be conveyed. When asked, I always answer as follows: "I know that I was there, but even I can no longer imagine the nature and extent of the horror." This does not, however, mean that one cannot or could not learn from Auschwitz, or even learn while in Auschwitz.

I have already described some of the lessons to be learned from how Auschwitz came about. What people learned *in* the camps depended largely upon their individual character traits or constitution, and what they had experienced and learned previously. Luck and the lack thereof played an enormous role as well. "I have a degree from the University of Auschwitz." This claim, frequently heard from concentration camp survivors who immigrated to the United States after the war, and who were able to reintegrate into normal society, is evidence that they believed they had learned a great deal.

LESSONS FROM PERSONAL EXPERIENCE

Among the lessons I learned from my personal experience in Auschwitz was that appearances are often deceptive. Out of fear of death a Jewish inmate might become a brutal Kapo capable of beating his fellow inmates to death. On the other hand, an SS man might, out of compassion, give an inmate a piece of bread, thereby endangering his own life. I owe my mental survival largely to an SS man who once spontaneously gave me a number of sandwiches.

Another thing I learned was that extremely strict but consistently applied draconian measures were better than anarchy. In our camp, there was a non-Jewish head Kapo who had been hauled out of prison where he was serving time for murder. In the absurd world of the camp, he did everything strictly according to regulations—which meant that his behavior was predictable. This gave us a paradoxical sense of safety. This also explains why arbitrary violence is so deeply disturbing, why European society reacts so strongly to senseless violence on the streets, and why Israeli society is so affected by the Palestinians' unpredictable suicide attacks.

An important lesson I learned about myself was that under no circumstances did I ever want to be like "them," the people who created and maintained the concentration camps—not even to save my own life. I sensed even then that such a moral downfall on my part would make my survival meaningless.

Among the highly personal paradoxes I experienced was that, in looking back, I consider it a stroke of luck that I so quickly wasted away to the point of starvation. I was little more than skin and bones. People in this condition were known as "Muslims" in camp slang. Such emaciation usually preceded death, but the mental numbness caused by my extreme weakness largely spared me negative emotions. This, I believe, also helped me to stay sane.

Another paradox was that, even under the most horrific circumstances, there were moments of comfort in Auschwitz. The music to which we inmates marched through the gate out of the camp each morning on the way to work was soothing, in a way. Even though it was marching music, it was well composed and arranged—and was played by excellent musicians.

An additional paradox that pertained to my personal experience was that one could draw strength even from a deep lack of religiosity. In other words, the understanding that there is no life after death could make it easier to endure one's fate. I firmly believe that everything that I was forced to endure in my life would have been for naught if I had died. In addition, by contemplating Nietzsche's dictum that "what doesn't kill us, makes us stronger," I realized while still in the camp that by virtue of my experiences in the camp, I would be better able to make meaning out of my life if I was liberated and survived.

Last but not least, I learned that friendship—in my case with a man named Jos Slagter—is of inestimable value. It enabled both of us to survive. It was the only and most effective cure for the almost unbearable loneliness. As head of the Dutch Auschwitz Committee, Jos Slagter dedicated his later life to spreading the lessons that he had learned there.

So much for the personal lessons that I learned in Auschwitz. Other survivors may emphasize other lessons, but I know that what I learned expanded my horizons. Still, nothing shaped my thought and emotions after the war as much as the recognition of the fundamental senselessness of suffering.

SUFFERING AND ITS CONSEQUENCES FOR THE INDIVIDUAL

Nietzsche believed that suffering could completely destroy the soul of a human being, but that it could also purify. This thought gave me much consolation in dark times. However, because the probability of damage is much greater than that of repair, it makes no sense to ascribe, *a priori*, healing or purifying qualities to suffering. In fact it would be immoral. In truth, suffering has no meaning in and of itself. Its negative effects can, however, be greatly limited if one is able to give meaning to what is essentially meaningless. This "attributing meaning to the meaningless" (*Sinngebung des Sinnlosen*), is the part of the title of a historical work by the German-Jewish philosopher Theodor Lessing, which in a few words describes quite effectively what one should do in the face of suffering.[11] Finding new meaning in life is probably the best way to regain emotional equilibrium after surviving trauma.

There is another important way of dealing with trauma, however, namely repression. This concept from psychoanalysis is much more real than some people think. I myself have experienced just how powerful this defense mechanism can be. It is not always possible to prove that a traumatic experience that has been repressed actually occurred. In my case, I have documentary evidence of this repression. Whenever people asked me, during the first twenty years after the war, whether I was in contact with my parents after my flight to Holland, I answered with a firm, "Hardly. The only contact was a monthly Red Cross letter of at most thirty words." I was absolutely convinced that this was the case, and was astounded when my elder brother, who was living in England at the time, told me during the 1960s that he had a stack of letters and postcards that I had written to my parents between January 1939 and March 1943. He had gotten them from a non-Jewish German friend of my parents who had kept them, at no small risk to him. I didn't count the letters, but

I had apparently written several each week. Contrary to my recollection, I had a very active correspondence with my parents up to the point when I was forced to go into hiding.

I have often pondered this remarkable case of repression. The explanation, I believe, is that immediately after the war I had no emotional energy left to grieve at the loss of my parents. By unconsciously denying that I had ever written these letters, I could hold fast to the illusion that I had already lost contact with them when I fled to the Netherlands by myself. By doing so, I effectively shut off grief.

In the late 70s and 80s, I served as a voluntary group leader in encounter groups with second-generation Holocaust victims under the auspices of a Jewish organization for psychiatry and social work in the Netherlands. During this period, I made a number of important observations that I later found confirmed and explained in the relevant literature. The people with whom I worked were fully grown up, and many had children themselves. They all suffered from the fact that their parents, who had been in camps or underground, were not able to talk about their experiences. Moreover, their damaged parents had given them too much responsibility at an early age, and they all felt guilty for their parents' suffering.

A late friend of mine, Dr. Theo K. de Graaf, served in the Israeli army as chief psychiatrist during a period of seven years. In this function, he had a unique opportunity to see and treat an impressive number of second-generation victims. What he learned there he reported in numerous articles, as well as in his book entitled: *Trauma and Psychiatry: The Role of Individual and Trans-Generational Traumatization in the Causation of Psychobiological Illness*. In his introduction to Chapter 3, "Family Dynamics in Trans-generational Traumatization," he wrote:

> Most of our knowledge about the influence of parental trauma on children's development is derived from case studies. During the '60s, Israeli psychoanalysts were among the first to report about serious psychological problems in youngsters that in their opinion could be tracked back to the parents unresolved traumatic Holocaust experiences… The case reports, which are mostly derived from psychoanalytic therapies, emphasized the child's perspective by means of its fantasies about the parents emotions and "secret" traumatic experiences, the child tries to fill the lacuna—"the conspiracy of silence"— in the survivor family's communications.[12]

De Graaf further expanded on the responsibility that such children tended to feel for their parents' suffering during the war:

> A prominent feature in many of these families is the strong and mutual-dependency relationship that continues to exist between the survivor parent and his or her child, even as the child matures. In these cases one may infer the existence of a secret dependency contract between parent and child.[13]

What I observed in my own sessions with second and third generation victims who tried to understand their parents' behavior was that these children and grandchildren of those who experienced the war in hiding or in the camps were often just as traumatized as their parents or grandparents, and in some cases even more so. My understanding of this phenomenon starts from the observation that they were brought up by deeply traumatized parents. The younger generation was thus continually confronted, from earliest childhood on, with the trauma of their parents. This took place during their most impressionable phase of growing up, in stark contrast to the experiences of the parents themselves, who grew up under what we would consider normal circumstances and had more or less normal childhood memories.

Consequences for the Jewish People as a Whole

The fact that an extremely high percentage (approximately 30-40%) of European Jews was murdered during those dark years means that almost all Jewish families in Europe, America, and Israel have been directly or indirectly traumatized. A contributing factor is the tenacity with which Jews continue to memorialize the Holocaust. Nietzsche noted how dangerous such traditions could be. In the second *Unzeitgemäße Betrachtung*, he writes:

> There is a degree of insomnia, of masticating, of historical rumination, which results in damaging—and finally ruining— a living element, be that one individual or one nation or one culture.[14]

This tendency of Jewish tradition to get locked into a preoccupation with suffering and trauma has, in my opinion, contributed to the way in which postwar generations have been drawn into re-experiencing that trauma. Terror learned by hearsay may leave a deeper impression than that experienced directly, since many of the people who were actually imprisoned in the camps had time to get used to the horrible conditions, and experienced a sort of psychic numbness that helped them survive. More important, perhaps, is the fact that members of the second and third generations were brought up by deeply traumatized parents. This is in contrast to the parents themselves, who in general grew up under normal circumstances and have more or less normal childhood memories.

THE ULTIMATE LESSON OF THE HOLOCAUST

For Jews, the most important lesson to be learned from the Holocaust is that we should never, ever become like our persecutors. It goes without saying that we must never build concentration camps with or without gas chambers, but more than that, I believe that we as a people, with our rich history and valuable tradition of ethics—a tradition of ethics that has profoundly influenced all legal systems in the West—should never even come close to behaving as our persecutors have toward us. If we do not soon internalize this lesson we will be in danger of betraying ourselves and endangering our very existence as a people with a common and valuable socio-cultural heritage. The meaning of 2,000 years of persecution in the Diaspora simply cannot be that now that Jews have their own state they may persecute others.

I make this claim, first of all, because Jewish ethics as set out in the Torah are absolutely clear about the treatment of outsiders. Leviticus 19:34 and Deuteronomy 10:19 state clearly that strangers may never be discriminated against. The reasoning in both books is based on the key phrase, "For ye were strangers in the land of Egypt," which is a clear statement of ethics. Making ethically positive sense out of senseless suffering is part of an ancient Jewish interpretation of history. Rabbi Hillel, one of the greatest rabbis in Jewish history, who lived in the 1st century B.C., exemplified this when he said: "That which is hateful to you do not do to your neighbor. That is the whole of the Torah."

There is another important argument why finding a positive ethical meaning from suffering is the only path that individual Jews and the Jewish people as a whole can take in coping with the effects of the Holocaust. This argument is connected with the question of whether the deaths of millions were merely senseless, or whether they may be given meaning after their deaths. To answer this question, we must understand that the Nazi criminals who created and maintained the death camp system had another goal in mind besides mass annihilation. They made the lives of those they did not gas immediately so wretched that they were reduced by starvation to little more than ghosts who fought with each other for a blanket or a piece of bread. By this means, the Nazis intended to prove how subhuman Jews were. The irony, of course, is that in the opinion of the civilized world, if there is such a thing as an inferior species of humans, those who invented that system of evil were the prime specimens.

If we Jews were to opt for an ethically compromised meaning to be gleaned from the Holocaust, according to which it would now be our turn to get revenge for all that was done to us—if we came to believe that now that we were in the driver's seat we could discriminate against those who didn't see things our way—then we would have sunk to the level of our former persecutors. We would, in effect, be proving them right. No, it would be appropriate here to practice a classical Jewish concept, the *teshuva*, which means the return from the wrong road. This implies a return to the deeply ethical Judaism characterized by Leo Baeck, the last great Reform rabbi in Germany, as follows:

> The respect that we owe other people is therefore not one single commandment, not a commandment among commandments. Instead, recognition of one's neighbor represents the entire content of morality, the whole richness of that which God demands from us for the sake of our God-given human dignity. It is the very essence of obligation. Hillel, and Akiba later, already emphasized this significance. They found in it the sum of the Torah, the all-encompassing principle.[15]

CHAPTER 2

JUDAISM IN THE AGE OF ENLIGHTENMENT
What the Modern History of the Jews in Europe Can Tell Us

THE TWO SIDES OF JUDAISM

TWO THOUSAND YEARS ago, the Jews were clearly recognizable as a distinct people. They possessed a common language and a common homeland, although Diaspora communities of Jews already existed. Since the sixth century B.C., there had been an important community of Jews in Babylon, and from the fourth century B.C. there was a huge community of Jews in Alexandria that greatly contributed to the Hellenistic culture. The members of this community already spoke Greek and wrote their works in that language.[16] What distinguished them from Hellenes was their monotheistic religion, which carried with it an entire socio-cultural heritage as well as an elaborate system of rules that determined much of their daily behavior.

After the destruction of Jerusalem in the year 70 A.D., the Jews were dispersed over the antique world much more widely than previously. They no longer spoke a common language, nor did their homeland exist. It is far from the truth that they share a common racial background. Thus, the claim of Zionists at the end of the 19th century that the Jews were a race had little to do with reality. It is debatable whether or not the Jews can even be considered a people. Without a doubt, they do share a common socio-cultural heritage as well as a common creed shaped during more than a millennium and a half in the Diaspora. Apart from this, perhaps their greatest commonality was the discrimination or persecution they experienced as outsiders in whatever culture they lived.

If, for the sake of argument, we grant that the Jews are a people, I have nevertheless dared to suggest that its foundation is primarily based on ethics. This radical view demands elaboration. While one may certainly raise doubts about it, it is nevertheless a conviction that is shared by a large number of Jews who still feel connected with their European background, and who were thus influenced, however indirectly, by the 18th century philosopher Moses Mendelssohn and his followers. As such an individual, I feel that Judaism reached its zenith following Napoleon's emancipation of the Jews in Europe and during the period of cultural renaissance that followed in Central Europe, and particularly in Germany.

It should be noted, however, that there have always been conflicting doctrines at the basis of Judaism. In contrast to the ethical side of Judaism, there has also been a dark side to Jewish thought, suppressed in great measure over the centuries by rabbinical tradition, but never fully eliminated. Today, expansionist Zionism has revived this strain of Judaism in support of behavior that would be considered by the enlightened portion of mankind to be barbaric. In this climate, elitist views of being "the chosen people" have been allowed to flourish, chauvinism and xenophobia have been accepted, ideas of a "better" race that is allowed to practice ethnic cleansing have been openly discussed, and the oppression, harassment, and humiliation of another people have been practiced and have obtained rabbinical blessings. Before coming back to the ethical side of Judaism, we must therefore first concentrate on the dark side of it.

THE DARK SIDE OF CLASSICAL JUDAISM

The more familiar aspects of the dark side of Judaism can be found in its isolationist, separatist tendencies. At their basis lies the idea of being the chosen people, the only people with which the only real God had a special contract. This idea was amplified by forbiddingly strict dietary laws that prevented easy contact with people of other creeds. This outspoken, separatist side of Judaism contributed to the origins of anti-Semitism, yet doubtless it was also instrumental in the survival of Judaism from antiquity to the present time. This is, however, not nearly the blackest spot of the dark side of Judaism. There is a spot so dark and threatening that with my background in the best tradition of German Judaism, it took me nearly my entire life to discover it and to acknowledge its existence. It is saddening to confess that my attention was drawn to this side of Judaism by remarks made in interviews with fanatically religious Jewish settlers in the occupied territories, who defended their harassment of Palestinians and their pogroms or murders of them through references to this dark side of the Jewish tradition. Only by reading these remarks did I come to realize that this black spot exists within Judaism from its very roots in the Torah.

I shall mention passages from the Old Testament in as brief a manner as possible in order to show some elements of this darkest side. It should be noted that in enlightened Jewish circles, as well in those Christian circles that acknowledge the Jewish Bible as their point of origin, all these quotations are suppressed. Thus, for instance, in an authoritative anthology of Talmudic comments only one of the Biblical texts below is mentioned.[17] In Joshua 7:24-28, an account is given of the death of 12,000 inhabitants of the city of Ai and the city's total destruction. In Joshua 10:28-39 a tedious enumeration is given of the total destruction of all the inhabitants of the cities of Makkeda, Libna, Lachis, Gezer, Hebron, and Debir. Time and again, it is repeated that not a single soul was kept alive. In Joshua 21:44, the blissful situation of living in a country where this ethnic cleansing has been successfully carried out is described: "And the Lord gave them rest round about… and there stood not a man of all their enemies before them."

There is a special reason why I am so shocked about this text that suggests how beautiful life is without a single enemy present. This is because of a Nazi song that I heard often as a Jewish boy in Nazi Germany, which contained the following verse:

> *Deutschland, Deutschland was bist Du so schön*
> *Weit und breit kein Jud mehr zu sehen.*
> *(Germany, Germany how beautiful you can be*
> *With nowhere around a single Jew to see.)*

Similar scenes of genocide including the scorched earth technique are described in Judges 9:45 and in 1 Samuel 15:3 and 18 as well as in 1 Samuel 27:9 and 11. And in Numbers 33:55, it is written:

> But if you will not drive out the inhabitants of the land from before you; then it shall come to pass, that those which ye let remain of them shall be pricks in your eyes and thorns in your sides, and shall vex you in the land wherein ye dwell.

As difficult as it is to believe, present-day religious Jewish fanatics use these Biblical examples for the purpose of defending their behavior. In a book entitled *Rabin: A Political Murder*," the fanatic murderer of Rabin is quoted saying: "If in Biblical times I had taken part in the conquest of Eretz Israel, I would also have killed babies and children, as it is written in the book of Joshua." [18] Discussion of the expulsion of all Palestinians from the West Bank takes place in large parts of Israeli society and has reached the highest political levels. It is a real tragedy that those who seriously consider such plans call themselves Jews. By doing so, they suggest to the rest of the world that they share the same socio-cultural heritage as those that initiated and greatly contributed to the establishment of the modern social welfare state, when in fact the difference between their interpretations of the Torah, or Old Testament, could not be greater.

JUDAISM'S GREAT ACHIEVEMENT: SOCIAL ETHICS

Without a doubt, Judaism has contributed positively and greatly to our modern world. There may be a deep reason for the historical fact that it was the Jewish people who formulated the laws regarding our dealings with our fellow human beings in such a way that it found acceptance in the Western world. In the Near East during Biblical times, a stranger automatically evoked uncertainty and fear. To him were extended the earliest rules of hospitality. As long as he remained within your four walls and shared your food with you, you were safe and he was safe. To violate these rules of hospitality of offering food and accepting food, thereby signaling non-aggressive intentions, was a deeply rooted taboo. Since the Jews, with their strict dietary laws, could not fulfill these very basic rules, something else had to be invented.

The rules Jews are expected to follow in dealing with strangers are clear and well motivated. They are laid down in Leviticus 19:18 and 19:34. Although (at least in the latter passage) the translation traditionally used in the Western world is probably not completely accurate, it was true enough to form the basis for our social ethics: "The stranger that dwelleth with you shall be unto you as one born among you and thou shalt love him, (and here the Hebrew text allows for, and actually asks to be translated as) 'in fact, he is' like you, for you (as well) were strangers in the land of Egypt." In view of the addition at the end, "For you were strangers in the land of Egypt" the translation as I give it here is logical. "Love the stranger; he is like you, as once you were a stranger yourself" is also the translation given by Hermann Cohen.[19]

It is also significant, and fundamental to our present day ethics, that in Exodus 20:10, it is commanded that the servant should also be granted his Sabbath rest. That this commandment should be taken seriously is evident from the fact that it is repeated in Deuteronomy 5:14. It was taken seriously in practice, at least in Germany before 1933 and probably in most parts of Europe. That is clearly imprinted in my memory. In my youth, when middle class citizens still had domestic help, it was common knowledge that servants in most cases preferred Jewish households to non-Jewish households, because the treatment there was generally more liberal and more caring.

The obligation of taking one day off from work, the Sabbath, has, via Christians on the one hand and Islam on the other, been adopted by much of mankind. The idea of having a day of the week without any obligation to work is an important one. Irrespective of the obsessive-compulsive interpretation that the orthodox have given this day, the opportunity to extend the human experience by enabling one to think, learn, and discuss—which in Judaism is nearly identical with learning—has been a great contribution to mankind.

Intellectual Tradition

The Jews have contributed greatly to Western intellectual tradition and to the techniques used to promote all sorts of learned endeavors. This can be demonstrated in many ways. According to Günter Stemberger,[20] it was the circle around Rabbi Jochanan ben Zakkai (Jabne, 1st century A.D.) who tried to introduce the study of the Torah as a substitute for the service in the Temple. Actually, the author says, they tried to define that study as being the most significant focus of life as a whole. In fact the Talmud says literally: "If you have learned much Torah, do not puff up yourself on that account, for it was for that purpose that you were created."[21] Anybody who thinks that this is intellectualism in an exaggerated form is certainly correct, but it is only one of many quotations in the same spirit. In line with this, all male children had to learn to read and also to write.[22] The general availability of schools for boys, once they were six or seven years old, seems to have existed from the second half of the second century onwards. In a country such as the Netherlands, the obligation to send children to school was not introduced until the second half of the 19th century. The Jews are not called "the people of the book" for a single reason alone.

Although until the start of the 19th century the contributions of Jews to fields outside their own culture were quite limited, there are at least two exceptions. In the first place, there was the completely non-dogmatic approach to the interpretations of the Holy Scripture. In the Talmud the contrasting interpretations of various Rabbis are all presented next to each other. This means that from the very start any new student is confronted with a variety of opinions. He has to think about the problem under discussion, himself, together with his teacher and colleagues. This training in not accepting an opinion on the basis of a particular authority, but only on the basis of thinking about it yourself and discussions with others, has certainly greatly contributed to the methods and practices of modern scientists. The principle is that different opinions and interpretations of acknowledged men of learning are valid, provided they are supported by disciplined arguments. It goes beyond even the peer group of the rabbis. In fact it also applies to discussions between a rabbi and his pupils.

While on the one hand no dogmatic opinion is accepted, every well-formulated and well-structured argument is worthy of attention. The methods of argument should be highly disciplined and follow the so-called hermeneutic rules. In the Talmud, an explicit commandment directed towards someone who wants to study Torah reads: "Set up a master for yourself, get yourself a companion disciple, and give everybody the benefit of the doubt." At the same time, it is acknowledged that a great master can also learn from a bright young student. A further injunction states: "Students take an active part in trying to work out a convincing interpretation."[23] The ready acceptance of the opinion of a brilliant student, so well known in modern sciences, is completely in line with the old learning tradition of classical Judaism.

In this context I am tempted to tell two anecdotes from my life in theoretical physics. I used to know some people who had been, at some time, assistants to the famous theoretician and Nobel Prize winner Wolfgang Pauli in Zürich. One of them, Ralph Kronig, later professor in Delft, told me this story. He had come to Zürich in order to be the intellectual sparring partner of Pauli's for a year. After arrival he asked him: "Herr Pauli, what do you expect from me?" At which Pauli answered: "Herr Kronig, your task will be to contradict me regularly but never without detailed argument." Pauli did, in fact, have a Jewish background.

The Jewish learning tradition is also reflected in my own experience with my theoretical physics teacher, Jan de Boer. He came from a non-Jewish family, but the influence of his many colleagues and teachers who did have a Jewish background was obvious from the following event. After I had passed my first academic examination, comparable to a B.S. degree, and had finished a first research task to the satisfaction of the professor, he said to me: "As I have accepted you as a pupil of mine, we will work together every Friday afternoon from 2 to 5 pm, just the two of us. Now it is obvious that, as of now, I know more about theoretical physics than you do. However, I am aware, and you should be aware, of the fact that my understanding can also have flaws or can be incomplete or even wrong. Thus, if in discussing things I make remarks which you think might be incorrect, you should say, 'Professor, I do not quite understand what you explained to me just now.' Then I will try to explain it again, and it is certainly possible that I myself did not have a full understanding of the matter. That might be the reason why you could not understand my first explanation." His instruction to me was an example of true Talmudic tradition practiced by a non-Jew in modern science.

It can be argued that the greatest impact of Judaism on the world as a whole was the introduction of monotheism and its influence on world history. The two most influential monotheistic religions, which from the year zero and from the early 7th century gave substantial shape to our world, both had their origin in Judaism. The doubt lies in whether, ultimately, their influence on world history has been more positive than negative and whether the introduction of monotheism into our world by Judaism should be placed on the good side of the balance.

From the purely philosophical point of view, at least as far as ontology is concerned, the idea of one single creator of the world, of one and only one *prima causa* can probably be considered as progress, compared to full polytheism. Ethically there is room for doubt, for at least two reasons. First, the idea of one and only one Creator-Father immediately confronts us with the eternal problem of theodicy—how a benevolent and just God can allow evil to exist in the world. Secondly, monotheism has been the cause of many wars and crimes against humanity. The Crusades, the Inquisition, the Thirty Years' War, and the Holocaust cannot be separated from their monotheistic Christian components. I have also mentioned the barbaric behavior of the Jews in antiquity in the name of the one and only God. In the modern age, crimes against humanity that are justified by invoking this same God are abundant on the part of Jews, Muslims, and Christians. Our conclusion must be that the introduction of monotheism can at best be described as a mixed blessing.

THE SURVIVAL OF THE JEWS

In view of the fact that before the catastrophe brought about by Hitler, the Jews in Germany had a long and at some times successful history, we will limit our focus to the events in this single country. In no other region of the Western Hemisphere, with the exception of Italy, have Jews lived over a longer period. In no other country have Jews been more successful and influential than in Germany before Hitler. Only in Germany did the Jewish community succeed at the right moment in formulating an adequate answer to the most important, and still acute, problem of modern Jews—how to be an emancipated, modern citizen and at the same time remain faithful to the most important and relevant Jewish values. Finally, it was in Germany where the greatest catastrophe ever to come over the Jews was concocted and executed.

The survival of the Jews is indeed remarkable, as one of the few peoples known in antiquity that has kept its identity from then until now. It has been caused by a large number of different factors. In considering these factors, we must distinguish between the period before the Enlightenment and the French Revolution, and that after this historic demarcation.

ADHERENCE TO RELIGIOUS PRACTICE

Before the Enlightenment, religion in general, and the Catholic Church especially, played a dominant role in European culture. In such a world, Judaism fit in rather well, albeit in a dialectical way. On the one hand, the whole idea of theocracy had its origin in Judaism. In addition, it must be said that the Church did not deny its relation to

Judaism, if only because at no time did it denounce the Torah as one of its two holy books. On the other hand however, the Jews were seen as the despicable murderers of the Son of God, Jesus Christ. Therefore, they had to suffer. They were discriminated against, such that only very few professions were open to them, but they were not to be annihilated. Their visible suffering had to serve as a warning to all those who could possibly be tempted to believe in God but deny that Jesus Christ was his only son.

This was a time when religion was the most natural structural element to which Jews could adhere. Indeed, the firmness with which, for various reasons, they remained faithful to their religious prescriptions laid down in the *Halacha* (the name of the body of these 613 ritual prescriptions) greatly contributed to their survival as a group during this period. Although physical survival was certainly difficult at times due to discrimination, poverty, persecution, and the resulting pressure to continually move to elsewhere, the closely-knit Jewish community also provided certain protection. The poor were supported, and the ailing cared for. Thus, for all those who needed this help from time to time, escape from the community was not an option. Due to tight social control, it was also nearly impossible. While it was certainly not easy to be a Jew, there was no doubt that you were one or as to what it meant.

THE REFORMATION AND THE THIRTY YEARS' WAR

At the beginning of the 16th century, the Reformation heavily challenged the dominant role of the Roman Catholic Church in the society in which the Jewish communities were embedded. In the wake of this decisive event, various developments took place. In the political world, it eventually led to one of the most important landmarks of European history, the Thirty Years' War. In the world of the mind, the loss of the monopoly of the Roman Catholic Church to prescribe what could be thought and expressed in public paved the way for developments of great importance in the second half of the 16th century, which were in effect the first steps towards the Age of Enlightenment. A hundred years later, the beginning of the scientific revolution occurred. This eventually influenced the everyday world to an extent that can hardly be overestimated.

Great cataclysms in history are the most effective means of bringing about perceptible changes. In the German countries, the Thirty Years' War was the great event that influenced the position of the Jews most perceptibly,[24] and eventually, as many believe, most dramatically.[25] According to Norman Davies, this cataclysm can be interpreted in at least three ways.[26] It was a conflict between the Emperor and the princes, as well as a war between Catholics and Protestants. It was also a continental power struggle between most of the states in Europe. Both the first two aspects of the conflict eventually led to less centralized power and thus, for the Jews, to enlarged possibilities to adapt to the new circumstances. The Treaty of Westphalia greatly diminished the power of the Habsburgs. It also made the German princes more independent. The huge material damage and the reduction of the population from 21 million to perhaps 13 million[27] required much activity on the part of these princes in order to rebuild their countries.

During the Thirty Years' War, the Jews played an important role in financing the various parties and providing them with necessary materials and equipment. In the reconstruction phase, they were called upon even more to mobilize their financial and trading potential. As the whole of Germany was divided up into a great number of independent petty states, there were a great number of rulers who needed the help of the financial and trading capacities of the Jews to rebuild their states or consolidate their power. Thus, the phenomenon of the court Jews (*Hofjuden*), which had already existed occasionally in medieval times, grew to impressive and significant proportions.

THE COURT JEWS

It is estimated that in the 17th and 18th centuries there were probably several thousand of these privileged Jews.[28] These men and their families provided the first and important window out of the ghetto walls and onto the surrounding Christian society. As well as these most privileged individuals, an increasing portion of the Jewish population came into regular contact with the world outside the ghetto, as a growing number of trading opportunities became available to them in such commodities as silk, metals, horses, and cattle. They also started trade as peddlers outside the cities. While in the middle of the 17th century only some court Jews were able to read and write letters in the normal German language, by the middle of the 18th century all the more successful and thus wealthier businessmen were able to do so. At home, they continued to speak the West Yiddish dialect until the beginning of the 19th century. From the beginning of the 18th century various Protestant universities also allowed Jews to study there.

These first steps into the outside world were probably facilitated by a dramatic phenomenon in the

Jewish world, namely the rise and fall of the charismatic false messiah, Sabbataj Zewi from Gaza, in the mid 17th century. In spite of his shameful end (he was forced to convert to Islam), his influence through Sabbatanic sects and works could be felt through the whole of the 18th century. According to Breuer,[29] this whole episode undermined the prestige of the rabbis and thus, dialectically, paved the way for the next important development in the Jewish world. This was the *Haskalah*, the Jewish version of the Age of Enlightenment.

THE ENLIGHTENMENT

According to Kant, one of the giants of the Enlightenment in Germany, this new way of interpreting the world could be defined by a quotation from the classical poet Horace: "*Sapere aude*," which in Kant's translation means, "Have the courage to use your rational brains."[30] It meant that one had to free oneself from all irrational dogmatic attitudes, including intolerance and superstition, which had prevailed in the previous period due to the overruling influence of faith and Church.[31] In accordance with this aim, the Enlightenment in general was not sympathetic to the Jews.[32] They were regarded as a religious community, and their religion (like every religion, but quite a bit more so) was seen as unreasonable and obscurantist. This criticism of the Jews was especially strong in France, where Voltaire wrote hatefully about them.[33] In his wake, with religion increasingly substituted by science (or pseudo science), it was here that the first theories about the inferiority of the Jewish race, as it was called, originated.

Interestingly enough, it was in Germany, of all places, where the Enlightenment looked upon the Jews from a much more favorable perspective.[34] As was most clearly explained by the American historian Fritz Stern, before the Bismarckian *Reich* there was no German equivalent of the nation-state that prevailed in France or Great Britain. The substitute for this binding structure was, at least until then, the German *Kultur* (culture). Irrespective in which principality or kingdom a German *Bildungsbürger* (educated citizen) lived, they all knew, read and quoted their Goethe, Schiller or Lessing, to mention a few. The Jews also had no nation-state, but substituted for this lack with their Torah and their eagerness for learning and knowledge. As a second factor, Poliakov mentions the frequent and close contact between the *Hofjuden* (including their offspring) and the surrounding world. They were economically well off, and directed their thirst for knowledge into the realm of German culture with increasing intensity.

MOSES MENDELSSOHN

One of the most important figures in modern Jewish history was Moses Mendelssohn (1729-1786). He was born in the ghetto of Dessau in 1729. There, he was a pupil of the then famous rabbi David Fränkel. In 1743, he followed his teacher to Berlin in order to continue his studies of Talmud and Torah. Soon he came into contact with two young Jewish university students, both descendents of established families of *Hofjuden*. Abraham Kisch gave him lessons in Latin, and Aaron Salomon Gumpertz had a vast general knowledge of humanities and sciences.[35] Through the latter, Mendelssohn perceived how one might be an observant and knowledgeable Jew and also be well versed in secular literature, philosophy and sciences.

In 1754, Mendelssohn met the great German

Enlightenment philosopher Lessing. By that time, he already had a firm grounding in philosophy.[36] Out of this meeting grew a lasting friendship between these men. The extent of Mendelssohn's influence on Lessing can be illustrated by two examples. First, Lessing's influential basic work on the aesthetics of the classical Laokoön group came out of a problem put to him by Mendelssohn.[37] Second, the famous stage play by Lessing, "*Nathan, der Weise*," was inspired by the friendship between the two. With this play, the public was able to learn about Jews for the first time as real human beings with admirable traits of character. At the time, this was a wholly new experience.

Of great importance in this context is the influential translation by Mendelssohn of the Pentateuch into beautiful *Hochdeutsch* (High German). In this respect, his influence on the German Jews is comparable to that of Luther on the Gentile world two hundred years earlier. The translation, still in Hebrew letters, appeared between 1781 and 1783.[38] Within a generation, the Mendelssohn Bible had found its way to the bookshelves of nearly every literate Jewish home in Central Europe.[39] By learning German, the Jews also became prepared to absorb the culture associated with this language. As we will see, they did this with great eagerness, zeal, and accomplishment.

Of the people who were highly influenced by Mendelssohn (and who influenced him), a few must be mentioned. In the first place there was Marcus Herz (1747-1803). Besides his medical studies, he had studied philosophy at Königsberg University under Kant, and earned his living as a physician. His wife, Henriette, fifteen years his junior, was to gain fame as the very first hostess of a Berlin cultural salon, in which everyone of note in intellectual and artistic circles came together, including the von Humboldts, Schiller, Heine, Schlegel, Schleiermacher, and others. A friend of Herz in Königsberg, also a student of Kant's, was David Friedländer; he became one of the best young friends of Mendelssohn. Friedländer was convinced that the Jews should become more westernized, in daily life as well as in religious practice. Together with his brother-in-law, Isaac Daniel Itzig, he founded the first Jewish school that also taught secular subjects such as French, German, geography and bookkeeping, in 1781.[40]

A HISTORICAL SHOCK WAVE

In 1789 the French Revolution broke out. According to Norman Davies, it was the event "which gave the word 'revolution' its full modern meaning: that is, no mere political upheaval, but the complete overthrow of a system of government together with its social, economic and cultural foundations."[41] The Jewish world was greatly affected by this event, the more so because over the previous fifty years its contact with the Gentile world had significantly increased. In particular, ideas about the nature of man were to influence the conditions under which the Jews lived. It would take more time than those who welcomed the Revolution and its new ideas had anticipated, but the change eventually came, even if it was not for long.

It is interesting to note that the definition of revolution given in a book by Davies in 1997 concurs with the description that the Jewish historian S. M. Dubnow gave in 1920 of the historical consequences of the French Revolution.[42] He described the events after the Revolution as an alternating sequence of emancipation and reaction to emancipation that occurred in two waves. He clearly distinguishes a first emancipation followed by a first reaction and then a second emancipation followed by a second reaction. The physicist in me sees here a description of a historical "shock wave" caused by the dramatic events of 1789.

Dubnow outlines the historical developments in more detail as follows: During the first emancipation (1789-1815), France emancipated its Jews, and other states under the influence of the victorious republic, and Napoleon's empire mandated the equality of all citizens. The first reaction (1815-1840) was of a general political nature. During this period, the rights previously granted to the Jews were nearly everywhere withdrawn. The second emancipation (1841-1881), which occurred in mainly in the Germanic countries, established the legal equality of the Jews, although not everywhere to the same extent. Finally, during the second reaction (1881-1945), which was anti-Semitic in nature, socially accepted anti-Semitism gained such strength that it prevented the practical realization of full social and political equal rights for the Jews.

The consequences of these two antagonistic trends of emancipation and reaction on the behavior of the Jewish community were also of a twofold and conflicting nature. On the one hand, in the ever more secularized world the promises of emancipation to a full and equal citizenship produced a clear trend towards quite far-reaching assimilation. Having been one of the early Zionists, it is interesting to note that Dubnow calls this process of assimilation "de-nationalization." It is to his credit that he was enough of a historian to explicitly mention that this process accompanied the Jewish people during many periods of their long history, for example and notably, the Hellenistic period and the period of the Arab renaissance. On the other hand, the rebuffs experienced by the reactionary trends led to some reawakening of Jewish nationalism. As we will see, however, this awakening of nationalist feeling on the part of the Jews was paralleled, and even surpassed, by a similar awakening of nationalist feeling in the non-Jewish population of Europe in which the Jews were embedded.

Besides economic and social factors, the French Revolution also got its fuel from spiritual sources. Rationalism led to Enlightenment, which also meant unproven authority was no longer accepted. In turn, this translated into anti-clerical and anti-royalist attitudes. One of the important consequences of this in the thinking of the times was that all human beings were created equal. Jews were also human beings. This thought, which had by no means been generally accepted at the end of the 18th century, meant that Jews had to be treated like all other people. These ideas were spread throughout almost all of Europe by Napoleon, and putting them into practice was sometimes even accomplished by force. It is therefore not surprising that after Napoleon's downfall in 1815, quite a number of measures to ensure the full emancipation of the Jews were not immediately enacted. This unexpected delay strongly disappointed many of those Jews who had already incorporated Western European culture into their mental outlook. In a new secular age, it was no longer an option to return to orthodoxy, and the Reform movement still had to gain momentum. Thus, many Jews converted to Christianity in the first few decades of the 19th century.

THE CHALLENGES OF EMANCIPATION

By the middle of the 19th century, however, Jews in most European countries were given the same rights as other citizens, and most professions became available to them. In former centuries, professional restrictions limited them to occupations involving various kinds of trade, especially in money. Now, for the first time, Jews could much more freely choose professions that they liked and for which they had a talent. In the Jewish tradition, learning was highly valued and followed from the earliest years on, as was professional skill. Because of this, by the end of the 19th century Jews had become highly successful as lawyers, physicians, entrepreneurs, scientists, as well as in their more traditional occupation of trading. This occurred particularly in the countries of Central Europe, where they were soon more than proportionally represented in such occupations.

They were equally successful in acquiring and internalizing the culture of their educated non-Jewish surroundings. This was such a striking achievement that the famous German author Theodor Fontane (1819-1898) wrote a poem describing this phenomenon. In it, he recalls that all his life he tried to depict the Prussian countryside and its inhabitants. But at the occasion of his 75th birthday, it was not so much the people whom he had portrayed in his books who came to congratulate him, but, unexpectedly, many Jews who were intimately familiar with his works. He thus wrote in his poem, "*An Meinem Fünundsiebzigsten*" (On My Seventy-Fifth Birthday):

> *Jedem bin ich was gewesen*
> *Alle haben sie mich gelesen,*
> *Alle kannten mich lange schon,*
> *Und das ist die Hauptsache… "Kommen Sie, Cohn."*

> (*To everyone a lot I meant*
> *They read my work from start to end,*

All of them knew me long quite well,
And that's what counts… "Come in, Mr. Israel.")

The Jews' rapid rise in society and assimilation of German culture naturally provoked jealousy on the part of non-Jews. This jealousy, combined with developments in thinking about society and man, would eventually produce a very dangerous mixture indeed. It took more than fifty years before the ideas that Napoleon had tried to introduce into large parts of Europe were, more or less, put into practice. At this point however, history played two tricks that were to have a large impact on the fate of the Jews. The first was that immediately after the Enlightenment, which had preached the equality of all men, modern nationalism began to flourish. This meant that the Jews were seen again as essentially different from the peoples amongst whom they lived. The second was that at the moment when religion as a discriminating characteristic was losing some of its previous importance, a new doctrine was born. This was the semi-scientific theory of races.

According to this race theory, the Jews were not defined as a people with a common religion, history, and culture, but as a race. This notwithstanding the fact that after two thousand years in the Diaspora they were probably, from the racial point of view, more mixed than any other people in the world. By this fact alone, the assertion that the Jews belong to a race of inferior quality had no scientific basis. This, however, did not prevent considerable parts of Europe from being seriously infected by this doctrine.[43] The late 19th century version of the race theory, which depicted the "Semitic races" as inferior to the Germanic one, inaccurately dubbed Aryan, found its way into practical political expression in the first years of the 1870s. This happened, significantly, following a stock market collapse in 1873. According to these ideas, people belonging to the Semitic races were lazy, cowardly, and parasitic, while those of the Aryan race possessed heroic and stalwart characteristics.

The most spectacular anti-Semitic event in Western Europe, which eventually would have consequences of truly historic importance, took place in France. The so-called Dreyfus affair kept French public opinion split into two camps between 1894 and 1906. On the basis of forged documents, Dreyfus, the only officer on the General Staff of Jewish origin, was accused and found guilty of high treason. Only the outcry of people as important and influential as the novelist Emile Zola eventually produced a revised verdict and the rehabilitation of the falsely accused Dreyfus.

EDUCATION AND REFORM OF RITUAL

Mendelssohn himself was aware that the Jewish community faced a problem, in that its knowledge of Hebrew was dwindling. The teaching of the language in Jewish schools had also deteriorated. While he still thought that he could change the people by education, one of his followers, David Friedländer, was convinced the Jewish religion had to be changed.[44] His view was greatly influenced by the ideas of the Enlightenment. He believed that mystic Kaballistic influences, which had penetrated the texts of the services, should be eliminated. The aesthetic shape of the ritual had to be made more attractive and purged of "oriental influences." However, there was great resistance to any change from the conservatives, and the followers of Mendelssohn realized that the way to bring about change would be through the education of the young.

Thus, between 1778 and 1816, ten modern Jewish schools were founded which taught a normal school curriculum alongside Jewish subjects.[45]

One of the prominent educationalists of the time was Israel Jacobson. He founded a school in Seesen in 1801, and then in 1809, during the reign of Jerome Napoleon, king of Westphalia, established an important school in Cassel. Here, as an innovation, some of the prayers were said in German. Songs were also sung in German, and a weekly sermon was given in that language. In 1818, the first true Reform congregation was begun in Hamburg with the building and dedication of the Hamburg temple. In the first decades, the Reform movement was primarily directed towards the aesthetic aspects of the service. It was more westernized, with more decorum and more dignity. In order to counter the opposition from the traditional part of Jewry, a new philosophical background of the new movement gradually evolved.

THE SCIENTIFIC APPROACH TO JUDAISM

One of the main foundations of this new movement was the work of the Reform movement on *"Wissenschaft des Judentums"* (the scientific study of Jewish history and religious literature), and in particular the book by Leopold Zunz, *Die Gottesdienstlichen Vorträge der Juden* (The Sermons of the Jews), published in 1832. Zunz showed that sermonic interpretations of the Bible in the vernacular had long been the custom in many Jewish communities.[46] He thus made it clear that such new ideas and patterns of expression, appropriate to the time and place of their development, had been perennially alive in Judaism and that change had been an established part of Jewish tradition.

On the other hand, the distorted views of the philosopher Immanuel Kant with respect to Judaism exercised tremendous influence. As Michael Meyer points out, Kant wrote that Judaism was "really not a religion at all," since it made no claims upon conscience. Biblical Judaism, he claimed, stressed only external acts and outward observances.[47] This, of course, is sheer nonsense, as the same social ethics espoused by Jesus, "Love thy neighbor, for he is like you," is an Old Testament text. Kant was thus only repeating the prejudices of his era.

In response to this, the Reform movement sought to present Judaism as the religion most exclusively concerned with morality, and hence most worthy of the future. One of the first to think in this way was Solomon Ludwig Steinheim. In his main work, published in 1835, *Die Offenbarung nach dem Lehrbegriff der Synagoge* (Revelation according to the Doctrinal System of the Synagogue), Steinheim argued that according to ideas often found in Jewish ethical literature, moral life was voluntary service that a free man gave to God.

ACCUSATIONS OF LEGALISM

During the first half of the 19th century, the Reform movement was still mainly influenced by the universalistic ideals of the Enlightenment.[48] The reformers were confident that a modernized Judaism could be part of the general progress of an enlightened mankind. However, as time progressed, the manifestations of nationalism and the pseudo-scientific revival of anti-Semitism became ever more visible. The emancipation of the Jews was not accompanied by a greater appreciation of them on the part of non-Jews. Thus, Reform Judaism faced an unanticipated crisis.

During the last two decades of the 19th century, the scientific study of antique cultures and languages had made great progress. It thus became increasingly evident how far Judaism had been influenced by laws and observances borrowed from Mesopotamia. Several of the scholars in this field stressed the preoccupation of Judaism with law. This they compared with the teachings of Jesus, who, according to their interpretation, was more deeply spiritual and put more emphasis on the importance of ethics. Certainly, even these people acknowledged that the Jewish prophets had also preached in favor of a moral life, but they went on to suggest that this message had been made a subordinate one, because the rabbis had superimposed on it an exaggerated legalism.[49]

This semi-scientific, semi-theological attack on Jews and Judaism had its origin in the new anti-Semitism, and ultimately provoked reactions from the Jewish side. For liberal Jewish thinkers, to whom ethics was the heart of Judaism, it was of great importance to show that individual and social morality reflected in Jewish tradition was not less potent than in Christianity. Not only did they wish to refute these semi-theological allegations on the part of their critics and potential followers, but they also wanted to give moral support to those Jews whose self-respect was in danger of being undermined. With this end in mind, *The Ethics of Judaism*, by Moritz Lazarus, was published in 1898. This was a detailed formulation of the central ideas of the Reform movement, which for some time had wished to shift the focus of Judaism from ritual acts to moral conduct. It was Lazarus who explained that Jewish ethics differed from Christian ones by their predominantly social character.

ETHICS AS THE ESSENCE OF JUDAISM

It is not my purpose to give a thorough survey of the Jewish thinkers and writers who, at the end of the 19th century and at the beginning of the 20th, occupied themselves with the role of ethics in Judaism. Nor do I want to explain their ideas. I simply wish to illustrate how central and essential these writers considered the place of ethical conduct within Judaism. According to Michael Meyer,[50] the most important Jewish thinker at the end of the 19th century was the philosopher Hermann Cohen (1842-1918), who founded the "*Marburger Schule*" of Neo-Kantianism. Meyer says this about his teachings:

> Cohen held that Jewish ceremony derived significance only from its capacity to serve as a symbol of moral values. [He believed] that one day the unity of God would be complemented by the unity of humanity. He called messianism the most significant and original product of the Jewish spirit. For Cohen the focus and significance of messianism lay not in the infinitely distant goal but in the unending task of moral improvement.

The very last of the great German Reform rabbis, and therefore a very significant person indeed, was Rabbi Dr. Leo Baeck (1873-1956). He survived the Holocaust, and after the Second World War went to Great Britain. In his main work, *Das Wesen de Judentums* (The Essence of Judaism), he is quite explicit about the role of ethics in Judaism. I quote from the first edition of 1905 a number of significant sentences:

Man has been created in the image of God… However large the differences between human beings may be, what they have in common and what characterizes all of them is that image of God in them… the most exquisite nobility that man can possess is possessed by all. To deny this nobility to anyone means robbing it from us all… It is impossible to express the unity of all human beings more clearly and more definitely… Simon ben Asai said: "This is the book of human history. When God created man he created him in his image"—in this sentence all of Torah is contained. [51]

The consequences of all this are still more explicitly expressed in the chapter under the title, "The Belief in the Fellow Human Being," in which Baeck writes as follows:

Together with this religious concept of "man," the implicit idea of fellow man is introduced. Also that idea is one of the great discoveries of the Jewish genius. And this again leads directly to the concept of humanity and to the very strictest interpretation of humanitarian behavior. That is respect for the innermost nature of a fellow human being, respect for his dignity and for the god-like nature of everybody who bears a human face. The respect we owe our fellow human beings is thus not just one commandment among many. No, it is in fact everything we need to

know. It is in its richness; in everything that
God has asked us to do. He asks this from
us because he, in return, gave us our own
human dignity. This respect for the other is
the very essence of all our obligations.[52]

THE INHERITANCE OF AMERICAN JEWRY

The extent of this ethical renaissance's influence on Judaism
can easily be appreciated by looking into the short texts
formulated as the basis for the strong American branch
of Reform Judaism.[53] In the so-called Pittsburgh Platform
(1885), well before the start of the Zionist movement, is
the following text:

> We recognize in the Mosaic
> legislation a system of training the Jewish
> people for its mission during its national
> life in Palestine, and to-day, we accept as
> binding only the moral laws and maintain
> only such ceremonies as elevate and
> sanctify our lives, but reject all such as are
> not adapted to the views and habits of
> modern civilization.

To me, this text defines in well-chosen words what
modern Judaism should really be. The co-responsibility of
modern Jews for injustice in society is addressed in the last
point of this platform:

> In full accordance with the spirit of
> Mosaic legislation, which strives to regulate
> the relation between the rich and the poor,
> we deem it our duty to participate in the

great task of our modern times, to solve, on the basis of justice and righteousness, the problems presented by the contrasts and evils of the present organization of our society.

The next Platform did not take place until 1937—a date that possibly reflects the terrible threat by then presented by Hitler's regime in Germany. The text was much more elaborate. It stated:

> In Judaism, religion and morality blend into an indissoluble unity. Seeking God means to strive after holiness, righteousness and goodness. The love of God is incomplete without the love of one's fellow men. Judaism emphasizes the kinship of the human race, the sanctity and worth of human life and personality and the right of the individual to freedom and to the pursuit of his chosen vocation. Justice to all, irrespective of race, sect or class, is the inalienable right and the inescapable obligation of all...
>
> Judaism, from the days of the prophets, has proclaimed to mankind the ideal of universal peace. The spiritual and physical disarmament of all nations has been one of its essential teachings. It abhors all violence and relies upon moral education, love and sympathy to secure human progress. It regards justice as the foundation of the well being of nations and the condition of enduring peace.

NATIONALISM IN EUROPE

History indeed played some nasty tricks on the Jews in Europe. The French Revolution had created real hope. Some of those parts of Germany that came under the direct rule of Napoleon between 1806 and 1812, such as Westphalia, allowed the Jews to be fully emancipated citizens. This progress, however, did not last long in most cases. On the one hand, Napoleon's expansion spread the liberal ideas of the French Revolution concerning the equality of all people. On the other hand, the French occupation and the wars against France evoked strong feelings of national identity. European nationalism was born with unanticipated virility.

This new awakening of nationalistic sentiment, thought, and political activity, would characterize the whole 19th and 20th centuries. It had a twofold influence on the Jews in Europe. In the first place, it aroused feelings in the general population in many countries of seeing the Jew again as a foreigner or stranger, but in a different way than before the Enlightenment. If he was a human being, as the slogans of the French Revolution had proclaimed, he was, however, not one of "our" people. The newly prevailing nationalistic ideas implied that France existed as home for the French, and that a homogenous, modern state could not tolerate another nation, i.e. the Jews, forming a nation within the nation. That this was intolerable was laid down in the famous words of one of the proponents of the emancipation, Count Clermont-Tonnèrre. During a session of the National Assembly in December 1789, he stated: "To the Jews as a nation, everything must be denied. To the Jews as human individuals everything must be granted." [54]

THE "HYPHENATED JEW"

Before the ideas of the Enlightenment and the French Revolution became part of the intellectual framework of larger parts of the European population, Jews had also been seen as strangers who adhered to another religion—not a completely unknown one, but a wrong one. In many countries or regions they were, in fact, the only foreigners. The awakening of national feelings on the part of nearly all peoples in Europe and their striving for the emergence of the nation-state required Jews to play down their separate ethnicity, the claim that they belonged to a different people than the majority. Many of them would even deny that claim. A Jew in France would be a Frenchman of the Mosaic creed. By analogy, a German-Jew (here the term "hyphenated Jew" comes into play)[55] would be a German citizen of the Jewish, or Mosaic creed. In Germany, a large number of Jewish citizens were members of the *Central Verein Deutscher Staatsbürger Jüdischen Glaubens* (Central Union of German Citizens of Jewish Faith.) This type of emancipation combined with the strong nationalistic tendencies in European countries, reached a dramatic peak during the First World War, which led to hyphenated Jews coming into deadly conflict with each other from opposite trenches.

THE BIRTH OF A NEW JEWISH NATIONALISM

The hyphenated Jew in the army uniform of a European nation was obviously not without problems. The false and frightening accusations of treason leveled against the French Captain Alfred Dreyfus, the terrible wave of anti-Semitism that swept France during his trial, and particularly the fact that people in high circles had used forgery to accuse someone who was an honest and completely assimilated Jew, made it a significant event, and not only in France. The intervention of Emile Zola eventually brought the case to an end, albeit not a very happy one. While Dreyfus was arrested in October 1894, it took until July 1906 before he was officially declared not guilty and was allowed to join the army again.

The whole affair had consequences out of all proportion to its own significance. They are still with us every day, and they are not pleasant ones. At the start of the trial in 1894, another hyphenated Jew, a highly assimilated Austrian Jewish journalist, happened to be the Paris correspondent of the Vienna *Neue Freie Presse*. His name was Theodor Herzl (1860-1904). The wave of anti-Semitism he saw sweeping across a country that was considered to be highly civilized made a deep and lasting impression on a man whose ties with Judaism were very tentative. He was conscious that his connection with the Jewish people was due to the shock of the anti-Semitism exhibited in the Dreyfus case, and expressed this in the following words: "The enemy forces us without any willful act from our side to become one people."[56] In fact, he saw no alternative to the Jews returning to a country of their own. In 1895, he laid down these ideas in a book entitled *Der Judenstaat* (The Jewish State).

When Herzl published this book, he was not aware that a Russian Jewish physician, Leon Pinsker, had published similar ideas as early as 1882.[57] While Herzl had been driven by the wave of anti-Semitism in France, Pinsker had written his book under the influence of the wave of Russian pogroms that began in 1881 in Elisawetgrad. They continued in 1882 and again in 1903 and 1905. These pogroms were supported by the repressive police state under Tsar Alexander III. This threat facing the Russian Jews was amplified by ever more restrictive laws limiting their chances for higher education. In consequence, more than 8,000 Jews immigrated to the United States in 1881 alone. Eventually, as many as three million immigrated to the U.S. up to 1914.

These numbers are illustrative of the despair that prevailed among the Jews of Eastern Europe, but this despair, mixed with new hope, also caused a much smaller stream of emigrants to head for Palestine. The ideological support for these first pioneers came from Moses Lev Lilienblum (1843-1910). He had made his name as a supporter of a reform movement of Jewish religious practice. As early as 1881, he published articles promoting the rebirth of a national home for the Jews in Palestine. At that time, this movement was known by the name "Palestinophily." The essence of his teachings was to pursue the colonization of Palestine so that within a century practically all Jews would have left hostile Europe to live in the land of their fathers, to which they were entitled.

CHAPTER 3

THE ALREADY-MARRIED BRIDE
What the History of Zionism Can Tell Us

THE FIRST ZIONIST PIONEERS

UNDER THE HIGHLY anti-Semitic rule of Tsar Alexander III, the number of restrictive laws in Russia continued to grow, making life for the Jews ever more difficult. In 1882, new restrictions about where Jews were allowed to live were introduced. Jews who lived in certain areas could be forbidden to return to their homes after they had been elsewhere for a time. This principle would often be applied even if the absence from the place of living were caused by military service—a highly cynical method of repression and humiliation. In many cases it was also forbidden to move from one village into another one. In 1887, more restrictive quotas were announced with respect to the number of Jews allowed to enter Russian schools and universities. Alongside the large emigration to the United States, the proponents of a national home for the Jews in Palestine also grew rapidly. In many places groups of Palestinophiles, or Friends of Zion, came into existence. The center of this movement was Odessa, where Pinsker and Lilienblum tried to set up an organization of territorial rebirth. In 1884, the representatives of these circles convened their first meeting in Katowice, now in Poland, but then part of Prussia.

In the spring of 1882, a number of Jewish young people, mainly students, started a group under the acronym

BILU, *Beit Ia'acov Lekhu U-nelcha* (House of Jacob, We Want to Depart) in Charkov. They had the idea of starting agricultural model farms in order to colonize the old home country. Soon, some hundred similar young people formed circles in other places in Russia, all with the idea of propagating the new colonization of Palestine. In June and July of that year, a few dozens of them left for Palestine. They were not welcomed cordially by the Arabs living in the country, let alone by the Turkish officials. In fact, the Turks prevented their landing in Jaffa, forcing them to disembark in Port Saïd, Egypt. Thus, they arrived in Palestine overland through the Sinai desert. As the Turkish government refused to provide these pioneers with a sufficiently large piece of land to begin the realization of their plan for colonization, most of them had to work as farm hands in existing settlements like "*Mikweh-Israel*," begun in 1870 by the Parisian "Alliance," a Jewish welfare organization. Others succeeded in acquiring a piece of land that would become the first agricultural settlement under the name "*Rishon le Zion.*"

The new-old homeland had to be conquered under harsh climatic and health conditions. For all of those idealists who had until then done only intellectual work, it was a difficult start. But it was also the very beginning of a new chapter in Jewish history. These first non-religious nationalist settlers were "the first sheep over the bridge" to enter Palestine. In Zionist history, this became known as the "First Aliyah," the first "move up" to a future in a Jewish homeland. The same year, two groups came from Romania, and in the next year new groups came from Russia. All this new agricultural activity on land that had not been cultivated for centuries required not only very hard work but also much capital. Fortunately, in 1884, the

Parisian banker, philanthropist and art collector, Baron Edmond Rothschild, helped by providing millions of francs of investment. Until the early 1890s, a difficult situation existed due to friction between the pioneers and the non–idealist administrators sent by Rothschild to supervise the way the money was spent.

Before Herzl published his epoch-making book, *Der Judenstaat* in 1896 and the First Zionist Congress in 1897, two events stand out. In Odessa, the two proto-Zionist pioneers Pinsker and Lilienblum were joined by Asher Ginsberg, who became famous under the name of Achad Haam through his writings on Zionist ideology. Unfortunately, or I should say tragically, his influence turned out to be all too limited. He had visited Palestine in 1891 and written an article under the title 'Truth from Palestine" in which one can read the following: "Jewish settlers treat the Arabs with hostility and cruelty, trespass unjustly, beat them shamelessly for no sufficient reason, and even take pride in doing so."[58] Chaim Weizman, one of the early pioneers of Zionism who was to become the first president of the state of Israel called it "a classic of Zionist history and literature."[59] Of the writer, he said: "For him Zionism was the Jewish renaissance in a spiritual national sense. Its colonial work, its political program had meaning only as an organic part of the re-education of the Jewish people." The other event was the foundation of an elementary school in Jaffa in the early 1890s, in which instruction was given in the New Hebrew language, *Ivrith*. This, together with the reconstruction and modernization of the old language, was mainly due to the huge effort of one man, Eliezer Ben Jehuda.

HERZL AS A CATALYST

In 1896, when Herzl's book appeared, the situation with respect to the Jews could be summarized as follows: In Russia, there was virulent anti-Semitism. It had already led to the emigration of large numbers of Russian Jews to the United States, and had also induced a small number of pioneering young idealists to start the colonization of Palestine. It also caused a relatively large group of young Jewish students with a middle-class background to escape the difficulties in Russia. They pursued their studies in cities such as Berlin, Zürich or Geneva, and formed Russian Jewish circles there. They cherished the ideals of the palestinophiles, whose centre was in Odessa. In Germany a strong but not yet virulent anti-Semitism was made intellectually acceptable by a popular professor of history, Heinrich von Treitschke, as well as by *Hofprediger* Stoecker and others. In Austria anti-Semitism was politically exploited by Karl Lueger, the leader of the Austrian Christian Social Party. Herzl, a completely assimilated and secularized Austrian Jew, had written *The Jewish State* under the impact of the anti-Semitic hysteria in France. Similarly, the book in turn made an immense impact on the young Russian students at the various universities of Western Europe. Chaim Weizmann describes this aptly in his autobiography:

> It was an utterance that came like a bolt from the blue. Fundamentally *The Jewish State* contained not a single new idea for us... We observed, too, that this man Herzl made no allusion in his little book to his predecessors, to Moses Hess and Leon

Pinsker and Nathan Birnbaum—the last a Viennese like Herzl, and the creator of the very word by which the movement is known: Zionism. Yet the effect produced by *The Jewish State* was profound. Not the ideas, but the personality which stood behind them, appealed to us. Here was daring, clarity and energy. There were also, as I have said, strong Zionist groups at the universities of Montpellier and Paris and elsewhere. It was from them that Herzl drew much of his early support. [60]

In August 1897, Herzl organized the first Zionist World Congress in Basel with two hundred delegates. Weizmann proudly quotes Herzl, who immediately after the Congress wrote:

> And then…there rose before our eyes a Russian Jewry the strength of which we had not even suspected. Seventy of our delegates came from Russia and it was patent to all of us that they represented the views and sentiments of the five million Jews of that country. And what a humiliation for us who had taken our superiority for granted! All these professors, doctors, lawyers, industrialists, engineers and merchants stand on an educational level that is certainly not lower than ours. Nearly all of them are masters of two or three languages, and that they are men of ability in their particular lines is proved by the simple fact that they have succeeded in

a land where success is peculiarly difficult for the Jews.[61]

Even so, according to Weizmann, there remained a deep rift in the approach to Zionism between the Western Jews and those from Russia. He wrote:

> Yet, with all this intuitive perception, this generosity of understanding, Herzl could not remake his own approach to Zionism. How much less possible was this for the smaller men who surrounded him! The Zionism of the Westerners was to us a mechanical and so to speak sociological concept, based on an abstract idea, without roots in the traditions and emotions of the Jewish people. We, the unhappy Jews of Russia, were to be sent to Palestine, by them, the emancipated Westerners. And if Palestine was not available, well—some other territory had to be found. We were vindicated in our attitude towards the Western leaders when at a crucial moment in Zionist history—following the Kishinev pogrom (1903)—Herzl attempted to substitute Uganda for Palestine as a temporary palliative measure. The fact that the heart of Jewry was fixed, by every bond of affection and tradition, on Palestine, seemed beyond the understanding of the Westerners.[62]

Jewish Nationalism

However true this sentimental tie of the Jews with Palestine might be, there is another truth not taken into account by these warm quotations from Weizmann's book. It cannot be illustrated more compactly than by the following anecdote related by Avi Shlaim in his book, *The Iron Wall*, as follows:

> After the Basel Congress the rabbis of Vienna decided to explore Herzl's ideas and sent two representatives to Palestine. This fact-finding mission resulted in a cable from Palestine in which the two rabbis wrote, "The bride is beautiful, but she is married to another man." [63]

In a time of ever-increasing nationalism, and with the last battle against Native Americans in the United States having occurred not more than twenty-one years before, such news concerning the presence of the Arab population of Palestine clearly did not make a decisive impression. As quoted by Dubnow, Herzl wrote that he considered the Jewish problem not as a social or religious one, but as one of nationality:

> We have to transform this problem into a political world problem that will be solved in consultation with the *cultured* [my italics] peoples. We are a PEOPLE. We are ONE people. [64]

To what an extent nationalism at that time was considered to be a positive force, and how far Herzl thought that this force could and should be exploited, can be seen from the following text quoted by Dubnow as an answer to Baron Hirsch, who doubted that Herzl would ever succeed in his endeavor:

> With a flag [as the symbol for a nation] you are able to lead people to any place you want, even into the promised country. They live for a flag and they die for a flag, in fact a flag is the only thing for which they are prepared to die in masses if they are educated to do so. Do you realize how the German *Reich* came into existence? It was constructed out of dreams, songs, fantasies and black-red-gold colored ribbons. [65]

With such nationalistic thinking, it is easy to understand that Herzl believed that the Palestinians would welcome the Jews into their country and bring prosperity with them.

JEWISH SOCIALISM

By the turn of the century, quite a number of secularized Jews in Western and Central Europe were active in various socialist parties. In particular, the Marxist versions were popular. The Divine messianism was now substituted by a messianism that claimed to be based on social science. It promised a beautiful world where social differences would disappear and anti-Semitism would be eliminated. It is significant that, in Eastern Europe, and to a certain extent also in the Netherlands, a Jewish Workers' union, the *"Bund"* was formed. Here, without giving up their own Jewish identity, socialist ideas could be pursued. In fact, the number of secularized Jews who believed that socialism would be the more promising way to bring about the elimination of anti-Semitism was larger than the number of those who thought that Zionism would bring liberation from this curse. Many of those who did embrace Zionism tried to combine it with the ideals of the socialists.

From 1903 till 1907 a number of new pogroms occurred in Russia, causing a second wave of immigration into Palestine during the years 1904-1914. This wave consisted of 40,000 mostly young idealists, collectively known as the "Second Aliyah." These highly motivated pioneers often combined the ideals of Zionism with those of socialism. They were convinced that only by working hard under the harsh conditions prevailing in the country could the Jewish people leave behind its problems. They no longer wanted Arab workers, paid by Rothschild's money, to do the hard work. They tried to realize their socialistic ideas in practice by establishing the first cooperative farming community, in the form of the Deganyah Kibbutz, in 1910.

JEWISH SELF-HATE

Until the second half of the 19th century, almost all Jews in central and Western Europe lived in sequestered quarters—the ghettos. In most countries, they gained full citizenship rights only toward the last third of the 19th century. The transition from a pre-industrial society, in large part controlled by the Church, to modernity was a complex historical process. This transition was borne along by the increasing awareness of national identity, which did not tolerate a Jewish nation within a larger national state, and pseudoscientific race theories, which were now coming into fashion. Hatred of Jews came to be grounded no longer primarily in religion, but rather in certain race-specific characteristics that were ascribed to them.

Thus, anti-Semitism during this period was based on the assumption that the negative and hateful characteristics ascribed to the Jews were a manifestation of their deepest nature. This was "classical" post-Enlightenment anti-Semitism. Whenever we rode the streetcar in Germany during the Hitler era, my father always said, "Quiet, children, or else people will say, 'Those Jews are always so noisy!'" He didn't realize that when we heeded his admonition and whispered to each other, the passengers would think, 'Those Jews are always so secretive!' For dyed-in-the-wool anti-Semites, Jews were simultaneously Bolshevist revolutionaries and capitalist exploiters, upstarts and parasites, filthy vermin and dandies.

The phenomenon of self-hate began to manifest itself in some emancipated Jews of the first and second generation, that is, among Jews who still had one foot in the old ghetto but who wanted to enter what appeared to be a larger, more open society. Relatively successful Jews were affected when their less successful colleagues and competitors responded to their success with envy and rejection. In fact, the rapid social rise of the Jewish *parvenu* was grist for the mill for "scientific" anti-Semites, who saw further proof of Jewish pushiness and ambition—both negative racial traits, among an arbitrary number of others—in the Jews' efforts at economic self-betterment. Their success was proof that they intended to rule the world. Jewish religious ceremonies, which Christians found alien, were perceived as oriental and primitive at the time. And the largely impoverished ghettos, in which the fathers and grandfathers of the first emancipated Jews continued to be rooted, elicited shame in them, and even disgust in some of them.

Life outside the ghettos brought the Jews into close contact with Western non-Jewish culture, and as a consequence, with the new racial theories, which distinguished between higher and lower human races, and from which racists derived the "fact" of Jewish inferiority. Some Jews actually internalized this defamation. Because, according to these twisted theories, every action taken by a person belonging to an inferior race was by definition a negative one, anti-Semites (and self-haters as well) had no second thoughts about ascribing the most contradictory characteristics to Jews. Thus, they could be simultaneously accused of pushiness and obsequiousness, slovenliness and dandyism, cowardliness and aggressiveness, ruthlessness and exaggerated patriotism.

Those whom we now view as self-haters accepted these prejudices as fact. They began to believe in their own inferiority. The problem lay not in their behavior, but in their nature. The self-hate of Jews who actually suffered from this self-doubt was an expression of their own internal conflicts. On the one hand, a new world was beckoning with all its novel possibilities. On the other hand, they encountered enmity based on ancient prejudices, fear and envy, and last but not least, the notion propagated by the new anti-Semites and their self-hating Jewish converts that Jews were by nature inferior beings.

THE JEWS: HELPLESS VICTIMS FOR NEARLY TWO THOUSAND YEARS

Much happened in the lives of Jews between the destruction of the Second Temple in 70 A.D. and the Israeli victory over the Arab states in the spring of 1948. But in one respect, their position remained the same throughout this period, in spite of all changes. They were always weak, oppressed, discriminated against and, above all, without any political power whatsoever. In Europe, they were a small minority, well educated but relatively poor except for a scant upper class. In the German conglomerate of small principalities, there were a scattered few wealthy court Jews who represented the financial interests of their rulers, a few of whom achieved prestige and personal influence.

Emancipation, when introduced in the mid-19th century, resulted in a slightly more prominent role being played in public life by Central and Western European Jews. In Germany, the percentage of Jews prominent in the sciences, literature, theater, music, journalism, self-employed professions, and the middle class was significantly higher between the final decades of the 19th century and 1933 than in the rest of the population. One or two percent would have been commensurate with their population figures, but in reality their numbers were much greater. The claim that they wielded more power as a result of their proportionally greater presence in the higher professions, however, is an old wives' tale that was effectively exploited in anti-Semitic propaganda. Many professions, many a career, and many a club or association remained closed to them. Their political influence was insignificant. The Auschwitz tragedy occurred in the context of this political powerlessness. No one in the world truly advocated for them during the Holocaust.

Thus, for nearly two thousand years, the Jewish people did nothing wrong. Classical anti-Semitism was primarily independent of what Jews did or did not do. What was despicable about Jews to anti-Semites was essentially their presence, not their deeds. In fact, for a real anti-Semite, everything a Jew did was bad simply because a Jew did it. If this statement is essentially true, and I am convinced it is, it follows logically that the onset of the Holocaust could not have been prevented by any action of the Jews. In other words, the Holocaust was the result of historical forces far beyond the Jews' control—the accidental mixture of the reaction to the Treaty of Versailles after World War I, the crazy German hyperinflation that followed, the economic world crisis, and personality of Adolf Hitler, all coming together with devastating consequences.

In contrast to this view of the Holocaust as an accident of history stands the Zionist myth that the high degree of assimilation of the German Jews contributed to the end result. It cannot be denied that this assimilationist tendency did create individual identity problems for a number of German Jews. But if the question is whether the Jews in Germany and other parts of Europe could have done anything at all to mitigate the tragic events of those years, the answer must be resoundingly negative. The only thing that might be said is that American Jews might have been able to do more for their co-religionists during the later stages of the Holocaust.[66] Plans to save their lives were rejected by the U.S. State Department, as well as by the Zionist organizations.[67]

Today, especially since the Israeli-Arab war of 1967, the situation has completely changed. The essential difference that alters the perspective of any real or alleged anti-Semitic event is the existence of a politically and militarily powerful state of Israel. For the first time in nearly 2,000 years, there is once again a Jewish political center of power that plays a not inconsiderable role in the political equilibrium of nations. Just think of the current tensions between the West and the world of Islam. The current influence of Israel upon the only remaining superpower, the United States, is disproportionately great. Jews, both in Israel and in the Diaspora gain from this a sense of security that may turn out to be false.

ZIONISM AS IDEALISM

The history of Zionism is complex. From its inception, it contained impressive positive elements, as well as equally negative ones. It is not my purpose here to provide anything approaching an adequate account of it. The idea of a Jewish state, which is the focus of Zionism, should be viewed as the reaction to the anti-Semitism that haunted Europe for nearly two thousand years. While Christian anti-Semitism dates back to the time of the Church fathers, in the wake of the French Revolution and the gradual secularization that followed, pseudoscientific theories became fashionable. From these, Hitler and his ideologues brewed their blood-and-soil ideology.

Zionism evolved into a vital idea when successive pogroms took place in Russia and Eastern Europe, one of the main centers of Jewish population, and when such occurrences as the Dreyfus Affair in France brought the virulence of anti-Semitism into focus. The early Zionists believed that only the founding of their own state would provide lasting protection to the Jews and put an end to anti-Semitism at last. From 1906 onward, the establishment of such a state was unquestionably approached with extraordinary effort, clever political scheming, and a considerable amount of idealism. This idealism, in particular, needs to be mentioned, since it ran counter to a deep stereotype about the Jews, explicitly expressed by the man who considered himself the greatest expert on this subject, Adolf Hitler. In *Mein Kampf*, Hitler wrote:

> For if the Jew's instinct of self-preservation is not smaller but larger than that of other peoples, if his intellectual faculties can easily arouse the impression that they are equal to the intellectual gifts of other races, he lacks completely the most essential requirement for a cultured people, the idealistic attitude.[68]

THE MASS CONVERSION TO ZIONISM AFTER 1933

Many Jews, like myself, who in their early youth were not educated in line with Zionistic ideals, eventually altered their views. We were still young, and living under the frightening measures taken by Hitler's regime against the Jews, so it was natural for our views to change. In fact, some of the restrictive measures of the Nazi regime were consciously enacted in order to stimulate the Zionist orientation of young German Jews, when anti-Jewish measures alone did not suffice for this purpose. Hitler didn't want young Jews in anything other than Zionist youth organizations. Thus, he prohibited the activities of non-Zionist Jewish youth organizations such as the one I had been associated with before 1936, which the German Jews who were proud of their achievements for the sake of their German homeland—the majority of whom had fought on the German side during the First World War—had founded.[69] These people, like my parents, were not able to change their anti-Zionist views so quickly. They could not imagine that the whole Hitler drama could last for long, but it did. By

1937, however, they ceased to show contempt towards me when I came home from my Zionist youth group, which by then was the only youth organization that I could attend.

The Zionist cause was naturally advanced after the Second World War when the dimensions of the Holocaust became known. The large majority of the Jews, wherever they were in the world, were more or less converted to Zionism, especially after the proclamation of the new state by its first prime minister, Ben-Gurion, on May 14, 1948. In that proclamation two important principles were explicitly expressed. At that moment, so soon after the shock of the great catastrophe, there was the extremely important announcement that the Republic would be open to all Jews who wished to enter. Here then, at last, was a safe haven for Jews who might be persecuted whenever and wherever in the world. An important part of the Zionist dream had come true. The other principle creating hope for the future was the stated intention that the new state would extend full social and political equality to all its citizens without distinction of religion, race or sex, and would guarantee freedom of religion, conscience, education and culture to all.

A RADICAL REMEDY: REVISIONIST ZIONISM

Lack of idealism was not the only anti-Semitic claim to be proven wrong by the Jewish pioneers. One of the key ideas of Zionism in general, and of its extreme right-wing in particular, and exemplified by the revisionist Betar youth movement from which emerged Israeli prime ministers Begin and Shamir, was the renewal of the Jewish race. As Martin Gilbert describes it:

The Betar youth movement, founded in 1923, was emerging as the principal advocate of a militant Zionism, and as an uncompromising opponent of the Zionist-Socialist youth groups. With its red-brown uniform, Betar was criticized by mainstream social scientists as having a "fascist character," reminiscent of Mussolini's Blackshirts.[70]

Evidently something must have been very wrong with the Jewish race for the leader of the movement, Vladimir (Ze'ev) Jabotinsky to include the song "Betar" in his songbook in 1932, a year after becoming its leader, with the following lines:

> *From blood and sweat a new race will arise,*
> *Proud, generous, and cruel.*
> *Lift yourself out of your comfortable freedom,*
> *Sacrifice your soul and blood…to win or to die*
> *For the sake of greatness never seen before.* [71]

The traditional tendency was for Jews to debate everything passionately down to the last detail, or as the anti-Semites used to say, "to fight it out like in a Jew school." Jabotinksy rejected this, saying:

What we Jews have to learn above all is to move in unison—to march in step, to strike as one.[72]

Or in the same vein:

However, the highest levels of civilization are reserved for those who, once having become aware and proud of their individuality, have the strength to control their will if necessary so as to fall in step with the nation, to act together with millions of others as if they were one single person, one single machine.[73]

This way of thinking is deeply at odds with what most Jews consider to be the fundamental values of Judaism, in particular, the ethics of brotherliness and humaneness, which the Torah expressed in its commandments. The ancient prophets, Rabbi Hillel, and the German Reform rabbis championed this ethical tradition. It incorporated concepts like sympathy, compassion, respect for others including strangers, freedom of thought, and the desire for peace, which comprise the most important elements of Judaism. Most Jews in Germany and in the Austro-Hungarian Empire supported this view during the hundred years prior to the Holocaust. Thus, there can hardly be any other interpretation of Jabotinsky's views other than that they were a gross over-compensation for the Jewish thinking that prevailed at the time, a radical form of self-hate.

It is striking that Zionists like Jabotinsky, in particular, opposed all attempts by Jews to assimilate completely. Even if assimilationism were itself a different form of self-hate, it would certainly have been preferable to the aggressive and racist variant represented by Jabotinsky and his followers. Today, however, we are faced with an Israeli state in which this aggressive variant of self-hate is widespread.

THE INVERSION OF STEREOTYPES

AS WE HAVE seen, one of the stereotypes about Jews quoted from Hitler's *Mein Kampf* was that Jews were incapable of acting out of idealism. If any assertion in history was ever false, it was this one. In fact, for many decades after 1910, the Israeli kibbutz was an object of admiration by a large number of non-Jews because there, ideals were often practiced with considerable success. Another stereotype that prevailed was the myth that Jews were too cowardly to be good soldiers (notwithstanding the good performances of Jewish soldiers in various armies during the First World War). It is a bitter irony that both these stereotypes have been completely inverted by history. The negative aspects that are always latent in any impressive achievement often win out, and in the case of the pioneering years of Zionism, many of its achievements have been subsequently distorted, perverted, and negated.

An example is the classical kibbutz. This was, before the occupation of the Palestinian territories, based on two separate principles. On the one hand, it was an idealistic commune in which personal interest was sacrificed for the common goal, a homeland for a dispersed people. On the other hand, it was also meant to be an armed, but defensive, fortification against intruders from neighboring Arab countries. Nowadays this has been changed by the ever-growing paranoia of the majority of Jews in general, and of Israeli Jews in particular (admittedly with somewhat more justification), so that the kibbutz exists mainly in a highly perverted form as an aggressive occupying settlement in Palestinian territory.

Also turned on its head with frightening thoroughness was the idea that Jews were unfit for military tasks. Evidence of the military craftsmanship and personal fighting spirit in battle among Israelis of all ranks had been demonstrated clearly in the various wars that occurred between 1947 and 1973, but the inversion of the stereotype that can be said to have laid the basis for the present vicious circle of oppression and humiliation through state terrorism by the IDF (Israel Defense Force) and the murderous terrorism of Palestinian desperados has an even longer history. The same acts of terrorism against unarmed civilians—including targeted assassinations of important people—so highly criticized as a threat to Israel today, were perpetrated by Jews years before Israel came to existence, and are nowadays a specialty of the Israeli Army.

With the exception of the most spectacular examples that could not avoid the light of publicity, little of this has become common knowledge. One of the spectacular cases was the huge bomb that the Irgun used to blow up a wing of the King David Hotel in Jerusalem on July 22, 1946,[74] an act of Jewish terror in which ninety-one unarmed civilians lost their lives. It is much less well known that that between 1936 and 1939, when the Arab uprising took place, the Irgun carried out terror attacks in Arab neighborhoods of the type that Israel nowadays criticizes with so much indignation. These are left out from most accounts of the early history of Israel, but are recorded in Weizmann's autobiography, although he tries to play them down as much as possible:

> It [a British report] looked very much like incitement of Jews to terrorism, and the human thing happened when a dissident Jewish minority broke ranks at last in the summer of 1938, taking its cue from

the Arabs—and from the administration.[75]

Simha Flapan, in his book *Zionism and the Palestinians*, is more explicit in his description of Jewish terrorism:

> Members of the Irgun launched terrorist attacks on civilians causing an escalation of violence at an unprecedented scale. It can be said that the Irgun established the pattern of terrorism adopted 30 years later by Al-Fatah. Among its actions was the wheeling of a vegetable barrow containing a bomb into an Arab market in Jerusalem, the firing at a bus, and throwing bombs into market places (Jerusalem, Haifa). [76]

Another military perversion, the "targeted killings," became notorious by the murder of Count Bernadotte, the United Nations mediator, on September 17, 1948.[77] It was performed on the order of a Stern Gang triumvirate, including Yizhak Shamir, who later became Prime Minister of Israel. Writing about this group in 1943, he stated: "Terrorism is for us in the first place part of the political battle which we fight under the present circumstances. It plays an important role...in our war against the occupier.[78] Less well known, a similar murder had been perpetrated four years earlier on the British Lord Moyne. At that time, one of the most prominent Zionists, Chaim Weizmann, said the following about this crime: "I can hardly find words adequate to express the deep moral indignation and horror which I feel at the murder of Lord Moyne. I know that these feelings are shared by Jewry throughout the world."[79] He further expressed his bitterness and frustration in the following words:

Here and there a relaxation of
the old traditional Zionist purity of ethic,
a touch of militarization, and a weakness
for its trappings; here and there, something
worse—the tragic, futile, un-Jewish resort
to terrorism, a perversion of the purely
defensive function of Haganah.

Thus wrote the man who a few years later became
the first President of the young Jewish state. In view
of these little known facts, the moral indignation about
Palestinian terrorism that is so often heard in Israel cannot
be said to be devoid of false notes.

ZIONISM IS AN ANACHRONISM

Zionism in its basic form is largely the result of three
confluent forces: anti-Semitism, nationalism, and
colonialism. A number of secondary forces and currents
also played a role. These included humanistic socialism, a
secular and nationalistic fascism, and an array of religious
tendencies, such as a form of fundamentalism that agitated
for a Greater Israel. After World War II, nationalism and
colonialism receded into the background on the world
stage, at least in their more aggressive and martial forms,
but 9/11 changed that. Within Western Europe, only
marginal politicians like Le Pen agitated for a return of the
19th century nation-state with slogans like "France for the
French."

Although the classical nation-state cannot be
revived, Zionism as it exists in the here and now (as
represented in the policies of the State of Israel) has
hardly separated itself from its 19th-century progenitors.

In fact the opposite has been the case, particularly since the 1967 Six Day War. According to former Attorney General Michael Ben-Yair, the Israeli government has since 1967 decided to openly and unashamedly reveal the colonial nature of its rule over the Palestinians and the apartheid regime it has set up in the occupied territories.[80] He and other critics of the Israeli government view the current situation as a massive regression compared to the first nineteen years of Israel's independence. Certainly, the Arab states played a considerable role in the deteriorating situation, beginning with their rejection of the partition of Palestine on November 29, 1947, and the dramatic lack of feeling for diplomacy, public relations, and propaganda that they have demonstrated ever since. Zionist leaders were able to skillfully exploit the Arabs' rejection of the partition, but in 1967, when Israel had the opportunity to decide on a less aggressive policy after the Six Day War, it consciously chose the road of permanent occupation.

A number of important critics of Israeli policies have come to the conclusion that even the fundamental idea of Zionism is an anachronism. The idea of a Jewish state in a Jewish country, a nation-state according to the ideals of the 19th century, is simply untenable for a country with pretensions to being a Western nation in the 21st century—particularly when the achievement of this goal requires ethnic cleansing. The examples from the Balkans are a horrifying example, and the perpetrators from that conflict are answering for their crimes before the International Tribunal in The Hague. Ethnically homogenous states such as Japan and Finland can, with some justification, still consider themselves nation-states, but in spite of the attempts of certain marginal groups, the multiethnic, multicultural society has become the standard model for the foreseeable future

In 1917, when the Balfour Declaration ceded the right to a national homeland in Palestine to the Jews, the percentage of Jewish settlers was less than ten percent of the population. In spite of the flight and expulsion of approximately 700,000 Palestinians,[81] and despite the massive influx of Jewish immigrants, even today approximately 20% of Israelis are Palestinian. Thus, the idea of a Jewish democratic state is a complete anachronism. A nation-state of the old type would only be possible after a new round of massive expulsions of Palestinians, and making Israel both Jewish and democratic could be achieved only by effectively denying the non-Jewish portion of the population democratic rights. That would mean maintaining a colonial regime of apartheid, as has been the state of affairs since 1967.

The Democratic Jewish State

The Zionist pioneers were passionately engaged people. Theodor Herzl, its spiritual progenitor, came from a completely assimilated family, and was interested neither in Jewish history nor in the Hebrew language. With only slight exaggeration, it might be said that the only thing he really knew was that Jews in the Diaspora had continuously endured persecution, even in modern times, in spite of the fact that the French Revolution had proclaimed equality and fraternity for all. It is interesting that he was born and lived in the only large European country that was then a multiethnic and multicultural nation. The Austro-Hungarian monarchy was a multiethnic state with German-speaking Austrians, Hungarian-speaking Magyars, Serbo-

Croatian-speaking Serbs and Croats, Slovenian-speaking Slovenes, and Czech-speaking Czechs. Many of the more educated Jews had studied in Vienna and appeared to be much more integrated than they were in fact. Just how serious the nationality problems bubbling beneath the surface were only became clear on June 28, 1914, when a Serbian nationalist assassinated Austrian Archduke Franz Ferdinand, triggering World War I.

Herzl apparently never sensed the undercurrent of tension between these nations, and therefore never anticipated the national antagonisms that might arise. In his 1902 novel *Altneuland* (Oldnewland), published six years after *The Jewish State*, he described an idyllic society in which Jewish immigrants lived in peace with the original inhabitants of Palestine. One of the characters, a Muslim named Rashid Bey, was introduced as follows:

> He studied in Berlin. His father was among those who immediately comprehended the advantages of Jewish immigration. He participated in our economic rise and became rich.[82]

And the same Rashid says to a Christian, who is amazed that Muslims do not view the Jews as intruders:

> Would you consider a person a thief who takes nothing from you but brings something? The Jews have enriched us, why should we be angry with them? They live with us as brothers, why should we not love them?[83]

THE FABLE OF ZIONISM

The fact that history did not turn out so idyllic is certainly not the fault of one party alone. It was a highly improbable event that the world at large might eventually accept the return of the Jews to their land of origin after nearly 2,000 years of exile. It required a human catastrophe of a hardly imaginable dimension to bring this about. After World War II and the catastrophe of the Holocaust, the survivors who found refuge in that country had deep psychological reasons to feel threatened. Palestinian resistance was completely underestimated from the outset, by the British, the Americans, and the Jews themselves, and this attitude reflected their contempt for indigenous non-European peoples—a widespread colonial attitude. To quote Martin Buber, another renowned early Zionist:

> When we returned to Palestine, the decisive question was: Do we want to come there as an ally, as a friend, as a brother, as a member of the coming community of peoples in the Near East, or as the representatives of colonialism and imperialism?[84]

In spite of the romantic ideals and elevated language in the new state's declaration of independence, a truly democratic structure was not created. The reason for this was that the overweening influence of Orthodox Jewish parties prevented the complete separation of church and state, that is, of religion and government. Even today, only a rabbi can conclude a marriage. A civil marriage, as such, does not exist in Israel.

The desire of most Jewish Israelis to have their own

state depends crucially on the existence of a clear Jewish majority in the population. A number of measures and laws were created to disadvantage non-Jews. For example, Jews all over the world enjoy a "right of return" to their "homeland," but a Palestinian born in present-day Israel does not possess this right. A non-Jewish foreigner married to a Palestinian Israeli has to clear all manner of legal and bureaucratic hurdles before he or she becomes an Israeli citizen. It is the declared goal of Israel to keep the Jewish proportion of the population much higher than that of other ethnic groups. However, the Arab birth rate is far higher than the Jewish rate, which creates a "demographic problem," sometimes referred to as the "demographic time bomb." As a result, within a few decades, Jews may be a minority in their own country.

This state of affairs is totally unacceptable to Jewish nationalists. It is shameful to note that right-wing politicians and radical rabbis have spoken openly about mass expulsions or deportations of Palestinians. The debate has been conducted in such sharp terms that close to 150 Jewish academics and scientists felt compelled to send an appeal to the international community, warning that the Israeli government might use the impending war against Iraq to commit further crimes against the Palestinian people, including comprehensive ethnic cleansing.[85] While this fear proved to be premature at the time, the mere consideration of such plans is the quintessence of racism. One need only read Israeli newspapers or listen to Israeli radio to understand the extent to which such groups have infected Israeli discourse.

However, the problem is anything but new. In an article published in *The Guardian*, well-known and once progressive Israeli historian Benny Morris explained that as early as 1895, Theodor Herzl, the prophet and founder of Zionism, wrote in his diary in anticipation of the establishment of the Jewish state:

> We shall try to spirit the penniless [Arab] population across the border by procuring employment for it in the transit countries, while denying it any employment in our country... The removal of the poor must be carried out discreetly and circumspectly.[86]

Future prime minister David Ben-Gurion in 1937 hailed the recommendation of the British Peel Commission regarding expulsions. According to Morris:

> A "clean and final" solution of the Palestine problem necessitated transfer, the commission ruled... By the end of the 1948 war, some 700,000 Arabs had been displaced—to become "refugees," in the jargon of the day.[87]

The idyll described by Herzl in *Altneuland* was never more than a convenient fable.

CHAPTER 4

THE BLINDING EFFECTS OF HISTORY
What the Experience of Trauma Can Tell Us

THE EFFECTS OF TRAUMA ON THE WRITING OF HISTORY

THE PROMINENT GERMAN historian Leopold von Ranke once asserted that that a historian, in recounting historical events, should neither judge nor lecture, but merely present things as they actually occurred. According to our modern sensibility, however, this is quite impossible. The British historian Arnold J. Toynbee recorded how his view of history was significantly changed by his experience in the First World War, and thus how differently he read and understood Thucydides' account of the Pelopponesian War after Great Britain entered the war in 1914:

> I was re-reading [Thucydides] now with a new perception—perceiving meanings in his words, and feelings behind his phrases, to which I had been insensible until I, in my turn, had run into that historical crisis that had inspired him to write his work. [88]

Von Ranke seems to have been unaware that one cannot avoid filtering the historical events of the past through one's mind. The mind is shaped and sensitized by historical events during a person's life. This holds even more true the more traumatic the events through which one lived were. Thus in appreciating, reading and, especially, writing about history, one must be aware of those experiences which influence one's judgment. In fact, one's mind may be sensitized to certain phenomena in history that are similar to traumatizing events, which one has gone through oneself.

In my opinion, however, another claim that Ranke and other historians make regarding the writing of history has a great deal of validity. Historians must try to locate themselves within the times they are researching. It is impossible to comprehend the past using the moral yardsticks of the present. Take, for example, the not inconsiderable role that the Dutch played in the slave trade. It would be ahistorical to base one's judgment of this phenomenon on present-day ethical norms, when in fact it occurred during a period in which the concept of the equality of all human beings was yet to be formulated. This concept of equality is based on ideas that were first articulated a hundred years later, during the Enlightenment, and did not achieve anything close to universal acceptance until after World War II. We therefore have to be very careful about judging, and particularly about condemning, people in the past based on today's norms, especially when dealing with the Holocaust, which was so utterly unimaginable an event. It is absurd, for instance, to accuse ordinary Germans of not having prevented something that they could not possibly have foreseen.

THE FORGOTTEN YEARS OF MARGINALIZATION AND HARASSMENT

Although it is unfair to judge situations and people of earlier times from the perspective of the present, it is completely justifiable and sometimes even useful to examine present-day conditions and political events on the basis of historical understanding. Because history never repeats itself precisely, however, caution is indicated when attempting to predict future developments on the basis of historical parallels. It is only natural for me, given my background and history, to compare current events with those that took place between 1933 and 1939. Of course, there are also certain risks and challenges associated with such an approach.

One such challenge is that it is difficult to convince people that the automatic association between "Germans" and "World War II" with "gas chambers" and "Holocaust" is ahistorical. The conventional view not only overlooks important parts of that history; but it also neglects how people actually experienced the period in which they lived. On the basis of my own experience and historical facts, I can claim that tragedies were played out even before the mass killings took place. I refer here to the lives of democrats, socialists, communists, and others who opposed Hitler, as well as, of course, the Jews. These tragedies are so bleached out by the systematic genocide pursued by the Nazis after 1942 that the terrible events that came before them are barely acknowledged. Hence, it is a challenge to raise any comparison between present-day practices of discrimination on the basis of ethnicity and the same sorts of practices that occurred under the Nazis before the great mass murders of the Holocaust took place.

The dramatic events during World War II have seriously and enduringly traumatized several generations. Although mass murders have been perpetrated on other peoples before, and some are occurring even today, the Holocaust was exceptional in its size, scope, and the rapidity and efficiency of its execution. Only tiny fractions of the sizable Jewish populations in Central and Western Europe survived. A very few survivors tried to build up a new life in their native countries, but many went to the U.S., Canada, or other countries overseas, and about 120,000 immigrated to the newly founded state of Israel.[89] Hardly any of these survivors were not severely traumatized, first of all due to their own experiences during the Holocaust, and then due to the realization that large numbers or all of their pre-war relatives had not, in contradistinction to themselves, survived. This engendered a new trauma known as survivor's guilt.

Those who survived the Holocaust in Europe were, in general, the ones with the strongest traumatic experiences. They were, however, not the only ones. Jews that had escaped Europe just before the war, or even decades before, also mourned the tragic loss of those relatives who had not escaped. This large-scale acute mourning by these survivors was in itself a traumatizing experience. The harmful effect was accentuated even more for those who felt, rightly or wrongly, that they had not done enough to help those who had remained in occupied Europe. Many Gentiles in the Western world also felt that they had not done enough to prevent or mitigate this tragedy. Thus, they too were traumatized to some degree by the events that led to the murder of so many millions under their very eyes. This was primarily true of many Germans, but also of quite a number of ethically conscious people throughout Europe.

This traumatization of Jews and Gentiles has led to a dangerous blind spot in the mind of today's public. Most people, when they think of Hitler's regime, immediately associate it with mass murder on an industrial scale. The first seven years preceding this mass murder, in which the

German public was systematically prepared to accept the increasing humiliation, pauperization and dehumanization of the Jews, are greatly neglected, if not totally forgotten. The Hitler regime is for all practical purposes fully identified with the gas chambers used for mass murder, rather than with the suppression, violence, discrimination, and theft practiced against the Jews and other political opponents in the years leading up to the so-called "final solution."

It is important to understand that the "final solution" of the Jewish question was planned and decided upon as late as the beginnings of 1942. While during the nearly nine years of Hitler's virulent anti-Semitic regime prior to that date, the discrimination and harassment of the Jews in Germany became increasingly humiliating and unbearable, it can be proven that at least until January 1939, Hitler's aim of this policy was no more (but also no less) than to make life for the Jews living under his regime so difficult that they would all leave Germany.[90] This gradual marginalization of the German Jews, from 1933 until the notorious "*Kristallnacht*" pogrom in November 1938, was very skillfully done. The significance of this is that if the methods used then to gradually rob the Jews of their status as citizens and reduce them to mere pariahs were more generally known, similar methods in use against other peoples today would attract more attention.

THE EFFECTS OF THE HOLOCAUST TRAUMA ON ISRAEL

The Holocaust was the unimaginable and unexpected end result of one and a half millennia of systematic anti-Judaism. The primary force behind this was the Christian Church, which determined the attitude towards the Jews for more than a millennium. This terrible outcome was, however, certainly not part of the original intentions of the Church. Many other historic forces had to come together for this to occur. Two of the most important contributing factors were the deep humiliation of Germany after the First World War and the devastating economic and social after-effects that came in its wake. The theologically based anti-Judaism of the Church was transformed into a racially based anti-Semitism at the end of the 18th century, and it was under the influence of this racial ideology that the crimes of the Holocaust were carried out.

The effects of the Holocaust have been devastating on at least three, if not many more, generations of the Jewish people.[91] This holds true for many Jews living in Israel, for a large part of those living in Europe, and also for an appreciable number of those in the United States. Most of all these traumatized people have a European background, if not themselves, then within one or two generations. They all come in some way from decimated families. They have either undergone unimaginable experiences themselves, or they have heard about the horrors that their relatives, some dead, some still alive, experienced. This second-hand information apparently leaves much room for fantasies, so that what is imagined is sometimes even worse than what really happened.

It is therefore understandable that trans-generational traumatization can often be at least as potent as that of the first generation. Those who experienced the Holocaust first-hand as adults or adolescents had at least experienced more or less "normal" formative years, while subsequent generations owed their upbringing to parents who had already been traumatized. The consequence of all these psychologically damaged individuals spawning new generations, which also carry the signature of their trauma, is so great that it seems to have engendered a collective paranoia in the Jewish people as a whole.

The trauma inflicted on both Jews and Gentiles by the atrocities of the Second World War, and successfully exploited by the leading Zionist politicians of the day, constituted the most important factor leading to the establishment of the State of Israel in 1948. Many Jews at the time, including myself, were convinced that if a Jewish state like Israel had existed in the early '30s, many of those German Jews who were eventually killed might have been saved. The guilt felt by many Gentiles caused them to agree at the end of 1948 to split the Palestinian mandate area up in two parts, one for Palestinians, the other one for the Jews. At the time the Arab countries did not accept this division—a historical fact that, in the Zionist narrative, is still brought forward today to excuse the present stalemate. After the convincing and definite victory of the Israeli army in 1967, Israel's policy shifted from a seemingly defensive to an overtly expansionist one.[92] Israel occupied the whole of Palestine and imposed an oppressive apartheid on the occupied territories.

That the Israelis were not really interested in a fair peace was exposed by its reaction to an initiative from an Arab summit in Beirut on March 27, 2002, which the Sharon government condescendingly rejected. The fact that there was no outcry against this from the Israeli public can be attributed to the suicide attacks carried out by Palestinians in Israel proper, as well as to skillful Israeli propaganda. Although these attacks represent one of the very few weapons the Palestinians have and are not nearly as murderous as the deadly Israeli incursions into the Palestinian cities, they are at least as counterproductive. As Napoleon's minister Joseph Fouché said after the execution of the Duc d'Enghien, in whose arrest he was instrumental: "It was worse than a crime; it was stupid." Similarly, the Palestinian suicide attacks are worse than crimes; they are extremely self-defeating, since they are exploited to the utmost for political purposes by Israeli propaganda.

In the same way that the "final solution" is seen as *pars pro toto* (a part taken as the whole) of Hitler's policy toward the Jews, the term "anti-Semitism" has also been taken as representing more than it actually does in today's world. As a consequence, many traumatized Jews are fearful when they hear that anti-Semitism is growing again. On the other hand, Gentiles fear accusations that they are motivated by anti-Semitic feelings if they dare to utter criticism of Israeli policies, however much those policies go against accepted humanitarian principles and international law. In this way, Israeli politicians manipulate both Jews and Gentiles, and influence world opinion. Israeli propaganda uses the fear of the still traumatized population by suggesting that, just as during the Holocaust, the whole world is against the Jews and that the Palestinians are the new Nazis who want to subject the Jewish Israelis to a second Holocaust by pushing them into the Mediterranean Sea. That this is indeed believed by large parts of the population in Israel and the world has nothing to do with reality and everything to do with fear and guilt, which in turn are the result of trauma. As the Israeli historian Idith Zertal writes in her book *Nation and Death*:

> With the help of Auschwitz—Israel's ultimate trump card in its relations towards a world, which time and again was defined as anti-Semitic and forever hostile—Israel immunized itself against

any criticism and allowed itself a status of quasi-holiness, in this way it closed itself off from any critical and rational dialogue with its surroundings.[93]

Those who think that all this is exaggerated should be reminded of the words of no one less than the former prime minister of Israel, Menachem Begin, who initiated the invasion of Lebanon in June 1982. He defended the beginning of this tragic failure in the Knesset, the Israeli parliament, with the following words:

> It is our destiny that in the land of Israel there is no other way than to fight with fierceness. Believe me, the alternative to that would be another Treblinka and we have decided that there never will be a second Treblinka.[94]

In my opinion, this type of talk represents a shameless and tactless exploitation of collective traumatic experiences by Zionist leaders, the aim of which is to cover up criminal deeds of aggression towards another people. It is also deeply ironic, since the large majority of those Jews who were murdered during the Holocaust were more antagonistic than sympathetic towards the whole Zionist enterprise. The majority of those coming from Central and Western Europe were enlightened modern citizens with humanitarian ideals who would turn in their graves if they knew how their suffering is being exploited for aggressive Zionist purposes.

THE HOLOCAUST AS THEOLOGICAL PHENOMENON

We have seen that traditional Judaism considers the remembrance of catastrophes that have been part of Jewish history as God's commandment. From the point of view of the mental health of the Jewish people, this is nothing less than a disaster. It has led to the collective paranoia of the majority of the Jews in Israel and the Diaspora. This paranoia in turn is probably the most important factor that has prevented Israeli politicians from having a clear view of the political situation there. Thus, the commandment to remember the mishaps of the Jews in history has led to a situation that may now be called disastrous. Eventually it will with great probability lead to even more calamity.

It should be noted that this remembrance is obviously an activity (and not a healthy one as we have seen) that requires a certain amount of religious practice from those who regularly obey this commandment. In a secularized age, their number is relatively limited. Much larger, however, is the number of those who characterize themselves as being Jewish, or as having a Jewish background, and who identify themselves without any publicly uttered criticism towards Israeli policy. They belong to a new type of Jew that was described by the French Jewish philosopher Alain Finkielkraut as early as 1980. His parents were Holocaust survivors and, as he writes, he saw himself as "doomed by identification, martyr by proxy, survivor through my parents." I quote from the German edition of his book, *The Imaginary Jew*:

> To be a Jew implied, at least for me, to have the right to usurp sufferings that I had not undergone and, due to the destiny of my people, to escape from

> the mediocrity of my actual life. Judaism
> for me meant just a bit of suffering and
> tragedy as a spicy addition to the banality
> of my everyday life. [95]

In this way, the Holocaust provided a new dimension to the life of post-war Jews and to the history of Jewish suffering.

One of the first thinkers to claim an absolute uniqueness for the Holocaust was probably Emil L. Fackenheim, a rabbi and professor of philosophy at the University of Toronto. In his 1982 book, *To Mend the World*, he wrote:

> The possibility that the Holocaust
> might be a unique and unprecedented evil
> in Jewish and indeed ALL HISTORY [my
> emphasis] I did not consider seriously until
> more than two decades after the demise of
> the Third Reich. [96]

In analyzing this sentence I cannot avoid the impression that here the theologian in him prevailed over the philosopher or historian. In fact, uniqueness is primarily a theological term, in that God is unique and every human being, having been created in the image of God, resembles Him in that they are unique, as well. As commentary on history, the remark is void of meaning, because, as any historian knows, history never repeats itself completely. Every historical situation is unique. One of the earliest Greek philosophers, Heraclitus, formulated this insight in his famous saying: "*pantha rei*," or "everything is always in flow," or, "you can never step into the same water of the river." As Fackenheim, a professional philosopher, doubtless knew this very well, it is clear that his remark about the uniqueness of the Holocaust can only be understood in a theological context.

The Holocaust has thus been transformed into a phenomenon of theological dimensions. Elie Wiesel has pursued this process of making the concept of catastrophe often epitomized by the word "Auschwitz" the basis for a new religion. In a book by Maurice Friedman, a good friend of Wiesel's, we find the following quotations from various parts of Wiesel's work, *Against Silence*:

> In the beginning is Auschwitz; it is the unavoidable starting point...
>
> For me as a Jew of this generation the Holocaust is the yardstick...
>
> Nothing should be compared to the Holocaust but everything must be related to it. [97]

It is possible that these short quotations from the work of Elie Wiesel were primarily meant to be very personal remarks, to illustrate how he sees the world after his traumatic experience in Auschwitz. Even so, they were not formulated carefully enough to prevent a number of followers making a religion out of his words. Thus the aforementioned Maurice Friedman writes: "The Holocaust is a unique and incomparable event that has never happened before and will never happen again." [98] This is a theological statement, which within the discipline of history is devoid of any meaning.

Critical historians and philosophers, such as the Belgian Gie van den Berghe, have come to the same conclusion. He writes in his book, *The Exploitation of the Holocaust*, about this claim of uniqueness:

In fact they [those who make that claim] just want to be granted a completely separate status, they want that the Judeocide be acknowledged as the worst thing that ever happened to human beings. They claim the role of the victim in the absolute and purest form. The Holocaust is in the words of Emil Fackenheim in 1977 the only example of the Absolute Evil. [99]

Finally, the theological dimension attributed to Auschwitz is very clear in this quotation from Emil Fackenhiem's *God's Presence in History*, which contains lectures he gave in 1968:

> Elie Wiesel has compared the Holocaust with Sinai in revelatory significance and expressed the fear that we are not listening. We shrink from this daring comparison—but even more from not listening. [100]

As previously mentioned, historical events have no intrinsic meaning and therefore do not, in themselves, contain a message. Any meaning one claims to read into such an event, or to hear from it, has to be attributed to the event by the "listener." Unfortunately, when I listen to the signals that this dramatic event in Jewish history sends out, I hear completely different sounds from it than large parts of the Jewish world do. Nor do I get the impression that the majority of Jews are listening. In my personal opinion, this majority has misread the message to be gleaned from this "new Sinai experience." They are following Elie Wiesel's recommendation to use the Holocaust experience as a yardstick in a wrong way. Using this yardstick, every crime against humanity so far perpetrated by Israel against the Palestinians seems smaller than what the Jews experienced. So, what they hear tells them to continue as they have been doing. It tells them that they can still have a clear conscience because they are not as bad as others have been.

What I hear is different. It tells me to see that I never become like the perpetrators, and to never use the Auschwitz phenomenon as a yardstick, because it is too extreme to be used like that. It tells me, instead, to be always aware of the most fundamental ethical command in Judaism, which is the famous summary of Hillel: "That which is hateful unto thee do not do unto thy neighbor. This is the whole of the Torah. The rest is commentary. Go and study."[101] How fundamental this saying was considered, even in Israel, as late as 1974, can be seen from the fact that an Israeli "Pocketbook" on Jewish values puts it on the very first page.

IRRATIONAL FEARS

A majority of the Jews in Israel, and also many in the Diaspora, firmly believe that the Palestinians, with or without the help of the rest of the Arab world, have nothing else in mind than "driving them into the sea." This fear, regularly expressed in Jewish circles inside and outside Israel, is only marginally related to reality. Of course, Palestinian or Arab extremists express this threat often enough, just as Jewish extremists and some of the members of the Israeli government utter corresponding threats about the deportation of all Palestinians. The Jewish fear is not realistic, however, for two reasons. In the first place, even if the Arab states were ever to unite, they would not have the military strength to carry out such annihilation when matched against the military might of Israel. In the second place, this fear ignores pertinent declarations of the Arab world to the contrary.

The last important one of these Arab peace proposals, by all means a fair one, came from the Arab summit on March 27, 2002, in Beirut. Given the intentions of Ariel Sharon, at that time head of the Israeli government, it is not surprising that his government reacted only condescendingly. What is puzzling, however, is that this important initiative did not lead to large public demonstrations in the streets of Israel's cities. The Israeli propaganda machine may be partly responsible for this lack of response, but it is certainly not the only cause. The Jewish public in Israel is so deeply steeped in its paranoid, yet comforting, conviction that "we always have been and we still are the victims," that the media remained relatively silent on this dramatic and historic step on the part of the Arab world. Public opinion in Israel can be expressed by the common assertion that "The Arabs want to drive us into the sea" and the equally ubiquitous myth created by Barak at the time of the above-mentioned Arab initiative, that "There is no one to talk to."

Two millennia of persecution leading up to the Holocaust caused many Jews to feel that no people suffered as much as they did. The Jewish tradition of memorializing plays an important part in this feeling. The constant, justifiable fear of Palestinian suicide attacks reinforces it, adding yet another chapter to the history of Jewish suffering. Claiming a monopoly on suffering automatically implies that the suffering of others is belittled. Concretely, that means the suffering of the Palestinians' fate is made even more oppressive. Recognition of an injustice suffered will diminish the suffering, while denying or belittling it makes it worse.

Claiming a monopoly on suffering also has a demoralizing effect on Israeli soldiers, making them even more brutal than they would be as a result of the permanent state of war. The frequently harsh and inhumane actions of Israeli armed forces, brought about by this combination of effects, has harmed their reputation beyond the borders of Israel. The same applies to Jewish citizens anywhere in the world who withhold all criticism, thus giving the impression of complete approval of any actions taken by the Israeli government and military. Meanwhile, the Israeli attitude that nothing is as bad as what Jews experienced in the Holocaust causes them to defend the harsh treatment of the Palestinians with the argument: "Sure, we are not always nice to them, but compared to what was done to us, they have it good."

REMEMBRANCE AND SEQUENTIAL TRAUMATIZATION

If I were forced to characterize the qualities of Judaism in a few words, one of them would certainly be "remembrance." As David Groskies writes:

> In Judaism, memory is a collective mandate, both in terms of what is recalled and how it is recalled. From the Deuteronomic injunctions to "remember the days of old" (32:7) and to "remember what Amalek did to you" to the persistent theme of remembering "that you were slaves in Egypt," the content of Jewish

memory has been the collective saga as first recorded in Scripture and as later recalled in collective, ritual settings. [102]

Jewish history is so full of persecution, exile, destruction and death, that this mandate of remembrance naturally signifies for many Jews an intense preoccupation with these negative experiences. It is significant that the most sacred place of Judaism is the "Wailing Wall" which is said to have been part of the Second Temple, destroyed by the Romans. Given this tradition of ritual remembrance of persecutions, expulsions, and pogroms, in addition to all the negative experiences recorded in the Torah, for an event of the dimensions of the Holocaust to occur was perhaps more than the emotional resilience of the collective Jewish soul could cope with. I presume for the moment that relatively little is known about the differences between an individual's coming to terms with traumatic events and the same process as undergone by a large, heterogeneous group such as the Jewish people. [103]

It is plausible to imagine, however, that the recent collective suffering, added to the tradition of ritual remembrance of old wounds, and including the mourning of new losses, could strongly amplify the traumatic effect. [104] This concurs with a theory based on clinical experience with Jewish Holocaust survivors after the Second World War conducted by a Dutch psychiatrist of German-Jewish origin, Dr. Hans Keilson. He called his idea the theory of "sequential traumatization." In brief, it states that the traumatizing effect of a threatening experience on an individual is greater in proportion to the number of traumatizing experiences that have preceded it.

A PROPOSED EXTENSION OF KEILSON'S THEORY

An extension of Keilson's theory is called for, however, in order to account for the truly pathological preoccupation with the Holocaust and other disasters from the past, as well as for the paranoid feelings and fears that haunt so many Jews. According to my proposed extension of this theory, so many previous sufferings of the Jewish people are time and again collectively remembered in ritual settings, that they serve the same role as the previous traumatic experiences. Collective remembrance thus acts as fresh trauma. Since the number of previous traumatic experiences that the Jewish people have suffered throughout history is so large, and as observing Jews have to remember many of them so often, the amplification of trauma is very great indeed. This, I feel, explains the strong tendency towards paranoid feelings on the part of so many Jews.

A somewhat amusing example of this paranoia can be found in *Ha'aretz*, which quoted the following conversation between then Prime Minister Ariel Sharon and Foreign Minister Shimon Peres. Israel's foreign relations were his responsibility, Peres said, complaining that the government's lack of policy was setting "the whole world against us."

"The whole world has always been against us," Sharon said.

"So maybe we should leave the world," Peres replied cynically.[105]

A less amusing example, which shows how deep this paranoid feeling has penetrated into the collective Jewish soul and how it is misused for political purposes, occurred in November 2002. A number of ultra-orthodox zealots had thought it necessary to pray in the "Cave of the Patriarchs" lying in the middle of the Arab quarter of Hebron. They had been protected by armed guards from the settlements and had all returned to their homes. As the last of the armed guards were returning, they were attacked in a well-planned ambush by a number of Palestinians. In the ensuing fight, twelve guards were killed. On November 19, 2002, *Ha'aretz* wrote about this event as follows:

> Ultra-orthodox newspapers concocted a description of a pogrom against Jewish worshippers, as if everything had happened in a small town in Galicia and the Polish officers had turned their backs while the Cossacks committed a massacre. The settlers are deliberately choosing terminology from the Diaspora. They are consciously creating a distorted comparison, between the distress of weak Jews in the face of cruel non-Jews who carried out pogroms, and the situation in the territories.
>
> Now they have once again succeeded in diverting the debate from the question of their residence in Hebron... via a frightening description of an attack on innocent worshippers [while no worshipper but only armed guards from the settlements were attacked] and there is nothing better than this for stirring up the nation's most painful memories. Brothers, the village is burning. The Jewish people are in danger. [106]

It is striking, in this example and the many similar

ones that can be found in the print media, how these frightening pictures from a hundred or more years ago are evoked and misused. That this can be done so successfully, it seems to me, can be explained by my proposed extension of Keilson's theory. Paranoia is a highly exaggerated form of fear. It is dangerous and self-defeating, even though in the case of the Jews, this fear has an indisputable basis in history. However, any fear (and certainly an exaggerated fear) leads eventually to reactions that are self-fulfilling, and therefore counterproductive. We should note that in the 1870s Nietzsche was aware that too good a memory could have devastating consequences:

> The joyfulness, the good conscience, the happy deed, the trust in what comes next, all that depends for the individual as for a people on the question whether there exists a line which separates the expected development, the bright side, from the dark side which cannot be foreseen. It depends on whether, on the right moment, one is able to forget as well as that one is able to remember when the right moment has come. It depends on whether one deeply feels when it is necessary to be aware of one's history and when it is indicated to forget about it... Both non-historic and historic faculties are equally necessary for the health of an individual as for that of an entire people or culture. [107]

Bearing this wisdom from Nietzsche in mind, there seem to exist real problems with the collective mental health of the Jewish people. The root of this may be buried deeply in the mandatory remembrance that is at the heart of the Jewish culture.

CRITICISM OF ISRAEL

Unfortunately, a majority of the world's Jews in the Diaspora uncritically support Israeli policies. An appreciable number of them work together with Christian fundamentalists who are as uncritical of Israel as the most radical extremists there. Together, these two groups have gained a considerable influence on the present administration of the U.S. and its current president George W. Bush.[108] Thus, it seems that there is little external influence to keep Israel's policy towards the Palestinians in check—a dangerous situation indeed. As pastor John Hagee proudly claimed recently, "The sleeping giant of Christian Zionism has awakened. There are fifty million Christians standing up and applauding the State of Israel."[109]

For those Jews who can no longer support Israeli policies uncritically, this situation poses deep problems. In many countries of Europe, such Jews have organized themselves in various national organizations that together try to gain strength via their coordinating organization, EJJP (European Jews for a Just Peace). Contact with similar organizations on the other continents is still in the process of developing. This movement developed primarily out of concern for the continued existence of Israel, but the increasingly egregious behavior of the IDF in the occupied Palestinian territories has led to greater shame and frustration on the part of the members of its constituent organizations. Unfortunately, the accusation that the majority hurls at those critical of Israeli policy is that they are "self-hating Jews," and in so doing, they ignore the old wisdom that only those who truly understand their strengths can have the courage to admit their weaknesses.

This accusation of self-hate is simply absurd. Many of the members of this movement are proud of their Jewish heritage and of the important contributions that Judaism has made to the key ethical and social ideas that animate Western civilization. They are convinced of the important and beneficial role that Israel could play in the Middle East. The prerequisite for this, however, is that both the Israeli state and Israelis themselves give up their paranoid ghetto mentality and respond in a more moderate and nuanced manner to Palestinian attacks. The fear in Jewish circles of criticizing Israel publicly because the *"goyim"* might exploit this supposed disunity, however, is a prime example of what I mean by a ghetto mentality.

Ultimately, I can't reconcile silence about the current state of affairs with my conscience. What is going on in Israel is painful, deeply tragic, and shameful. While the Dutch journalist Max van Weezel[110] has taken issue with the notion that Jews should feel shame at the crimes committed by Israel,[111] good, reasonable, and patriotic Dutchmen felt ashamed after World War II for their senseless and anachronistic war in Indonesia. The same holds true for many American citizens with regard to the Vietnam War. If one belongs to a community and crimes are committed in the name of that community, then shame—which develops out of a combination of connectedness with that community and human ethics—is not only legitimate but also called for.

CHAPTER 5

DÉJÀ-VU, OR THE NIGHTMARES OF A JEW BORN IN GERMANY
What the Situation in the Occupied Palestinian Territories Tells Us

A TRAUMATIZED PEOPLE TAKE POWER

IT IS DIFFICULT to bring up such a touchy subject as the parallels between the methods used by Israel to suppress the Palestinians and those that I experienced as a second-class citizen in Germany and occupied Holland at the hands of the Nazis, yet such parallels are inescapable. To understand these parallels, it is necessary to understand that they have their roots in the experience of collective trauma or perceived injustice. The German people among whom I grew up were stigmatized, if not traumatized, by their calamitous defeat in World War I, the economic exhaustion and political and social upheavals that ensued, and the forced signing of what they felt deeply was a shameful Versailles peace treaty. The conditions of that treaty were not only outrageous, but they were a grievous error. They paved the way for Hitler, who at the beginning of his regime managed by skillful maneuvering to achieve great economic and political successes. The German population responded to this with renewed pride and self-confidence. As a result of utter compliance on the part of the Western democracies that permitted Hitler one bold coup after another, such as the occupation of the Rhineland and the annexation of Austria, he and his henchmen, as well as a large percentage of the population, came to believe that they could do whatever they wanted in terms of forcing their will upon their neighbors.

Of course, the trauma inflicted on the Jewish people by the Holocaust was even more drastic and enduring. The guilt felt by the world for allowing this crime to occur led to the UN resolution of November 29, 1947, which provided for the partition of Palestine and created the preconditions for the founding of a Jewish state, whose independence was proclaimed on May 14, 1948. We now know that from the very birth of the new state, its armed forces were much better equipped and trained than all of the Arab armies put together. Moreover, the Israelis had prepared a plan to ethnically cleanse the area of the new state of its Arab indigenous population as thoroughly as possible. Still, the Zionist dream of being in possession of the whole of Palestine had to wait until June 1967. In that month, Israel won a decisive victory against its Arab neighbors and conquered the entire region up to the Jordan River. The Palestinian territories, which had been administered by Jordan and Egypt after the armistice of 1949, were now occupied by Israel. This convinced many Israelis, and in particular many politicians that they could do whatever they wanted. They could even force their will upon their neighbors.

ENCIRCLEMENT COMPLEX AND SACRED SOIL

One thing was clear to the Nazis: the deep humiliation of the German people caused by defeat and the Versailles Treaty must never be repeated. The new war, which Hitler and his cohorts were preparing, had to be made palatable to the German people. The slogan *"Volk ohne Raum"* (a people without space) was made to order. Germany, surrounded by enemies, had to fight for "*Lebensraum*" (living space) in Eastern Europe in order to ensure the necessities of life. The lost eastern regions had to be re-conquered. Historically, they justified this conquest by invoking the example of the Teutonic Knights, who rebuilt Krakow and other cities in the 13th century after the Mongols had sacked them.

The Jewish people in general, and Jewish Israelis in particular, also express the understandable wish never to experience anything like the Holocaust again. Unfortunately, this desire takes the form of an "encirclement complex." They feel that they are living in a country that is too small for them, just as the Nazis did. Even if this feeling is somewhat justified given their country's small size, the call for more space is morally indefensible in the world today. Moreover, with today's modern weaponry, it no longer makes sense on strategic grounds, either.

The National Socialist *Volk ohne Raum* ideology went hand-in-hand with the "*Blut und Boden*" (blood and soil) myth, according to which each square meter of earth is sacred. Such extreme thinking also exists in Israel, in particular among the settlers and their ideologues, the extremist rabbis. They, too, promote notions of the sacredness of the soil to resist peace initiatives such as the so-called Roadmap for Peace, while expanding their settlements to the east. The historical justification for annexing "Judea and Samaria" goes back to Old Testament times.

The Israeli resistance to the Roadmap for Peace is not in the least affected by the skimpiness of the concessions granted by this plan, according to which Israel must cede to the Palestinians what is, in essence, a collection of non-contiguous Bantustans. At a conference that took place in Jerusalem on June 23, 2003, which was attended by about 500 rabbis belonging to the so-called Federation for the People of Israel and Land of Israel, former Sephardic Chief Rabbi Mordechai Eliyahu stated:

> No one in the world, from drawers of water and hewers of stone to prime ministers, has the right to give up one grain of the Land of Israel. The Holy One, blessed be He, gave us the Land of Israel. There is holiness in every single grain.[112]

The Federation issued the following declaration:

> No government has the authority to declare the establishment of an alien state or to abandon parts of the Land of Israel to aliens, and everything that is done to this end is null and void in the name of God, the Lord of Israel, who has sworn this and in the name of the entire people of Israel throughout the generations.

EXAGGERATING THE THREAT

German propaganda and thinking in the 1930s ascribed to Jews a power out of all proportion to reality, when in fact their power was practically nonexistent. Nonetheless, Hitler was obsessed by the idea that Jews were planning to sweep Germany from the map by means of "plutocratic capitalism" and/or Bolshevism. Nothing illustrates the absurdity of this notion better than a joke that circulated among German Jews in the aftermath of *Kristallnacht* in November 1938:

--Have you heard? They've imposed a new collective punishment on us.
--No, what for?
--We Jews have threatened the German Navy. A Jewish baby carriage rammed a German battleship in the port of Hamburg.

In spite of the seriousness of the situation in which the Palestinians permanently find themselves, I thought about this old joke when I read what Chief of Staff of the Israel Defense Forces General Moshe Ya'alon said in an interview in *Ha'aretz* on August 30, 2002. Asked whether he thought "the goal of Arafat and of Fatah was to liquidate Israel by stages," Ya'alon replied, "Of course!"[113] Ya'alon's paranoid exaggeration of the enemy's power is comparable to the way German anti-Semites exaggerated the Jewish threat. Like any other delusion, it has tended to intensify over time. A mere three years earlier, Ya'alon's predecessor, Ehud Barak, Israel's highly decorated military commander and former Prime Minister stated that:

> The Palestinians are the source of legitimacy for the continuation of the conflict, but they are the weakest of our adversaries. As a military threat they are a joke.[114]

The fear, used to defend Israeli policies, that an independent Palestinian state could threaten the very existence of Israel, one of the great military powers in the world today, must thus be interpreted as little more than a ghetto reflex elicited by paranoia. Israelis, too, regularly talk about Jewish paranoia, as reflected in an article by Shulamit Aloni:

> "So who are we afraid of? The
> Palestinians? Isn't that a bad joke? But
> we aren't allowed to say that because our
> Jewish paranoia is very serious, and the
> public relations people of the army and the
> greedy of the Greater Land of Israel know
> how to manipulate it very nicely."[115]

In fact, Israel has one of the strongest militaries in the world. After roundly defeating Arab armies in several wars, it now inspires such awe that its neighbors don't dare come to the aid of their oppressed Palestinian "brothers." The only threat that Israelis really have to fear is suicide attacks, which cannot be addressed militarily. This by no means justifies terrorist acts against innocent civilians. What I am concerned about here is that while Israelis claim that Palestinians have both the intent and capacity to push Israel into the sea, with or without help from their Arab neighbors, the Israeli occupation, and the humiliation and oppression that go along with it, ensure that increasing numbers of Palestinians will be driven into the welcoming arms of extremist organizations. As Yishai Rosen-Zvi, one of the Israeli soldiers who refused to serve in the occupied territories, said after years of experience:

> "Fight terrorism? Don't make
> me laugh! Our army is ensuring that
> the occupied territories remain a
> breeding ground for misery, poverty, and
> hopelessness, a breeding ground in which
> terrorism thrives."[116]

Collective Responsibility, Punishment, and Blame

One of the most characteristic methods used by the Nazis to force their will on a population was the principle of "collective responsibility." What this meant can be easily illustrated by relating how it was put into practice by some teachers as a method of disciplining the pupils in the schools. If, for example, the principal of a school noticed something that he didn't like in a particular class, the entire class would be punished. In line with the Nazi doctrine, "All for one, one for all," the basic idea was that each individual was responsible for the behavior of all students in the class. If one student got in trouble, all of them were held accountable, because they should have watched out and prevented it. The collective responsibility of groups whom the Nazis viewed as enemies was a basic component of their totalitarian ideology. As a result, this notion became an essential part of the indoctrination that the regime imposed on the German people.

Collective responsibility contradicts the most fundamental principles of a democratic legal system, according to which each citizen is responsible for his or her own acts alone. One notorious example of this practice from the Nazi period was so-called "family arrest." If one family member did something that displeased the regime, an arbitrary number of family members would be arrested.[117] Unfortunately, Israel today frequently applies collective responsibility, and accordingly imposes collective punishment. For example, if a Hamas member blows himself up, all Palestinians in a particular region will be denied entry into Israel for several weeks or longer, or they will be placed under house arrest. As a result, completely innocent civilians are denied work and income. If the suicide bomber is identified, his house, in which three or more generations of his family may be living, is blown up.

Another form of collective responsibility is collective blame. According to this practice, an entire population is blamed for the crimes committed by their country. Jews and others who suffered directly or indirectly from Nazi violence still tend to attribute collective blame to completely innocent Germans, simply because of their nationality. According to J. L. Heldring, a longtime *NRC Handelsblad* columnist:

> There is still... a tendency to react to the suffering of innocent people who had anything to do with the Nazis—German women and children who were raped or killed in bombing raids, or children of collaborators—with the remark, "Serves them right!" or "They have only themselves to blame!"[118]

This tendency to allocate collective blame is extremely complex, but a few general observations with respect to it are in order. The collective responsibility of individual citizens for atrocities committed by their government is directly proportional to the freedoms that they enjoy. Conversely, the responsibility of individual citizens decreases as those freedoms are taken away—particularly where dictatorship has resulted not from democratic processes, but from military or political overthrow. The more freedom of the press, the more average citizens can learn about the offenses or even crimes committed by their politicians. The more the freedom of expression is guaranteed, the more easily citizens can express their dissatisfaction.

Conversely, it required extraordinary courage and even defiance in the face of death to express one's opinions in a police state like the Soviet Union under Stalin, China under Mao, or Germany under Hitler. It would be wrong to demand such courage of the average citizen. Those who have shown this kind of civic bravery—the Sakharovs or the Scholls, for example—are heroes in the finest sense of the word. We cannot condemn people who are unable to show such heroism. Only when a regime demands that a citizen commit a crime like murder or torture can we justifiably expect resistance.

Virtually none of the apologists for current Israeli policies—regardless of how questionable these may be or the extent to which they violate human rights—miss an opportunity to praise Israel as the only democratic state in the midst of despicable Arab dictatorships. Inasmuch as the democratic rights of the Jewish citizens of Israel are concerned, this is still largely true. A newspaper like *Ha'aretz* routinely reports on the cruel treatment of innocent Palestinian citizens in the occupied territories. Israeli soldiers can still refuse to take part in the oppressive occupation, although this stance is becoming increasingly more difficult in practice. Citizens can still read about excesses caused by the occupation, such as when a kidney patient or expectant mother is unable to get to the hospital because of a roadblock, often with fatal consequences, or—far less dramatic, perhaps—when young people are unable to attend school, which has terrible consequences for their future. Israelis may also read that Palestinian casualties are a multiple of those suffered by the Israelis.

Thus, precisely because of the media freedoms they still have, Israeli citizens share greater responsibility for the excesses of their government. Palestinian suicide bombings have played a major role in pushing Israeli public opinion to the right, but Israeli citizens can still read about the excesses committed by their own army and the suffering of Palestinians, and take to the streets in protest. If they fail to do so, for whatever reason (and here the suicide attacks almost certainly play a role), they will not be able to evade their share of responsibility for the misdeeds of their government.

The Dehumanization of the Enemy

We have seen how the Germans labeled the Jews as a foreign body in their culture, and that prominent Israelis promote the same view of the Palestinians. Still, as long as people are talking in terms of "another culture," the enemy is still a human being, even though of a different stripe. But demonization of the enemy goes much further. We know from Roseman, among others, that whenever Hitler talked about the Jews his language was "filled with metaphors of plague and parasites."[119] Hitler thought of the Jews as maggots, vermin, a toxic bacillus, and so forth. This form of demonization—the complete dehumanization of the enemy—crosses a line. Once this stage has been reached, leaders can authorize whatever discriminatory policies they want without significant protest because then, the people in the society assume they are no longer dealing with actual human beings who have human feelings and respond to the loss or death of a relative as they do.

Moshe Ya'alon, for instance, was interviewed while he was Chief of Staff. Questioned by the interviewer about why he saw "the Palestinian threat as an existential threat," Ya'alon's answer was: "The characteristics of that threat are invisible, like cancer… I maintain that it is cancer." Asked whether what he, as Chief of Staff, did in the West Bank and Gaza was chemotherapy, his answer was: "There are all kinds of solutions to cancerous manifestations. Some will say it is necessary to amputate organs. But at the moment, I am applying chemotherapy [to the Palestinians], yes."[120]

BETRAYAL FROM WITHIN

From the point of view of the Nazis, the traumatic defeat in World War I could not possibly have been caused by Germany's own failings, which is why the "stab in the back" legend was born. The only reason Germany lost the war was because traitors, weaklings, and profiteers within the Fatherland had fatally undermined the fighting spirit of Germany's brave troops.

Likewise, the Israelis do not attribute their own failure to strike a decisive blow against the Palestinians to any errors committed by the government or their military leadership. Although they are trying in vain to fight a popular uprising by conventional military means (something that has never been done successfully, by the way), that is not how Israel's leadership sees matters. In the interview cited above of August 30, 2002, Chief of Staff Ya'alon stated:

> You stand and try to contain [the other side], but they are shooting at you from all directions, and people from your side come and undermine you. Absolutely undermine you.

By "people" he meant members of the Israeli peace movement, and the Israeli peace bloc Gush Shalom, in particular. This is the classic "stab in the back" legend, transposed onto Israel almost a hundred years later.

THE THREAT OF DEPORTATION, ECONOMIC PRESSURE, AND HUMILIATION

All Polish Jews living in Germany were deported to Poland between October 26 and October 28, 1938. Many of them had lived for years in Germany and felt at home there. The alienation, existential insecurity, and humiliation of such deportation represented a traumatic experience that can hardly be overstated. My own forced emigration to the Netherlands, which literally occurred in the matter of a day, left deeper marks on me than did the ten months I spent in Auschwitz five years later. I still dream about hastily packing my things in my parents' apartment. Fortunately, by contrast, I almost never dream about the concentration camp. The deportation of Polish Jews from Germany so affected the son of a deported family who happened to be living in Paris named Herschel Grynszpan that he murdered Ernst von Rath, a diplomat with the German embassy there. The Nazis used this assassination as the pretext for their most notorious application of collective punishment, the countrywide pogrom known as *"Kristallnacht."*

Even aside from the deportations, the constant economic pressure brought to bear on the Jews to force their emigration from Germany became increasingly intolerable. The prohibition on practicing certain professions and the boycott of Jewish stores greatly exacerbated existential fear. SA members stood in front of stores and tried to prevent non-Jewish customers from entering. If we try to visualize this set of circumstances, we may be better able to imagine what the destruction of houses, the increasing threat of deportation, and the arbitrary limitation on their freedoms must mean to the Palestinians. Analogous economic pressure has been exerted on them, as well, as when fanatic Jewish settlers have prevented them from harvesting olives, which occurs quite frequently. Under the headline "Settlers Attack Palestinian Olive Harvesters, Kill One," *Ha'aretz* reported on October 7, 2002:

> [This is] the latest in a series of such attacks, Palestinian residents said.
>
> Speaking off the record, Israel Defense Forces officers confirmed that a group of young settlers in the area has been deliberately attacking Palestinian olive harvesters, and that the army has taken no real measures to prevent it.[121]

For me, this represents a truly distressing parallel to the behavior of the SA. Other memories from those years are stirred up when I read an editorial like the one below in *Ha'aretz*:

> Of all the grave and ugly developments on the fringes of settler society, none is more frightening than acts of Jewish terror, whose perpetrators attack Palestinian targets, primarily schools in East Jerusalem and the West Bank, without hindrance... The targets are chosen carefully—and abominably, they are children... In light of the impressive successes of the security services in foiling Palestinian terror attacks over the last two years, the failure of the Shin Bet's Jewish department demands a more convincing explanation than those that have so far

been offered.[122]

Such a report reminds me of a Purim celebration for children in 1935 or 1936 that was broken up by the SA. Complaints to the police didn't help at that time, either.

We are all too familiar with photographs of Germans in their immaculate uniforms making fun of destitute and frightened Jews. Jews in Germany could count on such humiliation at the hands of the authorities and their fellow citizens. The intimidation and harassment at Israeli checkpoints is not much different from what I experienced in my youth. I will never forget what I went through in this regard, even though it is no longer particularly painful. What I do find painful, however, is the knowledge that the Jews, who are my own people, are involved in similar humiliation of Palestinians. Salomon Bouman, the former Israeli correspondent for *NRC Handelsblad*, used the term "pogroms" to refer to the sweeping discrimination and collective punishment carried out against Palestinians in Hebron in the spring of 2001.[123] This event that, in itself, was sufficient to nullify the proud ethical tradition of Judaism. On November 1, 2000, *Ha'aretz* published an article by the Israeli journalist Amira Hass, entitled "The Mirror Doesn't Lie." The article concludes with the following challenge to Israeli Jews: "Take a good look at yourselves and see how racist you have become."[124]

ISRAELI POLICY AFTER 1967

In 1967, few saw that Israel, by erecting settlements and retaining the occupied territories, was following the wrong (one might even say fatal) path. The Oslo Peace Process, begun in 1993, caused even the few who openly criticized the settlement policies to hope for a positive outcome. In the Diaspora, a clear condemnation of Israeli policies was rarely heard from Jews. On the contrary, uncritical partisanship became a reflex for most. An important representative of this attitude has been Elie Wiesel who, as an Auschwitz survivor, world-renowned author, and recipient of the Nobel Peace Prize, is widely and highly respected. Although he should have known better, he did not wish to make public pronouncements about war crimes committed by Israel. In September 1982, he defended this stance in an interview, arguing that it was expressly not up to the Jews to evaluate Israeli policies. They should merely bear witness to what they have suffered.[125]

Such an attitude would, of course, have been perfectly understandable in the first decades after World War II. It would never have occurred to me, for instance, to criticize the policies of the young state before 1967. The great catastrophe of the Holocaust was still too recent to allow me to distance myself from it. Now that these traumatic events have moved farther away, however, it seems less and less acceptable to the non-Jewish world to cover everything with the cloak of charity. Anyone who believes that ethical standards need to be upheld in politics, even during a state of war, will find it increasingly difficult to accept the actions of the Israeli government without criticism, even if Israeli propaganda claims that this is a necessary and unavoidable reaction to Palestinian terrorism.

It goes without saying that the Palestinian suicide attacks on defenseless citizens are pure terrorism, and as despicable as any other kind of attack on unarmed civilians outside the occupied territories. But they have more than their counterpart in a cruel occupation, a containment wall built to run through the occupied territories, and a plethora of techniques employed by Israel's state terrorism. The latter include the collective punishment of Palestinian citizens by means of travel restrictions, curfews, destruction of crops, and the limiting of access to health facilities, schools and the workplace. They also involve more violent measures, such as the demolition of homes (sometimes with the occupants still inside), attacks with tanks, helicopters and F-16 fighter jets, and targeted assassinations.

It can hardly make a difference whether the deaths and injuries of innocent civilians, who often constitute "collateral damage," are intended or not. Since the Second *Intifada*, the total number of victims has been three times as high on the Palestinian side as for the Israelis. Using such overkill, the State of Israel seeks to fight independent militias such as Hamas and Islamic Jihad, which generally are beyond the reach of the almost completely incapacitated Palestinian Authority. This brutal, decades-long occupation, with no end in sight, means unimaginable suffering for the Palestinians. Yet the majority of Israeli citizens seem deaf and blind to it.

Since April 6, 1994, when the very first suicide attack ever was carried out in Afula, it appears to be impossible effectively to prevent Palestinian suicide attacks.[126] The continuing repression in the occupied territories creates the ideal breeding ground for an increasingly hopeless Palestinian people who are prepared to sacrifice their lives, while taking as many Israeli lives as they can with them. This murderous and suicidal technique came as an answer to the February 25, 1994 massacre of twenty-nine Arab worshippers, which was perpetrated by the fanatic Jewish murderer, Dr. Baruch Goldstein, in Hebron. To the great shock of the Palestinians, they, not the group around

Goldstein, were sanctioned by a curfew lasting six weeks. To this day, Palestinians are reminded daily of this fanatic mass murderer, and thus their feelings of frustration and revenge are stimulated. As Hirsh Goodman wrote:

> The grave of mass murderer Baruch Goldstein in Kiryat Arba has become a national shrine guarded by Israeli soldiers and police, as are those who come to pray at the killer's graveside. One wonders what they could possibly be praying for? What do we really think is running through the heads of those who come to Goldstein's grave for inspiration? In what other country is the grave of a mass murderer a tolerated national shrine? [127]

ILLEGAL SETTLEMENT POLICY

It should be noted that even of the Israeli's so-called "illegal" outposts hardly any, if any, have been removed permanently to this day. This shows that the Israelis want nothing other than to win more time to extend the settlements with the silent consent of the United States. As was stated in the highly respected Dutch daily *NRC Handelsblad* in July 2003, directly after Sharon's visit to Bush:

> Except the confirmation that Israel would welcome the coming into existence of a Palestinian state and the diminishing of military activities, Israel should have dismantled more than a hundred "illegal" settlements on the West Bank. Furthermore

all building activities in the 150 settlements founded before March 2001 should have been stopped. It is true, in order to give a show to the naive world, a few extremely decrepit caravans and containers had been removed, but after a good show of a staged fight, the settlers have come back. Stopping the building activities in the older settlements with a total of 220,000 Jewish settlers has not yet begun by Sharon. The reason being that many people in his government are against it and probably he himself as well. [128]

The reality is that none of this activity was halted. Instead of fulfilling his obligations as laid down in the "Road Map," on July 31, 2003, Sharon released a tender for building twenty-two residences in a settlement in the Gaza Strip.[129] This was all the more provocative as the Palestinians, and especially the extremists amongst them, had shown the greatest restraint during this period, and did not make any attacks on Israeli targets. That Palestinian patience came to an end after this increasing lingering by Sharon and the simultaneous construction of the Apartheid Wall was hardly surprising.

The Wall between Israel and the Palestinian territories is a subject in and of itself. It is concrete proof of the assertion that when it comes to consideration of the Palestinians, the difference between the mainstream political Left and Right Israelis, apart from the extremists on both sides, is ever so slight. The idea for the Wall came from the so-called Left and was strongly defended by Amram Mitzna, by now already completely forgotten as a politician. Those in favor of the Wall defend it by saying that a clear separation between neighbors is beneficial for peace. This, however, would only be true if the separation did not run through the garden and parts of the house of the neighbors, which is exactly the case in its present state and in its future planning. Of the Wall, President Bush said only the following:

> I think the Wall is a problem and I have talked about it with Prime Minister Sharon. It is very difficult to build up trust between Palestinians and Israelis if a wall creeps like a snake over the West Bank.[130]

Logically, the only conclusion one can come to is that it is exactly the end of Palestinian patience that the Israelis hope to bring about one day. The more massive and cruel the Palestinian attacks are, the more power and cruelty can be applied by the IDF, such that ever more Palestinians are prepared to leave their homeland in order to escape their ordeal. The Israelis call this "voluntary transfer."

LEARNING FROM HISTORY

While I have been pointing out these similarities for years, former Knesset member Shulamit Aloni has also cited similar and even worse instances. Aloni was a member of the Meretz Party, which was formed in 1988 out of an amalgamation of three left-wing groups allied with the Labor Party. She was also Education Minister in Yitzhak Rabin's cabinet. In other words, she is anything but an outsider to Israeli politics. On March 6, 2003 she published an article in *Ha'aretz* entitled "Murder of a Population under the Cover of Righteousness," in which she stated:

> We do not have gas chambers and crematoria, but there is no…single fixed method for murder, and not even for genocide. The author Y. L. Peretz wrote about "the righteous cat" that does not spill blood, but only suffocates…. Benny Alon, (a minister in the present government), already said: "Make their life so bitter that they will transfer themselves willingly."[131]

In the same article, Ms. Aloni also wrote:

> Many of our children are being indoctrinated in religious schools that the Arabs are Amalek, and the Bible teaches us that Amalek must be destroyed. There was already a rabbi (Israel Hess) who wrote in the newspaper of Bar Ilan University that we all must commit genocide, and that is because his research showed that the Palestinians are Amalek.

To the Jewish people, the Amalekites symbolize the archenemy, the personification of evil. Deuteronomy 25:17-18 states that one must never forget what the Amalekites did, that they did not fear God, and that they attacked the exhausted Jews during their escape from Egypt. The punishment that they deserve is set out in the Book of Samuel 15:3: "Now go and strike Amalek and utterly destroy all that he has, and do not spare him; but put to death both man and woman, child and infant." And in Exodus 17:14, God tells Moses: "I will blot out every trace of Amalek from under heaven."

It is not my intention to attribute genocidal plans to anyone other than complete fanatics. My point is merely that before the Holocaust even occurred, the Jews had suffered more than enough from discrimination, humiliation, harassment, and the threat of exile in Nazi Germany. In my opinion, the same may be said of the Palestinians' suffering from 1967 to the present. It is already more than a people should have to bear. I well understand that history never really repeats itself, and that the differences between two historical situations are often more important than the similarities. This does not, however, mean that we cannot learn anything from history. The manner in which the Allies dealt with Germany in the aftermath of World War II is a good example of wise politicians (yes, they really exist now and again) actually learning something from history. They avoided making the same mistakes, embodied in the Versailles Treaty, which had such catastrophic consequences after World War I.

The Israeli general staff discovered that they could learn something from history, as well. According to a report in *Ha'aretz*, written by Gideon Samet on January 26, 2002[132] and restated in the same newspaper two days later,[133] the commanders in the occupied Palestinian territories were ordered to study the strategy used by German troops when they stormed the Warsaw Ghetto.[134] By doing so, the Israeli Army would be able to minimize casualties when penetrating thickly settled Palestinian territory—which they in fact did a few weeks later.

In studying and following this strategy, the Israeli Army broke a long-held, self-imposed taboo against comparing measures that they employ against the Palestinians with those that the Germans took against the Jews. On the other hand, Israeli politicians have never been shy about comparing Palestinians to Nazis at every opportunity. At the end of July 2003, Ariel Sharon announced that the slightest breach of the so-called Roadmap for Peace on the part of the Palestinians would be severely punished. According to an article in *Ha'aretz*, in August 2003, Sharon said that this was because Israel's biggest mistake in the past had been its restraint in responding to violations of previous agreements with the Palestinians. As examples, he cited Europe's willingness to overlook Nazi Germany's violations of agreements prior to World War II. [135]

The comparison that Sharon made between the militarily weak Palestinians and Nazi Germany, which was a military power of the highest order during its era, was pretty far-fetched, to say the least. A much closer comparison can be made between the Palestinians and the German Jews prior to the Holocaust. Within Israel, the Palestinians feel like second-class citizens, and those in Gaza and the West Bank live in an occupied land. They are subject to collective punishment and other oppressive measures, just as the Jews were during the Nazi era.

Although the parallels between the Palestinians and the German Jews are close enough to serve as a lesson and a warning, the situations are not at all identical. To begin with, the Palestinians have a territorial claim that is recognized by the United Nations. The most important difference, however, relates to their ability to fight back. The German Jews were completely defenseless during the entire period of their persecution. Absolutely no notable examples of armed resistance occurred. In stark contrast to the posture of the Jews during World War II, the Palestinians use all means at their disposal to resist the their occupation by the Israelis. The most dangerous weapon that they possess, however, is the weapon of the weak—the cruel and counterproductive suicide bombings. Ironically, none are more critical of the defenselessness and passivity of the German Jews in the face of humiliation and persecution than today's Israelis, yet the Israelis fault the Palestinians' resistance just as they criticize the lack of it on the part of German Jews during the Nazi period.

MORE POWER: A DANGEROUS DEVELOPMENT

One of the accusations that notorious anti-Semites used to make was that the Jews were striving for domination of the world. The charge is not quite as laughable as it once was. In the last three decades, the influence of Israel and the Jews in the Diaspora on world politics and world affairs has constantly been growing, and this process has in the last few years attained a different order of magnitude. Ever since the American president George W. Bush and the Israeli prime minister Ariel Sharon formed a close friendship, the Israeli-Jewish influence on the strongest power in the world has taken on frightening and unhealthy dimensions.

Just how powerful Israel has become, and how radically the situation of Jews has changed, may be seen from the following examples. In June 2002, U.S. President George W. Bush gave a speech about the situation in the Middle East, after which Israeli Communications Minister and Likud Member Reuven Rivlin chortled in tasteless and provocative fashion: "It looks like it was written by a senior Likud official."[136] Agreeing wholeheartedly, Sharon bragged in an interview at the end of 2002 that the current Middle East policies of the U.S. government were largely the result of his influence.

Indeed, the Israelis show no restraint in boasting about the power they have acquired. Proudly, the most effective and largest pro-Israel lobby organization, AIPAC, has placed on its website quotations from the most prominent American politicians. The following quote by former Secretary of State Colin Powell is from March 2003:

> AIPAC came into being...to help the young Israel state meet the challenges of independence... You have a world-class reputation for being one of the most effective such organizations in that regard.[137]

Here is an older quote by Newt Gingrich, former speaker of the House: "You are the most effective group of general interest...on the whole planet."[138] As the well-known commentator Meron Benvenisti wrote in *Ha'aretz*:

> A powerful coalition composed of a right wing government in Israel, a Jewish lobby in the United States, the decisive influence of fundamental Christians and neo-conservative administration officials will make sure that the fate of the "road map" [the present plan to finally achieve peace between Israel and the Palestinians] will be like that of the Mitchell, Tenet and Zinni plans that...sank into oblivion.[139]

Consequently, *The Jerusalem Post*, which is a much more right-wing newspaper than *Ha'aretz*, wrote as follows about Elliott Abrams, then Condoleezza Rice's head of the National Security Council: "Elliott could always be relied upon to give clear expression of the Israeli line, and whether or not an idea would fly with the Jewish community."[140] Abrams received first hand insight into

Sharon's world when he made a secret visit to Israel with Hadley, the deputy national security adviser. According to Israeli sources, the prime minister took his guests up in a helicopter for a bird's-eye view of the Jewish settlement on the West Bank. Yoel Marcus of *Ha'aretz* commented:

> Sharon does not have to read the latest comments of Richard Perle—the spiritual father of the war on Iraq who says America doesn't owe the Arabs anything— to see that he has nothing to fear from a president who is running for a second term on the "National Hero" ticket. [141]

Perle was until shortly before that time not only chairman of the Defense Policy Board of the Defense Department in the U.S., but also director of *The Jerusalem Post*, now owned by extreme right-wing Zionists. This last description of Perle's position is from the pen of Uri Avneri, the leader of the Israeli peace group Gush Shalom, published in April 2003. He differed somewhat from Yoel Marcus, as he saw Paul Wolfowitz, the number two man in the Defense Department, as the father of the war in Iraq. That was a small difference of opinion, as both the American neo-conservatives belonged to the same closely-knit circle of influential Jewish neo-conservative hawks. Avneri writes further about this circle:

> Their big moment arrived with the collapse of the Twin Towers. The American public and politicians were in a state of shock, completely disoriented, unable to understand a world that had changed overnight. Only nine days after the outrage, William Kristol (the son of the

group's founder, Irving Kristol), published an open letter to President Bush, asserting that it was not enough to annihilate the network of Osama bin Laden, but it was also imperative to "remove Saddam Hussein from power" and to "retaliate" against Syria and Iran for supporting Hizbollah.[142]

The number of similar quotes—all taken from Jewish Israeli sources, albeit most from those critical towards the present Israeli government—could be much larger. The content of their messages is much in line with mythological assertions about the intentions of the Jews toward world domination, which in former times came only from notorious anti-Semites. Now they are uttered, well documented, by patriotic Israeli Jews who either see their country killing itself or brag about its newly acquired power. An article in *Ha'aretz* in 2003, entitled "Tehran Warns Israel Against Strikes on Bushehr Reactor," stated that according to the Israeli sources, Sharon and President Bush discussed this very issue.[143] Such adventurism would not be good either for Israel or for Jews in the Diaspora. But if it should come to pass, no one will be able to say that we were not forewarned.

From recent Jewish history it can be seen that having no political power at all can be extremely dangerous. Many more examples can be taken from world history to show that having too much power can also lead to the downfall of a nation. In the case of the Jews, a people extremely sensitive to the endemic disease of anti-Semitism, there is always the danger that this disease becomes suddenly virulent again. A trigger, which might cause such an event, could conceivably be any larger war that develops, for the outbreak of which the Jews and Israel can, rightly or wrongly, be held co-responsible. In such a case the disappearance of the Jews from world history might become more accelerated than even I anticipate.

.

THREE FUTURE SCENARIOS

To find a way out of this terrible situation, a few distinct scenarios can be imagined. These include a "Greater Israel" without Palestinians, a "cleaned up" Oslo Agreement, and a largely bi-national state. When the American war in Iraq began, the Israeli politicians thought that they could proceed with all sorts of radical initiatives because the world's attention would be focused elsewhere. What happened in Israel and the occupied territories would be out of sight and would offer a choice opportunity to carry out a large scale "transfer," i.e. forceful deportation and/or induced flight of most Palestinians from "Greater Israel." In this way, it was hoped that the whole area between the Jordan River and the Mediterranean would be free of Palestinians. Even if we overlook the crimes against humanity involved in such an ethnic cleansing operation, it would be an illusion to believe that the Jewish population of "Greater Israel" could henceforth live a quiet life in peace. The incredible amount of anger, frustration, and longing for revenge after such a second *nakba* (the Arabic word for disaster, which refers to the expulsion and flight of Palestinians in 1947) would offer an increasing breeding-ground for murderous suicide attacks on Jews in Israel and probably elsewhere. It seems inconceivable, however, that a physical wall, whatever its height and sophistication, could ever function as a hermetic seal around Israel to keep revengeful Arabs out indefinitely.

Another scenario, in my view extremely improbable,

is at the other extreme of the range of the theoretically possible "solutions" for the Palestinian-Israeli conflict. This highly optimistic projection would entail a return to a "sanitized" Oslo process. The term "sanitized" is added to indicate that the Oslo process was doomed to fail from the very beginning because the Israelis never considered their partners as equal to themselves, and cheated from the start by continuing to build settlements in the area designated according to UN resolutions as belonging to the Palestinians. Yasser Arafat and his officers gave to the Israelis, out of naïveté and/or his own personal interests in terms of power and money, the opportunity to get away with this.

The so-called "Road Map" to peace, launched by the U.S. administration under George W. Bush, and supported in addition by the UN, the EU and Russia, was hailed by some as a realistic proposal that could lead to the end of the conflict. Even if this plan were ever to be realized in practice, it would present a sort of peace that could never satisfy any Palestinian who cherished his national or even his personal dignity. However, as of now, it seems utterly improbable that this plan will ever be executed because Israeli leaders do nothing other than make promises that never are realized, and go on with extending the settlements.

In my opinion, in order to achieve a situation in which Israel and Palestine live next to each other as good neighbors, nothing less than a miracle would have to occur. In theory, this might happen if a charismatic leader were to rise up in Israel who would put real life into the Jewish concept of *teshuva*, inducing the Israelis to make a complete about-face in their policies. Such a leader would make it clear to his fellow Jews that a very first step in a serious effort for lasting peace really would be to ask forgiveness from the Palestinians for the way they have treated them. Obviously, such an important psychological gesture would have to be accompanied by material compensations for all the damage that has been inflicted on them. Paradoxically, the way in which the Germans tried to compensate for the harm done to the Jews could serve as a good example of how to go about such a difficult task—in principle impossible, but psychologically of extreme importance.

If such a miracle occurred, it would mean that all settlements, with the exception of those agreed upon between equal partners, would be cleared out of settlers. The houses would be transferred to the Palestinians as part of compensation for the damage done to the refugees in 1947-48, and (we are after all talking about a miracle) the two states would flourish in peace, side by side. As of now, however, about 20% of Israeli citizens are Arabs and their rate of growth is much higher than that of the Jewish population. Thus, unless a number of other miracles would occur, in fifty to a hundred years the Jews in Israel will be in the minority. Thus, the internal contradiction of a state that is at the same time Jewish and democratic could no longer be disguised.

There is, I believe, only one scenario that might result in a state that is stable and viable in the long run. This would be a democratic, multiethnic state, in which Jews and Palestinians constitute the main components. This would be, of course, contradictory to the Zionist ideas of most of the Jewish citizens in Israel who want a primarily "Jewish state," i.e. one in which the large majority of citizens is Jewish (whatever that means). On the other hand, however, such a multiethnic state would come very near the original ideas of some of the early pioneers of

Zionism, such as Herzl, who wanted the Jews to become like any other people.[144]

If this improbable scenario were to be realized, the ideal of the early Zionist pioneers would indeed come true. In fact, then and only then—in a multi-ethnic, democratic state—Jews would have a country of their own where they live in peace together with the Palestinians. Then, finally, the Jews would be similar to most other peoples. They would live in their country, Israel, just like the British live together with fellow citizens from the Far East, and the French with their fellow citizens from Africa. Only in this way could Herzl's wish be eventually realized, as expressed in his diary "such that the derogatory word 'Jew' will become an honorable word just like German, Englishman, Frenchman"[145] In our contemporary context, one hundred years after Herzl's time, the word "Jew" needs only to be changed to "Israeli."

It is interesting to note that already in 1985, *Ha'aretz* Editor-in-Chief Gershom Schocken called on Israel to encourage mixed marriages between Jews and Arabs for much the same reasons:

> For a sovereign nation that must achieve coexistence with the members of another group and create normal relations with neighbors beyond its borders, this prohibition [to marry within Israel an Arab or other non-Jew] which symbolizes alienation between the Jews and other groups, has become a curse. If it continues, it will contribute to making permanent the tension within the country and its isolation in the region. [146]

The irony, of course, is that if eventually such a multiethnic state were realized and the relatively large number of Jews in the Diaspora continued to disappear, the Jews would eventually be no different from other peoples. The early pioneers of Zionism attributed perennial anti-Semitism to just these differences, and they foresaw that anti-Semitism would disappear only when these differences themselves were erased and the Jews as a distinct people would virtually cease to exist.

CHAPTER 6

The Cudgel of Anti-Semitism:
What the Phenomenon of Cognitive Dissonance Tells Us

The Misuse of Ambiguity

I FIND THE widespread misuse of words as an instrument of deception to be profoundly discouraging and disappointing. U.S. President George W. Bush once called his friend Ariel Sharon a "man of peace," even though Sharon was on more than one count a war criminal. The most notorious case of his criminality was the mass murder of Palestinian civilians in the camps of Sabra and Chatila. Although Christian militias performed the actual deed, an Israeli commission under the chairmanship of Supreme Court Justice Yitzhak Kahan concluded that while Sharon had not personally ordered the mass murder, he did not prevent it from happening, which was his responsibility, and called for him to draw "personal conclusions."[147] In other words, this important commission held Sharon personally responsible for the mass murder and advised him to resign, which of course he didn't do.

More direct proof of his culpability as a war criminal exists from a much earlier time. It consists of an order signed by him personally on October 13, 1953, to kill 69 Palestinians, most of them women and children, and to blow up 45 houses in the village of Kibya. It reads:

> Objective: attacking the village of
> Kibya, occupying it and causing maximal

damage in lives and property. Signed, Major Ariel Sharon.[148]

To those who would argue that 1953 was long ago indeed, and that Sharon's desire for peace became evident by his "disengagement" from Gaza, I would cite a long interview with his closest adviser, lifelong friend, and lawyer, Dov Weissglass, conducted in October 2004 by Ari Shavit. This interview contains the following important words by Weinglass about the real significance of this disengagement plan, which show that the last thing Sharon wanted was peace via negotiations with the Palestinians:

> This disengagement is actually formaldehyde. It supplies the amount of formaldehyde that's necessary that there will not be a political process with the Palestinians... The disengagement plan makes it possible for Israel to park conveniently in an interim situation that distances us as far as possible from political pressure.[149]

That words and terms are rarely defined precisely in normal daily discourse makes it all the easier to use them for purposes of deception. Take the word "peace," for instance. "I want to live in peace" can also mean, "I want to be left in peace," the corollary to which could be: "That is why we need to toss everyone who disturbs *my* peace out of the country." For Sharon, peace was equivalent to a *Pax Israeliana*, a peace dictated by Israel. In contrast, when Uri Avneri, the head of Gush Shalom, the Israeli peace movement, speaks of "peace," he means a negotiated peace agreement with the Palestinians on the basis of equality and mutual respect.

Practitioners in the art of deception play fast and loose with the word "democracy" as well. Israel constantly insists that it is the only democracy in a neighborhood of corrupt dictatorships. The latter half of this statement is surely true. The states that surround Israel are mainly closed political systems. Nevertheless, merely because the *Jewish* citizens of Israel still live under a reasonably democratic system does not mean that Israel can justifiably call itself a "democratic" country. According to former Israeli Attorney General Michael Ben-Yair:

> The Six-Day War was forced upon us. However, the war's seventh day, which began on June 12, 1967 and has continued to this day, is the product of our choice. We enthusiastically chose to become a colonial society, ignoring international treaties, expropriating lands, transferring settlers from Israel to the occupied territories, engaging in theft and finding justification for all these activities. Passionately desiring to keep the occupied territories, we developed two judicial systems: one—progressive, liberal—in Israel, and the other—cruel, injurious—in the occupied territories. In effect, we established an apartheid regime in the occupied territories immediately following their capture.[150]

The use of euphemisms is also a common method of deception, useful for covering up crimes that are in the planning-stage or that have already been carried out. Since at least the end of 2002, for example, there has been increasing talk in Israel of deporting Palestinians, or at least driving them out by threats and the use of overwhelming force. The operative euphemisms are "transfer" or "voluntary transfer." If it proves impossible to deport or expel the Palestinian population, certain circles in Israel are prepared to accept a Palestinian mini-state. In order to maintain complete and permanent dominance over the population, the territory ceded to them is to be in the form of distinct ghetto areas that can be easily isolated from one another, with each to be encircled by a ring of Israeli settlements. Since the word "ghettoization" has certain unpleasant associations, the official euphemism is "cantonization."

In their attempts to win over world opinion, Israel, its neighbors—and the United States as well—have all been waging massive propaganda campaigns. These efforts, which aim at demonstrating the evil nature of the enemy, are pumped up in intensity by modern mass media. The power of the media to influence public opinion is demonstrated by the rapidity with which Americans are willing to call former enemies "friends," or vice versa. As a young man I saw how propaganda could seduce people into committing the most unimaginable crimes, or into wilfully ignoring them, and it is this indelible impression that has sensitized me to the deceitful and manipulative use of language.[151]

ZIONISM, RACISM, AND ISRAELI POLICY

Critics of Israeli policy are guilty of the misuse of language, as well. The old equation between Zionism and racism, for instance, resurfaced at the UN-sponsored World Conference against Racism held in Durban, South Africa, in 2001. Now, it is hard to claim that current Israeli policies do not have racial features. While Zionism and racism may have certain points of similarity, however, they are by no means identical. When, as happened during the World Conference, no sharp distinction is made between these concepts, the danger arises that this over-simplified and easily refuted claim will discredit all well-founded and absolutely necessary criticism of Israeli policies.

Zionism is the most important development in Judaism since Biblical times. In its original form, as enunciated by its founders, it bears about as much resemblance to racism as theft insurance does to theft. Its intent was to protect Judaism. It originated toward the end of the 19th century in reaction to the threats that Jews faced as a result of discrimination at the time. This discrimination increasingly came to have a racial component. In reality, however, there is no such thing as a Jewish race. Even if we accept the very idea of race as a valid category, there are probably no people on earth that are as genetically mixed as the Jewish people. Any attempts to identify features characteristic of the Jewish race are doomed to failure.

Zionism's original opposition to discrimination on the bases of religion, race, or sex is anchored in Israel's Declaration of Independence, according to which, historian Martin Gilbert writes:

> [Israel] would be based on "freedom, justice, and peace as envisaged by the prophets of Israel." It would ensure "complete equality of social and political rights to all its inhabitants, irrespective of religion, race or sex," and would guarantee freedom of religion, conscience, language education and culture.[152]

This can also be seen in the autobiography of

Chaim Weizmann, who was active in the movement after the second Zionist Congress in 1898, and who became Israel's first president. He wrote:

> I believed that a small Jewish state, well-organized, living in peace with its neighbors, a state on which the love and devotion of the Jewish community throughout the world would be lavished... would be a great credit to us and an equally great contribution to civilization.[153]

Recent Israeli policies have paid little attention to such niceties and good intentions. After more than 50 years, Palestinian Israelis still do not have equal rights as citizens. While it is wrong to claim that Zionism is racist, per se, the fact remains that Israel treats its Palestinian and Jewish citizens very differently. Because this inequality has only grown over the past few decades, the claim that "Zionism equals racism" has gained credibility.

ANTI-SEMITISM AS BOTH CHIMERA AND PALPABLE THREAT

One of the most glaring misuses of words as an instrument of deception involves the term "anti-Semitism." It will outrage many of my Jewish brothers and sisters that I refer to anti-Semitism as a chimera, even though it resulted in the terrible historical reality of the Holocaust. In the name of anti-Semitism, crimes were committed that remain incomprehensible to this day. Nevertheless, since the establishment of the State of Israel, anti-Semitism has to be viewed in a different light. As a result of such developments as Israel's 1967 victory over Arab nations and the subsequent, still ongoing occupation of Palestinian lands, Israel has become a significant power in the Middle East. While the new state gained widespread admiration throughout the world before 1967, after this date a reversal took place that entailed a fundamental change in the nature and perception of anti-Semitism.

To this day, the dimensions of the genocide known as the Holocaust elicit fear from many Jews—a fear that is easily exploited for the purpose of exaggerating actual or perceived anti-Semitic incidents. Consequently, while actual occurrences of this phenomenon have remained marginal or not turned out to be virulent, the combination of an admittedly real yet hardly dangerous anti-Semitism with the fear of a full-scale resurgence has proven to be nearly as bad as, or worse than, the real thing.

Although this fear is entirely understandable for historical reasons, in most cases it is unwarranted and engenders an unnecessary cycle of guilt and blame. Non-Jews fear being accused of anti-Semitism the moment they voice even the minutest criticism of Israel's politics. Such accusations can produce an anti-Jewish reaction, which in turn can lead to actual anti-Semitism, thus turning what was a chimera into a palpable threat.

THE ROOTS OF ANTI-SEMITISM

Until 1879, the word "anti-Semitism" did not exist. It made sense only after hatred of Jews became increasingly grounded in the pseudoscientific theory of races, which followed in the wake of the predominantly theological arguments of the Church. While the Church was thus primarily to blame for the continuous manifestations of anti-Judaism for more than two thousand years, the origins of anti-Judaism can actually be traced back to antiquity.

Any objective assessment of this history must set out with the realization—unpalatable to many Jews—that the earliest cause of anti-Semitism is to be found in Jewry itself, which offended other ethnic groups with its strict rules of conduct. The Jewish religion contains a rigid proscription against images. A sculpture of a human figure, whether representing a deity or a secular ruler, would thus have been repugnant to Jews, while non-Jews, on the other hand, would have regarded it with reverence. Judaism's dietary laws were presumably the most offensive, as they were ill suited to a world that regarded hospitality, the offering and accepting of food and gifts, as among the most important social virtues. In such a world, the attitude of the Jews was bound to arouse irritation or even aggression. The Roman statesman Cicero, for example, objected to the obtrusive presence of Jews in Rome around the middle of the first century B.C.[154]

In Alexandria, the hub of Hellenistic culture, peaceful coexistence of diverse nationalities and individuals was a fundamental feature of life. Yet even here, where Jews made up a large part of the population, there were riots almost to the point of pogroms during the thirties of the first century A.D.[155] As historian A. S. Rijxman comments in connection with this subject: "The Greeks were offended by the Jews' presumed or actual sense of superiority."[156]

THE CHOSEN PEOPLE

The Old Testament states that the Jewish people, in the desert near Mount Sinai, unanimously decided to distinguish themselves from other peoples.[157] In Exodus 19:5, God makes a pact with the Israelites: "Now therefore, if you will obey my voice and keep my covenant, you shall be my own possession among all peoples." Ever since, this decision has been reaffirmed again and again by every Jewish community. In this connection, Henri Atlan writes as follows:

> This perfect match, this mutual adaptation between a people and its god, had, of course, the immediate effect of differentiating that people from other peoples, separating it through the very act that established it and defined it. [158]

Commenting tersely on the continuation of this passage in Exodus, "And you shall be to me a kingdom of priests and a holy nation," Atlan states:

> The consequences of this plan could, however, be as unfortunate and catastrophic as they could be a blessing, depending upon the path taken by the [Jewish people regarding their] relations with surrounding peoples.

It is an undeniable fact that the Jews remain the only ancient people that still exist as a recognizable entity today principally because they kept alive a culture that is thousands of years old. Surely, many will consider this to be a blessing, but it was bought with much suffering. Things good and bad have been allotted the Jewish people in ample measure.

Hans Christian Andersen's tale of the ugly duckling that is shunned by the community of ducks because it is different is a good metaphor for any biological community's elementary reflex when faced with individuals of a different kind in their midst. The fact that the duckling ultimately discovers that it is a swan and is fortunate enough to be welcomed into a family of swans only heightens the analogy with the Jews in the Diaspora and their eventual incorporation into the State of Israel.

Isolated in the Diaspora by Choice

According to Jewish tradition, it was the famous rabbi Jochanan Ben Zakkai who shaped and led the process of renewal after the destruction of the Temple by the Romans. The Jews scattered all over the world were to find a community everywhere. It was of extreme importance to the preservation of Jewish identity to have Jews live close to one another, to make sure anyone destined or wishing to join a Jewish community would be subject to social control. Newcomers were keenly interested in the support of their religious brethren, for the community had the means and institutions capable of assisting them.

Two particular commandments have been a powerful factor in the close-knit living conditions of isolated Jewish communities in the Diaspora. The first is the rule that a prayer community must comprise at least ten adult men. Even largely assimilated Jews will honor this highly respected law for the sake of establishing a quorum for a service. In times when walking was the principal means of locomotion, Jews had to live in close proximity for this reason, if none other—a fact amounting to voluntary ghettoization for religious reasons. This was reinforced by means of the *eruv*, an enclosed area that made certain the members of the community remained within the ghetto even on the Sabbath when they were not required to work, thus rendering them incapable of escaping social control.

THE CHRISTIAN CHURCH AS THE DRIVING FORCE BEHIND ANTI-SEMITISM

It is undeniable that the Jews themselves contributed significantly to their isolation. This in itself aroused dislike and even disgust. From the 5th century onward, the Popes fanned these resentments for their own purposes. Considerably more vicious discrimination resulted from the Third and Fourth Lateran Councils in 1179 and 1215. They established the rule that, among other things, Jews could not employ Christian servants and that Christians could not live in Jewish quarters. Jews had to wear distinctive items, such as the pointed Jewish hat and yellow patch on their clothing. Seven centuries later, the Nazis would similarly stigmatize the Jews.[159] These laws had been preceded by the first two Crusades late in the 11th and in the mid-12th centuries, which entailed pogroms against Jewish communities, primarily along the Rhine, but elsewhere as well.

It is not my intention to go over the entire history of anti-Semitism from The Middle Ages onward. We can summarize its most significant characteristics in the last five centuries before the founding of the State of Israel, however, by noting that while the Church, which was the prime determinant of life in The Middle Ages, was conscious of having inherited the most essential portions of Jewish doctrine, it was of the opinion that Christianity was the true religion because it recognized Jesus as the son of God, the prophesied Messiah. Since the Jews rejected this belief, they were branded as the Savior's deniers and murderers.

To demonstrate to the population that denial of Christ would inevitably lead to damnation and misery, the

Church made life as difficult for the Jews as possible. They were not to be annihilated, as their miserable existence was intended to serve as a deterrent, but they had to live in separate quarters, were kept largely apart from the Christian community, and were neither allowed to own land nor to practice skilled trades. The Jews themselves, however, strove to keep their distance and avoid interbreeding, as did the Christians surrounding them, although it goes without saying that they would nevertheless have preferred better access to professions and fewer restrictions in their daily life.

THE COMPLEX CHARACTER OF ANTI-SEMITISM

The Church is obviously to blame for the most evil and shameful acts against the Jews. Myths were propagated among the people that portrayed Jews as deicides, poisoners of wells, and butchers of Christian children whose blood they would use for ritual purposes. Such myths became deeply ingrained archetypes in the Christian world, which could be mobilized again and again. For example, despite their lowly status in society, the Jews were a significant economic factor even in The Middle Ages. This was due to the fact that Christians were strictly forbidden to lend money for interest, and thus the chief livelihood open to Jews was money lending. The Jews were thus an important factor in any international trade, and were able to make funds available to Church and State. They were indispensable to temporal rulers, who readmitted them each time they had been persecuted or exiled.

Clearly, however, debtors did not tend to appreciate their creditors. In times of extreme economic decline, a pogrom would save these creditors from their indebtedness, and it was easy to soothe their conscience by invoking the stereotype of the Jew as deicide. Anti-Semitism thus arose from a multitude of external influences, at times occurring simultaneously and at times singly, including xenophobia, Christian theology, and economic tensions. In times of famine, epidemics or war, the need for a scapegoat was greater than in times of prosperity, and the manipulation of these factors by the Church and temporal rulers increased.

The evil of anti-Semitism afflicting the Christian world will probably never go away entirely. It is too deeply embedded in Christian thought. How any Jew processes anti-Semitic resentment depends on his individual attitude. A small dose of anti-Semitism can make some feel that they are different from the rest, or even better. It can also be an incentive, causing a Jewish person to make a greater effort than his non-Jewish competitor. This may increase his opportunities and even be beneficial for developing his talents. Thus, no matter how indisputably destructive anti-Semitism may essentially be, a mild version of it has, paradoxically, also had a protective effect and contributed to the continued existence of Judaism. The emancipation of the Jews following the French Revolution, for instance, did not mean that the Jews were suddenly free of all worries. Hostility against Jews persisted, and this may have helped limit the desire for assimilation, assuring that the majority would remain within the fold of the Jewish community.

The restrictions to which Jews are subject in social interaction differ just like the professions assigned to or withheld from them. The minute Jews are no longer—or only in exceptional cases—admitted to certain professions, clubs, or hotels, a more virulent form of anti-Semitism is at work. Naturally, the attitude of political decision-makers plays its part, too. They can have a moderating influence on the population, incite the masses, or silently tolerate a subliminal societal trend.

As long as anti-Semitism is not a threat to life and livelihood, or as long as it remains marginal and cannot count on widespread social acceptance, the remark once made by jurist and author Abel Herzberg shortly after he had returned from a German concentration camp, applies: Anti-Semitism is the anti-Semite's problem.[160] As a marginal phenomenon, it is restricted to minority groups, as well as the unsuccessful, the envious, and the embittered. Anti-Semitism expressed by such people is annoying, but as long as it is restricted to these groups, and as long as the number of their members remains relatively low, it is not truly threatening.

Thus, in Europe, we find anti-Semitism openly expressed by neo-Nazi skinheads on the one hand, and by Muslim youth who identify with the Palestinians suffering under Israeli occupation on the other. In both cases, these adolescents and young adults, unable to find a foothold in society, try to attract attention with provocative behavior intended to stir up anti-Jewish feelings. No matter how much Israel's existence may have complicated the problem of anti-Semitism, one significant motive for the conduct of marginal groups remains simply the desire to attract attention. Instead of rewarding such groups with publicity, thus spurring them on to even more such activity, it would be better to try to correct the behavior of their members through constructive social and educational methods.

ANTI-ISRAELI SENTIMENT

It is a bitter example of historical dialectics that the Jewish state, originally established in order to protect Jews from anti-Semitism, has spawned a new phenomenon often mistaken for anti-Semitism: namely anti-Israeli sentiment. While at times old anti-Semitic roots may partially feed this response, it is the current aggressive and shameful policies of the State of Israel that are chiefly responsible for its growth.

Anti-Israeli feeling and opinion are easily attacked as being linked with traditional anti-Semitism primarily because many Jews outwardly stand behind Israeli policies without voicing the slightest criticism, even when human rights and international law are severely and continually violated. Thus, criticism of the State can easily be interpreted as criticism of the Jewish people. It was understandable that the young nation, which seemed to be threatened on all sides, was practically above the law after World War II and the almost total annihilation of European Jews. Nor was it surprising that Jews outside of Israel identified with their potential refuge.

As we now know, however, the image of Israel as a vulnerable underdog in the coming political and military struggle was a myth. The important and revealing work of modern critical Israeli historians such as Avi Shlaim[161] and Ilan Pappe[162] has shown that from 1940 on, the Haganah prepared detailed plans on how every single Palestinian village could be conquered and the population evicted from their houses. The fact that these plans were successfully executed was due to the decisive militarily superiority of the Jewish forces, of which the Jewish leaders were already fully conscious before 1948. The image of a tiny, helpless

Israel being again attacked by superior forces in 1967 was a myth promulgated by Israeli politicians to gain the sympathy of the world.

How deeply this myth became ingrained in the minds of Israelis could be detected even in the reasoning of sincere critics of Israeli policy. According to former Israeli Attorney General Michael Ben-Yair, something went completely wrong after Israel's spectacular and complete victory over its Arabic neighbor states in 1967, when Israel opted for becoming a colonial power and setting up an apartheid regime in the occupied territories.[163] Until 2002, however, even Ben-Yair still thought that up to 1967 Israel was indeed in great danger. Based on what we know now, it would be more accurate to say that, after that date, Israel felt strong enough to display openly and without shame the colonial ambitions it had been nurturing secretly for years.

We have already seen how the racial theories of the 18th and 19th centuries, with their strict split between Nordic-Aryan and Semitic races, provided the pseudoscientific basis for modern anti-Semitism. According to these theories, Semites were lazy or overambitious, cowardly or insolent, but above all parasitic and depraved. The characteristics of the Nordic-Aryan race were supposedly the complete opposite. The response of the Jews was never aggressive, and they never conspired against the state, not even against Germany during the 1930s, where they had lived for more than a thousand years. Nevertheless, anti-Semites accused them of conspiring to rule the world, a goal that they would achieve with the help of their fabulous wealth.

This classic anti-Semitism is so European that it makes little sense to apply it to the Arab aversion to Jews. It makes more sense to say that the Arabs are enthusiastic recyclers of old European anti-Semitic stereotypes for propaganda purposes. A certain degree of congruence thus exists between the language and the images of Arab propaganda and that of classic anti-Semitism. However, the concept anti-Semitism, which emerged at a time when Jews had no political power, must be used very carefully under the present circumstances. Israel has been victorious in most of its campaigns against its Arab neighbors since its independence, and has been waging a low-level war against the Palestinians during this entire period.

Arab Anti-Semitism

Due to this continuing situation of conflict, the old concept of anti-Semitism can't be readily applied to Palestinians and Arabs. The demonization of an enemy with whom one is at war may be ethically reprehensible, but it is as common as war itself. The fact that the Arabs use stereotypes that are hundreds of years old in their anti-Israeli propaganda merely deepens the latent fears of many Jews that the darkest moments of their history might repeat themselves[164] and that Arabs are simply intent on their destruction—fears that are skillfully manipulated by Israeli politicians.

What is notable in this connection is the asymmetry between the two sides. On the one hand, Israelis complain about the hateful language used by Arabs, but at the same time it never occurs to them to end their repressive occupation policies, or to rein in the expressions of contempt that even their so-called moderate politicians employ. One can't hurt a person more deeply than by denying that he exists. Golda Meir, Prime Minister of Israel from 1969 to 1974, did just that with her notorious statement: "It is not as though there was a Palestinian people in Palestine, considering itself as a Palestinian people, and we came and threw them out and took their country away from them. They did not exist."[165] She herself was merely echoing Chaim Weitzmann, who in 1917 stated: "The current situation might lend itself to the creation of an Arab Palestine, if there were only something like a Palestinian people."[166]

The widespread nature of the contempt for Arabs on the part of Israeli Jews is demonstrated by an article by Yoav Peled at the University of Tel Aviv, published in *The Guardian*, in which he wrote:

> In Israel the public denigration of Arab culture was historically acceptable, since, like all colonial movements, Zionism had to dehumanize the indigenous inhabitants of its country of settlement in order to legitimize their displacement. Thus, as many studies have shown, depictions of the Arabs as conniving, dishonest, lazy, treacherous and murderous were commonplace in Israeli school textbooks, as in much of Israeli literature in general.[167]

The former Minister of Education, Shulamit Aloni, confirmed this demonization of the Arabs in Israeli schoolbooks. According to her, Rabbi Israel Hess wrote in the newspaper of Bar-Ilan University that his research had found that the Palestinians were the ancient Amalekites, and therefore must be destroyed.[168] And an article in the Israeli Russian–language newspaper *Novosti* called for the castration of Israeli Arabs as a means of fighting terrorism—without a single reader response! The article, incidentally, was entitled "How to Force Them to Leave."[169]

Compared with that, Minister and ex-General Effi Eitam responded mildly when asked whether it wasn't intolerable that the Temple Mount was not in Jewish hands. He answered, "Yes. Definitely. But that will be solved."[170] In language that is elliptical at best, Eitam made it clear that the current state of *tohu* (desolation), resulting from the presence of mosques on the Temple Mount, would be righted. The clear implication: they will be torn down. Is it any wonder that so many Palestinians or Arabs vent their rage, insecurity, and hatred in anti-Semitic tirades? The Israeli statements cited are at least as anti-Semitic as those in Arab schoolbooks, about which there has been such uproar. The irony, of course, is that the Arabs are also a Semitic people in the literal sense of the word, which only goes to show how carefully one has to choose one's words in attempting to write about this conflict.

LATENT AND VIRULENT ANTI-SEMITISM

After having barely manifested itself in the past five decades, anti-Semitism, always latent in the Christian world, is now finding a new foothold. Virulent, aggressive anti-Semitism needs no excuse for its expression, while latent, endemic anti-Semitism, found even among refined individuals, now surfaces readily in proportion to the overt actions of the Israeli Army after having been taboo since the Holocaust. Here, we encounter a complex phenomenon.

The fact that incorrigible anti-Semites condemn everything connected with Jews or Judaism does not mean that anyone remarking critically on Jewish affairs thus is automatically anti-Semitic. After all, they might be right.

Why, then, should they have to remain silent? It cannot be the case that the Holocaust forever makes all its survivors and their descendants proof against any criticism from now to eternity. Indeed, suppressing justified criticism may even indicate subliminal anti-Semitism more than expressing it. A reasonably intelligent person who realizes that he is not free from anti-Semitic influence is stopped by the memory of the Holocaust from stating his opinion openly. Since he cannot rule out that resentments of which he would have to be ashamed somehow influence his judgment, he chooses to avoid confrontation. On the one hand, this attitude has spoiled some Jews. On the other hand, it causes them to react hyper-sensitively to any sign of actual or perceived anti-Semitism.

The attitude on both sides is based on insecurity. In Jews it arises from a sense of being threatened, which clouds their judgment and triggers exaggerated reactions. Non-Jews who resolve to voice criticism, on the other hand, feel that they are unjustly accused of anti-Semitism. Since unjustified accusations tend to fan the urge to be critical rather than stifling it, a vicious circle is generated, and anti-Semitism evolves from a marginal manifestation into an actual threat.

DO SOME JEWS SUBCONSCIOUSLY WELCOME ANTI-SEMITISM?

An event in the Netherlands in 2003 illustrates the way in which some Jews feel it necessary to accuse non-Jews of anti-Semitism. Gretta Duisenberg, the wife of former European Central Bank President Wim Duisenberg, had hoisted a Palestinian flag on her house in protest of Israel's actions in the occupied territories. Her Jewish neighbors so inflated what she had done that it reached the columns of the *Nieuw Israelitisch Weekblad*, the oldest Jewish weekly in the Netherlands. It was not enough that a Jewish lawyer filed charges against her on behalf of a presumably fictitious organization, but he also approached the Jewish World Congress in New York with the request that Wim Duisenberg be declared *persona non grata* in the United States. This whole affair reflects a caustic, contemporary redefinition of the term "anti-Semite": *An anti-Semite used to be a person who disliked Jews. Now it is a person whom Jews dislike.*

Such an unreasonable reaction to an at most irritating occurrence is pointless. The intention is to fight anti-Semitism, but anti-Semitism is actually being fanned. It seems that people believe the Holocaust was made possible because the Jews allowed themselves to be led like lambs to the slaughter, and that consequently, even the slightest hint of anti-Semitism needs to be vigorously attacked. Twelve years of direct experience with anti-Semitism taught me that attack is not always the best defense. Anyone wishing to fight endemic anti-Semitism today must counter it in a manner that can be taken seriously, not by foolish innuendo and demands, seeing only the speck in the brother's eye but not the log (that is to say, current Israeli policy) in one's own.

People suffering trauma and feelings of guilt may sometimes be forgiven their overreaction, but the delusional ideas served up by statesmen and politicians should not. They usually veil a hidden agenda, if not criminal intent. Shimon Peres, who was considered a moderate, once said that European criticism of the actions of the Israeli Army in the Jenin refugee camp in the West Bank was an expression of anti-Semitism.[171] The same line was pursued by Shlomo Gur, the Israeli Secretary of the EU-Israel

Forum during a symposium in Tel Aviv in November 2002, when he spoke of a black cloud of anti-Semitism over relations between the EU and Israel.[172] Such remarks are heinous because they conjure up a specter with no other intention than to stifle any criticism. Or is there another reason behind this? Do these government representatives possibly use anti-Semitism in order to persuade disoriented Jews to immigrate to Israel, the Promised Land? It cannot be a coincidence that, immediately after Peres' accusations, Israel's Interior Minister Eli Yishai called upon French Jews to pack their bags as quickly as possible and immigrate to Israel.[173]

There is no lack of evidence to corroborate such a suspicion. For example, at a conference in Jerusalem during the week of August 4, 2003, Jewish organizations from all over the world, as well as representatives of the Israeli government and universities, developed a joint strategy for a "war against anti-Semitism." In this context, Natan Sharansky, Minister for Diaspora Affairs, Society and Jerusalem, wrote:

> The new anti-Semitism appears in the guise of "political criticism of Israel" consisting of a discriminating approach and double standards towards the state of Israel, while questioning its right to exist.

After deploring that ties between Jews in the Diaspora and in Israel had increasingly weakened in the course of recent years and some estrangement had occurred, he concluded:

> In a somewhat absurd fashion the war on anti-Semitism gives us a new opportunity to mend the rift... If we

succeed in overcoming the alienation,
if we manage to bring together the torn
shreds of the Jewish nation and make
them feel that we are brethren again—then
we have the chance. We cannot miss this
opportunity.[174]

THE EFFECTS OF COGNITIVE DISSONANCE

Unreasonable reactions, as in the Gretta Duisenberg Affair,
certainly cannot be attributed only to faulty thinking or
social envy. In my opinion, they are caused mainly by a
psychic behavior pattern known as "cognitive dissonance."
Uri Avneri of the Gush Shalom peace movement once
correlated this concept with the conduct of Jewish Israelis.
The term describes a feeling of unease that arises when a
person's self-image no longer corresponds to reality. In this
particular case, it means that Israelis would rather demonize
the Palestinians than think about the aggressive actions of
their own government.

Within Israel, many Jews have so internalized the
suffering of their families during the Nazi period that they
can barely see themselves as anything other than victims.
They are in denial about the often quite cruel actions taken
against the Palestinians. The constant fear of suicide attacks
reinforces the feeling of continued victimization, as well
as the conviction that the Palestinians have no goal but
to destroy Israel. Undoubtedly there are such Palestinians,
but the Israelis blithely ignore that the former have neither
the troop strength nor the equipment to follow through
with this intention. Whatever the Israeli forces do—
whether it is humiliating the Palestinians, destroying their

homes and infrastructure, targeted killings, or shooting at ambulances—Israelis do not consider it a transgression because two thousand years of persecution absolve them automatically of all guilt.

Indisputably, they have had to live in constant fear for many years, and this does generate real suffering. But it is also true that cognitive dissonance, the psychological impossibility of seeing themselves as anything but victims, renders them blind to the role of the oppressor that they have now openly been playing since 1967, and which is partly to blame for their precarious situation. To them, Jewish Israelis can never be war criminals.

That the equally tragic and comic events surrounding Mrs. Duisenberg occurred in the Netherlands is not only due to the fact that she owns a house in Amsterdam, but is also connected with the history of the Jews in that country during Nazi occupation, which was quite a bit harsher than in other occupied Western lands. Thus, although most Jews in the Netherlands have a good life, they regard themselves as victims as well, and this is not without reason from a historical point of view. Due to this shared history, they so thoroughly identify with the Jews in Israel that they have become uncritical apologists for Israeli policies.

Since Jews in the Netherlands cannot entirely shield themselves from television images of Israeli soldiers who act like vandals in Palestinian cities, however, cognitive dissonance arises once again. They feel this all the more strongly because their lives are rather safe compared to those of their Israeli brothers and sisters. If they believe that they are exposed to virulent anti-Semitism, however, the feeling of being a victim is reinforced, and relief provided. Thus, latent and virulent anti-Semitism both function as *Deus ex machina* for them. The fear of anti-

Semitism is historically understandable, but irrational, unjustified fear that escapes self-control or arises from a subconscious need can become a self-fulfilling prophecy.

A Storm of Controversy

"If a book and a head collide, and a hollow sound is heard, is it necessarily the book?" This question by the German aphorist Georg Christian Lichtenberg implies that our minds, as the receivers of communication, tend to be too empty, and that if they contained more substance, we would more easily assimilate information. In my opinion, however, the opposite is more likely the case. Our heads are too full—too full of prejudices that are the result of past trauma—and this is what blocks our receptivity to new information or points of view. This became clear to me after an exchange of articles that occurred between me and the Dutch Jewish journalist and columnist Anet Bleich, who accused me of comparing Israel's treatment of the Palestinians in the occupied territories with that which I myself experienced in Nazi Germany and occupied Holland.

I became even more aware of the storm of controversy that this comparison could cause when Ms. Bleich responded to an article of mine that had appeared in a daily paper, with one of her own. "Comparisons [between present-day Israel] and Auschwitz, the Nuremberg race laws, or the *Kristallnacht* is the last thing we [Jews] want to be confronted with," she wrote.[175] In fact, I never drew such comparisons, particularly not to Auschwitz. If Bleich had written, "with the onset of the Nazi period in Germany and in occupied Holland," she would have been correct. The identification of the Nazi period with Auschwitz was in her own mind. That most people tend to conflate these two completely different periods does not increase the validity of this mistake. The question here is: why do we keep falling into this error?

The fact is that I greatly underestimated the trauma suffered by most first-, second-, or third-generation Jewish readers of my article. This became evident not only in my exchange with Anet Bleich, but in discussions I had with others as well. At the time I had written as follows:

> In order to make anti-Jewish measures palatable to Germans during the early 1930s so that the social and economic life of Jews could be progressively strangled without creating perceptible disruption, an ideology had to be propagated that made it clear that Jews were different. In other words, Jews had to be demonized.[176]

In the 1930s, there were as yet no formal plans for annihilating the Jews. The idea was to make their life in Germany so difficult that they would want to emigrate. The reigning ideology stated that Jews did not fit in with German culture. The point I was trying to make when I wrote that article was that prominent Israeli politicians were promoting a similar demonizing ideology about the "Arabs" (the term "Palestinians" is traditionally avoided by Zionists so as not to grant them a national identity). They didn't belong to *their* culture. A good example is the following statement given in an interview by Ehud Barak, who was touted as the "moderate" candidate facing Ariel Sharon in the 2001 elections:

> Due to the nature of Arab thinking, their culture does not contain the concept

of compromise. Compromise is apparently
a Western concept for settling disputes. [177]

Somewhat later in the same interview, he stated:

> Those on the Left are divided. They
> see that their neighbors [the Palestinians]
> are not benign. They are not a part of
> Western culture.[178]

What I did in my article, and what I continue to
do, is to compare these two prejudices—one propagated
by the Germans against the Jews, and the other by certain
prominent Israelis against the Palestinians. In both cases, the
suggestion is made that the "enemy" understands nothing
of the culture of the dominant group. One reader wrote
in response to my article that in making this comparison I
placed Barak's stated opinions on a par with the degradation
of a people to be driven like cattle to the slaughter. Such a
reaction is typical of the mental short-circuit that causes so
many Jews conjure up "gas chambers" as soon as they read
or hear about "Germans during the Nazi period."

A Closer Look at the Short-Circuit

To show how illogical—although psychologically
understandable—this reaction is, we need to cast a brief
glance over some admittedly complex material. Recent
research has shown conclusively that as late as January
1939, Hitler planned nothing more than the deportation
of all Jews. Among other indications of this is Hitler's
comment to the Polish Minister of Foreign Affairs, Jozéf
Beck, in July, 1941, that he would "prefer to settle Jews in
a distant land" and that, "had the Western powers allowed

him, he might have chosen an African colony for the purpose."[179] According to the most recent evidence, widely disparate factors led to the decision to destroy the Jewish people. In addition, none of the statements and documents relating to the new policy is dated prior to the second half of 1941.[180] The demonization of Jews was unforgivable in and of itself—as is that of any people. The Catholic Church had been demonizing Jews for centuries before the Nazis enthusiastically took up the banner. Discrimination based on religion or ethnic origin is incompatible with human dignity. Even if such bigotry does not lead to mass murder, the experience can be extremely traumatizing and negatively impact a person's development.

The most extreme form of discrimination is genocide, although it can be seen as an entirely separate phenomenon that occurs only sporadically in history. The Holocaust is nevertheless a historical fact. For this reason, almost all Jews, and a large portion of the sympathetic world population, identify Nazi Germany exclusively with this program of systematic mass murder. They forget that for half of the twelve years that they were in power the Nazis did not contemplate such a methodical slaughter. Rather, what the Jews faced during this period was humiliation, discrimination and impoverishment. This was, in itself, more than enough to cripple them mentally and psychologically.

THE HOLOCAUST AS BENCHMARK

Thus, the Holocaust has, consciously or unconsciously, been transformed into a sort of benchmark that is applied in the new context of Israel's conflict with the Palestinians. In comparison to the Holocaust, sick Palestinians who die en route to a hospital because of roadblocks seem like a trifle. If, for example, Palestinian children are killed when the Israeli Defense Forces bomb the house of a suspected Palestinian terrorist, the Israelis view them as little more than collateral damage. This impulse to misuse the Holocaust as a yardstick to play down the suffering and injustice done to others overlooks the simple but fundamental truth that all suffering can destroy the life and soul of a human being.

The severe and widespread psychological damage caused by the Holocaust, intensified by feelings of guilt (whether justified or not), have served as the underpinnings of Jewish extremism. This extremism may manifest itself as religious fundamentalism or aggressive nationalism, as when Jewish settlers celebrated the anniversary of the death of a man who murdered twenty-nine praying Palestinians in cold blood in 1994, and received official sanction to do so.[181] Such abuses are justified by an argument, whether explicitly expressed or not, that essentially says: 'Until we Jews commit as many horrible crimes as non-Jews have committed against us, we can do whatever we want.'

This attitude was demonstrated in a most shocking way by the famous Harvard professor Alan Dershowitz, who either asked or allowed Henryk Broder, a well-known German Jewish journalist on the editorial staff of the prestigious German weekly *Der Spiegel*, to write a foreword for the German edition of his book, *A Case for Israel*.[182] Broder's foreword includes the following mind-boggling quotation:

> In the eyes of the general public, [Israel] has made the transformation from a victim to a perpetrator... This is true. Israel is presently more perpetrator than

victim. But that is good and it is right. After all, for nearly two thousand years the Jews were in the role of the perennial victims, and their experiences in this role were bad indeed. Perpetrators mostly have a longer life expectancy than victims, and *it is much more fun to be a perpetrator* [emphasis mine].

As a survivor of Auschwitz, I have this to say regarding Broder's appalling remark: I remember extremely well from my days in Auschwitz-Gleiwitz how much fun the camp commander, SS *Hauptscharführer* Moll, had when he ordered his big Alsatian to attack one of my comrades. He nearly laughed himself to death, especially when the Jew started to cry and to beg. After Moll's job as commander of the gas chambers, he was awarded the privilege to run his own concentration camp in the spring of 1944, and thus fully enjoy his status as licensed criminal. In one respect Broder is right. I, who had to look upon the scene in which my comrade was tortured, did not have the "fun" that Moll did.

From my experience, I have seen that individuals who amuse themselves by torturing people exist. A recent notorious example was the behavior of some of the military police in the Abu Ghuraib prison in Iraq. Such perpetrators who had no social ethics to start with may indeed have a long life. I suspect, however, that those who were decent human beings to begin with, and who were seduced into becoming something else, will have to cope with such psychological stress that they will not be able to live long without regular, and even permanent, psychological support.

A friend of Mr. Broder's, whom he explicitly mentions in his text, is the Dutch Jewish writer Leon de

Winter, also well known in the U.S. In an extensive interview some years ago, he said the following about himself:

> I didn't know, until a few years ago,
> that in the nineteenth century Jewish gangs
> of robbers were making the Dutch province
> of Brabant unsafe. Of these people I am a
> direct offspring. Robbing, blackmailing and
> cheating we wandered through the country
> of Brabant.[183]

Thus, in this interview, Mr. de Winter clearly portrayed himself as someone who consciously identifies with robbers and outlaws. Even when not consciously expressed, however, this attitude leads many Jews in Israel and elsewhere to such a level of moral insensitivity that Jonathan Sacks, Chief Rabbi of Great Britain felt compelled to express the following opinion in an interview with the British daily *The Guardian* on August 27, 2002. After pointing out that the Mosaic books repeat 36 times that Jews were exiled so that they may know "what it feels like to be an exile," this very conservative man, who had previously supported Israeli policies uncritically, stated:

> I regard the current situation as
> nothing less than tragic, because it is forcing
> Israel into postures that are incompatible
> in the long run with our deepest ideals.

Expressing shock at reports of smiling Israeli soldiers posing for a photograph with the corpse of a slain Palestinian, he added:

> There is no question that this
> kind of prolonged conflict, together with
> the absence of hope, generates hatreds

and insensitivities that in the long run are corrupting to a culture.

THE IRRESPONSIBLE USE OF WORLD WAR II AS A MORAL REFERENCE POINT

The misleading use of words is not always intentional or ill willed. The statements of some politicians or commentators are sometimes merely ill considered, and therefore easy to misuse. Here is an example from a talk given by the Dutch-Jewish journalist Elsbeth Etty, according to a transcript:

> But that does not mean that we cannot use the norms gained from our experience in World War II as a reference point in the debate about tolerance and discrimination.[184]

It sounds reasonable, but this formulation conceals a trap. The events of World War II represented a continuum that ranged from mere discrimination all the way to industrialized mass murder. Discrimination on the basis of ethnic origin or race must be condemned from the very outset, when it first begins to manifest, if we wish to prevent it from reaching its logical conclusion. Although I know quite well that Ms. Etty agrees with me on this point, she nevertheless felt justified in using the evil endpoint of World War II as the reference point for her criticism of the policies of Pim Fortuyn's populist party in order to show where such discrimination can lead.[185] It must be noted here that the situation facing Dutch asylum seekers and immigrants is fundamentally incomparable with that which Jews faced in Germany in the 1930s since most German Jews were highly integrated into German society—to such an extent, in fact, that they could have been characterized as more German than the Germans.

By using one of the most horrific crimes in the history of humankind for the purposes of comparison, Etty was on shaky ground. This is because the magnitude of the Holocaust dwarfs all other crimes. By so doing, one trivializes the suffering, in many cases traumatic, which the Jews suffered under Hitler during the eight years preceding the genocide. These included impoverishment, limitations on freedom of movement, and exclusion from education. In addition, one does an injustice to the approximately 300,000 German Jews who, although they escaped death in the gas chambers by emigrating in time, also suffered greatly in spite of their survival. A large number of them committed suicide, either in forced exile or in Germany. A suicide curve for German Jews shows that the Nazis' seizure of power, the "annexation" of Austria, the *Kristallnacht*, and the announcement of deportations all led to sudden increases in suicide. The conclusion would seem to be obvious—that the despair, social degradation, deprivation of civil rights, and isolation caused by these events triggered feelings of intolerable intensity in many.

Whoever makes light of all this does not understand dignity, what it means to have a country to call one's own, or how threatening existential fear can be. The humiliation that I experienced as an adolescent whenever I came into contact with German authorities, or with the SA, the SS, or the Gestapo has burned itself into my memory. It is precisely because this already occurred many years *before* Auschwitz that I am so deeply affected whenever I see Palestinian citizens being humiliated at checkpoints and mistreated by oppressors in the uniform of the Israeli army who have lost their moral bearings.

Because of their family history, the point of reference for many people of Jewish heritage is the gas chambers. Compared with this, almost all of the injustices committed by Israel against the Palestinians seem negligible. An illustration of this can be found in an interview with Dr. Arjeh Eldad, who was Chief Medical Officer of the Israeli army between 1979 and 2000, and is today Director of the Department of Plastic Surgery at Hadassah University Clinic in Jerusalem. As a supporter of such absolute solutions to the Palestinian problem as expulsion or deportation, Dr. Eldad said: "[The Palestinians'] small tragedies are always to be preferred to a greater tragedy, which is always ours." Interviewer Yossi Klein summed up Eldad's opinion: "We Jews can ignore world opinion because the world remains silent regarding our fate."[186]

Historian and Holocaust researcher Dr. Aryeh Arad, on the other hand, believes in human moral values. According to Klein, Arad "dismisses the concept of the 'voluntary transfer' espoused by Aryeh Eldad and Effi Eitam, because it is not practical." Arad, too, would like "the Arabs to disappear out of sight," but he knows that "the world will not let us do things like that." In the same article, the "moderate" Rabbi Adin Steinsaltz, a Talmudic scholar and professor of chemistry and mathematics at Hebrew University, states: "A transfer [of the Palestinians] may not be pleasant or nice, but it is not as bad as murder." Here, too, the end-stage of World War II is taken as the point of reference.

The fact remains that until January 1939 Hitler planned nothing more radical than the deportation of Jews still living in Germany. During an official discussion, he claimed to regret that the other countries weren't willing to take them in.[187] If we bear this historical fact in mind, shivers should run down our spine when we read the appeal, signed by 149 Israeli academics and scientists, which was sent out at the end of 2002 in an attempt to influence world public opinion:

> The Israeli ruling coalition includes parties that promote "transfer" of the Palestinian population as a solution to what they call "the demographic problem… Prime Minister Sharon has backed this "assessment of reality." Escalating racist demagoguery concerning the Palestinian citizens of Israel may indicate the scope of the crimes that are possibly being contemplated.[188]

RESPONSE TO CRITICISM

Joris Luyendijk, until recently Near East correspondent for *NRC Handelsblad,* the most prestigious daily newspaper in the Netherlands, made a name for himself with his clear and penetrating analyses of the difficult situation in the region, and is able to make this seemingly incomprehensible situation understandable to other people. For example, his article *"Nooit Veilig, Altijd Bang"* (Never Secure, Always Fearful) contains a series of sharp and expert observations.[189] He describes how the "sensitive triad of Holocaust-Israel-occupation" explains Israel's political behavior in many areas. In particular, fear of another Holocaust drives both the peace activists and the right-wing camp. Both parties agree that it should never happen again. Luyendijk continues, however: "When the peace movement says this, it means 'to people.' When the right-wing says it, it means 'to us.'"

Luyendijk has captured precisely the almost paranoid fear that many Jews both inside and outside of Israel feel, and that has a stranglehold on the behavior of virtually the entire Israeli public. In my opinion, however, what he overlooks in his analysis makes me wonder whether he doesn't overly identify with his Israeli friends. He has this, for instance, to say on the subject of why Israel is so severely criticized abroad:

> But again the question arises: Why is Israel so severely and relentlessly criticized? Given that human rights are trodden underfoot throughout the Mideast, why does Israel reap three-quarters of the criticism? After all, compared with the rest of them their record is really not all that bad. Is it any wonder that Israelis perceive a form of conscious or unconscious anti-Semitism in this selectivity? Why is it so much worse for a Jew, rather than a co-religionist, to oppress a Muslim?

Here it appears that he actually believes in the myth of a resurgent and malignant anti-Semitism, which is consciously being fueled against Israel. There are three things we can say in response:

First, the Israeli government itself abuses the word "anti-Semitism" in a completely irresponsible and almost reckless manner. For example, in April 2002, when Europe criticized actions taken by the Israeli army in the Yenin refugee camp in the West Bank, Shimon Peres, then foreign minister in Ariel Sharon's cabinet stated, "I regret the European reaction.... Where in Europe, at the beginning, anti-Semitism was against the individual Jewish person, today I am afraid there is anti-Semitism against the Jewish state."[190] This makes any critical remark about Israel's governmental policies suspect *a priori*. Israel is thus above criticism. The fact that Peres's remark was not merely a slip of the tongue is demonstrated by a statement by Shlomo Gur, Executive-Secretary of the EU-Israel Forum at a symposium in November 2002: "A black cloud of anti-Semitism hangs over the relationship between the EU and Israel, and stands in the way of open dialogue."[191]

Second, anti-Semitism has in one form or another been endemic in Europe for almost 2,000 years. The extremely negative connotations of this term should make us very cautious when accusing someone of anti-Semitic motives. Anti-Semitism has always been associated with discrimination, persecution, hatred, and finally with the destruction of a minority having absolutely no political power. The fact that Jews have for the first time since antiquity become a considerable political and military power, particularly after the Six Day War, and that they use, and sometimes abuse, this power, means that we must completely rethink how we deal with anti-Semitism. The mentality evinced by the statements of Peres and Gur, as well as Israel's military power, have led to a situation in which an important nation believes itself to be immune to all criticism. This trend can only be reversed by completely disassociating criticism of Israel's policies from the word "anti-Semitism." We must simply insist on the right to call clear violations of human rights by their name.

Third, the fixation on everything that Israel is doing wrong stems in part from a widespread identification of many non-Jews with their Jewish neighbors. The Jews are the oldest "foreign" group that has been largely integrated into European society since the second half of the 19th century. In the process they have made literary, cultural, and scientific contributions disproportionate to their numbers. In other words, for many civilized Europeans, the Jews living in their country are "their" Jews, and hence almost identical with themselves. Because a large part of the Jewish population of Europe still supports Israel's policies uncritically, at least outwardly, it would seem reasonable to assume that they share in the blame. On the other hand, as a direct result of their identification with their Jewish neighbors, many Europeans feel almost as if they themselves are in some measure responsible for Israel's human rights violations. Just as Americans demonstrated against the Vietnam War and the Dutch protested against the so-called "*politionele acties*," the military interventions carried out by their colonial administration between 1947 and 1949 in Indonesia, there is a strong critical interest in the war among non-Jewish Europeans because of their identification with "their" Jews.

Naturally, some of those who criticize Israeli policies do so either completely or partly because of guilt feelings, which they project onto the Jews. This may often look like a new version of old-fashioned anti-Semitism. I believe, however, that the majority of Westerners who criticize Israeli policies have positive motivations. Incorrigible anti-Semites do exist in small numbers, but because the taboo on anti-Semitism is still very strong, they tend to keep quiet if they still retain even a spark of decency. Open anti-Semites who attack citizens wearing the *kippah* and desecrate cemeteries and synagogues are a tiny fringe group. The wise remark made by the late Dutch writer and lawyer Abel Herzberg shortly after his return from Bergen-Belsen, that this type of anti-Semitism is more of a problem for anti-Semites than for Jews, applies here.[192]

Is Criticism of Israel the Same as Anti-Semitism?

Given the harsh occupation policies and the disproportionate reactions of Israeli state terrorism to attacks by diverse Palestinian groups, Israel's policy would, in the eyes of many, only be justified if Palestinian terror attacks would continue after the end of the occupation and the withdrawal from all Jewish settlements in Palestinian territory. Even then, however, a certain reticence would be in order. Yet Israel's ravages in densely populated Palestinian residential areas have often been barbarian, and its plans of using the war in Iraq to drive out or deport all Palestinians was so openly discussed that the Jordanian government demanded a denial from the government of Israel—which Prime Minister Sharon refused to do.[193]

Criticizing such actions and plans has nothing to do with anti-Semitism. Any claim to the contrary is a function of that flawed thinking described by Aristotle: *All white horses are horses, but that does not mean that all horses are white.* Even if all anti-Semites criticize Israel, not everyone who criticizes Israel is anti-Semitic. The above-quoted statements by Shimon Peres and Natan Sharansky are akin to a rule against criticism, but all they achieve is that Israel places itself outside the community of civilized nations. Jews, wherever in the world they may be, who unconditionally support Israel's policies, share responsibility for these policies and are included in the criticism, which in turn causes them to feel persecuted. They should realize, however, that they are no longer victims, but active participants in creating the situation that they face.

Non-Jews, for their part, need to gradually shed their feelings of guilt about the Holocaust and consider themselves free to criticize Jews who commit obvious crimes. No one should be exempt from accountability. Israeli-Dutch poet Tsavi Levi vividly describes every individual's shared responsibility: *For even the hands of those who look on as though paralyzed will turn red.* Anyone wishing to be known as a friend of the Jews will fail when withholding the critical truth from his Jewish friends. Not confronting criticism can have disastrous consequences in the long run. The illusion of being untouchable can only sustain the continuation of inhuman acts, with the resulting danger that real anti-Semitism will end up finding open doors.

In sum, we can state that at present the only reason to expect a revival of dangerous anti-Semitism is Israel's increasingly reprehensible policies. Justified criticism of the policies of Israel must be fundamentally and clearly distinguished from anti-Semitic words and acts. A real danger is that most Jews will, out of a misguided feeling of loyalty, continue to lend their unqualified support to Israel. As a result, it will become more and more difficult to distinguish between criticism of State policies and criticism of Jewish individuals. Those Jews who closely identify with the State of Israel will continuously and increasingly interpret any hostility as being directed against them, and will always brand any critic as an anti-Semite. Such a critic will in turn consider that accusation to be unjustified and unjust, and it will be increasingly difficult for him to suppress negative feelings toward his accuser.

Criticism of the State of Israel, no matter how obviously it only pertains to the matter at hand, inevitably refers to, or is felt in appeals to, Jewish individuals. With increasing criticism of this nature, a crisis situation arises because a nerve close to that of the old anti-Semitism is stimulated, even though criticism of the State of Israel has nothing to do with it in principle. It has to be possible to criticize a state, however, and Jews cannot afford to suppress their conscience. If they do so, believing it is their duty to defend wrongheaded and even inhumane policies and in addition raise unfounded accusations, then they should not be surprised if anti-Semitic sentiments are aroused again. Would it not be better if Jews throughout the world, or at least a majority of them, would immediately deny Israel the right to speak in their behalf? Jewish organizations need to publicly distance themselves far more from current Israeli policies, and Jewish citizens, wherever they may be, should actively and visibly stand with peace groups in large numbers.

CHAPTER 7

REFLECTIONS ON THE NATURE OF EVIL
What Goethe, Hannah Arendt, and Other Philosophers Tell Us

THE OPPORTUNITY FOR REINTERPRETATION AND NEW HISTORICAL PERSPECTIVE

DUE TO MY life experiences, particularly in those years leading up to and during World War II, I have witnessed evil and understood a few things about its nature. Moreover, it is clear at present that the diverse manifestations of evil are not relegated to the past, but are in full view again on various fronts, and not even very far away—in ethnic conflicts in Europe, in the Middle East, and in the war against the fundamentalist Islamic terrorism of Al-Qaeda.

In Goethe's *Faust*, evil plays a central role—not only in the character of Mephistopheles, but also of Faust and, less explicitly, the Lord in Heaven. That we can revisit this work two hundred years after it was written and still find it applicable to the issues of our own era is due to its classical grandeur, for the greatest works of art—those of eternal value—are precisely those that lend themselves to reinterpretation in any era. Truth, wisdom, ethics, or aesthetic principles are so universally and fundamentally stated in them that they permit ever-new interpretations appropriate to contemporary events. This applies to the Greek dramas and tragedies, Shakespeare's works, the music of Bach, and equally to the works of Goethe or Chekhov, to name but a few well-known classics. In the case of Goethe (1749-1832), it might be said that his genius was capable of foreknowledge of dangerous and inhuman events that were to happen long after his death.

The work of the 20th century philosopher Hannah Arendt (1906-1975) bears a relation to Goethe's *Faust* because Arendt, too, thought deeply about evil in the world—much more explicitly, in fact, than Goethe himself. She wrote her most important works at a time when a dramatic period in Europe's history had just passed—a time in which evil had attained a dimension not previously seen in the Western world. In her lifetime, the dust that had been stirred up by these events was still so dense that a full view of all-important aspects of them was practically impossible.

The war crimes trial of Adolf Eichmann was a major focus of Arendt's interest. The dust from that event has still not settled completely, by any means, but at least it is now less dense and permits us a clearer view. Moreover, since the events of September 11, 2001, we have experienced new and dangerous manifestations of world conflict. As a result, we now live in a world in which evil once again has made its appearance with great immediacy and in new forms of expression. This, in turn, opens up new historical perspectives. A re-examination of some of Hannah Arendt's principal ideas thus becomes both possible and necessary.

Enlightenment in a Kantian Sense

It cannot be denied that Goethe was almost excessively ambitious in attempting to symbolize in his tragedy the most important fundamental elements of European culture. Classical antiquity and the Renaissance, 19th century modern science and medieval alchemy, hell and heaven, devil and angels, damnation and redemption, and the use or misuse of both medicine and theology are all brought upon the stage in some manner. Goethe's viewpoint on theology, in particular, was modern for his era, even though he was critical of the Enlightenment as it expressed itself in France. It seems as if he fully subscribed to Immanuel Kant's philosophical views, and Kant must be seen as one of Germany's great Enlightenment philosophers in this context.

Kant's reply to the question "What is Enlightenment?" was *"Sapere aude,"* which he translated as: "Have the courage of using your own mind." [194] He goes on to explain that this autonomous thinking primarily pertains to religious matters.[195] Indeed, Goethe does think autonomously with regard to theological questions from the very beginning of his work—and quite thoroughly at that, as can be shown in any number of quotations. Early on, when Faust mentions all the disciplines he has studied, he adds the word *leider* (regrettably), to theology alone. [356] To further emphasize the entire nonsense of theology, he says a little later: "[*I*] *am not afraid of hell or devil.*" [369]

THEODICY: THE MEANING OF EVIL

Indeed, it is not only Faust who is unafraid of hell or devil. Goethe himself does not hesitate to offer an answer to the age-old theological question of theodicy, the meaning of evil in the world, when God, after all, is supposed to be benevolent. Judging by what is said on this point during the Prologue in Heaven, God himself (the Lord in Heaven) used, if not actually created, evil in the world—and did so with some degree of pleasure—to prod humans out of their natural lethargy. The Lord in Heaven:

> *Human activity slackens all too easily.*
> *People readily love unconditional rest;*
> *And so I like to send them that companion*
> *Who goads and acts and must be devilish.* [340-343]

Without the maturity in religious matters called for by Kant, such a bold step would hardly be conceivable. Indeed, Goethe goes one step further in shedding traditional theology. In spite of his aforementioned ambition to symbolize the basic elements of overall European culture, one gap is only too evident. One of the West's most significant cultural determinants, the Judeo-Christian ethic, is at best mentioned in passing. This ethic, without which our contemporary Western world would be unthinkable, and which comprises what Nietzsche called the transformation from morality of the master (*Herrenmoral*) to the morality of the slave (*Sklavenmoral*)[196], is notable in *Faust* by its almost total absence.[197] Primarily, this doctrine very plainly states our obligations toward our fellow human beings. This fundamental ethic in our Western world also implies an interpretation of evil, which addresses its most important manifestation: the evil done by one individual to another.

SOCIAL EVIL

In the Judeo-Christian tradition, i.e. in the Old Testament, social evil is primarily defined as that which is not good. What it means to do good is summarized not only in the Ten Commandments, but also in Deuteronomy 5 and Ezekiel 18:5-9, which demand, among other things, practicing justice, exacting no usurious interest, returning property that has been placed as collateral, refraining from robbery or adultery, feeding the hungry, and dressing the naked. Together with the law regarding the treatment of strangers enunciated in Leviticus 19:33-34, which stresses the essential equality of all people, these passages construct a baseline for the Judeo-Christian social ethic. The Bible's demand that humans should do only good deeds, thus creating a better world, is repeated and reinforced in the New Testament, most explicitly in Philemon 14.

It is important to note in this context that, according to the Bible, humans do know the difference between good and evil, and are endowed with the free will that allows them to decide which road to take. The first humans in this tale already acted contrary to God's will. Humans are, therefore, from the very beginning portrayed as being capable of judgment, and not merely as automata or puppets guided by God's hand. Human beings are the cause of social evil, and this evil is the price of human freedom. The mathematician and natural philosopher Gottfried Leibniz (1646-1716) appears to have arrived at this same conclusion, as well. Rüdiger Safranski summarizes this principle in his book *Das Böse, oder das Drama der Freiheit* as follows: "Hence, God is not responsible for the evil perpetrated by Man; he only allows it because he is giving Man the freedom [to do so]."[198]

In the Beginning Was the Deed

In *Faust*, Mephistopheles enters the stage as the manifestation of Evil. He is charged with goading Faust into deeds—that is, activity, per se, rather than necessarily *good* deeds. This obsession with activity for its own sake goes so far as to cause Faust to translate the New Testament in heretical fashion. "*In the beginning was the word*" [1224] is replaced with "*In the beginning was the deed*" [1237]. To understand what this really signifies, we have to recall that, in the Jewish tradition—the content of which was indeed preserved, and adhered to, by Jesus—the Word, which is the Torah, or Law, existed before the creation of the world.[199] In addition to many requirements hardly in keeping with today's idea of good deeds, it most importantly contains many commandments that specifically demand the practice of such deeds. With one stroke of Faust's pen, the place of this ethic, so important to our entire culture, is now taken by deeds—without the qualifying "good." This substitution fulfills the Lord's charge to Mephistopheles of inciting humans to action.

EICHMANN AND THE BANALITY OF EVIL

Coming from the satanic realm, Mephistopheles is not motivated by anything to do with social ethics, yet he nevertheless possesses a certain ethic, too—even a considerable one. In this regard, Mephistopheles' evil is comparable to Eichmann's evil as so painstakingly described by Hannah Arendt:

> Eichmann was not Iago and not Macbeth, and nothing would have been farther from him than to resolve with Richard III to "become an evildoer." He would never have killed his supervisor in order to attain his position.[200]

Eichmann, in other words, was by no means entirely without any ethics. On the contrary, he had a decidedly powerful moral consciousness in the sense of possessing strict discipline and great dependability, as well as in exercising care, obedience, notable diligence, and eagerness in the execution of his duties. He excelled in that which former German Chancellor Helmut Schmidt called "Prussian secondary virtues." Could Eichmann—the embodiment of the banality of evil according to Hannah Arendt—be considered a "virtuous" man? Yes, in the sense that dependability, eagerness, and attention to one's duties should also be counted among a person's virtues—even if they are only the above-mentioned secondary ones.

Thus, the "banality of evil" is in reality "substitution for the good." That is, potentially pre-existing humanitarian ethical principles are replaced by other values. When accomplished to perfection, as was the case with a man like Eichmann who was entirely reliable as a comrade and subaltern, this process of substitution results in "strictly disciplined evil." What takes the place of humanitarian, ethical values may differ from person to person, but it is always bound up with a perceived threat to one's country or people, instilled in the population by certain groups or membership of its leadership.

Examples can be found in slogans uttered in every dictatorship. The nation is surrounded by enemies and must be defended at all cost. All strangers must be expelled or exterminated because they weaken and undermine the nation. Only what the party, the ideology, or the *Führer* commands can guarantee the people a happy future. Nothing else counts, even if it implies mass murder on an industrial scale. As Arendt reported:

> Confronted in Jerusalem with documentary evidence of his extraordinary loyalty toward Hitler and the ominous order by the latter, Eichmann repeatedly sought

to explain that "the *Führer's* word was law"
in the Third Reich.[201]

It would be wrong, however, to assume that this
replacement of ethical values happens only in totalitarian
states. It takes place in any state that considers itself
threatened. In most cases, the intensity of the claimed
threat is exaggerated, even if the claim contains a kernel
of truth. This was true in the case of pre-First World War
imperial Germany, in Israel since its inception, and in the
post-9/11 United States.

What this was like in Germany in the years leading
up to World War I is well illustrated in the case of the
historian Heinrich von Treitschke, an intellectual of liberal
background who completely succumbed to the influence of
a charismatic demagogue, Adolf Stoecker. Together, they
wielded enormous influence upon the young intelligentsia
of the last two decades in 19th century Germany. Regarding
this pair, German-American historian Fritz Stern wrote:

> About 1879, it became clear
> that the atmosphere in the Reich had
> changed. It was in that year that two men
> with impeccable credentials warned in
> genteel manner of the Jewish danger,
> thus justifying the existence of a "Jewish
> question." One was Adolf Stoecker, Court
> Preacher and thereby representative of
> Crown and Church, the other Heinrich
> Treitschke, who was celebrated as Prussia's
> greatest historian and an adornment to
> Berlin's University. The great prestige of
> pastor and professor, guardians of national
> morality, gave the campaign against Jews'

and liberals' status and respectability. [202]

Of course, the substitution of humanitarian values is rarely as complete and enduring as in Eichmann's case. When a residue of average conscience remains in a corner of the self, it is capable of being stimulated again given sufficiently shocking experiences. We find such examples in Oskar Schindler, the subject of the book *Schindler's Ark* and the film *Schindler's List*. An opportunistic businessman, Schindler joined the Nazi Party in late 1939, and was one of many who sought to profit from the German invasion of Poland in that same year. At little expense, he gained ownership of a factory in Cracow from a Jewish industrialist named Nathan Wurz, and earned huge sums of money in record time. He is credited with saving as many as 1,200 Jews during the Holocaust by having them work in his enamelware and ammunitions factories. No one really knows what Schindler's motives were. However, he was quoted as saying that he knew the people who worked for him, and when one knew people, one had to behave toward them like human beings. He died in 1974 at the age of 66, and was buried at the Catholic Cemetery at Mount Zion in Jerusalem.[203]

Another example of incomplete substitution is that of *SS-Obersturmführer* Kurt Gerstein. He was a mining engineer by training and designed the first gas chambers for delousing at the Hygiene Institute of the *Waffen-SS* in Berlin. As soon as he found out what these chambers were being used for after 1942, he tried—due to a considerable residue of Protestant conscience—to warn the democratic world via contacts with Sweden and the Vatican. The world did not want to hear it. Goethe's words from *Faust* apply to people like Schindler and Gerstein, when, after commanding him to seduce Faust to commit evil deeds he has God tell Mephistopheles: "And stand in shame when you have to admit: a good man, in his dark urges, is quite aware of the proper course." [327]

MEPHISTOPHELES AS FIRST REPRESENTATIVE OF EVIL IN FAUST

Whether prophetic or merely coincidental, Mephistopheles, a member of the satanic world and archetypal representative of evil, has many of the qualities that could be considered virtuous in Eichmann. Mephistopheles punctiliously adheres to the contract made with Faust—in notable contrast with the latter. In other respects, he is dependable. While he is not a friend to Faust, he is nevertheless a good companion. Whenever the situation gets precarious, Mephistopheles does what he can to get Faust out of a tight spot. Naturally, he follows the orders of his superior, the Lord in Heaven, to the letter, but it is striking that he consciously fails to make use of opportunities that would make it possible to take Faust away to Hell earlier than strictly necessary. For example, he warns him: *"Pointless it was to make that promise carelessly."* [6188]. He then provides the means for Faust to retain his position with the Kaiser. Aware that Faust possesses magic powers, granted him by Mephistopheles, the Kaiser asks him to make the ghosts of Helen of Troy and Paris appear. Faust agrees to do this, but Mephistopheles warns him that this could have serious consequences, for he must confront the Mothers, who guard Helen of Troy:

Mephistopheles: *I don't wish to impart to you higher secrets. The Goddesses live alone. They have no place and no time. You cannot talk about them. These are the Mothers.*

Faust, startled: *Mothers!*
Mephistopheles: *Do you tremble?* [6212-6218]

Faust trembles at the mention of the Mothers, for having seduced the innocent Gretchen, and then murdered her along with her brother and mother, he remembers that Gretchen's mother had distrusted him from the start. Thus, it is actually Mephistopheles who reawakens in Faust a residue of conscience, which had hitherto gone almost entirely missing. Here, Mephistopheles stands archetypically for "reliable evil," a variant of the "strictly disciplined evil" of which Eichmann was an exemplar. Mephisto is reliable, but he also has a certain sense of humor. It is doubtful that Eichmann possessed that characteristic. He was Prussian discipline personified.

RADICAL EVIL

The disciplined evil of Eichmann and the reliable evil of Mephistopheles must be contrasted, however, with a far more potent evil, which Hannah Arendt referred to as "radical evil." In her great work, *The Origins of Totalitarianism* (1951), she states:

> Totalitarianism has discovered that there really is something that is radically evil and that it consists of that which humans can neither punish nor forgive. When the impossible became possible, it was found that it was identical with the unpunishable, unforgivable radical evil which can neither be comprehended nor explained via the evil motives of selfishness, greed, envy, lust for power, resentment, cowardice, or whatever

else there may be, and vis-à-vis which
any human reaction is therefore equally
powerless.... It is inherent in our entire
philosophical tradition that we cannot
conceptualize something that is radically
evil, and this applies even to Christian
theology, which attributed heavenly origins
even to Satan...[204]

This quote reflects, in part, Arendt's bewilderment
in the face of the Holocaust. It must be remembered
that she was writing in 1951, only a few years after the
immensity of the tragedy had become fully known. Thus,
she expressed the powerlessness of mankind in even
conceptualizing something that is so radically evil. As late
as 1981, the theologian Emil Fackenheim, who as we earlier
saw assigned the Holocaust to the theological category of
uniqueness, also claimed that because of this postulated
uniqueness he could no longer characterize it as radically
evil. I have already criticized this notion of a theological
category of uniqueness, however. Since history never
repeats itself, all historical events are unique. From my
viewpoint, the Holocaust is therefore no more unique than
any other historical event. It is, however, a manifestation
of radical evil.

What is needed here is simply a clear definition
of radical evil, and although this apparently confounded
philosophers and theologians such as Arendt and
Fackenheim, in my opinion it is not nearly as mysterious
and enigmatic as they perceived it to be. Radical evil can
be defined as any conviction in a person that denies that *all*
humans, as a matter of principle and at the deepest level,
have the same value, irrespective of race, creed, or
ethnic origins. Such a conviction can easily lead to the

demonization of certain groups of people. If applied to large population groups, the radical evil becomes acutely and plainly visible, stirring fear in the citizenry toward another distinguishable population group. At this point, any leader, given the right amount of charisma, can formulate the rules of behavior or patterns of thinking that can be substituted for fundamental social ethics. This points toward the culpability of such people as Hitler, in their supreme command position in a way that goes far beyond the banal criminality of individuals like Eichmann. The former represents the charismatic and pathological leader, the latter the obedient, though far from stupid, servant. As the Nazi leader Hermann Göring allegedly said while he was on trial in Nuremberg:

> The leaders can always seduce the population to stand behind them. It is quite simple. All one needs to do is make the people believe that they are threatened. Then you have to brand those who want to speak of peace and characterize them as unpatriotic rootless scoundrels who represent a danger to their country.[205]

Hence, the radically evil person is one who defines the threatening population group and formulates the doctrine that is to replace the social ethic. Not much more needs to be done to change the threatening population group into one being threatened. Limiting ourselves to the recent past, we can invoke the Stalins (all Kulacks dead), the Hitlers (all Jews dead and all Slavs enslaved), the Pol Pots (all non-Communists dead), and the list goes on. These are the psychopaths and charismatic leaders who indoctrinated the Eichmanns and set them to do their work.

In the wake of the Holocaust, the conscience of the world has acted as a restraining factor, yet visible symptoms of the demonization and segregation of certain population groups continue and may be merely preparatory in nature. We find such symptoms in the statements of Moshe Ya'alon, Chief of Staff of the Israeli Army from 2002 to 2005, who claimed in all earnestness in September 2002, when Arafat's headquarters was under siege and the Palestinian resistance at its nadir, that the Palestinians intended to "destroy the State of Israel step by step."[206]

As we have seen, radical evil is most plainly visible in totalitarian societies. It is by no means restricted to them, however. Arendt thought, even in her late work, that the totalitarian catastrophe of the last century was closely linked to secularization. For example, she wrote after a discussion with philosopher Hans Jona held in 1972:

> I am quite certain that this entire totalitarian catastrophe would not have happened if people had still believed in God or, rather, in Hell, i.e. if ultimate principles had still existed. But none did... There was no one to whom they could appeal. [207]

A little further on, however, Arendt hints at exactly the substitution of values that I emphasize so strongly as being the determinative factor in the appearance of radical evil:

> And if you want to generalize, then you might say that those who still very firmly believed in those "old values" were only too ready to exchange their old values for a new system of values, provided they were given one.[208]

Thus, any mass genocide, whether the Holocaust or the gulags of Stalin, could not have happened without the radical evil that preceded it. Hitler, Stalin, and their ilk personified this radical evil, thoroughly indoctrinating their followers by substituting inhumane, nationalistic values for the normal social ethics that are part of a healthy conscience.

FAITH IN GOD AS INSUFFICIENT SUPPORT FOR THE PRINCIPLE OF EQUALITY

It is true that some passages in the Old Testament, notably in Leviticus 19, indicate that all humans are equal, as does the principle that we were all created in God's image. As we have seen, however, there are also many Biblical passages to which a completely different and much less benevolent meaning can be attributed. These include the passages in Joshua, Judges, and Samuel, all of which command the most thorough ethnic cleansing in the name of God. It might be possible to consider these passages outdated, were it not for the many Orthodox Jewish settlers in territories occupied by Israel who invoke them to justify atrocities and attacks against Palestinians, and whose blood-and-soil theories also appeal to Old Testament passages in order to justify the theft of Palestinian lands.

Many of the Torah's ethical principles are emphasized in the New Testament, and thus apply to Christians as well. However, contrary statements in both the Old and New Testaments negate these ethical principles, particularly the essential equality of all humans, and it is quite certain that these statements follow the interpretation given them by the early fathers of the Church. This indoctrination by the Church over many centuries, in which

the Jews are represented as deniers and even murderers of
the Son of God and who therefore must be regarded as
being inferior, planted many anti-Semitic archetypes in the
souls of Christians. Such archetypes have been used again
and again by secularized anti-Semites. From today's vantage
point, the Holocaust catastrophe would hardly have been
possible without these deeply rooted prejudices. [209]

In this light, Arendt's statement that the Holocaust
would not have happened if people had still believed in
God or the Devil appears naïve. Even though the idea
that all humans are equally valuable is found in both the
Jewish and Christian faiths, neither of these faiths has
lent sufficiently strong and enduring support to this idea.
What we now consider to be the highest humanitarian
principle—the equality or human dignity to which every
individual is entitled—expanded from its seeds in the
Bible into the guiding principle of our values only when
stimulated by the egalitarian ideas of the Enlightenment,
which first culminated in the French Revolution. Thus, it is
a romanticizing error to assume, as does Rüdiger Safranski,
among others, that modern-day mass murders were the
direct consequence of secularization, although he puts it
very well:

> Hitler is the last remover of
> inhibitions in modern times. Since then,
> everyone has been able to know that human
> reality is bottomless... If you abandon your
> good instincts, then you must generate
> everything from your self. If you stop
> believing in God, nothing is left but to
> believe in humans. You may then make the
> surprising discovery that it may have been
> easier to believe in people as long as you

could detour through God.[210]

RADICAL EVIL IN FAUST

Having seen Mephistopheles as an example of "reliable" evil, rather than radical evil, the question arises whether or not there is radical evil in *Faust*, as well. In my interpretation, there is—paradoxically, in the "person" of the Lord in Heaven. After all, it is He who formulates the "new ethos" which is to replace the humanitarian social ethic. Mephistopheles merely conveys this ethos of "activity at any cost" to Faust, upon the Lord's orders. It makes no difference that this whole experiment that God orders Mephistopheles to conduct on Faust entails the sacrifice of numerous innocent people. Evidently, the end justifies the means. Primarily, these victims are the innocent young Gretchen, with whom Faust has fallen in love, her mother, and her brother. All three die simply to extricate Faust from his depression-related lethargy by means of sexual pleasure. Once he has become an "active" person, his ambition turns out to be much too great: *"I wish to rule and have possessions! Acts alone count—glory is nothing."* [10187-88] So great is this ambition, in fact, that innumerable other innocent people must be sacrificed toward this end: *"Human lives were sacrificed, groans of torment filled the darkness; fires flowed down to the sea—there, at dawn, was a canal."* [11127-31] All this occurs by order of the Lord in Heaven (or should we say, of the *Führer?*)

In this connection, it is extremely interesting that in his previously cited book, *Das Böse,* Rüdiger Safranski refers to a passage in Goethe's *Dichtung und Wahrheit,* which might point the way to understand why Goethe wrote such a cruel text.[211] There, Goethe gives the name "demonic" to the same thing that I, following Arendt, have called radical evil:

> But the demonic is most terrible when it manifests itself disproportionately in some person... These are not always outstanding people, neither in mind nor in talents, rarely recommending themselves by kindness of heart; but an immense power emanates from them, and they exert incredible force upon all creatures, even the elements, and who can say how far such an effect will go?

In this sense, the Lord in Heaven may very well be characterized as a representative of demonic power, and by extension, of radical evil.

FAUSTIAN CRAVING

Having examined the nature of evil in the characters of both Mephistopheles and the Lord in Heaven, we finally have to look at the nature of evil found in the protagonist of the tragedy, Faust himself. As we have seen, only very few people represent radical evil. Today's psychiatry would diagnose these charismatic individuals as psychopaths. Whenever such a personality enters the stage of world history, so many people are generally affected in a dangerous way that we can correctly call this the worst form of evil. Faust represents a kind of evil that is far less wicked in its discrete manifestations, but it nevertheless exerts great influence on society by affecting a large number of people from the very start. In a sense it is the simplest, and thus most frequently encountered type of evil, namely pure egotism. It could be called "egocentric" evil.

To the extent that Faust is also the prototype of a man truly striving for enlightenment—the very image of the progressive scientist and scholar—many generations, including my own, have idealized him, as have I. Can my goal as a theoretical physicist be more succinctly described than by Faust's statement of intent: *"that I may learn what holds the world together in its innermost reaches?"* [382-3] It is not possible to become a scholar, and certainly not a theoretical physicist, without some degree of narcissism of this type.

In Faust's case, however, this is so extreme that he thinks only of himself and of satisfying his own desires, not hesitating to walk over dead bodies in his quest. Even when he comes closest to despair and remorse, he still does not feel responsible for Gretchen's misfortunes. He blames Mephistopheles and is furious with him for having concealed her fate from him. Justifiably, Mephistopheles replies: *"Did we thrust ourselves upon you, or you on us?"* And, two speeches later, he asks: *"Who plunged her into ruin—I, or you?"* This type of evil is not examined in Hannah Arendt's work, but rather in Arthur Schopenhauer's. The latter wrote in clear terms:

> If a person is always inclined to commit a wrong as soon as a cause arises and no external power deters him, then we call him evil. In accordance with our definition of evil, this means that such a person not only affirms the will to live as manifested in his own body, but in this regard goes so far as to deny the existence of that will in other individuals ... The ultimate source thereof is a high degree

> of egoism…[deriving] from the fact that
> he alone seeks his own well-being, totally
> indifferent to that of all others, whose
> individuality is completely alien to him,
> separated from his own by a wide chasm,
> and whom he actually regards as no more
> than masks without any reality. [212]

As we have mentioned, the Faustian craving for knowledge
and for the comprehension of nature was a high ideal for
many generations of scientists and scholars—and it may
be so still. In this connection, it is interesting to note that
Hannah Arendt connected the rise of totalitarian society in
the recent past with what she called *"Wissenschaftbesessenheit"*
(obsession with science):

> Because the longing of the modern
> masses for scientific proof plays such a
> great role in modern politics as a whole,
> the idea has been conceived that the entire
> phenomenon [of totalitarianism] may be
> explained as a symptom of that obsession
> with science which has befallen the Western
> world since the rise of contemporary
> mathematics and physics. In this context,
> the totalitarian phenomenon seems merely
> to indicate that last stage in a process during
> which "science has become an idol which
> will magically expunge all the evils of life
> and change the very nature of Man." [213]

The profound crisis of the first half of the 20th
century was based on the substitution of nationalistic values
for fundamental humanitarian values, combined with an
incredible advancement in modern mass technology. In

this sense, Faust's combination of unscrupulousness and obsession with science can be seen as archetypical of this period in history.

ASPECTS OF EVIL IN TODAY'S WORLD

Social evil is evident today in various forms in many parts of the world, especially in its radical form. Its different manifestations, and the unpredictability regarding the time and place their occurrence, heighten the fear. The impossibility of localizing it to one region makes it much harder to fight, but in my opinion, not entirely impossible. These definitions that I have presented have been generated both by philosophic deliberation and personal experience. When we ponder the way in which we can fight radical evil, it is possible that they may point in the right direction. If so, this would also accomplish the task of "attributing meaning to the meaningless," for which I have striven throughout my life.

I have concluded that radical evil arises primarily when a tolerant social ethic is replaced by a system of values that denies the essential equality of all humans—a system that is in principle intolerant versus certain groups of people. It is also completely at odds with the Universal Declaration of Human Rights promulgated by the United Nations in 1948 and recognized by most of the world. As we saw, the Judeo-Christian Bible was by no means sufficiently unequivocal in its acknowledgement of the full dignity of all human beings. Neither the relevant Biblical passages nor even the Enlightenment and the dissemination of its values in the French Revolution sufficed for making the equality of all people the focal point of Western moral values. The Universal Declaration of Human Rights only came about as a result of the terrors of the Holocaust and the resulting guilty conscience of Western Christian nations. Since anti-Semitism did not entirely disappear in Europe even after World War II—in spite of the absence of Jews—most Christian churches in many countries came to realize that it was necessary to distance themselves from the anti-Jewish passages in the New Testament.

Although Holy Scriptures cannot be changed, their verbatim text can be interpreted in new, current, and—above all—less aggressive ways. By simultaneously explaining the historical, religious, and sociological background against which such a text was written, it can be understood as appropriate to its time. As already discussed in detail in the preceding chapter, there were such outdated, cruel, and Judeocentric passages in the Old Testament, and the Talmud as well, so that more gentle reinterpretation became necessary, and was indeed incorporated, even in Talmudic times, i.e. before the 6th century A.D. As Michael A. Meyer writes:

> Certain Biblical laws judged to be cruel by the Rabbis back then—and whose language therefore could not be in harmony with the spirit of the Torah, were reinterpreted: the law which reads "an eye for an eye and a tooth for a tooth" was explicated as merely implying a material retribution in proper proportion.[214]

As we have seen, under the influence of the Enlightenment, the emphasis in the German-Jewish reform movement finally shifted entirely to social ethics, while the Judeocentric and xenophobic passages in the Old Testament had already lost all relevance more than a thousand years before. This was perhaps due to the political powerlessness of the Jews who, living in the midst of European cultures, were forced to interpret their laws in a more benign way than that in which they were originally formulated. Today, however, extremist rabbis of fanatical settler gangs are using these same passages to justify cruel acts against the Palestinians.

This aggressiveness on the part of Israeli Jews toward the Palestinians in the Middle East, and the territorial claim to all of Palestine on the basis of Biblical sources voiced by a not inconsiderable number of right-wing Jewish Israelis unfortunately affects our entire world negatively. They are nothing but the outgrowth of a cruel, inhuman occupation explicitly approved and partly financed by the most powerful country of our times, the United States. The Western world, and Europe in particular, continues to watch this American support of Israel's policies of suppression from the sidelines. Since the suppressed individuals are members of an Arabic and largely Islamic people, the Middle Eastern conflict has become the geopolitical focus of tension between Islam and the widely secularized Christian West that goes back more than a thousand years. Of course, this is not to say that this conflict is the cause, or the only cause, of this tension, but it is a significant and aggravating factor. An ultimate end to the tension between the two worlds is entirely unthinkable without a resolution of this conflict.

Due to the high percentage of Muslim fellow citizens in most European cities, this tension is palpable and frequently frightening there. Particularly in the Netherlands, which used to be so relatively peaceful, the gruesome murder of the filmmaker and publicist Theo van Gogh—committed with intentional cruelty by a Muslim extremist—has given the question of how we can finally achieve a peaceful and mutually respectful co-existence with our Muslim fellow citizens extreme urgency. It follows from my remarks on the nature of radical evil that, as in the Judeo-Christian Bible, certain passages in the Koran could be moderated through re-interpretation. As long as that does not happen, not even the necessary first step will have been taken toward reducing the risk that young people facing existential problems will fall into the hands of extremist Imams. The latter can then invoke, unchallenged, cruel Koranic passages to assert that these anti-humanitarian passages represent true Islam when such individuals come to them for help.

These observations show that the extremist Imams, just like the extremist Rabbis among Israeli settlers, personify radical evil. It is therefore essential for our Western democracies to find ways and means of preventing, within the legitimate means provided by democratic constitutional States, such soul-destroying fanatics from continuing their attempts at seduction. Of course, that alone is not enough. The social conditions of young Muslims will also require enough attention and care to make them substantially resistant to evil elements. It is beyond the scope of this book to answer the question how our politicians should apply all this to actual practice. In Germany, most particularly, it should be self-evident what the fate of an inadequately self-protective democracy may be when a certain frustrated population group, for whatever reasons, falls into the hands of demagogues who promise to save it.

CONCLUSION

THE FAILURE OF JUDAISM
What the Loss of an Ethical Foundation Tells Us

THE FAILURE OF ISRAEL

I DO NOT intend to try to analyze here how it came about that the present state of affairs in and surrounding Israel is so vastly different from what was once hoped. The works of the so-called New Historians, such as Avi Shlaim and Ilan Pappe, have shown that the Zionist politicians in charge always intended to occupy the whole area that made up Mandatory Palestine, and saw to it that their military and political power was superior to that of the Arab countries. Doubtless both parties share responsibility for the ever-worsening enmity between the two peoples, but due to its proportionately greater power, Israel bears a greater share of the responsibility. The Israelis have refused to end the often-cruel occupation of that part of the country that was marked out by the UN for the Palestinians. They have also established ever more "facts on the ground" by building additional settlements, roads for Jews only, and a dividing wall that often deviates several kilometers from the official border, thus separating more Palestinians from one another. The Palestinians, for their part, have time and again murdered non-combatant citizens within Israel proper, causing the Israelis to counter with the bombardment of densely populated Palestinian areas, the destruction of crops and houses, the harassment of individual Palestinians, and other humiliating forms of collective punishment.

For both peoples, life has become hard—unbelievably hard for the Palestinians, but not easy on the Israelis either. Due to the formidable expenses required for security and the ever-growing settlements in the occupied territories, Israel faces a potential crisis. Even with the current economy booming, never before has the number of people living below the poverty line been as large. The post-traumatic stress syndrome of many young soldiers returning from duty in the occupied territories could be an additional destabilizing factor on Israeli society in the future.

In other words, the policies followed by the various governments of Israel have been ineffective with respect to coping with the Palestinian challenge. This also means that Israel no longer provides a safe haven for Jews from persecution. The provision of such a haven was one of the main reasons for the massive support by nearly all Jews and most people of good will for the new state in the first decades of its existence. Immigration to Israel continues, albeit at a reduced pace, fueled by nationalistic sentiments and religious motives, but in terms of achieving this primary goal of the Jews, the State of Israel must be considered as having failed.

THE FAILURE OF THE JEWISH PEOPLE

The history of the Jews in central Europe from the second half of the 19th century until the beginning of the Hitler era constituted the high water mark of Diaspora Judaism. The argument for this assertion is twofold. On the one hand, it can be said that never before since the time of Jesus (who, after all, was a Jewish teacher) was the emphasis on the ethical content of Judaism as strong as in those eighty-odd years. At the same time, the contribution Judaism made to the Western world via its recently emancipated members was impressive indeed: Einstein, Freud, Marx, Ehrlich, Disraeli, Rathenau, Kafka, Roth, Zweig, Werfel, Mahler, Menuhin, and Oistrach, just to mention an arbitrary selection of the most famous names from a list many times as long.

The prior, historically even more important, contribution of Judaism to mankind dates as far back as the first centuries of our era. At that time the two large monotheistic religions, Christianity and Islam, built on the basis of Judaism, established themselves in large parts of the world. In this way, much of the social ethics of Judaism was adopted by large parts of the world's population. The modern welfare state, adopted as the standard model in most of the Western world, would be inconceivable without its basic roots in Judaism. The difference between Christianity and Judaism in this respect is that in Judaism somebody who is in need of support has a right to receive this support from the community. For those who are well off, it is a religious obligation to provide the means to the community to enable it to give that support. In this way, the humiliation of the needy is diminished, because without them the wealthy would not be able to fulfill their obligation to the community. Psychologically, this ethic differs from the model of charitable giving common in Christianity, in which the rich distribute to the poor, with the latter in the position of grateful recipients. This difference reflects a distinct shift to the social welfare state that occurred in European society after the Second World War.

Obviously, not all those who call themselves Christians have kept up the extremely high ethical requirements that form an integral part of Christ's teachings. Probably one of the last people in the world you have to convince of this is an Auschwitz survivor. The criminals who ran the camps would practically all have called themselves "Christian" if asked about their confession. In spite of this, however, it is undeniable that the German people have learned from their extreme derailment. In the over sixty years since the end of the Second World War they have demonstrated time and again that they have understood, and to a far degree internalized, what democracy really means. Their response has stood in sharp contrast with a number of analyses after the Second World War that tried to prove that the Germans, due to their history, were predestined to live under regimes with highly autocratic, if not dictatorial, features.[215]

It is no exaggeration to say that the Germans have helped the State of Israel. Although German citizens faced a gigantic task in rebuilding their country, albeit with the help of the United States, they agreed to channel badly needed income to pay restitution money to the Jewish state, which numerous citizens received. This is in sharp contrast to the treatment of Holocaust victims in Israel.[216] Thus, that very essential Jewish way of feeling and practicing remorse for evil deeds, called *teshuva* (meaning return on the road of evil you went before) has been and is still practiced by the German people.

In contrast with this stands the way in which the Jewish people, if considered globally, have reacted to the enormous challenge with which they were confronted after the Second World War. This challenge has admittedly been made only harder by the Palestinians' response to decades of occupation in the form of murderous suicide attacks. Nevertheless, it is bitter and disappointing that a majority of Jews in Israel and the Diaspora seem to have chosen the hard, nationalistic, revengeful side of Judaism.[217] These feelings of bitterness and disappointment are shared by all those Jews (unfortunately a minority) who are consciously aware of the deep social ethics at the heart of Judaism. They include those active in the peace groups in and outside Israel, and the brave Israeli Army "refuseniks" in the occupied territories.

How all those mentioned who have adopted the ethical side of Judaism feel in detail about the state Judaism finds itself in today, I cannot judge, but I, myself—educated in the moral principles stressed so explicitly by the reformers of the last eighty years before Hitler—am deeply convinced that Judaism has betrayed itself. To those who think I exaggerate, I recommend the letters to the editor received by Rabbi Lerner, the editor of the American Jewish liberal journal *Tikkun*, after he tried to convince his readers that according to a basic law of Judaism every human being has been created in the image of God. Having had the temerity to argue that Palestinians were also human beings just like the Jews, and that therefore they should be treated as human beings, the death threats he received were frightening in their aggressiveness.[218]

THE FAILURE OF ZIONISM

From a purely pragmatic point of view, the present state of affairs in Israel is very problematic in nearly all respects. We have seen that at present the idea of a safe haven for Jews has vanished and that therefore one of the main aims of Zionism must be considered to have failed. Abba Eban is said to have formulated the observation regarding the Palestinians that "they never miss an opportunity to miss an opportunity." What the Israelis describe as being characteristic of the Palestinians, however, holds just as much for them. If less dogmatic Zionistic thinking amongst the prominent politicians of all parties in Israel had prevailed, then the proposition that neither colonialism nor the idea of a nation-state could be tolerated for long in the second half of the 20th century could have been taken into account, and history could have taken another turn.

The last opportunity for such a dramatic paradigm shift was probably after the June 1967 war. The former Attorney General of Israel, Michael Ben-Yair, describes in dramatic fashion what happened after the Six Day War ended in the following words:

> The State of Israel was born because the Zionist movement realized it must find a solution to the Jews' persecution and because the enlightened world recognized the need for that solution. The enlightened world's recognition of the solution's moral justification was an important, principal factor in Israel's creation. In other words, Israel was established on a clear, recognized moral base. Without such a moral base, it is doubtful whether the Zionist idea would have become a reality. The Six-Day War was forced upon us; however, the war's seventh day, which began on June 12, 1967 and has continued to this day, is the product of our choice. We enthusiastically chose to become a colonial society, ignoring international treaties, expropriating lands, transferring settlers from Israel to the occupied territories, engaging in theft and

finding justification for all these activities. Passionately desiring to keep the occupied territories, we developed two judicial systems: one—progressive, liberal—in Israel; and the other—cruel, injurious—in the occupied territories. In effect, we established an apartheid regime in the occupied territories immediately following their capture. That oppressive regime exists to this day. [219]

Although I agree in the main with what this prominent judicial expert says, I would go further. I don't believe that on the seventh day Israel chose to become a colonial society, but rather that on that day it chose to longer hide its colonial nature, and instead to make it shamelessly visible to the whole world. The seventh day could have been used to do away, once and for all, with the colonial attitude towards the Palestinians, and to begin considering them as equal partners from that point on. This, I think, is where Zionism as an ideology has fundamentally failed.

What adds an extra bitter note to this tragedy is the fact that the responsible politicians could have known how dangerous this disdain for the Palestinians was. Simha Flapan quotes Herbert Samuel, High Commissioner for Palestine who already in 1929 wrote to Weizmann:

> After a year in Palestine I have come to the conclusion that the importance of the Arab factor has been underestimated by the Zionist movement; unless there is very careful steering it is upon the Arab rock that the Zionist ship may be wrecked.[220]

To me these words sound rather prophetic. Those who neglected the importance of the Palestinians in practice, including all the Zionist and Israeli politicians in power before and after the establishment of the State, did not see, or did not want to see, the 19th century colonial roots in their thinking. In his article, "Explaining the Resistance to Colonialism in West Asia," Benjamin Beit-Hallahmi from the University of Haifa wrote:

> Colonialism is a formal system under which, in a defined territory, non-natives are entitled to political rights which natives are denied. A basic fact of colonialism, and actually what makes it possible, is the disparity between the two sides in power and technology.[221]

Thus, Ehud Barak, the one time Israeli prime minister became famous for his successful propaganda fraud, which represented his offer of a conglomeration of isolated Bantustans as a generous offer to the Palestinians. Even President George W. Bush, in a speech in the spring of 2002, said that eventually the Palestinians should be enabled to establish a viable state. This would be an achievement that Barak's "generous offer" would never have allowed.

Eventually, colonialism leads to a deep contempt of the natives. In August 2002 the new Chief of Staff Moshe Ya'alon used the metaphor of malignancy in saying, "The Palestinians are a cancer…an existential threat."[222] Another statement of his that appears in the same interview shows that this was not a slip of the tongue:

> There are all kinds of solutions to cancerous manifestations. Some will say

it is necessary to amputate organs. But at the moment [by reoccupying Gaza and the Palestinian cities on the West Bank] I am applying chemotherapy, yes.

In the same week we find in the same journal, under the title "Sharon backs Ya'alon Remarks on Cancerous Palestinian Threat," the following report: "IDF Chief of Staff Moshe Ya'alon's controversial remarks earlier this week were 'true and correct' and described 'the situation as it is,' Prime minister Ariel Sharon said yesterday."[223]

I wonder whether any human being that believes in the humanistic ideas of the Western world could ever be favorably impressed by the discriminatory and dehumanizing thinking of these most prominent Zionists. In early 2003, Sharon was re-elected by an impressive majority of the Israeli society, which obviously endorsed such thinking. I think that I am justified to conclude on this account that Zionism has failed, too.

THE WANING VITALITY OF JUDAISM

The end of Judaism, at least as far as it is represented in the European Diaspora, has been predicted before. Bernard Wasserstein's 1996 book, "Vanishing Diaspora," is an in-depth scholarly study concerning the future (or, more correctly, the non-future) of the Jews within Europe. Israel is mentioned only in the most optimistic terms:

[It is] a society that is unique because there the Jews constitute the majority. It has been created and is maintained with the preconceived aim to guarantee the survival of the Jews and of their creativity.

> Unless an unimaginable catastrophe occurs,
> there is no reason to doubt that Israel will
> survive.[224]

Wasserstein's conclusion is the more remarkable as the main tool he uses to bring him to his prediction of the vanishing European Diaspora is demography. And it is exactly on the basis of studies in this field that, at this moment, people within Israel are obsessed by what they call the "demographic bomb," which threatens the future survival of Israel. According to projections made by Prof. Arnon Sofer, the percentage of the Jewish population within Israel will drop from 71% now to 68% in 2020, due to the larger growth rate of the non-Jewish part of Israel's population.[225] It is obvious that this situation would become more extreme if those who are in favor of a Greater Israel get their way. In fact, according to studies by Prof. Sergio Della Pergola, this would mean that by 2010 only 44 to 47% of the total population will be Jewish, while by 2050 this percentage will have dropped to less than 37%.[226] Consequently, these nationalists are not ashamed to talk openly about "transfer" of the Palestinians from Israel and the occupied Palestinian territories, "transfer" being a euphemism for deportation or ethnic cleansing. The danger that the government might plan a major crime of this sort must not be underestimated.

THE GRADUAL DISAPPEARANCE OF THE JEWS IN THE DIASPORA

At the same time that the percentage of the Jewish population in Israel is shrinking, however, sociological and demographic forces are bringing about a gradual shrinking of the number of those in the Diaspora who are choosing to identify themselves as Jews. Prof. Sergio Della Pergola of Jerusalem's Hebrew University[227] predicts that in 2080, 81% of Jewish children under fourteen will live in Israel. He further says that intermarriage takes more children out of the Jewish people than it brings in.

Moreover, I believe that Prof. Wasserstein underestimates an important factor that may accelerate the disappearance of Jews from Western European society, namely that the multiethnic society has taken the place of the nation-state as it existed before the Second World War. Before the war, the population in most of these countries was ethnically much more homogeneous than it is now. That, alone, made it very difficult for Jews in most countries to just disappear in the society at large, unrecognized. While physiognomy and build alone could rarely be hidden successfully, there were other difficulties, such as the family name, which could not be changed as easily in former times as it can now.

Because anti-Semitism is no longer as virulent as it used to be, Wasserstein sees greater possibilities for the growth of Judaism, writing that "In the multicultural pluralistic society of Europe a Jew is no longer obliged to make his being-a-Jew invisible."[228] Rather, I would say that he is able to disappear as a Jew if he wishes. In the multi-ethnic society, those Jews who in this secularized age have no wish to adhere to the religion of their fathers can just opt out. They are no longer obliged by anything except their own personal sense of who they are to identify themselves as Jews. Before the Second World War, such a complete shedding of identity was for most Jews virtually impossible.

Thus, Jews can now identify themselves as Jews

or not, according to their own choice. In fact, in this day and age, a Jew is someone who identifies himself as such for whatever personal reasons he has. Before the war, such self-definition was nearly impossible. People could identify a Jew at a glance, and thus hinder his ability to blend in with society. At that time you were a Jew—even if you did not want to be so identified—as long as the people in your anti-Semitic surroundings saw you as such. The freedom of self-definition of one's identity was hardly available at that time for most Jews.

My view on the long-range future of the Jews in the world is thus much more pessimistic than Wasserstein's. His book appeared in 1996, when hopes for a solution of the Israel-Palestinian problem still seemed to have some foundation, so it is understandable that he still saw a long-range future for Israel as a Jewish state. An implicit assumption underlying my analysis is that the process of secularization that since the Age of Enlightenment has characterized our Western world will not be reversed for a long time.

Emil Fackenheim, who assigned the Holocaust to the theological category of uniqueness, feared that due to the decimation of the Jews in that event, the Jews might in the long run disappear as a distinguishable people. He reasoned, rightly, that this would mean that eventually Hitler would be given posthumous victory.[229] In fact, Hitler had, in notorious speeches in January 1939 and in February 1942, predicted that the Jews would disappear from the world. In order to avoid that, Fackenheim reasoned, a 614th command needed to be added to the existing 613 commandments of an observant Jew. This new command would say that it was forbidden for a Jew to leave the Jewish community, as that would contribute to

Hitler's posthumous victory. The flaw in this logic was that anybody who wanted, for whatever reason, to sever his ties with Judaism, would no longer be impressed by any of the 613 or 614 commandments, just as an army deserter would no longer polish the buttons on his uniform.

Indications exist, however, that the contrary might become true. As Samuel P. Huntington writes:

> Christianity, Islam, Judaism, Hinduism, Buddhism, and Orthodoxy, all experienced new surges in commitment, relevance, and practice by erstwhile casual believers. The fundamentalist movements are dramatic and can have significant political impact. They are, however, only the surface waves of the much broader and more fundamental religious tide that is giving a different cast to human life at the end of the twentieth century... The de-secularization of the world, as George Weigel[230] remarked is one of the dominant social facts in the late twentieth century.[231]

Throughout this book, I have systematically reasoned from a point of view that considers Jews to belong to the Western world and its culture. I have pointed out how the German Jewish Reform movement tried consciously to eliminate what they called "oriental elements" from the service. I do not expect that the revival of Jewish orthodoxy will take on really important dimensions. I cannot deny, however, that it is difficult to indicate how far that expectation is not influenced by hope and wishful thinking on my part. If this expectation should eventually prove untrue, then Judaism as I see it, and as I have tried to characterize it in this book, will have also reached its end, albeit in another way than the one I have predicted, and instead of passing away in a dignified fashion, the "end of Judaism" will culminate in the Jewish state's degeneration into a pre-Enlightenment fundamentalist theocracy.

THE LOST WILL FOR SURVIVAL

Wasserstein's prediction of the vanishing Diaspora is based on an unemotional, methodical, demographic analysis, taking in all areas in Europe where Jewish communities of any importance exist. In contrast with this, my prediction that Judaism will essentially disappear within the next two centuries is based not on a systematic scientific analysis but on qualitative reasoning. In this context, it is significant that on the second to the last page of his book, Wasserstein quotes the late president of the World Jewish Congress, Nahum Goldmann:

> Peoples have in the course of history disappeared...not through murder but by suicide... If the Jews of Europe do eventually disappear, this will occur because, collectively, they have lost the will for survival.[232]

This, essentially, is the basis for my reasoning. A people that has betrayed the basic ethical foundation of its long and astonishing survival will lack the vitality needed to preserve an identity of its own in the midst of an increasingly homogeneous world.

Faced with the possibility of the end of Judaism, it is justifiable to ask why the Jews deserved to survive for 2,000 years in the Diaspora in spite of all—or perhaps because of—all the adversities they had to face. From my perspective, the answer is that they had much to contribute to mankind with respect to intellectual and cultural endeavor, and particularly in the field of social ethics. For nearly 2,000 years, they were often the only distinct foreigners in many European countries, they had no political power, and they showed a remarkable instinct for survival as a group. Due to their lack of power, they could only rarely oppress others. On the contrary, after the emancipation they were at the forefront of humanitarian and socially constructive endeavors. The reform of an ancient religion to fit into modern, secularized society and the focus the reformers put on the ethical content of Judaism was a major achievement. It paved the way for the disproportionately large contribution that people with a Jewish background made to society, especially from the second half of the 19th century on.

Thus, if Judaism as a whole reached the highest point in its history in the eighty years before Hitler came to power, it is at present in decline. Due to the collective paranoia of an appreciable number (if not the majority) of Jews, they have returned—unnecessarily as I see it—to the dark side of Judaism. Israel is rapidly on its way to completely degenerating into a Middle Eastern power in the worst sense of the word. Those in the Diaspora who refuse to utter audible criticism of Israeli policies betray their heritage of being an enlightened people. If this trend continues—and there are no indications that it will change in the foreseeable future—Judaism will have nothing positive to contribute to the world any more. The number of Middle East powers with pre-Enlightenment regimes and views is large enough that the role of a degenerate Jewish state will be of no significance.

In this book, I have offered a pessimistic projection of the future of Judaism in the world. The way I have selected the facts, and the light that I have thrown upon them has been influenced by the dramatic period of Jewish history in which I lived my life. I cannot deny that I am disappointed. My disappointment is not with my life, however. On the contrary, in spite of the difficult times I have endured, I look with satisfaction on all that I have experienced. No, my disappointment is solely concerned with the way Judaism has developed as a body of culture and morals. It seems to me improbable that the pioneer experiment of Israel, which started out full of hope and ideals, can still be saved and that lasting peace and mutual trust between Israelis and Palestinians can still be achieved. The negative forces that were present from the start, especially the disdain with which the Palestinians were looked upon, have prevailed over humanistic idealism and social ethics.

However resilient Judaism has shown itself to be, however great the vitality which has enabled it to stand up to nearly two thousand years of challenges in the Diaspora, history appears to be proving itself stronger than this millennia-old culture. Although the long history of the Jews under unremittingly adverse circumstances since antiquity more than testifies to their fortitude, the impact of the Holocaust may have destroyed the innermost fabric, the deepest nature—in short, the essence—of Judaism forever. This should not necessarily be taken as a value judgment, however. I firmly believe in an aphorism coined by La Rochefoucauld that I learned in school, which says roughly: "If you can control your passions, this by no means implies that you have a strong will. It may simply be that your passions are weak." Similarly, one could say that if the essence of Judaism is eventually destroyed by the terrible impact of the

Holocaust, this does not imply that its strength was not great enough. It could simply be that the destructive impact of this cataclysm on the collective soul of the Jewish people was too powerful.

Endnotes

Introduction: Autobiographical Background

[1] These were local people who supervised damage control and rescue efforts after a bombing raid.

[2] Lion Feuchtwanger, *The Oppermanns*, New York: Carroll & Graf Publishers, 2001

[3] Weinreb was a somewhat dubious character that for a time during the Nazi occupation of Holland saved many Jews by using forged exemption lists, thereby allowing them to go underground. He became a controversial figure in the Netherlands after the war. Although he saved many lives, he may also have turned some people in. Personally, I am convinced that his intentions were good, and that he primarily tried to save people. When the Germans began to see through his tricks and forgeries, it may be that he betrayed some. His description of Master-Sergeant Koch largely agrees with my recollections, and in my opinion makes his autobiography believable.

[4] Friedrich Weinreb. *Die langen Schatten des Krieges*, three volumes, translated from the Dutch by Franz J. Lukassen, Weiler im Allgäu: Thauros-Verlag, 1989

Chapter 1: Lessons from Auschwitz

[5] Carl Friedman, "Niks Geleerd," *Trouw*, February 24, 2001

[6] Fritz Stern, *Gold and Iron: Bismarck, Bleichröder, and the Building of the German Empire*, New York: Knopf, 1977, 510

[7] Christian von Krockow, *Kaiser Wilhelm II. und seine Zeit*,. Berlin: Siedler, 1999, 76, 77

[8] Ian Kershaw, op. cit., Vol. 1, 390

[9] Gerald Reitlinger, *The Final Solution: The Attempt to Exterminate the Jews of Europe*, 1939-1945

[10] Ibid. 26

[11] Theodor Lessing, *Geschichte als Sinngebung des Sinnlosen*, München: Matthes & Seitz, 1983.

[12] Theo K. de Graaf, *Trauma and Psychiatry: The Role of Individual and Transgenerational Traumatisation in the Causation of Psychobiological Illness*, Tilburg University Press 1998, 94

[13] Ibid. 93

[14] Friedrich Nietzsche, "Unzeitgemässe Bertrachtungen II: Vom Nutzen und Nachteil der Historie für das Leben (1873-74)," *Nietzsches Werke*, Klassiker Ausgabe, Zweiter Band, Alfred Körner Verlag 1921, 134

[15] *Das Wesen des Judentums*, Nathansen & Lamm, Berlin 1905, 114

Chapter 2: Judaism in the Age of Enlightenment

[16] John Rose, *The Myths of Zionism*, London, Pluto Press, 2004, 30 f.

[17] C.G. Montefiore & H. Loewe, *A Rabbinic Anthology*, New York: Schocken Books, 1974

[18] Amnon Kapeliuk, *Rabin, Ein Politischer Mord* (Mit einem Vorwort von Lea Rabin), München: Droemersche Verlagsanstalt, Th. Knaur Nachf, 1999, 54. In her preface, Rabin's widow Lea writes, "Only the book by Amnon Kapeliuk reveals on the basis of thorough analyses all relevant backgrounds... Kapeliuk shows from which sources the murderer got the political and religious justification for his deed." As Avi Shlaim writes: "Rabin's murder was a religious murder, carried out with Orthodox rabbinical sanction." (550)

[19] Hermann Cohen, *Religion der Vernunft aus den Quellen des Judentums*, Wiesbaden: Fourier Verlag, 1988, 137

[20] Günter Stemberger, *Das Klassische Judentum*, München: Verlag C.H. Beck, 1979, 16-17

[21] Pirke Avot, *Torah from our Sages*, Translation and Explanation by Jacob Neusner, Dallas: Rossel Books, 1983, Ch.II No.8, 72

[22] Günter Stemberger, op.cit. 110

[23] Günter Stemberger, op.cit. 123

[24] Michael Meyer, *Deutsch Jüdische Geschichte in der Neuzeit*, Vol. I, Mordechai Breuer und Michael Graetz, 99

[25] William L. Shirer, *The Rise and Fall of the Third Reich*, New York: Fawcett World Library, 1962, 135

[26] Norman Davies, *Europe, a History*, London: Pimlico, 1997, 563

[27] Norman Davies, op.cit. 568

[28] Michael Meyer, op. cit. 107

[29] Michael Meyer, op. cit. 223

[30] Henriette Herz, *Berliner Salon, Erinnerungen und Portraits*, Frankfurt/M-Berlin-Wien: Verlag Ullstein GmbH, 1984, 221

[31] Norman Davies, loc.cit. 596

[32] Norman Davies, loc.cit. 598

[33] Léon Poliakov, *Geschichte des Antisemitismus*, Vol. V, Worms: Verlag Georg Heintz, 1983, 100

[34] Léon Poliakov, Ibid. 185

[35] Alexander Altmann, *Moses Mendelssohn*, London: Routledge & Kegan Paul, 1973, 23

[36] Alexander Altmann, Ibid. 27

[37] Alexander Altmann, Ibid. 70

[38] Michael Meyer, op. cit. 294

[39] Howard M. Sachar, *Modern Jewish History*, London: Weidenfeld and Nicolson, 1958, 49

[40] Alexander Altmann, op.cit. 352

[41] Norman Davies, op. cit. 674

[42] S.M. Dubnow, *Die Neueste Geschichte des Jüdischen Volkes*, Vol. I, Berlin: Jüdischer

Verlag, 1920, 66-74

[43] Robert M. Seltzer, op.cit. 628

[44] Joseph L. Blau, *Modern Varieties of Judaism*, New York and London: Columbia University Press, 1966, 28

[45] Michael Meyer, 344

[46] Joseph M. Blau, op. cit., 35

[47] Michael A. Meyer, *Response to Modernity, A History of the Reform Movement in Judaism*, Detroit: Wayne State University Press, 1995, 65

[48] Michael A. Meyer, op.cit. 200 ff.

[49] Michael A. Meyer, op.cit. 204

[50] Michael A. Meyer, op.cit. 205 ff.

[51] Leo Baeck, *Das Wesen des Judentums*, Berlin: Verlag von Nathansen & Lamm, 1905, 93-95

[52] Leo Baeck, op. cit. 113-114

[53] Michael A Meyer, op.cit. 388-394

[54] S. M. Dubnow I, op.cit. 88

[55] Joseph L. Blau, op. cit. 24

[56] S.M. Dubnow, *Die Neueste Geschichte des Jüdischen Volkes*, Vol. III. Berlin: Jüdischer Verlag , 1923, 331

[57] S. M. Dubnow III, op.cit. Section 122, 184 ff.; Göran Rosenberg, op. cit. Ch. 5

Chapter 3: The Already-Married Bride

[58] Tom Segev, *Elvis in Jerusalem: Post Zionism and the Americanization of Israel,* New York: Henry Holt and Company, 2002, 39

[59] Chaim Weizmann, op.cit. 36

[60] Chaim Weizmann, op. cit. 43 ff.

[61] Chaim Weizmann, op.cit. 53

[62] Ibid.

[63] Avi Shlaim, op. cit. 3

[64] S.M. Dubnow, III, op. cit. 333

[65] S.M. Dubnow, III, op. cit. 335

[66] David S. Wyman, *Das Unerwünschte Volk: Amerika und die Vernichtung der Europäishcen Juden*, Frankfurt a.M.: Fischer Taschenbuch Verlag, 2000, 287ff. (Original English edition: *The Abandonment of the Jews: America and the Holocaust*, 1941-1945, New York: Pantheon, 1984)

[67] In his *The Abandonment of the Jews*, which makes use of numerous Jewish sources, David Wyman details how on July 18, 1944, the Hungarian dictator Horthy offered to allow passage out of Budapest to all Jewish children under the age of 10 if they procured a visa from another country. About 230,000 Jews still remained in the city at that time with their children. The British government was prepared to let them immigrate to Palestine under the condition that they leave the country after the war. The U.S. State Department, however, rejected this plan because they were unwilling to accept these children after the war. The Zionist organizations objected to the proposal because they feared that agreeing to these conditions would undermine their

claim to Palestine.

[68] Adolf Hitler, *Mein Kampf*, Chapter 11

[69] Joachim Meynert, op.cit. 153

[70] Martin Gilbert, *Israel: A History*, London: Transworld Publishers, 1999, 68

[71] Göran Rosenberg, *Das Verlorene Land Israel: Eine Persönliche Geschichte*, aus dem Schwedischen von Jörg Scherzer, Jüdischer Verlag, 155

[72] Ibid. 161

[73] Ibid.

[74] Martin Gilbert, *Israel, A History*, London: Black Swan, 1999, 134

[75] Chaim Weizmann, op.cit. 397

[76] Simha Flapan, Zionism and the Palestinians, New York: Harper & Row Publishers, 1979, 116

[77] Martin Gilbert, *Israel: A History*, Black Swan, 228

[78] Noam Chomsky, *Offene Wunde: Nahost, Israel, die Palestinenser und die US-Politik*, Hamburg/Wien: Europa Verlag, 1999, 259

[79] Chaim Weizmann, op. cit. 437-39

[80] Ben-Yair, "The War's Seventh Day"

[81] Shlaim, *The Iron Wall*, 54

[82] Theodor Herzl, *Altneuland*, Haifa Publishing Company, 1962, 54

[83] Ibid. 100

[84] Martin Buber, "Old Zionism and Modern Israel," *Jewish Newsletter*, June 2, 1958.

[85] Avraham Oz, "A Message from the Middle East," University of Haifa, September 24, 2002.

[86] Benny Morris, "A New Exodus for the Middle East?" *The Guardian*, October 3, 2002

[87] Ibid.

Chapter 4: The Blinding Effects of History

[88] Arnold J. Toynbee, *Civilization on Trial*, London/New York: Oxford University Press, 7

[89] Martin Gilbert, Black Swan, 258

[90] Mark Roseman, *Die Wannsee Konferenz*, München/Berlin: Propyläen, 2002, 31

[91] For a psychoanalytic discussion of the connection between trauma, memory, and historiography, see two books by Dominick LaCapra: *History and Memory after Auschwitz*. Ithaca: Cornell University Press, 1998, and *Writing History, Writing Trauma*. Baltimore: Johns Hopkins, 2001.

[92] Ilan Pappe, *The Ethnic Cleansing of Palestine*, Oxford, Oneworld, 2006, 17-22

[93] Idith Zertal, *Nation und Tod*, Göttingen: Wallstein Verlag, 2003, 11

[94] Zertal, Ibid. 309

[95] Alain Finkielkraut, *Der Eingebildete Jude*, München/Wien: Carl Hanser Verlag, 1980, 7-9

[96] Emil L. Fackenheim, *To Mend the World*, New York: Schocken Books, 1982, 9

[97] Maurice Friedman, *Abraham Joshua Heschel & Elie Wiesel*, New York: Farrar Straus Giroux, 1987, 94, 95

[98] Maurice Friedman, op.cit. 95

[99] Gie van den Berghe, *De Uitbuiting van de Holocaust*, Amsterdam: Anthos, 2001, 147

[100] Emil L. Fackenheim, *God's Presence in History*, New York: Harper & Row, 1972, 84

[101] Geoffrey Wigoder, ed., *Israel Pocket Library*, Jerusalem: Keter Publishing House, 3. In my opinion, this well-known quote from the Talmud (Shabbat 31a), attributed to Hillel, comes nearest to expressing the essence of Judaism. It is a more practical recommendation than the Christian instruction to love one another.

[102] David G. Roskies, "Memory," in Arthur A. Cohen and Paul Mendes-Flohr, op.cit. 581

[103] Besides the prophetic words of Nietzsche's quoted below indications of similar thoughts can be found in Dominick LaCapra's work. He quotes from an article by Charles Maier: "I believe we have in a sense become addicted to memory… I think it is time to ask whether an addiction to memory can become neurasthenic and disabling. The present author answers: Yes."

[104] Dominick LaCapra, *History and Memory after Auschwitz*, Ithaca and London: Cornell University Press, 1998, 13,14

[105] Gideon Alon, "Angry Peres Slams Government, Says PM 'Has No Policy,'" *Ha'aretz*, September 30, 2002

[106] Avirama Golan, "Brothers, the Village is Burning," *Ha'aretz*, November 19, 2002

[107] Friedrich Nietzsche, *Unzeitgemässe Betrachtungen II*, op.cit. 135

[108] Uri Avneri, "The Night After," Gush Shalom's Weekly Essay, April 9, 2003. (Concerning the dangerous combination of evangelical American Christians and neoconservative Jews)

[109] "Christians for Israel," Editorial, *The Jerusalem Post*, March 17th 2007

[110] Max van Weezel, "De Schaamte Nog Niet Voorbij," in *Nieuw Israelitisch Weekblad*, August 1, 2003

[111] Various authors have described such shame in "*Een Ander Joods Geluid: Kritische opvattingen over Israel*," Amsterdam/Antwerpen: Contact, 2003.

Chapter 5: Déjà-vu, or the Nightmares of a Jew Born in Germany

[112] Nadav Shragai, "No Government Has the Right to Set Up a Foreign State in the Land of Israel," *Ha'aretz Magazine*, June 2, 2003

[113] Ari Shavit (interviewer), "The Enemy Within," *Ha'aretz Magazine*, August 30, 2002

[114] Avi Shlaim, *The Iron Wall: Israel and the Arab World*, London: Penguin Books, 2001, xii

[115] Shulamit Aloni, "Our Foppish Self-Righteousness," *Ha'aretz Magazine*, July 23, 2003.

[116] Yisahi Rosen-Zvi at a peace demonstration on February 9, 2002 in Tel Aviv, cited in *De Moed om te Weigeren*, Amsterdam: Stichting SIVMO and EAJG, 2002, 45

[117] As early as about July 13, 1933, relatives of Philipp Scheidemann, the first Chancellor of the Weimar Republic, who was living in exile at the time, were arrested for a "defamatory article" that he had published in a foreign newspaper.

[118] J. L. Heldring, "Mensen en Symbolen," *NRC Handelsblad*, December 4, 2002

[119] Roseman, op.cit. 10

[120] Shavit, op.cit.

[121] Arnon Regular, Amos Harel and Baruch Kra, "Settlers Attack Palestinian Olive Harvesters, Kill One," *Ha'aretz Magazine*, October 7, 2002

[122] "Blind Evil," editorial, *Ha'aretz Magazine*, September 19, 2002

[123] Salomon Bouman, "Hebron, Stad van Haat, Bloed en Angst," *NRC Handelsblad*, April 3, 2001

[124] Amira Hass, "The Mirror Does Not Lie," *Ha'aretz*, November 1, 2000

[125] Mark Chmiel, "Elie Wiesel and the Question of Palestine," *Tikkun* 17, No. 6, November/December 2001, 61

[126] Martin Gilbert, Black Swan, 569

[127] Hirsh Goodman, "Silence that Kills," *The Jerusalem Report*, September 9, 2002

[128] Oscar Garschagen, "Angst en Wantrouwen Nog Niet Overwonnen, Stappenplan Nog Geen Vredesplan," *NRC Handelsblad*, July 30, 2003

[129] *Ha'aretz* Service and Agencies, "U.S. on Gaza Tender: Settlement 'Freeze is a Freeze,'" *Ha'aretz*, August 1, 2003

[130] "Kritiek Bush op Bouwen Muur Israël," NCR, July 26-27, 2003.

[131] Shulamit Aloni, "Murder of a Population under Cover of Righteousness," *Ha'aretz Magazine*, March 6, 2003

[132] Amir Oren, "At the Gates of Yassergrad," *Ha'aretz Magazine*, January 26, 2002

[133] Gideon Samet, "You Won't Be Able to Say 'We Didn't Know,'" *Ha'retz Magazine*, January 28, 2002

[134] These troops were under the command of SS Brigadier General and Major General of the Police Jürgen Stroop. Of the 2090 men commanded by Stroop, at least 440 belonged to the SS. Reitlinger's accounting is the most detailed. The 228 security police he mentions were just as politically indoctrinated as the SS men. The security police were heavily involved in the massacres committed by the SS's Special Mobile Task Groups. Kershaw is more vague, and says that the total strength of the German troops was about 3000, most of them SS men.

[135] Amos Harel, "Arafat Calls for Urgent Quartet Meeting on Israeli 'Escalation,'" *Ha'aretz Magazine*, August 1, 2003

[136] *The Times*, London, June 26, 2002

[137] From The American Israel Public Affairs Committee Website, www.aipac.org

[138] Ibid.

[139] Meron Benvenisti, "The True Test of the Imperial Pretension," *Ha'aretz*, April 10, 2003

[140] Michael Dobbs, "Condoleezza's Right-Hand Man," *The Jerusalem Post*, May 30, 2003

[141] Yoel Marcus, "Unmasking the Real Sharon," *Ha'aretz*, April 15, 2003

[142] Uri Avneri. From a weekly article distributed by his organization, Gush Shalom, April 9, 2003

[143] *Ha'aretz* Magazine Service and Agencies, "Tehran Warns Israel Against Strikes on Bushehr Reactor," *Ha'aretz Magazine*, August 18, 2003.

[144] A similar analysis regarding a secured future for the Near East is Boaz Evron's article, "Demagography as the Enemy of Democracy," in *Ha'aretz*, September 11,

2002. He refers also to the large number of non-Jewish Russians in Israel, which makes the whole situation from nationalistic Jewish point of view only more terrible. He, too, comes to the conclusion that in the long run the only stable state can be one that is open, democratic, and provides for complete equality for all its citizens.

[145] Göran Rosenberg, op.cit. 91

[146] Tom Segev, op. cit. 110

Chapter 6: The Cudgel of Anti-Semitism

[147] Martin Gilbert, Transworld, 509-11

[148] Martin Gilbert, Transworld, 292. It should be noted that Martin Gilbert is a prominent, British Jewish, even Zionist historian. The journalist Haim Hanegbi exhibited the document from Kibya at a forum discussion that Gilbert moderated on January 9, 2002. Prominently present were former minister Shulamit Aloni, former Air Force colonel Dr. Yigal Shohat, and Brigadier-General (Res.) Dov Tamari.

[149] Ari Shavit, "The Big Freeze," *Ha'aretz*, October 8, 2004

[150] Michael Ben-Yair, "The War's Seventh Day"

[151] Victor Klemperer, *An Annotated Edition of Victor Klemperer's "Notizbuch Eines Philologen," Studies in German Thought and History*, Vol. 17, Lewiston, New York: Edwin Mellen Press, 1997

[152] Martin Gilbert, Black Swan, 188

[153] Chaim Weizmann, *Trial and Error: The Autobiography of Chaim Weizmann*, New York: Schocken Books, 1966, 386

[154] Robert M. Seltzer, *Jewish People, Jewish Thought*, New York: Macmillan, 1980, 175

[155] Ibid. 175

[156] A.S. Rijxman, "Het Anti-Semitisme als Reisgenoot in de Joodse Geschiedenis," in *Bijdragen en Mededelingen van het Genootschap voor de Joodse Wetenschap,* Amsterdam, 2002, 45

[157] Exodus 19:8

[158] Henri Atlan, "Chosen People," in Arthur A. Cohen und Paul Mendes-Flohr (ed.), *Contemporary Jewish Religious Thought*, Collier Macmillan Publishers, London, 1988, 55

[159] Hans Jansen, *Christelijke Theologie na Auschwitz*, Den Haag: Boekencentrum, 1982, 105

[160] Abel J. Herzberg, *Between Two Streams: A Diary from Bergen-Belsen*, New York: St. Martin's, 1997

[161] Avi Shlaim, *The Iron Wall: Israel and the Arab World*, London: Penguin Books, 2000, 16-27

[162] Ilan Pappe, *The Ethnic Cleansing of Palestine*

[163] Michael Ben-Yair, "The War's Seventh Day"

[164] Natan Sharansky, "Anti-Semitism is Our Problem," *Ha'aretz Magazine*, August 10, 2003

[165] Cited in Shlaim, "The Iron Wall," 311

[166] Simcha Flapan, *Zionism and the Palestinians*, New York: Harper & Row, 1979, 116.

[167] Yoav Peled, "Was Barak Telling the Truth?" *The Guardian*, May 24, 2002.

[168] Aloni, "Murder of Population under Cover of Righteousness," Ha'aretz Magazine,

March 6, 2003

[169] Lily Galili, "Israeli-Russian Journalist Calls for Castration as Anti-Terror Step," *Ha'aretz Magazine*, January 18, 2002

[170] Ari Shavit, "Dear God, This is Effi," *Ha'aretz Magazine*, March 20, 2002

[171] Reuters, "Peres Equates European Criticism of Israel to Anti-Semitism," *Ha'aretz Magazine*, April 22, 2002

[172] Salomon Bouman, "Een 'Zwarte Wolk' van Anti-Semitisme," *NRC Handelsblad*, November 27, 2002

[173] Yossi Melman, "Yishai Urges French Jews to Immigrate after Le Pen Advance," *Ha'aretz Magazine*, April 23, 2002

[174] Natan Sharansky, "Anti-Semitism is Our Problem"

[175] Anet Bleich, "Laat de Shoa Erbuiten," *Nieuw Israelitisch Weekblad*, May 18, 2001

[176] From an exchange of views with Anet Bleich in the *Nieuw Israelitisch Weekblad*, Spring 2001

[177] Ari Shavit, "Between Two Worlds"

[178] Ibid.

[179] Mark Roseman, *Die Wannsee-Konferenz: Wie die NS-Bürokratie den Holocaust Organisierte*, München/Berlin: Econ-Ullstein-List-Verlag, 2002, 31 (original English edition: *The Wannsee Conference and the Final Solution: A Reconsideration*, New York: Metropolitan, 2002)

[180] Kershaw recounts a conversation with Croatian Minister of Defense Sladko Kvaternik that took place on July 22, 1941. Hitler stated that it made no difference to him whether the Jews were sent to Siberia or to Madagascar—whichever, they needed to be gotten rid of in any case. Although Kershaw notes that deportation to Siberia would, in the final analysis, have been tantamount to genocide, the bottom line is that the decision to physically annihilate all European Jews, that is, the Final Solution, had not yet been taken. (470)

[181] Baruch Kra, "Police Allow Kach to Hold Purim Commemoration at Goldstein's Grave," *Ha'aretz Magazine*, March 8, 2001

[182] Original English edition: Alan Dershowitz, *The Case for Israel*, Hoboken, New Jersey: John Wiley & Sons, 2003

[183] *Ischa Meijer, De Interviewer*, Amsterdam: Prometheus, 2000, 348, an interview with Leon de Winter

[184] Elsbeth Etty, "Tweede Wereldoorlog Moet Moreel Ijkpunt Blijven," *NRC Handeslblad*, September 23, 2002

[185] Pim Fortuyn was a highly controversial, openly gay Dutch politician who was against Muslim immigration and wanted to close the borders to Muslims. He was assassinated just prior to the 2002 Dutch elections.

[186] Yossi Klein, "Displaced People," *Ha'aretz Magazine*, April 26, 2002

[187] Kershaw, *Hitler*

[188] Avraham Oz, University of Haifa, "A Message from the Middle East," September 24, 2002

[189] Joris Luyendijk, "Nooit Veilig, Altijd Bang," *NRC Handelsblad*, January 11-12, 2003

[190] Reuters, "Peres Equates European Criticism of Israel to Anti-Semitism," in

Ha'aretz Magazine, April 22, 2002

[191] Ibid.

[192] Abel J. Herzberg, *Between Two Streams: A Diary from Bergen-Belsen*, New York: St. Martin's, 1997

[193] Aluf Benn, "P. M. Rejects Jordan's Request to Rule out 'Transfer' in Iraq War," *Ha'aretz Magazine*, November 28, 2002

Chapter 7: Reflections on the Nature of Evil

[194] Immanuel Kant, *Werke*, Vol. 6: *Der Streit der Fakultäten und kleinere Abhandlungen*, Köln: Könemann Verlagsgesellschaft, 1995, 162

[195] Ibid. 169. Verbatim, he says here: "I have set the major point of Enlightenment, i.e. the emergence of humans from their self-inflicted immaturity, primarily in matters of religion."

[196] Friedrich Nietzsche, *Jenseits von Gut und Böse*, Fünftes Hauptstück, "Zur Naturgeschichte der Moral," Section 195

[197] Nietzsche's wording is: The Jews—"a people born to slavery," as Tacitus and the entire ancient world say, "the chosen people among the peoples", as they themselves say and believe—the Jews have accomplished the miracle of reversing the values... In this reversal of values (part of which is the use of the word for "poor" synonymously with "holy" and "friend") lies the significance of the Jewish people: In them, the slave rebellion in morality begins.

[198] Rüdiger Safranski, *Das Böse, oder das Drama der Freiheit*, 5th ed., Frankfurt am Main: Fischer Taschenbuch Verlag, 2003, 309

[199] *Jewish Values*, Jerusalem: Keter Publishing House, 1974, 96. Reference is made to the apocryphal book "Wisdom of Sirach" (Ecclesiasticus) and to the Talmud lines Gen. R., 1:4, Pes.54, et al.

[200] Hannah Arendt, *Eichmann in Jerusalem: Ein Bericht von der Banalität des Bösen*, 12th ed., München: Piper, 2003, 56

[201] Ibid. 246

[202] Fritz Stern, *Gold und Eisen*, Reinbek bei Hamburg: Rowohlt Taschenbuch Verlag, June 1988, 703

[203] Crowe, David M. *Oskar Schindler: The Untold Account of His Life, Wartime Activities, and the True Story Behind The List*, Philadelphia: Westview Press, 2004

[204] Hannah Arendt, *Elemente und Ursprünge totaler Herrschaft*, 9th ed., München: Piper Verlag, March 2003, 941 (Originally published in English as *The Origins of Totalitarianism*)

[205] G. M. Gilbert, *Nuremberg Diary*, New York: Farrar, Straus & Company, 1947, 278-9

[206] Ari Shavit, "Interview with General Ya'alon: The enemy from Within," *Ha'aretz*, September 2, 2002

[207] Hannah Arendt, *Das Urteilen: Texte zu Kants politischer Philosophie*, München: Piper Verlag 1985, 147

[208] Ibid.

[209] Hans Jansen, *Christliche Theologie nach Auschwitz: Die Theologischen und Kirchlichen Wurzeln des Antisemitismus*, Den Haaf: Uigeverij Boekencentrum, 1982

[210] Rüdiger Safranski, op.cit., 290

[211] Ibid. 267

[212] Arthur Schopenhauer, *Die Welt als Wille und Vorstellung*, Book 4, "Welt als Wille, " Section 65, in *Arthur Schopenhauer's Sämmtliche Werke in Sechs Bänden, Erster Band: Die Welt als Wille und Vorstellung*, Leipzig: Verlag Philipp Reclam jun, 466

[213] Hannah Arendt, *Elemente und Ursprünge*, op.cit. 736. Arendt quotes from a work by Erich Voegelein entitled "The Origins of Scientism" in the journal *Social Research*, New York, December 1948.

[214] Michael A. Meyer, *Response to Modernity: A History of the Reform Movement in Judaism*, Detroit: Wayne State University Press, 1995, 5

Conclusion: The Failure of Judaism

[215] See, for instance, The Rt. Hon. Lord Vanisittart, *Lessons of my Life*, London: Hutchinson & Co, London, circa 1943, and Erika and Klaus Mann, *The Other Germany*, Modern Age Books, 1940

[216] Alex Burghorn, "Many Holocaust Survivors in Israel are Poor and Neglected," in the Dutch daily *Volkskrant*, April 16, 2007

[217] Yitzhak Frankenthal, "Compromise for Peace," *Tikkun* 18, No. 4, July-August, 2003, 17; "An Open Letter to the Right Wing," *Tikkun* 18, No. 5, September-October, 2003, 24

[218] An example can be found on page 2 of the May/June 2001 issue of *Tikkun*, in which a reader responds to an article by Rabbi Lerner in *The Jerusalem Post* that was translated by an Arab newspaper, in which he expressed himself critically regarding Sharon. The reader's letter contains such expressions as: "No form of life exists which is lower than what you represent." Lerner's answer to this was: "The language which you use is typical of many other comments which I have received threatening my life."

[219] Michael Ben-Yair, "The War's Seventh Day," *Ha'aretz Magazine*, March 3, 2002

[220] Simha Flapan, op.cit. 61

[221] Benjamin Beit-Hallahmi, "Explaining the Resistance to Colonialism in West Asia," private printing, January 2003

[222] Yair Sheleg, "Palestinian Threat is Cancerous," *Ha'aretz*, August 26, 2002; Ari Shavit (interview), "The Enemy Within," *Ha'aretz*, September 2, 2002

[223] Aluf Benn, "Sharon Backs Ya'alon Remarks on 'Cancerous Palestinian Threat,'" *Ha'aretz*, August 30, 2002

[224] Bernard Wasserstein, *Het Einde van een Diaspora: Joden in Europa sinds 1945*, Vertaald door Tinke Davids, Baarn/Antwerpen: Ambo/Kritak, 1996, 289 (Original English edition: *The Jews in Europe since 1945*. London: Penguin Books, 1997)

[225] Avraham Tal, "How the Jewish Majority Can Turn into a minority," *Ha'aretz*, October 26, 2001

[226] Akiva Elder, "'Transfer' is Dead, Long Live Apartheid," *Ha'aretz*, October 23, 2001

[227] Yair Sheleg, "Intermarriage, Low Birth Rates Threaten Diaspora Jewry," *Ha'aretz*, February 13, 2002

[228] Wasserstein, op. cit. 246

[229] Emil L. Fackenheim, op.cit. 10

[230] George Weigel, "Religion and Peace: An Argument Complexified," *Washington Quarterly*, No. 14 (Spring 1991), 27

[231] Samuel P. Huntington, *The Clash of Civilizations*, New York: Simon & Schuster, 1997, 96

[232] Wasserstein, op. cit. 288

Index

For the fiftieth anniversary of the Summer of Love of 1967
San Fran '60s and *More San Fran '60s*
are combined here in

San Fran '60s:
Stories of the Hippies, the Summer of Love, and
San Francisco in the '60s, Volumes 1 & 2

"[A young man]... arrives in time to experience the 1967 'Summer of Love' and the zenith of the hippie movement. A series of nonlinear but connected stories follow as the unnamed protagonist takes plenty of drugs, attends concerts, hangs out with other hippies, has doomed love affairs, and wrestles with inner demons... He's smart, curious, a bit arrogant, and bedeviled by deep insecurity, sexual obsession, and family conflict... Jacobs' personal experience in the Haight-Ashbury district of the 1960s is apparent in his vivid depictions of the people of that time and place... Counterculture heroes, such as singer Janis Joplin and author William S. Burroughs, make appearances..." Kirkus Reviews

Reviews of the first volume are below.

"I really loved this collection ... In *San Fran '60s*, M.W. Jacobs brings the counter-culture of San Francisco in the 1960s to life through a sharply drawn collection of stories, which are frequently disturbing and surprising. Jacobs creates a montage of images and moments that capture the beat, sound and smell of the streets. ... This is an engaging half-forgotten

world of couch nomads, hipsters and the dispossessed in search of something that they themselves can't articulate." Douglas Field, Phd, lecturer in 20th Century American Literature at Manchester University, United Kingdom. He is the editor of *American Cold War Culture* (2005) and the author of *James Baldwin* (2011). He is also a regular contributor to the *Times Literary Supplement.*

"It's fun, with a quirky style... There's plenty of colour evoked and the language has a brisk and bold rhythm. There's an authenticity, an authority..." Simon Warner, PhD, author of *Text, Drugs, and Rock'n'Roll,* published by Bloomsbury, and Lecturer, Popular Music Studies, University of Leeds, United Kingdom

"Here's a book of tales ... from a guy who was there ... He's tellin' stories like they happened yesterday. Some of 'em are totally unbelievable, and some are totally, like, "That could happen to me," ya know? The stories are written with lots of dialogue, which makes the characters jump off the page ... Good stuff, man.- Nicholas Grizzle, *North Bay Bohemian* Oct 17 - 23, 2012, Vol. 34, No. 23

"It is a very good portrait of a period." Richard Olafson, editor of *Pacific Rim Review*

"A peek behind the idea of a hippy urban idyll. All very deeply personal. And it is very honest. There is no attempt to dress up the period. ... An encounter with William Burroughs, a fleeting meeting with Janis Joplin, a collision with murderous rednecks in a diner north of San Francisco ... A sober look at the city by the bay." Dawn Swoop, *Beat Scene #69* (a 25 year old glossy UK-based magazine dedicated to all things Beat Generation)

"It's entertaining to read. It condenses a complex reality into a fictional landscape that captures some of the rosy and bitter flavors of a time that continues to be mythologized." Nadya Zimmerman, author of *Counterculture Kaleidoscope: Musical and Cultural Perspectives on Late Sixties San Francisco*, teaches at Cornish College of the Arts in Seattle.

"Captures a particular time and place and youth very well." Jennie Skerl, author of *William S. Burroughs* (Twayne, 1985) and *Reconstructing the Beats* (Palgrave Macmillan, 2004), and founding board member and former President of the Beat Studies Association (USA).

"I found the stories colourful, evocative, beguilingly simple, and imbued throughout with a sense of the authority of witness. The portrayal of the seedier, more disturbing aspects of life in Haight-Ashbury during the 1960s ('The First Murder', 'Strangers in a Dark Room') was particularly compelling." Rona Cran, President of the English Graduate Society at University College London, editor of the journal *Moveable Type,* and contributor to the *Times Literary Supplement*.

"This book does an unbelievably good job of capturing the feel of the 60s. The pace is perfect. The rhythm is perfect... And some of the images are searing - they stick with you for days after you read them." Phil Kain, Phd, author of *Nietzsche and the Horror of Existence* (2009), Professor of Philosophy, Santa Clara University

"I... found it very readable. It certainly brings back the era with an inside look. I think it could find readers in Germany." Juergen Ploog, "Germany's last beatnik poet," novelist, author of *Facts of Fiction. Essays on Contemporary Literature*.

Amazon Customer Reviews of the first volume -->-->-->

San Fran '60s

Stories of the Hippies, the Summer of Love, and San Francisco in the '60s, Volumes 1 & 2

M.W. Jacobs

Escallonia Press
www.escalloniapress.com

Address all inquiries to Escallonia Press at
sanfran60s@gmail.com

ISBN-10: 0-615-88551-9
ISBN-13: 978-0-615-88551-3

This, my heart, my life for Nancy

Table of Contents

An old friend said of these stories, "But we all had experiences like that."

"That's the point," I replied, "They're not unique, they're representative."

I have lived in and around San Francisco since 1965 and present myself, lovers, friends, and acquaintances as prime specimens.

This is autobiographical fiction. The themes of many of these short stories are those of rock 'n roll, and the structure of the collection is modular; that is, all of the stories in both collections, *San Fran '60s* and *More San Fran '60s,* are interconnected. Yet each is self-contained, so they can be read in any order.

Rather than have an aspect of a larger over-arching story in each short story, each is invested as much as possible with the whole of that *San Fran '60s* experience, so the whole is in each part.

This book contains stories from *San Fran '60s* and *More San Fran '60s*, plus a new story, "The Land," the longest in the collection.

The Street

Haight-Ashbury District, San Francisco
Summer of Love, 1967

"I'm so glad, I'm so glad, I'm glad, I'm glad, I'm glad... I'm so glad, I'm so glad, I'm glad, I'm glad, I'm glad....." That's *Cream* in the inner distance while he strolls down Scott Street toward Haight Street. The midday sun pains his eyes as if he had just come out of a matinee, when actually he just woke up. The traffic on Haight Street up ahead tells him it's the weekend. Friday thru Sunday it's bumper-to-bumper in a five block radius.

Hey, Tim isn't at his post! Beside a stop sign where Haight intersects Scott, a sawhorse straddles a water department hole, and his roommate Tim sits on the sawhorse every Friday selling underground newspapers to the stalled tourists. He doesn't do it for the money, but the people he meets, mainly chicks. Sometimes, there're two. If he left the sawhorse this early, he must have met a groovy one, a very groovy one. Good for him!

It may be slight and subtle, but when you turn from a side street onto Haight Street, there is a click, and he feels it now as he turns onto the south side of Haight heading west. Haight Ashbury *is* Haight Street, and the Street is a village square, where the freaks bump into friends, are chosen by a possibility, answer the paradox

yes, trust chaos. When he was standing naked in his bedroom wondering what to do with the day, he knew that whatever else he did, he'd check-in at least once with the Street.

At Divisadero, waiting for the light, he's on display for a family in a station wagon. Two kids gawk behind the wife who smirks at him and says something to the husband who turns away from a braless chick on the other side of the intersection and looks at him. Should he flip 'em off? Wag his cock? Who was it told him about a cat that ran along side a tour bus holding up a big mirror? For the next eleven blocks, the length of the Street up to Golden Gate Park, he'll be walking beside a wall of idling cars, interrupted only at intersections, with windows up and doors locked, full of faces at an aquarium: aghast, tittering, grim, insulted, threatened, curious, ready…

The station wagon has to sit through a green light while he crosses …*glad, I'm so glad, I'm so glad, I'm…* The climb to Baker Street has him breathing heavily when he finally gets level with the plateau of the rest of Haight Street. Then a dash of sea breeze cools the sunshine, flutters his faded green tee shirt, streams through his sandals, jeans, and collar-length dark hair, and drags over his flesh like a long, airy tongue. Was that the acid? Already? No, it's too soon. Earlier he took a purple Owsley tab. Felt like the right day. Plus, he was lowering inventory. What he and Tim don't take themselves or give away, they sell.

Where Buena Vista Park slopes down to Haight Street, just past Lyon, he suddenly stops. Across the street, in front of the Christian Science Reading Room, are eight retarded men, walking in twos, hand in hand, with their familiar tousled hair and khaki uniforms. Some have smiles taut, nearly bursting with delight, while others have the distant amusement of someone being whispered a joke. They're a Haight Street fixture. Hey, the hooked-nose guy isn't smiling! He's not with the Mongoloid, maybe that's it. Their attendant herds them around the corner, out of sight, and down Lyon Street to a playground in the Panhandle, an extension of Golden Gate Park that runs parallel to the Street.

He crosses to the north side of the Street and turns left, continuing west. Crossing Central, he glances down two blocks to the Panhandle, a habit since last fall when free weekend rock concerts started there. Usually he hears about it through the grapevine the week before but sometimes not. He saw a magnetic unknown Janis Joplin at one. Nothin' there today so far.

Foot traffic thickens towards Masonic Street. This is where the bazaar really begins. To check-in with the Street, first he looks into the Drogstore Café on the northeast corner of Masonic and Haight. He can't see through the reflection so he makes a portal of shadow with a cupped hand. Nobody. Nobody anyway he wants to talk to now. He weaves through tourists and panhandlers to the curb and waits for the light-change. There's that chick. Selling underground papers on this choicest corner every weekend. Almost dutifully. Wearing jeans under a dress today.

Lanky and nineteen, he crosses Masonic copping a pose, stork-hunch and hands-in-jeans. When he reaches the sidewalk, he turns left. Traffic isn't moving, so he crosses against the light back to the south side of the Street. He then turns right, continuing west through a dense forest of freaks, huddling dealers, beseeching panhandlers, new arrivals with backpacks, and a few dazed, cringing tourists. The five blocks from Masonic to the park is a solid din of idling engines, music from windows, the crowd murmur and shouted greetings of freaks, some barefoot, some sitting on the sidewalk, some leaning against a wall, lounging on the thoroughfare as if at home. It's a livingroom with a street through it. The freaks bask in a liberation that keeps all-but-a-few tourists sealed in their cars.

He crosses Ashbury, which he knows is Ashbury Street from habit, not because there's a street sign. It's stolen every couple days. He glances down at the Panhandle again. Still nothing. Now two other checkpoints, the Psychedelic Shop, and across the street, the Print Mint, a cavernous room with hip posters covering all walls and the ceiling. And the usual crowd is in front of both. Some people seem

to never go anywhere else. See 'em down here every time. Though he passes through the Street at least once a day, he finds it boring to actually hang out here, as opposed to, say, a coffeehouse or the park or somebody's pad.

From the clothes of those just arriving from their pads, he catches whiffs of grass. Along his left, freaks mutter as he passes, "Hash, acid, grass... speed, hash, grass...spare change...grass, acid, hash..." This is an unpleasant new development. Christ! If ya hafta advertise...Obviously an inferior grade of dealer.

What the ...! That chick...! You can see right through her shirt! Wonder if ... of course she knows! A chick with swollen breasts stunningly visible through a gauzy blue blouse emerges in front of him from an apartment building. She checks to see if she is noticed, is overwhelmed by how much, then retreats back into the building.

The greasy aroma of a "Love Burger" reaches him. Across the street, beside the Print Mint, a cocktail lounge has cut a hole in the wall beside the sidewalk and installed a grill. A plump, middle-aged, straight lady cooks "Love Burgers" on it, and right now she is expounding, spatula in hand, on what was thrown off Tallahatchee Bridge in the lyrics of an AM radio hit. A freak passes in front of her wearing a cheap obvious wig. Every day sits higher on his head. Hair's growing. Just outta jail? Deserter? Conformist?

Anything is possible here, from the most deep-seated, improbable, foolish hopes to murder. Crossing Clayton, he can't resist a glance at the base of a fire hydrant. Still there. It's the blood stain from a racist murder he witnessed on a hot sultry night in the spring. A young black man squatting on the hydrant was stabbed in the heart by an extremely out-of-place chick, a redneck runaway. Can't walk by without looking. Another personal checkpoint.

Distracted, head down, he almost bumps into Peter, a friend from San Francisco State.
"Hey, man."

"Hey, man."

Peter smiles, granny glasses glinting from a black thatch of bangs and beard.

"Wha's happenin'?"

"Not much," Peter says. "You know Benny?"

He looks down first onto the part in the middle of the shoulder-length brown hair then at the smile of the short cat beside Peter.

"Oh yeah, hi. We met over at Illy's up on Downey Street."

"Yeah... Hi," Benny says.

"We're goin' to my pad to smoke some of Benny's Nepalese hash. Wanna come?"

"Uh... I took some Owsley acid and I'm walking to the park... waiting for it to come on..." He's flustered, as if someone barged into his room during a private act, in this case brooding. "Uh... I dunno... Nepalese hash sounds outasight but... I better not..."

"O.K. man," Peter says. "That's groovy."

What's he really thinking? Is he offended?

"I don't want to dilute the effect of the acid..."

"I can dig it," Peter says and starts walking again.

Yeah, he's offended. Or is he?

"See ya later."

"Yeah," Peter replies.

Benny smiles up at him and they disappear into the crowd.

Continuing west, replaying and analyzing the encounter with Peter, he's soon in a spiraling nosedive of introspection... Hash sounded nice, but... Can't get trapped in a social situation... Can't tell when it'll strike ... Don't want him to think I don't like him... Maybe I should tell him what's happening inside me... But... He recently took a devastating meth overdose, the worst experience of his life, beyond previous imagining. And he was already damaged from growing up as an irritating foreign object lodged in a redneck Sierra mill town. Now he can be ambushed any moment by a paralyzing paranoia.

He crosses the half-block to Belvedere and then the half-block to Cole before he's yanked out of himself. Across Haight Street, a

short, thin guy with delicate features and a corolla of ratted brown hair is going into the I-Thou Coffeehouse. Jesus Christ, is that! ...That asshole! See him a lot lately. Gotta be pretty low to make a career out of impersonating Dylan. Mmmmm... He smells piroshki, a pastry filled with spicy ground beef and costing ten cents at the Russian bakery he's stopped in front of. But for breakfast? Naw.

A few yards in front of him, a mountainous biker in a thick fatigue jacket in the hot sunlight stands on the sidewalk beside a pickup with a camper. He's teasing a couple of teenyboppers who probably snuck here against parents' orders.

"Oh yeah?" the biker says. "Let's see ..."
He starts unbuttoning the blouse of a pert, freckled blonde who's beaming ingenuousness. She looks at her girlfriend and giggles and blushes. He spreads open her blouse.

"Hey... hey... c'mere," he says to a biker friend nearby. "Look at these."

"Outa sight baby, yer really stacked," the friend says of two pink-tipped mounds. The girl's blush darkens and she turns her head to the side. The biker closes her blouse and kids her some more, then leads her by the hand to the back of the pick up. She exchanges a look with her girlfriend that says, I guess this is what you're supposed to do on Haight Street. She steps up, stoops, and, with a push on the ass from the biker, enters the low camper doorway. He then follows her in and closes the door. Wow, man! Well, she wasn't calling for help.

He's across Schrader and almost to the bowling alley when his stomach growls as if noticing the supermarket across the Street before him. Shit, that's right! He hasn't eaten yet. He jaywalks through stalled traffic to the north side of Haight. Oooooo.... that's nice. The acid flutters his nerves. Entering the supermarket, he sees in the glass door his giddy stoned grin, eyes all-pupil, and hair aflame from wind. Looks like he's holding onto a thousand watts. The automatic door swings open onto a frightened middle-aged straight woman.

Muzak! Sounds like there's an orchestra in the cheese section. In the fruit section, he puts some nectarines in a brown paper bag, then grabs-in-passing a pint of milk. On the way to the check out stand, he becomes absorbed in a show tune on the muzak and visualizes vast, petticoated chorus lines leaping and whirling. At the end of an aisle, he suddenly stops and looks around. Jesus! Was he dancing or just imagining it? He smiles at the idea of a freak dancing down a supermarket aisle, then he starts to laugh, and keeps laughing harder and harder, and just on the verge of blast off, catches himself. Cool it man!

The checkout line is a downer. The burly clerk eyes him warily. Chilling sterility, assembly line efficiency, telepathic ads, massaging muzak. If they could only eat it and shit it for ya...now that would be service. It's his turn. He struggles with a jeans pocket while the clerk rings up the items. The clerk has a flattop crewcut, and at the back, a long greased d.a. (duck's ass). His face is locked in a sneer. With his buddies outside the store, he's an authority on what's really going-on in the Haight. The clerk takes silver disks from him and puts them in a drawer with rectangular green paper. Now back to the real world...

The wind laves his face and he closes his eyes to ride the pulsation of conga drums in the park. He's waiting for the light-change at Stanyan. He bites into a nectarine. Kaleidoscopic nuances of texture and taste and ... Christ, has he gotta piss! He looks at the bowling alley across the Street. That's right, they've locked all the bathrooms around here. Too many junkies shootin' up. Could go to Steve's pad on Schrader. Naw, have to hang out and rap. Can't just piss and run. He looks across Stanyan at Golden Gate Park. He'll piss in the park somewhere.
    "Hey, man, can I have a bite of your peach?"
It's a psychedelic derelict complete with dirt-encrusted bare feet, raggedy soiled clothes hanging like Spanish moss, and the tangled, matted hair and beard of a saddhu. Excellent specimen. He's holding out a hand. The light changes.
    "It's a nectarine. Here, you can have the whole thing."
    "Thanks!"

Pedestrians fill all three crosswalks preventing cars from moving. In the empty intersection, heat undulates above the asphalt like an invisible wheat field. As he enters the park, a half dozen shirtless spades on a bench to his right are giving their own free concert in the park with conga drums, bongos, beer cans, and wine bottles. Walking down a sloping lawn between groups of prone sunbathing freaks, he sees Ashley Brilliant, in yarmulke and beard, at the foot of the slope, lecturing through a bullhorn on world peace or something. Heard it before, whatever it is. In the small cement pond at the base of the slope, in a spontaneous gesture of community spirit, several chicks wade about with rolled pant legs picking up debris in the gray opaque water and piling it on the side.

As he moves through the tunnel under Lincoln Avenue with its broken plaster stalactites, he's as light and transparent as a dandelion seed-ball. He emerges into trees and sun-spangles wobbling in the depths of shade and a swelling sound of new congas plus a calliope. On the left is a broad meadow with scattered clusters of sitting freaks. He's forgotten about the food in the bag and even begun to enjoy the pressure on his bladder. The paved path forks. Left to a merry-go-round, petting zoo, and play-ground (site of many a moonlit acid trip).

He goes right, to Hippy Hill, which he can see at the end of the path. On both sides of the path there's laughing, cuddling, reading, yoga poses, guitars, flutes. Overhead gulls and pigeons wheel and swoop. A short, goblet-shaped tree with freaks perched in its flat top passes on the right. And now, just ahead, on benches at the base of the hill, a dozen or so pounded congas with orbiting freaks who shimmy and pose and whirl.

A ways up Hippie Hill, he drops onto an unpeopled clearing. Farther up still is a cluster of twenty or thirty freaks. A Marlboro cigarette carton full of grass is going the rounds. The mammoth joint is grabbed, collapsed by a herculean toke that instills instant stupor, and then grabbed again. That's clever. Like the squirt gun

full of liquid acid. He drinks the sea breeze and listens to nearby conversations.

"...No man, I'm not an ice cream man anymore. I got fired. I went to work on mescaline and I was drivin' around in the uniform and the music was tinklin' and I was high and the kids were runnin' out .... I said, shit man, I can't take money from these people. So I gave all the ice cream away. The boss couldn't dig that at all..."

"Hey, what the...?!"
Suddenly a small boy is climbing all over him as if he were a tree. The boy drapes himself over a shoulder, hangs from his neck, slithers across his lap, and crawls under the arms he leans back on. Somethin' strange about 'im... He has the strength of a ten-year-old compressed into the body of a four-year-old. His features are pinched and oddly awry, and he makes distant grunting noises like intelligent baby babble. The kid's retarded! Thirty or so feet away is a thirtyish woman with the same chestnut hair as the boy, except hers is down her back and wind-wafted. She's beautiful, and she smiles at him as he submits to the child's gentle, ecstatic exploration.

Unlivable With

"What's that?" I asked of tablets in a baggie she held up to me.

"Acid," Ruth replied. "I took it from Ben's stash, when I knew I was really moving out. It's very good. Wanna take some tonight?"

Already her body was a miracle to me. She was my second lover.

"Yeah," I murmured.

We were in my cramped, dingy bedroom in the Mission District flat I shared with three other San Francisco State students. Tonight was the one-week anniversary of her moving in with me. I was just a year and a half out of a redneck Sierra mill town, and by comparison, Ruth, three years older and from New York, was a sophisticated woman. This invitation to share the acid was only the latest in what seemed unending surprises from her.

Like when she wouldn't give me her address, even after we started having sex. She said she was moving and would give me the new one when she got it. When I asked for her phone number she said she didn't have a phone. So I knew nothing about her home life. I accepted all this as just another inscrutable quirk of chicks, those aliens from another gender. I always knew if I really wanted it, I could find her address in the student directory at San Francisco State, where we had met in a philosophy class. And that

day I was ripped off for the ninety dollars she gave me to buy her a kilo of grass, I really wanted her address.

So I made a special trip across town by streetcar and copied her address and the number of the phone she supposedly didn't have from a directory for sale in the student bookstore. Then I took another streetcar to her house in Diamond Heights. Throughout these rides I was writhing and sighing with humiliation and despair. When I got off the streetcar at Castro Street, I didn't wait for the connecting bus but took off on foot, indifferent to the bite of the evening wind. Propelled by anguish, my long strides gobbled hills. When I eventually pressed the doorbell of her restored Victorian, I was panting.

"Ruth here?" I asked the guy who opened the door: blonde, lean, mid twenties, tie loosened.

"Yeah. She's in the kitchen." He turned toward the kitchen. "Ruth!" Then back to me. "C'mon in." Then back to the kitchen. "Somebody here to see you!"

I saw the kitchen and took off for it, stepping around him and through the tasteful living room and then through the tasteful dining room. When Ruth saw me, she stared an incredulous instant, and then threw her head back and laughed uproariously. I surprised even myself by taking her in my arms and kissing her. Her stifled laughter gurgled under the kiss as her eyes went to the enraged, speechless blonde guy pacing behind us.

2

"Husband?! Wow!" I said to her the next day across my kitchen table.

"Who did you think he was?" she asked with a broad grin, savoring the absurdity of the situation again.

"I dunno. A roommate I guess. Just a… nosey… ill-tempered…roommate."

She laughed. "He was furious after you left." A mischievous grin grew into more of that delicious laughter. Then she was suddenly serious. "He had no right to be mad. I've been telling him for a year I was going to move out."

After I stopped kissing her in the kitchen in front of her husband, she quickly and deftly walked me to the front door while I stuttered, "God, if. . . if. . . if I had any idea... I promise, I swear, I'll pay back every cent. I got burned. We got burned. The money for the kilo is gone. . . . "

All the while she said in soothing tones, "Don't worry about it. . . It's not important. . . I'll come over tomorrow and we'll talk about it. You'll see. There's no reason to be upset. . . Believe me."

Breaking the silence at my kitchen table the next day, I asked, "So you don't love him... or anything like that?"

"Him? No! He's. . . he's. . . un. . . unliveable... with..." she said, chuckling at the phrase.

"You've been planning to move out for a year?"

"Yeah, well, he's... comfortable. He puts up with my insanity."

"You keep talking about how insane you are, but I've never seen any insanity in you, not anymore than anybody else anyway."

"I know what I'm talking about. Remember my mother is a psychoanalyst. I could be committed for what goes on in my head."

"I still say you're the sanest person I know."

She thanked me with her eyes, and I took her hand.

"Why don't you move in here?" I asked.

She looked toward my bedroom and said, "It's kind of small."

"Then stay here while we look for our own place. I was going to move anyway. They raised the rent."

"O.k."

There was a ruminative moment when all this sunk-in.

"God," I said, "it must have blown his mind to have some stranger come in off the street and start kissing his wife."

She guffawed at the image and said, "Oh, he knew about you. I told him when I started seeing you. I don't think he believed me, and I didn't care enough to try to convince him."

"Well, I still want to pay him back for the kilo."

But I never did

3

The first night I noticed her in class my attention was caught by her extremely short skirt and extremely short hair. Then I noticed her pale skin, glowing the more for the dark hair and the startling blue eyes. After a couple high school crushes on them, I was especially susceptible to blue-eyed brunettes.

After class, we were standing next to each other, nose-to-nose with our reflections in the window, watching the bus stop across Nineteenth Avenue through the rain. We exchanged invisible acknowledgement of each other's presence. I glanced at her to confirm and then quickly looked back. I knew I would have to speak first.

"Uh, how... do you like... that class?"

"I like it," she answered, looking up at me but not lifting her head.

She was short and perfectly proportioned; I was tall, gangly, and hunched.

She added to her answer, with an impish grin I would come to savor, "I don't think I'll read any of the books, but the ideas are interesting."

"Yeah, I know what you mean. This is I think the third time I've been assigned Plato's *Republic*, and I still haven't read it. Are you a philosophy major?"

"No. Anthropology. Are you a philosophy major?"

"Not exactly. I just sign up for what looks interesting at registration. Most of my classes are in philosophy though."

I liked her a lot, and because of it choked. Now anything I said was a stall until the charm arrived, until the snappy repartee forced its way out of my mouth, as in movies. Of course, it never did. In the meantime, my conversation would resemble questions on a census form. But then I noticed a copy of *Jude the Obscure* among the books she hugged to her chest.

I asked, "You into Hardy?"

"Yes. I love him. I'm going to read all of his books. Do you like him?"

"Yeah. Especially his poetry."

"I haven't read it yet . . . "

Our bus splashed to a stop across Nineteenth Avenue. Everyone bolted out the door and stampeded across the street. She and I were among the first to reach the bus so there were plenty of empty seats. I stood behind her as she slid into one. I paused. She glanced at me. I accepted the invitation and sat beside her.

4

It was March of 1967, and the whole universe seemed crescendoing toward the coming Summer of Love in Haight Ashbury. Meanwhile, it was getting increasingly more difficult to drag myself out to State. As the absences, the untaken tests, and the unwritten papers piled up, I realized I wasn't going to finish the semester, which meant I wouldn't be able to make my extortion payment of grades to the draft board.

I didn't particularly like the philosophy class with Ruth. There were a couple of housewives who knitted in the back, wondering out loud annoying things like: "If Bishop Berkeley didn't believe in the material world, how could he eat?" Nevertheless, it was the one class I never missed and only because of the bus rides afterwards.

We talked hungrily. Every ride we experienced new clicks of agreement like the tumblers in a combination lock. I found it amazingly easy to make her laugh.

The first time I asked if she wanted to come over to my place, she put me off with a smile and said, "No, I've got to get home and practice my narcolepsy." I laughed hard and she liked that.

I had developed a finely-honed sense of hip and straight, becoming sensitive to latent straightness and the developmental stages of hip. I now automatically took a hipness reading of everyone I met.

One night, I leaned toward her in the bus seat and said,

"Ya know something? You're the hippest person I know."

She looked at me and smiled then looked back out the window.

"Wanna come over to my place for a while?" I asked. "Maybe get stoned or something?"

She searched my eyes, smiled, and said, "All right."

An hour later, stoned, with the kitchen table between us, I was wondering how I could kiss her.

"Really, my grandfather escaped from Russia In a basket on the back of a donkey," she said, giggling at the melodrama of the image.

"So you're Russian?"

"And Jewish. Where's the bathroom?"

While savoring her muted tinkle, I scrambled for a way of introducing sex.

"Uh. . ." I said, after she returned.

She looked at me expectantly.

"Uh. . .how. . . how did you come out to California?"

"I came out with a friend from Boston University. I told you about Cheryl?"

"Oh… yeah."

"And there was another friend, Alvin. The three of us came out together. Alvin's black. Kind of a hustler. He's illiterate, but he knows more about people, more about … living … than … anybody I've ever met."

I felt a twinge of jealousy. I wanted that distinction in her eyes. It was obvious that, years later, she was still feeling the force of Alvin's personality.

"Was he your ol' man?"

She shrugged and said, "We had sex."

"What happened to him?"

"The last I heard, he was back in Nyack, leading riots."

I had run out of questions. The moment of truth had arrived. "Geronimo!" I thought as I got up, stepped around the table, and bent down. She turned with deliberate slowness and looked up at my face now inches above hers. I kissed her.

The kiss ended and she said from a great stoned distance, "Kissing? I don't want to kiss."

5

She wasn't beautiful, not even pretty, but incredibly sexy. If I had encountered her intellect and subtle cynical wit in a guy, I would have eagerly befriended him. If I had encountered her exquisitely proportioned body with no intellect or wit whatsoever, I would have eagerly pursued it.

She seemed to always be laughing at some absurdity, seeing almost everything as a caricature or self-parody. Occasionally I sensed in her a vulnerability, the fear of the unarmed among the armed, and this made me determined to be her ally, and to that end I decided, when I invited her over the next week, not to so much as touch her. But then she went straight through the kitchen to my bedroom and sat on the mattress on the floor.

"Uh, don't you want me to hang up your coat?"

"Oh yeah."

She stood, removed the coat and handed it to me, then sat down again.

"Uh, do ya. . . uh, wouldjya like to smoke some grass?" I asked.

"Yeah," she chirped.

She removed her shoes, leaned against the wall, and pulled up her knees, showing me a wedge of panties under her miniskirt. I sat next to her, leaned against the wall and handed her the joint, already rolled for the occasion. I lit the joint then waved out the match and put it in a mayonnaise jar lid on the floor. Muffled shouts came from overhead.

"Sounds like gramps and grammy are at it again," I said. "Remember I told you about the old couple upstairs?"

She handed back the joint and exhaled smoke. There were more shouts and a thump.

"They're weird," I said. "I've only seen her. She was on the bus the other day holding up a newspaper at the side of her head, like she was trying to hide her face. And her skin is weird. It's all doughy and shiny."

"I have a friend who wants to buy a kilo," Ruth said. "Do you know where he could get one?"

"Sure. How much does he want to spend?"

"Is ninety enough?"

"No problem."

She rummaged in her purse for the money then handed it to me.

"Stop turning my copper cross to gold!" the old woman yelled above

"Oh, yeah," I said as I wedged the money into my jeans pocket, "she's always yelling these weird poetic things. Like that."

When the joint was finished, she rested her chin on her knees and fell silent. I too was silent and reconsidering my pledge not to touch her.

She looked at me and said, "Well, I guess I better go."

And that's when I kissed her. She didn't turn her body toward me, but she didn't take her mouth off mine either. Tongues met, saliva mixed, and lightly, hesitantly, I touched her breast. Her breathing leaped an octave.

A while later, when I put my hand on her thigh, she pulled her head back and said, "Why don't you turn out the light."

I did and there was only the brown glow of the window shade.

"I don't know if I should be doing this," she said without conviction, unbuttoning her blouse.

"Why?" I asked as I unlaced a shoe.

"I have a test tomorrow. I should be studying for it."

"Oh, I wouldn't worry about that. There'll be other tests."

She chuckled.

6

After that night I was in love, daydreaming about her moving in. So I was anxious to impress her by handing her a kilo of grass and twenty or thirty dollars change. Scoring a key was a measure of hip status and I was certain I had the connections to do it. But I couldn't.

My best connections were couch nomads who by definition didn't have an address and so I wasn't even able to find them. Other connections may have had addresses but not kilos or knowledge of any at that particular time. By the third day, I was

visiting people a second time and offering an exorbitantly high price that included a contribution of my own money. Still I couldn't find anything. And that's when I bumped into Ziggy.

"Heeeyyy....!" Ziggy called out. He struggled to remember my name but failed.

I had just left the Drogstore Café on Haight Street late on the afternoon of the fourth day and Ziggy approached wearing his standard outfit of gleanings from Goodwill throwaway bins. Today it was an oversize Hawaiian shirt, baggy pants, and scuffed shoes without socks or shoestrings. He was always a loud, slobbering spectacle, but today he was farcical. When black men had their hair chemically straightened ("conked"), they wore it in a colorful bandana, wrapped cylindrically, with hair showing at the top. Ziggy, who was white with sickly-pale cheese-textured junkie's skin, today wore his curly red bush in a yellow bandana as if it were being conked.

"Oh, hi Ziggy," I said.

"Wheh ya been?" he asked in his New York accent, as he put an arm around my shoulder.

His voice was full of sleepy junkie languor. A year before, Ziggy and his wife, also a junkie, had finessed their way into being my roommates. I enjoyed several weeks of mesmerizing close-study of Ziggy, a master burn-artist.

"Listen, I wanna tell ya how sawry me and Doreen awe about, about the shit comin' down at yoah place."

"That's o.k."

"Naw, we just came in an' laid owa hassles on you. We don't blame ya fuh cuttin' out."

"I was going to move anyway," I lied. I moved to a new apartment one night when they were out.

"We'eh sawry."

I was surprised when I thought I caught a glint of sincerity in those blue eyes at the bottoms of gray pits.

"C'meeuh, I wanna give ya somethin'." And he lead me east along Haight Street. "Heeuh, it's a lid." He deftly slid the baggy into my coat pocket while hugging me. "We owedjya."

"Hey Ziggy, um, do you know where I could score a kilo of grass?"

"Yeah, shooah."

"How much?"

"Hundehd an' ten." In response to my surprise, Ziggy added, "Things awe tight right now."

I certainly knew that to be true. "O.k.," I said, "but look, it's not my money. I want to be there for the whole transaction."

"Shooah."

We took the 6 Masonic bus. We sat alone in the back and the whole ride Ziggy kept up a friendly patter, exchanging gossip about mutual friends, describing big deals he had lined up. We got off at Laguna and walked downhill to Fell, where we slipped through a tear in a cyclone fence and entered an abandoned, crumbling apartment building with boarded windows.

We climbed to the third floor and walked down a long hall, shoes crunching plaster from the walls as we passed rooms with open or no doors. In one room, two male junkies were intent on shooting up. In another, there were only scattered stained mattresses. In the next, a couple was fucking on a mattress on the floor. Ziggy finally lead me into a room empty except for a folding chair.

"Sit down. Wait heuh. I'll be right back." In a few minutes he returned. "Everything's o.k. Just fine. 'Cept he doesn't wanna meetjya . . ."

I thought for a moment and said, "So bring the key here and I'll give you the money."

"I awready thought o' that and he won't do it. He's paranoid and I can't talk him out of it."

Alarms were going off inside me.

"I got a joint of it heuh, if ya wanna smoke it an' see how ya like it."

I didn't speak.

"Look, he's right upstaiuhs. Let me take him the money and I can have the key back heuh in one minute."

I didn't move.

"Look. If ya don't wanna do it, ya shouldn'ta brought me all the way down heuh. I'm just doin' a favuh fuh a coupla friends. If ya don't wanna do it, let's split. I gotta lotta things to do."

I thought about handing the money back to Ruth and admitting I couldn't do it. Ziggy would be my last chance. I searched his eyes. No, he wouldn't burn me, a friend.

"O.k., here," I said and handed him the envelope.

"Wait heuh."

Which I did. For a half hour. The couple I saw fucking walked by talking and adjusting clothing. Broad amused grins broke onto their faces when they saw me. Later, a tall, curly-haired chick walked by the door, stopped, backed up, and leaned her face into the room.

"You must be waiting for Ziggy," she said smirking. I nodded and she went on her way.

I finally realized I had been burned. I didn't bother searching the building or asking anyone about him. Ziggy would have already bought a week's worth of smack. I trudged down the stairs, devastated, reeling, and left the building. I walked toward Market Street and the street car that would take me to San Francisco State where I could get Ruth's address.

It was understood that if you were burned, it was your fault, and I knew the special contempt Ziggy reserved for his victims. As I walked, I remembered the contempt I came to feel for him and suspected that I may not have hidden it as well as I thought. I took the baggy from my coat pocket, heedless of who might be watching, but I had nothing to fear. It was oregano, as I suspected. And suddenly I saw the whole burn from Ziggy's perspective.

Ziggy heard that I was looking for a kilo. He even knew the exact amount of money I had with me, $110. While passing the Drogstore Café, which was all glass on two sides, Ziggy noticed me. Then, if he wasn't already carrying the baggie and the oregano, he could have gone to the nearest mom-and-pop grocery and lifted them. For Ziggy it was all in a day's hunt.

7

Two days later Ruth moved her clothes and books and records and other necessities to my place, and every afternoon the rest of the week, without hurry, we walked from one to the other of

the available apartments, often stumbling down the sidewalk arm-in-arm drunk with laughter.

As the week passed I enjoyed my first taste of conjugal life, an extended great date with a little crowding of some habits. She insisted on washing the dishes after dinner instead of the end of the week. I knew there would be vast stretches of time ahead to adjust. Then on Friday, she suggested we finish the week with a night of sex on LSD.

It would be the second time I had taken acid and she was the second woman I had had sex with. It was the first time for both to have sex on acid. We dropped after dinner.

"Hey," I asked while drying a plate. "Did you ever notice how we get weird looks sometimes on the street?"

"No," she said, looking up from the sink, interested.

"I mean, you have shorter hair than me, and I'm taller than you and if someone can't see your breasts, like if you have a coat on or something, then it looks like we're two cats walkin' arm in arm."

"How horrible! Two men actually touching."

"Yeah, once I saw this...Oh!" We locked looks.

"Is it coming on?" she asked grinning.

I could only nod. Delicious soothing tremors ran along my spine and I closed my eyes to savor them. When I opened my eyes, she was studying me, and when our eyes met, we laughed. I felt an increasing weightlessness which I tested with several slight jumps. Then I felt giddy and started laughing again.

And when I stopped, I said, "It's so funny."

"What?"

"Just. . . just. . ." I sighed deeply. ". . . Being here. . . "

We finished the dishes and dried our hands, then I reached for her and we began kissing. This was always somewhat ungainly while standing, because of the difference in our heights, so we unclenched and went into the bedroom. On the floor, beside the mattress, was a candle sticking up from an empty wine bottle that was layered with wax rivulets. Before dropping, I had put in a new candle and now, crouching, I struck a match and became so mesmerized by the match flame that it went out before I could light

the candle. And even with the second match, I didn't remember to touch it to the wick until I felt the heat of the flame on my fingertips.

With my swaying hard-on and the acid rushes, I was thrown off balance trying to take my jeans off while standing. When I was finally naked, she too was just finishing and I stared unselfconsciously, cock bobbing to pulse. By now, I had seen her naked lots of times but never like this. My first sex partner was skinny and flat-chested, so Ruth's Playboy-perfection was all the more startling. Globular breasts, narrow waist, luxuriant bush, and that creamy glowing skin, all of them were actually *there*!

She noticed my staring and let me look. Then our gazes met and we broke into giggles and lay on the mattress. In fluid motions hands roamed bodies and did whatever they felt like doing and it was exactly what the other wanted. I entered her slowly, savoring the friction as it reverberated through us. We stared into each other's eyes, pupils dilated to the point of no iris at all.

"I... I can't... tell... " she gasped, ankles crossed on my back, "where... you begin... and ... I end."

8

I don't know how many times we came, but when the gray overcast dawn was coming through the only window, I reached for her again and she got up and put on her panties.

"It's too much," she said. "The acid. This little room. I think we should go outside somewhere. Get apart for a while."

"You wanna walk in the park?" I asked as I stood up.

She bent to pick up her blouse and looked at me. I was gaping stupidly at her, erection undiminished. She stepped over, held my cock, and looked up into my eyes and said, "Put it away and get dressed."

I shriveled. While dressing, I tried to figure out if I had done something wrong.

"I thought I'd go down to that little store on the corner and call a friend," she said, angling arms through coat sleeves.
"Remember, I told you about Tim? He has a car. I was going to ask him to take us for a ride in the country."

I tested her mood by trying for what would now be a non-sexual hug, but she shrank and said, "I don't want to touch."

By the time Tim arrived the effect of the LSD had subsided to what would have been tranquil lucidity if I hadn't been so troubled by the suspicion that Ruth's change in mood was brought about by my having exposed some repulsive aspect of myself.

Tim left his wife for Ruth, who then left him for his friend Ben, who Ruth left to move in with me. Tim was a one-man cult centered on Ruth. He hadn't told her yet, but he was in the middle of a novel about her, furiously written in longhand on binder paper. His attitude toward her was that of a dog with the leash in his mouth begging for a walk. I would learn later that he was capable of a junkie-like obsession for particular women.

I was dimly aware of some of this when I met Tim. He had alert deep-set eyes and a handle-bar mustache framing an irritatingly constant smile. Because of the mustache and a gap in his front teeth, he resembled Teddy Roosevelt.

While I put on a coat and searched for keys, Tim studied me.

"How much is your rent here?" he asked.

"I pay fifteen for my room," I answered.

"I'm looking for a room."

"There'll be one available for twenty five next week."

Ruth got into the front seat of Tim's clunky old '53 Chevy and I surprised everybody by getting in the back. I felt cranky and annoyed by her distance, though I felt the same need for solitude. She looked into the backseat at me and smiled with amusement.

The car was one of those Tim frequently bought for under fifty dollars and abandoned where it died. As it warmed up, I was certain that I could hear the tapping of each valve in the engine.

The streets had the festive air of a sunny Saturday, kids playing on sidewalks and dads polishing cars. All the basketball courts in the Panhandle were full. By the time we reached the Golden Gate Bridge, Tim and Ruth were in the groove of an old rapport, discussing people I didn't know. While the wind through the window laved my face, I became absorbed in the faces of the tourists on the bridge passing like fluttered cards. When we were passing above Sausalito, I stared down absently at its steep green

slopes and the houses like box seats on the City. Meanwhile, I was also analyzing scenes from last night, searching for what I did wrong.

In Mill Valley, we climbed serpentine roads that tunneled through redwood forest, and at one point, I thought I caught Tim gloating in the rearview mirror. Ruth and I hadn't spoken once so far in the thirty minutes of the ride, and Tim was giddy with hope. He joined Ruth in a game of creating architectural cocktails: this house on that lot with those gables and that garden. Soon they were on a merry-go-round I couldn't jump onto.

We parked beside a fern-strewn slope with a vista of the bay. After a while, Ruth exclaimed of whirring crickets, "Oh, listen to the animals!"

I snorted, contemptuous of her city-ignorance. I was abandoned now in the back seat, glancing at Ruth, hoping our eyes would meet. But her eyes seemed to touch on everything but mine. Then I realized with a jolt that she wasn't pretending to ignore me. She had forgotten all about me!

"Look! There're freaks in that car!" Ruth exclaimed later as we crossed over the bridge back into the City.

A carload of freaks passed in the same direction, honking and holding up two fingers. Tim and I had dark hair just to the top of the collar, not long by Haight-Ashbury standards, but long enough to be recognized as part of the uniform.

She and Tim returned the sign and the honk and laughed at the cutting-up in the car as it passed. I noted that this was the third or fourth time I had seen that two-fingered salute. The victory sign from World War II was becoming a hip counter-sign. Significant when the velocity of change was such that many fads lived only weeks.

At the booth, the toll taker said our toll had been paid by a car up ahead. The car with the freaks honked, rear window full of V signs, and then it disappeared into traffic.

9

That impenetrable silence stayed wedged between Ruth and I even after Tim dropped us off. We ate in silence and then went to bed and lay back-to-back. For hours after Ruth fell asleep, I

could still feel traces of the acid, stirred-in with nearly forty hours without sleep and the sudden withdrawal of her affection.

The next morning I was awakened after a couple hours sleep by her clatter in the kitchen. I lay in bed remembering the previous day and wondering about her attitude now. I got dressed, and when I entered the kitchen, saw that she too was fully dressed.

"Hi," she said without a smile.

"Good morning," I said with forced cheeriness.

Toast popped up, she moved a skillet with fried eggs to a cold burner. I knew I should wait but I had to know. I walked up behind her as she scanned the shelves for plates, turned her around, and took her in my arms. She went limp.

She said, "It's not working with us. I'm moving back with Ben."

I was stunned. Trouble, even crisis, that I was prepared for. But this was death. I said nothing. I was flummoxed and befuddled, so much that I couldn't think of a thing to say to save us. And so it ended, just like that, no accusations, no arguments. It just collapsed, shot in the head.

Tim and his smirk arrived around ten to take her and her things back to Ben. Tim and Ruth must have arranged this the day before. As I closed the door behind her, I timidly said, "See ya." But I didn't. Not for years.

I never went back to our class either. Within days, I became resentful of the breakup, and in case of a chance encounter, I polished some lines that would show her how little the whole thing meant to me. In the end, it seemed a normal affair of months crammed into days.

A few nights after Ruth left, I couldn't sleep, still fidgeting with outrage, and when the couple upstairs started in about one o'clock, I was agitated enough to confront them. The rickety back stairs creaked under each step.

"You're a crow on my shoulder!" she screeched.

On the landing I paused, watching through gauzy curtains as the old woman at the kitchen table yelled, "You scarecrow in knight's armor!"

She was addressing an empty chair.

Bernie's Big Secret

"You mean," I said, lowering my voice, "you think that guy back there snuck into the kitchen and put poison in your food?"

Bernie glared hard at me, not speaking.

"That's why you're not eating?" I asked.

I looked over my shoulder at the man, the only other customer in the restaurant. He actually was somewhat sinister looking: gaunt, middle-aged, in a dark overcoat. But that was a coincidence. I turned back to my best friend, terror-stricken across the table from me, and stifled a guffaw.

"He was looking for the bathroom," I continued. "I heard him ask the waitress. He went into the kitchen by mistake. Bernie, that's ridiculous. It's just more paranoia."

But he looked away, not convinced. He was lean and hunched and had thick glasses with black plastic rims and a helmet of thick reddish-brown hair that went from the top of the glasses to the bottom of his collar.

"If you're not going to eat it . . ." I said, stabbing my fork into a potato on his plate, "I will," and put the potato in my mouth.

He looked at his food. He was hungry, but pride was involved now.

"Are you sure you don't want it?" I asked.

He nodded not looking at me. I scraped his plate onto mine. We were in David's, the best Jewish restaurant in San Francisco, and I was treating him to dinner the night before he emigrated to Israel. His emigration was the desperate act of someone convinced he was under constant surveillance by the F.B.I. In his mind, his watchers had followed him, bugged his phone and those of his friends, and eventually, bugged most rooms he entered. But they had never before threatened to kill him. It was logical they should attempt tonight because this might be their last chance.

There was nothing particularly unusual about paranoid delusions in the early Seventies in San Francisco. Many of my friends had been in a psychiatric ward at least once, as had I about five years before, when I scorched my mind on methedrine. Insanity was an inconvenience like the flu. However, Bernie was *not* one of those friends who had been in a mental hospital. He had the greatest strength of character, the surest sense of himself, of anyone I had ever known. This made his breakdown the more unnerving.

One cause of his strength was in his every spoken "l" "r" and "s." He had a speech impediment, an exaggerated lisp, which was further distorted to my California ear by a strong New York accent.

In five years of close friendship, the only things he ever said about his childhood were that he was very close to an older brother and they grew up in a working class, Jewish, Bronx neighborhood. What wasn't mentioned but implied by his strength of character was a childhood spent crashing through torments.

"Look, Bernie," I said, chewing his going-away present with conspicuous impunity, "I'm still alive. And I bet I will be for... days. Past that, who can say? Next week the planet may not be habitable. But this whole melodrama about government assassins is just... like the poison in this food."

"Theyoo awe thing-th (*There are things...*) I can't teh-oo (*tell*) you . . . but they would ekthpwain evewything (*explain everything*)."

He was abandoning his wife and infant son, his career and his country, and he wouldn't tell his best friend why.

2

I knew Bernie was fleeing a delusional threat, but I also knew it had to be huge and overwhelming, as big as the federal government, because Bernie's physical courage was extraordinary, impressing me the more for my lack of it.

For instance, the night we were driving home from a movie, and while waiting at a red light at Masonic and Fell, Bernie suddenly yelled at me, "Get down! Get down!" and he dove to the floor. I was behind the wheel and looked toward him and saw in the car in the adjacent lane a cat my age with a long Beatle-cut and a crazed leer pointing at me something like the barrel of a gun with cloth draped over it. I dove to the floor too. Then waited. Nothing happened. The light changed and I raised my head to watch the loony drive off.

"I'll bet that's not a gun?" I said.

"That thun-of-a-bitch."

"Let's follow 'im."

And we took off.

While our rage grew, we followed him down Masonic, across Oak and uphill, then across Page, and as we were about to cross Haight, he made a u-turn at Waller, a short block ahead, and came back toward us.

"Maybe it is a gun," I said.

The light was yellow. I had a second to decide. I made a quick left turn, cutting in front of the loony, who then turned right, coming up behind us. I pulled to the curb and he went around us, leering and pointing something, like before, except on my side. Like before also, he seemed to be satisfied with our cowering on the floor. But unlike before, he did the same to a taxi double-parked in front of us, and I knew we had him. The taxi would have a two-way radio.

Bernie and I got out and, in the chilly wind, paced in circles on the sidewalk. Macho indignation was gone now and I just felt fear. Bernie was still muttering his outrage, showing no fear at all. After a few minutes, my knees suddenly became wobbly. I thought for a moment I wouldn't be able to stand but recovered. Then a police patrol car came toward us and I ran into the street to stop it.

"The guy with the gun in a tan Chevy?" the cop in the passenger seat asked.

"Yeah," I said. And the patrol car shot down the street.

I was impressed not only by Bernie's lack of fear, while I trembled, but also his quick thinking when he first spotted the loony.

This was during the emergence of the first celebrity homicidal maniacs, like the never-caught Zodiac killer, who preyed on random strangers in the Bay Area. When the City was being terrorized by the Zebra killers, a murder cult of black men, most of whose white victims were pedestrians, Bernie walked the nearly deserted streets with a pistol in his coat pocket. He saw this as a civic obligation as well as a personal challenge.

3

His courage reached mythic proportions one night in a greasy spoon on Haight Street near Fillmore. It was the kind of place, in a poor black neighborhood, where hippies could feel safe from pigs and/or rednecks.

Bernie stopped our conversation in a back booth by staring over my shoulder then suddenly leaping out of his seat. I turned around to watch him head for the front, where a muscular young black man in a raspberry colored bellbottoms-and-vest combo with matching cap, stood inside the open door, looking down at a hippy couple at a table by the window, who, terrified speechless, were looking up at him.

On the sidewalk outside, another young black man watched the couple intently then glanced quickly up and down the street then back at them. As Bernie approached, the young man in the combo turned toward him, revealing that he had a knife in one hand and money in the other. Bernie raised a finger toward the ceiling as if about to make a debating point.

"Bwuthuh, thith ith countuh wevoluionawy (*Brother this is counter revolutionary*)," he said in a gently scolding tone.

Alarm flashed across the thief's glistening sweaty face. He thought Bernie was going to challenge him but Bernie stopped at a tactful distance.

"You can thee theeth awe hip peepo (... *see these are hip people*)," he said gesturing toward the dazed couple in their long hair and indigo pea coats. "They haven't got any mouh (*more*) than you."

The bewildered thief stared hard at Bernie, the least frightened of them all. Outside, the lookout stared down the street.

"You and them and me, we'uh awe (*we're all*) fighting the thame (*same*) enemy. If you hafta do thith (*this*), at leatht (*least*) do it to thtwaight peepo (*straight people*)."

Bernie always had a messianic attitude toward the counter-culture, often referring to the moral obligations of "we hip people."

Fear switched to anger as it occurred to the thief that he might be the butt of a joke. A mean smirk slowly appeared. Then the lookout opened the door, leaned in, quietly spat an order, and retreated. The thief followed the lookout through the door, but before he disappeared, the thief glanced back through the window at Bernie, anger having reverted to confusion and suspicion.

The kid with the lisp, a magnet for bullies, became the man who could not be intimidated. Except that he *was* being intimidated. He was fleeing to the other side of the world, and his plane was leaving the next morning, and I had invited him to David's in a last ditch effort to get him to change his mind. Jenny, his wife, a close friend of mine, and the mother of their son, was counting on me. But he countered all my arguments by repeating that there were things he couldn't tell me.

4

I knew a government official had indeed once threatened him. He told me about it one afternoon when we were hanging out in the kitchen of a flat across from Dolores Park that I shared with some college students.

Due to a rent strike, he hadn't paid rent on his own place in nearly a year. With no legal training whatsoever, he was representing himself in lawsuits against landlords and banks – and winning. He had been a math prodigy who walked away from scholarships to become a radical journalist and help bring about an anarchist utopia. During research for an article, he discovered that

the City that burned down in '06 now had a deliberately impenetrable thicket of a fire code, which he had mastered and was now using to advantage in court.

"You th-ee (*see*)," he said, chuckling at the wickedness of the scheme. "It wath cweated (*...was created*) back when evewy thity guvooment wath cowupt (*...every city government was corrupt*). It wath dethigned (*...was designed*) to be unenfothable (*unenforceable*)."

He always had an esthetic appreciation for a good con. Friends of his once started a literary review in order to sell the review copies to used bookstores. This review accidentally evolved over the years into a pillar of the West Coast literary establishment.

He was laughing hard now. His sense of humor was my favorite of his traits. We spent a lot of our time together simply laughing. Now as he spoke, his boney, square-tipped fingers sculpted the air between us with his awkward grace.

"It wath dethigned to genewate bwibe-th (*It was designed to generate bribes*)! Evewy beeooding in the Thity mutht be viowating thum pawt of the code (*Every building in the City must be violating some part of the code*)."

Doubled over with laughter, he staggered a step to the side. Suddenly I understood.

"That's how you've been winning these rent strikes?!"

He nodded vigorously, unable to speak from the laughter, then he wiped spittle from his lips and red mustache.

When the laughter subsided enough, he said, "Yeth, if they'oo viowating the fiuh code (*yes, if they're violating the fire code*), then the went thtwike ith leegoo (*...the rent strike is legal*), untiyoo they cowect the viowation-th (*until they correct the violations*).And that can be ekthpenthive (*expensive*)." He suddenly became serious and said, "They don't have compwete wecodth (*complete records*)!" Face lit with inspiration, he turned to me and explained, "I caught one of the bank'th lawyeth twying to wead my note-th (*...bank's lawyers trying read notes*). Ah'll (*I'll*) bet they don't have compwete wecodth (*complete records*) on that beeooding (*building*) . . ."

He stepped over to the kitchen table and sat, lost in thought.

After a while, he said, "Ah'll make thpecial note-th fowuh them to thee nekth time *(I'll make special notes for them to see next time)."* Then he turned to me, "Lithen, you can do thith too. Move into any ohd Victowian apawment in the Thity , like thith one *(...old Victorian apartment in the City, like this one),* and I gawontee at leatht thikth month fwee went *(I guarantee at least six months free rent).* All we do ith decla-oo a went thtwike *(...is declare a rent strike).* Would yohwuh woommate-th join a went thtwike *(...your roommates join a rent strike)?"*

Not only was this a blow against the System, not only did it save him rent money, but it was also an exhilarating game. He was the cartoon mouse toying with the cat.

Then one day, just after leaving the courtroom, going down the echoing marble hall, swinging his briefcase and strategizing, Bernie was stopped by a beefy sheriff's deputy (the Sheriff's Department handled evictions). The deputy told him, in a confidential tone, if he didn't lay off the rent strikes, he could expect jail "or worse." It wasn't clear if the deputy was acting on his own, on orders, or for money on the side, but Bernie quit anyway. His attention was already flitting off to other campaigns.

5

So, he was indeed capable of drawing threats from government officials, and I knew he had recently started focusing on the federal level. He mentioned once that he was maintaining his own surveillance on the home of a regional official of the FBI. Another time he gave me a hilarious description of a clandestine meeting in a Chinatown restaurant with an FBI agent. When I asked him why he was meeting with the FBI, he wouldn't tell me. Another secret.

Actually, I never knew him when he didn't have some dangerous grandiose secret. And indeed he had shared secrets that, when I heard them, seemed to have historical significance. Once, when I was living in the bucolic farm town of Petaluma in Sonoma County, he drove fifty minutes at night from the City (I deliberately didn't have a phone) to share something monumental.

Inside my cottage, he convinced me that he indeed had something worth hearing, but he wouldn't tell it to me except

outside in the parking area. I knew without being told that he feared my cottage, because he was a frequent visitor, might have hidden government microphones. I was barefoot and expecting him to go only a few steps over the gravel. Instead, I had to follow him in the dark, my irritation increasing with each step, to what he decided was the suitable distance of sixty or so feet.

Wind jangled eucalyptus trees and a spray of galaxies arched over head when he leaned toward me and whispered: "I found a thpeech Nikthon *(speech Nixon)* made to a bunch of bithnethmen in Dallath two dayth befoh Kennedy wath athathinated *(...businessmen in Dallas two days before Kennedy was assassinated)*. He thaid, I quote: 'We weeoh do whatevuh ith nethethawy to weemove the Kennedy-th fwom offith *(We will do whatever is necessary to remove the Kennedys from office).*' "

I was impressed. "How do you know this?" I asked at a normal volume.

"I wead *(read)* it in the New Yohk Timeth of Novembuh *(New York Times of November)* twentieth nineteen thikthty thwee *(sixty three)*," he answered, also at a normal volume.

"What in the world were you doing with a New York Times from way back then?"

The only light was what dimly reached us from my kitchen window, but I could see his face well enough when he caught himself before answering me and smiled a familiar smile that said he couldn't say. This information about Nixon was very impressive though and I would have stayed impressed if I hadn't read it in a story by another writer in Esquire a month later.

6

So if I knew he could draw threats from government officials and he could uncover threatening government secrets, why couldn't I believe he was a target of the FBI? One reason was a faultline of political paranoia I could trace all the way back to the first night I met him, on the night shift at Rincon Annex, the post office hub of the Pacific mail routes. Hippies worked at the post office for the same reason black people did: it was the federal government and it couldn't discriminate against long hair any more than dark skin.

It was when conversation drifted to Nixon, for whom we shared a loathing, that I got a first glimpse of the depths of Bernie's political paranoia. We were on adjacent stools sorting mail on the night shift. We leaned toward each other, shouting in the rhythmic clatter of the huge automated sorting machines all around us.

"Oh, c'mon . . ." I said, incredulous of an assertion that Nixon was about to incarcerate the anti-war movement.

"No, it-th twue *(it's true)*," he insisted, his eyelids half shut. It was his third day without sleep. "They declayoo an emuhgency *(declare an emergency)* and then they wound *(round)*-up the whole anti-wah *(war)* movement . . ."

"Congress would never let him," I countered, placing a letter in a slot in front of me.

His eyes closed and his head slumped forward. Instead of sleeping, he spent his days working full time as an underground journalist, usually sleeping only a few hours every other day.

After a couple seconds, he sprang awake. "Pubwic *(public)* opinion wiyoh fohth *(will force)* them to."

He lowered his head toward me, furtively looked from side to side and then up. Rincon Annex had floor space the size of a football field and suspended over it from the high ceiling were enclosed catwalks. They had strategically placed slots covered with dark glass through which the workers below were watched

He said in a lowered voice, "He aweady hath plan-th dwawn up *(He already has plans drawn up)*. . ."

"How do you know that?" I asked at normal volume and inserted another letter.

Rather than lift his eyelids, he titled his head back to look at me from under them.

"They can yuth the pwithon camp-th *(use the prison camps)* they put the Japaneeth-Amehwicanth *(Japanese - Americans)* in in Wuhld Wah *(World War)* Two."

"Naw. The public might go along with it, but not the Congress. There are still some decent people in Congress."

While I was speaking, Bernie stared at a letter in his hand, figured out what it was doing there, and put it in a slot.

"Didn't you evew notithe *(ever notice)*," he asked, then lowered his voice, "how Nikthon thuwoundth himthelf with

Guhmanth *(...Nixon surrounds himself with Germans)* . . ."

"What?"

He took a pen from a shirt pocket and wrote on the back of a letter "GERMANS."

"Guhman thuhname-th *(German surnames)*: Haldeman, Eulekman *(Erlichman)*. That-th a methage to the wuhld *(That's a message to the world)*. Nothing at that levoo ith cointhidenth *(...level is coincidence)*."

I thought about that for a moment, and then, when I turned to rebuke him, I saw that he had fallen dead asleep holding a letter in front of a slot.

It was inevitable that Bernie and I would meet. Each on his own homed-in on the easiest job in the building. Payments on oil company credit cards had their very own sorting machines and the sorted envelopes had to be collected. For the oil companies, two people worked all night at something one could do in half a night. We had each maneuvered through the bureaucracy to get ourselves permanently assigned this job.

I occasionally had articles published in the underground press, usually book reviews, and we discovered that we knew some of the same people. I was at the fringes of circles he was at the center of. He had a column in the most popular Bay Area underground newspaper, *The Berkeley Barb*, and in the early sixties, he published the largest radical newsletter on college campuses on the West Coast. He had written or collaborated on several books with radical themes. He knew Jerry Rubin and Abby Hoffman and was himself something of a minor celebrity. Only a few days before I met him, I had read his interview with a well-known, mainstream journalist who had just returned from Hanoi.

But what really cemented our friendship that first night was his sharing of a secret.

Most of my free time on the job, half a shift, was spent reading in a lavatory stall. Suspended from the coat hook on the inside of the door of each stall was a white cardboard dispenser of paper covers for toilet seats, "ass-gaskets." I discovered that on the blank backside of many of the dispensers, which were about the size of typing paper, there was a periodical full of dirt on Rincon Annex handwritten by an anonymous representative of the people.

As a loyal reader and occasional contributor to "The Ass-Gasket Gazette," I was thrilled to meet the founder and publisher when Bernie confided, upon my guarantee of not telling anyone, that it was none other than he.

7

So I knew he was somewhat cracked from the first night we met, and over the next couple years, his condition evolved into full-fledged insanity. I first noticed this one night when we were stoned on grass and discussing politics on the floor of a small, candle-lit bedroom with the ambience and half the size of a railroad boxcar. We were visiting Duffy, an old friend of mine from earliest Haight-Ashbury days. We had bumped into each other the week before at a demonstration against Nixon's invasion of Cambodia and the killing of demonstrators by National Guardsmen at Kent State.

Duffy and I quickly resuscitated the outrage we felt at the demonstration. Bernie was unusually somber, quiet, and preoccupied.

"And I'll bet the guardsmen aren't even tried," Duffy said, handing me a joint. He was short and hunched and so malnourished that he got out of the draft without even trying.

"Oh hell no!" I said and took my toke. Bernie turned down the joint so I returned it to Duffy. Holding–in the toke, I breathlessly whispered, "Those guardsmen did something millions of people, half the country, wanted somebody to do." I gushed smoke.

"Yeah, it was like this tribal... ritual... killing thing," Duffy said.

Bernie suddenly leapt to his feet and, facing a wall (and supposedly, hidden microphones), announced for the record, "I compweetwee dithagwee (*completely disagree*) with that. They-oh ith no evidenth yet that thith wath anything but an acthident, a mithtake... (*There is no evidence yet that this was anything but an accident, a mistake...*)."

"O.k., o.k.," I said, cutting him off. "I'm sure they heard you."

Embarrassed, I looked at Duffy, who didn't know Bernie. Duffy's beady eyes, between bushy eyebrows and a bushy mustache, were amazed, then delighted.

"Bernie, goddamit!" I shouted later while driving. "They couldn't have bugged that room! You'd never been there before and they couldn't have known we were going there. Remember how we decided to go? We were driving down Guerrero and I said I owed a visit to a cat that lived over there and you said you didn't mind stopping. We didn't know ourselves that we were going there, so how could the government?"

He said nothing but turned and looked out the window.

But there was even stronger evidence that his problem was psychological and not political. He let slip one evening in a coffeehouse, in the closest to a confessional moment I had ever known with him, that he had taken a lot of LSD the last year or so. Though he didn't actually say that was a mistake, he knew he didn't need to. He even admitted that many of the times he and I had been together he had been on acid while I knew nothing about it.

8

I was still chewing his going–away dinner at David's when Bernie went into a familiar routine: with his arms crossed tightly over his chest, tongue smacking on his palate, he acted-out a straight-jacket struggle of indecision about whether or not to share the Big Secret, which he was certain, would convince me he was worthy of assassination and that he indeed should leave the country. I was supposed to interrupt this performance with pleas. Instead, I concentrated on my (his) meal.

I thought again of the times he and I had been together, evenings or afternoons, at a movie or a coffeehouse, when he had been stoned on acid and I hadn't known about it, and I felt angry and betrayed. It was a ridiculous thing to hide, like all his other secrets. Months of resentment welled up in me.

Before he mentioned the poisoning of his food, I was on a mission to save him. Not any more. He had ruined the evening by bringing along his bogeymen and I didn't give a damn if he emigrated or not, or what the Big Secret was. I put the fork on the plate.

"Let's go, o.k.?" I said as I pushed the chair back.

He was surprised. He thought we were still negotiating over his telling me the secret. The bill hadn't been totaled yet, so I put a tip under a plate and walked over to the cash register. While I paid, he just sat at the table, not moving, still considering. I pocketed change and looked at him.

"I've got to get home," I said. "It's late." Then I went through the front doors onto the sidewalk, where I waited for him.

Good-byes were curt, shaking hands beside my car. There was a moment of awkward silence when he let me see some of his continuing struggle over the secret.

"Wanna a ride?" I asked with only as much conviction as felt decent.

"No," he said with a shake of the head.

"I'll stop by and see Jenny once in a while. See if there's anything I can do to help," I said as I opened the door.

"Yeah. . . thank-th. . . "

He continued standing there as I started the car then pulled into traffic. I saw him in the rearview mirror watching me drive away. After a half dozen or so blocks, my mind drifted to Jenny, and I suddenly realized that, if she knew the Big Secret, I might be able to get it out of her.

9

When I met Jennie and Bernie, they were at that stage of a break-up where they were getting separate apartments. Both spoke with absolute certainty that the relationship was dead, though they saw each other nearly every day. Bernie seemed reconciled, even relieved that it was finally over, and that was why I was so surprised when, responding to a casual question about Jennie one afternoon at my apartment, he said:

"Don't athk *(ask)* me about huh *(her)*. I want to kee-oo huh *(kill her)*."

"What's wrong?" I asked.

He stared at me a moment then turned away and punched a palm and spat: "I could kee-oo huh."

I knew better than to ask again. But his vehemence stunned me into almost believing he meant what he said. I thought

their relationship had cooled beyond that, and jealousy seemed unlikely in light of all their sexual experimentation.

Bernie was one of the founders of the Sexual Freedom League, mainly a front to help the founders get laid. Once Jenny told me with a chuckle that she couldn't keep up with Bernie's sexual experimentation. They once had an arrangement where each would have a lover come to their apartment, the four would have dinner, then Bernie would take his lover to one room and Jenny take hers to another, and later the lovers would leave and Bernie and Jenny would go to bed together.

Jenny and I had a friendship independent of Bernie, so there was nothing unusual about my visiting her the night after Bernie declared his desire to kill her. She had moved out of the place she shared with him into a lower Haight Street flat she now shared with a couple roommates. While she and I were rapping on the living room couch, I was alert for an opportunity to ask her about Bernie's rage. Then we were on our way to her bedroom, away from the kitchen and her roommates' chatter, so I could hear her poetry.

The room was richly decorated with the best of the Haight Street paraphernalia store where she worked. My scan of the books on the bottom shelf of the nightstand lowered my hopes for the poetry: Ginsburg, Lenore Kandel's *The Love Book* (beat sex poems that were convicted of obscenity), the *Baghavad Gita*, *Autobiography of a Yogi*. No serious poetry. She got a sheaf of poems from a bureau drawer and we sat side by side on the bed and she read a couple. It was just as I feared: free-verse rock lyrics. When she finished, I scrounged for comments.

Eventually I blurted out, "Ya know, Bernie came over the other day, and he was so angry with you . . . "

"Oh, I know . . ."

"I've never seen him so upset . . ."

"I know . . ."

"He was . . . crazy. Or, at least, crazier than normal. What happened?"

"I don't know. Really. I don't know what he's angry about. He won't tell me." (That she wouldn't even guess made it seem she was holding something back.)

Suddenly, with inches between us on her bed, I had a realization, and I knew she was having it at the same time: there was no reason why we couldn't have sex. There had always been an ignored mutual attraction. Sex wouldn't have even occurred to me while they were together, but they weren't. A stuck door between she and I suddenly swung open.

The silence became noticeable. She was looking up at the ceiling with a slight, expectant smile. She wore hip hugger bellbottom jeans and a low-cut imported blouse that hung in folds over her braless breasts. I could have sworn I heard my jeans stretch.

She was plain-pretty with a plumpish body. Her pale skin was finely freckled and her eyes were cornflower blue. Her long fine straight brown hair was all bangs and stray strands. She had a girlish, vulnerable smile that could suddenly turn impish as prelude to a witty, barbed aside. Any man of worth would have to be at least a little in love with her. One who was quite a bit more than a little in love with her was her boss, owner of the first Haight-Ashbury coffeehouse and now the owner of the largest head shop on Haight Street.

Then, as if it was something to do while waiting for me to make my move, she leaned over and slid the folded pages of her poetry between some books on the bottom shelf of the nightstand. Her blouse, of the same material as the bedspread, now hung open on the bottom revealing a hanging breast and a conical, pink nipple.

It was only later that I thought of all the good reasons not to have sex. If Bernie hated her that much then he still loved her, no matter what he said. I felt too much for her to have just casual sex and being in love with her would have been even more complicating.

Jenny and I didn't make love, not because reason triumphed and I persuaded myself not to, but because I couldn't. I had a debilitating panic attack. I "tuned out." This was a paralysis that could ambush me anywhere, anytime, even without provocation. A condition that had changed little in the several years since I left the mental hospital.

The pressure of the situation caused a bottomless vacillation, making decision impossible for anything except flight. I became encased in a tense silence, finally managing a gulp. She broke the tension by standing up. I too then stood up and I could see she was surprised. Was this the opening or the closing act?

"I have to go," I murmured. "I have to be . . . I'm late . ."

I backed away, erection at a painful angle. I struggled not to reach down and fix it. I opened the door and stared at her, trying to think of something to say, certain it would be the wrong thing. She recovered herself, smiled ruefully and then nodded, not so much in goodbye as in agreement that she and I were unworkable.

From that day on, every time we were alone, there was clumsiness and charged glances, and we were around each other a lot because, within a couple months of that night, Bernie and Jenny were married. I was best man. It was winter and their honeymoon was a train loop through western states, a couple days of sex on LSD in a private car with snowbound America flowing by the steamed windows.

After such a rupture, their marriage seemed a raising of the dead. That Bernie loved her, he proved by the intensity of his hate. But what about her? What kind of feelings could she have for him after all that? I knew she wanted a child, and she became pregnant almost immediately. But she also seemed to be fleeing that bone-chilling loneliness I saw in myself and others in their mid twenties. Also, at about the time of the wedding, she joined the "Family." More commune than cult, it centered on "Father," a self-declared god-realized Indian who peddled a generic Hinduism.

The Family took up several apartment buildings on the outskirts of the Fillmore District. It was a measure of their mellowness that Bernie and I, who openly mocked them, were accepted as unofficial members. With his love of a good scam, Bernie started a running joke between he and I about Father.

"Owa big mithtake wath *(Our big mistake was)* that we didn't claim to be God," he would mutter.

10

Of course, as a master manipulator himself, when Bernie left for Israel, he had Jenny and the baby safely on welfare as well

as supported by the commune. So she didn't really need my help when, as promised, I went to their apartment to offer it. It occurred to me while I drove there that evening, a week or so after he left, whatever illusory assassins he may be running from, Bernie might also be running from his wife and child. He was almost thirty, with few marketable skills and no degree, and for the first time in his life, he really needed money.

I didn't know if Bernie had shared the Big Secret with Jenny, but I would try to get as much as I could. It had been nearly two years since our near-miss in her bedroom. My mental state had only slightly improved in that time. I had had an ol' lady but we broke up months ago. I was sexually starved and emotionally desperate and couldn't connect with even one of the pack of acceptable single chicks in the Family, some as desperate as Jenny had been.

"Everything go o.k. at the airport?" I asked from the kitchen doorway. "He get off o.k.?"

She was at the sink making tea. The baby was asleep and the apartment was empty of other Family members, which was unusual.

"Yes," she threw over her shoulder out of the clatter of tea-making.

Then she sighed in exasperation. This trip was a burdensome indulgence of Bernie's that she would just have to put up with. In ways, he was her firstborn. Throughout the chat that followed, which included too little news about Bernie and too much gossip about the Family, I watched for an opening to ask her about the Big Secret.

"How's Janet?" I asked when we were sitting over steaming cups at the kitchen table.

Janet was a short busty blonde with a great laugh, the sexiest of that pack of single chicks. I felt tremendous attraction to her and had blown it miserably when I came on to her. I suddenly felt depressed.

"Oh, she's alright, I guess," Jenny said and then smiled. "She came home late last night really drunk in her underwear and this morning she couldn't remember what happened."

The singles in the Family were notoriously wild partiers. This news about Janet depressed me even more.

I asked, "Was she one of your roommates in that flat down on Lower Haight Street?"

"No, I met her when I joined the Family."

"Oh."

"You might be thinking of Cindy, she was sort of like Janet."

"Oh... yeah."

That's when I fell through a trapdoor in time. I landed in that same Lower Haight Street flat and in the very moment we were sitting side-by-side on her bed, *before* I decided not to kiss her. I felt again all the desire and all the potential of that moment. This happened while I was looking across the table into her eyes. It took a while but she found her way to what I was thinking and she answered with an expression of horror. I had asked her for sex. And I was as surprised by it as she was.

After the shock wore off, I felt humiliated. If I had thought about it, I wouldn't have said I was at that moment hornier than usual. A few times I had masturbated over what might have been between us, still I hadn't once thought consciously about approaching her. But if it was a measure of my sexual desperation that I would try to seduce Bernie's wife, it was also a measure of my anger with him.

"Uh, do you know why Bernie left?" I asked in order to distract her. "Do you know exactly *what* he was running from? I couldn't get him to tell me."

We were both grateful for a change of topic. Nevertheless, I could see by her smile that she did know Bernie's secret and didn't want to tell me. Then she frowned and began searching inside herself to see if she had in any way led me on. She was blameless, of course, and I should have relieved her by withdrawing the question, but I didn't.

Then, in lieu of her body, she shared the Big Secret with me.

"Oh, he sold some information to the F.B.I.," she said with the smile of an indulgent mother. "Nothing important."

"I remember. . ." I said. "He told me about this meeting he had, in a restaurant in Chinatown . . ."

The baby cried out and Jenny got up from the chair.

"That was it?" I asked.

"Yes. That was it," she said stepping away from the table.

"He never told me what it was for," I said. "I guess I just figured it was... some... intrigue of his I would read about later."

"I don't know what he told them," she said from the doorway, "but I know it wasn't important. He just wanted to see what it was like – you know what I mean? – to have that experience." She left the kitchen.

I remembered how he told the story with such relish, repeatedly punching his thigh and shaking his head as he laughed. He held up his hand to silence me as I was about to ask him a question. Then he overcame the hilarity enough to tell one more nugget. Watching from a corner table in the Chinese restaurant, he had been delighted by the spy-movie corniness as an agent came in and checked the place for an ambush and then left and wasn't seen again. Then a few minutes later, Bernie's "contact" came in and joined him.

Jenny thought what Bernie had done was a goof, a tweaking of the System, like the rent strikes. And it seemed to me too that this was just a grand prank gone awry. He ripped off the FBI and now feared detection and retaliation.

Or did he rip them off? And why wouldn't he tell me about it? I would have expected him to be crowing. Maybe he gave them valid information and the assassins were projections of his guilt. Could he have been less concerned with the prank than the money (for his new wife and child)? His extreme extroversion and insensitivity to psychological nuance made him seem more liable to fooling himself about his true motives.

He had recently humiliated himself trying unsuccessfully to sell a collection of old articles and columns to book publishers. Also, he was resentful of incompetent friends who had money and the media spotlight dropped on them. Plus, he had a model of betrayal and corruption in an older brother who went from being a Berkeley radical to a corrupt official of the Lindsay administration in New York City. The brother and others surreptitiously bought the

future site of a hospital before it was made public. Bernie accepted this as simply the way things were done in the Big Time.

All of this mixed with too much LSD could produce convincing government bogeymen.

Jenny returned, cooing to the baby yawning in her arms.

"Don't tell him I told you that. O.K?" she said.

I was so anxious to ask more questions that I was twitching, but I had to say, "Oh yeah, no, no, I won't say anything. I promise."

She felt uncomfortable about having told me and wanted to drop the subject. I never again found a way to reopen it and I never knew for sure whether he ripped-off the FBI or his ideals. But then something happened that made it all irrelevant anyway.

11

A couple months later, in a supermarket aisle, I bumped into Alfredo, a pudgy, affable Latino who was one of the true believers in the Family, and who informed me that Bernie had been back in San Francisco for a couple weeks. This surprised me, but what followed floored me. When I asked why Bernie had come back, I was told, with a glint of vindication for Bernie's and my mockery, that Bernie had a vision at the Wailing Wall in which Father, the Hindu charlatan, told him to go home. I immediately went to see Bernie.

As I crossed the livingroom, my hand extended, he looked away. Then, as we shook hands, he met my eyes.

"I'm really glad you're back." I said, putting his apprehension to rest.

He had an awe-shucks grin as he pumped my hand some more and then gestured toward the sofa. Jenny was beaming as she hugged and kissed me, and soon, with characteristic tact, she went to the kitchen to make tea. I asked him about Israel and he began the travelogue. We both knew it was filler and that we were stalling to avoid the painful part. Jenny brought the tea and left to go shopping. And then I asked the big one.

"Is it true?"

"My hoh wife *(whole life)*, fwom euhwy adowethenthe *(from early adolescence)*, I've theen mytheh-oof ath an atheitht *(...seen*

myself as an atheist), an atheitht wevowutionawy *(atheist revolutionary)*. . . I wath compweetwy thupwythd by thith *(...was completely surprised by this)*. I wath jutht anothuh touwitht going to the Wayooing Wa-oo *(...was just another tourist going to the Wailing Wall)* and then . . ."

I didn't hear exactly what the vision of the guru said to him there. I had withdrawn into contemplating the grotesque pairing of Father and the Wailing Wall. But soon enough my friendship with Bernie was almost back to normal, except now there were subjects we didn't discuss. I never asked him that question that I also never asked Jenny: do you really believe this guy is God? Nor did I ever bring up to Bernie those phantom government assassins.

12

I moved to Marin and we naturally drifted apart, infrequently seeing each other. For the first time in his life, he was pursuing money and, compared to his heroic pursuit of political chicanery, it was squalid and he was inept. He drove a cab and, when a real estate boom hit the city, he went for the sucker ads on the radio for licensing courses, and the former recreational rent-striker became a real estate salesman—who never sold a single building that I knew of. He didn't abandon politics altogether, often sneaking into big Democratic Party powwows when they were held in the City, where he was about as likely to mix as he was with real estate investors.

A trend in movies at the time was children born of the Devil, and Jenny and Bernie's son was a case in point. When he was three or four, I visited and was treated to a gymnastic tantrum in which he fled them like a squirrel until he wound up hanging by his hands from the top of a door. He couldn't have been more oblivious to their threats and pleas if he had actually been deaf. He was a capsule concentrate of Bernie's explosive energy with the added impurity of a sadistic streak. At one point, he leaned on my knees and, while I tried to engage him in a conversation, he drilled a fingernail into my leg, staring into my eyes to savor the discomfort.

A few years later, I was living back in the City and bumped into Jenny at the Tassajara Bakery. I was shocked at the change in

her. She seemed stuporous with exhaustion and covered with a gray dust-film. That, and the devil-child pulling her arm taut, made the once appealing thatch of her hair now seem emblematic of her frazzled life.

Not long after that, I bumped into Bernie – or rather, he saw me and pulled to the curb in his cab. We went to the Owl and the Monkey, one of a new Seventies generation of City coffeehouses. This one was just outside the Haight in the Inner Sunset District.

"Do you hear what you're saying!?" I asked, in disbelief.

Nixon had just resigned and I was shocked when Bernie started defending him. (And this time he didn't have the excuse of fearing hidden government microphones.)

"We don't know the puthpective fwom up theuh (...perspective from up there)."

"The whole world thinks he's a crook, even the right wingers, and *you're* defending him?!"

"Theuh could be awoo kindth of weethenth (*There could be all kinds of reasons*) why he had to do it..."

"When we met, you told me you thought he was sending a message by having advisors with German surnames. Well, you were wrong about that, and you're wrong about this."

Later, as he drove me to my basement apartment, the argument continued. I kept expecting him to snap out of it. But he didn't.

"It-th a diffewent wuhld at that levoo (*It's a different world at that level*)."

We were still a few blocks from my place when we stopped at a light and I decided I couldn't take anymore.

"I'll get out here," I said as I opened the door. "Bye Bernie."

He leaned across the seat as I stood. The light changed.

"But theuh awe tho many thing-th they have to conthiduh (*...there are so many things they have to consider*)."

I shut the door. A horn blared behind him. He drove off and I never saw him again.

Amateur Insanity

The First Murder

My Summer of Love was bracketed by murders. The second murder, in which my roommate Tim and I were marginally involved, marked the historical end of the Summer of Love, as much as any single event could.

The first murder occurred a little after we moved into our pad on the edge of the Haight-Ashbury. Like the murders that drove Tim out of the South, the first murder was racist and, ironically, committed by an unlikely redneck right on Haight Street a block from the intersection with Ashbury Street.

Throughout that summer there was a brown bloodstain on the sidewalk around a yellow fire hydrant on the southeast corner of Haight and Clayton Streets. Through the room-spin and slow flash of that summer, I never once walked by that stain without remembering what I witnessed there one sweltering night.

A hot night in San Francisco is rare any time but especially in spring. Around nine on this one, I was coming from friends on Schrader Street where I had gotten very stoned. I was seeing through the wrong end of a telescope and hearing through a warped-wavy phonograph record while navigating a sidewalk clogged with more people than I had ever seen on Haight Street at one time. They were weaving around each other, leaning against walls, sitting on the sidewalk, laying on the hoods of cars with radios blaring. It was a spontaneous party for spring.

I was wearing a sky blue, stylized military jacket like those worn by high school marching bands. I had marched in one myself only a couple years before. The Beatles would make them well known in a few weeks on the cover of *Sgt. Pepper's Lonely Hearts Club Band*. I had a scraggily full dark beard and collar-length hair, was tall, lean, and hunched, and was ascetic in clothing style, usually wearing sandals, Levis, and a T-shirt.

So the coat felt like a costume. I had tried it on at my friend's, who got it in a thrift shop, and when I was about to take it off to leave, he insisted I wear it and bring it back next time I visited. And now I was in it, vibrating to the festive atmosphere of the luxuriously tropical night. Though at first I recoiled from the attention the jacket drew, within a block or so I relaxed into it. A block more and I was reveling in it. Eventually, though sweating and uncomfortable, I didn't take it off.

I was in a crosswalk on Haight Street more than halfway to Clayton, when a chick yelled, "I'm tired of you niggers buggin' me!" And then a different chick screamed. I froze.

Twenty feet to my right, on Clayton Street, a mountainous young black man, maybe three hundred pounds, squatted on a fireplug, hands wedged in Levis pockets. He wore a white tee shirt that glowed purple in the lunar street light, and at the center of his chest was a black hole, the apex of a triangle of blood. His bulging eyes were stunned... unbelieving.... fading......

A short blonde teenybopper in faded Levis ran east down Haight Street with a hunting knife in her hand, which she threw into a pile of shredded newspaper in the gutter. The scream had come from one of the dozen or so people around the victim. All, like me, were frozen with shock. It may only have been a second or two, but it was a noticeable length of time before anyone recovered enough to help the victim lay down on the hood of a car.

Meanwhile, the teenybopper disappeared into the milling crowd on Haight Street, which was unaware of what had just happened around the corner on Clayton. A freak stopped a cruising cop car, which then pulled onto the sidewalk. One cop ran to the victim, the other talked on the car radio. After both examined the victim, one ran back to the car radio and the other, taking a pen and tablet from a breast pocket, started talking to witnesses. A

chick, perhaps the one who screamed, pointed at the corner where the assailant had escaped and where I was now standing, able to look down both Haight and Clayton Streets. I looked around and realized I was the only one who had seen the knife tossed.

I stepped over to it and pointed down at it and looked at the cop with the pen and tablet about thirty feet away. I didn't speak. I knew he would look in my direction eventually, which he did. He then came over and looked down at the knife. I stopped pointing and headed home. A couple blocks east, an ambulance shrieked west. Later that night, the radio reported the black man died on the way to the hospital and the chick turned herself in at a church.

Even in the most sympathetic neighborhood in all of white America, a black man could be killed for his race, in this case by an out-of-place redneck runaway (aside from being incapable of the act itself, no middle class girl northern or southern would have used the word "nigger.")

65 Scott Street #2

Tim and I shared a pad in that sympathetic neighborhood. 65 Scott Street #2 had a livingroom view over the rooftops of the Fillmore District and across the bay to the Berkeley Hills. I filled the small bedroom with a mattress on the floor, orange-crate bookshelves, and cardboard boxes full of clothes. Tim filled the livingroom with brick-and-board bookshelves, a stereo, a burgundy velour couch, a large double bed, the back seat of a VW van, and a wicker wheelchair. On the walls were genuine Soviet propaganda posters he bought somewhere in Eastern Europe. On the inside of the bathroom door was a poster of Ho Chi Minh that smiled at you just above your knees while you took a dump.

When I was a couple haircuts overdue and tensions were rising, just before summer, I quit my part-time file clerk job and started full-time living. At about the same time, Tim lost his job as a draftsman because of too many unexplained absences (acid trips the night before). With money from my tax rebate and the sale of my car, Tim and I became dealers, which meant we had an unlocked drawer that might contain lids of grass, tabs of LSD

and/or STP, tinfoil-wrapped gems of hash, peyote buttons, and occasionally opium, among other things.

Day after day of doing only what you wanted. No appointments, no authorities, no schedules. There was little difference between day and night, one day and another, one week and another. The biggest decision of the day was what drug to take and who to visit. Of course, the drug that always had priority was the one we hadn't taken yet. We sniffed glue, drank cough syrup, crushed and ate morning glory and wood rose seeds, gagged then giggled on peyote (it has the taste, texture, and color of dehydrated garden slug), and of course, took LSD and STP. Marijuana was the staple; it goes with anything. We greeted the dawn on some kind of drug a couple times a week.

Added to all of this was my draft status. It became increasingly more difficult through the spring to drag myself out to San Francisco State and doodle or daydream through a class when there was always a friend who needed visiting or a sunny day that needed savoring in the park. So, I dropped out and therefore became eligible for the draft. I would have eagerly fought the Fascists but I wasn't going to feed myself to this kill machine. It was the sentence for a crime I hadn't committed.

Throughout that summer, I was running down a steep hill with the only alternatives being fly or crash.

Sawhorse Over a Water Department Hole

Tim did have a job ... of sorts. Where our street, Scott, intersected Haight, there was a water department hole beside a stop sign and the hole stayed there all summer. So every Friday Tim perched on the sawhorse that straddled the hole and held out the Berkeley Barb, an underground newspaper, to the cars stopped beside him. And they were bumper-to-bumper for blocks in every direction, all coming to gawk at these mutants with their fantasy-life licentiousness. And here was one right in front of them!

Through much of that summer Tim was the very first Haight-Ashbury "hippie" many tourists saw. The whole of Upper Haight Street for a dozen-or-so blocks to Golden Gate Park was

lined with hippies at thirty-or-so yard intervals selling underground newspapers to the stalled week-end traffic. Tim was the first in that line.

Which was an invitation to a car full of straight white teens that pulled up beside him one day. A fist shot out and sent him flying. The car then slowly drove off to guffaws and the bass burble of the muffler. There was nothing to do but stand up, brush himself off, and return to his post.

Once, a cop car pulled up and Tim waited to be told to get off city property or get over to the sidewalk.

Instead, the cop at the passenger window asked with blue-eyed sincerity, "Are you a communist?"

Another day, a car full of young blacks pulled up, pointed a gun at him and demanded all his money. Handfuls of change into outstretched palms and then they drove off. Nothing to do but sell the rest of his papers and try to break-even, which is not to say he did it for the money.

No, he sat on that griddle of summer pavement for the people he met, especially chicks: teenyboppers, topless dancers who were also groupies, secretaries with art degrees, etc. He rarely came home alone on Friday evening.

There was Brenda, a peroxide blonde in her late twenties who was a pill freak and early Jesus freak, who didn't eat meat or wear leather, and who once remarked the only book she ever saw in her father's house was *Mein Kampf*. She had a passably coherent personality until, in the middle of a conversation, she would jump up from her chair and talk to an invisible entity somewhere above her left shoulder. She would come up from L.A. with no money or even a place to crash trusting that whenever she needed food, clothes, shelter, or pills, the Lord would provide, and he did. Tim inexplicably became obsessed with her. Then, to jolt another lover, she killed herself on a whim by diving head-first onto the sidewalk from a fourth floor apartment.

And there was Diane, a buxom groupie with eyeliner so thick it could have been applied with a canoe paddle. She moved in for a week with her clothes and a portable TV, and every night the Fillmore or Avalon Ballrooms were closed, we watched old movies, stoned on the couch, Diane in the middle, Tim and I

alternating handfuls of popcorn with handfuls of tit, but no more than her tits, since we weren't musicians.

Race Traitor

Tim and I got to know each other through nightly conversations at the kitchen table.

"We had known for a while that I was being followed by the Klan," he said during one of them, then took a drag on a cigarette. "Schwerner, Chaney, and Goodman had just disappeared... "

"The guys they tortured and killed?" I asked.

"Yeah," he said nodding, then exhaling smoke. "Though at first we didn't know what had happened to them." Quietly, slowly, precisely, he continued. "Carol and I had a friend at C.O.R.E. She was a negro but could pass for white. One night, she and I went to a White Citizens' Council meeting."

These were memories stirred by grass he and I smoked half an hour earlier. His gaunt face was framed by longish dark hair that slanted across his forehead and flared out both sides of his neck. Over deep-set eyes was a prominent brow now pinched hard.

"We sat at the back...God it was hot ... It was night ...and it was televised and the lights made it even hotter."

He took another, harder drag on the unfiltered cigarette.

"All of a sudden, this guy sitting next to me ..." His hands mime pushing against the guy.

"He starts yelling 'Help! Help! He's hitting me! Help!' Then *he* starts hitting *me*. And then... almost instantly... cops appeared."

He becomes a cop disposing of a troublemaker at arms' length.

"...And they hustled me out of the meeting. Then out on the street they let me go."

He picked a fleck of tobacco from his tongue and ruminated on it. I became impatient.

"I don't get it," I said. "What was the point of *that*? Why did they attack you in the meeting? Why not on a deserted road or some place like that?"

"The whole thing was on television, and the attack was an excuse to show my face. It was like a... a wanted poster. The idea was that some random Klansman would recognize me somewhere, maybe in a convenient place... "

"Oh, I see..."

"They have a special hatred for 'race traitors'."

He stubbed out the butt in a saucer.

"Like a white southerner in the civil rights movement?" I said, describing him.

"Yeah," he said and took a pack of cigarettes from a breast pocket and dug out another. "A little while later, they found the bodies of Schwerner, Chaney, and Goodman."

He put a cigarette in his mouth and picked up a book of paper matches.

"Carol knew Schwerner pretty well. They had worked together."

He struck a match and touched the flame to the cigarette.

"Anyway, after that attack on me, and then their deaths..."

He whipped out the flame.

"She insisted we leave the South."

He tossed the smoking match onto the saucer.

"I insisted that, if we did, we come here."

Rednecks were a bond for Tim and I. We both grew up among them, though I recognized our California descendants of the Gold Rush losers weren't as lethal as his descendants of the Confederacy. Tim was twenty-five, six years older than me, and I would always wonder: had I been old enough, would I have had the guts to face *his* rednecks in the great crusade?

"Did you see that Art Hoppe column yesterday?" I asked during another stoned kitchen table conversation.

"I don't like Art Hoppe," Tim said with surprising vehemence.

"Why, what's wrong with him?"

"I don't like his . . . cartoon segregationists . . ."

"Yeah, but . . ."

"They are *not* stupid! That is a serious miscalculation."

I recognized the frontline veteran's respect for a formidable enemy and felt chastened and kept quiet. Tim was a hero of the only war that mattered, the last front, the home front against the fascists. And because of this status, inspite of his occasional buffoonery and selfishness, he was always, ultimately, for me, a hero.

Only child of two PhDs, Tim attended Quaker elementary schools in Philadelphia until his father, a liberal activist minister, was made president of a seminary in the South. Tim had a jeweler's eye for the facets of a political issue and a sober, calculating savvy that prevented him from becoming an actual communist, even though, by the time he graduated from college, he idolized Mao Tse Tung. He was inevitably drawn into the civil rights movement, and whenever he talked about it, he displayed an utter seriousness, a lucidity of purpose, that reminded me of my father and my uncles when they talked about their experiences in World War II.

That seriousness was paradoxically at odds with Tim's most distinguishing characteristic: a child-like glee, an ability to hit the high notes of joy. Tim in the Haight was righteousness stepped out of its armor and awkwardly learning to gambol. An eager conduit of the smallest enthusiasms, he could be as excitable and unrestrained as a puppy and as graceless. He was always stumbling over something or spilling it. In short, he was totally devoid of cool, which isn't to say he wasn't hip, because he was the living essence of that.

And he was always at the center of the action. After high school, he hitchhiked to Venice, California, then a thriving beatnik capital. After college in California, he and his wife returned to the South at the beginning of the civil rights movement and were among the first white members of the Congress of Racial Equality in New Orleans. And now he was in the Haight-Ashbury for the creation of the Counter Culture.

Chicks were the first ten or fifteen reasons Tim and I got the pad together in the Haight, so appropriately we met through a chick. Ruth was three years younger than Tim and three years older than me. Even more than politics or a childhood among

rednecks or an intense love of literature and art, the friendship between Tim and I was founded on awe for Ruth and her unique, askew wit set in a dazzling female body. We were a cult of two. Tim left his wife, Carol, for Ruth. Six months later, Ruth left Tim for his friend Ben. About a year after that, she left Ben for me, and when she returned to Ben, Tim was there, helping to move her belongings and hoping to intercept her on the rebound. He didn't, but he was looking for a room to rent and there was one available in the flat in the Mission District I shared with other San Francisco State students.

There was a dark side to Tim's talent for enjoyment: oblivious selfishness. A pampered only child, he could not deny himself or his sharkish appetites. An intimate was someone he could take advantage of; for instance, his ex-wife.

"The Blues Project was playing at the Avalon and I really, really wanted to go..." he related another night at the kitchen table. "We were supposed to meet Ruth there but Carol didn't want to go. Well, why couldn't I go alone? Carol got upset, and we argued and argued for a long time."

"Maybe she sensed what was beginning between you and Ruth..."

"Maybe... But she became completely irrational. Oh, and I was on acid."

"Was Carol on acid too?"

"No."

"Did she know you were?"

"Uh... no... I had timed it to come on while we were at the concert but she kept arguing and she made us... made me... late. So it came on while we arguing there in the kitchen."

"Sounds like she might have been trying to save the marriage."

"Yeah, I guess... Anyway, the acid kind of made me irrational too. She started crying and I... I couldn't help laughing... It... It wasn't about her... A random thought about... something made me laugh..."

"Jesus..."

"Yeah, and there were dishes and cutlery drying in the dish rack... I was trying not to laugh and she got hysterical... and...

Anyway, she grabbed a steak knife." He acted it out, grabbing the invisible knife and then raising it above his shoulder. "... And she tried to stab me..." He became himself and raised his left forearm. "...And I blocked her, but she still got it into my arm..." He held up the bottom of that forearm so I could see the inch and a half scar. "She got it in at an angle." He showed the angle by miming the stab. "... And it went fairly deep... Hurt like hell." He lowered his arms and looked into the memory and showed sympathy for the first time. "She dropped the knife right after she stabbed me. She was horrified at what she had done."

"Did you call an ambulance... or go to the ER?"

"Oh no, no... I just put some iodine on it and gauze and bandaged it up tight and it was fine... Then I went to the Avalon and met Ruth and we heard the Blues Project... It was a great night."

"What about Carol?"

"Well, she was crying on the kitchen floor when I left..."

Amateur Insanity

Tim had many accomplishments besides his participation in the Civil Rights Movement, among them: sneaking into a Beatles concert, standing within stabbing range of Nikita Khrushchev when he was touring LA, smuggling a copy of *Naked Lunch* into the States when it was banned. But, for me, his greatest accomplishment, the ultimate imprimatur of hip, was his being a recurring mental patient.

"Ya know what I want to be when I grow up?" I asked him during a kitchen table conversation. Before he could, I answered, only half in jest, "Mentally ill."

There was an intellectual fashion then, reflected in the books of Norman O. Brown, R.D. Laing, David Cooper, and others, declaring madness latent or awry enlightenment, suggesting links between schizophrenia and mysticism. Madness, the ultimate pariah-hood, was actually heroic battle against dark forces on the frontiers of consciousness, certification of being deep, in another league, non-middleclass. Also, having been in a mental hospital at

least once was a badge of profundity among the hippest chicks. Even more important for Tim, it was how he stayed out of the draft.

Before the summer began, and through its whole bacchanal, Tim and I suffered from recurring episodes of drug-induced psychosis (with no holiness in it). Tim's were always triggered by police paranoia, and fear like that is a cop-magnet. His rap sheet spanned from civil rights sit-ins and anti-war demonstrations to pissing in the bushes of a park and lifting cigarettes (they didn't bust him until he had paid for forty dollars worth of groceries).

Still he was capable of fits of "reckless abandon," like the time he carried a kilo of grass in a shopping bag the entire length of Haight Street to our Scott Street pad. But there were other times when drugs (likely acid) and circumstances (friends recently busted) ganged up on him and gave him a whopping police paranoia of hallucinatory intensity. Though caused by drugs, its obvious connection to his experiences in the South gave Tim's psychosis at least an aspect of the heroic. I had no fear of police and considered any authority figure a stooge to be manipulated. My unheroic phobia was others' secret opinion of me.

My psychosis started a couple of weeks after we moved into Scott Street in the next door kitchen. Our apartment became an annex to Christine and Cookie's with the doors to both kept open most of the time. The two chicks would occasionally come over to listen to Tim's stereo and dance on our hardwood floors or savor the view, while he and I used their phone. So, it was routine for me to wander into their kitchen that morning.

Occasionally a stranger would be there, picked up by Christine the night before at the Fillmore or the Avalon ballrooms. Few were seen more than once. This morning, he was tall with a dark Beatle-cut and handlebar mustache and, as I entered, he was sitting at the table eating and rapping with Cookie's youngest nephew, Danny, and her ol' man, Don Ed.

I exchanged nods and "hi man"s with those two and a nod with the chewing stranger. Groggy and bedraggled, Christine entered and went around me, radiating bed-warmth, wearing only a guy's t-shirt. I read her guest's fate in her resentful offer over her shoulder while reaching into an overhead cupboard.

"You want some coffee…uh…Brad?"

He shook his head and turned back to his cereal bowl. He'd caught her tone and wasn't bothered. Christine reached deeper and her shirttail rose on an electric glimpse of pubic hair. I was in the kitchen to check in and to see if they had plans for the day that were anymore interesting than my own, such as a drive in the country or to the beach or walking to a free concert in the Panhandle or taking acid in the park…

"What're you guys doin' today?" I asked, half-sitting on a padded barstool that was leaning against the wall.

"I gotta go down to the hiring hall," Danny said then finished rolling a joint with a-lick-and-a-twist-of-the-tip. He was short and wiry with a reddish handlebar mustache and a buoyant, infectious grin.

Don Ed, a sprig of goatee at the end of a long chin, shrugged and said "Nothin'," and then took Danny's joint and lit it.

"I've gotta go to work," Christine said glumly as she poured coffee. She worked at the Post Office. The only one with a regular job, her name was on the lease. "I don't have any sick leave left and I'm losin' money when I call in now," she added.

"What about you?" Don Ed asked me, holding in a toke, then handing Danny back the joint.

"I don't have anything planned," I said. "Guess I'll head up to Haight Street" (The last resort).

"What's Tim doin'?" Danny asked.

"I'll go with ya," Brad said to me and shoveled in the last of the cereal.

"Uh, he just got to sleep," I said, sliding off the stool. "He took acid last night with Gail."

"Who'zat?" Danny asked, holding-in his toke, handing me the joint.

I took it and paused to say, "Remember those two chicks at our place night before last? She was the dark haired one."

Brad put the spoon beside the bowl and got up. I handed the joint to Don-Ed and started out the door holding in my toke. As Brad approached, Christine raised a steaming coffee cup to her mouth blocking a kiss. He touched her shoulder instead and raised a hand and said, "Later," to the room then followed me out.

Our conversation as we walked the five blocks to Haight and Masonic confirmed a first impression that he was a loudmouth blowhard. But I stuck with him, where I might otherwise have left him at Masonic, because a couple times sexy chicks came up to him and enthusiastically hugged and kissed him. Then, after each passed on, he described in graphic detail his sexual adventures with her. At the end of Haight Street, I continued with him into the park, and he made it a tour of locations where he had had sex. We were approaching a nearly-deserted Hippie Hill when I finally pried myself loose. He rewarded my patience with a folded paper containing a spoonful of methedrine.

Strangers in a Dark Room

Later that afternoon, I stood before my kitchen sink with the paper containing his meth unfolded on the counter. I really didn't know how much to take. I had taken it only once about a year before so I was about to take a cautiously small amount, then hesitated: I knew speed freaks who took a whole spoon at a time. If I couldn't take that amount, did that mean I somehow wasn't up to the cut? Did it mean that in spite of living in and around the Haight for a year and a half, I wasn't hip?

I didn't choose to be the scornful nonconformist, I was driven to it. I desperately tried to conform in that redneck mill town but failed. I picked up the paper and chuted the powder into my mouth, gagged on the bitter, metallic aftertaste, then washed it out with quick glasses of water. Later, I would estimate it to be six to eight times as much as would have been safe for me. I had just fallen through a trapdoor into years of nightmare.

Tim was still sleeping off an acid trip and, while I waited for the speed to come on, I drifted back over to Christine's kitchen. Though it was now afternoon, the same people were passing in and out. I sat at the table and joined the conversation, and soon noticed that whenever I spoke someone would interrupt me. So consistently was I interrupted that it eventually occurred to me that it might be deliberate. But then something else happened.

"Hey I was at this pad over on Waller and Steiner," I said, "and they said they had the lead guitarist for Big Brother and the lead singer for the Doors over there a couple nights ago and I know Blue Cheer lives down there somewhere too and god man at the Fillmore last week I was watching Blue Cheer and there was this chick you know how loud they play this chick was leaning her head against a speaker on the stage and sleeping god man . . ."

"Wanna beer?" Danny asked me, the open refrigerator glowing behind him.

"No," I replied and the room fell suddenly and conspicuously silent.

Danny, Don-Ed, and Christine all turned toward me with surprised, defensive expressions. I was shocked. They seemed to be reacting to a tone in my voice that I wasn't hearing. Danny became defensive and moved about the kitchen warily. Gradually conversation resumed.

"We're out of peanut butter," Christine said then licked the last of it off a spoon, bent over and placed the empty jar in the paper bag under the sink.

I saw an opportunity for an apologetic gesture and offered, "Take some of ours."

Again, a chilly silence fell on the room. Don-Ed gave a sharp cough and adjusted himself in his chair. Danny shot me a sidelong glance, quick and accusing. Christine suddenly straightened up and stabbed me with the pain in her eyes, then quickly looked away. It was as if she had been hit by a sniper. Again, I couldn't detect in myself what they were reacting to. My entire body was vibrating and I finally realized the speed was coming on.

Conversation resumed and after awhile a lull developed. I hadn't spoken in some time. It was clearly my turn. The lull was an invitation. But I couldn't. I couldn't trust myself. I withdrew far into myself, sitting still and rigid, both the clutch and the accelerator to the floor. It seemed I should have been able to just open my mouth and speak. Come on, there's nothing to it! But I couldn't. The only sound I made was an occasional loud, tense gulp of saliva.

One by one everybody finished their business in the kitchen without speaking and left. I was certain that my vibes had

driven them away. The torrent of energy created by the speed was funneled into my mind as I analyzed and re-analyzed and re-re-analyzed everything I had said and done while in the kitchen. My body was ringing with tension while my mind ran in circles like a dog biting a bullet in its haunches. I seemed to be exuding an emotional force-field that warped everything passing in and out. I don't know how long I sat there, ten minutes or sixty or more.

Afternoon became evening and it was dinner time yet the kitchen was empty except for me. I knew there were any number of explanations for the emptiness that had nothing to do with me, but as I sat there, alone, in near-dark, I couldn't resist feeling avoided, quarantined. Throughout my childhood, it was communicated to me in countless subtle ways, from family and peers, that there was *something,* unnamed but clearly sensed, wrong with me. I couldn't help wondering now if the drug hadn't simply highlighted or exposed an innate and ineradicable repulsiveness.

Cookie came into the kitchen and turned on the light and went to the phone and read a note from Don-Ed. She looked up and noticed me with a start.

"Oh, hi ..." she said.

I said nothing. I was afraid to. She went back to the note and then started out the door.

"Cookie. . ." I said. She stopped and looked at me. I was desperate. "Uh, have you ever taken a lot of speed? Too Much?"

She studied me for a moment, trying to figure out what was behind the remark. Then she discovered it and answered, "No," and walked out of the room.

It finally, belatedly, occurred to me that I would be safer in my own apartment. I waited through Cookie's boot clomp down the stairs and the closing of the street door, then I crossed the hall and closed my apartment door behind me. I could feel my heart thumping and my skin was clammy and I ached to piss and I was amazingly thirsty.

But when I entered the dark livingroom I noticed two human figures on the couch silhouetted against the dusk-lit window and I could just make out they were both male. I heard Tim clanking in the kitchen. To the confused, tentative "Hi" from the

couch, I muttered a syllable, made a sharp right, and almost ran to the kitchen.

"Hi," Tim said looking up from a chuck steak sizzling in a crusted pan. Occasionally he treated himself to a shoplifted one. "I met those cats on Haight Street, when I was coming back from the store," he said gesturing a fork toward the living room. Then he added, "They obviously needed a place to crash." He poked the meat. "I was hungry, so I'm fixing something. Want some?"

"There's something wrong," I began. "I took some speed... And my head... I, I can't... Everything's, uh... It's like... my vibes... I can't control them and everybody gets offended by everything I do..."

"That's self-consciousness," Tim said poking the steak. "Just... don't pay attention to it."

"No, no... you see it's... it's taken over... I mean, my vibes are... infected..."

"Well, I don't know what to tell you," he said with a shrug. "Just try not to think about it."

I realized I couldn't penetrate Tim's indifference and I looked down the hall to the living room which was totally dark now. He said it was all in my head. There was nothing wrong, no unmentionable defect, no disfiguring personality scar visible to everyone but me. Just ignore it and it'll go away. I could feel that the speed had peaked. I decided to go down that hall and rap with those cats, just like normal. I walked down the hall. After all, what's to fear in a dark room with strangers?

"Hi," I said into the darkness as I entered it.

"Hi," two voices said.

"I better turn on the light," I said as I felt the wall for the switch and flicked it on.

Typical of Tim to leave guests in the dark while fixing himself a meal. They were ordinary freaks, about my age: one lean, clean-shaven, and blond with shoulder-length hair; the other cherubic with a wiry scribble of dark hair and dense beard. Their backpacks were on the floor at their feet. As I crossed the room toward the empty side of the couch, I caught from the corner of my eye their faces crumpling with helpless panic as they scooted

deeper into their side of the couch. I sat down, telling myself I was misinterpreting that. Then I scrounged for something to say.

"Uh. . . wha. . . what happened on Haight Street today?"

Both sat looking straight ahead. The one farthest from me, the lean blond cat, leaned forward and as lightly as possible met my glance and then looked away.

"Not much," he said. "It was kinda windy and cold."

Their fear was subsiding to wariness. Judging by their reaction and the reactions in the next door kitchen, I was radiating a threat. But, my god, I didn't even know these cats! There was phlegm in my throat but I didn't dare cough or gulp or move, not even scratch my nose, for fear of sending a hostile signal. I eventually had to gulp down the phlegm, and simultaneously, both freaks coughed. I tried talking again.

"Where're ya from?"

The pudgy dark-haired one, closest to me, crossed and recrossed his legs, while the other readjusted himself on the couch and coughed sharply into his hand. Tension had downshifted.

"Ohio," said the lean one who spoke before.

This time, he scornfully looked down his nose at me. He had just figured me out. I realized there was no chance of undistorted human contact, so I sank back into myself. Tim came into the room and sat in the wicker wheelchair and rolled a joint while talking to the guests. I moved my head slightly from side to side when offered the joint. Though I felt sealed off, paralyzed, I monitored everything said and done, picking up double entendre quips, with exchanged loaded looks, crypto-comments on my weird vibes. A couple times, Tim tried to draw me into the conversation, but all I did was look at him and smile weakly, as if I didn't speak English. Anything I said would be taken wrong. Finally, it dawned on me that I could leave the room.

So I got up and, without looking at anyone, said, "I'm gonna crash," and went into my room and shut the door. On my mattress on the floor I listened to the conversation and stared at the light under the door, reliving, reexamining the day until about 4AM. I was trapped in that day for weeks.

John Groupie, Speedfreak Extraordinaire

Most days: a replay of the speed disaster. Some days and parts of days, normalcy. Paranoia in waves though, and every time it ebbs, I'm certain it's gone for good. But the next day or the day after... Never sure when I'll be staggering through the minefield. And each time it's just different enough to invalidate conclusions from the previous time.

Any crowd not large enough to hide in is a threat. So only one person at a time if possible. If paranoia strikes and I can't escape, I tense to flee, withdraw, "tune out," hide behind my face. A zombie. Then everything said around me is code, possibly crypto-comment on my odd vibes. Anything said directly to me, I can't understand, but try to fake it, and comment on a topic dropped minutes ago. Confused listeners exchange glances. I get tenser. The avalanche begins. I'm buried under self-hatred, humiliation, bewilderment, rage, contrition, fear, all the while staring vacantly at the floor, paralyzed, mute, fleeing, like a turtle on its back.

After the speed crackup, I slogged through used paperbacks of Jung, Freud, and other seers, eastern and western. The search party. Those trying to see things as they really are. Whole afternoons spent in the Humanities enclosure of the San Francisco State library scribbling notes until my wrist hurt, eyes blurred, and head ached from hunger. Mining. Building a theoretical model of my condition. It had elements of schizophrenia, psychosis, and lots of other things. One day I was sure that it was "the dark night of the soul." A couple days later, *angst*. Yes, that's it, *angst*.... A couple days after, an identity crisis... No, no, it's a weak super ego... An imbalanced anima and animus... It's... It's... spiritual hypochondria?

One part of me was always bolstering and reassuring another part that it must now finally be over, or soon would be anyway. It certainly couldn't last much longer, definitely not months or years or decades.

What I feared most was becoming a drug zombie, a psychedelic derelict, a fly-eater like those I had seen, even before summer, talking to themselves in coffeehouses. In February, I had to leave the I-Thou one morning when I was confronted with Howie,

one of my first Haight mentors, in a corner angrily arguing with himself and avoiding my eye, if he was even aware of me. A similar burnout haunted 65 Scott Street, obsessed with Christine.

John Groupie was a speedfreak with an impenetrable rap, whether high or not. Late one morning, going next door to use the phone, I almost collided with him as Cookie, Don-Ed, and Danny were backing him out the front door of their flat.

"John," Cookie says with controlled annoyance, "she doesn't want to see you."

"Oh yeah?!" he replies, chewing air, fumbling for a comeback. He is whippet-lean and hunched, with a skimpy blond goatee, and often, as now, shirtless and barefoot. "She wants to see me... I know... I just... I have... two things, no three things I want to tell her. When we were up in the mountains, down in Santa Cruz, uh, a year ago – no, it was thirteen, fourteen months ago – I told her..."

"Joooohhhnn! Go awaaaay!" That's Christine, at the opposite end of the apartment, behind the closed door of her bedroom. "Please! Leave me alone!!!"

"Hey man, John, you should split," says towering lanky Don-Ed through a marijuana stupor.

"John, she doesn't want to see you," Danny adds, exasperated by the obviousness. He steps forward, hands raised in supplication, saying, "So cool it man and just leave. O.K.?"

John backs several steps to the head of the stairs that lead down to the street door.

"Jooohhn!!! Please!! Please John . . ." Christine's distant yell again, this time choked-off by a sob.

Don-Ed crosses the foyer, stands beside Danny.

John steps down the first step and says, "I have to tell her something. Lemme see her. I have a right to see her." He takes another step down, stops, and switches on hyper-rap. "She-was-my-ol'-lady-in-Santa-Cruz-and-we-hadda-cabin-and-a-white-dog-named-Peyote-a-German-sheperd-he-wasn't-all-white-he-had-some-brown-patches. . . " Head down, eyes down, he fends off Danny and Don-Ed with a desperate furious rap. "...And-we-hadda-psylocibin-factory-and-we-got-busted-and-I-just-did-six-months-actually-five-months-and-twenty-three-days-actually-it-was . . . ."

Jail explains the short hair. I stand to one side, unnoticed. Danny and Don-Ed are experienced street fighters from the lower Mission District. Plus, Danny has survived merchant ships. They stand determined and ready, though not angry. Then, without a pause in the rap, John swivels to his left and starts up the stairs toward me.

Growing up a coward among rednecks, I have developed a finely-tuned bluff for situations like this, but there is no opportunity for bluff here, and so, when Danny and Don-Ed turn and look at me, I step into the breach and block John. He looks up and for the first time ever, our eyes meet. I stand firm and he stops, turns around and goes down a step.

"Leemee alone," he snarls over his shoulder, through clenched teeth.

Then he slowly turns, facing us, but looking at the wall. Face, neck, and chest dark purplish-pink. Fists quiver with a rage he sputters through.

"Fuck you! Goddamnit! I'm not afraid of you. I'll kill you! Fuck you! I'm not afraid. God ... God said I can see her... I can see her. She loves me... Fuck you!"

Danny is usually easygoing and quick to laugh, so I am surprised to see him now angry. I look at Don-Ed just as Cookie's hand touches his shoulder.

"C'mon," she says. "Come inside."

And she backs through the apartment door watching Danny and Don-Ed as they turn and follow.

John reacts by going a few steps down the stairs and yelling, "I can see her... I can see her... whenever I want!!" Cookie closes the apartment door as John, spraying spit, threatens, "God told me he was gonna destroy San Francisco tonight if I can't see Christine!!!"

I go behind my own door, while John descends, making the stairwell resonate with ever more bizarre threats. That first meeting was the most coherent I would ever see John Groupie.

I didn't know for certain, but it seemed likely that "Groupie" was a nickname given to him for his favorite anecdote: the time he met Dylan on a sidewalk in the East Village and carried his guitar for him. Too much speed and jail had scrambled his mind so that,

by that summer of '67, he was a walking filibuster, inflicting his rap like miles of life-line tied to nothing. It was as if to stop talking were to die. Those who knew him avoided him. It usually took just minutes for John in a room with people to be ignored, talked around. He would retreat to a corner and babble to himself, sometimes into a mirror, and become like a TV turned on in another room.

A human presence, an excuse to rap, was all John needed, and I often provided it. The rare times he would look me in the eyes, I thought I caught a glimpse of a possibly interesting person buried alive under the rap. Every time he came over, he had pockets full of dope samples others had given him, probably bribes to stay away. I felt the same as the bribers but I couldn't help responding to his being ostracized, his pariah-hood, even though he himself seemed oblivious to it.

Ziggy and Shob

Crossing redneck territory with longhair, while holding, was best done at night. So one midnight, Tim and I and another friend, Rob, left for LA in Tim's car, stoned on acid and STP which is as more powerful than acid as acid is than grass.

We were carrying acid to sell down there, where we heard there was a shortage, and then we were going to buy grass to bring back to the City, which we knew to be running low. It felt good getting away from Scott Street and the Haight generally, but when we returned about eight in the morning a week later, I was also glad to be back. After the all-night drive back, I was too charged to sleep, so I walked up to Haight Street.

I needed to check-in with the Street even though I knew it would be deserted at that hour. I went up the north side and down the south, my usual circuit, nodding to shop owners and stepping around puddles glinting on the hosed concrete. With each step, the backs of my knees hurt. The whole back of my body was sun-burned from an afternoon passed-out on Venice Beach. Most of our time in L.A. I was stooped like a chimpanzee.

We sold our acid down there and, more importantly, met a big grass dealer in Venice, and now we would try to arrange a deal

between a big Haight dealer and the Venice dealer, hoping for maybe a two kilo commission out of a fifty kilo deal. I spent that first day back visiting every dealer I knew, and everyone who might know an interested dealer, and returned to the pad late that afternoon, adrenaline-drained, exhausted, and very stoned. Among the half dozen I visited, there wasn't even a vague possibility. But it wasn't necessary. Tim found an interested dealer.

He was the acid dealer to the Hell's Angels, and a couple nights later, he came over to Scott Street. Tim had already told me his name, but it wasn't until I saw him that I realized I already knew Shob.

The year before, I tagged along for a few weeks of field-study and chauffeurship with Ziggy, junkie, master burn-artist, and friend of Howie and Art who gave me my first methedrine for letting Ziggy and his wife crash with me. Actually, I didn't know Ziggy was a junkie until the evening I drove him to score smack from Shob. We went to a huge, elegant, white Victorian with dormers and stained-glass windows on the north-east corner of Clayton and Page.

The doorbell was answered by an attractive long-haired teenage chick who led us through what was a type of boardinghouse where a bedroom is rented along with access to a common kitchen and bathroom. On the third floor, while Ziggy and I sat on pillows on the floor and leaned against the wall, the chick disappeared. Across the room, Ziggy and I could see a vista view over the roofs of that part of the Haight. A towheaded boy of five or six stared placidly out at the view.

When the chick returned, Ziggy asked her in his thick New York accent, "That yuah kid?"

"No," she cooed. "I'm just babysitting him."

"Oh. He's a cute kid. A vehry cute kid."

She looked down at the boy with a warm, indulgent smile. The child blushed and squirmed with shyness. That was as close to a normal human sentiment as I would ever hear from Ziggy. He was awkward with it.

"We're coming down from acid," the chick said.

"Hi Ziggy," said a cat who had just entered.

He was tall and lean, with light brown hair, thin on top but reaching to his shoulders, and mutton chops.

"Hi Shob," Ziggy said and then stood. "Wait heeuh, I'll be right back," he said to me and followed Shob out of the room.

At that time, I had only taken acid once, when it was still legal, and loved it. Little was known about it yet. For me it was just one of an array of unexplored drugs. But I was repulsed by the idea of giving it to a small child, and so I didn't bother to make conversation with the chick. Instead, I listened to the light traffic on the street below. A few times I exchanged smiles with the boy in his post-acid calm. Ziggy returned and led me downstairs and into the street.

After we got into the car, he was the first to speak.

"Man that cat is weeuhd," he said, tossing his head back towards Shob. "Ya know what he does fuh kicks? He drives old caws down to Big Suh and rolls 'em off cliffs. Fuh kicks!"

So on a Wednesday night, Shob limped into the Scott Street pad with one foot in a dirty plaster cast. It was a stale submarine-sandwich of toes and an excuse to sport a cane. He also wore a Smokey-the-Bear hat and a suede vest and leather pants, all in manly brown. He was stylish, self-assured, commanding, with no time or inclination for small talk. He glanced over the room including me, without greeting or recognition, and I felt relieved, not wanting to be remembered as Ziggy's mute sidekick.

"Hi Shob," Tim said.

"Hi."

"What happened to your foot?" Tim asked.

"Had some trouble with some spades. . . It's nothin'. What's this deal?"

Tim explained the L.A. dealer's terms: fifty kilos, forty dollars each. Shob smoked a sample joint, a few feet inside the door, looking down, evaluating, running through timetables and capital, ignoring Tim's offer to sit.

Eventually Shob said, "Yeah. O.k. I'll do it."

Tim and I exchanged a thrilled glance.

"*But* here's how it's gonna be," Shob continued. "We'll meet out in the desert, at night, like he wants to, but I'll pick the spot. There'll only be two cars, his pick up and my pick up."

"Great! We'll contact him right away," Tim said.

The roller coaster of a Really Big Deal was starting down the tracks.

"O.k. man, I gotta split. I'll talk to ya later," Shob said, then pivoted and, hobbled by that monument to whatever point he made by fighting the spades, started out the door. It wasn't a new cast, yet, I noticed, it was conspicuously free of graffiti or autographs or even psychedelic doodling.

"Yeah," Tim added, "Yeah, we'll, we'll let you know what he says as soon as we talk to him."

Just then, Christine appeared outside our door. She came in and greeted Shob and it was immediately apparent they had been lovers and not long ago. She tucked hair behind an ear and asked in a low voice how he was. He told her and asked her the same and, at her bidding, explained the cast. I read their mime across the room.

All through this nonsense her eyes pleaded and she melted with contrition. He had to look down, and then when he looked back up, he showed her his stern resolution. She had apparently violated some section of his code and, painful as it was, he was going to have to abide by his earlier ruling in the matter.

I knew she had recently given up for adoption an out-of-wedlock baby and I wondered if he was the father.

"Hey Tim," Shob said, about to step out of the doorway. "I'm gonna have my piece with me. And if there's any trouble, I'm gonna use it."

Apparently, recent events had driven the ex-Marine to resolve not take shit anymore from anybody. He said good-bye to Christine then clumped down the stairs. She watched him until he was out of the building then she turned and went into her apartment, hurt, and seemingly oblivious to the gun comment, which was probably meant for her.

Tim and I were stunned. "Piece" hit us like a bomb. Neither said good-bye to Shob.

"Hey man," I said. "We've gotta talk."

"Yeah," Tim replied.

"Man, I don't wanna . . ."

"Yeah, I don't either," he said.

I understood that he agreed but I still couldn't keep from venting fear.

"The game of dealing is fun but... " I continued. "The kind of mind that sees a need for a gun can distort a situation for an excuse to use it... If enlightenment was even a remote possibility... but this is ... this is just ... *money* ... and he's taking money *too* seriously..."

We were both incapable of that. Each had decided separately and simultaneously to back out, regardless of what the other did.

The Hell's Angels were, then, a redneck gang on motorcycles, a California cousin to the Klan, though more bandits than terrorists. They were the darkest part of the dark side of the Haight and their acid dealer, just after he left, reminded me of the first time I had heard of the Angels: when they beat up anti-war demonstrators.

In the following days, Tim looked for Shob to cancel the deal but he couldn't find him. Gradually, Tim started worrying that Shob's scarcity was due to an intense campaign to raise the money, and the more trouble invested, the angrier Shob would be when the deal was cancelled. Tim asked everyone he could think of whether they had seen Shob or knew where he was but still couldn't find him. So Tim became desperate, a pest, asking the same people over and over.

By Wednesday, when one freak saw Tim coming toward him on Haight Street, he preemptively said, "No, Tim, I haven't seen Shob."

Vietnam

Those days of Tim's search, I lolled around the apartment brooding over my parents and the draft. While we were in LA, a letter arrived from my parents and another from the draft board. I had to have a pre-induction physical. I was an expert on the draft and knew this was too early for a physical. The draft board

shouldn't even have my grades yet, but even if they did, I was supposed to have a semester of failure before losing my deferment. In that redneck milltown everyone knew I had become a hippie, no doubt confirming suspicions. Drafting me may have become a patriotic obligation.

My parents' letter made them seem innocents from the perspective of Haight-Ashbury, which had surfaced in the media since the last time I visited at Christmas nine months before. In Haight-Ashbury, for the first time in my life, I felt part of something bigger than myself. The future's welcoming committee. A group who, though vastly outnumbered, were inevitable. The winners disguised as losers. Volunteer niggers.

Nevertheless, media exposure had made hippies living smut. Juvenile delinquency with a twist of degeneracy. A consumer item of bigotry. "For the very first time! All together in one compact portable unit! A combination sex deviate, dope fiend, communist, & welfare loafer!"

At my parents', the Haight would have been another trip wire for shouting matches, for another eruption of that ongoing argument that began with atheism at fifteen, continued through my long hair, and now was about Vietnam and the draft. It could only culminate in exile, from home and soon probably country. I couldn't blame my parents for the exile from home because I wouldn't have returned there during that time anyway. I feared as much as them whatever the shouting matches were crescendoing towards.

"The Vietnamese fought the French, the Japanese, and now us, 'the good guys,'" I wrote in the latest of the letters the argument was now confined to. "The U.S. broke the Geneva Accords of 1956 by not allowing elections that would have put the communists in power like the people want... The North Vietnamese and the Viet Cong are nationalists before they're communists anyway... I'm including a clipping of an article by Walter Lippman that makes the argument that, since the U.S. hung Nazis for obeying immoral orders, they can't expect us to obey orders we consider immoral..."

Letter after letter I watched meticulous arguments die bug-deaths-splat! against incomprehension and/or indifference. The letter accompanying the draft notice was written by my mother and

I skimmed it on the livingroom couch, cringing in anticipation of the first shot.

A classmate I didn't like much was killed in Vietnam… Something about "our boys" over there… Hi from my cousin, the son of her twin sister and like a brother to me, whose letters from Vietnam coincided with mine from the Haight… (He would later tell me, not them, about grooving on the light shows of nighttime artillery duels while on acid.)

My mother's letter avoided the argument completely, and at the end I found out why. "I know you're busy but it does seem like an awfully long time since you visited." My father hadn't told her that he had asked me to "not come home for a while."

I dropped my hands holding the letter finally admitting to myself that I couldn't possibly go into the army. I saw now with stabbing clarity, there was no way to avoid the public humiliation of my parents… and after all their pride in my scholarship to a prestigious private college (from which I transferred to San Francisco State, where the action was). I saw the scholarship was an installment payment of compensation for a freak son.

And now I would also be a draft dodger. I loved them, which didn't keep me from feeling like a space-alien foundling. Still, I loved them, and their love for me was granite, and I ached at the thought of hurting them. I thought conscientious objector status might be a solution but they were horrified, having the WWII attitude that C.O. status was a ruse for draft dodging. Which, in my case, it was. Far from feeling the requisite pacifism, I carried a heartworm of rage against rednecks.

"Please realize things have changed since World War II," I had written. "I am more intelligent, better educated, and more sensitive than the majority of Americans whose opinions you defend. Please remember I am sincere and I am doing all I can not to hurt you."

While putting my mother's letter back in the envelope, I wondered: so, what next? My instinct was to go on the lam, like others I knew, maybe to Canada or Sweden or Mexico. Just a few weeks before, a young F.B.I. agent appeared at the door of a shaggy bearded friend and showed him a picture of himself short-haired and shaven and asked the whereabouts of the guy in the

picture. The young agent must have known it was him but went away, instead of busting him, apparently tipping him off. My friend immediately disappeared. Eventually I would have to also.

Learning the Lab Rat's Prayer

Late in the morning of the fourth day of Tim's search for Shob, John Groupie dropped by.

". . .—Up-on-Haight-Street-and-I-told-'im-I-haven't-seen-Shob-since-I-saw-'im-on-Waller-and-Masonic-talkin'-to-Beast-and-this-cat-named-Fropo-or-Frodo-who-drove-out-from-Kansas-with-a-pickup-full-o'-grass--. . ."

He was standing in the middle of the sunlit livingroom. I went about my business trusting him to keep me informed. As I was about to leave the room, he stopped me mid-stride. He had tugged a paper packet from a jeans pocket and unfolded it.

"...White-really-pure-white-like-this-crystal-Amy-laid-on-me-right?"

Methedrine. I hadn't seen any since that last time, the effects of which were behind me now. I was sure of it ....

I couldn't have explained why I was taking methedrine again even while I was doing it. Was it that I didn't like the idea of a human experience that was forbidden to me? In any case, I had to get over my speed problem, and I was confident that if there was any trouble this time, I could handle it, ride it into submission. Also, I wanted to know if the monster was still behind the door. So I took the same amount as before, a spoonful, and as I stood over the sink gagging and washing down the aftertaste, it occurred to me that, actually, I didn't *like* methedrine.

The monster was still there. I first noticed it in suspicious eye contact, masculine ego-grappling, with John. I was sitting on the couch, my head in my hands. He was jabbering in front of me. It was familiar territory, except something was magnified that was muted last time: imminent violence. The air was charged with it, overloading my receiver. I was a bomb that could be detonated by a glance. Every time I looked up at the human being in front of me, he shifted to a counterattack pose, and behind the babble, I caught

in his eyes a glint of wild alarm. The hand facing me was a rigid fist. He was used to fending off jail rapes.

What the fuck was it? I wasn't mad at John, so why should I be hostile to him? And where was the hostility? I couldn't hear it in my voice or find it anywhere in my demeanor. This time I knew what to do though. I got rid of John by telling him I didn't feel well and needed to be alone. I walked him to the door, opened it, and waited for him. He was babbling as I shut and locked the door. I decided to ride out the speed hidden in the apartment.

Throughout the afternoon the usual traffic of friends and customers wended its way by our door. I sat in a catatonic daze, afraid of breathing too loud, while one after another knocked once, waited, knocked again, waited, and, after a quick, tentative third knock and a slight pause, headed down the stairs. Late that afternoon I heard Tim's key in the lock and leapt up and waited in front of the door. He came in with a worried expression.

"Oh hi," he said, surprised with me suddenly in front of him, then he continued, "I didn't think you were here. Cookie said you were gone. I couldn't find Shob. I've asked everywhere... " He sighed and tossed his jacket and a *Village Voice* onto a chair. "Is something wrong?" he asked.

"Yeah, yeah... I... I... Everthing is... I'm locked in this... this..."

"Okay. What is it?"

"It's, it's... I dunno... Okay... It's like... behind everything I say or do is.... " my eyes pleaded, ".... violence."

"That's just your self-consciousness again." Groceries in hand, he started down the hall to the kitchen. "I told you, there's nothing there. It's all in your head. Forget it."

"I know it's in my head. I know that." I started after him. "I keep telling myself that, over and over, but it doesn't do any good." While he set the bag on the table and took a crusted pan from the stove to the sink, I continued, "It's like I'm offended or angry or something all the time. I can't.... I mean... I feel so..." He concentrated on the pan under the faucet. "It's infected my vibes, other people see it and react to it, and I can't stop it!"

"It's all in your head, okay? It's not out here."

He took the pan back to the stove and turned on a burner. I looked down at the floor and made my decision and then headed down the hall and out the door and onto the street, on my way to a mental hospital.

Langley Porter Neuro-Psychiatric Institute is embedded in a eucalyptus forest, on top of a steep hill, overlooking a football stadium, and when I hit the sidewalk headed for it, the sun is almost down and the wind has the bite of evening, reminding me that I'm wearing only a tee-shirt and sandals. Then I notice, thirty yards down Scott Street, coming from Haight Street, another freak.

He has dark bangs and an Abe Lincoln beard. I study him hard for any sign he is the least receptive to my vibes. When he notices me, he almost stops in his tracks. Then he does a double-take. Assured now, he leans forward, hardened and ready, continuing toward me. I ready myself in turn: lower my head, square my shoulders, but force my gaze away from him. When we are abreast, I growl as if to hawk phlegm. Then immediately I wonder if I have actually done it or imagined it. We've passed and I look over my shoulder. He is looking over his shoulder at me, bug-eyed with fear and bewilderment.

I continue toward Haight Street, but even before I reach it, I know I can't use it because of the crowds. So I cross it, and a block further, turn left onto Page Street, heading west for the hospital now parallel to Haight Street, a block over.

But on Page Street there is still foot traffic. The instant anyone comes into sight, I track their least gesture, glance, turn of the head, for signs they are receptive to my vibes. Anything said anywhere around me, every cough, scraped heel, slammed door, I take for granted is really a coded comment, a response to my odd, hostile vibes.

If the other pedestrians are males around my age, alone or in a group, there is added tension. My intense stare is a dominance challenge. Each time it is a variation on the freak with Lincoln beard and bangs. As the sidewalk diminishes between us, I bend my gaze down, stiffen, afraid of what brushed shoulders might detonate. In the climactic moment, as we pass, invariably they cough and I can hardly keep my balance, as if bumped by the cough.

I can't believe this is happening again. I feel like a lab rat tortured by electric shocks, frantic to surrender, if only he knew how. Whatever I've been doing wrong, I'll stop. I'm sorry. But there is no appeal, no relief, no retreat, no shelter. Is this the ultimate, snarling, gristly, lacerated nub of myself?

My only goal now: encountering as few people as possible while getting to the hospital as quickly as possible. The speed gives me tremendous energy, fuel for a full-heat walk up the hills, gaze always bent down. Each step on the concrete is a blow to the bottom of my feet.

Langley Porter is on one of the City's steepest streets. When I clear the top, gasping and limping with gut-pain, I'm shoved backwards by numbing, night ocean-wind. I look down Parnassus Street to the hospital. The speed energy is spent. And with it, resolve.

Tim said there was no taint and it was all my projection. Suppose the hospital staff doesn't see anything wrong with me either, then what? Am I certifiably nuts? Paranoid. What's that? I know the meaning of the word but I can't name a single great artist, mystic, or philosopher who has suffered from *paranoia*. This is an intrusion, a meteor crash, into my script. There is no glory in this at all. It seems an aberration even from the aberration of madness. God, Enlightenment, the Divine Light are still lightning strikes in the next county. My problem is no more than a personality kink in a middle-class adolescent. I look again at the hospital. Committing myself now seems like a melodramatic gesture.

Now I feel isolated and exposed and just want to get back to my bedroom. An eastbound bus approaches. I find a quarter in my jeans but don't take it out. Can I survive a bus ride? The least time with the least people, that's all I care about. The 6 Masonic pulls out of a stop a block away. An icy wind-lash sends me sprinting across the street between honking cars to the bus's next stop. If I'm wrong, I get off. The paranoia may have ebbed a little with the effect of the speed. Maybe I can make it.

The coin counter crunches my fare, the bus pulls into traffic, and, while we're slung forward and back, I thread the crowd. Rush-hour has ebbed and I'm able to make it, without a brushing, to a standing space by a pole at the backdoor. I chance looking up

and scan the bus for another freak. Reflexive whenever in public. None. The leaden public silence is scratched by coughs and sniffs, tooth-suckings and throat-clearings.

Below my left elbow, an intern in green surgical garb hawks phlegm. A young Asian nurse in the front sniffles and wipes her nose with tissue paper. Behind me, a short, sharp cough from a middle-aged suit with a briefcase shielding his chest. Then three passengers get on and are greeted with a cough from a seated old Slavic lady in a thick coat. Almost simultaneously one of the new passengers, a chubby young Mexican with a glossy spit-curl, coughs a reply. I gulp. Three coughs answer. Patterns of unconscious call and response crisscross the bus, as between caged animals. And logically, what else would they talk about but the freak at the back, the foreign body?

Blocks creep by. This is all so banal and pointless. Instead of a noble philosophical dilemma, the central issue of my life is whether or not I can make it to my stop without screaming. Each time the door opens, I ask myself: can I make it just to the next stop? If I think I can, I let the door close me in again, and with head down, eyes closed, and with sweat-slick palms, I clutch the chrome pole tighter. I'm holding in a murder or a suicide. No difference. I am poised to destroy the single perpetrator of all my pain, whoever that is. Finally, I can't make it even one more stop and jump out two before my own.

The Second Murder

I felt relief, even joy, as I nearly flew down the steep and delightfully deserted Waller Street. Flailing sycamores made a light show of the street lights. I started to feel almost safe. Then guilty. None of the people around me deserved my hostility. I had been on a rampage, attacking strangers with my vibes. It was a tantrum, a rage binge, and I was a powerless witness.

I turned onto Scott Street and was relieved that it was deserted as far as my pad, in which I noticed the light was on. Shit! Tim at the very least was there, possibly others.

When I entered the pad, I immediately saw Peter, the junkie boyfriend of Ruth's best friend Cheryl, and I felt a panic

surge. He sat on the couch, his solemn face embedded in a dark thatch of beard and hair. It was unusual to see him outside of his own apartment. He said nothing to me, just looked at Tim, who was in the wicker wheelchair, frozen in a catatonic stare.

When Tim didn't look at me, I turned back to Peter, who offered, "Hey man, they rubbed out Shob."

"What?"

"Yeah man, they found his body in his apartment. He was stabbed."

My first feeling was irritation with Peter. He was prone to affectation and "rubbed out," crime-movie slang, grated. I felt nothing for Shob. But I understood Tim's condition and became concerned for him.

I leaned over into his face and said, "Tim?"

He looked at me, pupils enormous.

"They don't know who did it or anything," Peter said. I turned to him as he continued, "When I found out, I came right over to see if Tim knew about it. I knew he was asking around for Shob." He looked at Tim and added, "When I told him he freaked out." I looked back at Tim. Peter stood up and said, "I gotta split man."

"Yeah," I said absently, studying Tim's abandoned body. "Yeah, thanks Peter. I can take care of him now."

"Later man," he told Tim, with a small wave. Tim didn't look up.

"Hey Peter," I said as he held open the door. "Was he stoned before you got here?"

He considered a moment then said, "I dunno. I don't think so."

"O.k."

He closed the door.

"Tim?"

He looked at me.

"Did you take any drugs before Peter came, before you found out Shob was . . . before you heard about Shob?"

He moved his face to the side and back as a half "No". I had seen Tim this far gone before but always stoned. This was serious. I knew how to talk him through a bad trip, but *this* . . .

"I . . . I . . . I was . . ." he said, "I went around . . . I asked everyone . . . about Shob. Everyone will tell the police I was looking for him."

I was about to tell him not to worry but realized he should. He refixed his enormous pupils on his thoughts. I could hear him breathing. He seemed capable of anything and I had to suppress my own alarm. Though we were about the same height and weight, I wasn't sure I could handle him hysteria-fueled. A man's body charged with mortal panic and nobody behind the wheel.

"Tim, what's your parents' phone number? Do you have it memorized?"

He stared at me a moment, processing my words, then shook his head.

"Uh, ok. . ." I said, "let me see your wallet then."

He leaned to one side in the wheelchair and struggled to get the wallet from his back pocket, but couldn't. So he tried to stand, but the chair rolled, and he couldn't do that either. He looked at me with a weak, apologetic smile, a film on the surface of fear. I held the chair for him as he tried to stand, but his knees buckled and I caught him by the armpits.

"I don't know what's wrong," he said with more embarrassed cover-laughter. "I can't stand up."

I walked him to the couch and sat him down. He got out the wallet and I took out the address book and found the number then tossed the wallet onto his lap.

"Tim? Tim, look at me. I'm going to call you parents, ok? Don't go anywhere while I'm gone. Stay right here, o.k?" I walked toward the door. "If someone comes to the door, don't answer it. Just sit and don't say anything, o.k.?" I locked the door behind me.

Christine's door was unlocked as usual. As I turned from the hall into the kitchen, Christine crossed the living room toward her bedroom. She gave me a quick, indifferent glance and sniffled. Her eyes were red and her cheeks glistened with tear streaks. Obviously, she'd heard about Shob.

"The End of the Dance"

The next day Tim's father flew up from L.A. where he and Tim's mother lived in retirement. This was Tim's father's second trip north for a breakdown and this time he wanted to take Tim back to Southern California. At first, Tim didn't want to go.

"C'mere," he said to me and went down the hall into the kitchen, leaving his father in his dark suit in the middle of the livingroom.

Embarrassed for Tim, I said to his father, "I'll be right back."

His father was stocky and severe with wire-rimmed glasses, an old liberal-activist, protestant minister, a friend of Upton Sinclair. I wanted to establish myself as an ally but instead caught a glint of outrage and accusation.

Tim was standing in the center of the kitchen, staring at air with those enormous pupils, not only forgetting what he wanted to say but where he was. So I spoke first.

"Tim, you've gotta go with him man."

He woke and said with confused desperation, "No, no. . . I don't want to. . I . . . No . . . Do you think so?" His skeptical, plaintive eyes searched mine.

"Yeah, you've got to go. Suppose the police come? If you go home with your dad there'll be no way to find you. Nobody around here will tell them where you live. They know you had nothing to do with. . . what happened to Shob. And I won't be here."

He was surprised.

"The draft, man," I continued. "I might be paranoid but paranoids can have real enemies and... you know where I grew up, everybody knows everybody, and I think they've been waiting for a chance to get me ever since my first weekend home from college with long hair. I think they're determined to draft me. So I've gotta split man. I can't stay here and take care of ya. And if you leave, that's the best way to avoid any problems with the police."

While he considered this, I started toward the doorway.

"Besides," I added, "it may not be that bad. You can hangout at Venice Beach. That place is groovy. I'll visit ya as soon as I can." He stared at me a moment. "C'mon," I said and started

down the hall to the living room where I could see his father, stiff as rigor mortis on the couch.

Tim eventually followed me. After we agreed on how to dispose of the apartment and its contents, Tim and his father left, each with the last of the cardboard boxes of indispensable books and records and clothes.

The next day, Monday, Shob's death made it into the media. He was murdered on the previous Thursday, the day after he talked with Tim and I, but his body wasn't discovered for a couple days. Stabbed twelve times, once through the heart, he was dead the whole time Tim asked around for him. The murderer, a biker friend of Shob's, on acid at the time, was caught in Shob's car, with thousands of Shob's dollars (probably intended for our grass deal), Shob's pistol, and Shob's left arm cut off at the elbow, which, in a silly, early street-rumor, the murderer was caught gnawing.

Then, a couple days later, the body of another major dealer, Super Spade, also an acquaintance of Tim's and mine, was found in a sleeping bag hanging down a cliff near picturesque Point Reyes Lighthouse. At first, there was speculation that the same guy murdered both, and then the newspapers swallowed an old street-rumor about the Mafia taking over the Haight drug business.

In all, the conservative *Examiner* squeezed four days of headlines out of the Haight's first big murders. Shob got his picture in *Time* magazine, described as an "unemployed flutist," in a story titled, "End of the Dance." Though it was only the first week of August, for Tim and I and for the media, the Summer of Love was over.

But I lingered on, in part, because I wasn't sure where else to go. Obviously, there was no place for me in Nazi-Occupied-Territory. And just as threatening was the speed overdose after-effect. I feared now that I might be stuck in that day and somehow couldn't get out.

This second speed crash also showed me that, to my shock, on some level, in some way, I believed the red necks' unremitting message that *something* was subtly, fundamentally, and unmistakably wrong with me. Could I be a mutation locked out of the unconscious wavebands of human love?

Also, I'd found a volcano of self-hate and murder. Shob's murderer couldn't hold it in. I could.

Missionary to the Rednecks

A couple days after Tim left, a direction, a destination was provided by crashers, a couple from New Orleans. The first night, after the chick fell asleep on Tim's bed, the cat and I got deep into a stoned conversation about the spreading hip scene. We sat on the floor next to a lit candle, KSAN barely-audible.

His dark hair was brushed into flames by San Francisco wind and his eyes dilated with visionary rapture as he said, "I know that New Orleans is ripe for a scene like this."

He held his toke as he handed me a joint. His ol' lady was cute and had hair shorter than his, which reminded me of Ruth and I.

He gushed smoke and said, "All they need is someone to show them how."

"The cat who used to live here with me was down in the South a few years back. He and his wife were members of C.O.R.E. in New Orleans."

I was boasting about Tim, and also testing this southern cat, seeing how he reacted to, or if he even knew about, CORE. I couldn't read him.

"Some friends of his were killed ... and tortured ..." I added. "The Klan started following him around and he had to get out of there."

I handed back the joint, holding in a toke, noticing a favorite on KSAN, Big Brother and the Holding Company's instrumental *Hall of the Mountain King*.

"Yeah, that's true, it is kinda dangerous outside of New Orleans. But the city is kind of an island and I know they're ready for this," he said, gesturing out of the apartment to the Haight.

Well, I did have to get out of there, and I was curious to see Tim's old battleground for myself. Of course, I knew that I was also running away from my state of mind, running panic-stricken and directionless, like my clothes were on fire. Also, I had nothing better to do.

The cat picked up on my interest and said, leaning toward me, crossed-legged, "I guarantee you'll have a free place to crash."

"How much is acid goin' for down there?" I asked.

He was surprised, then delighted. "They're desperate for it. It's about ten bucks a hit."

I knew some messianic dealers who would front me a few dozen hits. I had enough money to get there by hitchhiking, and with proceeds from the acid, I could support myself for a while.

My new role as missionary to the rednecks would require a haircut. Hitchhiking without a haircut, I probably wouldn't make it alive out of California, let alone across the Deep South, where I would be crossing real Nazi-Occupied-Territory. I was depressed but not suicidal, so I went to the only remaining barbershop on Haight Street.

Needless to say, there was no wait and the barber was smug. My hair grew more out than down, but it was almost shoulder-length. As his scissors bit into it, a freak couple stopped in front of the shop window, and for a shocked moment, stared at me, the parade of Haight Street flowing behind them. Then they mimed a plea of "Don't do it!" but I could only shrug and look apologetic.

Cutting my hair had no other significance for me than as a survival stratagem. As I told my parents when I wrote announcing my trip to the South: "The Haight is rotting into a circus. I'm tired of giggling, ogling tourists bumper-to-bumper for blocks in all directions. This doesn't mean I'll stop being a beatnik. I was born for that (though I know you don't agree)."

I was eager to tell Tim about my trip to New Orleans, but when I called, his father told me, voice taut with anger, that Tim was in Camarillo State Mental Hospital. I shouldn't have been, but I was surprised, and though I wanted to know more, I was afraid of his father's anger, so I just thanked him and got off the phone. I found out later his parents blamed me completely for Tim's drug problems.

Tim would spend the rest of his life, long after both parents died, in and out of major mental hospitals on both coasts. I would live about seven years with an ever-present though diminishing ambush-threat of paranoia paralysis, a flashback to the speed crashes. I became fluent in coughs, snorts, sniffs, throat-clearings,

gulps, shoe-sole scuffings, all the freighted nonverbal communication. A loud gulp in a crowded silent elevator, every time without exception, provokes an answering cough.

I was saddle-broken. I was fleeing pain more than pursuing truth.

After I left the barbershop, I did my rounds of the Haight one last time, feeling the wind in places I hadn't for a year and a half. Though I felt uncomfortable disguised as a straight in the Haight, I needed to walk and think. It was the afternoon before the morning I would hitchhike south. I had already collected the other elements of my straight costume: a plaid shirt, a duffle bag, shoes from an Army surplus store. The duffle bag was packed at the pad, which I was giving to friends, furniture, food, kitchenware, and all.

At one point, I stopped and sat on the sloping lawn of Buena Vista Park, across Haight Street from the Christian Science Reading Room, several blocks from the center of the action. After a while, a big, late-model, family station wagon with fake-wood side-paneling parked in front of me. Four straight, shorthaired teenagers got out, donned headbands, wrapped themselves in blankets, and walked single file along Haight Street toward the action.

Junkie Love

Ziggy and Doreen

What do I do now? I'm standing in the livingroom of our illegal basement apartment, my limbs vibrating with the stallion-energy of methedrine (methamphetamine). I know! Of course! I run into my bedroom and take off the clothes I wear as a part time file clerk and quickly put on old jeans and a dirty sweatshirt.

The night before there was a fire in the illegal attic apartment. Nothing of ours burned because we stashed our portable property in our cars, but our walls, floor, and furniture got soaked. So I start the cleanup in the bathroom, which took the most damage.

I toss charred boards and other debris through the black hole of the window into the black airshaft. Between crashes I can hear through the airshaft the soughing of traffic and distant lone footsteps, the night sounds of Waller Street, on the edge of the Haight-Ashbury District of San Francisco. I'm struck by the contrast to last night when, before the firemen arrived, the airshaft contained a roaring cyclone of flames, and I and one of my roommates (Mike: six feet six, curly red hair, razor wit) lobbed pots of water from the filling bathtub at the board-snapping fire-dragon.

When I finish clearing debris, I sweep the bathroom floor, scrub the walls and floor, and then get down on my hands and

knees and chase the least dirt crumbs into the tightest crevices, all the while roaming far into my thoughts. A voice from the livingroom yanks me back.

"Yeah?!" I call and stand up.

I'm expecting several different visitors but when I reach the livingroom it's none of them. It's Cappy, a friend and couch nomad (someone with a personal list of available couches who sleeps on the most convenient when he's tired). He's already standing inside the front door.

"Hi, man," he says, a nicotine-stained smile spreading under a bushy moustache. "Heard about the fire. Man, you can really smell it."

"Yeah and it's cold too. Everything is soaked and it's kind of...refrigerating the place. Hey ya want some tea?"

"Yeah."

"The stove doesn't work but I've got a hotplate," I say on the way to the kitchen. "They condemned the building and turned off the gas and the electricity, but we figured out how to turn the electricity back on."

"Are Francine and Mike still here?" he calls from the livingroom.

"Francine left town with Ralph last night," I call out while searching for a clean pot. "They went to Fresno to stay with his parents. And Mike went home for a couple weeks before shipping out."

Cappy is short, skinny, and hunched, with a spoon-shaped torso. He lives on candy bars and beer and an occasional can of beans and always carries a bottle of aspirin for the pain in his teeth. Without even trying, he beat the draft on malnutrition. I'm envious. At that time, late summer of 1966, I was eighteen and moving into the advanced stages of draft-obsession.

"I thought Francine's husband's name was Larry," he says.

I step into the doorway of the kitchen to see his face as I tell him, "It is. Ralph is Larry's best friend."

"Oh, I met him."

"She's been sleeping with Ralph for a couple weeks now and she told me she's in love with him."

"Shit."

"Yeah."

"But I thought Ralph was gay," he says.

"Yeah," I say and look at the pot of water on the hotplate. I want to go into the livingroom and talk to him but I'm reluctant to be out of sight of the hotplate. I decide to trust myself to remember it and announce, "He *was* gay."

"No shit," he says grinning as the soap-opera plot unfolds for him.

"I thought you might be Larry," I say as I sit opposite him in a stuffed chair which like most of the furniture was culled from the sidewalks. "She's been expecting him for a couple of days. They're gonna send him to Vietnam, so he's supposed to go AWOL and then run off with her. I think she used the fire as an excuse not to face him."

"So I guess Mike gave up trying to get her back?"

"Yeah. He needed to get out of here too."

Cappy reflected on the situation some more and then said, "Shit."

He was a gifted story teller, and for sharing your dope or letting him sleep on the couch, he would tell a tale about the time he fled the FBI in a high speed chase through downtown Denver, or the time he hitchhiked to New York, immediately met a chick in a coffeehouse, and two hours later was hitching back to California with her.

"You know a cat named Ziggy?" I ask.

"No."

"Ya know Art and Howie?"

"Yeah."

"Well they were just here and they asked me if this Ziggy and his wife could stay here and I said yeah and to thank me they shot me up with methedrine just before they left and I've been cleaning up the bathroom and my mind has been going like a squirrel in a treadmill and I think I've come up with the most basic question of western philosophy." I was a philosophy major and my head was buzzing with theories most of the time but right now it was near exploding. " 'Is the glass half full or half empty?' Yeah. That's it! That's what the philosopher asks. The scientist asks 'How does this work?' The mystic is just into the fact of existence not

how or why something is there but *that* it is there at all. Ya see? Now-the-truth-of-the-mystic-especially-the-Eastern-mystic-is-a copout-to-Western-Faustian-man-with-his-search-for-meaning-which-is-to-have-a-self-which-is-to-have-allies-and-enemies-something-to-defend-to-be-in-some-camp-either-that-of-your-own-ego-or-some-cause-substituted-for-it-that-is-a-substitute-ego-an-identity-now-identity-has-to-do-with-the-basic-archetypal-universal-duality-which-is-exponential-and-an-exponential-duality-proves-that-identity-is-provisional-and-relative..." I sniff. "Hey, something's burning."

"It's in the kitchen," Cappy says.

I get up and go in there and see that the pot that held our tea water is black and smoking on the hotplate. I quickly unplug the hotplate and am about to grab the pot handle but catch myself and instead take up a threadbare dishrag and carry the pot to the sink and hold it steaming under the tap.

"Hey we're gonna hafta wait some more on that tea," I shout over the hissing.

Then, instead of his comment, I think I hear the door close. I turn off the tap and go to the kitchen doorway and see that the livingroom is empty. That's strange, I think, he must've suddenly remembered some appointment.

2

"Hey, anybody heuh?" a male called from the livingroom the next morning.

I was already awake, lying in bed, analyzing a distant muffled trilling in my nerves, traces of the speed. Perhaps because I didn't yet know about it, I felt none of the notorious depression of the methedrine come-down.

I got up and slipped on my jeans and headed for the livingroom. I expected to find Larry and dreaded having to tell him that my ex-roommate, his wife, had run off with his best friend. But instead, there was a curly-haired man and a short woman.

"Awt oha Howie heuh?" the man asked me.

"No, I don't know where they are. They haven't slept here in a long time. I saw them yesterday afternoon but they didn't say where they were going."

"Oh... I'm Ziggy," the man said.

The woman, now seated on the couch behind him, interrupted a worried frown with a too cute, too friendly smile, and said, "I'm Doreen."

"Hi. They told me about you," I said.

"They said we could stay heeuh," Ziggy said. "They said theuh was a fiuh and everybody split."

"Well there was a fire and most everybody left but I'm still here. . ."

"Could we stay just for a couple days? We really need a place," Doreen asked delicately with a desperation that made it nearly a plea. "You wouldn't even know we were around."

"OK, sure. I already told 'em you could stay here," I said. I was greedy to increase my savvy by studying Ziggy, described by Art and Howie as a master junkie burn-artist.

"Oh thanks a lot," she said. "We brought some food. Would you like a bologna sandwich?"

"No thanks, I'm going to have some yogurt. Do you know what time it is?"

"A little after noon," Doreen said carrying a grocery bag into the kitchen.

"What happened to Mike and, uh, Francine?" Ziggy asked a while later through an open mouthful of churning bologna and white bread.

"Mike went up north for a while. To Vancouver," I said from the recliner. He was on the couch. "And Francine went down to Fresno."

"It certainly is clean here," Doreen said from the kitchen.

"Yeah," I said with a smile, "I was up on crystal last night and went on a scrubbing binge."

"You into crystal? I'll bring ya some. Ya dig marijuana? I'll bring ya some," Ziggy said.

"I like to clean house. I'll keep this place real clean," Doreen said.

"Baby, yuh a great housekeepuh. You keep a vehry clean house. She keeps a vehry clean house," Ziggy said. "Hey, you into poetry?" He nodded at a copy of Wallace Stevens' "Selected Poems" on the improvised table of a fruit crate on-end. I had read it till dawn, savoring how previously insoluble knots untied at a touch.

"Yeah, sorta."

"Ya know Fehlinghetti and Ginsbug? I used to sell grass to them. I had a cabin down in Big Suh wheuh I grew it. Hey, Howie said you gotta cah. Listen, we could make a lot of money with yuh cah. I got connections down south. We could bring pills and grass and all kindsa shit up heuh and make lotsa money."

"Sounds good," I said.

3

Ziggy and Doreen were married. She was an ex-nurse and in her late thirties and seven or eight years older than him. He was the precocious son of a professional family in New York whom he hated and avoided.

Doreen usually wore a faded cotton dress. She had a tired, wrinkleless face framed by bobbed, brown hair. Incongruously girlish charm shown through puffy eyes over brown trenches. I calculated that she would have been starting high school when I was born. I found her attractive though and could tell that she liked me by her lingering gaze and her touching me at every opportunity.

Ziggy's hair was closer to orange than red. A mangled, kinky bush tapered to nothing by ear level. An auburn crescent of moustache tightly framed bulging pink lips. His skin was pale and cheesy. His spine was so concave that it seemed sometimes as he walked that the top half of him was trying to catch up with the bottom half.

The next day, after I returned from my part-time file-clerk job, I discovered Ziggy and Doreen were junkies.

"Hey," Ziggy asked shortly after I got in the door, "will ya drive me somewheuh. It's vehry impohtant or I wouldn't ask ya."

I drove him to an elegant white Victorian with stained glass windows and turrets at the corner of Page and Clayton. When we got back to my apartment, Ziggy went straight into the bathroom. I

changed clothes and was fixing a sandwich when Doreen came in with a bag of groceries.

"Did he get some?" she asked me. "He got some, didn't he?" She shouted, "Ziggy! Did you get some stuff?!"

She put the bag on the table and ran to the locked bathroom door and gave it a few desperate tugs.

"Ziggy, baby, please honey, please save me some, please," she cajoled softly. She pressed her cheek to a square panel of the translucent glass door. "C'mon honey, pleeeeeze..."

He was conspicuously silent.

"Ziggy!!!" she screeched. "You gimme some! That's not fair."

"OK, OK" he said.

"You're taking it all yourself," she whined. "Ziggy, baby, please honey, please save me some, please. *Ziggy !!!*"

She grabbed a broom and banged the handle on a square section of glass on the door cracking it. Ziggy pulled the door open and came out. In his left hand he held over his head, beyond the reach of his straining wife, an eyedropper full of a syrup-tinted liquid with a needle attached. He led her into the living room.

"Awright, awright, I toldjya I'd give ya some, heeuh, heeuh."

He handed her the prize in the middle of the room. She took it, pulled up her dress, pushed panty off a buttock and slid the needle in just under the skin. I got a hard–on of course from the sight of the buttock. I had followed them from the bathroom, shocked, repulsed, and fascinated.

Ziggy could hardly stand up. He stepped backward and forward in a fitful rhumba as if trying to get his balance on a rolling ship's deck. With his left hand he would yank up his pants while his right hand ran down from the top of his head over the drooping eyes, over the tiny blood-filled craters of picked scabs, and over the gaping mouth.

"We'uh. . . we'uh. . .we'uh. . . we'uh gonna make soooo much money. .. with yuh cah. . . I'm. . . gonna. . . make yoooouu money... I'm gonna make you money. . . make you ... "

4

That summer William Burroughs' *Naked Lunch* came out in paperback for the first time. I bought it and devoured it. Burroughs was a homosexual, criminal, and junkie who accidentally killed his wife in a William Tell stunt gone awry, shooting her instead of the glass on her head.

I left the Sierra mill town where I grew up as though shot from a cannon. Destination: as far as possible from rednecks. Burroughs was already there. His books were dispatches from an interstellar outpost. He was the "objective correlative" of my alienation, and I identified with him immediately and completely. He also had a romantic appeal for an eighteen-year-old eager to be one of those guys who's seen too much.

At that time, before the full emergence of psychedelics, junkies were the aristocrats of the drug culture. Surrounded by consumer zombies, the junky had guts enough to lock himself in a cage with utter need and accept social ranking near the child molester. He stood alone like an upraised middle finger at the world. From physical necessity, he lived a day at a time, determined to give meaning and direction to the chronic low-grade emergency of being civilized, at any cost to himself or anybody else. He ran red lights.

Ziggy was my opportunity to study one. He lived an urban version of living off the land. One day he would have several hundred dollars, the next day be broke. And if he needed food then, he'd go to the farthest aisle in the nearest store and stuff whatever was available under his belt, then walk out. He got his clothes from garbage cans, people's closets, or stole them from stores. He was a carnivore among herbivores. He may have gotten away with much of his shoplifting simply because he was capable of murder and it showed on his face.

When he wasn't using his wife for recreational torture, they might lapse into playing house: she the mommy, and he the spoiled brat, complete with tantrums and baby talk. Ziggy: the six-foot tall baby with the mind of a cobra. Once he threw a loud tantrum in a supermarket aisle during rush hour when she wouldn't agree to his flavor of ice cream. They were exhibitionists who flaunted, instead

of immoral body parts, grotesque deformities: themselves. When they would perform one of their routines in public, it seemed as if they were mugging passers-by for their attention.

5

Ziggy and Doreen could also be proud craftsmen. One day we parked on Haight Street near Masonic while Ziggy went into a deli. A couple of beat cops noticed him and sauntered up to the door and waited for him to come out.

"Hey, hey, d'ya see the heat over there?" Doreen asked me from the back seat. "Watch this, watch how Ziggy handles 'em."

Today Ziggy wore a ratty sport coat over a flowery Hawaiian sport shirt, plus baggy trousers and scuffed shoes without laces. Plus he had his hair conked. When black men chemically straightened their hair, they often wore bandanas on their heads with a little of the hair visible at the tip of a silken topknot. Ziggy was the only white daring or crazy enough to wear one.

This and his general circus clown demeanor had the cops homing in on him right away. When Ziggy eventually strutted out with a crotchful of booty one of the cops stopped him by holding a night stick across his chest.

"I've got his outfit here so they can't get him for that," Doreen said, narrating the silent vignette.

Ziggy smiled and kidded the cops while one of them patted the pockets of his sportcoat.

"See? They're gonna ask him to roll up his sleeves."

Ziggy pushed up both sleeves of his coat and held up the inside of his elbows.

"See?" she said with a note of admiration. "He's been using the veins on the underside of his forearm."

Ziggy lowered his sleeves, kidded the cops some more, then crossed the street to the car. As he dodged traffic, the cops chuckled and commented to each other and shook their heads. Ziggy had successfully used his protective buffoonery.

6

Late one night, Doreen came into my bedroom. I was awake still wandering among concepts from William James' *Varieties of Religious Experiences*, which I had just turned out the light on. My bedroom, between the kitchen and the bathroom, had two walls of damp concrete and clothes hanging from overhead pipes.

"You awake honey?" she asked tentatively.

Little of the streetlight that came through the front window made it as far as my room. I could just make out her silhouette.

"Yeah!"

"Where are ya honey?"

"Over here."

"Listen, Ziggy went out. I think he's gonna be gone all night and I'm kinda lonely. D'ya think I could get in bed with you?"

"Sure!!"

"Where's the light, baby?"

"Here, I'll get it."

I got out of bed and crossed barefoot to the middle of the cold concrete floor and swatted the darkness for the string hanging from the bare bulb. Finally, I grabbed it and yanked dim light into the room.

She was standing closer than I realized, wearing only black bikini panties and a bra, both several sizes too small. I was wearing only underpants stretched of course by an erection (my sidekick).

She looked down at it and back up with a bashful, hopeful smile. Then she stepped toward me and stopped, looking up, expectant. I looked at her body. Most of my knowledge of the female body had come from *Playboy*.

Doreen's flesh was gray, doughy, and lumpy, pinched into rolls by the underwear. Little mounds protruded through the grid pattern of the panties. Her legs had several large abscesses, usually just black and blue pot holes in the flesh, but in the dim light of the room, they were filled with what seemed a bottomless shadow. Even the collapsed veins in her arms seemed to catch shadow.

"What's wrong honey?"

"Uh..."

"Doncha... Doncha wanna...?"

"Uh, I guess I don't, uh... feel like it... tonight..."

She was surprised, then disappointed, and then, in her expression of weary resignation, I caught a jolting glimpse of the desolation of her life. My hard-on wilted. I looked down at it and then she did too.

"Uh, I have to get up early for work..." I said.

"Oh...O.K," she said and then turned around and walked slowly out of the room.

7

A few days later, I was parked alone in front of the Double Eagle Hotel reading *Varieties of Religious Experiences*. It was a routine foray into the Fillmore for smack or to promote a deal.

I was now spending all my time waiting in the car instead of inside observing. I wanted to watch a con from beginning to end. A couple times I asked if I could come with him and his standard reply was that the others involved wouldn't like it. Maybe. At first Ziggy liked me (as much as he was capable) and wanted me to become an apprentice, but I think my disgust and revulsion, since his first stoned rumba in the livingroom, snuck out.

Now, around my car, blacks of both sexes and all ages milled about the sidewalks in the warm sunlight, joshing and guffawing. Ziggy came out of the hotel and casually got into the car. I broke off my reading, inserted a bookmark, and put the book under the seat. A tall lanky black teenager strode up and put his face in Ziggy's window.

"Staht the cah!!" Ziggy shouted frantically. "Get outa heeuh!! Staht the cah!!"

I started the car.

"Hey, man," the black kid drawled, "I know some cats wanna kill yoh ass."

Ziggy pulled a foot length of lead pipe out from under the seat. I had never seen it before.

"C'mon get outa heeuh!!!" he shrieked.

I pulled the transmission into first and checked the side mirror. There was a space in traffic so I pulled out and we shot down Fillmore Street. In the rear view mirror, the spade watched us.

"What the fuck was that about?!" I demanded with the vehemence of my fear.

"Theh's these cats that wanna kill me," Ziggy explained as he replaced the pipe under the seat. "That's why we hadda move into yah place. They'eh lookin' all oveh town fuh us. These cats will kill me on sight. I buhned 'em. They found awe pad and we hadda split right away. Left awe clothes theh and everything."

8

It had never occurred to me to ask why they were so desperate for a place when they came to me. I remembered the times I had seen Ziggy with his shirt off. His skin was pale as a fish's belly and dappled with abscesses and scars from what looked like knife wounds.

This incident in front of the Double Eagle Hotel suddenly made urgent what, since the fire, had been a casual search for a new apartment. That afternoon I found a studio two blocks away at Page and Scott, and that evening, while Ziggy and Doreen were out, I loaded up my car and moved my things to the new place. I thought I got everything in one load but then remembered leaving behind my copy of *Varieties of Religious Experiences*.

I left the car with the engine running double-parked on Waller Street for a quick search and escape, but then, when I opened the door, I found my former roommate Mike filling the livingroom.

"Hey man. How's it goin'?" he asked in his baritone and in the characteristic pose of his 6'6" height, head bent to the side against the low basement ceiling.

He was a merchant seaman who, after the fire, made a family visit to Vancouver and now was about to ship out of San Francisco. His duffle bag was on the couch.

"Oh sweet Jesus, am I glad to see you," I blurted. "You know Ziggy?"

He nodded, listening intently.

"Well, he and his ol' lady have been staying here since you left. And it's been a madhouse. Today I found out somebody is looking for him to kill him. I got a new apartment and took stuff over there and... hey, wait a minute. The landlord owes me money which he 'says' he doesn't have. The new place doesn't have a refrigerator. Will you help me steal this one?"

"Of course."

The landlord lived upstairs and I don't know what he thought of us taking the refrigerator but he had to know about it, because we banged it against the door and then the walls of the outside passageway. Eventually, we got the heavy end into the trunk of my car, but it was too long, and without someone holding it up, the protruding end tilted onto the ground. Mike was unanimously elected.

I drove the car two or three miles an hour, slow enough for him to waddle behind with arms full of refrigerator. Pedestrians and drivers were laughing and I was trying not to. Mike couldn't spare the breath. Besides, he could be sensitive about his size.

Some black kids shouted at me, "Hey man, someb'dy tryin' to steal the refrigerator outta the back of yoh cah." They yelled at Mike, "Hey, hey man, how much you chawge foh that? I gotta house needs movin'."

At Scott and Haight we had to wait behind the stop sign for our turn to cross the intersection like anybody else. Eventually we got to the new apartment and were grateful it was on the ground floor.

I never saw Doreen again, but bumped into Ziggy about nine months later when I was desperate to buy a kilo of grass to impress a chick. I gave him a hundred and ten dollars after looking into his eyes and deciding, no, he wouldn't rip off a friend, a teammate. Of course, that was who Ziggy would rip off first.

Junkie Love

Peter and Cheryl

I knocked on the door of a couple friends I visited regularly that summer of '67. The door started to open but went only a few inches and stopped. At eye level was a shiny brass chain lock, something I had assumed was as extinct in the Haight as a bow tie.

Cheryl appeared in the crack and murmured, "Hi," but didn't unlock the door.

"Hi," I murmured, bewildered.

Peter appeared suddenly behind her.

"Hey man," I said to his glower.

"Hi," he grunted.

"What's the lock for?"

"We got robbed!" Peter said with a laser-glare of scrutiny.

"Yeah, it was the shits," Cheryl said.

"What happened?" I asked. "What'd they take?"

"Six kilos of grass," he said. "Four cats came in here with guns. They knew exactly how much I had."

"They didn't even leave us anything to smoke," she added.

Silence. I realized the meaning of the glare.

"Somebody told them about those keys," he said. "You didn't say anything to anybody did you? You know, just casually mention it?"

"No. No, I didn't even know you had six kilos."

"Yes you did. I told you that day we bumped into each other in that crosswalk down on, uh, Haight and Central."

"Oh, well, I dunno... Maybe I forgot. I'm sure I didn't tell anybody though."

But I wasn't sure.

However, if I didn't remember the six kilos, another part of that day was certainly memorable. It was the first time they had sex in front of me.

2

In that crosswalk at Haight and Central I reversed my direction after accepting his invitation to go back to his pad and smoke dope, and it was while on our way there that he supposedly told me about the six kilos.

I did remember that, while walking beside me, he said at one point in a blasé, husky whisper, like someone talking while holding in a toke, "Shit man, I'm outta bread. Hafta get my ol' lady to turn a coupla tricks."

This was a ludicrous comment made only for effect, like everything else about him: his clothes (found art from the Salvation Army free bin), his gestures, his conversation, and this comment, it all contributed to a meticulously calculated impression, a style, an ongoing impersonation of his ideal self-image. I loved it.

He walked beside me, a head shorter, in his best imitation-spade, customized street-strut. He wore granny glasses and a thick black beard and sandals, baggy khakis, and an oversize sport shirt. It was a tasteful version of Ziggy's more utilitarian costume. Peter added a dark brown hat with an upturned brim á la Burroughs.

Peter was a socialist and aspiring junkie. He was a new wave junkie, inspired by the kamikaze dedication of junkies like Ziggy, but saved from Ziggy's viciousness by a conscience. Peter would only burn capitalists. He talked about the dope market and revolution with equal intensity.

Currently, he was having a hard time getting addicted. He couldn't afford it. And his socialist ethics kept him from using the standard criminal methods to raise funds. He had planned to retail the stolen six kilos of grass to get the money for heroin.

Contrary to popular misconceptions, getting addicted to heroin is not easy, requiring not just deliberation but determination. Burroughs said in *Junky* it usually requires twice daily use for three months to get a habit. It took Burroughs six months to get his first.

"Hey," Peter says and stops, looking into a garden beside the sidewalk. "Those are poppies. Over there." He points at some flowers with stalks bent by fat tulip-like bulbs at the top. "Those are opium poppies."

I look at them doubtfully while he steps over the wrought-iron fence and goes between roses to the poppies.

"Yeah, that's what they are," he says standing beside them and looking down at them. "They're legal. For the gardners. Because they're so beautiful. Whatchya do is..." He bends down and moves his finger like a blade across a bulb. "... Slit'em right here. And ya get this goo...Hey!" He looks furtively around. I'm already nervous about his traipsing around somebody's garden in plain sight. He says in a stage whisper, "I'll come back here. When the poppies are ready." Then he straightens up, gingerly steps back to the fence and over it, and we continue on.

It's doubtful Ziggy could even identify a poppy. He definitely wouldn't know how to harvest it.

3

One thing I knew Peter *wouldn't* do for the money he needed to start a habit was have his ol' lady, Cheryl, turn a trick. Theirs was one of those romances right out of the rock n' roll lyrics. Both were studying to be social workers at San Francisco State when they met and moved in together on the same day.

Cheryl was the best friend of a former ol' lady of mine, Ruth, who dumped me some months before and today will be the first time I've seen Cheryl since. She always had a knowing smirk that unsettled me and I can't help cringe a little as I step through the door into their pad. But she greets me with a warm coy smile and I relax.

Cheryl is a short sultry blond with swollen pouty lips and big brown spaniel eyes and she is wearing a satiny white slip that

might have served as an evening gown for Carol Lombard. She is on her way to the bathroom and stops to greet me.

"Hi. How have you been?" she asks.

"O.k"

She assumes I haven't been and her smile sympathizes. Until this moment I thought I had gotten over Ruth in the swirl of the Summer of Love.

"I'll be right back," Cheryl says and goes into the bathroom and shuts the door.

Peter puts away the groceries that were the purpose of his errand to Haight Street. I notice their small apartment is stifling and, on this hot sunny day, the shades are drawn over closed windows. Cheryl's muffled tinkle reminds me with a pang of Ruth's in my pad.

Cheryl comes out of the bathroom as Peter comes out of the kitchen. He passes behind me into the main room of the studio apartment and I look at Cheryl and am stunned by her slip as she walks toward me. It's a shimmery white liquid flowing over the soft roundness of breasts, tummy, and pubes. I am jolted by raw, unadulterated lust. I pry my eyes free and focus on her pleased seductive smile.

As she passes me going into the main room, she asks, "Peter said you have hash?"

He is now sitting cross-legged on the floor and searching through his stash in an open shoebox on his lap. I savor the jello-wobble of her ass as she walks to a mattress on the floor and sits.

"Yeah I have some," I say and look for a place to sit and choose a chrome kitchen chair next to the mattress. "I have grams for ten."

"I'd love some hash," she says and just let's the invitation hang in the air.

I can tell through her slip that she isn't wearing panties and as she resettles into a pillow pile, she flashes her crotch. She does that a lot, which is fine with me. But right now it's dark in the room and darker in there and I can't be sure of what I saw.

"I don't have any hash on me but I'll bring ya some."

It's left unresolved whether this will be a gift or a sale.

"How's Tim?" she asks about my roommate.

"Fine...O.k."

Peter has found a roach, nearly half a joint, which he lights, tokes from, and hands to Cheryl, who takes a dainty toke and then hands it to me. The only light comes from the dimly glowing ochre rectangles of the drawn shades. A portable TV sits on another kitchen chair at the foot of the mattress. As in so many other pads, my own included, Peter and Cheryl seem camped out, on their way elsewhere, another pad or another hemisphere or the Apocalypse.

"Hey the *Velvet Underground*," I say after exhaling my toke. The album cover is among others piled beside a portable record player on the floor across the room. I hand the roach across the mattress to Peter.

"We got it yesterday," Cheryl says. "I haven't listened to it all yet."

"Heeerooooiiinnn," Peter croons, imitating Lou Reed on the song *Heroin*.

Peter takes a toke of what is left and when he offers her the last toke, Cheryl waves it off, then I do the same. He puts a finger to his tongue and then taps out the roach with saliva and tosses it into his mouth.

"I saw them last year at the Fillmore," I say. "On the same bill as Frank Zappa."

"How was that?" Cheryl asks.

Peter gets up from the floor and sits beside her on the mattress.

"Great! At least Zappa was... I don't think I ever saw a skinnier human being."

"But how was the *Velvet Underground*?" she asks. They were Andy Warhol's foray into rock and would naturally appeal to her.

"Well...the album is a lot better than their stage performance, that's for sure."

"Wanna listen to the album?" Peter asks me.

"Yeah!"

"Put it on," he says and I stand.

"I want to watch Mike Douglas," she whines about a singing talk show host. "He's on now."

I look at Peter and he shrugs, so I go to the TV instead and turn it on. As I don't own one, and few people in the Haight do, this will be as much of a treat as listening to the Velvet Underground album.

4

We sit in a stoned silence only occasionally broken by Cheryl's ridicule of the TV show, which, it becomes apparent, is why she watches it. I drift off into thoughts of Ruth. There were numerous parallels between Cheryl and Peter as a couple and Ruth and I. For instance, Cheryl and Ruth were the same age and both were three years older than Peter and I. I had the stoned epiphany that Cheryl and Peter had the relationship I wanted with Ruth.

That was when Peter started nuzzling Cheryl's neck. Then he started kissing it. Had he noticed me noticing her? Was he marking territory? Eventually he kissed his way to her mouth, and after a moment's hesitation, she got into it.

Then she pulled away from him and said about a strain of music in a commercial, "That sounds like Mahler!" She turned to me with drooping eyelids and languorously asked, "Do you like Mahler? I lo-o-o-o-ve Mahler." Each word is lugged with a breathy groan up a steep slope. "I don't know anyone with good taste who doesn't have Mahler in their record collection."

Peter put a hand on a tit. She slowly removed it by pushing against his forearm. He sat up and leaned back against the wall. There's something else going on here besides his staking a claim, but I don't know what yet. I turn back to the TV and wander through corridors of thoughts.

Just a few weeks before, I had taken speed. It was the first time since the previous summer, when Ziggy and Doreen moved in, and it was disastrous and I was still feeling shaky. The mysterious way Ruth pulled out of the relationship with no clear explanation reinforced fears carried from that redneck mill town where I was resident space alien. I suspected there was something deeply wrong with me, unnamable but repulsive.

"I heard Che sniffed coke before addressing the UN," Cheryl called out from her own thought maze, breaking a long silence and bringing me back.

It was night outside now and the lunar glow of the TV was the only light in the room. In the dimness, I could make out Peter nuzzling Cheryl again and this time, when he put a hand on her tit, she let it stay. In a while, she started to pant, audibly. I realized we were playing a three way game of chicken: loser is the first to admit there is anything going on in the room besides the television.

I turned back to the TV, but couldn't get lost in it. The whole time I had been in their place, I was acutely aware that she wasn't wearing panties. I was anticipating his next logical move, when she suddenly slid a hand into his pants and started giving him a hand job. Maybe she was trying to shut him off altogether or just raising the bet between them or maybe calling his bluff, but it was a brilliant strategic stroke. He didn't seem to like it but leaned back and allowed it. Eventually, before he came, he stopped her. She won.

Like Ziggy and Doreen, Peter and Cheryl were dueling exhibitionists. But Peter and Cheryl were younger and not yet junkies, so they still had a full sex drive. Their stage was a mattress instead of supermarket aisles.

5

Cheryl and Ruth had shared several lovers including my present roommate, Tim. (They were two of the four women he had sex with serially in one day, his personal record.) And before Tim, they shared a spade they came to California with and who returned east last summer "to lead riots."

Ruth was my second lover, and Cheryl's already considerable attractiveness was only heightened by her association with Ruth. This was despite Cheryl's being a hypochondriac who kept the blinds permanently drawn and only left her apartment when necessary. She also wore dark glasses at night, sported a cigarette holder, and was the first person I heard use *ciao* who wasn't in a Fellini or Antonioni film. Most of the times I would see

her she would be on a mattress in a slip watching television. Being bedridden with an illness would have hardly changed her life-style.

Peter and Cheryl were on my visit-list mainly because of their erudition and their style of nomadic, exiled aristocrats. Visiting them usually consisted of sitting beside their mattress-on-the-floor, TV interspersed with sophisticated conversation, and sometimes they would have sex of some kind. I learned that they did it in front of others too when I arrived one afternoon just as three foxy college friends of Cheryl's and Ruth's were leaving.

6

Purses in hand, they were standing by the door as I entered it. I was introduced but only one name stuck. Conversation resumed but I was too busy checking out the chicks for much to register.

They were sleek and sexy and sophisticated. They exuded money. They inherited it and they wore it. That was the problem. Their clothes were expensive not hip. Mini skirts and bouffant hair. They were just stylish. They didn't stand a chance against Cheryl.

On their way home to LA, the chicks had stopped in SF to check out the Haight and visit Cheryl and Ruth. I noticed they were discussing getting together again before the chicks left and the best looking of them, Barbara, was stunned. She had just caught Cheryl's hesitation (or was it even reluctance?) about getting together again. And it was too obvious not to be deliberate. Cheryl kept her head down and said nothing to dispel Barbara's suspicion. The hip-straight chasm then cracking open the country just ran through that apartment.

Then, as Cheryl was thinking out loud in an unconvincing effort to find free time, Peter started nuzzling her neck. She was surprised but she didn't pull away. Then suddenly he pulled her housecoat aside exposing a circular brown nipple. She jerked the housecoat closed and turned a sour scowl on him and almost spoke to him but instead turned back to her friends. She set a tentative time for the next day and goodbyes resumed and the chicks left. Nothing was said about the nipple.

7

There did seem to be a trajectory to Peter and Cheryl's sex, going further each time, and it all climaxed in the middle of the summer, on the evening I stood before their front door, opened only the length of the chain lock, waiting to see if they believed that I hadn't mentioned their six kilos to the wrong people. Our friendship was in the balance. I was poised to turn around and leave when Peter finally shut the door, undid the lock, then reopened the door all the way.

As I stepped through it, Peter said, "Sorry, man."

"Yeah, that's o.k. Were you hurt?"

"No."

At least not physically. I could sense the experience through his fear and outrage.

"Djyou ever see any of 'em before?" I asked while he went passed me toward the mattress where Cheryl was already sitting watching TV.

"No," she said.

"I'd offer ya some smoke..." he said, rage welling up again. "But they even took my stash!"

"I brought some hash," I said, pulling a foil-wrapped chunk from my Levis coin pocket. They stared at me a moment dumbfounded. Then they exchanged glances and broke into beaming grins.

"But I didn't bring a pipe," I continued. "I knew you had one in your stash. We could improvise a hookah with tin foil and a glass of water. You know that one?"

He didn't, which surprised me. He brought me a half-full glass of water and enough tin foil to cover the top of the glass. On one side of the foil, I made a slight indentation with my finger and in that indentation pricked tiny holes with a safety pin. That was where the hash burned. On the other side of the foil, I made a single finger-poked hole for inhaling the smoke over the water.

We smoked and then fell into the familiar pattern of TV and talk. I began to feel anxious, confused, and guilty. Maybe I did

mention the six kilos to someone and it got passed along to the thieves. I must have done *something* wrong.

The hash and the accusation jarred me into a flashback to yet another disastrous speed crack-up, the second that summer, and by the end of that one, I was standing across the street from Langley-Porter Neuropsychiatric Hospital talking myself out of committing myself.

8

The only light in the room now was the TV and I stared vacantly into its gray cave-fire while it emitted canned laughter. When the rhythm of the conversation required something from me, I said one or two words, the minimum.

Peter picked up the glass with the tinfoil and offered me the smoldering last toke but I shook my head. I was struck that he *didn't* then offer it to Cheryl and I think she was too. He lit the ember and took the toke, but then, holding it in, he put the glass and lighter on the floor, turned to Cheryl and kissed her and blew the smoke into her mouth.

Of course, the hard-on I carried up Delmar Street on the way to their place had wilted in front of that chain lock on their front door.

Panic was welling up inside me and my mind raced, analyzing, weighing, tracking, as it would compulsively for years to come, trying to understand what was happening to me. I had to get alone, and for the thousandth time, try to break free of this thing, whatever it was, that had its fangs in my neck. I had to get back to normalcy, my old self, resume my life…

Cheryl exhaled the smoke Peter had given her and then he resumed the kiss and she didn't pull back. And then he started slowly moving his hand up her leg and again she didn't stop him. It occurred to me that she might see a sex show as a return favor for the hash.

But I was free-falling through what was becoming a familiar and recurring catatonia. I was immobilized by countervailing urges to cry out for help, and/or attack, and/or flee.

His hand was now the distance under her slip and rotating slowly with her hand resting on his wrist. She started panting.

Flight won. Often since the speed crash and still more often in the years ahead, I would be tensed and ready for flight and unable to leave for any of numerous reasons, none of which was present now. So I stood up. They froze in-place and looked up.

"I've gotta split man," I said.

"OK," Peter said, pulling his hand out of her crotch.

I added, "I'm... late... to meet someone..."

"Oh... OK."

Cheryl smiled up feebly, then sighed deeply. I turned around and headed for the door.

9

The theft of the six kilos didn't prevent them from becoming junkies. Within weeks Cheryl received an inheritance, and in the middle of the Summer of Love, too hip for the Haight, they headed for South America, where it was cheaper to maintain a heroin habit.

She returned a few years later, pregnant, broke, and alone, except for a lap pet: a rare, hairy, pygmy pig. She and Peter weren't just temporarily separated but broken up. When the CIA sprang its coup against democratically-elected Chilean President Salvador Allende, Peter covered it as a stringer for *Time* magazine. That was the last I heard of him.

Becoming a journalist implied that he probably wasn't a junkie anymore which may have been the wedge that split the couple. I saw Cheryl about a half dozen times over the next few years but never asked her about it. She was like her pet: exotic, shivering with vulnerability, and full of ravenous appetites. If you called before visiting her, you risked having to pick up groceries along the way, and it was more or less understood you wouldn't be paid back.

The one time sex came up between us, she made it clear that she wanted some kind of commitment and that was unthinkable. After the psychedelic dawn of '67, "drugs" meant psychedelics, and for me, as for most of the drug culture, junkies

became as antiquated, boring, and irrelevant as aristocrats. I eventually developed a deep revulsion toward them.

In the Seventies, Cheryl and I lost touch and I heard about her only through mutual friends. She had a second child who died of exposure after being left overnight in a car while Cheryl was passed out where she had supposedly made a quick stop to score smack. Cheryl's mother then got a court to give her custody of the child Cheryl had had with Peter. In the mid Eighties, Cheryl was beaten to death in a Tenderloin hotel room by a boyfriend.

10

Burroughs made the same change as the drug culture and turned away from junkies. By the late Sixties, in a round table discussion sponsored by *Playboy* magazine, he asked, "So what can we do to keep these junkies from breaking into my hotel room and stealing my typewriter?"

He had had a foot in the new drug culture before it existed. He was, among other things, a psychedelic scientist, himself his own guinea pig. His field reports became great literature.

In the early Seventies, I scored a half hour alone with him in New York.

Junkie Love

Burroughs

Yage (Yah-hay)

"Yage? You have yage in there?" I ask. "You know who William Burroughs is?"

"Yeah," he says.

"Have you read *The Yage Letters*?"

"No."

"It's a collection of letters that Burroughs sent to Ginsberg while he was searching for yage in the jungles of, uh, Colombia."

"Yeah, I've heard about it."

"He said yage was like witnessing the first day of creation."

I'm in the kitchen of a wealthy friend, Henry, and I'm standing before his magic refrigerator. He started the first Haight-Ashbury coffeehouse and later the biggest and one of the earliest head shops, and his refrigerator is legendary for its drug exotica. I bought a rare African mushroom from there a few months ago.

We're casual not close friends. I've partied here at his remodeled Victorian on a hill above the Haight. My best friend's ol' lady is one of his employees, and Henry is desperately, hopelessly, pathetically in love with her.

"You can have it if you want," Henry adds.

"You're *giving* it away?"

"Yeah, I'm not sure how good it is. I've had it for a while."

I've never known him to give away drugs. But then I realize he's showing off for the two comely chicks I brought along. Maddie and Yvette are clerks at the San Rafael Post Office, where I'm a carrier. I've also brought my roommate, Doug, an assembler of automatic pool-cleaners and a rock bassist. We've come to score some super hash I've heard about.

"Yeah, God, Henry, thanks so much, that's... that's so generous..." I say and look over at the chicks.

I invited them along in part to impress them and this is pretty impressive. To me anyway. They've got blank expressions. But my luck with them is about to get much better.

"Sure, you're welcome," Henry says. "But you don't have to get it now. You can take it when you leave. You wanna use the sauna?"

EUREKA! That's what I was hoping for. I look at the chicks and then at Doug whose eyes are twinkling.

"You want to?" I ask the chicks.

"Yeah, sure," says perky red-headed Maddie. "Sounds... groovy."

She looks at Yvette who is less sure and who says "Yeah...o.k....sure..."

"O.k.," I say leading the way down the hall to the sauna at the back of the house. "Thanks again Henry!"

The chicks are pretty young, about seven years younger than me, and, though eighteen would be a fairly old virgin in the early Seventies, I'll learn later that both are. It occurs to me now they may not realize they're going to have to be naked. Saunas are not common at this time. So, when we reach the dressing room, I immediately start unbuttoning my shirt, and, if they didn't already know it, they get the message.

Conspicuous silence as we undress. There is an awkward moment for Yvette before she begins, but Maddie is naked before Doug and I. And he and I don't even pretend not to look. She has bulging, bobbing breasts, and a shout of orange bush below.

She absorbs a jolt of our awe, then, flattered, blushing, asks "In here?" while gesturing toward the door to the sauna.

"Yeah," I say, dazed.

She opens the heavy door and, after a quick glance at our dicks, goes in. Yvette meanwhile has misplaced her shirt and stumbles over clutter looking for it. She wants to place it on top of her jeans and panties.

Doug is short, pale, and skinny with a dark shaggy Beatle-cut and goatee, and right now, he has a grin radiant with idiot glee. But he's not sure which chick he's supposed to be with. Neither am I. I invited him along as a favor to him and to take care of whichever one I didn't want. I don't know which that is because I haven't dated either. Right now, we're just friendly co-workers getting together one night after work. Doug nods toward the sauna silently asking if he should follow Maddie. I nod yes.

I'm feeling a host's responsibility to watch over Yvette. We're all quite stoned on a sample of Henry's high-quality hash. She eventually puts her shirt on her jeans then I lead her into the sauna. Her breasts are small whip-cream waves with brown-dot nipples and her bush a brown wisp.

We silently sit together, me, Yvette, Doug, and Maddie, in the smothering heat, not completely sure what to do besides sweat. It's time for the host to step in.

"Oh yeah," I say and stand. "If you're interested, he's got all these ointments and oils. That's what those bottles are on that shelf. He sells that stuff in his store. It's for...rubbing on..."

I fall silent, suddenly realizing the sexual potential. But I can't focus on that too hard. Doug and I are already fighting erections.

"And those heated rocks over there... Have you been in a sauna before?" I ask the chicks.

They reluctantly shake their heads.

"Oh, well, if you want it hotter, you put the water that's in that bucket on those heated rocks. Or if it's too hot, you pour the water on yourself."

Fortunately, the wood bench is a little short for the four of us and I have an excuse for pressing against Yvette when I sit back down. I can now finally see beyond her nudity. She is confused and

uncomfortable. I am involved in the prolonged ending of a multi year relationship, and that ol' lady and I had a term for my sudden, inescapable psychological dislocations (paralyzing flashbacks to my disastrous speed trips of '67). We called it "tuned out." You can't connect with your surroundings no matter what you try. Eventually, in my case, panic and paranoia set in. I recognize that Yvette is tuned out from the hash.

If she doesn't have a body of Maddie's quality, she does have what I noticed earlier tonight is an extraordinary face. Though she is naked, I'm stealing glances at the face. She is beautiful, that is immediately obvious, but tonight I get lost in the nuances and subtleties of her features.

"Where's the bathroom?" Doug asks.

"Huh? ..." I say. "Oh, uh..." Yvette turns toward me so I have to leave the face. I concentrate to remember and then say, "Oh, that way." I point. "End of the hall and left."

Doug gets up and leaves, letting in a chill, and I am alone with the chicks. But so what? What do I do next? I'm too hot, so I get up, step over to the bucket, scoop the wooden ladle full of water and pour it on my back. I pour another ladleful over my head. Then I return the ladle to the bucket and turn around to face the chicks, who are staring at my dick.

Maddie raises her eyes and smiles at me, eager, inviting. Yvette turns away scowling. That does it. I'm going after Maddie. I gesture toward the shelf and start to ask if she would like me to rub-on an ointment but Doug reenters and sits next to her. I pause, hand in the air, considering.

Then Yvette stands and says, "I don't feel good," and rushes out the door.

Maddie watches her, concerned, and seems on the verge of following her when I say, "I'll see if she's alright."

I sigh with exasperation and go out. Yvette is going into the bathroom as I enter the changing room. I'm suddenly cold and think about going back into the sauna but realize I should give Doug his chance with Maddie. So I stand and wait and shiver. The toilet flushes and eventually Yvette comes out.

"How are you feeling?" I ask.

"Not so good. I threw up," she says and reaches for her panties.

"Oh," I say and feel foolish when I ask out of desperation, "Wanna go back into the sauna?"

"No, I better not," she says, stepping into the panties.

I realized the evening was over and, disgruntled, went back into the sauna and told them about Yvette. I also told them to take their time, then, like the dutiful host, I went back out to keep Yvette company. Doug and Maddie emerged minutes later and I distractedly dressed while Maddie hid away that body.

Later, when he and I were driving home alone in my VW bug, Doug laughed about my confusion when we dropped the chicks off. Standing in the parking lot between our cars, saying good night, I knew a hug was in order and evidently my head comically went back and forth and back and forth. Maddie ended the indecision by leaping into my arms, kissing me on the lips, then hugging me. When she released me, I turned to Yvette … who was already walking to the driver's side of her Volvo. She said thanks and good night.

I was pissed. But only until I remembered I had yage, Burroughs' grail drug. For a few nights I jerked off to fantasies of Maddie, but within weeks I was in love with Yvette, desperately, hopelessly, pathetically. For four years. Actually, though love may have been mixed in there somewhere, it was more like a pathological obsession. She was the long-missing high school steady, among other things. Throughout the whole ordeal, I was detached, analytical, and helpless.

Of course, it wasn't an addiction as bad as junk but at least with junk you have the option of kicking.

Some weeks after that night in the sauna, I took a long-planned vacation trip alone to visit friends on the East Coast. That was when I accidentally scored a half hour alone with Burroughs. And the yage made it possible.

Tim in New York

I stayed in the Greenwich Village apartment of an old roommate from Haight-Ashbury days, Tim. We hadn't seen each other in a couple years, not since we shared an apartment on the Lower East Side of Manhattan and my father died in California and instead of forwarding my last paycheck to me there, Tim forged my signature and cashed the check so he could chase his latest female obsession to Europe.

"Look, I'm sorry," he said. "I ... I ... I looked at my needs and your needs and I figured... you could probably handle it better than I could..."

"That's such bullshit! That's like the cat I let stay at my place who stole some grass and when I confronted him, he said he only took as much as I would have given him if he asked for it and I was a decent person."

"O.k., I know I was irresponsible," he conceded. "I did send you *some* money though...Ya know I had money problems too. Greg from Kozmic was supposed to send me $75 in Barcelona and he never did."

That was Kozmic Messenger Service, a hippie bicycle messenger service we worked for in downtown Manhattan. The only business where a bad acid trip the night before was a valid excuse for missing work.

"It's just that it was...sleazy," I said. "It was like... junkie-behavior. I was broke, no job, and my mother could barely pay for the funeral..."

"Yeah, I know, but...but... Janey and I were at a very critical juncture..."

It was the afternoon of my first day back in NY and we were talking at the kitchen table in his cramped, dingy studio apartment. It was furnished with the usual sidewalk gleanings and indistinguishable from countless identical ones I'd been in on both coasts except that in this one the bathtub was immediately adjacent to the kitchen sink.

His rip-off had to resurface at our first face-to-face meeting, though actually it was all settled by letter over a year ago.

I asked, "Whatever happened to her?"

"Janey? She's back in LA. Back at Camarillo too."

That's Camarillo State Mental Hospital, which was where he met her. Tim broke down more or less yearly. When his deep-set eyes would get a tell-tale vacancy and become all pupils, and when his breathing became audible and he was conscious but almost paralyzed, catatonic, then it was time to go in. Sometimes in that state he would make gnomic utterances.

Here are a few of Tim's Greatest Hits: "We never made love to the extent that either of us will get pregnant;" "If I wasn't here I'd be somewhere;" "If you want an abortion don't go out asking for tomatoes." But the one that applied to my own psychosis and indeed it became something of a motto for my own insanity, was "Help! I'm surrounded by people."

Often Tim came out of a mental hospital obsessed with a female fellow patient, attaching himself lamprey-like for a year or two. After they had both been released from Camarillo, he followed Janey to New York. But before he could follow her back to California, he crashed into Bellevue, which was where he met his latest.

"How's Liz?" I asked about this latest.

"I don't know. She won't see me," he said from sudden dejection. "She's stuck and doesn't know it." He paused. "She's got a new boyfriend or... lover anyway. His name is Len and he used to be a chick. Or anyway, he started taking the shots for a sex-change operation. He still wears a bra and still has a cunt." Then he added with a relieved grin, "No cock yet."

Liz was a sexually daring, svelte blond. Neither of us knew her when she lived in San Francisco in the Sixties, but like a lot of hip chicks then, she had been a topless dancer in North Beach, with the distinction that she was also Phi Beta Kappa. In some of his brilliant soaring letters, he described their threesomes and other adventures.

"Liz was always bi," he said. "But now she seems to think she's a lesbian. I asked her, do you want me to get an operation? So my big swollen cock won't get in the way?"

I laughed and said, "Tell her you'll change into anything she wants except a Republican."

He chuckled and said, "Yeah, I draw the line there that's for sure..." Then after a while he added thoughtfully, "Actually, she always responded best manually... God I love the smell of her cunt. She's got this... natural body fragrance... I called it 'Eau de Liz.' Sometimes I wish she was still dancing topless. I'd go watch her every night... She's my absolute fleshpot dream queen... We're lust-mates."

We had been celebrating with some of his expensive, bad grass and maybe because of the grass and the time since we had last seen each other, and maybe because of his relief that we were still friends, he was venting on me. And sometimes, as in his letters, he could soar into a Ginsbergian riff.

"She is without doubt the most challenging woman of my career," he said. "She's got this notion now that women are superior... Well, of course they are! But no one, male, female, or reptile, will ever love her like me. I have never loved another woman like I love her. And never will. I'm so far in love with that woman I'm never comin' out. She is the last best love of my life. Actually she's the first *real love* of my life because I feel things with her I've never felt with anyone before. We are lifetime psychic allies. I am absolutely certain that I'll marry her... I hope." Then after a long stoned pause he added, "Priapus unpredictable."

"Sounds like a Kenneth Anger film," I said. "Why won't she see you?"

He frowned, shrugged, and reluctantly admitted, "Sudden subway materializations."

He was stalking her.

"Then last week..." he added. "I tried to get into this lesbian bar up on Nineteenth Street, but they said it was private or something. Then they got mad. I just wanted to see if she was there! I asked if they knew her... She might have found out about that..."

"I'll bet you owe her money too, dontchya?"

"Yeah."

"How much?"

"Uh...ummm..." He didn't want to tell me. "About a year of borrowing."

I picked up a facedown paperback collection of Sappho and saw Tim's handwriting in the margins.

He commented, "Liz's perversity is vastly educational."

Suddenly, the doorknob turned and stopped. We both froze and looked to see that the doorknob and the three bolt-locks were all locked.

Tim yelled, "Get the fuck out of here!!! You fucking junkies!!!"

"We've got a shotgun in here!!" I added.

In the hall, there were urgent whispers then footsteps departing down the stairs.

"Christ, you're this far west on Ninth Street and you still have that problem?" I asked.

I could tell the junkies had worn Tim down since I was last here. He swore at them with the same vehemence, even used the same words that he chided me for using back on the Lower East Side. New York was a city under siege by an underground army of junkies, and that doorknob brought back my nine month sojourn in the bad parts of NY, "the behavioral sink" (the center of the action in overcrowding experiments with rats).

In our first month, we were burglarized three times. If you didn't have "police gates" on your windows you could, at any time, return to an apartment cleaned out down to a bare floor. One night I was bringing a chick home and we were robbed at knifepoint in the hall. Actually, the sidewalks seemed safer than the pad. That may have been because the cops were so visible, walking around in threes.

The neighborhood was made up of hippies, Puerto Ricans, a few blacks, and some elderly Jews and Ukrainians, and lots of dogs, the size of their owners' paranoia. The stench of the dogs' shit, like the crime threat, was ever present in the background.

Our pad was at the back of our building and had a view of a quarter acre enclosed by other buildings and full of garbage in some areas a couple yards deep. There weren't as many rats as I expected but the cockroaches were unrelenting, like the thumping Puerto Rican jukebox in the ground floor cafe, and like the mosquitoes and the smothering heat in the summer.

Eventually, everyone in NY seemed a junkie to their own tyrannical desires. It was America concentrated, and heroin was the ultimate consumer product: effortless ecstasy.

Yet, here I was in NY again, like the other rats, for more of the sweet, and to sniff around old haunts and old girlfriends. At one point in my first evening back, Tim and I moved to the window, which overlooked Ninth Street, and people-watched.

I broke a stoned reverie with, "Hey, in San Francisco, I had two different New Yorkers tell me the same thing word-for-word when I told them what neighborhood we lived in: 'Ya gotta carry a machine gun to walk around down there.'"

"That's good. Mingus used to live down there and supposedly when he would take walks late at night he would carry a big butcher knife openly in his hand."

"How's Ruth doin'?"

"Great. She's working at Bellevue in intake and doing some study there for her anthropology thesis. When I was in there it was easy for her to visit. By the way, we're invited to her place Tuesday for dinner. She'll tell you about some of the amazing patients she knows in there."

"Oh, I heard something third hand about Cheryl," I said. "She's pregnant again."

"What?! Since when? I mean, how far along is she?"

"I dunno. She could have had it already."

"I had sex with her... possibly at the right time. She was back here trying to get money out of her family, and Liz and I had broken up. That was the third, uh, second break up." He paused and considered. "Usually I'm very careful but... we were really drunk... It depends... I know she hadn't been with anyone in a long time... I don't know if she fucked anyone else later... I could be a father... I want to see that kid! I guess it's about time I had one. I'm thirty."

We fell silent for a while. I noticed a junkie go by. I had a radar for them. I could identify one by the strut, the languor, the tics.

Tim said, "Tell me about this chick you met..."

"Yvette?"

"Yeah, she sounded amazing in your letters," he said and then added with his own knowing smirk. "You're a braver man than I to give your heart to an eighteen year old."

"Yeah, but what an eighteen year old," I countered. "Actually... she doesn't feel the same way about me that I feel about her but I'm confident that... we'll work it out. Sometimes we don't have a lot to talk about... She's not intellectual... Sometimes I feel self-conscious... like I'm auditioning and forgetting my lines. But, hey, did I tell ya I got a hold of some yage?"

"You wrote about it."

"She wants to try it. I figure if we don't bond after taking that...well... We haven't taken it yet because we'll need a couple days free and neither of us has had the time yet... "

"Oh, that reminds me!" Tim interrupted. "Guess who's in town? Burroughs. I was at a party at Ginsberg's the other night and heard about it. He's teaching a writing class at CCNY. I knew you would be excited by that."

Liz was a friend of Peter Orlovsky, Allen Ginsberg's long time lover. From hints in letters, I learned that Liz somehow coerced Tim, either to torment him and/or shake free of him, into having homosexual sex.

He guessed the drift of my thoughts and said, "I know you haven't had any experience with homosexual sex, so take my advice... It's boring."

I liked Tim tremendously but would never fully trust him again, and I had almost no respect for him. I couldn't respect such a groveling fool for love. My years with Yvette were ahead of me.

He was right that the news about Burroughs would excite me and I decided to sit-in on his class at CCNY. I was only recently a college student myself and still felt comfortable on a campus. But as I thought more about meeting him, I became concerned. Around my heroes I froze. So I worried about being discombobulated with Burroughs, such that I even considered not going to his class. Then I realized that I had a conversation starter: yage.

The Meeting

I called City College of New York and got the day, time, and room number of Burroughs' class. There were only about a dozen students in the classroom when I arrived and sat at the back. Burroughs arrived a few minutes later, looking just like the photographs, *el hom
bre invisible,* in the signature hat with the turned up brim. As he conducted the class, he seemed unsure of himself, harried, ill at ease. And the kids didn't help. They were disrespectful and ignorant about his work and literature in general.

I connected with his nervousness and this weakened my resolve to talk to him. As I envisioned approaching him after the class, I felt panic and searched for an excuse not to do it. I would just be another irritant and one that hadn't paid the fees. But then I remembered what a once-in-lifetime opportunity this was and steeled myself. He closed the class by reading a draft of an article about his new obsession: language and authority as viruses. I liked it and had read other similar writings of his recently.

Most of the kids filed out and a few stood around Burroughs with questions. I waited behind them. He broke off with a chick by telling her to come to his office during office hours. Then there was just one guy between us. He had shoulder-length dark hair and beard, and he said in a soft southern drawl that he had just hitched up from Alabama to see him. I didn't catch Burroughs' reaction, but I was impressed. I always had a special respect, even awe, for Southern freaks. Tim was one.

While the Alabaman and Burroughs talked, the mention of his office hours reminded me that I could go to Burroughs' office and maybe have him alone, and it would be safer and therefore easier to bring up yage. The Alabaman was running out of conversation. I took advantage of my excuse and left.

A couple days later, I was walking down a long wide corridor in some basement somewhere at CCNY, scanning the names on the office doors. Kurt Vonnegut's got a reverential pause. Burroughs' door was open and he was sitting behind a desk. The room was the size of a large walk-in closet and its bare walls were

an institutional gray. He looked up from a student paper, pen in hand.

"Hi..." I said. "I, uh...I'm not a student... in your class. I'm just a... big fan...of your work. I think you're... unique... in world literature."

"Well...Thank you." He seemed slightly less uncomfortable than in the classroom.

I didn't have anything more to say and would have preferred to just silently study his face. There were countless photographs of it and I had seen it in some art films. (He was something of a ham.) Granitic, inscrutable, it was the face of a man with a self-proclaimed talent for invisibility.

But I'm expected to speak! And not a thing comes into my head. Then I remember the yage.

"Uh, I have some yage..." I said.

His discomfort was instantly replaced by interest.

"...And I was wondering if, uh ..." I said, "maybe you could, uh... give me some advice..."

"Sit down," he said gesturing toward the only chair besides his.

"Uh, I got it from a friend in Haight Ashbury," I said as I sat. "I'm from San Francisco. There's a cat there... he's made a lot of money from head shops and he's got this... amazing refrigerator. And with all the exotica he's got moving through there, I wasn't too surprised when yage popped up."

"You've got to be careful. There're a lot of people *claiming* to sell yage."

"Oh, yeah, I thought of that..."

"There's a blue light..." he said and paused. "*If* it's yage you'll see this... blue light."

"Yeah, you mentioned that in *The Yage Letters*..."

And we were off. With Burroughs, it was "know the work, know the man," and I knew the writings so well that he didn't have to explain, so he picked up momentum. We became like a couple of heads (users of psychedelics) meeting anywhere. Then, at one point, he mentioned there was intermittent interest in a movie script he had written. Among Burroughs' odd interests were the delirious rantings of the gangster Dutch Schultz during the days it took him

to die from gunshot wounds. The rantings were transcribed and Burroughs had fashioned from them *The Last Words of Dutch Schulz*.

He sighed and looked off into his thoughts and said, "They've been jerkin' me around about this for a couple of years…"

"It's hard to believe they wouldn't be eager to buy a script from *William Burroughs…*" I gushed.

Was it possible? Did he blush? But then he paused. He seemed to be examining a note in my tone of voice. Sarcasm? I could be taking a potshot at him. He didn't know me. Since the speed disasters of '67, I could never be sure what was communicated in my tone of voice.

But he wasn't offended. He considered my comment and replied seriously, "They don't care about… literary reputation."

I was glad that I hadn't offended him but I realized I wouldn't be able to relax again. I was locked on-guard for an outbreak of tuning-out or any other alienating behavior.

So, reluctant and relieved, I said, "I've got to leave."

He was surprised and clearly wanted me to stay longer. We had been together about a half hour. He stood and we shook hands. I thanked him for sparing me the time, when in fact he was glad for the company, and left.

It was only later amid the rumble-clatter and flashing chrome of the subway that I realized my accomplishment. It was in his body language. I got him to lean back and put his hands behind his head. I was hip enough to relax with. For a while, I prized an invisible trophy with a gold statuette of William Burroughs reclining in a chair with his hands behind his head.

Junkie Love

Yvette

A couple weeks after I returned to the West Coast, I took the yage with Yvette. We sat in my livingroom for an hour or so of mostly strained silence, waiting to be transported. But nothing happened. Maybe, as Henry had warned, it was too old.

Gilroy

We entered a low, thick, obliterating fog and my attention was confined to the thirty-yard pie-wedge of light in front of the car and the dipping swerving asphalt treadmill underneath it. After enough miles of oncoming traffic shooting out of the fog and whooshing by a few feet the other side of a painted line, I realized with a shudder, in my LSD hyper-clarity, the extreme vulnerability of anyone, even a driver who wasn't high, on a California highway at night. It was Russian roulette and every car that didn't hit us was an empty chamber.

I was driving, Tim was in the back, and Rob at shotgun, and they, like me, had a sleeping bag wrapped around them because the rear window didn't have glass. But unlike me, they were on STP which is as much more powerful than acid as acid is than grass.

Each time I adjusted myself in the seat I felt the baggy of purple acid tabs I carried in my underwear. Tim and I were roommates of convenience in the Haight-Ashbury who became friends and partners in a small dealing business. That meant we had a full and eclectic dope drawer and what was in it we either took ourselves, gave away, or, when we needed money, sold. The purpose of this trip was to sell our excess acid in LA.

I noticed the muted distant trilling of an alarm bell in my nerves. It was left over from a trucker's cafe now miles behind us where we had nudged the latent lynch mob in rural California. As I would learn in similar encounters that summer and afterwards:

when the adrenalin drains the fear surfaces. I let out a boulder-heave of a sigh.

The whole episode had been like that long moment at the beginning of a car accident when you're not yet sure how serious it is, and, if it isn't bad, whether you can enjoy it. Except this time, instead of two or three seconds, it lasted a fast meal.

We had spotted the trucker's cafe around 2:00 AM, just below Gilroy, a small town an hour and a half south of San Francisco. The LSD and the STP were still at full strength. I was lying on the back seat looking up through the sucking rear window lost in the stars. Rob was driving. Tim was riding shotgun.

In the parking lot, eight or ten mammoth trucks, like sleeping chrome dinosaurs, were parked in a couple loose rows. Rob pulled up next to one and our beat old '53 Chevy wasn't much above the trucks' fender level.

We got out, as if from a packing crate, unwrapped, unfolded, and stretched. Then we walked toward the café. The gravel was sharp and lights suspended from tall poles glinted off the chrome like flashbulbs. Gradually, as we approached the door, we realized where we were going. Then Rob had pulled back the screen door and I was opening the wooden one.

The Haight-Ashbury District of San Francisco was something of a frontier fortress at that time, July 1967. Tim and Rob and I had abandoned its safety and launched out into a dangerous primeval unknown. It was reflexive long ago to be on guard outside the Haight, but now, after the recent months-long global eruption of publicity about "hippies," it was common to have people stare and point you out on the street. Rob had shoulder-length reddish hair, Tim's dark brown hair was down to his collar, and my black hair was just short of my shoulders. Plus, after an hour and a half of lying on the back seat, my hair was armpit-scraggly.

We were accompanied into the restaurant by a gust of mild night wind that, somehow, turned eight or ten truckers into ice sculptures. Not one spoke the entire time we were in their presence.

The acid and STP curdled as we walked to the end of the counter closest to the door. We sat on revolving padded stools, plucked plastic menus from behind a napkin dispenser, and

pretended to read. A shriveled old Chinese guy shuffled up and waited silently for our order.

"Uh, I'll have a bowl of clam chowder," I said.

"I'll have a grilled cheese sandwich," Tim said.

"Bowl of chowder," Rob said.

"Coffee?" the waiter asked.

"Yeah."

"Yeah."

"Yeah."

The waiter left. We folded and reinserted the menus. Loud silence. I was in the middle, Tim was on the end, and on the other side of Rob the rest of the counter was empty. Each of us casually shot an over-the-shoulder half-glance around the room. Experienced eyes registered mild disgust to tense outrage. Most of the truckers resumed eating, a couple though were transfixed by us. We meanwhile were studying the counter top. I was still stoned enough to drift off into the formica pattern.

One trucker with a greased whorl of brown hair and a dented nose was so bug-eyed with rage it looked as if he might shoot us with his eyeballs. Clearly, it was one thing to cluck and curse these bold new perverts when they were on TV or in the newspapers, but it was something else again having them right there in front of you.

The bug-eyed one left his table and joined us at the counter, turning his stool, three down from Rob, to skewer us on his glare. He looked like he was in the presence of three people who had just shitted on his mother's grave then wiped their asses with an American flag. He was wiry and short, while each of us was over six feet, but he was tensed to spring and oblivious. There was no doubt about sympathies in the rest of the room.

Normally, I might have made a hollow show of defiance but I couldn't on acid. Though I did surprise myself by how easily and firmly the sober driver wrested control of the wheel. There was a head-on collision anyway between ecstasy and murderous hostility.

By the time the food and coffee arrived, I felt like someone with St. Vitus' Dance neck deep in concrete.

"I don't think I can eat," I said quietly, staring into my bowl of chowder.

"Why?" Rob asked.

"The vibes. They've taken my appetite away."

"Ignore it," he said and shoveled in a spoonful of chowder.

He was a merchant seaman and months at sea with crews interchangeable with these truckers had hardened him to bigot hostility. Tim had faced even worse rednecks while in the Congress of Racial Equality in the South during Freedom Summer of '64. Though I was nineteen, five or six years younger than them, I had grown up in a redneck Sierra mill town. So, we weren't novices.

Nevertheless, we ate as fast as we could. I forced myself to taste the soup and was glad of it. It felt good against the lingering chill of the car. Still, there was no enjoying it. Each spoonful had to be slow and controlled to avoid spooking the bug-eyed cat down the counter.

Finally, we finished, got up, and walked, as if under water, to the cash register. I didn't think about being the first, I just somehow moved faster than Tim and Rob. They stood around while I paid my bill. Then I stood by them as they paid. I was a little embarrassed for being first to the cash register.

Rob paid last and then led us out. This was the last chance for bug-eyes and the others, which made it a remarkably long thirty feet or so, but we eventually reached the door and passed through it.

We all vented at the same time, after we were safely across the parking lot and getting in the car.

"Christ…"

"Did you see that guy down the counter…"

"And that fat guy in the corner, when we first came in, with his mouth open, full of food…"

"Shit…"

"I thought for sure we were gonna get jumped…"

"Me too…"

"Fucking rednecks…"

"Chowder was good…"

If none of us was particularly heroic in that café, Tim was nevertheless a hero to me. He had been driven out of the South by Klan threats and was a veteran of the only war that mattered. Rob was the former shipmate of one of our neighbors. His most

impressive accomplishment was smuggling five pounds of hash through twenty borders. He was so relaxed his arms hung down like empty sleeves. I particularly relished an expression he got as if everything he was witnessing was an unnatural phenomenon. I thought of him as a purebred existential man, resigned to the Absurd, and I liked and respected him immensely.

And that's why I was so surprised and then hurt when he suddenly attacked me. Though the effect of the drugs was declining, if three psychedelicized minds are locked up together in a shooting metal box for hours at a stretch, well....

Tim was driving. Rob was at shotgun. I was in the back again but sitting up. The radio didn't work so except for gray engine drone there was a long ruminant silence. From the sleeping bags, we watched exit signs file through the headlight beam: Salinas, Soledad, King City, Paso Robles, Atascadero, Nipomo, Lompoc.

"Hey, didjyou see that?!" Rob asked, breaking the silence.

"Yeah," I said.

Tim roused and asked, "What? What did you see?"

"A sign back there," I said.

"Yeah, it said, 'Correctional Facility, Keep Right,' " Rob added, awed.

There was a suspended moment when nobody explained or commented.

Then I said, "The right that isn't right...that suppresses the right...that can't get it right...right?"

They laughed. I saw it as an opportunity to vent philosophical insights roiling in my brain. I was a philosophy major and my guiding passion, second only to sex itself, was philosophical debate. I was still only a couple years out of the intellectual desert of that redneck mill town. (Where there was the unmistakably communicated sense that there was something indefinably wrong with me).

"Ya know... I've been sitting back here thinking... and ya know what is the key insight, the bedrock insight, the rock of ages if you will, of all philosophical traditions?"

"No, what?" Tim said absently. He had limited interest in philosophy but he would put up with my babble and even listen on occasion. Rob was silent.

"The identity of opposites."

"Hmmm..." Tim said.

"Of course, it's the key insight of Taoism but it's everywhere. God and the Devil are just Yin and Yang broken out of the shell. Now Nagarjuna says..."

Rob suddenly turned around in his seat and demanded of me, "Look!" His left index finger was poking an indentation into the vinyl on the top of the front seat. "There's you." Then the right index finger poked an indentation a foot or so away. "And there is what *is*. And... and nothin'... you say *about* it... matters man!"

Tim and I were startled, not just by the act but also its vehemence. Neither of us spoke. Rob turned to face the road. I decided to shelve Nargarjuna for a while.

Then, moving us on, Tim asked me, "You didn't tell me what happened with Natasha last night..."

He had deftly chosen a guaranteed distraction. I leaned forward, and, on the back of the front seat, crossed my arms and rested my chin on them and sighed. She was my first passion, as opposed to lust, in months. Fantasies about her would be the soundtrack to this trip.

"Not so good," I said. "Actually... it was a disaster."

"Oh... Didn't you say you were 'in love' with her?"

"Yeah, I'm...I'm...knocked down, but I'm not out yet. We had a bizarre... misunderstanding... I still have hope to..."

Suddenly Rob turned toward me and snapped his fingers, twice, inches in front of my face. Then he turned back and stared at the road.

I was shocked and intimidated. What was I doing? I had no idea. It had to be something in my voice. We didn't even have eye contact. I leaned back and shrank into the seat and then into myself and stayed silent. But it didn't do any good.

Within a few minutes, Rob turned around in his seat and looked me in the eyes, then loud and hard, clapped his hands, once, inches from my nose.

"Knock it off!" he growled. "You're trying to get into my head, man. Knock it off."

I was stunned and flustered. It was long seconds before I could mumble, "I don't know what you're talking about."

"We have to remember," Tim interjected, "we're all stoned and tired and we're cooped up in this car. There're bound to be... clashes."

"Yeah," Rob agreed, then turned around and faced the road again. "Yeah. I'm sorry man. It's just... three cats in a car... on STP... I'm sorry man."

"That's O.K." I said.

But it wasn't O.K. There I was again doing something, I didn't know what, that was causing trouble. What could it be? I took off on a jag of frenzied self-analysis. Then I remembered a monkey.

A couple weeks before, on an outing to the zoo with friends, I had just joined the crowd in front of the monkey cage when a monkey leapt from a corner and, hanging by an arm from the wire mesh ceiling, swung low over a brimming water tub, dragged a few fingers on the surface, and with a screech, shot the foul water through the bars into my face.

Was I inherently repellant on some animal level? Now, in the back seat, I was free-falling through the void, not the liberating one of the Zen masters but that of acid depression, and it was worse in its way than the fear in the truckers' café. I was locked in a skid. I reached out and gripped the armrests at both ends of the backseat and held on as if we were taking a sharp turn too fast, though the car was on a straight away.

Summer of '66

One night, I arrived home and looked up to see on our roof man-sized flames, twisting and jabbing at the sky.

I ran to the open window of our illegal basement apartment, pulled back the bedspread that served as the curtain, and yelled, "The fucking building is on fire!   Call the fire department!"

Then I thought of the Negro family in the illegal attic apartment. I ran down the passageway under the building, emerged into the backyard, and ran up the back stairs, heart pounding in my throat. On the stairs I met a Negro man coming down in his underwear carrying a frightened little girl, his wife and son were in bathrobes behind him.

"You O.K.?!" I shouted over the fire roar.

The man nodded.

"Everybody down from there?!" I asked and was ignored.

He kept going followed by his family. I turned around and bounded down the stairs behind them, glancing at the shifting light that the flames on the roof threw onto the weedy back yard. Then I remembered we didn't have a phone. But I heard a siren anyway. I thought about warning the landlord and his family who lived between the attic and basement apartments then remembered they were out of town.

"Put everything in that tan Pontiac across the street," Francine instructed as she came out of our door with arms full of clothes.

Seconds later, as I approached the Pontiac with arms full of sheets and blankets, the first fire engine stopped with a brake squeal, siren wail tapering off like an unplugged phonograph. Then another truck arrived, then another. Bystanders collected on the sidewalk. The negro family stood in blankets among them.

A few more trips and we had all of Ralph and Francine's clothes and records and other valuables in the car.

.   "Did you get my pea coat?" Francine asked Ralph. "And my paintings on the kitchen wall?"

He nodded. "Yeah, they're all in here," he said.

She and I and Ralph were standing beside the car.

"Let's not bother with my stuff. It isn't even worth the effort," I said, boasting about the disposability of my estate. "Hey, who's car?"

"Mine. I bought it today," Francine said.

"I thought you were broke," I said.

Firemen hooked up one end of a hose to a hydrant and carried the other end through the open front door of the owner's unit and up a stairway to the fire, which could be heard snapping lumber and smashing windows.

"Remember when I got raped?" Francine asked. "Well, they caught the guys. I went down to the police station and identified them. They've raped a whole bunch o' chicks. Anyway, one of 'em is German. He just immigrated here. His mother said he just... fell in with a bad crowd. He was the one who couldn't get it up. She offered me five hundred dollars not to press charges. So I took it."

"Oh," I said and pondered for a moment the moral ramifications. Then I asked, "Hey, where's Mike?"

"I dunno," Francine said.

Ralph shrugged, lost in watching the firemen.

Mike

On my first morning in that illegal basement apartment, I woke up and looked across the room at my new roommate and

was startled. He was huge with the curly red mop of Harpo Marx and the bulbous nose of W.C. Fields, which he snored through in fitful hog-snorts. His right hand was bandaged.

He weighed over two hundred and thirty pounds and was about six feet seven inches tall. Whenever standing in that basement apartment he had to cant his head to the side. Yet he was very sensitive, with small wispydelicate handwriting. He also had a cobra-quick wit and nearly total recall. He had quit high school in Vancouver and joined the merchant marines, and by the time I met him, when still in his early twenties, he had already been on all the habitable continents.

He was Chandler Hampton Crawley III, poet and communist.

"But we just call him Mike," Francine explained in the kitchen after I got up and while he was still sleeping.

My freshman year of college had just ended and an apprenticeship under Mike was beginning. Actually, our friendship had a rough start, because I was gullible and willing to believe any evidence of the insanity of society and Mike was an incorrigible prankster.

"In another week or so it's going to be Eskimo hunting season," he casually mentioned one evening in his resonant baritone.

We were home alone reading, he in the recliner and me on the couch, with the Stones' new album *Aftermath* playing.

"What?" I asked, not sure I had heard all that was said.

"Eskimo hunting season. In Alaska."

I looked at him blankly, processing the comment.

"Don't you know about that?"

Did he mean when Eskimos start their seasonal hunting?

"Christ, Americans are a bunch of children. Every year oil barons and corporate executives and cats like that go up there and hunt Eskimos from helicopters."

"Are you kidding? I don't believe *that*."

"Sure, man, everybody in Canada knows about it. The authorities in Alaska don't care. It makes it easier for them to take the land. It's called 'recreational genocide'."

"My God! That's incredible," I said and put down Jean Genet's *Thief's Journal.* "Well... if the federal government won't do anything then... the United Nations should step in... or someone."

"Most imperialist empires are founded on genocide," Mike said. "Alaska is just a hold out of the old frontier spirit. Dontcha know what kinda injun is the only good injun?"

"My God " I slapped my forehead.

Eventually I caught on.

And then there was the night of the fire, when I decided to look for Mike and left Francine and Ralph watching the firemen. I squeezed through spectators, jumped over hoses, and crunched glass, going back into the apartment. He wasn't in the livingroom or the kitchen or our bedroom. But when I pushed open the bathroom door, there he was squatting beside the tub which was half full of water, the faucet shooting in more. He smiled up and said hi.

Then he scooped a large pot into the tub and tossed the water into the maw of the airshaft window. Through it, I could see a roaring cyclone of trapped fire. Shards of the blackened window glass were scattered on the white tile floor. I started to help him then caught myself. Uh oh, Eskimo hunting season again? This was obviously futile.

Mike tossed the pot into the water and shut off the spigot. As I started toward the door, he produced a joint from a breast pocket and held it up to me. A test of cool? I accepted the challenge.

"Wanna hear a poem I wrote the other day?" he asked then stepped over to the window. "It's an epic."

"Sure."

Small flames writhed on the sill. He touched a flame with the joint. Upstairs sounded like a gymnasium for poltergeists.

"Ready?" he asked. He held the joint before his mouth, toked, and then, handing it to me, held-in the toke while he said, "It's called *San Francisco.* 'Lots of wind in lots of hair'."

"Very good. I like it," I said and took my toke and held it as I added, "Iambic pentameter, isn't it?"

And that was when a jet of water hit the bottom of the airshaft spewing dense black smoke and large flakes of ash and

spattering hot gray mud on the white bathroom and Mike and I. We left. Water was dripping from every crack in the ceiling and trickling down all the walls. Ahead of the water down the kitchen walls cockroaches skittered in the broken lines of routed cavalry.

A couple of firemen entered the livingroom at the same time as Mike and I. The firemen, in yellow rubber suits and fire helmets, looked around at the shabby furnishings, barely able to conceal their disgust. They were in the lair of alien life forms. Cautious nods were exchanged.

"Nothing's burning down here," I said. "Just the airshaft. It's back there." I pointed the way to the bathroom.

The firemen left the livingroom. Then two others appeared at the front door and scanned the room with morbid fascination. The first two returned and one said to the second two, "There's nothing down here," as he and his partner passed between the second two who then left also. Mike and I joined Ralph and Francine across the street.

Hanging Out

Nevertheless, Mike and I shared a passion for literature that became the basis of a friendship such that he would one day show me his proudest possession: a letter of reply to a letter he sent to Norman Mailer. It was just a few paragraphs complimenting Mike on some points he made about Mailer's essay collection *Advertisements for Myself*.

After Mike finished reading it, I stared at Mailer's letter and in hushed awe said, " 'The White Negro...' " That was the title of Mailer's most influential essay, the classic exposition of hip, making him the Aquinas of Hip.

Mike patiently answered my endless questions about drugs, slang, and hip mores, plus he introduced me to some indispensable books: William Burroughs' *Junkie*, Jean Genet's *Thief's Journal* and *Our Lady of the Flowers*, George Orwell's *Down and Out In and Paris and London*, Jean Cocteau's *Opium*, and other explorers' journals.

Burroughs descended to "rolling lushes," robbing passed-out drunks on the subway, while Genet descended to mugging beggars. Like Genet, Burroughs was a homosexual, but more than

Genet, Burroughs was also a junky. We celebrated and read together the literary event of that summer, Burroughs' *Naked Lunch* in paperback. Only a couple years before it had to be smuggled into the country.

Throughout that summer, Mike and I practiced that grand old folk art, refined in village squares for millennia, hanging out.

The day began by eating whatever was available and smoking the previous night's roaches. After that everything was in slow motion, as if performed underwater. Appointments and errands took hours to prepare for and even then we were invariably late. We passed languorous, stoned afternoons with our feet on the sill of the open livingroom window, warmed by the sun, cooled by the breeze, entertained by the negro kids playing on the sidewalk. Meanwhile the tinny scratchy portable phonograph played Dylan or the Beatles or Miles Davis or the Stones and we caressed each note as it drifted by.

Or we might read or Mike would write poetry or I would draw or we might just engage in a little intellectual whittling. We were both connoisseurs of outrage, anything to goose the tight-assed puritans. But ideas that Mike relished because they were crackpot, I tended to take seriously.

"All through your childhood," I said one day, "you have these civil defense drills. Once a month or so you crouch down under your school desk and practice the end of the world. Of course, this is supposed to have no psychological effect on you at all. Those assholes."

"I have a new stand on nuclear disarmament," Mike said. "Everybody knows it's hopeless, even Bertrand Russell gave up. So, I've gone the other way. I think we should have pocket-sized, transistorized doomsday machines. They should be free to anyone, all over the world. Any moment the whole planet could be turned into a smoking cinder, so every second that it didn't happen would seem like a miracle."

"I have the answer to all of America's sex problems," I announced another day. "There is this contrived mystery based on ignorance about the body of the opposite sex. Now puberty is the most crucial phase of sexual development, right? So, we have to have co-ed shower rooms in junior high schools. It's the only way."

"Mailer says in 'The White Negro' that southern crackers have a better idea of what's really at stake in integration than northern liberals," Mike said with a smile another day. "That's a good point. You can always trust reactionaries to know what to fear. You could make it a policy standard. Whatever they fear most you advocate most."

"Yeah. . . Yeah!" I said, ignited by the idea. "Then, then we should advocate miscegenation. I mean there should be organizations that do nothing but push it. It's obvious the trend of history is toward world unity, a blending of all races and nationalities ... Yeah ... Yeah, there should be special tax breaks for interracial couples . . ."

Conversations usually weren't as lofty when Ralph and Francine were around. Topics then might be drug allusions that had snuck by the public in popular songs, or the latest fluctuations in the drug market, or have the Beatles smoked grass, or does the lipstick and fingernail polish Dylan is wearing on the cover of *Highway 61 Revisited* mean he is gay?

And when Francine and Ralph were around, when the four of us were in the livingroom together, there was a noticeable tension. Besides being my mentor and roommate, Mike was also Francine's spurned lover. He was hanging around in stupefied disbelief that she preferred Ralph (who he considered a dolt) and waiting for her to come to her senses. I never got the full extent of Mike and Francine's relationship, whether they just slept together a few times or actually lived together for a while. I didn't feel comfortable asking either one of them about it.

Mike's frustration no doubt contributed to his general irascibility. There was enough passion on his end so that it all culminated in an argument, before I arrived, in which Mike put his fist through a panel in the glass door of the bathroom. Hence the bandage on his hand. He was certainly love-gored, and more even than that, he seemed to be railing against the deformity of his brute, oafish appearance.

With dimples and an overbite and perfect features framed in straight black hair, Francine was undeniably pretty, probably the prettiest girl he had ever had. And I could see how she would be attracted to his wit and personality, at least for a while.

Francine

She and I grew-up in and fled the same redneck Sierra mill town, so she was one of my oldest closest friends. Nevertheless, when I stood outside the door of her Waller Street pad the night before that morning I first saw Mike, I was desperate and anxious and uncertain.

She had invited me to move in when I visited about six months before, but I hadn't seen her in those six months and suppose she had forgotten the invitation or now didn't have enough room? School had ended and I couldn't afford my own apartment, and the only alternative was going back among the rednecks, which I couldn't possibly do, even just for the summer.

So, standing between two apartment buildings in a deep narrow passageway that funneled the sea wind, I knocked on Francine's door.

She swung it open and I timidly said, "Hi."

"Hi!" she yelled, a smile instantly replacing a scowl. "What's happenin' man?" She hugged me, and then as we parted said, "C'mon in."

I followed her in, reassured somewhat by the smile and the hug.

"I would have called but you don't have a phone," I said. "Classes ended at St. Crispin's weeks ago and everybody left and I've been sort of … camped out in my old dorm room."

We were standing in the livingroom, its white walls lit by a bare bulb in a ceiling inches above my head.

"No shit?" she asked with a laugh as she sat in a creaking, threadbare recliner chair. "They let you do that?"

"Not exactly," I said, sitting on the swaybacked sofa. "But nobody's said anything… It's weird."

"Maybe they don't have a rule against it because nobody's done it before," she said delighted with the irony.

"Yeah… maybe. Anyway, I have to leave. There's going to be a convention or something. A groundskeeper told me yesterday. Any day now I'm going to be surrounded by hundreds of nuns."

She laughed her signature whinny and repeated, "*Nuns?!*"

Hanging over a doorway opposite the front door was a bedspread that parted and a short, drowsy guy with tousled brown hair emerged and stopped, staring at me.

Francine introduced him as Ralph.

"We went to school together," she told him about me. Then she added, "He's moving in."

Ralph and I shook hands, him grinning uncertainly, me gushing relief and gratitude.

"So you grew up together?" Ralph asked me.

"Yeah," I said.

He seemed to relax. He had probably been wondering whether I was yet another cast off lover he had to contend with, but, two years older than me, Francine was the older sister I never had and I the younger brother she never had. She was also a spoiled adopted only child with iron whimsy, and, like a younger brother, I had been ambushed often by her foul moods. But we had been close friends immediately and ever since with an effortless rapport. She had a defiant, mischievous iconoclasm and was always quick to laugh.

"We were the resident weirdos of Tuolumne High School," she said as if reading a trophy inscription.

"We met at Twain-Harte Elementary School...in the band..." I said.

"Yeah..." she said. "What did you play?"

"The clarinet."

"That's right."

"And you played the tympani drums... about two feet behind my head."

"Yeah," she said with a grin and then suddenly a distasteful memory surfaced in a scowl. She hated the place too, another of our bonds.

After a pause, Ralph looked up at me and said, "That's... that's groovy."

I took note of *groovy*. I was hearing it with increasing frequency.

"C'mon, I'll show you your room," Francine said as she stood up.

The only other time I had been in the apartment, I hadn't gone beyond the livingroom. I followed her into the kitchen where there was another single bare bulb in the center of a low ceiling. She pulled the light string and said, "Kitchen." The walls were glossy, loud yellow. The dirty dishes in the sink provided an aerial view of a cockroach metropolis during an air raid. We continued into a dank, fetid, windowless room. Francine pulled the string to that bulb but the light seemed only slightly to dispel the darkness, perhaps an effect of the damp gray concrete walls.

"Bed," she said.

We were standing beside an old-fashioned iron bed-frame conspicuously missing a mattress.

"You'll need a mattress," she added.

"I have one in the back seat," I said. She looked at me, surprised. "I stole it from St. Crispin's, just in case."

I noticed an open door at the opposite end of the room, and Francine said, "That's the bathroom."

I walked over to the door, which was sectioned translucent glass with a missing pane at chest height. Beyond the door, an old fashioned bathtub rested on its knuckles. Beyond that, the toilet sat beside a window onto an airshaft with deep debris. Then as I left the bathroom, I saw, around a corner from my new bedroom, Francine's bed and dresser. That was the bedroom Ralph had first entered the livingroom from. I now had the layout of the place: the thin, single-board walls of the livingroom and kitchen were surrounded by a basement, and they were lovers.

A Kids' Secret Clubhouse

I was moving from an adolescent bedroom adrift at St. Crispin's to a kids' secret clubhouse in the Haight.

Carrying-in boxes of records and books and clothes, I passed several times through the livingroom, which was furnished with cullings from Francine's previous apartments and from furniture left on the sidewalks. The kitchenware was stolen from restaurants and cafeterias. Noticeably absent was a television.

Dylan's new album, *Blond On Blond*, played on the portable record player on the floor. Francine was in the old recliner. Ralph sat in the lotus position on the couch with the dual album

cover open on his lap. He was emptying grass from a baggy into the crevice.

I put the last box on the floor and shut the door and asked Francine, "How is it?"

"Huh?"

"The album. I haven't listened to it all yet."

"Oh. Fantastic! ... Beautiful."

"How're the lyrics?"

"I don't know. I haven't gotten there yet. I'm just digging the beauty of the music."

I sat on the couch and joined Francine in watching Ralph pick seeds and stems from the grass while listening to "Leopard-Skin Pill-Box Hat."

Suddenly she said "Oh! I almost forgot to tell you! I got married!"

"You're kidding!" I said.

"No."

"Congratulations," I said to Ralph.

"Not to Ralph," she said, amused, "to Larry. He was my ol' man. He said it would help him get out of the Army. But it didn't. He's in the army now and he's trying all kindsa shit to get out. He even went to one of their shrinks on acid the other day... We thought getting married would make him feel better and maybe help him get out somehow ... Anyway I didn't see how it could hurt anything, so... we got married."

"Oh."

"He kept telling me about his best friend Ralph," she said looking lovingly at him "... and how groovy he was and all that..."

"He gave her such a good sales pitch that she bought the product," Ralph said, proud of the line.

"We were both visiting Larry at the same time, down at Fort Ord," she continued. "And we tried to hitch back together, but we couldn't get a ride, and it was late, and then it started to rain, so we got a motel room... Can you believe they were in a military academy together?"

"Wow, what was that like?" I asked Ralph.

He thought for a moment then said, "I'm not sure. I was stoned the whole time."

"He was queer before I got hold of him," she boasted as if he were a Rembrandt found in a thrift store.

He grinned at me sheepishly and gave an apologetic shrug. I returned the grin. I didn't care about his sexual denomination.

"What does Larry say?" I asked her.

"About what?"

"About you and Ralph."

"Oh...I dunno... I haven't told him yet."

There was a long ruminant silence. *Blonde on Blonde* ended and Ralph gingerly placed the album cover with a small mound of cleaned grass and a larger mound of seeds and stems onto the overflowing coffee table. Then he got up and went to the record player.

"What's your draft status?" Ralph asked me suddenly and bluntly.

"Huh? ... Oh, I'm still a student. I've got a deferment ... or ... well ... I had one." I exchanged a glance with Francine. "I lost my scholarship to St. Crispin's..."

She knew about my parents crowing pride in my scholarship. I considered it the first installment in compensation for having a freak for a son. But obsessive reading got in the way of my education and the scholarship starved on Cs and Ds. In the Sierras, the closest we had to a bookstore was a revolving rack with paperbacks in a bait-and-liquor store. Then I was released into the bookstores of Berkeley.

"I don't know yet if I've been accepted at San Francisco State," I said to Ralph. His worried expression told me his draft status. I added, "Actually, that's the only reason I'm in school."

"Yeah, school's a drag," Francine said.

Ralph lowered the phonograph needle onto the Rolling Stones' *Aftermath* and the room filled with the ragtime intro to "Flight Number 505."

"Yeah, school is a waste," I concurred.

Ralph returned to the couch and the lotus position and then gingerly placed the album cover back on his lap.

"American schools should be banned by the United Nations," I said. "Really. I'm just putting in my time. I've either

already read or will read on my own everything they assign. And that sports shit..."

I was working myself into one of my tirades. Francine and I had had variants of this conversation for years.

"It's just training in how to be part of an organized mob. Love your country. Be true to your school. Be loyal to your row in study hall. What's the fucking difference? I think you have three choices in life, and school is relevant to only one of them. You can become a businessman, put your mind in formaldehyde. You can go into a monastery and become a Trappist or a Buddhist monk. Or you can become a criminal."

Ralph deftly sprinkled a pinch of cleaned grass into a trough of wheat-straw rolling-papers resting between his extended forefinger and thumb.

"What's your choice?" Francine asked, amused by my earnestness.

"I'm going to combine the last two. I'll violate every inhibition I have and every taboo they have. I'll wallow in everything repulsive, degenerate, and immoral. I'll become a... drooling, mangy pervert." I was gaining momentum now. "Like a dried up turd you kick out of your way on the sidewalk, I'll be so low I'll be outside the social spectrum. Humanity dips toward the center. When I'm farthest from their values, their reality," I gestured toward outside, "then I'll be free and near the truth."

"Be yourself," Ralph chirped.

"That's not a choice," I snapped. "You are yourself every instant you're alive."

Ralph shrugged and then licked the tapered ends of a joint and handed it to Francine. I knew I had taken a mollifying suggestion as if it were a serious philosophical proposition, but I was worked up. And besides, I was a philosophy major.

Francine lit the joint then asked me, "Have you smoked grass before?"

While I spoke, I studied her holding it between thumb and forefinger before the oval of her lips, sucking its tip red.

"Yeah, a bunch of times, but I've never felt high from it," I said. "I took acid *before* I smoked grass."

She said, holding in the toke, "Oh... that's ... weird."

She handed me the joint trailing an undulant ribbon of smoke.

"The first time I smoked it was at the first Fillmore dance," I said.

Anxious to get the effect this time, I sucked the harsh dry smoke deep, and then immediately coughed it out, jerking spasmodically.

"Slower. Do it slower," Francine cautioned. "Don't take so much in. Try it again."

When the coughing stopped, I more carefully imitated Francine and drew in a small amount of smoke and held it and then exhaled.

"How was that?" Francine asked. "The first Fillmore Dance. I wasn't in town for it."

"It was really something... I went with some friends from St. Crispin's... There was a double line a block long out front ... and there were these musicians carrying in their instruments, the, uh, Warlocks . . . I never saw shoulder length hair on a guy before. I thought, Jesus, these guys probably can't go outside in the day time or they'd get arrested."

I suddenly remembered that I was holding the joint and handed it to Ralph.

"The hall was like a musty old attic. But huge. Even the, uh, mezzanine was big. It had a snack bar... There were these big signs on the walls saying 'LOVE' and stuff like that... The stage was at one end with beat out old couches and stuffed chairs around it and there was this huge cloudbank of smoke in the middle of the hall... And the light over the stage was like . . . well, with the cigarette smoke drifting through it... and the darkness pressed against it, it was kinda like the light over a backroom poker game, or something else that had to take place in a backroom."

Ralph exhaled a toke and then handed the joint to Francine.

I laughed at a memory and said, "I was standing next to some Negroes... and we were all laughing at the way people were dancing... so gawky and awkward... more like calisthenics... Oh, and the clothes... really, they were more like costumes. Some of the guys had long hair and wore fringed buckskins and the girls

wore old clothes that maybe they borrowed from their grandmothers or something. They were yippin' and hootin' and whoopin' like at a hoedown. That's what it was like, a rock n' roll hoedown."

Francine expelled a toke and handed me the joint and I held it in my hand as I said, "It wasn't like a public dance. I mean, you know, anybody could pay their buck fifty and walk in. But it was more like a party. Like the annual convention of a secret society. I kept thinking, who are these people? Where are they hiding out? How can I join 'em? When it was over, all I could think about was when is the next one?"

"Hey man, don't Bogart the joint," Ralph advised with a nod at it.

"Oh," I said and took a quick but careful toke and handed it to him.

"What time was it over?" Francine asked.

I exhaled and said, "I dunno. We left around six in the morning and it was still goin' strong. Everybody was giddy and sweaty and slaphappy... It was the night before Christmas vacation too... When I went back among the rednecks it was like... like... coming from another planet..."

"It's not easssaaaay..." Jagger crooned and Ralph handed off to Francine.

I broke a long silence with, "We smoked grass in the car, before we went in, but I didn't feel anything... " Then, as I watched Francine sucking the joint tip red again, I said to myself out loud, "Ooohhh, I see . . ."

I had just identified the grass high. Everything was in sharp focus, flexing a new dimension. I had expected to be, as I had been during LSD, skydiving in my seat, instead this felt so... subtle and light...

"Ya know," I said. "Its... it's like... after you put on the special glasses at a 3-D movie..."

Larry

One night in the middle of the summer, Francine came home and announced that she had just been raped. Ralph and I stood up.

After a stunned pause, I asked delicately, "Are you O.K.?"

"Yeah, they didn't hurt me."

She slumped down on the couch. Ralph sat beside her. She took his hand. The toilet flushed and I searched for something to say during the time it took Mike to reach the livingroom. He looked at Francine and Ralph, then at me.

"She got raped," I said.

Silence, while he absorbed it.

"Can we do anything for ya?" Mike asked. "Can we get you something?"

"No... I was down at the beach watching the sunset. I hitched a ride back with these two cats on motorcycles. We stopped in the park and they pulled a knife and told me to strip..."

"Did you go to the police?" I asked.

"Yeah. I'm going back down to the police station tomorrow."

We felt like we should be dressing a wound. But it wasn't physical.

She got up and walked toward the kitchen saying quietly but not facing us, "It wasn't that big of a deal. One of 'em couldn't even get it up." Then she entered the kitchen and called, "Anybody else want tea?"

Meanwhile, every few days a letter arrived from Larry, her husband. Seeing the shrink on acid hadn't worked so his next ploy was swallowing a bottle of sleeping pills. But that didn't work either. She still hadn't told him about her relationship with Ralph. I didn't bring it up because it wasn't my business and I was afraid of getting bitten. After every letter, Francine was sullen for a while and seemed about to write to him but then would get stoned or go on a lark with Ralph.

Once they met me at the bus stop on my way home from work with Francine in a supermarket shopping cart that Ralph was pushing. Another time I walked into the apartment and found them

holding open the front of each other's pants and sprinkling talcum in and giggling.

"We shaved off our pubic hair," Francine said. "We got crabs."

"What's that?" I asked.

"You don't know what crabs are? You'll find out."

Then a letter arrived that she had to share with us. She and Mike and I were in the livingroom. Ralph was in the kitchen.

"It didn't work," Mike said from the recliner chair as she opened the letter, sitting beside me on the couch. "Or he'd be here instead of the letter."

"What didn't work?" I asked. "Seeing the army shrink on acid?"

"No, we already know that didn't work," he said, watching her silently read the letter. "He said he was going to slash his wrists."

"Yeah, that's what he did. And it didn't work," she said then continued silently reading the rest of the letter. Eventually she put the letter down, sighed deeply, and said, "His unit goes to Vietnam soon... and he says he's going to go AWOL... and come up here and get me and we'll go to Canada together."

"Shit!" I said. "When?"

"He's not sure. It could be any day... or weeks."

"Fuck."

Ralph stood in the doorway of the kitchen exchanging glances with Francine. He shrugged and looked down.

There was a ruminant silence, and then Mike suddenly leapt from the recliner and angrily spat, "What a fuckin' soap opera!"

He opened the front door and added, "And a couple weeks after you leave, the FBI will be here!"

The door slammed behind him. I noticed the bandage was gone from his hand.

So now, the days passed waiting for a knock on the door.

Amy

In the meantime, we had to pay the rent. That was $65 a month, and on the day it was due, everyone put in whatever money they had and Francine took it upstairs to the landlord.

Three times a night, two nights a week, she "volunteered" from the audience then went to work as an "amateur" topless dancer. Ralph got an allowance from his rich parents. Mike worked at The Blue Unicorn, the first Haight coffeehouse. The little I had saved from garden work in the suburbs around St. Crispin's was gone by mid July, so I was forced to get a part time job as a file clerk for an insurance company, from 9 a.m. to 1 p.m. five days a week. That meant a haircut. I started growing my hair long before I ever heard of hippies or beatniks for that matter. The fad started by the Beatles just gave my natural slovenliness an excuse. Outside the Haight, long hair first symbolized nothing more than slob and/or queer, as I learned when I visited my parents in that redneck mill town. Shock, anger, and then taunts. By the time I applied for the job, long hair was starting to be recognized as part of some sort of uniform, still only local but vaguely threatening.

Among chicks in the Haight, male hair-length established rank, which was driven home to me one afternoon when my friend Howie took me to a garage that had been converted into an apartment, sort of. It was on Lyon Street just below Haight Street and, as usual, while Howie knocked on the door, I stood behind him, shyness compounded by self-consciousness about my file clerk costume.

A skinny frizzy blond let us in. There were two double beds and three couches taking up most of the floor space. There were no windows. Five very attractive young women lounged about, languidly discussing musicians. In another couple years, they would be known as "groupies," priestesses providing fellatio for rock idols.

Howie left the room for a few minutes with the frizzy blond. The room was lit by a couple lamps and I stood in the shadows against the wall by a console phonograph heaped with records the sheaths of which were scattered about the room. None of the girls noticed me, or if they did, they didn't consider me worth acknowledging in my slacks and short hair. One of them was in a slip and another had the front of her jeans unbuttoned displaying a white triangle of underwear. When they moved their arms for lethargic gestures I could tell by the jiggle of their breasts under their shirts that they weren't wearing bras.

Mysterious, self-contained, and awesomely blasé, they were discussing musicians with the same tone of conspiracy and cold appraisal that I had heard girls talked about in shower rooms for years. I knew there were girls like these and Francine all over Haight-Ashbury. They weren't shaving their legs or armpits, had doffed girdles and bras, and were getting comfortable in public. They didn't give a damn about the wobble under their clothes. They were throwing away what men everywhere were trying to steal.

And they had black lovers. Francine had had several. It was the litmus test for hip. No truly hip white chick would reject a black man solely because he was black, and no hip white cat would think less of a chick because she had had a black lover.

Howie returned with the frizzy blond and we left. I couldn't even imagine one of those sirens desiring me or what I would do if one did. They were roughly my own age though seemingly years more sophisticated.

Three particularly attractive ones shared the illegal basement apartment of a building next to ours. I embarrassed myself in front of one of them one night in our living room when she chatted with Francine while watching out the window for a date to arrive. She herself had boy-short brown hair and wore a miniskirt and was remarkably sexy. I kept staring at the toothbrush so prominently sticking out of her purse beside her on the couch. I was stoned and not sure of what I was seeing and came late to its meaning. She noticed my noticing and got a bemused smile and let me see her panties. Then her date pulled up outside and she left.

I had an age-appropriate enflamed libido and hair-trigger hard-on and was constantly frustrated. I felt sealed-off from these enchantresses by my ignorance, timidity, and hair length. I was stranded in my horniness. Francine had a friend named Elizabeth who I liked a lot but she was obese and homely and when she asked Francine to ask me if I would have sex with her, I said no. About then Amy Purtle's letter arrived.

In high school, I could never get a redneck girl to go steady with me, but every summer I had a string of two-week steadies from among the prettiest city girls in the nearby tourist resorts. Amy was one of those. We lost our respective virginities together next to the Tuolumne River, afterward sharing poison oak on our genitals.

Though I didn't attend my own, I accepted her invitation to her prom. She was thin and blond and had huge startling blue eyes and I liked her personality a lot. We drifted apart more than broke up.

Then my parents forwarded a letter to Waller Street inviting me to visit her in the Sierras where she was working at a summer camp. I drove up, we had a couple fun days and fun nights, then I drove home, contented. Then I got a letter that in essence said, "Don't write, don't call." With no explanation. But I figured it out.

The turning point for her was almost certainly when I was gushing about the wonders of this secret world I had discovered in the Haight (the word "hippie" hadn't surfaced in the media yet).

"… And I'm even going to try heroin," I had said.

Though I never did.

Janis

Another of those sexy Haight-Ashbury chicks, and someone who did try heroin, was Janis Joplin. Everybody was at least a little bit in love with Janis. I always associated her with the Panhandle, a strip of park that jutted east out of Golden Gate Park. Eight blocks long and one block wide, running parallel to Haight Street and two blocks north of it, the Panhandle was spanned by irregular rows of eucalyptus trees that were as thick as cathedral pillars and had high jangling leaves.

In one of the earliest of the free rock concerts there I saw a group called Big Brother and the Holding Company. Usually a flat bed truck was the stage, but on this overcast day, the band was on the ground. The restless crowd flowed around and even between the musicians as they played. I was circulating too until I stopped in mid stride and then turned around to watch the lead singer. Her long brown hair and purple shawl flared as she whooped and swayed to the music, tearing off notes oh so slowly and wringing her face into the microphone.

Gradually everyone realized there was a band somewhere among them and settled down and started watching her. After the usual poker-faced guitarists and wind-up Mick Jaggers, we weren't sure at first what to make of someone bleeding in public like that. She played the Fillmore and Avalon Ballrooms a few times and the first "I Love Janis" lapel buttons started appearing.

It was about then I bumped into her, again in the Panhandle, about six months after that first concert. She was still only a local star but clearly going to hit nationally. She was kissing another local star, Country Joe MacDonald. They parted and he crossed Oak Street and she continued toward the stage, right behind myself and two friends. Normally I wouldn't smoke grass on the sidewalk but the crowd provided enough cover so my friends and I were passing a joint.

"Hey people! What are you up to up there?" came from behind us.

We turned toward the voice and she came up by my right shoulder and I handed her the joint. She was in love, or radiantly happy anyway.

"Are you playing today?" I asked.

She nodded and said through a held toke, " 'Bout three..."

She exhaled and said, "Hey!" to a friend heading in the opposite direction. She handed back the joint and joined the friend.

I saw her often on Haight Street wearing some flamboyant thrift-store collage, and when she started appearing on TV, especially the Dick Cavett talk show, we were proud when she wore her Haight Street costumes. In that setting, in her boas and dyed plumes, she was like a rare tropical bird. She was just as rare, in that setting, for her absolute integrity and intellectual sophistication and radiant charm.

Once, she was the only one on the show, besides Cavett, who had read the current best seller *Zelda* about Scott Fitzgerald's wife, and you could see Cavett's attitude toward Janis change. A couple months later, after she died, he gave a somber, stricken speech about her at the beginning of a show.

Howie

The Panhandle had other associations besides Janis. It became routine for Howie and I to meet there about 1 PM, after I got off work. He was a bottom-feeding drug dealer and another Haight mentor under whom I would serve another apprenticeship.

Often in the morning, when I left for work, there were strangers sleeping on the couch and/or in the recliner chair. They were couch nomads who slept in whichever available pad was

closest at the time they were tired. Our dope and food were community property and as available as if they were stored on the sidewalk. Our door was never locked. So, we were on the circuit for quite a few couch nomads. The two I got to know best were Howie and Art.

Art was a dark-skinned negro who spoke with the precision of a Shakespearean actor. He wore a tall narrow-brimmed hat of the style made popular by Thelonious Monk. Art made his own woodwind instruments and claimed to have jammed with Coltrane. He also claimed to know Dylan (as did about every third person in Haight-Ashbury then) and he was one of numerous messianic speed freaks who interpreted each new Dylan album as a personal message from Bob to him.

Art let me know that he had some new religious message based on drug insights but that neither I nor mankind was yet ready for it. I was fresh from kills in late-night dorm debates at St. Crispin's where I sabotaged the faith of jocks and novice brothers with ease. So I licked my chops over Art. Such pretension was a delicacy. But Art was crafty and evasive and eventually I gave up trying to get his "message" out of him.

"I met a woman from India at a party," he pronounced one night, "and she said I was fifty years ahead of my time."

Howie was Art's first and still sole disciple, who had his own life on the side and who let me tag along with him in it.

Howie was short with short curly brown hair and plastic-rimmed glasses and a yarmulke. He was never seen without a sketch pad and rapidograph pen, with which he filled the pad with paisley patterns, and he always had a wooden recorder flute on which he was never known to play a coherent melody.

He had quit school at fourteen to become a gambler, then an apprentice bookie. Then he was converted to the realm of ideas where he was as much a novice as I would've been in a Brooklyn pool hall. Howie just knew what he liked, be it from Hegel or Dale Carnegie.

When they were together, he was Art's backup man, wearing the smirk of the saved while the master spoke. But when he was alone, Howie was soft spoken, humble, with a gentle wit, and an almost formal politeness. I liked him and was curious about

him. He was flattered. He also enjoyed riding in my car, a treat for a New Yorker.

The first thing Howie did whenever he entered our pad was check the refrigerator. The second thing was offer to share whatever dope he was carrying. Besides an extended tour of pads of the Haight and an introductory course in the dope market, I picked up miscellaneous urban survival techniques that had long been habit for Howie. He never passed a phone booth without checking the coin return slot. He kept track of which of his friends was in need of soap or toilet paper then appropriated it from gas stations and restaurants. He always kept his head down as he walked, scanning the sidewalk with expert eyes, frequently stopping to pick up a coin or a bus transfer. He knew where all the free eats were in town, such as St. Anthony's Dining Room. If your appearance was passable, you could sometimes scarf hors d'oeuvres at the conventions downtown. Once every three months you could sell a pint of blood for $20.

He was also a gentleman of laundromat society, those bleareyed or plugged-in people who could be seen between midnight and dawn in all-night laundromats exchanging pills and gossip or drawing or strumming guitars. Tracy's Donut Shop, between Ashbury and Clayton on Haight Street, was another stop on that circuit. It was an intersection for people coming from all points of the psychic compass on every conceivable and available drug. Mostly speed.

Howie always knew how much who was willing to pay for what and where it was cheapest. There was an unstated understanding that he would get a commission of dope for any deal he arranged. Since he had much more dope than he could use, he bartered most of it, rarely using money.

Haight Street

But one afternoon late in the summer he was trying to make some money by finding a kilogram of grass, the wholesale quantity used by retail dealers. I knew enough to know that scoring a kilo was difficult and conferred some rank among dealers. It was generally above Howie's level but he apparently already had a buyer and just needed the kilo.

We met in the Panhandle as usual and he went about his visits with me tagging along. Though a head and a half taller than Howie, I was essentially invisible in my short hair, slacks, white shirt, and tie, my work costume. He never introduced me and I rarely spoke. I loomed in the background.

To everyone we saw, whether in their pad, on the street, or in the park, he slipped into their hand a small wedge of incense as a gift as he asked if they knew where he could score a key. They all said no.

It was afternoon before we emerged onto Haight Street, and at about Clayton we heard someone call, "Hey, Howie!"

"Hi, Phineas," Howie called back to a burly, bearded guy with a headband leaning out the corner bay window in a third floor apartment.

We crossed Haight Street, went into a building, up some stairs, and in through an open apartment door. In a bedroom at the end of a hall the Beatles' latest album *Revolver* was playing on a stereo. We went into that room and joined five people sitting on the floor like unstrung marionettes. The only furnishing, besides the portable phonograph, was a mattress on the floor. Phineas sat on that beside a window at the far end of the room.

"Hey, man," Phineas said, "sit down. What's happenin'? Wanna smoke some hash?"

He handed Howie, who sat beside him on the mattress with his back to the wall, a makeshift hooka, a half full glass of water with tinfoil on top and pin holes at one end of the tinfoil on which crumbs of hashish smoldered, and opposite the pin holes, a sucking hole.

Howie sucked the hash red then handed the glass to me sitting beside him. This was my first hash. I warned myself not to over do it, and then at the last instant panicked that I wouldn't get high, and sucked hard at the hole. I was overwhelmed by the harshness of the smoke and coughed a roiling cloud into the slanted sunlight.

"Hey, man, that's from Afghanistan," Phineas pointed out. At that time hash was a rare.

When the coughing subsided, with my eyes watery and throat raw, I scanned the room to measure the effect of my faux

pas. No one was aware of anything but the Beatles. I handed the glass toward Phineas.

"Go ahead and take another hit. But do it slow," Phineas said. "Oh, this is my favorite cut," he said of "Tomorrow Never Knows."

I smoked it again, as instructed, and soon joined the stoned silence, losing myself in a ballet of the dust motes.

"Anybody know who's at the Fillmore this week?" Phineas asked of the room.

"Uh-uh."

"Uh-uh."

"Uh-uh."

Howie quietly asked Phineas, as he placed incense in his hand, "Do you know where I can cop a kilo?"

"Grass?"

"Yeah."

"Let's see," he twisted his beard with his right index finger. "Ya know Rolly? Lives up there across from Buena Vista Park? Used to live at 1090 Page? Short. With a beard."

"Yeah, I knew him on Page Street."

"He had some friend come in from New Mexico with a whole panel truck fulla keys. Try him."

"Ok, man, thanks," Howie said, smiling and confident for the first time that day.

A strong breeze blew through the open windows as if the room were flying. Howie and I turned around, folded our arms across the window sill, rested our chins on our arms, and looked down onto Haight Street flowing by below.

On the other side of the street in a black overcoat, a stooped, whiskered old Slavic lady waddled along muttering to herself. She was passed from the opposite direction by a tall sullen young negro walking a doberman pincer on a taut leash. He was passed from the opposite direction by an even younger negro bopping to the portable radio at his ear. On the sidewalk beneath Howie and I, a teenage white girl in a faded blue work shirt and bell bottom jeans, a bell tinkling at her ankle, skipped barefoot between the dog turds, smiling at the people and the lamp posts and the fire hydrants.

Howie and I hovered there with the Beatles then Dylan then the Stones wafting over our heads and down to the street. We returned smiles, zoomed in to read faces, invisibly joined friends bumping into each other. Howie knew many and had gossip about some, especially the chicks. Eventually sunset tinted the light.

I would pass that summer dazed, gaping, and blinking. This was more than a street, more than a neighborhood. It was an enclave, a colony of rejects, a camp for refugees from affluence who got support from each other and their counterparts in other ages.

They called themselves "freaks." The very word was an exposed nerve for me, naming my worst fear about myself: that I was a mutant, irrevocably outside the human fold. And these people in Haight-Ashbury made a joke of that, a badge, a banner, a secret society.

A police patrol car cruised by like a cancer cell. They were an occupying army of middle class mercenaries and the most persistent reminder of that other world, and a justification for a paranoid glance over the shoulder in public. Jail, for some reason or another, was inevitable.

That night I arrived home and looked up and saw flames on our roof.

The End

After the contest of cool between Mike and I in the bathroom on the night of the fire, and then the encounter with the firemen in the livingroom, we joined Francine and Ralph beside her new Pontiac.

Francine announced, "Hey, we're gonna split. We've been talkin' about it for awhile anyway, and the car is all loaded so we might as well leave now."

"Where ya gonna go?" I asked.

Mike watched the firemen and pretended not to listen.

"I think we're gonna go down and visit Ralph's parents in Fresno."

"Well, I guess I'll see ya when I see ya," I said.

"Maybe before then," Francine said as she stood on her tiptoes to kiss me on the cheek and hug me. "You can have the kitchen stuff and the furniture," she added. "See ya, Mike."

Mike stood with his arms crossed and conspicuously didn't bend down.

"Yeah, see ya," he growled.

"So long," Ralph said as he got in behind the wheel.

Francine got in the passenger side, the engine started reluctantly, and then slowly the car pulled away from the curb. Francine and I waved to each other until the she was around the corner. And that was when I realized I had a question for her: what was I suppose to tell Larry if he showed up?

When I turned back to the fire I discovered that Mike was gone again. I found him in our bedroom stuffing clothes into a duffel bag. Somehow our room and everything in it stayed dry.

"I'm gonna split too, man," he told me.

"Oh."

Picking up on my sense of abandonment he added, "I'm just going up to B.C. for a couple weeks. I'll be back."

He zipped the bag shut.

"If ya leave here leave a note on the door where you're at, or at the Unicorn. Oh, and if you go by the Unicorn in the next couple days tell 'em I quit, will ya?"

I followed him out to the sidewalk. The fire was almost out now. Wispy smoke floated under the street lights.

"O.K., man, later," Mike said shouldering his bag.

"Yeah, see ya."

I watched him step over the hoses and through the gawking, chatting crowd, the duffel bag on his shoulders passing over their heads.

The Blue Unicorn

In the coming months, Mike would stay with me for a few days a couple times while passing through. We exchanged a few letters but then lost touch. Francine married a truck driver and had a son with Downs Syndrome. The last time I saw Howie would be five or six months after the fire, January or February of '67. He was talking to himself out loud in a corner of the I-Thou Coffeehouse.

I never heard how the fire started. The day after it, I went to the Blue Unicorn and told some middle-aged beatnik behind the counter that Mike had quit and then ordered my fourth coffee that day and sat with it alone at a table.

This was my first chance to reflect on my new living situation.

My education had continued with Mike and Francine and Howie and now they too were behind me, and for the first time in my life, I felt truly alone and truly free and finally at large in the real world, where the characters of novels and movies lived.

I could afford my own place now and, though I would start classes at San Francisco State within weeks, it seemed here in the Haight Ashbury as if there would be a permanent spree of summer vacation, that crack in the sidewalk where childhood grew.

More coffee had me running yet again to the bathroom. There was only one and I liked to keep up with its graffiti. Nothing new today. Same quotes from everybody from Heidegger to Kahlil Gibran, comments and comments-on-comments and slogans from the emerging ideology of Love. Throughout the city, but mainly in the Haight, anti-war slogans, Hindu incantations, metaphysical formulas, even physics equations, glimpsed at the peak of acid trips, were spray-painted on outside walls, etched on tables, or penned on coffeehouse bathroom walls.

Near the front door of the Unicorn there was a bulletin board. I checked that on my way out. There were poems and drawings, some of them on napkins, a few notes to runaways that were found poems.

WENDY HAMLIN
Please call your father.
I'm sorry. I understand now.
I've been terribly worried about you.
Call me collect at the office.

Oaxaca

September 15, 1967
somewhere in northern Mexico

Dear Tim,

I'm writing this beside a highway in the desert. I've been meaning to write for quite a while and now I have the time. And then some. I'm hitching and there hasn't been a car for I-don't-know-how-long.

"Mexico! What-the-fuck is he doing there?" I'm glad you asked because that will force me to explain, to myself and you what-the-fuck I'm doing here.

How are things in the loony bin? Your dad told me you were back in Camarillo. I'll send this letter through him. I know you were always fond of Camarillo because Bird was in there.

Whoa! I was just about to explain what-the-fuck I'm doing here when a campesino approached me out of nowhere with a machete in his hand and a hard glare on his face. I saw his shack and the *milpa* far back behind him in the pocket of an arroyo (somehow I hadn't seen it before) and I understood the situation immediately. He's out here without a phone, miles and miles from cops, and he's got a family back there and a tall gringo suddenly appears... Anyway, I nodded and buenas tardes'd him and

backed away, which seemed to satisfy him. Now I'm about a quarter mile down the road. Hours ago I got dropped off out here by some drunk *vaqueros* in a pickup who then turned off the highway onto a dirt track across the *llano* into low hills ... It's getting too dark to write and dark gray clouds are drifting in ...

September 16, 1967
Saltillo

Man! Talk about luck ... just as it started to rain last night the first car in a long time came along and stopped. It was an Avanti. (Studebaker's answer to the Corvette. Actually, I kind of like it.)

A hulking Chinese guy gets out of the driver's side and asks me in English, "Can you drive a car?"

"Yeah," I say.

"Then drive. I have to sleep," he says and squeezes into the backseat.

I get in behind the wheel, look over at the other end of the front seat, and see a beautiful middle-aged Mexican woman. The Chinese cat goes to sleep and I start flyin' this spaceship through the black void, rain bending into the windshield, distant mountains silhouetted against lightning. I'm driving for hours. And the whole time the chick doesn't say a thing or look at me once. She seems to be pouting. I keep sneaking glances in the dash light and god she's gorgeous ... I'm fantasizing like mad of course.

The Chinese cat eventually wakes up and takes back the wheel and we talk and I learn he's a doctor and she of course is his wife and man is she pissed because she doesn't talk to him either. Up to when I fell asleep in the backseat anyway. We drove all night through the rain and they dropped me off here in Saltillo a couple days south of the border.

September 17, 1967
on the way to Tampico

Came downstairs this morning and the lobby was knee-deep in floodwater. I'm writing this on the bus to Tampico on the Gulf Coast. (You can tell by the jerky handwriting.) I'm going there for no other reason than I remember it looked interesting at the beginning of *Treasure of the Sierra Madre* and there was a pop

song about it when I was a little kid and I can't think of any place else to go. Maybe I can sleep on the beach, fish, maybe find coconuts. We'll see...

September 17, 1967
Tampico

Christ! Tampico has been an unmitigated disaster so far. I'm writing this in a room in a brothel where I have a chair wedged against a door that doesn't lock.

When I got to Tampico in the evening, exhausted, I decided to go straight out to the beach. The night was warm and clear with a nearly full moon. So, I got a cab and told him to go the beach. And all of a sudden I got attitude. Snide, contemptuous. It was nothing he said just his tone of voice and some fleeting expressions in the rearview mirror. Of course, the first thing I ask myself is: is that real or my projection or hypersensitivity? Or is this an ambush by that crippling paranoia I dragged out of the Haight? (I should mention I got a haircut so long hair is not a factor.)

He drops me off at the last stop on the streetcar line and with a nod indicates the direction of the beach which I can hear through some trees. After I pay him, he sneers and speeds off, tires spitting stones. Maybe he really really hates gringos. Or maybe my secret fear is real that my vibes are infected and I radiate an undefinable but palpable offputtingness, and that on some animal level I am inherently repellant. I know it's not rational. I know it's some warp I got from growing up among rednecks but still... sometimes there's the evidence staring you in the face.

The streetcar stop is deserted, except for a Mexican about my age on a bench.

I walk by him carrying my duffel bag and nod and he says in perfect English, "Hey man, wanna get high?"

"Sure," I say with a chuckle.

As I sit down beside him, he takes a joint from a breast pocket. He has an unusually round head topped with a shock of black hair. He starts to strike a match but looks down the road. I follow his gaze to an old gray '53 Chevy crossing at an intersection seventy-five yards down.

"Hey, c'mere," he says leading me by the hand behind a low building with a fenced yard with tools and equipment for track repair.

"Cops?" I ask.

"Mexican cops are a joke, huh?" he asks. He lights the joint, reddening the end, and says, "I know those cats. They wouldn't bust us." He takes his toke and hands me the joint and says with held breathe, "I just don't wanna share it." He speaks English like a native but with a Spanish rhythm.

"You live down here or up there?" I ask and then hold in my toke while handing back the joint.

"Both. Everywhere."

I exhale my toke and ask, "What do you do? I mean for money."

"Smuggle."

"Really?!"

"Yeah. I smuggle stuff from the States into Mexico."

"What kinda stuff?"

"Oh, lately it's been levis and transistor radios. I sell 'em to rich kids in Mexico City. It's a nice safe business."

He takes a black case from a breast pocket, opens it, and takes out a chrome-plated harmonica. I'm staring at nothing intently. The grass is excellent. The Mexican launches into something I think could have been from Vivaldi's *Four Seasons* but then he veers into blues harp smooth as a banking jet. And that's Muddy Waters' "Seventh Son" no doubt about it. I become the percussion, slapping the stucco wall that hides us. Man, he's good! We were jammin' under the stars and taking turns singing lead and passing the joint back and forth and it was fantastic! We could've gone on for hours but something happened.

I feel a hand sliding down the inside of my thigh. My first thought is that he's an extremely inept pickpocket. Then I realize this cat is a homosexual. I've had doubts about my own sexuality. After all, most of my heros are homosexual: Burroughs, Whitman, Genet. But, as you well know, I am certifiably pussy-crazed. I have a voracious fascination with the female body and have never felt sexual attraction for another male.

I look at the Mexican who keeps playing the harmonica with his eyes closed.

Before he reaches my dick, I step backward and say, "Hey, uh. . . ya know, uh, . . . I'm not a . . . I mean I don't. . . I'm sorry but, uh. . . Oh, hey, I gotta crash." I stoop and pick up my duffel bag. "I'm really beat. Thanks a lot for the grass."

The Mexican looks up and nods, the harmonica jerking back and forth across his mouth, a flash of hurt in his eyes. When I'm out of earshot of him, I cut my pace down and focus on the ocean still hidden behind trees that are now all around me. The deep trail is easy to follow even in this near total dark. Then suddenly there's a clearing and loud surf roar.

The whole hideous scene is shades of gray in the bright moonlight. The water is very shallow. At fifty yards, logs a foot wide aren't even covered in water. It looks like it wouldn't be over your waist at the horizon. The logs, which are bare and straight and might be abandoned telephone poles, are jostled and tossed and their banging blends with the waves' booms. Some logs roll onto the beach.

Suddenly a shadow flits behind me and to the side through the trees. Then there's another on the other side and another directly behind me. And a guy runs by in front of me and whistles and holds up an exaggeratedly limp wrist. Suddenly I realize what's going on. The cab driver's attitude and the gay blues harpist and now these gay cats pirouetting all around me. This is the gay pick up spot.

I turn around and head back to the streetcar stop. The blues harpist is gone and I notice a sign with the hours of service that indicates the streetcar stopped running for the night. I'm exhausted from a day on a bus and too little sleep for nights before that. I start trudging down the dusty, rutted road, duffle bag on my shoulders, gradually getting angrier and angrier at my situation. That's when the cops arrive.

Their headlights throw my shadow on the trees and I hear the squeak of car springs. I turn around and see bouncing headlights slowing toward me. It's that old gray '53 Chevy. It stops.

"Tenga cuidado, señor. Está peligroso aqui," (*Be careful, mister. It's dangerous here*) a guy in the front passenger seat says, thick arm hanging out the window.

There are four of them, two in the front, two in the back. They're not in uniform and somehow they don't feel like cops. I see the handle of a pistol poking out of the pocket of one in the backseat whose face I can't see.

The one in the back on my side opens his door and steps out saying, "Es mejor que venga con nosotros." (*It's best that you come with us.*)

He steps aside and I get in the back seat. I was going to ask for a ride anyway. The car lurches forward and I hear "gringo" muttered in the front seat and then the burly guy in the front passenger side turns around and asks, "Que hace aqui... tan tarde?" (*What are you doing here... so late.*)

"Uh, primero..." I say still pissed at my situation, "uh, muestrame su... uh..." (*First... show me your...*) but then I can't think of the Spanish word for "badges."

"Placas?" the guy to my left, with the pistol, asks.

"Yeah... si... sus placas..."

The car stops suddenly, throwing us all forward. All four doors fly open and all four get out as I hear addressed to me, "Venga, venga." (*Come here, come here.*)

We go to the front of the car and stand in the headlights. The burly guy takes out his wallet and opens it in the swirling dust of the headlight beam.

He says of his "badge," "Mire... Somos policía... de veras," (*Look... We're police... really.*)

That's when I fell in love.

Each takes out his "badge" and insists on showing it to me. The "badges" are old World War II medals like you can buy for a quarter in army surplus stores in the States.

It turns out these cats are some kind of neighborhood crime watch on wheels. There is something endearing about them and as we drive into the city (my head occasionally banging on the ceiling) I discover that they're husbands and fathers and this is a guys' night out while doing the necessary work of protecting their neighborhoods in the absence of reliable cops. I ask them to take

me to the bus station and I'm enjoying them so much that when I finally get out and thank them and say bye I have to remind myself of why I'm getting out: I'm drunk with exhaustion and there are bound to be flophouses around the bus station.

After they drive off, I notice a place across the street and down a couple buildings. I cross at an angle and enter. There are a bunch of chicks mid twenties to mid thirties sitting around the lobby. Daughters of the owner I figure. I ask for a room and after I eventually get the key and start for the stairs, one of the chicks stands up to lead me. She's thirty-ish kind of plump in a rumpled black dress. It's not until the top of the stairs that I see her face well and I like it … a lot.

We emerge onto the roof where there are joined concrete boxes the size of small rooms. As we walk to the end of a row of them I can hear the moans and gasps of fucking. We enter a room and she turns on the single bulb in the ceiling. The room is stark and gray.

There is a basin on the table next to the bed and I ask her what it's for and with a quizzical look she rubs her hand over her crotch and I realize where I am.

I stammer "No mas … ahorita… gracias" and she shrugs and leaves. I shut the door behind her and discover that it doesn't lock. There is only one chair in the room and I wedge it firmly between the door handle and the floor.

Now…I've finally got it down on paper and I'm feeling an adrenalin crash and I'm going to go to bed. Though I'm concerned about the sheets I know all I have to do is lay down and close my eyes …

September 18, 1967
highway to Mexico City

Tampico was just a big greasy industrial port city and I got out on the first available bus, just ahead of a hurricane. I'm in the middle of a thirteen-hour ride to Mexico City, where I'll mail this to you as soon as I arrive. Reading over yesterday's incidents I'm a little embarrassed. It just didn't occur to me that there would be a whorehouse across the street from the bus station. Nothing happened that night after the prostitute left by the way. Hey, I'm

nineteen and this is the first time I've been out of the country or even out of California!

Guess it's time I came up with a reason for being here. Well, first and foremost is my psychological condition. I know better but that doesn't keep me from running here to escape the … that problem with paranoia I had at the end in the Haight … after those speed overdoses. You seemed not to notice it but it was a hell that could erupt and swallow me at any moment without warning. The question is can I escape it down here? It occurs to me that Mexico may be my Camarillo.

We really haven't talked much since Shob's murder. After we found out about it, you were incoherent most of the time, that is when you were even capable of speech, so I don't know exactly what you know. Do you know they caught the cat who did it?

I didn't tell you at the time, because you were so freaked out, but you were right to be freaked out. If they hadn't caught that cat, they would have questioned you for sure. The real murderer by the way was a biker friend of Shob's, on acid at the time, and he stabbed him twelve times, once through the heart. He was caught in Shob's car, with Shob's pistol, and with Shob's left arm cut off at the elbow. The arm was handcuffed to a briefcase with a couple thousand dollars in it, probably for our big grass deal with him. Early on there was a silly street-rumor about the murderer caught gnawing Shob's arm.

A couple days after your dad took you back to LA, Super Spade was killed. All I really knew about him was that he was a big dealer. Didn't you know him? They found his body in a sleeping bag hanging down a cliff out at Point Reyes. At first, there was speculation that the same guy murdered both, and then the newspapers swallowed that old street rumor about the Mafia taking over the Haight drug business.

Hearst squeezed four days of headlines out of it and Shob got his picture in Time magazine, described as an "unemployed flutist," in a story titled, "End of the Dance."

Also a couple days after you left, a crasher and his ol' lady offered me a place to stay indefinitely in New Orleans with some Tulane students to help create a hip scene there and I was curious after all your Freedom Summer stories so I hitched

through the Southwest and across the dirt ocean of Texas (got a ride in the middle of the night outside a bar from a drunk trucker who almost killed us a couple times) into Louisiana where I arrived broke but Ollie had fronted me some of those purple acid tabs which I sold in a bar (that I was told later was riddled with undercover narcs) and I took a tab myself a couple nights later on the banks of the Mississippi envisioning a philosophical unified field theory but I finally got busted trying to hop a freight train and spent three days in a segregated parish prison where I met cats serving years and years for grass and then I faced a judge who was courteous and sympathetic and reprimanded the cop and somehow I got through the whole time in the parish prison never having to take off my socks which was where my stash was and that bread bought my bus ticket to El Paso and that's what I'm living on down here. But all that is for another time. I'm in Mexico now and I found something here, I don't know yet what it is, but I like it.

By the way, when I talked to your dad on the phone I got the distinct impression he blames me for your being in the loony bin. Set him straight will you? Christ man I'm six years younger than you!

See ya, Your Haight Roomie

P.S.

September 23, 1967
Mexico City

Hey, I didn't mail this yet because I didn't have the time to get stamps because I've been so ...entranced. This place is amazing. I think I'm in love. Not with a chick but a country. Every day I come back to the hotel delirious with exhaustion from walking all day. Today I explored some place that felt familiar, the campus of the University of Mexico. It's an architectural masterpiece.

There's so much here and it's all so fascinating ...You grow up in California and you're surrounded by Mexican place names and Mexicans and you think you know something about Mexico. I knew nothing. Mexico is the most American of the countries of the Americas. Those 80% mestizos are the biggest

grafting of Europe onto the Americas. What happened to the Indians you ask? A lot of them became Mexicans. They celebrate this. It's right there on their flag. They created a Mexican answer to the great questions of the twentieth century in that remarkable revolution, the first great war of the century. I've been reading this incredible book about Mexico, *Labyrinth of Solitude*, by the poet Octavio Paz.

I'm staying in the Hotel Rosalina, a couple blocks from a beautiful downtown park, the Alameda. The first word that comes to mind about my room is "cavernous." The ceiling has got to be 12 feet high and the bed occupies about a fifth of the creaky old wood floor. In fact, the whole place is old and creaky. And musty. The hall carpet smells. The glass doors onto my balcony go up to the high ceiling and the balcony looks from the fourth floor down onto a roaring street.

P.P.S.

September 24, 1967
Mexico City

One summer in high school, I worked with an old Mexican digging trenches for the water department. We just called him Mexican Joe because that was the name of the restaurant he ran with his wife and kids. He was a smart businessman who did other work on the side and spent half the year in Mexico where he was rumored to be wealthy.

There was something soothing just in his presence, a radiant calm that felt good just to stand next to. And there was something in the way he would look directly into your eyes when he spoke to you.... He just had ... something that shamed the silliness out of you. Something that I would like to have some of. No, a lot of. After reading Watts, I see there was Zen in Joe's calm deliberation, his mindfulness, his being totally in the moment.

I always thought of him like a favorite uncle and I loved his big brown face with the pocked hook nose and warm, wise grin full of gold-framed teeth. I've seen that face or variations of it in some of the historical murals that are everywhere. University of Mexico has whole walls of 7,8 story buildings covered with mosaic paintings and murals, same with some of the ministry

headquarters. Some of them, you walk along beside them, reading them, and it's like a movie. After the revolution, murals were a way to teach the illiterate indigenous population about this new thing: their country.

This city has so much more than the usual gray canyons.

Hey this letter is going on and on like our conversations at all hours at the kitchen table. Except I get to hog the airtime. And it may be mutating into a travel journal too.

September 25, 1967
Mexico City

The chicks! They're utterly amazing. I stagger around the streets dazzled by them. I don't know how many times I've gone around a busy corner and almost bumped into a stunning beauty who I could only stare at dumbstruck and gaping until her laughter brought me back and I apologized.

The other night I was out on the sidewalk after a cooling rain and it was packed and I did something I used to enjoy sometimes in the City, get on a crowded sidewalk, or in a hallway out at State, and drift down the rapids. I was stopped for the light at a crosswalk when I heard a small voice beside me.

"Do djyou…. like…. Mexico?"

I looked down and saw a chick about my age with a sly little smile looking up at me.

"Yes… very much…" I said. "You speak English?"

"I … am … lehr-ning … in … school … for …. Olympics."

"That's right … You're having the Olympics here next year."

"Yes …"

The light changed and the crowd swept us into the crosswalk.

She is Nélida Rojano. Very short, *moreno* (dark skinned), with a classic aquiline Indian profile. Though she's not pretty, I like her looks a lot. She has in her gestures and intonations a special … manner… a delicacy or maybe finesse… or…?????… that I really like.

For nearly an hour we talked and walked and sat in the Alameda Park. She's middle class. She even has a sister who is a

lawyer, which is really far out. She really loves her English language night class. Her English is better than my Spanish but still our conversation involves a lot of passing back and forth of my little red pocket traveler's dictionary.

I can cobble together sentences from three years of high school Spanish, growing up among Mexican families, and Joe. That and a lot of "Despacio, por favor, muy… muy… muy despacio." (*Slowly, please, very … very … very slowly.*) And, of course, a lot of hand gestures.

September 26, 1967
Mexico City

There's another chick I need to tell you about. Her name is Chencha, short for Inocencia, which she most decidedly is not. She just showed up at the door one morning when I was expecting someone to pick up laundry and I assumed that was her.

While I was putting stuff in a paperbag, she noticed my bedside reading and said, "Oh, Tagoré!!"

There's another *extranjero,* foreigner, who apparently is also reading Rabindranth Tagore and staying somewhere on the other side of the hotel. It seems likely but not certain that he's a freak.

She was giving me the eye the whole time she was in the room. That afternoon she returned with everything clean and folded, and then she lingered, chatting, waiting, sending vibes through long intense stares. I never had a chick come-on so hard … She did everything but take off her clothes … Actually she did take off her clothes but later, after I was certain of the message and kissed her and told her she was *bonita*, pretty. Which she isn't. She is cute though. And plump and *morena* and sixteen. And really energetic in bed.

September 28, 1967
Mexico City

I've been spending a lot of time with Nélida. That first night in the Alameda she asked if I would like to come and talk to her English class, which I did and it was a gas answering their questions and correcting their English. The next day I went over to her house for dinner where I sat at the end of the table and ate

alone while she, her younger brother and sister, and her mother watched me. Her father is dead and her other four siblings are adults.

After dinner, we watched TV together and talked and at one point her mother turned to me and said, "¿Sabes... dicen que los mejores esposos son los norteamericanos?" (*Did you know ... they say that Americans make the best husbands?*) She wasn't talking about wealth. The Rojanos, with a big house, a car, and a TV, are wealthier than me. She meant American men treat their wives best.

I think my Camarillo is working. I haven't had a paranoia attack since I got here.

September 30, 1967
Mexico City

Went out to Teotihuacán today. It's this amazing city of ancient ruins about an hour or so by bus outside Mexico City. Its pyramids are bigger than those in Egypt but nobody knows the name of the people who built them and abandoned them or why. We went out with Nélida's brother and sister and she and I talked more than ever. I'm starting to feel a little guilty because I really like her and, of course, there is no chance that I am going to marry her. At one point, she said proudly that she wanted me to see Teotihuacán because it was built by "mi gente," my people.

I was definitely impressed. At its peak in the 6th century A.D. it may have had 200,000 people and been the 6th largest city in the world. The climb to the top of the Pyramid of the Sun was grueling and endlessly up ... steep ... stone .... stairs ... under pounding sun. And when I finally got to the top ... there was a Mexican kid with a pocket-sized transistor radio playing Beatle music.

Hey, remember Brando's *Viva Zapata*, about the great peasant general of their revolution ... There's a scene where he's courting his woman, who has Spanish lineage, and she insults his people, and he tells her something like, when her people were living in mud huts in Europe, his were living here in magnificent stone cities.

October 1, 1967
Mexico City

There is of course no chance for sex with Nélida. We're icebound in the same exact sexual morality as our parents'. I really like her though... a lot. I would really like to kiss her, just kiss her. Just a kiss nothing more. And I think she wants to ... but no ...

Something really weird happened earlier tonight. Nélida took me to a friend's house. I guess she was showing off her gringo. I just go where I'm led. So, I was introduced to some parents and chatted a little and eventually we wound up in the girlfriend's bedroom behind a closed door, three teen age girls and a large male foreigner. I thought ... What the fuck?! This would never be allowed up there. Then I realized that the parents allow this because sex, or anything close to it, is so remote, so completely unthinkable ... That's how a nice middle class girl like Nélida could pick up a guy waiting for the light to change at a crosswalk.

I was sitting on the bed and I could see that some of the excitement was not only because there was a gringo visiting but because I was Nélida's *novio*, which can mean either boyfriend or fiancé.

When her girlfriends were talking among themselves, I decided I had to try to get through to her about how marriage wasn't possible.

"Conoces tu..." I said to her, "... jovenes en el norte ...uh, llamada ... 'hippies'?" (*Do you know about young people in the north called hippies?*)

She thought a moment and shook her head.

I gesture from my head to my shoulders as I say, "Uh, muchachos ... tienen ... pello largo," (*The boys have long hair),* and I rub my chin as I say, "... y barbas," (*and beards)* "... Uh, fumen, fuman ... marijuana ... uh, lucha ... contra ... la guerra en Vietnam ..." (*and they smoke marijuana and fight against the Vietnam war.)*

She shook her head again and then seemed bewildered by the question.

"*Soy... hippie...*" (I'm ... a hippie.) I said.

"*Oh, 'existencialistas'!*" erupted a girlfriend who I didn't know had been listening.

"*Oh, si... existencialistas!*" Nélida said.

I think it's less the philosopher than your basic bearded bohemian intellectual. But since I am neither bearded nor long-haired I don't think she could connect it with me. Anyway I dropped it...

Meanwhile, every couple days Chencha shows up. Apparently she has a few times when I wasn't here, but I have no way to get in touch with her... I'm not even sure how she's connected with the hotel. I haven't understood her explanation the couple times I asked.

And she has never asked for money. I was feeling a little guilty about just fucking in the room all the time and told her we could go to a movie but she wasn't interested. Which surprised me a little because she has occasionally struck poses and made breathy declarations as if she was acting-out or impersonating favorite movie scenes.

Thought about going out to find my "Tagore" doppelganger on the other side of the hotel. I'm pretty sure Chencha had sex with him.

I have started practically living on something they call "elote." It's a fat corn cob on a stick sold by sidewalk vendors from steaming vats on wheels. It's smothered in butter and sprinkled with grated cheese and salt and red chili powder. It's delicious and cheap. Good thing, because I'm running low on money.

October 4, 1967
Mazatlan

I'm on the west coast in Mazatlan. From Mexico City just pushed myself, hitching night and day to the coast, stopping only for a night in a dingy motel outside Guadalajara.

Though it has the usual *mercados*, churches, and leafy plazas, culturally Mazatlan is a letdown after Mexico City. It seems to exist on fishing and increasingly tourism. The sunsets are pretty dramatic against the *islas*, rocky islands just off the beach. But I've

only been here a day and a night and I'm ready to move on. Maybe take the ferry to La Paz and go up Baja.

Good bye with Nélida was... weird. When the clerk told me at my door that she was waiting down in the lobby, I just followed him back down the stairs... barefoot. That's what she noticed first when I approached her. She smiled but didn't like it. I thought after being in her girlfriend's bedroom it would be no big thing for her to come up to my hotel room... But no...

Then I thought, well here's the big parting I should be able to get at least a peck on the cheek... But no... when I moved toward her she stiffened and backed away.

Finally, we shook hands and she asked when I thought I might be back and I told her sincerely that I hoped it would be soon. We promised to write and she said, "Buen viaje," and I said, "Adios," and she turned and went out the door.

There was no good bye at all with Chencha of course. She could be knocking on my door right now.

October 4 still, but a couple hours later, 1967
Mazatlan

There's a noticeable community of gringo freaks here. Couple hours ago passed a couple chicks in the hall of my hotel and we stopped and did the "where-ya-from-where-ya-been-where-ya-goin'." They're Canadian. Gena is stocky with straight brown hair and a sweet smile. Adrienne is short, perky, and sexy with a corolla of tight blond curls.

Still October 4, but it's 9:30PM, 1967
Mazatlan

I was returning from another exploratory walk when I passed Gena and Adrienne's room. The door was open and they were sitting on their beds talking.

I nodded and said hi and was going to keep going but Adrienne said, "Come on in."

I enter the room, lit by a stark dim ceiling bulb and crammed with two double beds. I sit on one, beside Gena, so I can face Adrienne on the other.

"I was just walking around and I noticed there're a lot of freaks here," I said "You see'em everywhere."

"Some of them have friends or family who have been busted," Gena said.

"This is the state capitol and there's a big prison here," Adrienne added.

"Oh..." I said. "Do you have someone... uh...?"

They both nodded.

"My brother," Gena said.

"And he's my ol' man," Adrienne added.

"They caught him with a bunch of kilos," Gena said.

A cat comes in who looks something like John Groupie, skinny and hunched with a skimpy goatee. We're introduced. His name is Brad. He sits next to Adrienne.

"How were you going to get the grass back to Canada?" I ask.

The chicks know I'm from Haight-Ashbury and hip but Brad glares at me.

Adrienne answers, "We have a friend with a yacht who came down."

"I was involved in a big Mexican grass deal up in the Haight in August," I say. "We met a big grass importer in LA and we knew the Haight was getting low, so my roommate set up a deal with him and a friend who was the acid dealer for the Hell's Angels in San Francisco, and we were suppose to get a couple keys out of it. But then he got murdered ... for reasons that had nothing to do with the deal. His name was Shob Carter. It made national headlines as the murder that ended the Summer of Love."

"Oh I read about that," Gena said.

"Yeah, I heard about it too," Adrienne said.

"Things really got weird after we found out about the murder because... Well, Shob was an ex Marine and he could really be violent and the way the deal was supposed to go down was we, that is my roommate and Shob and I, and the grass importer, were supposed to meet out in the desert at night in pickups. But just before he walked out the door at our last meeting, Shob said he was going to bring his piece and if anything

happened he was going to use it. Later, my roommate Tim and I decided that we wanted out of the deal."

I see the chicks are hanging in there and even Brad, reluctantly, so I keep going.

"So then Tim went around the Haight looking for Shob so he could tell him we were backing out of the deal. But he couldn't find him and he was afraid it was because Shob was working hard to raise the money. For days, Tim went all over the Haight asking for him, while Shob was laying dead in his apartment. So when we found out about the murder, Tim freaked out ... he has an exaggerated fear of the police because of experiences in the South during the Civil Rights Movement.

"So, he thought he was going to be accused of the murder ... that pushed him over the edge, that and maybe too much acid in the days leading up to the murder. Now he's in Camarillo State Mental Hospital."

Chicks're impressed. Not Brad though. Bad vibes there.

There was one last thing I wanted to tell them, the most important.

"On my way down here I went through New Orleans....you know about the American South... how dangerous it is?"

Blank stares.

"Well anyway, it would be suicide to hitchhike through the South with long hair. That's why I got my hair cut before I left."

Except for the day I got my hair cut on Haight Street, this is the first time I've been around freaks when I had short hair. I don't like it. I don't know if it bothers you that I told them so much... Remember you're not likely to ever meet any of them.

I had talked long enough about myself so I changed the subject and broke another brooding silence and asked, "How did the bust go down?"

"They waited till after Nathan paid for the weed, of course" Adrienne said. "He got it in a village up in the hills and it filled the trunk and the backseat of a car we rented. Then just outside the city they pulled him over and busted him."

"I was supposed to be with him," Brad added. "But I'm in another hotel across town and I couldn't get here on time so he had to leave without me or be late for the meet."

"We heard it's usually the grower who turns you in," Adrienne said. "And the police give the grower back the grass after the bust."

Another long silence while we all meditated on the unfairness and despair.

"Can you bribe him out?" I asked.

"We're workin' on that," Brad said," and other things..."

His tone closed the door on the subject so I tried to lighten the atmosphere by asking, "What'd you guys think of Mexico City?"

October 6, 1967
Mazatlan

O.K., been spending more time with the Canadians. There is a fairly close-knit group (Canadians along with Americans) of those with loved ones inside. The horror stories from in there are making everybody outside edgy, at times even frantic. When you're around them, there's a suppressed air of desperation like in a hospital waiting room. You can see it on their faces. It's never far from their thoughts. If they're able to laugh or get into some music, soon enough that same preoccupied frown comes back.

Adrienne seems an exception. She doesn't seem that devastated by her ol' man's predicament. Though Gena told me that Adrienne cries uncontrollably after every visit.

Doubt if Brad has slept with Adrienne yet but it's pretty obvious that he wants to. I wondered at first who he was focused on. Adrienne is by far the more attractive of the two but she is also the ol' lady of a friend and a friend who is in prison. But he warned me off her with his vibes and now is becoming openly hostile and more so all the time. This is a pretty good sign for me. His disliking me probably grows in direct proportion to her liking of me.

The asshole is trying to sell me a kilo. He's desperate for bread. What the fuck am I supposed to do with a kilo of grass down here?!

October 7, 1967
Mazatlan

I was just in Adrienne and Gena's room (where I seem to be spending more and more time). I'm finding that Gena and I easily fall into intense conversations that exclude everyone else. And I'm more and more attracted to her plain-prettiness especially those blue eyes. Adrienne is so dazzling that it takes a while to notice Gena and her quiet magnetism.

We were discussing Mexico in general while Adrienne was showering ... with the bathroom door open.

I was telling Gena a lot of the stuff I've already talked about in here to you and she was talking about her similar impressions. She's read the Octavio Paz book too.

I finally had to blurt out, "Isn't this place incredible? I mean Mexico."

"Yes it is. I love it."

"I mean... I had no idea before I came here..." This is a conversation I've wanted to have for weeks.

"Me either ..."

"I mean the art, the murals, the colors everywhere, the people, their graciousness..." I'm leaning in toward her as if sharing a secret.

"Yes, yes, yes..." she says.

"There's so much...uh...it's...um...it's..." There's so much I want to say that I'm tongue-tied.

Then we stare at each other a frozen moment, realizing that the other feels exactly the same thing, this love for Mexico, and that we've never shared it with anyone else, not quite like this anyway. Then each realizes that the other realizes it. Then I realize I want to kiss her and she realizes it too and lowers her eyes and waits. And that's when Brad comes in. Right on cue to be thoroughly useless.

He and I nodded. I leaned back and there was an awkward silence while Gena and I tried to get our bearings.

"That's really beautiful," I finally said of a black vase with an unusual dull luster sitting on the chest of drawers across the room.

"Oh, I got that in Oaxaca," Gena said. "It was made with a special glazing technique they developed in a village down there. They call it *barro negro*, black clay."

"I keep hearing about Oaxaca," I said, "and the way people talk about it... They get this kind of dreamy expression... They make it sound... mythical, or even mystical... or something..."

"Oaxaca... is... so groovy..." Gena said trailing off into that same revery I had seen before.

"Oaxaca is soooo... far... out!" Adrienne called out, voice reverberant in the bathroom. She was out of the shower now and toweling off.

"Yeah, it's pretty fine," Brad added. "It's a bitch to get to though."

"The bus ride from Mexico City was... endless..." Gena said.

Then Adrienne stepped out of the bathroom into the bedroom wearing nothing but the towel she was using to dry her hair.

She said, "You know what Nathan said? He said Oaxaca was 'the distilled essence of the mystery of Mexico.' Isn't that far out?"

Nobody answered her. She's been sunbathing nude and that little blond bush stood out nicely against the brown skin. Of course my eyes drank the deliciousness of her body in micro seconds and then returned to her face so I could listen attentively just as if she were standing there fully clothed.

Man was Brad pissed!

It's only now, hours later, that I appreciate Nathan's comment and yes it is far out. It neatly sums up all I've been hearing about Oaxaca. That comment has changed my opinion of Nathan. I wasn't too hip on anyone who would have Brad as a friend or partner but this makes me want to meet Nathan. His sister is clearly very intelligent. Nathan's comment also gives me more respect for Adrienne, if she can be the ol' lady of a cat like that...

She may have gone skinny dipping with Brad (I once saw them disappearing into the woods together at the far end of a

beach) but I see now there is simply nothing there for a chick in love with Nathan. She would be defiling herself with Brad.

"I heard there's a lot of Indian influence down there," I said, trying to keep the conversation going and to keep Adrienne in front of me naked. I could smell her skin.

"Oh, yeah," she said, her little brown nipples jiggling as she fluffed her hair with the towel. "There're a whole bunch of different tribes and the women wear this amazingly beautiful, um..."

"*Traje*," Gena added with exasperation. She clearly disapproves but has accepted Adrienne.

"*Traje...*"

"It's their traditional tribal costume," Gena said. "And they weave them themselves and they put in these brilliant colors and complex geometrical patterns."

Brad is too furious to talk. First he is angry with Adrienne for... this charitable contribution, and then with me for receiving it.

"And there are ruins everywhere," Adrienne continued, missed drops glistening on her neck and shoulders. "They've been right there in that same place for thousands of years. You feel how deep and ... and ... ancient their connection with the earth is. The vibe there is really groovy."

Her hair was dry and she lowered the towel onto her shoulders.

"There are a number of different Indian cultures there," Gena said, "and their folk art generally is quite remarkable. Their pottery," she nodded toward the black vase, "these woven rugs they call *tapetes*, and even their toys which are these really imaginative little carved wooden animals they call *alebrijes*."

Then Gena suddenly became sullen and distracted and I think it was the mention of her brother. Adrienne turned around to go back into the bathroom.

When they left to visit Nathan a little while later, I was thinking about how I could get alone with Gena.

October 8, 1967
Mazatlan

Earlier today bumped into Brad sitting with a couple freaks at a sidewalk café on a plaza. He surprised me by inviting me to sit down. There were three at two small tables pushed together. He didn't introduce me and I was already self-conscious because I was the only one with short hair. So immediately, I started thinking of an excuse for a graceful exit.

"Think anymore about that kilo?" Brad asked in a low voice, revealing why he invited me to join them.

"Not really."

Long silence while we all people-watched. The three freaks were stoned. Brad turned to one of the other cats and continued a conversation about a mutual friend who regularly walks kilos through customs.

"It's all about controlling your vibes," the other cat said to Brad with authority. "He's really good at that." He has long brown hair and a dense beard, and his legs are crossed so a foot pokes out with a worn huarache sandal. "They don't go into his bags 'cause he's standin' there with a big grin not sweatin' it. Like a big contented baby."

The third cat had long scraggily dark hair and a couple days of beard and a squinty challenging stare.

He said, "It's like those pictures of those cats with thousands of bees crawlin' all over 'em."

He grinned broadly, proud of his insight. The rest of us stared at him waiting for an explanation.

"Whaddaya mean?" Brad asked.

"Well, how come those cats don't get stung? ... They're controllin' their vibes."

I was listening with interest and Brad noticed.

"You ever walk a kilo across?" he asked me.

I shook my head.

"It oughta be easy for you with short hair," he said in a taunting tone. "I've done it with long hair." He turned to the cat he was talking to before and asked, "You have too haven't you?"

"What?"

"Walked a key through customs."

"Yeah."

Brad looked at the third freak who glanced at me and then said, "Naw."

More long silence and people-watching.

"Look man, I'm desperate," Brad said suddenly, leaning in close to me. "How about twenty dollars U.S.?"

He was radioactive with contempt for me and this should have been a moment of delicious revenge but instead I said, "O.k."

"What the fuck?!" you exclaim. And that would be appropriate if my decision had anything to do with Brad. But it was more about you than him. Of course, the asshole thinks he talked me into something.

First off, it's an incredible deal, a key for the price of two lids! It would be worth a hundred, hundred twenty in the Haight. (Actually, though, it's not very good grass.)

Second, remember that time you carried a kilo the length of Haight Street in a shopping bag, and for what? It was much safer just a block over on Waller or Page, but you said you just wanted to see if you could do it. Same here. Rob got five pounds of hash through twenty borders when he was a merchant seaman. The challenge here is controlling your vibes. I think I can do that. This sleazy weasel Brad walked a key through with long hair and mine is short. (Actually, he looks more like a possum.)

Haven't seen Gena since midday yesterday and I'm anxious to see if I can pry her free of Adrienne and Brad and we can be alone for a while.

October 8 still but 10:30 PM
Mazatlan

As I move north it seems the paranoia is returning. In Mexico City I was totally serene but I just had my first serious attack since Tampico and the cab driver.

Earlier tonight, I was in a tourist bar across town, in a neighborhood I don't know, with some of the Canadians. I'm too young for bars in the States of course but this place seemed like an imitation American bar for the tourists. Dark and windowless, with loud music and loud neon signs on the walls.

There were five of us. Nobody was talking much. They were generally too bummed out, and besides, the Mexican music was deafening. I think we were there in a (futile) effort to escape their concerns. They seemed even glummer than usual and at the same time slightly nervous and agitated.

Since I don't drink, I ordered a beer and sipped it just for thirst. We were at a table next to the dance floor, I was seated on the far right side, Gena was next to me, then Brad, Adrienne, and a cat named Ian I had seen a couple times before.

We were sitting there like a wax museum when a freak comes in who I'd never seen before. He goes up to Ian and says something in his ear and then they confer and then the cat leaves as suddenly as he appeared. Ian then leans across the table and says something to Brad who has been watching carefully.

I think the whispering is because of the loud music and I start to lean in to hear what's being said but suddenly get threatening glares from both of them. They quickly pull apart and I sit back in my chair. Brad then turns to Adrienne right next to him and she hears what he says and quickly glances at me and away. Gena then leans in and Brad and Adrienne tell her something and she also quickly glances at me and away.

What have I done?! Are they talking about me? Of course I examine and reexamine and re-re-reexamine everything I've said and done tonight while with them. Am I doing it again without realizing it: involuntarily radiating a toxic psychological force-field? I can't find anything in my behavior or in anything I've said … If it's not about me, what could they be whispering about like that?

The roof has just collapsed on me and I am buried in the debri while reliving those days of the accidental meth overdose. I can't move. I can't do anything but stare at the floor. A tornado of thoughts trapped in my head.

Then Gena said something to me. I couldn't tell what she said but I sensed that she was concerned for me and was trying to pull me into the conversation. But I couldn't ask her to repeat it for some reason. Maybe I was too tuned out. I wasn't stoned. I looked at her and shrugged slightly. When it strikes, there's no telling how long this paralysis will last, seconds or fifteen minutes. I can hear what's around me but can only stare at the floor. The Canadians

leaned together and asked each other questions and made comments but I couldn't tell what about. Eventually I realized I could simply stand up and leave ... If I could think of an excuse.

"... Don't feel well," I said to the wall as I stood, not loud enough. "And I'm tired..."

I turned and left without looking at anyone, including Gena, and went out into the night with only a vague sense of where across town my hotel was. I don't know why I didn't grab a taxi. It just didn't occur to me. I avoided the busiest streets, going into areas where half the streetlights were out and the dust was suffocating. I had to decipher the headlight beams sweeping the dust clouds from behind me to know when another car was going to buck ruts passed my left elbow. Underneath me, the sidewalk appeared and disappeared block to block. And on the right were occasional telephone poles tilting into the street that I had to squeeze around while sheering away from the passing cars. But I kept pushing, pushing.

Finally the hotel sign was visible a block down, then the front door, then the desk clerk, the key, the stairs, the hall to my door, my door, and now I am inside and the door is shut and locked.

Felt the first waves of fatigue and am now finally ready to crash but had to get this down first.

October 9, 1967
On the train headed north

Late this morning, I was on the street and heard a distant muffled explosion and after a few seconds saw drifting up into the sky a thin ribbon of black smoke apparently at the edge of town. A half hour or so later, I bumped into an American freak I'd talked to a couple times and he told me someone had tried to blow a hole in a wall of the prison and killed a guard. The Mexican police are (understandably) freaking out.

I knew immediately that every freak in town was in danger and rushed, as fast as I could without actually running, back to my hotel, packed in a couple minutes, and rushed-almost-running all the way to catch this 1:08 PM northbound train.

That's all I know. I don't know if the Canadians were involved. I didn't see any of them this morning. It seems like an incredibly stupid thing to do. Like an idea somebody got from a bad Hollywood movie. It's tempting to think the whispering last night was about that. But I'll never know for sure ...

As for last night, I remembered this morning how you once so eloquently put it during one of your own crash landings into the loonie bin, "Help! I'm surrounded by people."

There are a couple freaks on the train right now but I've never seen them before. Ever notice how you automatically scan an enclosed public space for another freak? And how you relax a little (no, a lot) if you find one? Must be the same for negroes in the States.

I brought the kilo. I'm thinking about what to do with it.

There are some Mexican Army troops on the train. They're about my own age, so it was easy to talk to them when we stopped at a little town and got out and stretched. At one point I asked where they were going and they said there were horses in some of the train cars and they were headed into the mountains to chase "banditos."

That was a couple hours ago and I've been thinking: "bandits," isn't that what reactionary governments have always called rebels? Not that I've heard of any in Mexico, that kind of thing would be hushed up anyway. But would they really have to send the army after bandits?

Hey that reminds me of something groovy I forgot to tell you. About mid afternoon one day in Torreon I was hungry and noticed that I was on a street in which every building was a restaurant. I randomly picked one in the middle of the block and entered.

I'm the only one there. I sit down and a foxy waitress comes up and I'm reading the menu and digging her smile, but when I speak, placing my order, she suddenly turns around and walks away.

She comes back leading a tall frail ol' geezer in his late seventies, at least. He was Irish and spoke with a thick brogue and said he didn't have much chance to speak English and "relishes" it. (Actually it had been some days since I spoke any

English.) I invited him to sit down and we started talking and slowly, as I waited for chicken enchiladas with mole and then ate them, his story came out.

He participated in the Easter Rising of 1916 in Dublin that started the Irish Revolution. He knew De Valera personally. He was involved in a political assassination of a British official around that time (even now fifty years later he wouldn't get into details) and he had to escape to New York as a stowaway and was almost captured there but then ran all the way to Texas where he got arrested just for being foreign. He broke out of jail with a bunch of Mexicans, some of them revolutionaries, and with them he joined Pancho Villa's army. He started a family and businesses here and he never went back to Ireland even for a visit, and I could see how that pained him now that he was too old to make the journey. His name is McGowan but he's called "El Greco," the Greek, because he married a Greek immigrant. She runs the restaurant.

I can see how someone could arrive here and just immediately become Mexican.

I can barely write this for trembling. I just saw... We just stopped in another town, called Benjamin Hill ("Bain-ha-meen Eel"). I got out and went to a little stand selling candy and toys and comic books and bought a Spanish language Tarzan comic. I walked back to the train and stood reading it by the steps up to the car.

"Le gusta el libro, heh?" (*You like the book, huh?*) someone asked me.

I looked up from the comic book and standing in front of me was a middle-aged Mexican, grizzled and weathered, no higher than my shoulder, in over-sized torn clothes as dirty as the soles of his unraveling sandals. His bindle was a sack over his shoulder that could've been a pillowcase. He had a broad happy smile. A wretch noticed only by the flies. And me. I started trembling.

He was the most perfect specimen of a Holy Fool that I have ever seen. Like Han Shan, the Tang poet Gary Snyder translated in *Riprap*. The dishwasher at the Taoist monastery who's wiser than the abbot.

He took the comic book from my hands without saying a thing and started at the first page, commenting frame by frame. He found something amusing if not hilarious on almost every page.

"Mire!... El mono!... " (*Look... The monkey...*) he said pointing at a frame and holding up the book for me to see.

I followed his finger and then looked at him and smiled and nodded. I was gradually relaxing into this visitation. Then a gaggle of kids fell on him almost knocking him over. One draped on each shoulder, the rest crowded at his sides. I had seen a couple of them earlier playing in the area. They looked from the comic book up at me to make sure it was alright to look at it. I just smiled. They smiled and went back to it.

"Ay, aqui! El leon!!" (*Hey, here ... The lion...*) the Fool exclaimed and pointed at another frame.

The kids, open-mouthed with awe, followed his finger and jostled to see better. Probably none of them, including the Fool, could read, so they were following the story by interpreting the pictures. There was nothing condescending in his attitude; he didn't even find the book silly – just funny. Physically he was perfect but that wouldn't have been enough without the ultimate certifying trait: the purity of his delight. He had deep smile lines around the eyes. The Fool sees what's there and speaks profundities too obvious for the adult, sometimes not fully understanding himself what he's saying. Most important of all, he's happy. Emerson says the wise man is content.

A bell clanged a couple times and the train engine sounded its horn and people started getting back onto the train. I moved reluctantly toward the steps. I thought about giving him money but I had less than two dollars left as it was. Besides, he might not take the money any more seriously than the comic book.

As I moved up the steps, he looked at me and we locked gazes.

"Guardelo," (*Keep it.*) I said.

He didn't thank me and didn't wave or even nod good-bye but went back to the comic. If I had taken it with me he would be just as happy right now but for a different reason. I watched them through the window while the train slowly pulled out. One of the

194

kids pointed at a frame and a different kid made a crack that broke them all up.

He was the real thing, avatar in direct descent from Han Shan, Ryokan, and the others. Now I've seen one and there can be no doubt that they're out there.

Just now, back in another dusty little town we stopped in, I saw a dog like no creature I have ever seen before. Some boys were idly pelting it with rocks or trying to. None of the rocks hit the dog though it made no effort to avoid them. It just trotted evenly away from its tormentors.

It seemed as much rat as dog, with torn ears, corrugated ribs, and the permanent snarl of the cornered. It was knee high, with sparse gray fur, lifetime mange, and patches of pink flesh stippled with welts and scabs and scarlet craters. It had probably spent its life just skirting starvation.

It trotted away down the middle of a broad dirt street and pothole obstacle course. Guts dangled from its asshole and above that was the shit-encrusted remnant of a tail. Rocks bounced and skittered around it.

It may be getting to me. The dirt-smeared urchins staring the train along. They would be happy to live off our garbage. Is it because their skin is too dark? Remember the Ron Cobb cartoon with the businessman who says, "Poverty is God's punishment for not believing in capitalism enough"? I see it so clearly now: they're our niggers. California's niggers.

Christ I'm trembling again! But this time from fear.

It's hard to sleep on the train, the noise and the jostling (I'm in an aisle seat), so when I finally succeeded in drifting off this afternoon and was knocked hard by a passer-by, I was really pissed and ready to snap at somebody. But when I opened my eyes, there was a square-handled pistol in a holster right in front of me, moving away. It was on the hip of a federale in a khaki uniform.

There were two of them going down to the front of the car, knocking whomever they pleased. At the front, each reached up into one of the overhead luggage racks and, without a word to anyone, started opening and searching luggage. Those gringos I saw earlier complained but the federales ignored them. The

Mexican passengers kept quiet. Before a wake of spilled luggage, the federales were searching their way back toward my end of the car.

Then I remembered the kilo in my duffle bag in the overhead rack opposite. I held myself back from jumping up right away. When I did get up, I held my stomach and walked a ways haltingly down the swaying isle holding onto seat backs. I stopped and backed up as if I had forgotten something and reached into the rack, unzipped the duffle bag, and inside it, wrapped the kilo in a shirt, and took it out. Without once looking at the approaching federales, I continued down the aisle away from them toward the bathroom, savoring each instant they didn't call out to me.

The bathroom was occupied... of course. I stood there waiting, clutching the key to my stomach, while the federales came on. I couldn't resist a quick glance. They were almost here. There were only two or three unopened bags left in each rack. Should I turn around and go into the next car? Could draw too much attention.

Then the lock clicked and the door opened and a woman came out and smiled and I quickly went in around her and locked the door. The toilets don't flush, they're just a hole in the floor and the shit goes down onto the tracks.

I opened up the bag containing the key which was glued together with sugar, as we've seen them before up in the City. In seconds, I broke it up and dropped all the pieces and the bag down the hole.

I then celebrated with a piss.

I wonder if this sudden search by the federales is normal or related to what happened back in Mazatlan?

Hey, I just realized something as we're approaching the border: I'll be in LA before this letter. I might as well hand-deliver it myself. Are there specific visiting hours and all that? Christ, I hope you can lend me enough money to get back to San Francisco. I used my fall-back emergency stash to buy the key. Five bucks would be enough.

Long Hair

"We have to talk," he said.

She looked at him. She was hunched, tensed, and cornered.

"You must know how I feel about you by now," he began. "It would be hard to miss. But I don't know how you feel about me."

She relaxed and turned away from him to stare over the steering wheel. They were in her rickety Corvair (he didn't own a car) parked beside the six-lanes of 19th Avenue in front of San Francisco State. Packs of cars intermittently whooshed by a couple feet from the door beside her.

He followed her line of sight out the windshield and then said: "I mean, we're together almost everyday, so you must like my companionship. But you also seem. . . I dunno. . . " He turned to watch her response. ". . . Repulsed by me."

She turned toward him with a tiny smirk of admiration for the aptness of his word.

"What's wrong?" he pleaded. "You act sometimes like I have leprosy or something. Am I . . . physically . . . unattractive . . . to you? What is it?"

"Your hair," she said quietly. "It's your hair."

He ran his fingers through his short-cropped hair. It had grown somewhat since they met, but it was still a straight's haircut.

"What do you mean?" he asked, though he already knew the answer.

"Your hair, it disgusts me," she said firmly. "Short hair is sexually repulsive to me. It just looks ugly."

Silence except for the engine whine of passing cars. He was stunned and reeling.

She was gaining momentum. "And your clothes... What *are* you? Your personality is hip, but your appearance is straight. No, not even straight. Straights don't even dress like that." She gestured dismissively at his saggy corduroy coat and baggy khaki pants. "You're a. . . you're a. . . non-entity."

He sprang upright and said, "That's right! That's exactly what I am. When I got out of the mental hospital, I cut my hair and threw away my bell bottoms and Beatle boots, because I was through belonging to a camp. I wanted to erase myself. To be invisible. I like it that way."

"Well I don't. It's ugly."

She had been a groupie in high school, often staking out the airport with girlfriends on the off-chance of catching a passing rock band. He knew her type well. Teenie boppers, nymphet refugees from suburbia, were always hanging out on Haight Street, hoping to be picked up by an incarnation of their rock star fantasies. He also knew cats who played-up a resemblance to a rock star to pick up these chicks. One night in a dark corner of the mezzanine at the Fillmore Auditorium, while she was still a virgin, she sucked the cock of such a guy. Because of his "regal demeanor."

She had managed to transfer an obsession with the Beatles and other English rock groups into an obsession with English literature and now she was a straight-A student aimed point-blank at a PHD with a groupie lodged deep in her libido.

Sltting beside her in the car, he realized the absurdity of his predicament. He had had many sex partners but never a girlfriend. He had never so much as touched a girl he was in love with. He didn't go steady in high school because no girl would have him. He was too weird. And here he was again, in love, and again, thwarted from living out the rock songs, those ad jingles for romantic love. And this time, he was thwarted by a frivolous,

adolescent fetish!!! He had held strategy sessions with a couple chicks from his outpatient therapy group and hair didn't come up once.

"This is some kind of sick joke!" he suddenly roared with outrage. "I don't believe it. I. . . it's. . . this is incredible!"

Thrown onto the defensive, she snuck an embarrassed glance at him, then bent her head and stared at her fidgeting hands.

"You mean to tell me, you're going to let **HAIR** keep us from getting together?! I mean. . . we have so much. We've always got something to talk about. We're always laughing. We have the same values. It's a perfect match."

"I know. I know. I don't know what to do." He realized this had been a gnawing problem for her. "It's the way I feel. I can't help it. I love long hair."

He saw that she was a victim of this no less than he was. All the same, when he thought about being thwarted again, a shiver of rage ran through him, and he slammed his fist on the dashboard and shoved his face to within inches of hers and yelled, "But I love you goddamnit, can't you see that?!"

He noticed a fleck of his saliva on her cheek and sat upright.

"Yes," she replied in a near-whisper. Then she crumpled into sobs and said, "What can I do? What can I do?"

He wanted to comfort her but was afraid to touch her. Instead, he leaned his head against the cold, wet window. The windows were translucent with condensation (as if they had been making out) and glowed gray with the afternoon overcast.

He felt another surge of outrage and this time decided he would never see her again. But that wasn't feasible. Due to an accident of scheduling, they shared one class Mondays, Wednesdays, and Fridays, and another Tuesdays and Thursdays, and it was too late in the semester to transfer out of the classes and dropping them would endanger his draft deferment.

Then he admitted to himself that he wouldn't have left the classes anyway. He still had a nub of hope.

*

One night the previous summer, the Summer of Love of 1967, he stood across the street from Langley Porter Neuro-Psychiatric Institute. He was shivering in the ocean wind and panting because he had just climbed one of the City's steepest hills. He thought about how to explain his problem to the hospital staff and balked. Maybe he wasn't sick enough, or didn't have the right kind of sickness. Eventually, he convinced himself that he somehow wouldn't qualify for admittance, and anyway with enough time he would master the problem himself. So he didn't go in. But six months later his condition hadn't improved and he went there to ask for help.

Those few weeks weren't a particularly unpleasant experience. The therapy groups didn't seem to accomplish much. The panic and the chaos and the withdrawal into a barricaded dungeon cell deep inside himself and the urge for panicked flight from anything resembling a human being, they all seemed to dissipate by themselves.

After he left the hospital, at the beginning of the spring semester of 1968, he felt a calm, crystalline lucidity. Demagnetized and socially erased by a straight's costume, he also felt a giddy anonymity, savoring college like never before. He drifted on the current of bodies jostling through the halls during registration, savored the chicks sunning on the quad lawn, watched the debates
beside card tables hung-round with posters and heaped with pamphlets.

Then she shattered his serenity.

*

They had a class together every weekday, nevertheless it took some weeks before he noticed her. But for a couple days after he did, he just watched her, in awe.

And then there she was, during a break, approaching him down a corridor, about fifty feet away, in conversation with another

chick. Her over-sized army-surplus jacket was open for the first time and he saw her breasts, small but firm, pointed and freely bobbing under a sweater as she walked. The pockets of the jacket drooped within inches of the knee-high black boots her pants were stuffed into. Her clomping reverberated down the corridor.

He stared unconsciously. She had lank brown hair that hung to mid back and bounced with her stride, and as she passed, she signaled him by tucking a strand behind an ear. She had a thin-boned frailty and the hunch of someone expecting an explosion. Her skin was the hue of milk glass and her laugh-ready eyes were light blue.

Normally he would have settled for furtive glances and a nod and a smile as they passed in the hall, but he was only a couple weeks out of the mental hospital, and her attractiveness and his jarred inhibitions shoved him at her when he saw her after class in line at a water fountain. With her right hand resting on a cocked hip, she was staring into thoughts, and smiling. He got immediately behind her.

"Like that book?" he asked of a book by philosopher Alan Watts in her back pocket.

She turned around after the surprise of his voice.

"Yeah," she said, pleased. "He's great. He's so... articulate." She took the book from her pocket and held it with both hands. "Some of the things he says. . . Wow. . . He's too much." She shook her head in wonder. She had bangs over an oval face with a pointed chin and an aquiline nose.

"I had lunch with him a couple weeks ago," he blurted out. Immediately he cringed with regret, but he was careening downhill with no brakes.

"Oh yeah?" She was impressed. "This is the first book of his that I've read. I don't know that much about him. I just discovered the cosmos a couple months ago." She threw up a hand in happy exasperation at the overdue arrival. "Did you like it?" she asked, holding up the book.

"Uh, well I haven't exactly read that one . . . yet. But I looked it over."

It was her turn at the fountain. Afterwards, she straightened and stood aside for him.

"Where did you meet him?" she asked, while he gulped water.

"In a mental hospital," he replied with a slight smirk of pride, then returned to the water.

When he stood up and wiped his mouth with the back of his hand, he noticed with relief that she was waiting for him. Her expression was solemn but sympathetic. He now knew the degree of her hipness.

"I was a patient at Langley Porter, up at U.C." He said it as if reciting the inscription on a trophy. "Watts used to come around and talk to the patients every once and a while. Joan Baez came once too."

He was confident now.

"What was it like?" she asked delicately as they slowly began walking down the hall.

"The hospital? Oh, it was o.k. I learned to play pool, and the food was alright. The rest of it was a waste of time."

"What was Watts like?"

They had reached the end of the hall and he could see she was starting down an intersecting hall in a direction opposite to his.

"Uh, feel like a cup of coffee?" he asked.

She stared at him a moment, then said, "Yeah, sure."

It was late in the afternoon and the cafeteria was empty enough so that they could have one of the padded booths. They each sat behind a white, institutional mug with steam wafting up.

"Actually, I have a confession to make," he said. "I did meet Watts but. . . I blew it with him."

"How?"

He was scrambling to shade it, tilt it in favor of himself, but he was too keyed up, and instead an outburst of suicidal candor escaped him.

"I got defensive and provoked an argument."

He was surprised and delighted to see her grinning.

"He wasn't very, uh, elevated," he went on. "In fact, he had a hangover."

She chuckled.

"He really wanted to seem hip, so he kept talking about his drug experiences. I thought he was phoney, and I didn't try to hide it. He didn't like me much."

She threw her head back and laughed uproariously.

"That's great! That's fantastic! That's just what I would have done," she said, shaking her head at such a coincidence.

She liked him. He saw it in her eyes and relaxed.

After a pause, she asked gingerly, "Why did you go to the hospital?"

"Oh, I took too much speed, about six times normal, and I freaked out. Got real paranoid and catatonic. I was glad to be there after a while. Nice quiet place to come down in."

About an hour later, they slouched in contented silence, digesting biographical data. She lived with her parents in working class San Bruno. Until she escaped to the livingroom couch in early adolescence, she shared a bedroom with an older schizophrenic and sedated sister. So she grew up in a one-patient mental hospital, and as a result, her own stability was so fragile that, despite her hipness, she was terrified of all drugs, even alcohol.

He broke a silence by asking the question, as casually as he could while trembling, "You have an ol' man?"

She searched his eyes quickly and answered, "No."

In her eyes, he caught a glint of anger, as if she was threatened. In his eyes, she saw eager desire, and softened.

"I had an ol' man, sort of, for awhile. I'm not into that anymore. I don't like to feel all freaked out over somebody. I don't need that. I'm really into serenity."

"Yeah, I know what you mean. I feel the same way," he said, and then leaned forward on his elbows, over clasped hands. "But I also like ecstasy." She flashed a warning glare, a step-back order, and he leaned back, but added, "You can have both ya know."

"No," she said, then turned toward the window, now opaque with night, and stared into her thoughts. "No... I don't want that now."

He knew it was time to retreat, so he kept quiet.

She finally broke a long pause by asking, "You didn't have your hair that short in the Haight, did you?"

*

That night, he entered his tiny studio apartment in the Mission District and immediately started to rehearse asking her for a date. Through dinner and afterwards, and for hours after he went to bed, he polished his lines.

The next day she was late for class, blowing away his poise. She finally did arrive, but he had to wait for the class to end, and when it did, she got up and left without acknowledging him. He caught up with her in the hall.

"Oh. . . h-hi. . ." he said as if he just happened to bump into her.

"Hi," she said with a polite, distant smile.

She kept walking and he struggled on wobbly knees to keep up.

"Uh. . . I was wondering if. . . how are you?"

"Fine."

"Good."

He felt like he was holding in a seizure, as if he might scream or explode or laugh hysterically. His tension arced onto her and she became nervous, not knowing why.

"Uh. . . could. . . do you wanna. . . would you like to go to a movie this weekend?"

"What? I don't think so. No, I can't. It's my nephew's birthday and we're throwing a party for him."

"Oh. O.k. Well, have a nice weekend. See ya next week."

"Yeah. You too."

He released a deep sigh. She went to her car and he to a bench in a nearby garden nook to calm down. It wasn't until late in the weekend that he realized he didn't have to worry about getting a date with her. They would be together an hour a day, five days a week, for months.

Something this important brought out in him the patient, meticulous strategist. Not only did he not ask her out again, he

didn't even try to strike up a conversation. He was friendly, and after class they occasionally exchanged quips on discussions or classmates or the teacher. Gradually, he made himself safe, familiar, comfortable. Within a few weeks they had started a habit of spending every afternoon sitting over coffee and talking, ravenously.

She was sassy and opinionated and quick-witted and all of it incongruously packed into an anemic-looking sparrow of a girl. He savored every flick of her boney wrists, every wry sidelong half grin, every one of the deft impersonations that illustrated her anecdotes. She obviously enjoyed their special rapport, but she was very troubled about her feelings for him. He noticed this and dismissed it as fear of getting hurt.

He waited three weeks before even attempting physical affection. Then he occasionally made his hand brush hers, sat so close they touched, and even several times lifted a stray strand of hair from her face. Each time he was rebuffed by a scowl. But he was determined, and he was sure this irregularity of hers could be overcome in time.

Then one afternoon as they were leaving campus together, he followed her through a door and placed his hand on her back. She vehemently swiped it off with an elbow. The rest of the way to her car neither mentioned her reaction to his touch, but it lurked under the conversation. After they got into the Corvair, parked on the roaring six lanes of 19th Avenue, she put the key in the ignition but didn't turn it. Each waited for the other to speak first. He did.

*

After she declared her revulsion that afternoon of the steamed windows in the parked car, they still hung out together most afternoons but witty banter was replaced by a sullen silence, punctuated by his sighs. His brooding was no longer on how to win her love but how to escape his own. He wanted to dig it out like a bullet.

Conversation inevitably degenerated into her defense of her taste (embarrassed at first, then haughty) versus his vitriolic attacks on an inane but implacable nuisance. A train was being

derailed by a pebble. He still loved her but now he also hated her. It would take at least a year for his hair to grow as long as she wanted it, and anyway, out of spite, he told her that he was going to keep it short.

One sunny Friday afternoon they went to a free promotional rock concert in Golden Gate Park, common in 1968. The grass was boggy in places from a spring rain, and it sucked at his shoes and her boots as they crossed the meadow toward the stage where a crowd of about a hundred milled around in the pre-concert lull.

"Want to sit here?" she asked him of a dry spot on the outskirts of the crowd.

"I don't care."

"Wait. How about over there?" She pointed to a slope on the opposite side of the crowd.

"Yeah. That's fine."

They sat on the slope, at about head level with the crowd. He sat in the pose of his despair: legs pulled up to his chest, arms around knees, brow pinched, staring into himself. She stretched out beside him, leaning on an elbow, watching the crowd. Neither spoke. He wanted to get up, go home, and never speak to her again. But he couldn't stop hoping.

Musicians tuned guitars. Roadies scurried over and around the flatbed truck that served as the stage. He looked at the crowd and was somewhat pulled out of himself by familiar faces. It was testament to the small town character of the San Francisco hip scene that he never went downtown or to a public event without seeing someone he knew. Even in a crowd this small, there were a few he could visit with, if he had been capable of conversation. Instead he heaved a deep sigh.

She was flattered. No one had ever reacted to her with this much intensity. She studied him, curious. She felt no sympathy for him though. He deserved it for his ridicule of her. It penetrated his daze that she was staring at him. Slowly, he turned toward her, then stopped, stunned by the expression on her face: a gloating sneer. She was enjoying his pain.

Then, with the silent thunderclap of a mini-satori, the love vanished. Just clicked off. He was free. Now he stared right back at her, savoring her sudden ordinariness.

Guitars, bass, and drums detonated together as the first number began. She didn't notice his transformation until he smiled. It was a joyous upwelling of relief and it stunned her. Her sneer crumpled. He stood up and stretched and looked down onto her upturned face.

"I'm going to circulate and talk to some friends," he said, then went down the slope and disappeared among the bodies.

An hour or so later, as they recrossed the meadow toward her car, he walked at his own brisk pace, silent and smiling, and she trotted beside him, grinning weakly, suspicious that she was the brunt of a joke. He wanted to get home as soon as possible and never speak to her again and not even bother to explain. He thought she deserved it; still he couldn't do it. It would be like abandoning an accident victim. He would tell her what had happened, then go home and never speak to her again.

When they were standing beside her car and she was rummaging in her purse for the keys, he said to her, "I don't love you anymore."

She stared at him in disbelief. His casual indifference brought it home. When she didn't speak, he felt compelled to.

"It happened back there," he said, gesturing toward the distant, tinny guitar smudge on the wind.

He had expected when he told her that she would be sore and defensive. Perhaps for awhile she would even miss him, miss his companionship anyway, but certainly it wouldn't be anymore difficult for her to forget him than vice versa.

Instead, she threw her fists at the sky and wailed: "Oh no, I did it again!"

Then tears started down her cheeks. Shit, he thought, where did this come from? Then she walked passed him and passed her car. He didn't know where she was going and didn't care, except that she was his ride home, so he followed her into a eucalyptus grove, where they waded through knee-high grass to a clearing.

"What did you expect?" he asked.

"I don't know," she blubbered.

"I didn't know you felt like this."

"I didn't either."

They started walking along the perimeter of the clearing, around and around, trudging an oval rut in the grass. He looked up and saw that the tops of the eucalyptus trees, flung back and forth in the ocean wind, were lit with last sunlight.

"As usual, you're right on time," he said, referring to her insulting habit of being late for every meeting.

She smiled, almost laughed. The old, easy rapport resurfaced. Then was gone.

"You should've shown it earlier," he said with glum resentment.

"I know. I couldn't."

"You said I was physically repulsive to you."

"I know."

"I've been miserable for weeks . . . ever since that day in the car... "

*

An hour or so later, they were facing each other in their oval rut.

"Do you think you could love me again?" she asked without looking at him.

He was numb with fatigue and his head ached from hunger. He just wanted to go home. She now leaned against him and he understood it to be a cue to embrace her, so he did. He didn't want to deceive her, but even more, he didn't want anymore crying.

He looked up and noticed there was only a hint of day left in the sky. Through the eucalyptus trees, he saw the Lincoln Avenue street lights come on. Now she turned her face up to his and he recognized a cue to kiss her and he did.

The rest of the night he was on automatic pilot. She drove them to his studio apartment and he invited her to stay for dinner.

"Oh shit!" he said looking into the small near-empty refrigerator. "That's right... I was going to go to the grocery store. How about breakfast cereal?"

After the cereal dinner, she sat in the stuffed chair, he on the bed. He was afraid to make his moves because he wasn't yet convinced she would accept his touch, so he started an empty chatter.

"Yeah, didn't I tell you about that? I got out of the hospital and got this place and everything I needed was already here. Furniture, dishes, utensils, even sheets. And it's *not* a furnished apartment. There was an old lady living here before and she died. Her family took her clothes and a few other things but they left all this. Even a jar of coins... Yeah, this is a weird place... There're these Russian Orthodox priests living here and I see them in the halls all the time with these long beards and long black cassocks down to their shoes... And across the hall is this creep who listens to records of Ku Klux Klan meetings. Swear-to-god! ... Yeah, it's really disgusting. And whenever he leaves, a friend of his comes around and the wife greets him at the door with a kiss..."

Which brought him around to sex. It occurred to him that he didn't really care if she turned him down. At least then she would leave and he could go to sleep. So he got up and knelt beside her chair and kissed her. She not only didn't stop him but tilted her head and ground her mouth against his. O.k., but she had already done that much in the park. His hand went straight to a breast. After the shock wore off, he waited, and she didn't remove it. So he slid it under her sweater. Still no resistance.

"Let's sit on the bed," he said and stood and sat on the bed.

She got up uncertainly and sat next to him.

"There's something I need to tell you," she said cringing with embarrassment. "I'm a virgin."

"O.k.," he said, surprised, but not turned on or off by it. "You weren't much of a groupie, were you?"

She laughed and said, "No, I wasn't."

She was now just another one night stand that he knew wouldn't go anywhere. Better than masturbation though. So they started kissing again. He slid his hand under her sweater and then into her pants. Courteously, dispassionately, he explored her desanctified body. Then he unzipped his fly and put her hand in it. So far she hadn't shown even reluctance at any point.

"You want to get undressed?" he asked.

She pulled her hand out and thought.

"I dunno... "she said. "I... I..."

"Forget it... It's o.k... No big deal," he said then zipped his fly.

He realized from her relieved smile that she had mistaken his indifference for kindness. She kissed him.

Then she announced she had to go and he walked her to the head of the stairs that lead to the street door. They pressed their bodies and lips hard against each other then parted with a few light pecks. Already they were exchanging the small affections of a couple.

"Wanna get together tomorrow?" she asked. It would be the first time they were together on a Saturday.

"Sure," he said.

"O.k., I'll come around . . . how's eleven?"

"How 'bout one?"

"O.k."

They kissed again and parted, her face radiant with the quiet joy of someone in love and loved. She slowly started down the stairs, releasing his hand reluctantly from the third step. Then she turned and ran, boots clomping, hair flaring. He had never seen her so happy. When she was outside, she turned and gave him a quick, playful little wave through the glass in the street door, then disappeared.

He turned and walked back to his apartment. The cereal had revived him somewhat, but now he was depressed. True, he was no longer pinned under crushing frustration, but he had conclusively missed, yet again, the Big Bliss.

As he went inside, he remembered that he hadn't answered her question in the eucalyptus grove, "Do you think you could love me again?"

Six weeks later, they got their first apartment together, and he didn't answer the question in those six weeks, in the two years they lived together, or in the two years it took them to break up.

Satori

It started in my stomach and then became a muffled tickle climbing my spine, rising slowly, up, up, up, gradually, inevitably, casually, until it reached the skull, entered the central control room, and then, as suddenly and nonchalantly as the flicking off of a light switch, the universe was no more. Satori.

But it really started hours earlier....

"A description of what is is an explanation."

"Hey that's pretty good!"

We were walking on Haight Street late at night.

A while later. "Reality is a quality of perception."

"Tasty."

I was with an old roommate and friend, Mike, a merchant seaman back in San Francisco for a few days. It was winter 1966 and this was the first acid trip for either of us since it was made illegal just a few weeks earlier.

A while later. "The mystic hears the roar of the shoreless river."

"Uh... Ok... nice."

This was also the first time I had had someone else along for one of my ritual late night walks. These ecstatic rambles frequently followed hours of ecstatic reading in Alan Watts, D.T. Suzuki, Buddhist philosophers, and Norman O. Brown, among others. Insights that used to just swirl around in my head now were flying out my mouth, refined and compacted by the acid.

A while later. "When you see the road is endless then you're home."

"O.k ... kinda ... zen."

Ours was a literary friendship and he wanted to participate and compete but he couldn't, and I knew in my acid clairvoyance that it was in part because he was stunned by my brilliance, as was I. I had no idea where these things were coming from. They were meteors from the depths of inner space.

"In a few blinks, we won't even be memories. A few blinks after that, anything we can imagine will be as if it never existed."

I expected him to say, "Wordy..." but instead he said, "The cloud-capp'd towers, the gorgeous palaces, the solemn temples, the great globe itself, yea, all which it inherit, shall dissolve and leave not a rack behind. We are such stuff as dreams are made of, and our little life is surrounded by a sleep."

The only way he could get into the game was by enlisting Shakespeare. Mike was always good with quotes.

A while later, I lobbed at him: "Death is nothing to fear / You won't know that you're not here."

I was starting to feel somewhat avenged for his merciless teasing last summer. He had been one of my mentors and initiators into the ways of the Haight and hip culture generally but he was also tormented by thwarted love for the high school friend of mine with whom he and I and her newest ol' man shared a basement pad in the Haight. He had been cruelly goaded to cruelty.

That was another reason he couldn't compete with me: he was growing increasingly bummed as my company and the Haight generally and the acid particularly were bringing back that pain. We had dropped the acid after ten and talked for a couple hours before deciding to get out of my cramped studio apartment. The warm dry nights of the fall were over and this night was full of that cold heavy fog that is just short of a drizzle and that sets the fog horns groaning.

Now we had been on Haight Street for seven or eight blocks and were approaching the intersection with Masonic, the gateway to Haight Street proper, the part that would be world famous in a few months. The lights of the Drogstore Café were coming up on the right.

"This world is a copy without an original."

"Hey man, I'm gonna split."

"Oh..."

He was six six and one of the few men I had to look up at. I recognized in his coarse features, under spilling red curls, acid depression, a freefall crashdive inward.

"Uh, ya wanna go in the Drogstore?" I asked.

"Naw, I'm cold ... I just wanna go back." And though he couldn't say it, get away from me.

"O.k ... You got that key to the pad that I gave ya?" I asked.

"Yeah," he said.

"O.k., well... I'm gonna keep walking for a while."

"O.k.," he said and turned around adding, "See ya."

"Yeah see ya."

I watched him walk away and then turned around and went up to the edge of Masonic Street. The light was red for me but there was no traffic so I could have crossed but instead I looked to my right into the Drogstore Café and immediately knew it wasn't for me ... not tonight ... not on acid, even though there were various habitués in there with whom I had often closed the place at a cluster of small tables pushed together during intense philosophical debates.

I turned around and my eyes were drawn to the streetlights across the street, and just above them, the ceiling of churned fog. I could see individual drops and the pulsing rainbow at the center of each... Weeks later the traffic light changed and I crossed Masonic.

I had no destination. I just knew that the Drogstore was not for me tonight. I was immediately struck by the emptiness of Haight Street, the palpable absence of milling throngs of freaks. Then I noticed the quiet that was occasionally broken by cars with tires that sounded like tearing glue, and was broken even more occasionally by the bass thrum of a foghorn that I now felt in my belly. A freak passed, aimlessly wandering, wrapped in a blanket, vaguely familiar, though I couldn't find a name. My crumpled old leather jacket would be warm enough, at least while I was pumping out the strides.

*

Some of the most enjoyable hours of my boyhood were spent with my dog wandering in the wilderness behind our house. And now in San Francisco I was continuing the habit. A couple nights a week I would slip on hiking boots and take off in any direction they chose. And the blocks I ticked off not only measured my progress through the City but also into myself.

I would walk along ruminating on readings until I was giddy with exhaustion and then start laughing for no reason and keep laughing, harder, until my eyes teared. Then I would sing rock songs, playing all the instruments and singing all the parts simultaneously, while gobbling blocks on the most deserted streets. Sometimes I ran or skipped. I was filled to bursting with a wild, spontaneous, aimless rapture. I was free, alone, and happy, fascinated by everything around me and exultant before a future that could only be fantastic.

One night I walked through a race riot. The cops killed a Negro kid. Shot him in the back while he was fleeing. And the whole Fillmore erupted. "Racial disturbances" were sweeping the nation that fall and it was San Francisco's turn. I had been at the Drogstore Café only a few minutes when the 10PM curfew hit. I was tired after hours of walking, and was looking forward to some rest and socializing and had forgotten about the curfew.

I split when the first patrol car pulled up and parked across Masonic. It was the middle of September, the hottest month of the year, and this was one of the hottest nights of the year, so I would be sweating the whole 8 or so blocks back to the pad which was at the other end of the Haight and into the Fillmore District. I stretched my legs full-stride and pushed to a near-run along Page Street avoiding Haight Street, which ran parallel a block south. All the while I was tensed for a patrol car, even though I was entering the riot area with only an idiot's grin for protection.

At one point, two Negroes my age passed me from the opposite direction and one stopped and turned around and muttered something about white people but his companion briskly scolded him and they went on. I wondered: was it becoming

known in the Negro community that these young whites with long hair were okay?

Finally, only a block from the pad and pushed by momentum from going down the last steep hill, I was crossing Divisadero. This normally busy four-lane crosstown thoroughfare was completely empty, not a car in sight in either direction. When I looked south though, up the hill, I was stopped in my tracks. A block up, in the middle of the intersection with Haight Street, right under a streetlight, was a canvas covered military truck. Pimply dazed national guardsmen were jumping from it onto the street, helmets and carbines glinting.

I kept pushing. Now under thin smoke drifting high in the still air, I heard multiple distant sirens. My street door was in sight, and as I was searching for the key, I noted a garbage can had been emptied into the street. As I closed the door, I heard a distant smashing of glass.

After these long late walks, I got back to my place exhausted, clear, and tranquil, and I would lay on my mattress on the floor in the dark studio, and with a broken transistor radio held together with rubber bands laying on my chest, I would writhe off to rock music the last bits of energy.

*

Before that night on Haight Street with Mike, I had never taken acid for one of those walks. And as I now bolted the familiar blocks, I got lost in studying the sidewalk unrolling underfoot, that narrow strip for people between the street and the buildings, daily growing richer with the stains of living.

"Prepare for the coming of the Lord, for Jesus is thy Savior!"

Suddenly to my left was a short middle-aged woman wearing rolled bobbie socks and with thick long dark frizzy hair, dewed with fog. She was a mechanism that errant souls tripped to release her spiel, which lasted just as long as it took to pass in front of the recessed doorway in which she huddled.

But I stopped and faced her. The first and biggest surprise about her was how good-looking she was. She lit up with a warm friendly smile.

" 'Not how the universe is is the mystical, but that it is' " I said. "That's not mine ... That's Wittgenstein ...."

" ... Oh ..."

I turned and continued west. She made me miss Mike for the first time. He had kept me focused. Now I was drifting.

In puberty I read books of advice to teenagers by Ann Landers. By junior year of high school, I had moved up to Sartre, Kierkegaard, and Nietzsche. There was practically nothing I enjoyed more than those rapt hours in my bedroom or in the darkest corner of the school library submerged in some treatise full of subtle distinctions between essence and existence or being and becoming.

Philosophy became second only to sex itself (and this was at a time when a hard-on was noticeable mainly by its absence). Philosophy also became an ego investment when I drew the attention of attractive girls in after-school catechism classes by asking sophisticated questions that befuddled the young priest. I got a scholarship to St. Crispin's College where I cavalierly annihilated opponents in late-night dorm-debates, sabotaging the tooth-fairy faith of jocks and novice brothers with ease. Now I was living alone for the first time and a sophomore at San Francisco State and just able to provide the grades necessary to avoid the draft while attending to my real education, the slow explosion in my mind through obsessive reading of philosophy.

Eventually and inevitably I discovered eastern religions and easily accepted their basic premise: if you don't see god everywhere, there's something wrong. Then I discovered Nagarjuna, one of the patriarchs of Buddhism. *The Central Philosophy of Buddhism* by T.R.V. Murti was a published doctoral thesis full of arabesque logic and untranslatable Sanskrit terminology. In recent days I had struggled with it in the Humanities enclosure in the San Francisco State library. I could now make out the outline of Nagarjuna's system for destroying all of one's premises in order to free-float in the void, enlightened.

Zen was the ultimate refinement of Buddhism and I was especially struck by the apparent randomness of Satori, the enlightenment experience, the goal of Zen. Even though I knew that satori usually required decades of za-zen meditation, I found in the small but rapidly growing literature of Zen a few anecdotes in which non-monks had the experience dropped on them. So I lived now hoping for an ambush.

*

There was so little pedestrian traffic on Haight Street that I made it to Schrader in record time though I didn't have a watch and couldn't find a clock in a shop window. It was late enough so that there were few lights in the apartments and flats above the shops. A block ahead was Stanyan Street and then Golden Gate Park, where I didn't want to be. I looked to my left, south down Schrader, and saw a light in a familiar window a couple blocks down.

I headed toward it and then suddenly a guy appeared at my elbow.

He asked, "Hey, uh ... wanna earn some money?" He was a pudgy nervous middle-aged pharmacist-looking guy, and he fell into step beside me.

"Doing what?"

"Oh, just ... let a guy fool around with ya."

I snickered and said, "Get outta here."

He looked as if he had just been bitten by a product on a supermarket shelf. He hurried across Schrader and got into a glossy Buick.

I walked a couple blocks then knocked on the street door to Ollie's studio apartment and after a few seconds he opened it and said, "Oh ... Hey man!"

"I was up on the Street ... And I saw the friendly light ..."

"Groovy! C'mon in ..." he said holding the door open.

I continued my prepared lines as I passed through the door, "...And I thought I could escape the fog and wind for awhile."

"Of course... I'm glad you did," he said and closed the door. "I took some deximil and I'm makin' somethin'."

"No shit?"

"Sit down," Ollie said indicating a stuffed chair.

"I took some acid," I said tossing my coat onto the arm of the chair.

"Oh yeah?"

Ollie was short with a weightlifter's build and he made himself stand out in the Haight by having a shaved head. At times he was surly and spoke with authority on every subject, but other times, he was a fawning host which was just what I needed now.

The studio was one good-sized room with a kitchenette and bathoom. His project was a stained-glass lampshade made of plastic on a table in the center of the room. It was a heap of colored, translucent plastic fragments which he was cutting and gluing together. Wafting up from a stereo in a corner was the Blues Project, one of the best of the new hip rock groups, like San Francisco's Grateful Dead and Jefferson Airplane, except the Blues Project was from New York.

"Hey, I've got somethin' for ya," Ollie said with a delighted grin. He turned and went over to the kitchenette. "I've been workin' on it and I think I've perfected it and you'll be the first to try it. I'll warm it up again… It'll just take a second."

He turned on a burner and placed a tea kettle on it. I was leaning against the wall, supporting myself on one hand, with my head canted so far to the left that it was uncomfortable. I was reading an episode of *Xorfuck, God of Rock*, an incoherent meth-epic by an anonymous folk poet written in randomly arranged square-foot blocks of miniscule longhand squeezed into available space on three walls.

"Did you ever hear of Han Shan?" I asked Ollie as I straightened upright.

"No."

"He was a dishwasher in a monastery during the Tang dynasty," I explained. "And also a great poet, and he went around scratching poems on the sides of cliffs and places like that. After he died, some Prince sent servants around the countryside to write the poems down."

"Far out," Ollie said not looking up from his measuring and pouring of dark foamy liquids. "The speed freak who invented

Xorfuck is Haight-Ashbury's Han Shan. Too much ... Hey, it's ready!"

He handed me a steaming cup. I slurped some and felt a bursting rush of warmth.

"What is it?" I asked.

"It's Dr. Pepper, Mu tea, and grass tea."

I sipped the concoction again and said, "Mmmm it's good ... thanks."

Ollie returned to the table and, with his face just inches above blue triangles and red squares, quietly talked as he worked. It seemed he wasn't so much talking to me as allowing me to eavesdrop on his talking to himself. My attention drifted away and his soft speed-babble became part of the audio landscape like the thumps from other apartments and the music.

The phone rang.

"I know who that is..." Ollie muttered on his way to the phone.

Whoever it was, at this time of night, it must have been urgent.

"Hello ... Yeah ... No, it's o.k. I wanted you to call ... "

He took a business course at State so that it would make him a better dealer and he had a grim determination that no one would take advantage of him.

"He *says* he got busted... but..... but .... but why didn't he at least have his ol' lady call me?"

My attention drifted into the music just as "Flute Thing" began. Each note dropped into a glassy sea, and as the ripple passed over the horizon, the next note dropped. I wondered if I had digested the grass tea yet. Then a muffled soothing tickle started up my spine and I slumped deeper into the seat and closed my eyes. Slowly, it ascended my back, rising up, up, up gradually, inevitably, casually ...

Later, I would describe it as "seeing pure energy." It was like driving through snow at night with the flakes flying into the windshield at you, except there were billions and they were microscopic and every conceivable color. It might have lasted one five-hundredths of a second or fifteen minutes.

*

So this was enlightenment... As I walked home in the chilly overcast dawn, I explored this new state of being. I wondered briefly whether this was an official satori experience and I was certifiably enlightened. Then I didn't care. It wasn't so much that I had any answers. I just didn't have any more questions. Everything was so obvious, so immediate, so real. Everything was the only way it could be. Philosophies, theories, and proof were completely irrelevant. Explanations and justifications were pointless. It seemed I would never have to think in the abstract again. Briefly, I felt that I had lost something and I wasn't sure of its value or whether I could find a replacement. But that passed and I felt a rush of joy. This was what I had been preparing for: satori, nirvana, making the two one.

When I got back to the pad Mike was asleep and snoring like he used to when we were roommates. Then, as I was undressing, I looked across the room, and in the dim light of an overcast morning through a drawn shade, I discovered the true price of being a sage. My books were haphazardly arranged on cinder block and board shelves and I stood before them in my underwear realizing I would have to give them away. Their vexations, speculations, stepping stone conclusions, the whole printed colloquy was part of that world I had now transcended.

When I laid down on the mattress on the floor, I felt the full weight of my exhaustion and fell asleep almost instantly. It was almost that quickly after I awoke in midafternoon, that I realized the "enlightenment" was gone. Gone the weightlessness, the lucidity, the detachment. I was still here, weighted-down in the vale of tears.

For a few minutes I became depressed then I remembered those on the path must persevere. This no doubt was one of many failures before I finally made it. And anyway, now I wouldn't have to give away my books.

Mike was gone. He left a terse note, and I never saw him or heard from him again.

The Fantasy Faire and Magic Mountain Music Festival

It's the usual party on wheels in the car: radio rock thumping in open-window wind-roar, a jug and a joint going the rounds. Danny is driving, Cookie and Don-Ed beside him. In the back seat, Tim is sitting next to Sherry who he doesn't really know very well. He bumped into her on Haight Street earlier that morning and invited her to come with us. I'm sitting next to Christine.

Grass and wine eventually kick-in. Knees wedged against the back of the front seat, we four slouch deeper and deeper. By the time we reach the Golden Gate Bridge, Tim has his arm on the seat above Sherry's shoulders. I'm still reeling with disbelief and awe, suspecting that I'm misreading this and afraid. Cookie occasionally peeps over the front seat and exchanges a knowing smile with Christine.

It is while she and Christine and I are ranking favorite cuts on the Doors' album that Danny suddenly lets out a panic-charged whisper, "Cool it man, the heat! Right behind us. "

"Don't turn around and look!!!"

"Relax!"

"Keep the jug down!"

A highway patrol car creeps by in the next lane. We turn with wooden casualness and answer the cop's tired scowl with that smile prey gives a predator. But today, this stretch of Highway 101, the descent to Richardson Bay and the turnoff to Mill Valley, is four lanes full of our type, so he pulls ahead.

It was a June morning in 1967 and we were headed north of San Francisco to The Fantasy Faire and Magic Mountain Music Festival at the top of Mt. Tamalpais in Marin County, the first rock festival ever. It will be the biggest hip gathering since the "Human Be-in" in January, the founding event of the Counter Culture, and it will be the first big event of the Summer of Love. Monterey Pop will be on the next weekend and become more famous because of its stellar line-up and a documentary about it.

The Haight-Ashbury apartment I shared with Tim had become an annex to the only other apartment on our floor, that of Christine, her best friend Cookie, Cookie's ol' man Don-Ed, and Cookie's nephew, Danny, a merchant seaman between ships, who was older than Cookie. Whenever it was suggested that we go for a drive, whoever happened to be in the two apartments (including visiting friends, chicks met on Haight Street, friends of Christine and/or Cookie) filled up whatever car was available.

Haphazard seating often threw together random cats and chicks. An arm over her shoulder, significant nudges or hand-brushings and, if the signals were right and the road clear, you started kissing. Backseat foreplay might be consummated behind trees or bushes, at the beach, or in the redwoods, or wherever. If a cat and a chick were on speaking terms and mutually attracted, there was no reason not to have sex. And if they did, their acquaintanceship might end cordially or they might move-in together, with one or both covering expenses.

If I thought about how Christine and her apartment-mates thought about Tim and I, I would have guessed they saw us as likeable, bumbling eggheads. Hardly glamorous enough for Christine. She was a couple years older than my nineteen, yet decades more sophisticated. Occasionally in the morning there would be a good looking stranger in her kitchen who she had picked up the night before at the Fillmore or the Avalon ballrooms. Few were seen more than once.

This morning as I sat onto the back seat and slid down to the end, Christine surprised me, and probably everyone else in the car, by cutting in front of Sherry and plopping down beside me. Then she was pushed against my shoulder, and after a pause, she glanced up at me with a coy, shy little smile. This was bold for

a chick so extraordinarily attractive. I was surprised that she felt that way and not yet convinced she did. It was too incredible. There had been calculation before in choosing seats, but never so blatantly as Christine just did. Next to her sat Sherry, then Tim of course was next to Sherry. His calculation.

Sometimes while just standing near Christine, I would lose my balance. She was long-necked and willowy with fine straight brown hair that slanted across her forehead and hung in silky folds down her back and often with a single motion was flung over a shoulder and tucked behind an ear. She also had a radiant, infectious smile, and when she laughed, her brown eyes and long lashes squinted deliciously into crescents. I had never enjoyed a chick's laugh more. When she wasn't laughing, she sometimes seemed distracted, bruised, melancholy, even mournful. A few years before, she had given up for adoption an out-of-wedlock child.

The adrenaline rush from the cop gives me the courage to put my arm on the seat above Christine. As the car switchbacks up Mt. Tamalpais we slide back and forth, throwing her against me. Then, after we turn a sharp curve and go straight along the crest of a ridge, she stays pressed against me. That's it. No mistaking it now. I'm going for a kiss.

Through the car window there is a break in the trees, and where I expect a panorama of gray scintillate ocean, there is instead a cotton prairie of fog, walled from the bay by the hills. In front of that, Tim and Sherry are already going at it. I drop a hand onto Christine's shoulder and she looks up at me, ready, expectant, aware of Tim and Sherry. I lean down and we kiss.

She is much smaller, lighter than I expect, almost fragile, with a delicate kiss. We part and she looks up and I see she too is pleased. So we do it again. Then we part and she puts her head and hand on my chest and I clutch her. Then we start kissing again, and if we were alone, I would touch her breasts. I see Tim feeling Sherry's, but I don't want to move too fast. In my elation, I am patient.

Half way up Mt. Tam, we arrive at an overflowing parking lot where buses are taking people to the concert at the top. It's crowded and we're late and a bus is filling-up as we pull-in.

Because I am the only one familiar with the area, having hiked in it, I feel obligated to help Danny find a parking place. And besides, I want to get away from Christine for a while and savor her in my thoughts.

Tim gets on the bus arm-in-arm with Sherry, then Don-Ed and Cookie. Christine and I part at the door. Caressing gazes, brushed fingertips. After parking the car, Danny and I walk beside creeping traffic back along the road to the parking lot. Occasionally we speak, but most of the time I stumble along in a daze, stifling a whoop, a guffaw, a cartwheel, a leap-and-tapping-together-of-heels.

Among the dozen or so bands playing on Mt. Tam this day, we're eager to see one that won't be at Monterey Pop but has just leapt from the hip cognoscenti to a #1 AM hit, the Doors. "Light My Fire" is all around Danny and I coming from the radios of most of the cars we walk beside. On her own, before they were famous, Christine found their album and bought it before anyone else I knew. One night she invited Tim and I to her bedroom to hear it, especially that last cut on the first side, "Light My Fire." With some chicks, their bedroom was their art form, and I had seen enough to recognize Christine's virtuosity. It was an eclectic, exotic showcase: pomegranate-red paisley bedspreads covered the walls, bead curtains hung over the windows and closet, multicolored Afghani fabric billowed down from the ceiling over an enormous double mattress on a box spring surrounded by incense holders and candles and a hookah. Across the room in orange-crate shelves was the stereo, records, and copies of Siddhartha, The Lord of the Rings, and the I Ching.

While Tim and I drifted in the music, laying on the bed, Christine knelt on the floor and colored in a coloring book on the bed. By the end of the album, she had switched to stringing beads. The next album, Fresh Cream, was equally exciting, still, the whole time I was on her bed, my mind never got far from the realization of where I was.

After Danny and I get off the bus at the top of the mountain, we cross the road and walk down a crowded paved path through overhanging fir trees to an amphitheater. Like a Greek ruin, it has stone-slab seats that terrace down to a stage

behind which is a gleaming vista of the Bay and the City. Danny and I stand to the side scanning the crowd. It's a Sunday on Haight Street teleported to the top of Mt. Tam complete with booths from hip stores, milling teenyboppers and Hells Angels, speechless tourists and swaggering straight short-haired Berkeley frat boys pathetically trying to blend in by going shirtless. There is one thing on Mt. Tam not found on Haight Street though: dazed, starched forest rangers in Smoky-the-Bear hats.

All this is sprinkled on a great sun-warmed mass of freaks. I will find out later that twenty thousand are on Mt. Tam today, still it doesn't feel as crowded as I expected, so I am surprised when I can't see Christine. I see Tim and Sherry sitting and snuggling thirty yards away and I start toward them. Danny then spots Don-Ed and Cookie uphill and starts toward them. As I approach Tim and Sherry, I notice Christine sitting twenty yards beyond them, some cat talking to her. I stop, stunned. She is laughing. The cat crouches on one knee. I anxiously read their poses. Though it doesn't seem he is settled-in or she is exuding more than normal wattage of charm, I sit beside Tim and Sherry.

While watching the crowd, I frequently throw quick, sidelong glances at Christine. The cat stands, says good-bye and leaves. Eventually she notices me. I try to maintain convincing interest in the crowd and/or the stage which is crawling with roadies. Now, she'll have to come to me. Our eyes never meet. In snuck glances, I see her face go through surprise, then bewilderment, then hurt. She stares-off into her thoughts for a while, then I see that familiar rueful expression. She becomes resentful, resigned, and finally she stands and goes uphill.

And that was the end of that. It was over. Stunned and dazed as by a bomb, I immediately regretted it. Instantaneous total irrevocable change. A groan of self-disgust welled up. I hadn't the slightest idea why I did it. It was only days later that I thought about how sticky things could have gotten if Christine and I had become a couple. Also, I avoided possibly sharing the trash heap with those bewildered cats seen once only in her kitchen the morning after. Though if she had dumped me, she would have been justified. I didn't lover her and couldn't. I could desire her

overwhelmingly, fantasize and masturbate about her, but I knew I couldn't love a chick without an intellect.

So, for the heaven of Christine's bed, I would have had a doomed relationship that would have kept me out of circulation during the Summer of Love. Which explains why, after a couple days of self-flagellation, I felt relieved that it had ended.

Later that afternoon as we were leaving the concert, Tim and Sherry and I walked back along the paved path, the music receding behind us. We had lost the others and now were finding our own way back to the City. Sunlight had left the amphitheater and a cold wind had come up. I had watched the concert from farther than the distance to the stage, noticing the performances only intermittently. My head was swarming with replays, castigations, and stifled cries of despair.

Then I noticed, going around us off the path but in the same direction, **JIM MORRISON!!!**

He wove through the crowd quickly, the hub of stares, evoking hush, even the other Doors were walking at a distance from him. He seemed smaller and, now without a shirt, scrawnier than he had on the stage, from which he had fallen while trying to swing around an upright two-by-four. I found him annoyingly affected.

When I saw the Doors at their first Fillmore gig, at one point, instead of singing, Morrison let the intro go on and on while he staggered and reeled back and forth across the stage, provoking Ray Manzarek to slam his hand on his electric piano and vehemently shout into Morrison's face, "Sing!!!" This kind of thing went on throughout the performance. The next day on Haight Street I saw Morrison in a store and it seemed from the desperate way he scanned the crowd for recognition that word may have already gotten around about his outrageous onstage behavior. Now, on Mt. Tam, as he passes Tim and Sherry and I, Morrison lifts his chin, breasting the awe.

A few minutes after that, just before we reach the road, I see Christine for the first time since our "breakup." She emerges from the woods just as I am passing. It's too neat and I suspect she's planned it until our eyes meet and I face her weary indifference. She doesn't care enough to plan anything. A goateed

cat, lean and good-looking, emerges behind her. He leans toward her and tells her something he finds amusing which she ignores. She says nothing as she turns onto the path in front of me and heads toward the road, causing the cat to hurry to keep up.

I feel a pang of desire just as I would have before she sat next to me in the backseat.

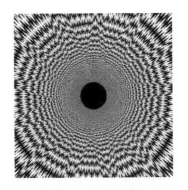

The Land

I have waited years to see that smile. She is dazzled.

"How do ya like it?" I ask, unnecessarily.

"It's…" she says and searches for the right word, then in defeat whispers "… beautiful."

She is radiant with love – for the land. Then we both realize that we haven't hugged. But I can't move. She gets a wry smile and walks over and we embrace. Friendly but warm, no kiss. But I give her a quick hard squeeze, bodies flush, as an answer to the big question: do I still feel the same?

"It's good to see you, Yvette," I say after we unclench.

A door of the VW bug slams and Maddie, who has just tossed her blouse onto the front seat passenger side, stands there naked from the waist up.

"This is *sooooooo* beautiful!!" she exclaims and rushes at me that blue-eyed, freckled face set in carrot-colored hair. We kiss and hug.

"Glad you like it," I say as we pull apart.

I look down at her breasts, swollen and pendulous with nipples like pink cookies. I had always enjoyed looking at them, and she had always enjoyed showing them off. She and Yvette have been best friends since early girlhood.

"Jesus Christ!" Maddie's ol' man Gordon says as he comes around the hood. We shake hands as he adds "You told me about it… but… this is…"

He's burly and relaxed with a big pleased grin set in a thick beard under wavy brown hair. I've seen his expression on the faces of other friends up from San Francisco, eyes devouring every detail while they calculate: how can I get this for myself?

For a silent moment, the four of us take it in together, the twenty-acre shoulder on the side of a steep wooded mountain in the Yolla Bolly-Middle Eel Wilderness, in the northeastern corner of Mendocino County, ten-or-so miles from electricity and asphalt down a dirt-and-gravel logging road. From most points on that shoulder, there is a vista view of about fifteen-or-so miles southeast across the forested granite valley of the Eel River. There has been nothing but the soughing of the pines for a while, when we hear the far, fading screak of a red tail hawk.

"It's even better than I expected," Yvette says to me and hooks behind an ear a strand of the fine chestnut hair that hangs to mid back.

I didn't know how I would react to seeing her again. As I waited for her and Gordon and Maddie to arrive, I monitored my feelings and was relieved to conclude that I didn't need her. When her image came up, I felt indifference; at most, lust. Then, there she was in front of me, and I felt an overwhelming rush, and realized, of course, I was fooling myself, and the old feelings were there under the scar tissue. I heard that she had split with the most recent guy, and I had sent an open invitation through friends to come north and see the land.

Even if Yvette hadn't been in my life, I would have done everything the same regarding the land; at the same time, there was nothing that would attract her more than the land. She would be even more at home here than me.

"It took a year and a half to find it," I say, then gesture toward the shaded stream that is part of the northern boundary, adding, "It had to have year round surface water..." And then I gesture beyond the stream, "... and at least one boundary with National Forest..." I turn and gesture toward the dozen-or-so acres of gently sloping meadow at the center of the forested parcel, "and open land with Southern exposure."

I say to Yvette, "I'm starting to feel like a docent..." Then for her blank expression, I add, "the guide... in a museum... I keep

giving the same spiel over and over. It seems like I'm hardly ever alone on week-ends anymore, now that the weather is so good."

"And there's a pond!" Maddie cries, looking toward the bottom of that sloping meadow.

We all look down at the half-acre pond, and I notice there are long jagged late afternoon shadows crossing the meadow toward it.

"Yeah, I paid a hundred bucks to have a small bulldozer come in and make the dam. It took less than a day."

"And that's going to be... the garden?" Maddie asks.

"Yeah, that's the garden," I say and then we start walking down toward it, which is about half way between the parking area and the pond. "I had to put up this fence first. Against the deer. It's supposed to be seven feet high but I made it eight. Hardest part was the postholes. The posts are just the straightest trunk branches that I could find... which could also hold the weight of the chicken-wire."

We stop outside a twenty-five-by-forty-foot rectangle of chicken-wire nailed to spaced, upright, gray, bent branches, the tip of each pointing in a random direction.

"Those are... planting beds?" Gordon asks about three five-by-twenty-foot rectangles of turned soil, side-by-side, each eight inches high and covered with the floppy, bright green leaves of young plants: corn, peas, lettuce, tomato, and squash.

"Yeah... Eventually there'll be ten beds... a thousand square feet."

Just outside a corner of the garden, I have a mattress and a box spring on a level plywood platform under a bay tree. I dash over to the mattress, and from the tangled sleeping bag, pick up a banged-up oversize paperback and hold it up.

"I'm using this," I say. "It's called the biodynamic French-intensive method. It specializes in raised beds and double digging for the roots."

He doesn't ask for it but I know to go back to the garden and give the book to Gordon. He immediately goes to the table of contents.

"And listen to this," I continue, "the guy who invented it, that gardening method, lives in that little town back in the valley,

Covelo. Isn't that too much? I knew I wanted to use that method, even before I came here, and then I found out the guy who invented it just moved here from UC Santa Cruz. He's this scrawny, eccentric old Englishman who works in his garden wearing only shorts... He's browner than the Indians..."

Do I detect a note of cabin fever in my rambling?

"I saw an old woman fishing with a net in the river..." Yvette says. "She looked Indian."

"Yeah, she is. I've seen her too," I say. "They're the only ones who can legally fish with nets in the rivers."

"There're little fish!" Maddie exclaims standing beside the pond.

"They're mosquito fish. They eat the larvae," I say and start walking toward the pond, Gordon and Yvette following.

When we all arrive at the pond, Maddie asks, "O.k. now, how about the cabin? You're going to build a cabin, right?"

That gently sloping meadow at the center of the parcel is creased down the middle by the shallow ravine of a seasonal creek that empties into the pond.

"There. Over there," I say, pointing to the opposite side of that ravine, pointing south from the south-facing side with the garden. "It'll have the best view and never cast a shadow on the garden."

"Whadda ya think it'll cost?" Gordon asks clutching the book.

"I'm working on that now. My plan is to hire one carpenter and I'll be his crew, and I think we can throw something up within... I dunno... a week... ten days at the most?"

I realize that I've been avoiding looking at Yvette.

I turn to her now and say, "It's just going to be a box with a loft and a wood stove... at first."

She nods, slightly but eagerly.

It's the eyes, huge, brown doe eyes with long lashes, not only beautiful but incredibly expressive. Her eyebrows are perfect. After the eyes is the flawless olive skin. Then the lips: full, sensuous, á la Jeanne Moreau. Then the teeth, perfect and glowing, and right now, filling a huge joyous grin between prominent dimpled cheeks. It's all in an oval face, framed by

shoulder-length chestnut hair, parted in the middle, with a widow's peak. She's medium height, slender but sturdy.

"In the meantime, there's the milk truck," I say and gesture uphill to my beat-up milkman's delivery truck, parked beside Gordon's VW. "After I got here in March, I got snowed on... And it's rained... I've had to spend whole days in the truck in the sleeping bag reading."

"Do you have enough money for the cabin?" Gordon asks. He wants me to succeed, to prove it's possible.

"Not yet... but I couldn't build now anyway. The rednecks are trying to push out the freaks by condemning all our buildings. They claim none of 'em meet code. So, everybody hip who's built something is just waiting for their turn to get red-tagged. We're fighting back, and I think we have a real good chance of beating this, but I don't want to start building until it's decided... So, it's o.k. for now... But I will have enough money. Follow me."

I lead them single file around the pond, out of the meadow, and into the forest at the eastern edge of the parcel. The trail we follow winds between thick pine trunks, then suddenly ends against a dense manzanita thicket. I step up to two six-footish manzanita bushes standing on top of the ground side-by-side, and lift and set aside each in turn. Before us is the hollow inside of the manzanita thicket filled with a couple dozen marijuana plants in rows, a couple feet high.

"If the problems with the building code are worked out, I'm gonna start the cabin right after harvest," I say. "I've read everything available on growing grass. I've picked the brain of every experienced grower I could find... " Then I revert to my docent spiel, "There are no tall trees immediately around the thicket. That's to maximize sunlight. It's already facing south... sort of... southeast. The soil right here is terrible though. I had to dig a wide deep post hole for each plant and then fill it with soil and manure from the vegetable garden... I had to fill-in some gaps in the manzanita wall too... That's more for the deer than the sheriff... This isn't my land. It's National Forest. So I'm not automatically liable."

Maddie says, quietly, "You've thought of everything."

Then I turn to Yvette and say, "I planned and prepared for almost three years... and now... well... I lay down every night after 12 or 14 hours of labor, and can't wait to get up the next morning and start all over again."

Yvette looks up at me, transfixed, grinning and nodding.

"Wait till you hear the coyotes," I tell her.

*

After the tour, I started a fire for dinner. Ten or so feet from the plywood platform with the mattress, there was a fire ring of fitted boulders, and covering a corner of the ring was a steel screen, blackened and encrusted with drippings from recent meals. My furniture was ultra minimalist, for seating there were three thick old logs, stripped of bark and gray, that I rolled down hill and dragged to the fire ring, putting one on each of three sides. On the ground beside the fire ring was a plastic ice chest, the kind used for picnics, providing slight refrigeration and sealed food storage and serving as a table for food preparation. On the bay tree beside the mattress, four orange crates were attached to the trunk and limbs with wire, at chest height, one on each side. The crates served as shelves for dishes, utensils, cups, pots and pans, toiletry articles, and books.

During the dinner of Dinty Moore canned beef stew, with cookies for dessert, and throughout the whole evening, sex with Yvette was at the back of my mind. She must have been expecting sex, logic told me, but logic had been wrong before. So, after a couple hours of smoking grass and rapping by the campfire, when it was time to sleep, I resolved not to risk humiliation by inviting her to sleep with me.

Gordon and Maddie took their sleeping bags to a far edge of the big meadow. After a short while, Yvette and I, sleeping forty feet apart, heard them fucking. I realized this was the single moment of the night with the best chance for me having sex. But I had to risk getting up and walking over to Yvette in her bag. Though we were close enough for conversation, neither had spoken since we lay down. Gordon's rhythmic grunts and

Maddie's gasping tremolos crescendoed to the high note, and dropped.

I lay there in my bag, drifting in the stars, as I had contentedly for so many nights. Nights when, by now, I would have been jerking off to fantasies of Yvette. For the first time in our almost three year off-again-on-again, again-and-again relationship, I had leverage. Yes, I would like to own that beauty again, but I didn't need to, and I was happy without it. Then I started to feel resentful, even invaded. Before she arrived, my life had been as close to perfection as it had ever been. But horniness prodded me. Can we fuck without it being an implicit invitation to live on the land? No. Can I be strong enough to let her go home with Maddie and Gordon? I think if she went back south, I might have a chance to forget her up here. Or would I just run after her the next day?

Certain that I wouldn't be going to Yvette that night, I rolled over and went to sleep.

That was in June of 1975.

2

About two years earlier...

"Nineteen? Nineteen years old?!"

"She was eighteen when we started."

"How old are you again?" she asked. Her voice was sultry and raspy and so low that on the phone she was sometimes mistaken for a man.

"Twenty-six," I answered.

Bree burst into her signature, wild, crescendoing guffaw. It was flamboyant, brash, and now, full of mock outrage.

"I know, I know," I said. "I feel the same way... Some of my friends are disgusted..."

"Well I don't feel *that* way..."

"Chip... Dave... Peter... Peter said, 'Anybody who gives his heart to an eighteen year old is gonna get what he deserves.' And I'm in complete agreement. If it was someone else in my

predicament, I would be disgusted too... It's obviously a... neurotic... delusional... arbitrary fixation... I mean... someone so young and naïve who has all the power... I deflower an eighteen year old and instead of her falling in love with me, I fall in love with her."

"She was a *virgin*?!"

"Yeah..."

"Holy shit!" she said tilting her head down, looking up from the tops of enormous bemused blue eyes.

"I didn't want her virginity... I would've preferred to have her... more experienced... I was even annoyed by it..."

"Wait a minute, what's this chick look like... Is she good looking?"

I had to look away before I said, "Stunning... Her face is..."

"Oooooooh, now I see..."

"But there's more to her than that..."

"Of course... Hey, have you read *Lolita*?"

"Yeah..."

"I loved that book," she said gazing off into pleasant memories.

I avoided talking to Bree about Yvette. I don't know why, because I was always eager to talk about Yvette. It helped me figure it out. I was essentially thinking out loud when I talked to close friends about her. Tonight, also, I tried to avoid the subject with Bree, but then she brought it up and kept asking questions.

Bree suddenly stood up from her chair and announced, "O.k., it's tea time!"

"Huh? Oh... chamomile, please."

She went into the kitchen from where she announced in a raised voice, "Oh, and this evening, we're being visited by none other than Mr. Toshiro himself."

"Oh, yeah?" I said and stood up. "I'll come and say hi."

I entered the kitchen and saw near the backdoor, his back to me, eating from a bowl, an enormous alley cat, the color of an over-washed gray sweatshirt. I didn't approach him. Nobody but Bree would think of petting him. He was the only cat I was ever physically intimidated by. She named him after the great Japanese

movie star Toshiro Mifune for a samurai gravitas the cat earned the hard way. He was a lump of scar tissue, with ever-fresh gashes around the eyes or on the ears or somewhere on the torso, all from bad luck in the alleys. I looked from the cat through the reflection in the kitchen windows into the night-dark of the alley behind Bree's cottage.

"Speaking of your strays," I said. "What happened to your heavy breather? You were going to talk to him..."

"Oh, Emmett... the obscene phone caller," she said and then sighed. She adjusted the gas burner under the teapot. "O.k., well, like I told you... after just yelling at him and hanging up all the time, I decided to talk to him, and... well... we decided to meet."

"You're kidding!"

She burst out again with that guffaw, but this time it was aimed at herself.

"I had all these silly fantasies..." she said as she took two cups from the cupboard, "so I had him come over..." She placed the cups on the counter.

"You met here?!"

"Yeah... but he was ugly... and dumb... and... boring..."

This was a woman who could have almost any man she wanted. Bree was easily as beautiful as Yvette, though in a different way. Bree had black hair, boyishly short, pale skin, perfectly proportioned features, and a light stipple of Irish freckles across the cheeks. She was thirty-ish, about five four and compact. (If her body were proportional with her personality, she would have been over seven feet tall.) Crowning it all were those delicious blue eyes. Set in long lashes and eyeliner, they were huge, startling, and seductive. An expert technician, she fluttered them and hid them, beckoned with them and skewered with them. You did not want to stop looking at those blue eyes.

Toshiro finished dinner and Bree let him out into the alley, and then we returned to the livingroom, she carrying an antique silver-leaf tea tray arrayed with tea things. Tea was an elaborate ritual for Bree, a habit she picked up in Morocco. She set the tray on the table to the side of a large beautiful stained-wood chair, her throne, which fit across a corner of the small livingroom. Then she would sit and put the tea bag in a cup and pour the steaming

water and then hand you a cup on a saucer. You then put it on the small table next to the guest chair and let it steep.

"O.k., so she's good looking and young... sooooooo young..." Bree said as she poured the water into her cup. "So..." She replaced the pot on the tray.

"Are you really interested in this?" I asked skeptically.

"Yeah."

"If you are, you're about the only one left. Everyone else is so..."

"I'm just curious... So how'd you meet this chick?"

She picked up from an ashtray a cigarette holder with a smoking cigarette.

"At the post office. She was a clerk where I'm a carrier... Actually, ya know what? You two have a lot in common."

About to take a drag from the cigarette holder, she froze, the tip inches from her lips, and looked at me and said, "Oh, yeah?"

"Yeah... You're both hip to the ultimate degree."

Big, pleased, cynical grin. She took the drag and then tilted her head back and exhaled upwards.

"You're both beautiful."

She looked at me blankly and raised her right eyebrow.

"You're both the most honest, frank people I know... She tells me everything... If it pops into her head, it comes out her mouth... Her older sister is gay, and Yvette had sex with a lesbian friend of that sister, and she told me everything, every detail, and I didn't ask one question."

"Did she like it?"

"Yeah."

(I *didn't* mention that both Bree and Yvette had alcoholic fathers.)

"You have your differences too," I added. "In some ways, you're absolutely antithetical."

"Such as?" she said, tapping the tip of the plastic cigarette holder on her teeth.

"Where you're loud and flamboyant, she's soft-spoken and reserved."

I picked up my cup, tested the tea, and started sipping. She put the cigarette holder back in the ashtray and followed my lead with the tea.

"Oh... something else you have in common," I said warming my hands on the cup. "Traveling right after high school. When they changed the law, making eighteen the age of consent, she was graduating from high school, and she and her girlfriend were some of the first out of the gate. Have you heard of the 'Hippie Trail'?"

She shook her head.

"That's after your time... Actually, you were one of the trailblazers... It's an overland route that freaks take from London or maybe Amsterdam all the way to India. Anyway, she's on the Hippie Trail now. Except she and Maddie are gonna keep pushing and come back through Thailand, Malaysia, Indonesia, East Asia. So, when they get back, after a year or so, they'll have gone around the world. They're taking trains and buses and flying when they have to, but they're also hitchhiking when they can."

Both sipped.

"She gotta a mind... an intellect?" Bree asked.

"Uh... no... She's definitely a B student... Make that C plus..." Long pause... "She breaks all my rules... But we share something big. I told you about the land I'm saving for? She worked and saved for this trip while I was working for the land. But she's as much into the land as I am..." Long pause... "She has other qualities though. She has this amazing... I dunno... Call it... There's a whirl of words around it... emotional... sensitivity... or... or... intensity... And she has this preternatural gentleness... She doesn't know how to fight. I've watched her being bullied by her younger sister and she was utterly defenseless. I've never seen anyone so incapable of aggression or causing harm, even in self-defense... Yet she's strong... fearless... Look where she is now... at nineteen..."

It was gushing out of me now and I realized how much I had needed to talk about it.

"She's the only hip chick I ever knew," I continued, "who didn't like the Stones. She reacted instinctively to their misogyny, or anyway, she wouldn't overlook it for the music."

"You're making a study of her," Bree said in a low voice.

"Yeah? ... I guess so..."

She slouched into a corner of the throne and, while I rambled, aimed an intense stare at me over the teacup.

"I don't know if I really love her though... I mean, love might be mixed in there somewhere with neurosis... lust... loneliness... boredom... and who knows what... Sometimes I think there's contempt in there too. She can be insipid... What I take to be her unplumbable depths... Maybe she's just an air head with nothing to say and a personality like... weak tea."

"Is that too weak?" she asked nodding at my cup.

"No."

I paused to watch her put her teacup back on the tray and pick up the cigarette holder from the ashtray.

"But whenever I'm around her, I'm a puddle..." I said, then sighed, and continued. "The whole thing is so... humiliating... like it's this dark secret on display to the world... And I can't blame her for anything, not even when she causes me overwhelming pain. I'm not her victim. She's my victim. I imposed this fantasy on her. She even said once, 'You want something from me that I can't give you.' "

I paused again to watch Bree exhale a drag to the side, away from me.

"Sometimes," I went on, "I can watch the whole agonizing show as if it's twenty years from now... I'm completely detached... but at the same time, I can't affect anything. I can't change anything. I'm a helpless bystander. No attitude of mine, no... thought process has any effect on how I feel or what I do... Ya know what Chip calls her? My 'fetishistic attachment.' "

"Oh I like that!" she said pointing the cigarette holder at me. "Has he met her?"

"Yeah, he said she reminded him of the girls in the underwear ads in the Montgomery Ward catalogue... wholesome but sexy."

I had talked the limit about Yvette, at least it felt like that, even though I could have gone on for hours more. So I brought up another topic.

"Hey, are you acting in anything now?"

"Yeah, a Tennessee Williams one act, *The Gnädiges Fräulein*. We're doing it over at the Goodman Building... on Geary and Van Ness..."

"Nothin' goin' on with the Hussies?"

"Not now."

I was proud that I was the one who talked her into stage acting. Bree was all id with an outsized, theatrical personality that was a natural for the stage. She had already acquired "stage experience" when she put herself through nursing school as a topless dancer. She even appeared in some primitive early porn shorts.

"Oh, I only showed 'em my pussy..." she once said from the throne with a dismissive wave of the cigarette holder. "Not like today! When they actually fuck!" she added, mock outrage mixed with real.

With no training and little discipline, the quality of her acting performances varied. I saw her brilliant, when she was inspired and focused, and wretched when she wasn't. Eventually, she joined a popular feminist theater company, the Shameless Hussies. In one of their biggest hits (they toured Europe with it), Bree played both an old lady in her seventies and a teenage girl. Friends who saw the play, but didn't know Bree, couldn't believe that those two characters weren't played by two different age-appropriate actresses.

*

That was in 1973. Eight years earlier, I was a college freshman, a scholarship boy at an all-male Catholic college, St. Crispin's, in the Bay Area, sharing the top floor of a four-floor dorm with the Jews and the Negroes. And while at St. Crispin's, I fell in with a group that in a few years would be called "hippies." Then, we were just a bunch of weirdos, concentrated mainly at San Francisco State and UC Berkeley, wearing Beatle haircuts, listening to Dylan, opposing the Vietnam War, and taking LSD, which was legal still and plentiful, and smoking marijuana, when we could get it.

One night four of us huddled around a candle on the floor in a dark dorm room with a towel stuffed under the locked door, and the two windowshades pulled and taped to the inside of the windowframes. To anyone knocking on that locked door, it was just another uninhabited dorm room. The other three guys were older than me.

"One night we dropped acid and fucked," one guy said just above a whisper.

Needless to say, he had our attention. He looked off into the memory, and then he took a joint that was handed to him. Behind us, our elongated shadows wavered with the candle flame.

"Jeez..." he said, "the look in her eyes... while we were fucking... I, uh... It was just... uh... I dunno..." He shook his head. "I mean... the things she's done... where she's been... since high school..."

Then he looked at the joint, which was starting to come apart. We were all novice joint rollers then. He took a hurried toke just before it fell open. He exhaled the toke then handed-off the pieces in cupped hands to another guy, who asked, "She's the one whose parents died?"

"Yeah... both in the same year... her junior year of high school... Her dad was driving drunk and her mother had cancer. She's an only child and it rattled her pretty bad... of course. I mean it devastated her... obviously. But it also freed her. She got a passport with one of those letters you have to have if you're a minor. Somehow, she talked her aunt and uncle into it, and she took off for Europe right after high school with some of the insurance money... She lived in Morocco for... I dunno... a long time... And when she came back, she smuggled in a manuscript that she thinks might have been the original manuscript of *Naked Lunch*."

"I read that it might be legal pretty soon," I contributed, too eagerly.

Throughout the rest of the school year, I heard more about this mysterious chick, and she lodged deep in my libido as the ideal, ultra-hip chick. Then, five years later, I met her. Brianna "Bree" O'Shaughnessy was from an old San Francisco Irish family, and I met her at a party thrown by a mutual friend, Bernie, an

underground journalist with a column in the *Berkeley Barb*. Over the course of the evening, Bree and I talked our way to discovering that we had mutual friends at St Crispin's, and that she was that legendary chick.

She had a short affair with Bernie that ended amicably and then it was my turn. Fucking with her was wild and loud, and I especially liked her body, a flourish of black bush and dark nipples on breasts that just filled a hand. But I had just moved to Petaluma and had to hitchhike an hour or more to get to the City, so the logistics of our relationship were strained. Plus, I was in the midst of a grueling slog through the break up of a multi-year relationship. And with a personality as vibrant and barely contained as Bree's, a relationship with her would be work anytime. Plus, she had a fickle volcanic temper. So, I stopped calling her.

But then, months later, we bumped into each other at another party in the City, where we spent most of the evening in a corner talking furiously only with each other. If she was sore about the ending of the affair, she never showed it or mentioned it. Anyway, we became close friends. She talked to me like her girlfriends and I talked to her like my buddies. I did the things with her I did with buddies: parties, movies, plays, poetry readings, gallery openings, protest rallies, coffeehouses. Over the years, she worked her way with short affairs through my friends, and I worked my way through her girlfriends, including one of the Shameless Hussies, an even better actress than Bree. I lost a tug-of-war with that actress's lesbian lover who was also in the troupe. The former would go on to have a lead role in a one-season TV series and then become a professor of theater; the latter would have minor roles in a couple big-budget Hollywood films and become a successful stand-up comedienne.

Most of Bree's lovers were artists. There was the pioneering conceptual artist who would hike out into the woods, extract a cylindrical section of earth - four or five inches wide, a couple feet long – and then reinsert it reversed. That was his artwork. (Bree claimed his real talent was for oral sex.) There was one who scratched film stock to create moving abstract images, plus he created an accompanying nonmusical soundtrack. It was a

hybrid of abstract painting and film. I liked the ones I saw at the Roxie Theater in a program of experimental shorts.

*

Eventually Bree settled down with a friend of mine, a former poet. Chip had a disheveled appeal in his rumpled clothes and thick light-brown hair that, after the wind got into it, would point in three or four directions at once. He had a dense light-brown beard that he fingered when lost in thought. He could get an abashed Stan Laurel-ish grin that was quite effective. A pampered only child, Chip was passive with women and that left extra room for Bree's oversize personality. They were complementary. What put a lock on the relationship was their shared passion for jamming on drums. That and the rev of his sex engine.

Bree had an extensive collection of drums, but the three gems were from Morocco where she picked up the habit of drumming, whether alone or with a roomful of friends. There were never complaints about the noise because she lived in a classic mother-in-law cottage behind a large house on Church Street in Noe Valley, and the owners, a middle-aged gay couple who lived in the main house, adored her. In the middle of a conversation, Bree might reach from the throne for one of the Moroccan drums, one was usually within reach, and without saying a word, she would close her eyes and start drumming herself toward a meditative state. She was extraordinarily spiritual. One of her favorite anecdotes about herself was about the time she was broke and lugged a sewing machine up a steep San Francisco hill to barter it for admission into a Gurdjieff group.

It would have been logical, after they started living together in the mother-in-law cottage, to assume that I would see more of Bree and Chip, since whenever I visited one I was also visiting the other. But I actually saw less of them. That was when I was searching for the land on my days off, sent by realtors wending over crude dirt roads into the nether reaches of Mendocino and Sonoma Counties. After I found the land, most of

my free time went into preparing to move there. Neither Bree nor Chip had any interest in the land. They were the exceptions among my friends for not coming up there at least once that summer. So, when I visited them, just before I left to live on the land in early spring, I didn't even bother to extend the open invitation I had offered everybody else.

We were in the livingroom. Bree was on the throne and Chip had a smaller, padded, stained wood chair to the side.

As I started to sit in the guest chair, Bree said, "We're getting married."

That stopped me. They had been living together about a year and a half, and the subject of marriage never came up in conversation with either or both.

I slowly lowered my butt onto the seat and said, "Oh..."

"It's his idea," she said sarcastically, waving the cigarette holder at Chip.

I looked at him and he looked at the floor, then resettled himself in the chair, and then cleared his throat. I expected an explanation but he just crossed his legs and kept looking down and didn't say anything. Why would he want to get married, of all things? And if he's not volunteering it, the reason must be embarrassing.

"Groovy," I said. The word had acquired pejorative overtones by 1975. "When is it? I'll be here 'til... uh, next Thursday."

"It's next Tuesday, but we're not going to have a party or anything like that," Chip said. "It's just a civil ceremony at city hall and that's it."

"Oh..." I said again.

One side of Chip's family went back to the Gold Rush. There was even a mountain somewhere in Marin with his family name on it. His father, a dentist, died a couple years before I met Chip, who was set to inherit the fortune his father amassed from Marin real estate. Chip would never work a day in his life. But for now, his mother controlled the money and she was very religious, so I speculated that she wasn't fond of her son living in sin. For Bree, the marriage was just a matter of indulging Chip's whim.

"Hey, the last few times I've been over, I haven't seen Toshiro, and you haven't mentioned him," I said. "When was the last time you saw him?"

She handed me a saucer with a cup of steaming rosehips tea.

"About seven or eight months ago?" Chip asked Bree.

I savored the tangy aroma while she handed Chip his saucer and cup. He kept holding it, and I did too, for some reason, even though there was a small table next to my chair. Bree left her own steeping on the tea tray. She slouched into the throne and looked at me expectantly.

"Oh... that's not good..." I said about Toshiro.

"He used to come around a couple times a week..." Bree added glumly.

A moment of silence for Toshiro...

"How's your Béatrice?" Chip asked with a smirk, giving it the Italian pronunciation, "Bay-uh-tree-chay."

"What's that?" Bree asked.

"Dante's love interest," I said, "his 'fetishistic attachment'... She's ok."

"Is she back from her trip?" Bree asked.

"Oh yeah, she's been back for nearly a year."

"How was it?" she asked.

"Completely positive... There was none of the rape and... hair's-breadth... death-defying escapes that you had."

"Is she going up north with you?" he asked.

"No."

"What happened?" she asked. "I thought that was the plan."

"Well... She came back, and... I hadn't seen her for more than a year, and I thought this was a good time to let it go. I saw her a couple times but I just kept it friendly, no sex. There were plenty of other guys who wanted her of course. My fast lasted three or four months and then I started seeing her again and having sex. Then she announced she was going to move in with one of those other guys... which she did..."

Bree picked up her cup and tested her tea and then began sipping it. Chip and I, already holding ours, followed suit.

A long pensive silence ended when Bree asked me, "Can you see... now... finally... that all her 'other qualities' are... just fantasies... excuses... so you can... jerk off to that face?"

I felt an impulse to contradict her but caught myself. I wasn't sure she was wrong. Actually, she had just put into words my main fear with Yvette, that there really was only the face. At first, I felt the stab of what Bree said, but then I focused on the note of vehemence in her voice. I turned to Chip and saw as he stared at her that he too noticed. He always was a little suspicious, maybe even a little jealous, of the friendship between Bree and I.

" 'I hate and I love,' " I said to Chip, trying to distract him. " 'Why? You may ask but It beats me. I feel it done to me, and ache'... Catullus."

"... Via Ezra Pound," Chip said.

"Yeah..."

" 'We are lived by forces we pretend to understand'... Auden," Chip said.

"Oh I like that," I said. "I like that a lot."

Our friendship was based on poetry. He was one of the few people I knew who was on my level of sophistication and passion, as I was one of the few he knew. But our tastes were antithetical. He tended to hate what I loved and love what I hated, so it was a contentious friendship. We were prone to loud arguments in restaurants.

Once, he had been a celebrity of the poetry world. Just out of high school, he had his first poetry collection published by one of the most prestigious hip publishers in the world. His poetry was a clever hybrid of the styles of William Blake's prophetic books and Allen Ginsberg, and his book was touted as the *Howl* of our generation, and he the new hippie Ginsberg. Chip was a dynamic reader who performed more than recited his poems. Once he performed from the same stage on the same night as Ginsberg and acquitted himself well. Chip might indeed have been the new hippie Ginsberg, if he wrote more books like that first one. But he didn't. The second was a dismal failure, so he crashed and burned after one book. That was now many years in the past. Whereas he once had a business card that identified him as

"poet," now it said "metaphysician." But he still loved to pontificate about poetry.

"Hey, Merwin has a new book coming out," I said.

"So does Ginsberg,"

"You're not still... seriously?... comparing Ginsberg to Merwin?"

He didn't answer but he didn't have to.

"Oh, c'mon, Ginsberg Is for middle brow bohemians..." I said.

"... Yeah, yeah, who don't really want to *read* poetry but want to *have read* it."

This is the first time he and I have had one of these arguments in front of Bree, or rather had an eruption of the ongoing argument. Literature for her was a handle on life, not life itself, like it was for Chip and I.

I explained to Bree, "I like a school of contemporary American poetry called the 'Deep Image' school..."

"Word puzzles..." Chip muttered, addressing the air, twisting a hank of beard.

"Yes, some of their stuff is very difficult..." I continued to Bree. "The best of the Deep Image poets is a guy named W.S. Merwin. He's just... When I read 'im... I don't know how many times I've been reading him and thought, 'Wait-a-minute, language can't do that!'... But nobody else I know likes him."

"Ok, ok, I get this," Bree announced. "This is a little boys' pissing contest over poetry."

That closed the door to poetry, so I brought up another topic and asked Chip, "I haven't seen you since you went to the Philippines. How was that?"

Like many hypochondriacs, Chip was sickly and actually had several obscure disorders, so obscure that I could never remember the names of them. But, recently, he had been traveling to far-flung destinations pursuing exotic cures for things as vague as "impurities." A few years before, he had gone into the Sierra Mazateca mountains in Oaxaca, Southern Mexico. He was seeking Maria Sabina, a Mazatec *curandera* (healer), who used psilocybin mushrooms and who had been the subject of a well-known anthropological study. He found her village, but dozens of

seekers had been there before him and the villagers were now turning away outsiders. Since then, it seemed spiritual seeking had mutated in Chip into psychosomatic hypochondria.

He shifted in his chair and became the most animated he would be that night.

"I witnessed something... incredible in the Philippines," he said looking at us, then at the floor and the memory, then back at us. "This guy was an actual shaman from some tribe on, uh... Mindanao, I think..." He gestured toward that island on the other side of the world. "And, in Manila, in this small auditorium, I saw him reach into this guy's side, below the ribs..." He mimed what he saw, inserting a flattened hand, perpendicular to the floor, into an invisible man's side. "...And take out this... stuff... It was sort of a..." He looked at the invisible stuff in his hand and rubbed fingertips together feeling for the right description of it. "... Viscous... fatty stuff... that was causing paralysis of some sort..."

"Was there a hole in the guy's side?" I asked.

"No!" he exclaimed, wide-eyed with awe. "It closed right up after he pulled his hand out!"

"Did this... shaman... reach into you?" I asked.

"No, no... I just watched. I talked to him later though, alone, except for the interpreter, but I can't talk about that."

The scene was easy to imagine: a highly skilled con man using sleight-of-hand and chicken guts before an audience of true believers. Chip was always at the cutting edge of the cutting edge of New Age quackery and had espoused some pretty nutty "cures:" urine drinking, aura reading, colonics, chakra enhancement, crystal healing, etc. My favorite among the most recent featured pine needle tea. It was as if gravity were slowly letting go of the "metaphysician" and he was about to float up into the sky and disappear.

I looked at Bree and she was staring at him and I could see she was having a realization about him. Then it suddenly occurred to me: the marriage could be for placating the mother in order to get the money for these pilgrimages around the world to these bogus "cures."

3

Two months later, May of 1975, and a month before Yvette, Maddie, and Gordon visited the land the first time…

"C'mere Memphis!"

The German Shepherd perked up at his name and stood rigid, staring at me, wagging his tale. The stick was in his mouth of course. That dog lived to chase the stick and would choose it over food.

"C'mon Memphis!"

He didn't move. He didn't want to stop chasing the stick. But I knew how to get him into the milk truck. I got in behind the wheel, started the engine, and then slowly jounced down the steep rutted driveway toward the logging road. Memphis had been staring intently at me the whole time, but as soon as the truck moved, he barked, dropping the stick, and ran for the truck. I slowed a little and he leapt into the open side door. I leaned over and slid the door shut to keep him in and the road dust out.

Fortunately, the land had a section about thirty yards long and so steep that it was almost a cliff, and sometimes I would throw the stick down there. After returning it a few times, Memphis would literally fall over with exhaustion, and let me do my work. Not that Memphis wasn't hugely entertaining. In our favorite campfire pastime, he would face me, within arm's-reach from where I sat on a log, with the stick in his mouth, and keep it out of my grasping hands with flagrant ease. And just to show off even more: he did it without ever moving his paws. No matter how hard I tried, I couldn't get ahold of that stick. It was as if he were saying, "You may have the brain, but look how I can best you."

I had a German Shepherd the whole time I was growing up in the Sierras, and spent countless hours with him exploring our corner of Stanislaus National Forest. Here in the Yolla Bolly–Middle Eel Wilderness, Memphis made me feel more attuned to the woods, and at night, a little safer. There were

black bear and mountain lions in this forest, though I didn't worry about them, having grown up in a similar forest. If I knew a bear or mountain lion to be in the vicinity, I could easily sleep in the milk truck. Of course, there was an extra element of vulnerability sleeping under the stars as I did every night. But I also had the "Screamer."

That was what I named a painfully loud air-horn, a canister of compressed air that fit in my palm and let out a metallic screech like a punch. Smaller versions can be heard in the bleachers of college football games. I bought mine in a nautical supply store. It would also be useful in the fall during hunting season for scaring away deer and alerting hunters of my proximity.

Plus, the Screamer was field-tested. I was backpacking with friends when a bear suddenly appeared beside the trail. We were in the northwest corner of the state, in Marble Mountain Wilderness, the area in the state with the densest bear population. Suddenly, there was a fat old shaggy bear growling at us from thirty yards away in a manzanita thicket. I quickly swung off my backpack, got the Screamer out of an outside pocket, and blasted the bear a couple times. It terrified him, and his breakneck rippling waddle as he crashed through brush was comical. He stopped at sixty yards and looked back at us out of curiosity. Another blast sent him disappearing behind trees.

The Screamer was always within quick easy reach of my bed, whether Memphis was with me or not.

And if Memphis protected me at night when he was here, I once protected him, or at least soothed him, during a mountain lightning storm. I had been in similar ones but nothing nearly this intense. As soon as the first raindrops pocked the ground, I covered the bed and the rest of the camp with plastic tarps, and then backed the milk truck into the trees at the edge of the meadow. The lightning exploded low over the meadow and was stunning each time, but it was the thunder that terrorized Memphis, making him howl and whine and press himself into the truck floor. If it could be called thunder. It wasn't a distant muffled rumble, or even majestic cannonade, like bowling balls rolling over a rough plank floor overhead. This was

more the sharp crack of a blast, simultaneous with the flash, which was random, all around us, far and close, a bombardment. I stroked the head and back of the trembling dog. I felt safe in the trees and on top of the truck's rubber tires. The barrage went on long enough so that I started to feel exhilarated. Then it suddenly stopped and the storm swept on. I remembered how John Muir would ride out a storm in the Sierras on top of a whipping pine tree.

The milk truck was almost as big a coup as the land. Boxy, dented on a couple sides, and covered in smog-gray paint primer, the milk truck had had numerous lives since it delivered milk, and now it was my car, shelter, and pick up truck. I could almost stand up in it, and with the shelves removed, it was almost spacious. Its simple fifties engine was easy to maintain and there was plenty of windshield, plus a large window in the sliding right side door, for seeing pedestrians in the dawn light while delivering milk. The driver's seat was problematic, high-perched and wobbly, and the steering could be ornery. The milk truck wasn't built for highway speeds, and even less so for the logging road, at any speed. The normally three and half-hour drive back to San Francisco took closer to five hours in the milk truck.

Now with Memphis beside me panting, and behind the truck, a roiling dust plume, I recalled one of my favorite aspects of Memphis: he wasn't mine. I was just his baby sitter and now I was taking him home. About once a week, for one reason or another, I made this same 30-minute drive down into Round Valley and its only town, Covelo, population less than a thousand.

As we rolled due west down the logging road, the milk truck shuddered and rattled, an earthquake on wheels, and I could feel all of it in the tall gearshift stick with the black plastic knob that I gripped with my right hand while steering with the left. There was a hard sun in a clear sky, and it was mid afternoon, prime time for logging trucks, the drivers of which might have been on the offshoots of this road for hours without encountering anything but squirrels. Also, this road would be like a super highway compared with some they had just been

on. Fortunately, the milk truck had a large side-view mirror on each side.

I was constantly checking those mirrors while swerving back and forth through an obstacle course of ruts and potholes and washboard. Plus, I had to be vigilant about the steep canyon on the left plunging three quarters of a mile down to the Eel River. Both sides of the canyon are covered with a dense emerald carpet of trees: fir and pine along the ridges, oak and scrub oak below. On the forested side of the road, opposite the canyon, I occasionally caught a glimpse of a logger's small trailer home just visible in the trees.

Plus, I was resisting the hypnotic repetition of the looping curves. Usually I tried not to drive stoned. Today I failed.

At around the half way point, we arrived at one of my favorite parts of this drive, when the Eel River came into view way, way down there at the bottom of the canyon. At first, it was just a small green curvy ribbon, but as we descended, it went in and out of view every five or so minutes, and each time it appeared, it was closer, and each time, I stole more glances from the road. In most places, the river was shallow and clear, but in a few places, it was freakishly colored. There were a few pools where a luminous light turquoise phased into light jade shallows and navy blue depths. The first time I saw one of these pools I thought there had been a chemical spill. Actually though, they're frequently good swimming holes.

We hit asphalt with the first level ground, and for a few miles, we drove parallel to the river, which was a few dozen yards to the south. This section of the road had the best access to the river and to some of its best swimming holes. One in particular had a broad sandy beach, was hidden from the road, and was frequently occupied by skinny-dipping freaks. Indeed, it was becoming something of an unofficial community center for the nascent freak community of Round Valley. I recognized a couple cars among those parked at the closest point to the beach. There were members of that community I had never seen clothed.

Most of the friends visiting the land from the City were naked soon after they arrived and most of the time they were here. That included me too, of course, though I didn't like to work naked.

254

Chicks frequently doffed their blouses immediately. There's something about being engulfed in nature that returns you to your flesh, makes you want to remove all barriers, even the material, the easiest to remove, and savor the wind and sunlight with your whole body, your whole being. Not to mention that savoring the sunlight on a naked chick's flesh and the breeze on her pubic hair could be a minor sex act.

Friends who came just for the weekend didn't have to work, but the occasional few staying through the week or longer, testing their own back-to-the-land fantasy, had to do some work on the place. If enough eventually accumulated, we might have a commune... or not. I was fine either way. This week I was alone with Memphis and that was fine. The perfection of my life now included a perfect balance between solitude and companionship.

It wasn't until after I started it that I fully realized homesteading my own twenty acres was the unseen target of my life, the culmination of years of obsession with Henry David Thoreau and Beat poet Gary Snyder, who was himself then homesteading in the Sierras. Which was where I grew up and acquired the skills and taste for country living. So, for me, going back to the land also had an element of going back to childhood. Plus, even with the little work I'd already done, I was beginning to feel something primitive but powerful, something I didn't think I could feel, love of land.

Almost daily, I recited to myself part of a poem by Beat poet Brother Antoninus, about working in the garden of a monastery: "The mind loosens, the nerve lengthens, / All the haunting abstractions slip free and are gone; / And the peace is enormous."

*

His name was Alan Chadwick and he was very British. He was a Master Horticulturist, and according to some in his field, a genius. He was a professional stage actor for much of his life, knew George Bernard Shaw, and was a close friend of T. E. Lawrence, "Lawrence of Arabia." During World War II, Chadwick was commander of a naval minesweeper. Then in the late

nineteen sixties, amid the redwoods of the UC Santa Cruz campus, in a barren, poison-oak-covered clearing, he created a "miracle garden." But he had a falling-out with the administration (he was cantankerous), and then was offered free land in Covelo.

And here, he hath wrought a thing of beauty. Called the Round Valley Garden Project, or sometimes just the Covelo Garden, its perfection extended from the compost piles, to the plate-sized dahlias that grew along a border of the vegetable and herb gardens, to the military precision with which the entire place was laid out. For the freaks, like me, living in the mountains around Round Valley, and even outside, in the rest of Mendocino County, Chadwick's was the homestead supreme, the model. (Not that I seriously believed I could replicate the Covelo Garden but it was always inspirational.) It was an incredible stroke of luck to have it nearby, and it was even luckier to have Chadwick here to answer questions about his method.

I just walked up to him one afternoon while he was working in the vegetable garden, and told him how much I liked his method and that I was using it in the mountains east of Round Valley. He asked a lot of questions about the land and seemed favorably impressed. After that, I stopped by every-so-often with questions about growing vegetables (and grass, without ever mentioning it), and he was always pleasant and forthcoming.

Finally, Memphis and I arrived on the valley floor where there were broadly-strewn cattle and a few horses and fewer deer grazing in a vast green meadow with scattered oak tree clusters, and here and there, barbed wire section fences. It was a straight shot with one turn across the valley to Covelo. Chadwick's was just west of the tiny town.

When I pulled up in the milk truck with Memphis, I was glad to see Chadwick working alone, turning over compost with a d-handled spading fork. I made a point of only approaching him when he was not with assistants and students. I was always afraid of him suggesting that I should talk to So-and-so about paying the fees and joining the apprentice program. After all, I was getting free what others were paying for. That I already had my land and was working it, not preparing to, might have given me privileges in Chadwick's eyes. There were about a dozen students here in any

given time, coming and going in three-week shifts. Most of what I knew about Chadwick, outside of the little mentioned in the book on his method, came from the students and assistants. I would see them around the town but spent more time with them at the swimming hole than anywhere else.

Getting out the sliding side-door of the milk truck, and keeping Memphis in at the same time, was tricky. Immediately after the door clicked shut, Memphis started whining and whimpering, and he kept it up the whole time I talked to Chadwick.

He was in his mid sixties, tall, wiry, with a boney, etched face, and a high shock of gray hair combed back. Now, working in nothing but his usual shorts and a deep tan, and with his large aquiline nose, he resembled a big bird. There could hardly have been a more exotic presence on the few streets of the town than when he rode around on his bicycle, as I saw him do several times.

"Suppose... you suspect root rot?" I asked after we exchanged the usual greetings and pleasantries.

"Root rot? Now?" he said and stuck the spading fork in the ground and rested his right boot on it.

"Yeah, some visiting friends over-watered..."

"You shouldn't have to wuh-ry about root rot now, in this heat... And you double-dug the beds?"

"Yeah."

"Then you shouldn't even think about root rot now. Especially with the excellent drainage you have up theh-uh. That's my problem down hee-uh in the valley... drainage... What made you suspect it?"

"A discoloration in some leaves... this dark stain..."

"That could be any numbuh of things...Is it widespread?"

"No."

"I shouldn't wuh-ry about it... If it spreads, tell me."

"I have that problem up there too... drainage," I said with that trepidation I always felt when I talked to him incognito about the grass; that is, without him realizing that was the real subject. "A couple things we're trying to grow outside the beds... tomatoes... a special breed of tomatoes that needs more sunlight... So we're growing them in holes in clay and we had to

put garden soil in the holes... but the clay holds the water. And like I said, some visiting friends were... over enthusiastic about watering."

"I still wouldn't wuh-ry about it in this heat... even hee-uh, with this tehrible drainage, I don't even think about it."

He pulled the D-handled spading fork out of the ground and turned and stuck it into a compost pile. I silently watched him turning the compost for a while.

"I wanted to tell you ..." I eventually said, and then he stopped, frozen in place, and turned to face me, "... how beautiful I think your vegetables are... the ones you sell..." I gestured toward the kiosk, a tiny rough-plank building beside the road, where he sold his excess vegetables. "I've never seen anything like them. I had no idea that a vegetable could be so... beautiful... so... perfect...in shape and color... and taste ... In their way, they're as beautiful as flowers."

He stared at me, waiting for me to finish, and then he turned back to turning compost. No nod, no smile, certainly no thank you. One of his assistants described him as being "like something out of the Old Testament... a raging prophet" with an organic gardening gospel.

I saw for myself that he was prone to wild tangents. His property had old apple and walnut trees, and once I was talking to him while he was harvesting apples, picking them and placing them in a cloth sack hanging from his shoulder. He railed on and on about the low quality of American pears.

He ended with, "Yestehday, two chaps from the Ministry of Agricultuh wuh hee-uh, and I told them theh-uh is not a decent pe-uh in the whole of Nohth Amehrica."

I returned to Memphis, still whimpering in the milk truck, after thanking Chadwick and saying good-bye. I was always mindful of not overstaying my welcome with him. Through the summer, his help would be indispensible to the success of the vegetable garden and the grass.

*

As for the rednecks in Round Valley, about half the population, mostly cowboys and loggers, I was as familiar with them as I was with the bears and mountain lions and ignored them the same way. I had only a single encounter with a redneck in the valley, and he was a bartender. I avoided bars usually and definitely redneck bars, but I had just driven the milk truck back from the City and had a mighty hankerin' for a beer. So I pulled into the parking lot of "The Best Bar in Town," the only bar in town, and discovered that on this weekday night at about nine, I had the place to myself, except for the bartender. We were both about the same age and took one look at each other across the room, after I entered the door, and his greased dark forelock hanging over his forehead and the fringe of my hair hanging over my collar told each of us all he cared to know about the other.

But I really wanted that beer, so I crossed the room and sat at the bar and asked for a draft. The bar was indistinguishable from any other mountain bar: dirty windows, dim light, neon beer signs glowing on the wall, a jukebox glowing in a corner, and thumbtacked to the wall behind the bar, snapshots of patrons posed with dead bucks and prize trout. The bartender and I were the only human beings in the room, so each knew he was going to have to make conversation with the other.

I told him about the drive up north and he mentioned he was from west Marin County. I remembered how dangerous it was back in the Sixties for longhairs in that same area, where I liked to hike, though by now, spring of 1975, it had improved. I asked him why he left and his answer was the plaint of rednecks everywhere, and a possible explanation for why it was now safer in west Marin.

He said with a contorted sneer, "Too many people from New York."

I wasn't in the bar more than ten minutes, finishing the beer and paying for it as quickly as possible.

*

Memphis liked me well enough. He whimpered and barked and pranced in a circle by way of greeting whenever he first saw me. But Memphis loved Bill, who raised him from a pup, and Memphis showed that love by whining and shuffling his paws after we left Chadwick's and headed north out of the valley toward the hills and Bill's land.

Just before we left the valley floor, we passed two drunk middle-aged Indian men, laughing and stumbling over each other in a roadside ditch. The other half of the population of Round Valley was Indians. I had heard that this reservation was a dumping ground for survivors of various tribes from around the northern end of the state.

Bill's was the best hippie teepee I'd ever seen. A dozen tips of the straight poles radiated out of the top at about ten or twelve feet high. I, who had searched unsuccessfully for straight trunk branches for my vegetable garden fence, knew how much patient, attentive searching was required. But the whole teepee showed the same patience and attention to detail. The waterproof canvas was flawlessly wrapped taut around the poles and pegged into the ground. Bill's was like the sample a professional teepee builder would have in front of his shop.

I pulled off the road and headed toward the teepee at the edge of a clearing. Bill's land was right off a paved road on a plateau, nearly level and thickly forested with firs and pines and some redwoods. He was going to have to cut some trees to get a clearing large enough for a vegetable garden. He had a seasonal stream in one corner of the parcel, but was going have to dig a well, probably not too deep.

Memphis whimpered louder and jumped up and placed his paws on the shelf below the windshield so that he could see Bill as we approached him. Bill was standing in front of the teepee, wearing only his usual baggy denim overalls and sandals. Memphis barked. I pulled up beside Bill's old red Ford pick up, and immediately after turning off the key, I slid back the door and Memphis shot out. Bill squatted on his haunches and Memphis ran

at him full speed, barking and wagging his tail. On reaching Bill, Memphis started licking his face furiously.

"Hi Memphie! Hi Memphie!" Bill said, laughing under the rain of licks. "Miss me?"

I approached, Bill stood, and we shook hands, clutching thumbs. Then I handed him a big paper bag of dog food.

Bill was scrawny and almost concave-chested with a scraggily dark blond beard and lank hair parted in the middle and hanging to six inches below his shoulders. His lean, narrow, sunburnt face looked closer to adolescence than his thirty-two years. His overalls looked like clown pants or hand-me-downs from somebody obese. There was almost room in there for a second Bill. They were ideal for labor in the heat though, protecting while letting the breeze through.

"Thanks again, man" he said.

"Sure... My pleasure... We always have fun up there," I said as Memphis and I exchanged glances.

Then I noticed for the first time, off to the side, a small teepee, a perfect replica of the big one and about half the size. I walked over to it.

"Bill, man... you've really got a talent for this stuff."

He said nothing, just nodded and grinned, hands in pockets, because he knew it was true and he was proud of his handiwork.

"It's for the girls, right?" I asked.

"Yeah... They haven't seen it yet."

These were the 9 and 7 year old daughters from a previous marriage of his new ol' lady, Bonnie.

"You're gonna make a good dad," I said.

"Hope so... I'm workin' at it. Want somethin' to drink? Water? Celery juice?"

"No, I'm o.k. thanks. I carry a canteen in the milk truck."

Without thinking about it, we wandered toward the fire ring. That was the area where we usually talked. Beside the ring of blackened boulders were a folding poolside lounge chair of plastic webbing stretched over chrome tube. There were also two matching folding chairs and a card table covered mostly with cooking utensils and bags of food. Bill placed the bag of dog food

on the table. Even more than my own, his was the standard California car camp, but permanent.

He knew what I wanted to talk about, and I was encouraged when, as he sat in the poolside lounge chair, and I in a poolside regular chair, I saw calm satisfaction in his face.

"So..." I asked. "How'd it go in Ukiah?"

"You're gonna like it... I think," he said petting Memphis, panting beside him. "We've come up with a pretty good strategy... In fact, I think we've got 'em by the balls."

One of the things he did while I babysat Memphis this time was attend a meeting at the county seat of United Stand, the hip homesteaders' association fighting the red-tagging campaign.

"O.k.," he continued. "This was a meeting about... what exactly we're going to say to the Board of Supervisors... The state has been sayin' we're violating the building code and the county was happy to go along. But, it is our constitutional right to have a jury trial for each red-tagging, and that would mean hundreds and hundreds of trials that the county cannot possibly afford."

Having grown up among rednecks, I knew their aptitude for bigotry, and easily pictured the smirk of the county leadership over their red-tagging strategy. I now savored the collapse of that smirk as they learned of our counter-strategy.

"You're right, I like it..." I said. "But are they still red-tagging?"

"There hasn't been anything official yet, about stopping it, but they're nuts if they start up again. I mean... we can flood the court calendar any time we want... So, one immediate goal is to get the county to pressure the state to ease up and start negotiations. And listen to this..." He adjusted himself in the lounge chair and leaned forward, sharing a confidence. "We found out that the inspectors don't get a salary, their payment is the permit fee. They don't make the law, but it's in their interest to loosen the code for us. They sure as hell would rather be giving out permits and collecting fees than giving out red-tags."

"Yeah, that's good..." I said.

"I brought up the point that, if we let 'em drag this out passed fall, then we won't be able to start building till spring, and they'll win a delay. So, I'm sayin'... let's be aggressive and force

their hand early and not give 'em time to come up with a counter-counter-strategy..." Then he said with a gloating smirk, "We've got 'em by the balls," as he closed his hand on an imaginary scrotum in front of him. "Anyway... you can read about it in the next issue of the Grapevine... They'll have all the details."

That was the Mendocino Grapevine underground newspaper, the Berkeley Barb of the redwoods, and the hip community's only means of communication. It had an elaborate logo designed by R. Crumb and occasional cartoons of his commenting on the red-tagging campaign and the destruction of the redwoods.

Bill was the union rep for the carriers when I worked for the post office, and he took it on himself to occasionally visit at home some of the broken lonely people who worked there. Shared politics and the shared dream of homesteading our own land made us immediate and fast friends. He left the P.O. before me and moved to Willits, where he worked as a carpenter while making the move into the country gradually. After nearly a year of fruitless searching, I finally followed Bill's lead and searched for a land parcel around Round Valley and found my exact ideal.

Before the P.O., Bill was a union organizer who had become a socialist from something he read while serving a term in a juvenile detention center. His involvement in the anti-war movement included fire-bombing a draft office from the back of a motorcycle. His involvement in the Civil Rights movement included driving to the safety of the Mexican border one of Los Siete. They were seven Chicano activists from San Francisco who were being framed by the cops for the murder of a cop. Bill had a loaded pistol under his seat the whole way to the border.

He was unusually aggressive for a freak. Maybe it came from having two bullying older brothers who were outlaw bikers. There used to be something deep in Bill that was cocked-and-ready to fling him kamikazee-like at an enemy. Then he found Bonnie and her daughters and they replaced the Revolution.

We fell silent and my attention wandered back to the small teepee replica.

"When are Bonnie and the girls movin' up here?" I asked.

"Not till after school ends."

"They gonna stay the whole summer?"

"They'll be goin' back and forth to Willits."

Bonnie was plump and blowsy, a decade older, and the original earth-mother. I was tremendously fond of her and found her easy to talk to and when we were alone once waiting for Bill, I unburdened myself about Yvette. Bonnie was fixing me up with some of her single girlfriends in the area.

We lapsed into silence again. My eyes wandered to the hammock hanging between two young redwoods and then to the nearby clothesline, also hanging between young redwoods, with light gray boxer shorts and cotton socks drying.

"Hey," I said breaking the silence, "when we were coming out of the valley, I saw a couple of Indians, drunk, in a ditch by the road... It was painful..."

"Yeah, I know... I probably even know who that was... You and I chose to come here, but they're prisoners out here. This has been their concentration camp for almost a century. Lots of them don't have the skills or connections for a decent job outside, so they're stuck out here, sentenced to life on welfare... You know about this place right?"

"You mean about the Indians here?"

"Yeah..."

"Well, I heard the reservation was a dumping ground for the survivors of various tribes..."

"Yeah, it's that, but... Look... in the whole of North America, Indians were treated worse in California than anywhere else. And in California, they were treated worst of all here, in Round Valley. Whites shot 'em any time they felt like it for decades in the middle of the last century.... At one point there was even a bounty on Indian scalps and heads, men, women, children, it didn't matter. The counties paid for them and the state reimbursed the counties and the feds reimbursed the state. They even had something they called 'The Mendocino War,' but of course, like most of those Indian wars, it was just another slaughter. Anyway, they wiped out about ten thousand Indians here over about twenty-five years..."

"How many?!"

"It's possibly as high as ten thousand. About eighty per cent of the population. And that's just around here. Of course, there was slaughter all over the state."

"... My god..."

Pause...

"Jesus man," I asked, "how do you know all this shit?"

"I talk to the Indians... They know about this stuff. They make a point of remembering it.... They told me some radical young historians are working on the history of this place. They came up and talked to the Indians. They said the historians learned things from them and they learned stuff from the historians."

Pause...

"God..." I said. "I feel... unclean..."

"Hey man, the whole hemisphere was stolen from Indians."

"Yeah, I know, but this... It's... It's too close..."

Pause...

"You wanna smoke some grass?" he asked.

"Uh... I better not. I got high before I left and I've gotta long drive back... and I just remembered, I've got to get back to Covelo before the store closes."

I stood and we started slowly walking toward the milk truck.

"How are you feelin' these days?" he asked me.

"Ok," I answered, confused by the question.

"Hey man," he said slapping me on the shoulder, "we've all had our turn bein' a doormat for love... Comes with the territory."

He was referring to things I had told Bonnie.

4

About a month later, June of 1975...

"So, Eve comes to Eden, huh?" Gordon asked, shaking my hand, proud of the quip, and knowing my fear.

I didn't answer because I was too rattled. Yvette and Maddie were standing on the passenger side of the VW bug, hugging and laughing. Gordon got into the driver's side.

"I want another hug," Maddie said as she ran around the front of the car and into my arms. She pulled away and placed her right hand on my chest and looked up at me and said, "I'm so happy for you both."

She looked from me to Yvette, who was smiling, and then back at me. Then Maddie ran over to the passenger side and got in. As they bounced down the driveway, Yvette and I waved and called "bye," and as I waved and called, I felt with near certainty that this was a mistake. Then I looked at Yvette, smiling that radiantly happy smile back at me, and I became a puddle.

Their first morning on the land, I knew I wouldn't feel comfortable with Yvette until I could get her alone, so I invited her to go exploring with me. I hadn't yet followed the year-round, border stream to where it met the Eel River. She knew it was also an invitation to sex and said yes.

It was a hot, late morning, and we were hiking without a trail beside the creek in dappled shade. We were both in cutoff jeans and hiking boots and shirtless. I was getting turned-on by the jiggle of her small breasts as she jumped from boulder to boulder or their hang as she bent to get under a log, though it was nothing compared to the spectacle of Maddie just walking around the camp.

Soon we were beyond the few hundred yards that I had already explored. We stopped in a big clearing, in harsh sunlight, where the creek met another and where there were large gray logs strewn like spilled matches. For at least one long ago winter, my humble five-foot wide creek had been a bulldozing torrent.

I mentioned this and she looked around and said, "Yeah."

We returned to silence. Both had a lot to think about, most immediately sex. I was unsure of how to start. I was scarred from the Sixties, when sex was readily available but dependent on the unlikely coincidence that both participants were sufficiently sane at the same time. Most daunting of all, sex between Yvette and I would be the seal on a commitment. There could be no

casual sex between she and I. And always at the back of my mind was the near certainty that having her on the land would be a mistake. Yet, I had to make a move soon, if only to put an end to the hike. We kept going and going because I couldn't figure out how to begin, and because I was so afraid of the rejection, however unlikely at that point, that I feared like death. Plus, we were getting tired.

"You wanna rest? We could sit over there," I said gesturing toward a grassy area in the shade of some douglas firs.

"O.k."

The cool of the shade was a relief as we sat on the grass. I knew she was wondering what was taking me so long... or was she? I was torn between overpowering desire for her and fear of even touching her. Then, with an attitude somewhere between panic-stricken and perfunctory, I leaned over and kissed her. She didn't stop me. I fondled her breasts awhile, then slid a hand along the inside of a thigh, then squeezed a finger under her cutoffs. She didn't stop me. I laid her back onto the grass and laid beside her and unbuttoned and unzipped her shorts. She didn't stop me. I fingered her for a while, until she squirmed and panted.

"D'you... wanna fuck?" I asked, my face over hers.

"Yeah..." she said, uncertainly. She was reacting to my own ambivalence and confusion.

"Here, lay on our shorts," I said and stood and took off mine.

I wanted her comfortable, but also wanted her to see my hard-on. It might be just that little bit more difficult for her to turn back. She glanced at it while she took off her own shorts. I put both pairs side-by-side on clumps of grass and she laid down on them. I laid down beside her and followed standard procedure: massaged her breasts, licked her nipples, and fingered her vagina, and soon she lost herself in the pleasure and became wet enough. Then I entered her.

She was now officially living on the land.

*

And on the land, Yvette was completely in her element. The land answered her extreme sensitivity and calm. More than anything she said, I could see it in that smile. Here, even more than me, she was being released into the wild.

Each night we fell asleep to the crickets and the frogs in the pond, and real late, a couple owls, and about every other week, the coyotes. Each morning we awoke in the gray predawn to the wall of bird song, what sounded like millions of birds calling the sun up.

The hardest work on the land I had done through the spring, digging holes for the marijuana and for the fence posts around the vegetable garden, and double-digging the garden beds. There was still the daily routine of chores: watering the grass and the vegetables, gathering firewood, preparing meals and cleaning up after. The vegetable garden started providing edibles a few weeks after Yvette arrived, and over the course of the summer, she and I added three more beds, but we took our time. She fit into the routine perfectly, and her enthusiasm showed in her hard work, though the pace slackened after she arrived. There was a reason now not to go to bed exhausted.

Whereas Bree and I could talk nonstop for hours at a time, Yvette and I didn't talk a lot. She never talked just to fill the silence, and was more comfortable with silence, allowing more of it, than anyone else I knew. That quality lent her mystery, especially beside a chatterbox like Maddie. It wasn't that we didn't have things to say to each other, but nothing we said had the charge of some of those shared silences. We had a rapport outside of language, using "hard squeezes," gestures, glances, even the lyrics to idly hummed songs.

Beside the campfire, she talked about her trip around the world more than anything else. By the time of her trip, 1973-74, the action wasn't in San Francisco anymore, with the Haight long over, or in New York, or any place else in the States. The action was on the Hippie Trail. And she migrated instinctively right to it. The campfire crackled in the background, flame light wavered over her face, when she began at the beginning, then over the

summer, took me along on her trip, adding to and expanding on things mentioned in letters.

"We landed in Paris... Took our time, doin' regular tourist stuff goin' down through France and Italy... In Rome we heard about this island in Greece that had a village that was practically all international freaks... We were naked on the beach most of the time...

"...We crossed Turkey in a 'freak bus' that came from Amsterdam and it had a stereo that played the music of each region as we went through it... It broke down in Iran, and after waiting a couple days and it still wasn't fixed, we decided to hitch... We were hitching to Mashad across the Great Salt Desert ...It was really weird... white talcum powder as far as you could see..." She stopped to stare off into a memory and started laughing. "We got picked up in the middle of the desert by a VW bus that was driven by friends from Greece. They pulled up and when we recognized them, we started screaming..." When she laughed hard, as now, pain was visible in the curve of her right eyebrow.

"... There weren't many freak chicks, and there were almost none traveling without a guy... We were told a couple times that it was too dangerous for women traveling alone in the Muslim countries east of Turkey... We were always careful in those countries... There were lots of places where women weren't allowed. It's called *purdah*... We saw freak chicks in shorts and halter-tops. That's underwear there... We didn't wear *chadors*, the black bag those women live in, but we always wore head scarves, covered our arms and legs, never made eye contact with men, always said we were married... We imitated the local women as much as we could...

"... A border guard tried to sell us hash when we were going into Afghanistan..." She shook her head. "Can you believe that? The cop was a dealer... Kabul is really pretty. It's surrounded by snow-covered mountains... The freaks hung out on Chicken Street... Outside of Kabul, some *Kochi* were camped, Afghan gypsies... The chicks..." She looked off and smiled, delighted at the memory. "Some of 'em were beautiful...

Their eyes... glowed... and they wore bells on their ankles, like chicks on Haight Street used to...

"... In Pakistan... there was some kind of tribal war, and one night, in the middle of the night, the owners of the hotel woke everybody up and took us down to the basement, and then put a guy with a gun in front of the door...

" ... Of course you're always talkin' to other freaks, gettin' tips... We met a guy who hitched from Istanbul to Bombay on eleven bucks... We met a guy who was robbed of everything except his pants and his passport... In the restaurants and the inns where freaks hung out there were guest books with messages and comments that you could learn a lot from... As we moved east, every once in a while, we met freaks goin' home, goin' west, and some of 'em were sick... or broke... or both... but they were always smilin' and glad they went... and encouraging... There was somethin' in that smile...

"... In India, they greet like this," she said as she made a slight bow, hands pressed together, close to her chest, fingers pointing at me. "They call it *namaste*. It means 'I bow to the divine in you'... It seemed like the small animals, the birds and squirrels were less afraid of humans there... I dunno...

"... We learned that when you're hitching in India you want to ride only with truck drivers... Some of 'em are Sikhs who carry pistols against bandits... We saw a lot of India from the roof of a truck cab... Sometimes we rode on trains, third class... If you were goin' overnight you slept up in the luggage racks... The trains could be so packed that you had to get on and off through the windows..." She got excited and shifted her weight on the log as she described a special memory. "There were these tea-sellers, and they would come through the windows carrying a tray with clay cups and a big teapot on charcoal burners... They would go back out the windows, while the train was running, to sell tea on the roof. And we never saw 'em spill a single drop... or a crumb of charcoal... They were like acrobats...The train stations could be insane, no lines for tickets, just a crowd pushing and shouting and reaching over you. On the streets around the stations, the sidewalks were full of people sleeping, living there... and..." She stared transfixed

at a disturbing memory, then lowered her voice, "... and there were babies with flies all over them and no one brushed them off..."

"... In Allahabad we took a ferry, just a big row boat, and there were a lot of pilgrims on the boat and they sang hymns to the river goddess... Giant fish, carp, came up to the boat and some pilgrims fed them these little balls of dough. Some pilgrims threw money into the river, and others put flowers on leaf boats and sent them off on the current...

"... In Benares we stayed with some German freaks in a houseboat on the Ganges... They had some acid... It wasn't bad..." It was one of the rare moments of inhibition from her. The way she looked at me, I knew she and one of the Germans with the acid had been lovers, and she saw I knew it.

She usually spoke freely about her other lovers, and I surprised myself by not being jealous, which made me suspicious of my true feelings for her. Did she and the German fuck on acid? I never asked her, and she never volunteered it. Somehow, Yvette and I never got around to fucking on acid, though at the beginning of the relationship, we took yage together, the grail drug William Burroughs took deep in the jungles of Colombia. It failed utterly for us (an omen for the relationship?), probably because it was too old, as the guy who gave it to me suggested.

"... We took a boat from Bombay to Goa. It took a day and a night. Most of the freaks were at the back playing guitars and smoking chillums. We stayed up near the front... We didn't even try to sleep because the engines made the deck vibrate... The stars... god, the stars... There were dolphins following beside the boat... There were flying fish on the deck in the morning that got stranded there in the night... We spent Christmas in Goa ..." She became wistful. "From the roof of our hotel, I used to watch against the sunset the kite fights of boys yelling in the street." Then, suddenly alert, she sat up. "And all the while, ya had to watch out for monkeys... in gangs. They would just swoop over the roof, grab whatever they wanted, especially food, and get away into the trees before anyone could do anything...

"... In Nepal, we went over a pass that was 16,000 feet high... The bus... the bus was falling apart and the road in some places was just a... big trail, and there was this cliff, right there, that went down... You couldn't see the bottom down there... And there was this boy whose job it was to jump out and put rocks under the tires when the driver stopped to change gears. All the other passengers would get out too, but we couldn't, because we had such bad altitude sickness... The freaks' favorite restaurant in Kathmandu is the Blue Tibetan, the favorite hotel is the Matchbox and it's on..." She started to laugh. "... Freak Street, of course... and across the street are these hash and ganja shops that are licensed by the government... Oh, and there was also the Bakery that supposedly had the best stereo in Nepal... We got up at 3 AM one morning and hiked in the dark up to the rim of the Kathmandu Valley, and we got up there just-in-time to watch the sun come up over the Himalayas... It was..." She fell silent, and while staring off stoned into the memory, started to tear up.

"... There was no road through Burma, so we just skipped Thailand and flew directly to Malaysia... I was kinda lookin' forward to Burma. They're supposed to have a far out kind of Buddhism. I like the Buddhists ... They're... uh..."

"Hipper?"

"Yeah..."

She had that coy little smile she got when she had wandered into the foreign territory of abstract concepts and their attendant difficult words. But, as always, her instincts were unerring.

"It's a lot of things..." she said. "I like the uh... uh... what they believe in."

"The philosophy?"

"Yeah... but mainly I just like the vibe... It's so... so..."

"Accepting?"

"Yeah... but also deeper than the others... mellower... In French there's a better word for it, *doux*..."

"...In Penang, we went to the Snake Temple, and there were thousands of snakes there, and there was a Buddhist monk who spoke English... Malaysia used to be a British colony

so a lot of people spoke English there... and he handed us each a snake... We were already holding them, when I asked him if they were poisonous and he said yes they were very poisonous, but they were holy snakes and very well fed and cared for, so they were safe to handle..." She smiled as a shiver ran through her. "What could we do? We didn't want to offend him, so...

"... Everywhere in East Asia, we saw some version of a guy on a motor scooter, with his wife and a newborn, a couple little kids, a grandmother, and some chickens, all on the same scooter...

"... In Java, we found out that we could ask a policeman to find us a ride and he would go around and ask drivers stopped in traffic or parked beside the road, and usually he would find us a ride... to the next town at least..." (Often, as now, I became distracted by the way those lips slid over those teeth while forming words.) "Indonesian trains were big and comfortable compared to Indian trains, but the buses ... It felt like they didn't have springs and the roads were full of potholes, so we were bounced around hard at the back of those buses for... days it seemed like... When, we had to walk with the backpacks, in village after village, we were mobbed by kids..." For the first time, she recognized the beauty of that image. "... Curious kids..."

"... Bali..." she said slowly turning her head from side to side while staring at me. Though she talked more about it, she didn't need to, that radiantly content, Buddhistic half-smile said it well enough.

"... We thought about comin' back through Japan, but it's so expensive, and we were runnin' low on money, so we flew to LA from Jakarta..."

*

The land was also a refuge for Yvette from the high-decibel chaos of an alcoholic home. She grew up in a small town in Marin County (from which it was easy for two bold thirteen-year-old girls to sneak off to the forbidden Haight Street during the Summer of Love).

Her father was an insurance salesman, half a head shorter than his wife, and a maudlin drunk. I may never have seen him sober. He was prone to dramatic, embarrassing scenes, and made Yvette cry numerous times when I was with her.

Her mother was something else, gracious, inviting, a French Canadian, hence Yvette spoke French. The mother was also a Julliard-trained classical pianist who gave up a career to raise three daughters. I saw immediately after meeting her mother that Yvette's beauty was a further refinement of her mothers'.

Here on the land, I was 28 and Yvette was 21, and I had been obsessing over her for almost three years. Whenever we had been apart, I noticed the subtle changes in her, and here on the land, she had never seemed more the confident young woman, so far from the eighteen year old, essentially still a high school kid, I became fixated on. It occurred to me one night beside the campfire that I had been the privileged witness of her transformation from callow beauty to fascinating woman. A woman who was still strikingly innocent, even for her young age, still ignorant of the world inspite of having gone around it. But at the same time, a woman often wise beyond her years, because she always spoke from her depths.

What I was also noticing now, on the land, stronger than ever before, were her emotional needs. Before the trip, she enjoyed exploring sex with various partners, but was focused on the trip and not interested in a relationship. It was a measure of how much she now wanted a relationship that, after she returned from her trip, she went all the way to Wyoming to see some guy she met on the Hippie Trail (note: he didn't come to California to see her). Apparently, back on the ranch, he was too much of a redneck, and she came home disappointed. Then there were a number of guys in quick succession, including the one she had just lived with. She wanted to be in love.

The land was also what was missing between she and I. Gradually, through the summer, we relaxed around each other to a degree we never had before. We were naked around each other every day and even got used to pissing in front of each

other. Of course, throughout the summer, there was lots and lots of sex. Most of it was on the mattress under the bay tree. But we both enjoyed swimming, and it was also a bath, and of course, we couldn't be that close to each other, naked and alone, and not fuck. There were few if any swimmable ponds or river pools in the area that we didn't fuck in at least once that summer.

One day, while we were swimming in a pond, a couple boys yelled from the bushes, "Put on your clothes!" and laughed. So, we didn't fuck there that day, but we did see a single otter sunning on a log on an island. I found out later from Bill that the otter had had a mate but a redneck boy killed it with his .22 rifle thinking he could somehow sell the hide. The carcass sank to the bottom of course.

Another time, we were in a pool in the Eel River and saw actual fresh water eels, which had become rare. Fucking in that pool later, we were surprised then embarrassed when a logging truck shot by on the road we had forgotten went alongside the river there. The delighted driver, who had an unobstructed view of us from about thirty yards, gave a long staccato blast of the horn that echoed down the granite canyon.

We heard about a place where the river narrowed into a stone bowl creating a natural jacuzzi. When we arrived there, several groups of freaks were nude sunbathing on nearby beaches. So, we didn't fuck in the river that day. We did talk about going up river to find our own pool, but by then, we were getting blasé about fucking in the river.

We asked for directions to the jacuzzi pool and then went toward it. We were walking with difficulty alongside the river in huarache sandals, over large gravel and around granite boulders, when a freak on the opposite side and fifty yards down river started staring at us. He too was naked, older, lean but muscular, very tanned, and with dark brown hair in a ponytail. The stare was so flagrant that it was a male dominance challenge. Except that it wasn't really. I knew exactly what he was staring at: radiant beauty, naked. I looked from him to her, but she was already turning away, bored with his attention. When we met, she was still learning about her beauty, now it was a

dead subject. That guy's stare reminded me though what a liability her beauty was when every third guy was smitten with her. Plus, I was a little embarrassed by her beauty. It seemed vaguely shallow for a man to have physical beauty in his lover. Thoreau wouldn't.

We continued clumsily picking our way toward the jacuzzi pool. It lived up to its reputation. Part of the river was pinched between boulders into a deep granite bowl where it became a powerful whirlpool of massaging currents and tickling fizz. It was just big enough for one at a time and you had to stay alert to avoid drifting directly under the bone-crunching gush.

*

Yvette was too shy to be a good party mixer, and when I was with her, I wasn't a very good one either. Even so, that summer we went to a few potluck picnics with other hip homesteaders from the hills around Round Valley. One was also a wedding.

It seemed an excellent parcel, a large clearing in dense pine forest, almost level, with a year round stream in the middle. I was impressed, at first. Parked on the edge of the clearing was a converted school bus. On the side facing the clearing, it had an awning of blue plastic tarp, and under that, two long tables on end consisting of plywood on sawhorses. The tables were covered with sheets and scattered foodstuffs and surrounded by casually busy chicks in aprons. The bus stood out for not being covered in psychedelic swirls of color. Instead, it was a dull, institutional middle-blue, probably former military or correctional. Inside, it was now a home, like a huge trailer.

Near it, in the woods, was a chicken-wire enclosure with half a dozen chickens and a black she goat. A few yards from the awning, toward the creek, was a small scraggily vegetable garden, and even nearer the creek, were a few large backpacking tents belonging to visiting friends. Kids and dogs were swirling around and between the tents.

The day was sunny and breezy under a clear sky. The milling chatting crowd was bunched near the bus and a nearby fire ring. A St. Bernard dog sat apart, in the shade, on his haunches, panting and watching. One guy was naked. Most guys were bare-chested, a couple chicks were, one was nursing a baby. A clothed chick was in late pregnancy. Of course, there was lots and lots of hair, everywhere, hanging from heads and faces. In the shade, beside the fire ring, musicians on a guitar, a banjo, one conga drum, and a resonant wooden box were stumbling through the simplest Beatle songs. A couple teenage chicks, in full gypsy, were trying to dance to the halting music, twirling about, skirts flaring, upheld arms writhing with self-conscious grace.

All the elements of a hip mass gathering were there, just fewer of them. Around a third of the three or four dozen wedding guests were familiar. And, as usual, there were a couple times more males than females.

We arrived late and parked beside the road among a dozen or so old pickups, jalopies, and a VW van. We then walked fifty yards through dense pine forest to the clearing. As we crossed the clearing, I noticed that the crowd was sending wisps of dust into the wind and that made me focus on the sandy alluvial soil. That creek occasionally flooded this clearing. This parcel wasn't such a prize after all.

We didn't know the hosts, who were also the bride and groom, but that hardly mattered. We immediately saw Bill and Bonnie and Bonnie's daughters on the outer edge of the crowd. As we walked toward them, the girls as usual became entranced by Yvette. She saw it and broke into a broad grin. Before we reached Bill and Bonnie, the girls came out, each took one of Yvette's hands, and they led her toward the bus to see some newborn rabbits they were sure she would enjoy as much as they did.

Of course, Yvette easily charmed Bonnie and Bill, but for their girls, she was a fairy tale princess come-to-life because of her beauty, her poise, her adventures, and most especially, her purse. That was a Tibetan woven pouch with multicolored, finely-detailed flame designs that she wore hanging from her

neck onto her chest. She bought it in a market in Dharamsala, India from Tibetan exiles. In it, she had carried the Holy Trinity of the Hippie Trail: passport, money, and tickets. Now it served as an exotic purse that enchanted Bonnie's daughters and symbolized Yvette for them.

I said hi to Bill and Bonnie and then walked over to the the long food tables and placed on one an unopened gallon jug of cheap red wine and a brown paper bag partly filled with tomatoes, carrots, and snow peas from our garden. As I tore the bag and rolled it open, I couldn't help comparing the quality of ours with similar contributions and felt good that ours were up with the best.

As I walked back to Bill and Bonnie, another couple that I didn't recognize joined them. We were introduced, and while we chatted, Yvette appeared, coming around from the far side of the bus. The sunlight was on her face, the breeze in her hair, and she was chuckling to herself about something that happened with the girls. She always handled their veneration with grace and humor.

She was dressed in her usual utilitarian hip. Today it was khakis, and for the occasion, an imported, embroidered peasant blouse, and of course, the purse around the neck. She never wore make-up or jewelry. I never saw her in a dress or wearing a bra. Utterly without vanity, she placed little value on her appearance. When she focused on the effects of her beauty, more often than not, it amused her.

When she reached us, Bill introduced her as my "ol' lady." I looked for her reaction. She took it in stride and was just smiling and nodding to the couple. My ol' lady. I hefted the phrase. Yes, she was my ol' lady, and that was what I had been working for all this time. But, I was still cautious. Though it was fading, I could still find that knot of dread that I felt the day Gordon and Maddie left Yvette on the land. I had avoided discussing "our relationship" or our feelings for one another, and she didn't bring it up. So, we never openly discussed it.

Two chicks and a guy suddenly came out of the woods, laughing, dripping wet, and naked, except for sandals. They fast-walked passed us, tits and dick waggling, and across the

clearing toward the chilling creek. The guy of the other couple with Bill and Bonnie started a joint around and his ol' lady mentioned a makeshift sauna in the woods, a tent made of white plastic tarp, and she pointed to where the nudists came from.

Over a clearing near the fire ring, hanging by rope from the high branches of surrounding pines, was a five-foot-in-diameter peace symbol made of tied green branches from willows near the river. Standing under the peace symbol, a freak with straight dark hair and beard and granny glasses announced that the ceremony was about to begin. The musicians stopped playing and the teenage chicks stopped dancing. The freak under the peace symbol said he was an ordained minister of the Universal Life Church. Founded by Kirby J. Hensley in 1969 and having as its sole doctrine belief in "that which is right," The Universal Life Church was somewhere between a prank and conceptual art. Inhabiting that space where a tradition of absolute religious freedom intersected civil law, its marriages were actually legal. Though that may not have mattered so much in this case.

The bride, a cute skinny frizzy blond with a mega-watt grin, led by the hand her dazed groom to the willow-branch-peace-symbol. He had a silly bearded grin beneath plastic frame glasses. The bride had also gone full gypsy, wearing a gauzy white blouse with sleeves that billowed at the elbows and a print skirt to her ankles. Bill said they had lived together for years and had two kids, the proprietors of the newborn rabbits.

The minister, wearing a tattered old sport coat to symbolize his office, raised the paper on which the bride and groom had written their vows. Just before he spoke, the bride turned to the whole assembly and told us, giggling, that she and her groom were on peyote. Cheers and applause.

*

As the summer wore on, there were fewer and fewer visitors on the land. Gordon and Maddie came a couple times

and that was special, but the novelty wore off for most of our friends in the City. We did have one recurring visitor throughout the summer though.

His name was Ed, but either Yvette or I could always get a chuckle out of the other by calling him "Mr. Ed," as in "the Talking Horse" from TV. Ed was short, muscular, and barrel-chested with an especially elongated jaw that made him look like a cartoon horse. Actually, we may have associated him more with coyotes than horses, because we saw him most often when he came by on a horse hunting coyotes. Usually, we'd hear the clopping hooves first, and then maybe the snuffle of the horse's nostrils, and that announced Ed. Then I had to check that Yvette was not bare-breasted or even naked. Fortunately, it took the horse awhile to make it up the steep driveway.

One day, in early September, Ed showed up and Yvette was already fully dressed. She was reading something in the shade on the mattress. I had just secured the filter box on the end of the main pvc pipe in the stream and was coming into the parking area, headed back to the camp, when I heard the hooves. Yvette heard them too and put down the book and walked up to the parking area. We were both standing there when Ed arrived on his swayback old chestnut.

"Hi Ed," I said.

"Hi Ed," she said.

"Hi," he said, halting the horse between us.

"Shoot any?" I asked, nodding at the hunting rifle with a scope he held erect, butt on the saddle.

"Naw..."

"We haven't heard any in a while ..." I turned to Yvette asking, "maybe seven, eight nights?"

She nodded vaguely.

"I found some fresh skat over there," he said, twisting around in the saddle, making the leather creak, pointing at a treed slope in the direction of his ranch, east on the logging road, away from the town. "Sons o' bitches..." he said as he turned around and looked across the meadow, scanning the edge of the woods, "Ate a calf as it came outta the mother... coupla nights ago..."

She and I looked at each other.

"That's... horrible," I said.

"Yeah..." she said.

Two crows flew over the clearing, caws like rusty hinges.

His cattle ranged freely in these mountains throughout the summer. We occasionally ran into them while hiking. He told us once that, "in the old days," ranchers set fire to a whole mountainside in November and walked away, trusting the winter to squelch the fire. The following spring there was grazeable grass in the burn area. He was resentful the Forest Service wouldn't let him do the same now.

"Anyway..." he said, "I got some more manure piled up for ya."

"Oh... great... thanks Ed," I said.

"I raised the blade a couple inches off the ground this time... So there won't be as many stones."

"Oh, thanks Ed... You didn't have to do that... but it is better with fewer stones."

"Yeah, I figgered..."

He had a small bulldozer at the ranch for all the horse and steer manure, and though what we took in large plastic bags in the milk truck didn't diminish the manure much, Ed seemed to enjoy helping us. He seemed to have an appreciation for what we were trying to do out here.

"Want some water?" Yvette asked.

Ed too was smitten with her, and he always became slightly flustered whenever she spoke to him.

"Naw, I'm ok... Got a canteen," he said and nodded at it, hanging from the saddle horn down one side of the horse, on the other side hung binoculars.

"How 'bout the horse?" she asked, raising a hand to shade her eyes as she looked up at him. "I can put some in the big pot."

"He drank down there where the crick crosses the road."

"Are your wife and kids at the ranch?" she asked.

"No, they're in town, but they'll be out here at the end of the week."

"Ok, we'll come out then to get manure," she said, looking at me for confirmation, "and we can finally meet 'em."

"Sounds like a plan... Hey, remember that song we couldn't remember the title of?" he asked me, "Dun-dun-duuunn-dun-dun-dun? That's 'Look at You, Look at Me' by Dave Mason."

"Oh, yeah... yeah..."

"It's from *Alone Together.*"

"That was his first solo album... Wasn't it?... That was a great album... Hey, I'm surprised you like Dave Mason. Did you like *Traffic?*"

"Yeah, they made some good stuff."

Ed spent part of the winter snowed-in on his ranch linked to the wife and kids in Covelo by a ham radio run off truck batteries. When I asked him how he passed the time, he said by playing guitar and writing songs. He was an aspiring country western songwriter who liked many of the new hippie bands. Our shared love of the new rock n' roll helped bridge the hippie-redneck divide.

"Hey, when we come out to the ranch, can we hear some of your songs?" I asked.

"Yes..." Yvette chimed in. "We'd like to hear some."

"Yeah, yeah, sure... I'd like that."

He turned the horse's head south, tapped its haunches with his heels and it lurched forward downhill into the meadow.

"Ok... We'll see ya then," I said.

"Bye," Yvette said.

"Bye," he replied.

"Good luck with the coyotes," I said.

"Yeah, thanks... the bastards..."

Yvette went back to the mattress and the book but I stood there watching Ed cross the meadow. As he went over the dry creek bed and started up the other side, I became anxious. I knew there was a spot at the top of the rise where he would be able to see, poking out of the manzanita thicket, the tops of the marijuana plants, now dark green, tall, and shaggy (thanks in part to Chadwick's unwitting help.) Ed was headed due south so he would have to look almost ninety degrees to his left, east, to

see the grass. Like most of the rednecks, he must have at least suspected something, and a quick glance would be enough to confirm suspicions. But when he got to that spot, his gaze went to that same edge of the woods he scanned when he first arrived and which he was now closing-in on. Still, I didn't relax until the horse's swaying rump disappeared along a deer trail and behind trees.

I didn't mention this to Yvette. There was no point in alarming her. As I approached her, I noticed for the first time *what* she was reading and was amazed. My scant library, sharing an orange-crate shelf with pots and plates, was made up of the book about Chadwick's techniques, the *Whole Earth Catalogue*, Gary Snyder's *Earth House Hold* and *The Back Country*, and a couple books of very difficult poetry by W.S. Merwin. She was reading Merwin. I had never said a word to her about him. It never occurred to me. I normally wouldn't have interrupted her now but I had to know.

"Do you like him?"

"Yeah... a lot."

"Do you understand him?"

She thought for a moment, then said, "Not everything, but... what I do understand is... far out..."

She went back to reading, with my own enthusiasm.

*

We weren't honest with Ed about the coyotes. He assumed we shared his hatred, but actually, we loved them, inspite of their fondness for newborn calves. Sometimes they sounded at night as they did in the western movies: yip-yip-yip-yip-ow-ooooooo. But more often, they created a sustained, high-pitched, piercing, harmonic note, a choral wail. It was a special night when we heard them, and just a few nights after Ed told us about the devoured calf, we heard them, and it was the most special night of the summer.

We fucked and caressed and kissed good night, then she rolled over and seemed to be sleeping. It was one of the

hottest nights of the summer and we just lay naked on top of our sleeping bags. I was drifting in my thoughts and staring at the stars. Shooting stars, those brief white scratches on the black, were common enough to barely be noticed. But a satellite, a star steadily creeping in a straight line across the sky, was entertainment. I had been following one for awhile, when a bright light in the treetops caught my eye. It was the moon rising over the eastern ridge. I watched it come out of the trees into the open sky, a classic harvest moon, pale ochre, perfectly round, and enormous. I sat up and looked toward the pond and then swiveled around, stepped into my sandals, stood, and tiptoed toward the top of the sloping meadow.

When I got up there and turned around, I was surprised to see Yvette standing beside the mattress, looking up at me. I motioned with an arm for her to come up, and she put on sandals and started toward me. When she reached me, I pointed down at the pond and she turned around and looked. The moon was mirrored in it and the water was so still that even the stars were reflected. We stood for a while, staring into the glare of the dual moons and listening to the frogs and crickets. Then, on cue, the coyotes started. I enclosed her in my arms from behind and locked my hands on her waist and she rested her hands on mine.

5

A couple days later, on a withering afternoon, Yvette stood with her back to me, looking at the ground, staring far into herself, sounding her emotional depths.

Then, as she turned around to face me, she said, as if answering a question, "I don't love you."

But I hadn't asked her that. We weren't even talking. All day the heat had been crushing, and it still was, and we had just gotten back from a cooling swim in the river and were now late watering. I could see the vegetables were limp and drooping, and I had learned over the summer, the grass would be in even worse condition. We had just gotten out of the milk truck and I was on my way to the stream to divert water to the vegetable garden,

when she suddenly spoke. She was speaking to herself as much as to me, and that she did not love me was a revelation to her as much as to me. I could see she was deeply disappointed.

I stood frozen, while the realization sank through me. Then suddenly sobs gushed out of me, and I shuddered and gasped and tried to stop crying, to get ahold of myself, but couldn't. Almost instantly, a foot long streamer of mucus was dangling from my nose. Finally, I was able to stop crying. I wiped the streamer onto my right forearm and looked at her. She was staring at me, stunned. Before I quite realized it, I was headed down the steep driveway in long bounding strides. At the logging road, I turned left, uphill, and started pumping out more strides.

After a while, I stopped and realized: she has to leave. I knew that was too harsh and would look like petty vengeance, but that breakdown shocked me as much as her, and it may have jarred me open to doing things to protect myself that I might not have done otherwise.

"I can't have you here," I told her. "It'll destroy me."

Again, she was stunned. This hadn't occurred to her, even as a possibility. She just blurted out the truth as she was discovering it (which gave authority to what she said). How typically guileless and uncalculating... She might not love me but she loved the land. I could see how stricken she was and felt an impulse to reach out and comfort her. It might have been as difficult for her to give up the land as for me to give up the idea of her loving me.

I should have watered before we left, but didn't. I wanted the pain to stop now, and I concocted a desperate superstition that when she left the land, she would take the pain with her, and I could go back to that life before her. Neither of us spoke for the hour and fifteen minute drive to the highway. What was there to say? We arrived at the junction, and I stopped the milk truck in a gravelly pullover forty feet from Highway 101, which cut through dense pine forest and was now deep in afternoon shade.

"I'd take you all the way down to the Bay Area," I said turning around to face her sitting behind me. "But I have to get back to water... It'll be late as it is... and in this heat..."

She nodded, staring out the windshield at the whooshing traffic. Was there anything that either of us could say that would prevent her from having to leave? No.

"And it's harvest season... and there are thieves..." I continued.

"Yes, I know..."

She slid the door back, got out, then lifted out her backpack and placed it on the ground, then slid the door closed.

"Here..." I said as I dug it from a jeans pocket. "I've got some money..." I held it out through the door window. "Hitch to Willits and stay in a motel and take the next bus south."

"No."

"Please..."

"I hitchhiked around the world, remember?!" she shouted, voice crackling with anger and hurt.

Then she lifted the very backpack she had taken around the world, put her arms through the straps, settled it onto her back and then turned around and walked to the edge of the highway.

"I'll give you some money..." I called, "after the harvest... for your labor..."

She ignored me, looking back and forth for a break in the traffic that would let her cross to the southbound side.

I turned the milk truck around and headed east back to the land.

"O.k. now... to somehow get back to the peace before she came...I think I can get back to that peace... Yes... There might be a few bad days... weeks maybe... but I think I can do that.... Yes, I feel like I can do that..."

I didn't stop in Covelo but shot through it to get back to the plants. Still on the valley floor, I was closing in on the ascent of the logging road, when I remembered a phone conversation with Bree, about seven months before, the night before she was to get married.

*

"Hello."

"Hi..." Bree slurred.

"Oh, hi... What's goin' on?"

"I… uh… uh… Why don't we fuck?"

Pause…

"Is Chip there?" I asked.

"No…"

"You've been drinking."

"Yeah, so what?"

"You're drinking alone? I never knew you to do that."

"This is the first time…"

Pause…

"Aren't you getting married tomorrow?"

"Yeah… but I don't want to marry him… I want to marry you…"

Long pause…

"I have strong feelings for you too… I even love you… but like… my best friend…"

I waited for her to speak, but she didn't, so I had to…

"You're such an important friend… I can't risk losing you… Our friendship is too valuable to risk ruining it… by… trying to turn it into a… a … trying to make you my ol' lady."

Pause…

I continued, "Suppose we had a bitter break up?… We'd risk losing this friendship that we both need…"

Long pause…

"Look how many guys you've gone through in the time we've been friends…"

Pause…

"Is this about Chip's… breakdown?" I asked.

"That's part of it… and other things…"

Pause…

Then she mumbled something I couldn't understand ending with: "…your chick."

Pause…

"I don't know why I am telling you this now," she said. "I could have told you anytime…"

"Because you're getting married tomorrow?"

"Oh, yeah…"

Pause…

"This is ridiculous," she said and hung up.

I put the phone receiver in the cradle, but left my hand on it, as I realized that she was waiting for me to call her back and tell her I felt the same way. But I didn't feel the same way, so I couldn't call her back, and I lifted my hand from the receiver. I remembered how patiently she listened to me ramble on about Yvette.

This was also a call for help. One of my best friends was in great pain and I didn't respond. Maybe I was too shocked, or maybe too selfish. Or maybe I was the one of all her friends who couldn't respond. I thought about Bree often when I was living alone on the land, but forgot her after Yvette arrived.

I hadn't been in touch with Bree or Chip for months, when I heard through mutual friends that they didn't get married.

Bree and Chip, Yvette and I were all part of the food chain of love.

*

Back on the land, I park the truck and get out, and I'm about to walk to the stream to divert water, but stop…

Yvette did nothing more than be honest…

What have I done?

I am suddenly overwhelmed with guilt and remorse.

I've got to go to her and apologize… Maybe I can still get her on the highway…

I turn around toward the truck but don't move. I notice the caged tomato plants, some nearly as tall and bushy as the marijuana plants. The leaves of all the vegetables are hanging straight down, pointing toward the ground. Though I'm already dangerously late, immediate watering should bring them back.

I've got to water…

I turn around toward the creek but stop.

If I water now, it'll be dark by the time I get back to the highway… It'll be a lot harder to see her… I've got to catch her on the highway… If I let her get down there… there's no telling where she'll go… maybe his place… I at least have to try to find her on

the highway... I might have to go to her parents' house... It'll be late... Can't help that... I'll water when I get back...

I turn around toward the truck and stop.

But this will be ten straight hours of driving there and back... Couldn't get back before dawn... And with another hot night... They'll be dead... the grass and the vegetables...

I turn around toward the creek but stop.

I misjudged... This is an opportunity, not a disaster... She doesn't love me, so I know now what I'm up against... I can work with this... Lily didn't love me either... And I turned her around... together four years... If I can get Yvette back up here, I'll have her here to myself. I can really focus on her... She was that close... Look how long it took her to decide. That's a good sign... And we've never been together this long, known each other this well... I can do this... If I can get her to come back... She may not want to... She might run back to What's-his-name... She could even be on her way there now...

But I have to water first... real fast...

I take a couple steps toward the creek and stop.

Then I turn around and run to the milk truck, get behind the wheel, start it up, back it around, and head down the driveway.

Be-in

I realized if I was conscious and mobile, I had to be there. But I barely qualified in either category as late as 2PM, an hour after the starting time. I had the flu or a very bad cold and had told friends I wasn't going, but as I laid on my mattress on the floor of my Page Street studio reading *One Flew Over the Cuckoo's Nest*, the importance of the day, the full weight of the occasion suddenly hit me, and I realized I was going, despite having a sandpapered throat and lead clothes.

I trudged the three or four blocks to the bus stop and caught the 5 Fulton. After I sat down, I was struck by the lack of a crowd and felt a panic surge. But, though it had been going more than an hour, it was certain to last well into the afternoon. Still, the bus crept.

I wore a wool scarf around my throat, even though it was a warm clear sunny Saturday in January, 1967. There used to be a brief preview of spring that regularly occurred in San Francisco around the last two weeks of January, and it was planned for that interval. Astrologers and mediums also were consulted. There was a lot of talk about it beforehand and lots of declamations of purpose from the organizers and the underground newspapers. Though there were numerous posters by different artists all over the Haight, there seemed almost no publicity outside the Haight other than the grapevine. Its full title was *The Human Be-in, a*

Gathering of the Tribes. It was the founding event of the Counter Culture.

Allen Ginsburg and Timothy Leary and, most importantly, Gary Snyder, whose classic poetry book *Riprap* I had nearly memorized, were all going to be there. Plus, there would be the best of the new local rock bands: the Grateful Dead, the Jefferson Airplane, Quicksilver Messenger Service, Big Brother and the Holding Company. But these were people you could see at the Fillmore or Avalon Ballrooms or an anti-war demonstration. I was going to the Human Be-in for the crowd. How many of us were there? What would we look like all together in one place at one time?

Finally, the bus reached 30th Avenue and I got off and entered the north side of the park along a short extension of the avenue. A distant rock band blended with ocean wind in the trees as I walked amid scattered clusters of hippies. In a few minutes, I was going up the last slope, between massive eucalyptus and fir trunks. The music got louder, I walked faster, and then I reached the crest and there it was. Or rather, there we were.

The Golden Gate Park Polo Fields is a huge grassy oblong basin ringed by trees. It's about the size of three or four adjacent football fields and lies west-southwest. Today, also ringing it, were refurbished old school buses and VW buses with the loud swirling colors of psychedelic paint jobs. Like bison on a prairie, a vast teeming herd of hippies, us, covered the northeast half of the field. Later estimates ranged around twenty thousand. More late arrivals flowed around me as I stood taking it in.

There were costumes familiar from Haight Street: Mad Hatter top hats, magicians' robes, fringed buckskin, gypsy blouses and skirts and jangling anklets... Here and there on poles above the crowd floated peace symbols, multi-colored god's eyes, undulant banners with marijuana leaves or paisley patterns or tie-dye rainbows, and there were balloons, some saying "Dizzy Gillespie for President."

I descended the slope into the basin, skirting the edge of the crowd, weaving among dancers and players of finger cymbals, tambourines, kazoos, harmonicas, flutes, mandolins, Arabian drums, bongos and congas, a tabla and a sitar... I dodged and

greeted distributors of oranges and flowers and smoking incense sticks and bay leaves and soap bubbles... Of course, there were photographers everywhere shooting other photographers and the crowd.

I waved and nodded to friends and acquaintances but I didn't necessarily want to join anyone because I expected to leave any minute. Just as I was noting how painful it was to swallow, I was clobbered with a wave of deep fatigue. I could have lain down on the grass and immediately slept.

The rock band I heard when entering the park was the Grateful Dead, and they were still playing and more and more freaks were getting up and dancing where they stood or rushing to the edge of the crowd... I was drifting around the outer edge of the crowd without having thought about where I was going... At about half way around, at the farthest point from the stage, I stopped to groove on a couple of chicks dancing in that gawky white-people style that floats with undulant arms above the beat, familiar from the rock ballrooms and concerts in the park. This was like a concert in the Panhandle, only fifty times bigger.

Suddenly, as I was watching the stage, people sitting on the ground in front of me were pointing up at the sky behind me. I turned around and looked up at a guy descending in a parachute. I didn't see or hear a plane anywhere. More people noticed, some started cheering, then some started running to the other end of the oblong field where the parachutist was landing. I noticed for the first time two teams were playing a ball game of some sort at that end.

The Dead finished their song and I realized I had to leave immediately. I completed my semi-circumnavigation of the crowd by heading toward the closer south side of the park where I could catch a bus on Lincoln Avenue. Instead, I couldn't wait and splurged on a cab.

Newspapers in London and Paris carried long stories with photos about the Be-in. It inspired imitations in New York, London, Los Angeles, Denver and other cities. From then until and through the coming summer there were film crews from Germany, France, and England in the Haight and around the City. Then in May, "San Francisco (Be Sure to Wear Some Flowers in Your Hair)" shot to

the top of the record charts. The Mamas and the Papas wrote it, one of the hottest pop music groups. Kids adopted it as an anthem even in Communist Central Europe, and it was widely played during Czechoslovakia's "Prague Spring" uprising against the Soviets. In the States, the song served as an ad jingle for the coming Summer of Love, the anticipated mass migration of kids to the Haight.

As I was climbing the slope out of the basin, I noticed a couple of nuns at the outermost edge of the crowd, which reminded me of the last time before the Be-in that I saw Beat poet Michael McClure, who I had just seen up there on the stage with the musicians and other Beat Poets. I saw him the previous fall at a rock concert in the Panhandle where he was sitting on the grass between a Hell's Angel and a nun.

Night of
the Synchronized Paranoias

I was already agitated when the chicks arrived. They were both in their late teens. My age. My roommate Tim was in his mid twenties. I had been alone for hours, sealed inside myself, reading and thinking, studying my psychological condition. When they came in, I was lying on the floor, a speaker at each ear, listening to *Absolutely Free*, Frank Zappa's latest scolding of the hippies. I quickly stood.

"Let me introduce Jan," Tim said gesturing toward the prettier with a hint of his Southern courtliness. She had a thin nose and dark blond hair that was parted in the middle and hung straight down to her shoulders. We exchanged nods and hi's and I shot her in her big blue eyes with the Stare.

"And Jan," Tim said with a giggle gesturing toward the other.

"What...Oh, you're both named Jan?" I ask the second.

Ripe zits and bleached hair with dark roots. She nodded, and I saw in her even darker blue eyes that she liked me as much as I liked her friend.

"May I get you some Mu tea?" Tim asked them.

"Yeah."

"Sure."

I didn't have to ask where he met them. It was a Friday during the Summer of Love and I knew he had been sitting all day

on his sawhorse over a forgotten water department hole beside a stop sign selling underground papers to bumper-to-bumper tourists while trolling for chicks. Sometimes he came home with two.

Tim left for the kitchen with the tea orders and I felt a panic rush, but immediately got distracted by the chicks, who were looking over the pad while I was looking over them. They belonged to Tim so he got first choice, which he had clearly signaled was the prettier, Blond-Jan. It was she who saw the picture window first and walked to it, Roots-Jan following.

"That's Berkeley on the left, with the tower," I said behind them of the view over the rooftops of the Fillmore District. The phosphorescent pink of sunset had left the Berkeley Hills and the scattered first house lights of evening were appearing. I remembered Zappa and went over and turned down the stereo and remained standing there.

The chicks stared in silence at the view and Roots-Jan murmured, "That's groovy."

"Yeah," said the other.

Roots-Jan stepped over and stood in profile against the window. I couldn't avoid noticing through her translucent paisley blouse her only assets competitive with her near-beautiful but flat-chested friend. She let my stare linger. She too realized we were to be paired.

Her breasts were swollen and pendulous and just as I got to the nipples she turned her back to the window and scanned the room again. I liked what I saw, including her mischievous chipped-tooth grin. Then she really got my attention by noticing the books on the board-and-cinder-block shelves and then walking over to read the titles.

She picked up Alan Watt's *Nature, Man and Woman* and said to me," I loved this book."

"You're into Watts?" I asked with too much doubt showing.

"Yeah. Djyou read *The Joyous Cosmology*?"

" Yeah."

"I loved that one too... Remember 'the eenie weenie' "?

"Oh yeah," I chuckled remembering it. "Yeah ... the 'eenie weenie.' The ultimate node of being. That was too much."

A chick who could talk philosophy! And then, like a puppie lolloping off to play, I felt a leash-yank of panic: I'll have to make conversation. I was certain that I couldn't function socially after I had spent the better part of an hour on the floor stoned drifting in albums. As tempting and delicious as Roots-Jan was becoming, it would have to be another day, another place, but not here, not now.

Then she noticed the records stacked on edge on the floor by a wall and went to them and bent over them. Her blouse hung open and she smiled at my blatant stare and stayed bent over, flipping through albums.

"Oh, Donovan!" she said and stood up with the album.

I pressed the reject button on Zappa and said, "Why don't you pick the music," and then headed down the hall to the kitchen.

"Wanna listen to Donovan?" I heard Roots-Jan ask.

"Yeah... Oh, ya know who he always reminded me of?"

I didn't hear anymore except, as I entered the kitchen, conspiratorial giggles. Tim was arranging cups and tea bags on a tray.

"Where're they from?" I asked with forced casualness.

"Montana," he said then headed out of the kitchen, adding over his shoulder, "At least, that's what they claim."

That took a few moments to register. I heard him ask, against Donovan's tepid crooning, if they wanted honey in their tea. They did. Soon he reentered the kitchen. As he took the kettle from the stove and poured water into cups, I noted the absence of his usual whinnying giddiness at the prospect of sex.

"Listen," he said, ending an extended preoccupied silence, "don't let them know how much dope we have, o.k.?"

"Why?"

"I just don't think it would be a good idea to advertise it around. I mean, we don't know them. We don't know who they really are."

"OK."

He carried a tray arrayed with tea things to the living room.

You could share your home with them, call them friend, perhaps even love them, until one day they disappeared, you were busted, and the next and last time you saw them was when they testified against you at your trial. In San Francisco in the 60s, there was no cop more insidious than the undercover narc.

My roommate Tim and I had a thriving business selling mostly grass and acid and this ever-present narc-threat fueled occasional episodes in Tim of crippling paranoia. He had been in the South during Freedom Summer of 1964 when civil rights workers Schwerner, Chaney, and Goodman were tortured and murdered by the Klan. Eventually Tim himself was driven out of Louisiana by Klan threats.

When the searing fear from that police state combined with too much acid and too many friends recently busted, he went over the cliff. As a consequence, he would eventually become a connoisseur of the major mental hospitals on the east and west coasts.

Throughout that summer of '67, the Summer of Love, Tim and I both suffered from random ambushes of drug psychosis. I had taken a massive overdose of methedrine in the middle of the summer, and like any philosophy major in good standing, I could still expound passionately for hours about whether or not existence preceded essence, but I could also suddenly and without warning become scared speechless of chitchat, and then, if I couldn't immediately escape, I became almost physically paralyzed with blocked panic.

Then any crowd not large enough to hide in was a potential threat, and if I couldn't escape, I withdrew, hid behind my face, all the while staring vacantly at the floor, paralyzed, mute, fleeing like a turtle on its back. Anything said around me seemed like coded comments on my odd vibes. This dislocation was all too reminiscent of my predicament growing up as the resident space-alien in a redneck Sierra mill town.

Though I had no fear of cops whatsoever (they were just another stooge authority figure) on occasion even I could get spooked. As I was the night Tim and I discussed a rumor we each had heard from separate sources about the screams of hippies being beaten in isolated basement cells of the county jail.

But it was insane to suspect those chicks! They might not even know the meaning of the word "narc." Then it hit me: he was having an attack of his paranoia while I was having an attack of mine. I relaxed slightly. He might provide cover.

I reentered the living room shortly after Tim. Roots-Jan was sitting on the floor against the couch. I sat beside her, as expected. Tim and Blond-Jan sat on the floor facing us.

Conspicuous silence.

Etiquette required Tim and I produce grass, but I was afraid of how he would react.

Roots-Jan saved me when she took a joint from her purse, held it up, and asked, "Wanna smoke some grass?"

"Sure," I said and looked for Tim's reaction.

He shot her a quick glance full of hurt, fear, panic, and anguished disbelief. I reached under the edge of the couch for a mayonnaise-jar-lid ashtray, took the book of matches out of it, and handed them to Roots-Jan. Neither she nor Blond-Jan seemed to have noticed anything in Tim. He grew more sullen but I relaxed. Now I could mention dope. A well-worn topic with only literal meanings and no dangerous ambiguities.

"What're lids going for in Montana?" I asked Roots-Jan as she handed me the joint.

Tim scowled at me.

"Oh," she said looking at Blond-Jan. "Fifteen?"

"Yeah. . . fifteen," Blond-Jan said then added, "I've even seen 'em for twenty-five."

"Are they hard to find?" I asked, and so on, and so on . . . I felt relative safety now.

Somehow a half hour passed, with me and occasionally Tim plugging a hole with another routine question. The chicks were tense. Eager but uncertain. This may have been their first sexual experience in Haight Ashbury or anywhere.

I was still hoping to find a graceful escape, but I was also getting increasingly more turned-on to Roots-Jan. And she knew it. I handed her a joint that Tim and I had contributed, and instead of returning my hand to my lap, I laid an arm along the edge of the couch. Behind her neck, but not touching it. I knew the timetable called for that.

On the stereo, we had gone through Donovan and were now well into Judy Collins. Then, after handing-off the joint, Roots-Jan laid her head back onto my arm and blew smoke at the ceiling. I knew now that, after a suitable pause and the tribute of a deep fascinated stare, I could get away with a kiss. But, inspite of the hard-on stretching my jeans, I couldn't make my move. Her head seemed to have me pinned, held from flight. So, instead of kissing her, I dodged the moment with another meanIngless question.

"How long have you been in town?"

" 'Bout a week," she said then turned those enormous blue eyes on me. Highdivers' pools. I gulped.

"I thought you said two days," Tim blurted.

I realized the grass was affecting him. They still didn't seem to notice his suspicion. It was too preposterous.

"Uh, lessee," Roots-Jan said looking at Blond-Jan, "how long have we been here?"

"Five days," Blond-Jan replied, her arms around her knees. Tim put his hand to his forehead and sighed.

Silence.

"Uh, did you go to the concert in the Panhandle yesterday?" I asked in a knick of time, then continued, "Was it Country Joe and the Fish?"

"I don't know," Roots-Jan said. "I don't know who that is."

Tim moaned, got up, and left the room.

"Uh, why don't you change the records?" I asked as I stood. "D'ya want some more tea?"

Each looked up at me startled and confused and slowly shaking her head. I followed Tim into the kitchen.

"We've gotta get all the dope out of the house," he urgently whispered.

"What?"

"Didn't you hear her?!" he shouted in a whisper. "She said she never heard of Country Joe and the Fish! Everybody's heard of Country Joe and the Fish…"

His eyes were mostly pupil.

"Tim," I said delicately, "they're just chicks. They're not narcs."

He searched my eyes.

"Man, this is all in your head," I said. "I'm positive, I am absolutely positive, those chicks are not narcs. You have to trust me on this. They're just chicks. Really, really groovy chicks. And definitely not narcs."

No, I thought, they're something much more dangerous than narcs: human beings. Then I caught myself on the brink of asking him to go back into the livingroom, my desire for Roots-Jan momentarily causing me to forget my first priority: escape. Tim had presented me with the opportunity.

"Look, uh, we've blown it with them," I said. "Why don't I tell 'em... you're not feeling well and ask 'em to leave?"

He looked at me and looked away and drifted off.

"O.k.?" I asked.

He looked back at me and nodded.

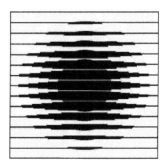

The Neocon

The first time I saw him he was reciting poems while a very attractive young woman in translucent turquoise tights danced beside him. She was a curly brunette with freckles and nubbin breasts and of course my eyes, like those of the dozen-or-so men around me, went to the darkness of her nipples and bush. This was going on just beyond the fringes of the crowd at a free rock concert in the Panhandle of Golden Gate Park. It was a windy overcast afternoon in the fall of 1966. I was leaving the concert when I was stopped by the spectacle.

The chick wasn't very good, improvising her gawky writhing to the arrhythmic recitation. The reciter was tall, hefty, and jowly with dark straight hair to just above his hunched shoulders. He had a scarf wrapped around his neck.

When I had my fill of her body, I moved on, deeply troubled. He was an unintentional parody of a bohemian poet and I was a bohemian poet. To make matters even worse, I had had a similar idea myself.

Furthermore, the poems were from Pablo Neruda and I loved them and saw the reciter as defiling them. It was as if he were reading in a topless club and expecting a serious attentive hearing. And he was completely oblivious to this.

I felt a deep, intense, instinctual revulsion toward him.

*

Not long after that, I saw a similar though much longer scarf on Richard Burton in a role parodying a poet in the movie version of Terry Southern's *Candy*. The living caricature I first saw that day in the Panhandle would be at poetry readings and other literary events that I also attended over the next decade or so. A face familiar enough to speak to but which I avoided. We shared mutual friends in the world of those avant-garde literary journals that were funded by grants and had more contributors than readers. The mutual friends didn't feel the same as I did about him so we avoided the subject.

Then one day, a decade or so after that first encounter, he raucously invaded a quiet coffeehouse in North Beach where I was reading a newspaper. As soon as I recognized him, I went back to my paper. He started talking excitedly to the guy behind the counter.

His babble blended with the traffic noise until he loudly said, or rather detonated, the name "Francis." The filmmaker Francis Ford Coppola, then at the height of his fame, had just opened offices in the neighborhood and was rumored to be starting a literary journal. The name-dropping didn't bother me as much as the hunger in his expression as he scanned the room for the effect on the half dozen patrons.

I went back to my paper again having discovered new depths of loathing. That would be the last time I saw him in the flesh. From that point on I would encounter him only through the media.

*

But about a decade after the North Beach coffeehouse, in the mid '80s, I had occasion to feel sorry for him.

The emergence of cable television had introduced the phenomenon of the community access channel on which anybody could broadcast anything. The cable company couldn't turn down anyone and there was almost no censorship. A lot of San Francisco looniness made it onto this obscure cable channel, but

also, occasionally, there were some worthwhile independent documentaries and arty shorts.

One night, I was channel surfing and stopped there for a crude documentary made with the new technology of consumer video. The subject was a young woman in her early twenties, aimless and flippant, not pretty but lithe and blond and with a winsome charm. She was trying to break into the pornographic movie business.

The camera operator seemed smitten with her, and while the wind was mussing her hair at the beach and I was looking for a reason not to change the channel, it cut to the dim interior of an apartment, and there he was, sitting at a typewriter, thicker with living and officially middle aged, like me.

The camera operator asked him what he thought of the young woman's ambition to be a porn actress. He grinned and shrugged and muttered something while she made a disparaging remark about him that I couldn't hear (the sound quality was awful), but it caused an outburst of laughter of several people off camera. He kept grinning, red-faced, wounded, and helpless.

From what little was said that I could understand, plus body language and facial expressions, I gathered she and he were in some sort of uneven romantic relationship in which he was hopelessly at the losing end. He was her hulking pet bear. I felt a sting of recognition.

Mine had been about seven years younger than me, his looked to be about ten-or-so years younger than him. I always thought of mine as a belated and pathetic attempt to make up for the high school steady I never had. Close friends referred to her as my "fetishistic attachment." I had spent much of the previous decade trying to make an impossible relationship happen and then recovering from it in Mendocino, Mexico, New York, and now back in San Francisco.

I knew everything he was feeling: the raking relentless pain, the galling humiliation. I felt like we shared a shameful secret. I felt sorry for him.

*

About a half decade later, I discovered that he was a "red diaper baby" and that one day in the late '80s, he had a revelation

of the intensity of a mystical experience that "communism is bad." It turned him into a pathological anti-communist, just in time for the collapse of communism. But, like many another good commie-hunter, this poor hapless doofus wouldn't let their mere non-existence get in the way of his crusade. And that would be his downfall.

I pieced together his biographical facts from several sources but mainly a girlfriend at the San Francisco Chronicle. I was then a free-lance journalist, just a bottom-feeder. She said he had gotten into rarefied far right circles and there met the owner of the paper who ordered his editor to hire him. But he was shunned by co-workers for the way he was hired, for his politics, and for his obnoxious personality. Eventually it became scandal enough to be the subject of an article in the paper itself, including a photograph of him standing in the middle distance, isolated, hunched, and scowling.

Over the following years you could tell in the infrequent appearances of his by-line that he was getting table scraps for assignments. They eventually got rid of him during layoffs.

*

"Vivan derechos humanos!" (Long live human rights) I shouted into the silent street.

It was May first, "Workers' Day," and the trade unions were having a parade which I watched from a crowded sidewalk in Quetzaltenango, the second largest city in Guatemala.

When, at the end of the parade, there appeared suddenly a small contingent of indigenas, Mayan Indians, an electric jolt ran through the placid onlookers. The Indians were anti-war and human rights protesters and, among banners calling for peace, a replica of a child's coffin was held aloft with a paper sign on the side demanding in crudely lettered Spanish "Punishment for violators of the law."

That was a euphemism for the death squads that had reigned in Guatemala for twenty-five years. The Mayans were the victims, and their courage in this street demonstration, and that coffin, caused "Long live human rights!" to burst from me in Spanish, startling me as much as those standing around me, who

were mostly expressionless Indians and appalled *ladinos* (hispanicized Guatemalans of any ethnicity). There followed a pall of disapproving silence except for the shuffling of the demonstrators.

A few of the Mayan women in their brilliant multi-colored *traje* stared at me a moment after my outburst, startled and uncertain, and then looked away as they continued on. One young woman smiled thanks. The protesters were mostly women and children because so many of the men had been killed or drafted.

The army was conspicuously absent, which meant that the government, by allowing this, was trying to show how *really* democratic it was. Nevertheless, scattered among the bystanders were plain-clothes agents of paramilitaries or the government or both (by night, they were all death squad members). They were here to intimidate and made sure they were noticed. And this time they were not just stifling reform or stealing land but trying to keep themselves from being prosecuted for their crimes.

This magnified the courage of the Indians. Just being relatives of previous victims put them at risk, but here they were almost arms-length from some of the very men for whom they were demanding punishment. Death squad activity and army atrocities had abated for the latest negotiations (which the protesters were trying to influence) between guerrillas and the government.

Ten-or-so yards to my right were three death squad members absurdly conspicuous with their thick expensive wristwatches and designer dark glasses. They were glaring at the Indians and intently studying faces, finding familiar ones and memorizing the unfamiliar.

After I blurted out my support, one of these three death squad members turned to stare at me, which drew my attention away from the Indians. He was the shortest by far and that made him seem even more menacing. He sneered from behind huge dark glasses and I sneered back. Then I raised my camera and clicked his picture.

He didn't know who I was other than a well-off gringo. I could be an observer for a human rights organization or even for the State Department (there was a Democratic administration at

the time). Eventually, he turned away. Whoever I was, I was more trouble than he wanted. What I wanted was to smash his face.

I was bluffing of course because I was nothing more than a student at a language school where I was spending a month in deep-immersion study of Spanish, plus the culture, politics, and agony of Guatemala.

Believing it was fighting communism while protecting corporate interests, the U.S. had backed the Guatemalan government in a ferocious, sadistic ethnic cleansing of the Mayans. Europe showed its disapproval by awarding the Nobel Peace Prize to Rigoberta Menchú, a little-known Mayan woman author and human rights activist. This made her the anti-communist voodoo doll of conservatives, as I discovered on a visit to the old colonial capital of Antigua.

While exploring its cobbled streets with their rococo architecture set against distant volcanoes, I came upon an apparently empty store, without an identifying sign, but which nevertheless had people entering and leaving, mostly gringo tourists. Of course, I investigated.

It was empty except for placards on the walls and on easels in rows and the only sound was the shuffling feet of the tourists. Few spoke because few had any idea what the point of the show was. The door was wide open and people came in because people came out.

The placards attempted a less than coherent rebuttal to the country's human rights reputation. Some Guatemalan conservatives, no organization was credited, had blown up and mounted photostats of articles from around the world sympathetic to their cause.

Among them was an article from *National Review*, the most prominent conservative magazine in the U.S. at the time. It was written by him. It was a half-decade-or-so since I first heard about him at the *Chronicle* and now here he was writing for William Buckley Jr. But he had chosen a radioactive topic. Even most right-wingers avoided, when they could, "human rights atrocities in Central America during the Cold War," which provided an opening for him.

His article was an attack on Rigoberta Menchú for some minor inconsistencies in her autobiography. The article propelled him into the national media and, for his own twisted exorcistic reasons, it was also a blow struck at the dead god. About a quarter million Mayans had been murdered in the worst human rights atrocity in this hemisphere in the twentieth century, and he was defending the perpetrators.

Before the nation, he had put himself morally on the level of a Holocaust denier.

*

About a decade later, I was checking out the week-end book shows on CSPAN2 and there he was being interviewed and flogging a book. He was gray and paunchy, like me, and naturally, he was a neocon and vigorously defending the recently begun Iraq War. At one point he referred to himself as a "minor celebrity."

And he had reinvented himself even further. The hippie-and-red-diaper-baby-turned-rabid-anti-communist was now an Islamicist.

Then he disclosed something that made him an unintentional self-parody yet again just as in the Panhandle decades before. In the process of becoming an Islamicist, he, a Jew, had converted to Islam.

I changed the channel.

There is Only One Misfortune

I had God on the telephone and I couldn't think of a thing to say.   My friend Dan, a mystic and a successful businessman in his mid-thirties, was the telephone, sitting across my kitchen table, silent, staring into himself, in a trance.

I couldn't think of a question for God because of my stupor from fatigue and hunger. I looked up at the clock and realized we had been talking for eight hours without a break. It wasn't over yet and it was already our longest session. Of all the trances I had seen Dan enter in the year and a half I had known him, this was the deepest by far, and I knew he was as exhausted as me and could shut down any moment and the opportunity lost. But instead of coming up with a question, my mind wandered.

I noticed how much my butt and back hurt from sitting so long. Also, my head ached from the hunger. We had talked right through mealtimes, not that there was anything appetizing in the place to eat. We were in my cottage in Petaluma, a farm town north of San Francisco. It was about eight on a warm spring evening and overhead a bare bulb diluted the darkness. After hours of listening to his voice, the quiet was palpable, just crickets and the distant highway.

There had been something different in him when he arrived around noon.

2

He usually quit work in San Francisco about one in the afternoon and, a couple times a week, dropped by to see me on his way home. That day, he arrived an hour early and was already charged, shirtsleeves rolled and tie loosened. Usually there was preliminary chitchat. He was, after all, a salesman. But today he got right to an important sighting on a sidewalk as he was leaving the City.

"You know that old lady, the skinny one?" he asked, shoes crunching the gravel between his car and my door.

"The one with the baseball cap?" I asked. "And she's always angry?"

"Yeah. I saw her today."

I shut the door behind him. My cottage was a hundred and twenty-year-old water tower that a farmer converted when a state college was built nearby. It was a stack of three square one-room floors, connected by ladders, and narrowing toward the top. Dan accepted a cold soda and sat at the kitchen table on the ground floor.

At that time, 1970, communities around the country expressed their opinion of San Francisco by sending to it their indigent mentally ill via a one-way bus ticket. The City had become the national outpatient clinic. On every block downtown it seemed there was someone crying out from their delusions. On every other bus, it seemed there was someone babbling to himself, oblivious to the nervous titters around him.

Among my favorites was the short, gentle-eyed, well-dressed black man I saw on buses who made calls to FBI Headquarters, intended to be overheard, on a regular pocket-sized transistor AM radio. And then there was the old guy who appeared every morning in a clean suit and tie on the same corner downtown where he stood under a traffic light and directed traffic with balletic grace.

But that old lady Dan spotted was a masterpiece, and he and I were connoisseurs. Scrawny, late middle-aged with cropped brown hair and soiled khaki pants and cap, she was

always in a hurry, furiously striding along, swinging straight arms, face contorted with rage. Once, as we were driving out of the City, he went around the block to get a second look at her.

"She was walking around, like she does," Dan said and then leapt up from my kitchen chair, taking center stage. "Tear it down! Tear it all down! Tear it down!" he crone-shrieked, goose-stepping across the kitchen, impotently waving away Mammon.

I laughed hard. This was early for impersonations. He really *was* revved up.

He saw in her a courageous, thwarted prophet. I agreed but also felt her fear. Once, without him, I saw her melting before puppies in a pet shop window, and when she noticed my stare, she instantly switched to a protective scowl and took off. I knew he genuinely envied her, and I understood the feeling. My operating assumption then was: if you're not seeing God everywhere all the time, there's something wrong. I agreed with the Muslims who said that there was only one misfortune: not to see God.

Instead of returning to the chair as he usually would, he stood with his hands on his hips, waiting for me to stop laughing.

"We should listen to those people," he declared. "They have the spirit-fire. We build walls between ourselves and the Source, but they stand in the Source and build a wall between it and the world - the superego."

"Best of all would be to have the source and the superego," I added.

"There are people who have both," he said. "I remember this old man, kind of a hobo, all bent and crooked. I saw him as I was coming out of a supermarket in Tokyo."

He became the old man, hobbling across the kitchen.

"All there was, was a quick glance between us. That's all."

He threw a furtive glance over a hunched back.

"But that was enough. I could see he had it."

He straightened back into himself.

"And he saw that I saw, and he hurried away. He told me more in that glance than he could've in years of conversation."

3

We were connoisseurs of crazies because of a shared personal experience: we had both been patients in a mental hospital. We felt an instant bond because of that initiation. To Dan though, being in a mental hospital was an embarrassment with no meaning other than as the aftermath of encountering God. While to me, the mental hospital was the most extreme reach of hip, a certification of profundity, though I was driven there by the paranoid hell of a methedrine overdose.

When we met, I had recently dropped out of San Francisco State a few credits short of a degree in philosophy, in the course of which I had read most of the scant literature available on mysticism. Living around San Francisco in those years, I frequently met people who had had incomprehensible, sometimes disabling, mystical experiences (with drugs playing no part at all). But I had never met anyone who had that experience and also had Dan's intellectual gifts.

Part of the charm and authenticity of his philosophy was its homemade quality. This came out in a mispronunciation of terms and names that academic training in philosophy would have corrected. Also, he was completely oblivious to the fads on campus. While reading them to his children, he discovered that fairy tales were a metaphorical code, unaware that the same discovery had arrived in lit departments decades before.

His conversation was peppered with allusions to the Giant, the Witch's Brew, the Magic Sword, and the Rose, among others. None of these were ever explained and I knew exactly what he meant.

"There is this world community, people chosen to protect the Rose," he said. By now he was pacing the kitchen like a cage. "They can be on any level of society, have any occupation. Like that old man outside the supermarket in Tokyo." He gestured toward the ocean. "They have a natural

aversion to the Giant and they don't necessarily know each other. They may not even know they've been chosen. They just hang loose, committed to noncommitment, awkward, a little off balance, not quite with it. At all costs though, they stay open. They're like the first apes to walk on the ground."

Now he became an ape looking down from a tree limb, one arm dangling below his knees, the other attached to an overhead limb.

"Hey, ya jerk," he said, addressing an ape on the ground, "Whaddaya doin' down there? Yer supposed to be in the trees. Whaddaya think yer doin' anyway?"

Then he became the ape on the ground. Assuming a slouch and a dopey expression, he looked up into the tree and replied:

"Huh? Uh . . . I dunno." He looked around on the ground, as if for an explanation, scratching the top of his head like Stan Laurel. "It just . . . seemed . . . like the thing to do . . ."

He became Dan again and returned to pacing while he explained: "In evolution, those are the freaks who initiate the new. They're mouthpieces of the Spirit."

He wasn't referring to hippies. He knew nothing about the counterculture nor was the least interested in it. Though we lived in the same town, indeed were natives of the same state, we lived in different worlds: he was straight and I was hip. Though this was never an obstacle, it was always present, from the day we first met.

4

It was not unheard-of for a businessman to pick up a hitchhiking hippie, so I was not too surprised when he motioned me to get in while stopped at a traffic light on Lombard Street in the City. As I got in, I noticed a briefcase and a suitcoat on the back seat. I stretched my legs to full long length and inhaled the luxury of the plush American car.

It was about two of a glistening summer Friday as we soared north over the Golden Gate Bridge. I was living then by jiggling the system for unemployment benefits and food

stamps, while getting pocket money from selling underground newspapers from a street corner in the City every Friday. The rest of the week I spent reading, writing poetry, drawing, writing an occasional article for an underground newspaper, walking, staring, recuperating.

He didn't say much at first, but I knew what was coming: "What's *really* goin' on with these hippies? What's this all about?" Just picking me up was a peace gesture. Satisfying their curiosity was the fare. They get to talk to the freak and I get a comfortable ride.

But instead of starting the interview, he kept throwing glances at the paperback in my hand, then grinning at me with a glint of idiot-glee, then shifting in his seat. I got a lot of my reading done between cars while hitchhiking, and for some months now, beside freeway entrances, I had been percolating with epiphanies brought on by my second or third reading of an apocalyptic, visionary book of philosophy, Norman O. Brown's *Love's Body*.

"How do you like that book?" he finally asked.

I took this as a clumsy attempt at conversation. Nevertheless, I was bursting with enthusiasm for the book and had no one else to talk to about it. It was too sophisticated for most of my friends, and I was so desperate that I was willing to vent my feelings even if to an uncomprehending straight.

"This is the most fascinating book I've ever read. But it's very difficult. Kind of like great poetry. Like Eliot. Ya know? T.S. Eliot?"

"I thought it was alright."

"You read this?!"

"Yeah." He smiled at my amazement. "He and I exchanged letters for a while."

"You . . .? With . . .? What's he like? What did you talk about, in your letters?"

"I wrote a book and I sent it to him."

"Did he like it?"

"Yeah. He seemed to."

"Did you ever meet him?"

"I was living in Japan at the time, so there wasn't a chance."

I was also currently smitten by Japanese culture, having found my way to it through Zen.

"Ah, land of 'the fine arts of moon-watching and cricket-listening'," I said, quoting Gary Snyder.

Instead of parting, when we reached Petaluma, we had coffee at a diner. We became a mixture of friends, master-and-disciple, and intellectual sparring partners. This was despite the hip-straight mismatch to which he was completely oblivious; as he proved conclusively the day I went to his office.

5

Frequently, when I was in the City, I met him for lunch or a ride back to Petaluma. Only once did I get beyond the lobby of the building where he worked, and that day in the elevator, surrounded by buffed chrome and edgy suits, I expected at every floor to be suddenly grabbed by security guards. The doors eventually opened onto his floor and a vast, fluorescent-lit room crawling with more suits. I couldn't have been more conspicuous if I had been naked. "Hey! There's a hippie over there!" lit up face behind face down the rows of desks to the back of the room.

Dan was thirty feet from the elevator when he saw me and nodded and then slowly disengaged from a conversation. He got into the elevator, the doors closed over gawks and smirks, and he and I immediately fell into conversation. That he had off-handedly invited me up there on the phone, when he thought he would be delayed, showed his indifference to our uniforms. But even more, he showed no awareness at all of the reaction of his colleagues surrounding us in the elevator or in the office. This probably confirmed some suspicions about him. He never worked past midday and for three years in a row had turned down the top sales prize of a Caribbean cruise.

6

But, if we were able to overcome sectarian divisions, nevertheless we argued from the start and vehemently. I believed there was a lot of truth - blended with delusion - in the experience that sent him to the hospital. I didn't believe in anything to do with the telepathy he mentioned, but something had definitely happened to give him an extraordinary metaphysics: original, highly sophisticated, and in some areas, just plain wrong.

Our ongoing tension peaked only three hours into that longest, most intense day, the day I had God on the phone. Afternoon sunlight was slanting through the kitchen window. He was slumped in the kitchen chair, too exhausted for impersonations. I was in the same condition. We were both snappish, and argument was crescendoing toward violence.

"No!" he spat and leapt from his chair into the middle of the room. "You don't understand . . ."

"I think I do. I just don't agree . . ." He reached toward me with a rhetorical hand gesture while launching into another foray, but I cut him off. "I think the experience, as you're describing it, is fundamentally identical to satori in Zen. You say it isn't, but you haven't produced a single fundamental difference."

He sat down, ready to engage me face-to-face, somewhat more conciliatory.

But I continued, "I understand your vision of dyadic change as opposed to dialectical change. Theses, antithesis, and instead of synthesis, intervention of God in history through scattered visionaries. That's it, right?"

"Yes, but . . . "

"So I understand it. I just disagree when you say it is unprecedented. I think that it is compatible with Hegelian dialectics. You say it isn't, but you can't make the case. So..."

I gave him the airwaves but instead he pondered what I was forcing him to face. I had him and we both knew it.

There was always more at stake than our egos, though they were never absent. During that particular historical

moment, the Sixties, the human mind lay open on the operating table. It seemed mankind, and Dan and I, had an opportunity to shift the foundations of thought.

"Look," he began with his best salesman's agreeability, "I'm not saying that dyadics contradicts dialectics. It subsumes it. Redefines it. It doesn't negate it. Like satori. Western mystical experience doesn't negate satori, it just subsumes it, includes it in a broader context of historical change. History is not an illusion. There is scientific evidence. Look, when a fetus is developing, there are opportune moments which, if they're lost, can't be made up..."

"But that denies the infinite nature of satori," I said, cutting him off again. "It's outside of time."

His expression soured. And here he blundered: he mistook convincing me for being right. He was constantly trying, subtly and unsubtly, to bend me into a disciple. Also, there was something crucial to the integrity of his vision that demanded it be unprecedented. And he now felt driven to intimidating me into submission. He leaned across the table.

"Look," he hissed, "I've been given the Magic Sword to protect the Rose . . ."

"I don't doubt the authenticity of your vision. It's just ... I don't think you're articulating it well."

Just inches from mine, his purple-pink face was moist from sweat and tensed for action. I could feel his body heat. That close, that intense, was an undeniable physical threat.

"Maybe . . ." he said, "you . . . can't . . .*hear* it."

We teetered an instant on the edge. Coming from rednecks, I learned early how to face down a bully. I stayed still, unyielding but relaxed. He was no church-mouse mystic but tremendously energetic, playing pickup basketball every weekend with teenagers at the school across from his house. I decided if he made a move, I would hit him with the chair next to me.

"If it's beyond someone like me," I asked quietly, "then who's going to understand your book?"

That deflated him. He realized what he had done and felt embarrassed and slumped back into his chair.

7

Dan no more believed in God than a man believes in the train that has run over him. I wasn't toying here with tooth-fairy faith. While I had doubts about his philosophy, I never doubted the authenticity of his experience. He had the Vision, saw the Source, however imperfectly he articulated it. I was never able to get a coherent narrative of it because whenever he talked about it at length, he drifted into a trance-state. I had to piece together a jumble of dropped references.

He was a probation officer and a graduate student in behavioral psychology, and the mystical experience occurred while he was attending a psychologists' conference in Oregon. He went into the conference on a creative tidal wave, presenting papers on three different studies. It was the early Sixties and he was on the verge of having the god-experience that Leary, Alpert, and probably some in the seminar audience would soon be chasing with psychedelics.

His papers were all poorly received and the resulting crash seemed to have been the catalyst. One thing that made him unique: he had virtually no religious training either in school or at home, other than some respectable generic Protestantism. Indeed, before the experience, he would have described himself as an atheist.

During the experience, he had sensitivity heightened almost to telepathy, a god-like overview of history and humanity, and intense love for everyone around him. ("We humans are heroic," he told me once. "We carry around so much pain..." And I could see as he said it that he empathetically felt the secret burden of pain in all humans.)

The experience varied in intensity during its roughly four-days. At some point, he was in a crowded restaurant and felt that he was an intimate of everyone in the room. When he got to the cashier, he discovered he didn't have any money (earlier he had blindly emptied his pockets to pay a cabbie). Somehow by looking at the cashier, he got her to let him leave without paying. There was a woman in a bar who said talking

to him was better than sex. There was skinny-dipping at night with a Catholic priest and some teenage girls. There was an aimless train ride in an open boxcar through the night and the voice of God telling him that was enough, now go home.

It ruined his life. He was committed to a hospital and diagnosed with a nervous breakdown. Every time he tried to explain the days he was missing, he fell silent. He said later that was the experience protecting itself. The admitting psychiatrist reported his "unsettlingly passive aspect."

Later, when that same doctor annoyed him, Dan made him cry. Whether he thought he did it telepathically or with a calculated comment, I could never get straight. After the hospital, he took his Japanese wife and two children and moved to Japan. His father-in-law gave him the job of running the Tokyo English Institute, a language school for executives.

8

His wife Helen supported him and nursed him and believed his explanation over the doctors'. She was an extraordinarily beautiful woman, gracious, personable, and generous. I was smitten from the first time we met. She gave me bags of groceries whenever I visited and I had a standing invitation to dinner. We had our own long conversations about our parents, our childhood, and especially R.H. Blythe, the greatest translator of Japanese poetry and an early western exponent of Japanese culture who wrote his best book while in a Japanese prison camp. So, while Dan and I were colleagues, Helen and I became friends.

I was the first person Dan had ever told about the experience besides Helen, and it was never clear how much she understood. (His own father was convinced he had found the root cause of Dan's mental problems when he found the Communist Manifesto from a college course among Dan's books.) I was Dan's conduit, facilitator, straight man, and sidekick.

For me, he was a consolation prize. I was a loser in the vision lottery. "And your young men shall have visions" went a warning from Ecclesiastes often quoted at the time. I seemed to be constantly meeting young men, young women, middle-aged men, and middle-aged women who had had visions (having nothing whatsoever to do with drugs). The visions seemed as random and plentiful as rain. I stayed dry.

And by the time I met Dan, I suspected that if there ever had been a chance for me, I probably lost it after methedrine. I was always aware that intellectual investigation was sublimation, a substitute, yet I compulsively pursued it, in part because there was nothing better to do. So, I was a prison convict, a lifer, who became an expert on travel.

The death of Yaweh in the Holocaust, ended all possibility of belief. Nihilism could not be avoided with a creed or a philosophy but only with an experience that can only be given. Like Dan's.

He told me only a little about a few of the many inexplicable occurrences in his experience. He said that telling more would dissipate power. Often when I pressed him for a particular detail, he would listen far into himself and then come back with a decision, usually not to share that detail. But, at about five and a half hours into the eight of that longest day, I decided not to accept no and pushed him with great effort to a definition of God.

9

"But it's a lie," I insisted.

"No, it isn't," he calmly retorted. This was not a vital topic for him. We were both worn down, still at the kitchen table.

"Just by being there," I continued on the offensive, "you're lying to the guy in the church pew next to you..."

"No, that's not true..."

"Yes it is. You don't share his conception of God..."

"That's not..."

"Yes it is." I was exhausted enough to not care and pushed past where usually I would have backed off. "You believe Christ is a . . . meta-shaman. You use Christianity the way you use fairy tales. It's a symbol system . . .You draw sustenance where you find it: Christian mysticism, fairy tales, science, even atheist existentialists..."

"Yeah but . . . "

"That guy sitting next to you would be outraged. . . " I said.

"They think he's *the* Christ," he said quietly," instead of a Christ . . ."

"O.k., that's the son, what about the father? You don't believe in the grandfather in the sky. By their definition, you're almost an atheist . . ."

"I am *not* an atheist . . . "

"You don't believe that God recognizes individuals... What kind of God do you believe in?"

He stared inward a long moment and after a while whispered, "It can't be described."

"What's your definition of God?" I challenged.

He thought a moment then snorted at the preposterousness of fitting *that* into words. He was always disdainful of theological hairsplitting. He shifted in his chair as if catching himself from running away.

Finally he said, "It can't..."

"Try!"

He stared inward again, trying to unscramble a dim message.

"Just...put a word there," I said gently. "Any word."

"Oh . . ." He raised his hand dismissively. "Call it . . ." Then he drifted off again.

"What? Call it what?"

He shifted in the chair and said, "Call it the... the . . . call it the 'wisdom of the whole.'"

10

Then I heard car tires crunch gravel. I didn't have a phone, so friends had no alternative to dropping by unannounced. I tried to identify the timbre of the engine before it switched off. Then I stood up and stretched to see out the kitchen window. Sure enough, my number one suspect was getting out of a jalopy I had given him as a wedding present.

This was the rarest moment of the day so far and there was no telling where Dan and I could have gone if we hadn't been interrupted instead by the most bizarre confrontation of the day.

I opened the door and saw Bernie approaching warily, studying Dan's sleek car.

"What's happening man?" I asked.

"Hi," he said and smiled but I could see his disappointment.

I knew he had just driven forty-five minutes from the City, and while he might come that far just for a visit, usually he arrived with some revelation that he urgently needed to share, unearthed while researching a story for the *Berkeley Barb*.

"I'm glad you came," I lied. "I've got a friend here that I want you to meet."

Bernie entered the kitchen door and Dan advanced wearing his salesman's smile, hand extended. Suddenly I changed my mind. This was going to be fun. I couldn't imagine two people more antithetical in temperament and worldview, yet both were brilliant, outspoken, and aggressive.

Bernie was a math prodigy who had walked away from scholarships to become a radical journalist. He had a speech impediment that made his childhood, in a working class Bronx neighborhood, a gauntlet of torment. As a result, he couldn't be intimidated.

As he shook Dan's hand, Bernie was clearly uncomfortable. He had something he was burning to tell me and would have been thrown off by anybody being there, but a *straight?!* I introduced Bernie as a journalist. Then I introduced

Dan as the author of a book of philosophy. I realized I would have to find common ground.

"What kind of philothophy (*philosophy*)?" Bernie asked Dan.

"It's similar to Whitehead's philosophy of organism," I said and looked at Dan for confirmation. He just smiled. Whitehead had also been an important mathematician.

"Whitehead, huh?" Bernie said.

Bernie wore his thick reddish-brown hair in a longish Beatle cut and had a handle-bar mustache, and he stood now with his left hand tucked under his right armpit and his right thumb supporting his chin, studying Dan.

And under that withering scrutiny, Dan just grinned, stoned on God, relaxed and happy as a baby.

"Bernie, you want some tea?" I asked.

"Yeah, shoo-uh (*sure*)."

I asked him if he was working on any interesting stories. He relaxed his stance, looked at his enormous feet, abashed, and said no. He wasn't going to open up in front of a stranger, especially not a straight.

Though Dan wasn't the least interested in Bernie, he knew he would have to take a turn with him, so he asked Bernie what kind of journalist he was. Predictably, Bernie answered evasively. Then, as I handed Bernie the tea, I saw through his thick glasses and knew what he was thinking: could Dan be a government agent trying to get some information about him, Bernie, by befriending me? I stifled a laugh. In recent months, Bernie had been wrestling demons of political paranoia.

Though Bernie gave intellectual recognition to things outside of the political realm, he had no real understanding or interest in them. He couldn't be brought into what Dan and I were doing. Another time I might have been able to find enough common ground between them to have had an entertaining encounter, but Dan and I were nearly six hours into the day and I just didn't have the energy. I was too tired to maneuver in a sticky social situation, just as at the end of that day I would be too tired to think up a good question for God.

We sat around the kitchen table, each with a steaming cup of tea in front of him, and the awkwardness became like an odor. Soon I could see Bernie was searching for an opportunity to exit. It came in a dramatic culmination to the tension.

As I watched them in conversation, verbally circling each other, tiptoeing between volatile topics, I remembered that, to the degree Dan had a political viewpoint, he was a liberal who had canvassed for Stevenson in the fifties. So, I wasn't afraid of Bernie being set off by a political comment, at least not a serious one. Unfortunately, the detonator was an unserious one, in response to a passing comment of mine on nuclear war.

"I'm not afraid of nuclear war," Dan announced smugly. "In fact, I welcome it. It would give us a chance to start over again."

Bernie stared at Dan as if he had declared himself to be a space alien. He didn't know, of course, that Dan himself didn't believe in what he had just said, that it was a form of exhibitionism. Dan sounded to himself like that old crazy lady in the baseball cap ranting on the sidewalks of downtown San Francisco. His lack of fear of nuclear war was a frequent boast of his, meant to demonstrate the depth of his commitment to his vision. And though he might have been capable of flippantly sacrificing his own life, I knew all those times he declared his readiness to "Tear it down! Tear it all down!" that he didn't include his wife and children. Many times I passed up the opportunity to remind him of this.

I had to stifle a laugh again, savoring Bernie's expression. He was flustered and wondering if this could be a joke, or if not, could the man be mentally unstable, and therefore could he be set off by a wrong comment. But then the full magnitude of the inhumanity of the statement sank in, and Bernie felt it a challenge to his moral integrity to declare himself against it. He said it slowly, almost in a whisper, studying its effect in Dan's face.

"That ith the motht (...*is the most*) inhuman thing I've evuh hoouhd (*ever heard*)." He paused, ready for a reaction. "It ith compweetwee inthane (...*is completely insane*)." He turned

to me. "I have to go. I planned to thtop-by jutht foah (*stop-by just for*) a moment anyway."

This was silly. He didn't know another soul north of the Golden Gate.

I followed him to the door, where he turned around and said to me, "Theuh wath thumthing (*There was something*) I wanted to talk to you about. When we have moah (*more*) time..."

He nodded, frowning, at Dan, who replied, grinning, "Bye."

11

Other friends had reactions as strong against Dan.

Barbara was attractive enough to support herself as a topless dancer while going for her degree in philosophy, which was how I met her. She also did typing jobs: stories for the creative writing department, theses for others. When I brought her the latest draft of Dan's book to type, she and I had known each other for a couple years.

We started out lovers and then spun apart after a few months. Yet we periodically bumped into each other at school, occasionally having sex, if we were between lovers. I was never in love with her, if I was even capable of love then, still it was an ideal relationship in some ways. She was completely undemanding, extraordinarily sexy, with the pendulous breasts and dark nipples that provided most of her living, and when she didn't want to have sex, we always had a lot to talk about.

When she handed me Dan's manuscript in the doorway of her apartment, I anxiously asked what she thought of it.

"Oh that is such a bunch of crap!" she said with stunning vehemence.

"Wh... why? Wh-what didn't you like about it?" Her response couldn't have been further from what I expected.

"Oh c'mon, you don't take that stuff seriously, do you?"

"Yeah, I do. I think you're probably taking it too literally. You've got to read it kind of like...poetry. It's ..."

"Oh, c'mon. That stuff is just ...egomaniacal... delusional... rantings."

"Wh-what about Nietzsche! He wrote the same kind of thing. Are you calling Nietzsche, er, rantings?"

That was the last time I ever saw her. But if some of my friends weren't able to appreciate Dan, others were. The most important of these was a former professor of mine from San Francisco State.

Newman was not only brilliant, getting his PHD in philosophy from Harvard in his early twenties, but also exceptionally personable. He had the openness, candor, and sincerity of a true seeker. After several courses, I saw him as a friend as well as a teacher and started sending him some of my "finds," the visionary lottery winners, those who, like Dan and unlike me, had gotten wet in the Sixties rain of visions. Newman seemed flattered and bemused when I sent him a frumpy, middle-aged beatnik poetess who pleaded that she had exhausted all the psychiatric nostrums for getting rid of intrusive, inexplicable, semi-mystical episodes.

About a year later, I sent him Bernie's nubile, nineteen-year-old sister-in-law. If she wasn't quite pretty, she was very sexy, especially in hiphugger jeans with a gauzy blouse pressed against her breasts by the seawind of Point Reyes, where we were hiking one day. We were on our way to an isolated sylvan pond where, as part of my plan of seduction, I hoped we would go skinny-dipping. But half way there, she decided I was the right person to tell about a certain troubling and inexplicable experience. That dominated the rest of the afternoon and we didn't even reach the pond.

Both women only met with Newman once yet both seemed to have gotten something out of it. I suspected that he might be feeling imposed upon when I showed up at his office one afternoon, but that suspicion was dispelled when I saw his fascination grow as I described Dan and his experience. When I was sure the hook was set, I brought out the manuscript.

In the years I was taking classes from him, Newman wrote a bestseller about the booming interest in exotic religions. This was soon followed by his becoming the editor of a series on religion for a major international publishing house. So I left the manuscript of Dan's book with him and, as I had

hoped, when I saw him a few weeks later, he was impressed enough to want to meet Dan.

12

The book wasn't so much written as it coalesced from hundreds of pages of notes taken during Dan's rummaging through literature and the sciences, fairy tales and mythology, religion and philosophy for concepts and images to express his vision. While managing his father-in-law's language school, he spent afternoons and evenings devouring about a book a day, with notes. Late nights, he tried to unwind by drinking, carousing, and whoring all over Tokyo. Eventually he was stung awake by guilt for betraying his loyal wife. He had been her lapdog since.

Eventually he discovered Norman O. Brown and adopted Brown's aphorisitic style and condensed the thousands of pages of notes into a hundred and forty-six pages of dense aphorisms, written in a spare, plain, utilitarian style, all message. He titled it *The Creative Advance: From History to Mystery*.

He sent sections to various writers of philosophy and religion. Brown had responded favorably and Alan Watts requested a meeting. Watts was responsible for the introduction of Zen into American culture and was able to fill auditoriums for his lectures. Dan decided within minutes that Watts was a huckster (I met Watts also, when he visited the mental hospital, and had a similar reaction). Dan barely kept himself from walking out of the bar where they met. It was just that touchy impulsiveness that had me concerned as Dan drove us out to San Francisco State to meet Newman.

"I'm not going to have my name put on a book," he said abruptly breaking a long silence.

"Why not?"

"Too much satisfaction for Ego-Dan. I don't want to be tempted into defending something I might not believe tomorrow." He shifted in his seat. "At all costs, I've got to stay

open. The apocalypse is imminent, and the only way to get through it is to stay open, deny no possibility."

For days I had noticed his growing tension over this meeting. He was in an octopus-wrestle with his ego: ashamed of his desire for recognition, then accepting of it, then overwhelmed by it, and then again rejecting it. With Bernie, he had been poised, detached, and imperturbable. But Newman, or rather what he represented, instilled alarm, even panic.

When we arrived at the coffee shop adjacent to the student cafeteria, Newman was waiting alone in one of the semicircular padded booths, tea steaming in front of him. I introduced them. They shook hands. Dan and I sat and slid squeaking along the vinyl upholstery.

"I like your book very much," Newman opened. He was tall and thickly built with a cherubic face. His wavy brown hair ended in a flip on his collar, daringly long for a man in his mid-thirties in 1970.

Where there should have been a thank you or, at least, a nod, Dan stared, taking a reading of him. But Newman didn't seem to notice. He immediately launched into the first of some stored up questions. His genuine interest and enthusiasm for Dan's vision and philosophy started softening Dan, who gradually became the cordial salesman. We wended our way to what I was most anxious to talk about: publishing the book. Newman could see this and went mercifully to the point.

"With your permission," he said. "I'd like to send the manuscript to my publisher."

There it was: Newman's commitment and the answer to the question that had been gnawing at Dan and I for weeks. I was excited. I looked over at Dan and saw troubled ambivalence.

"But I can't make any promises," Newman continued. "For one thing, I can't publish it in my own series. It just doesn't fit in with what we're doing. So, I wouldn't be the editor. But I'll give it the strongest recommendation."

The whole time Newman talked, I watched Dan go through wariness and now arrive at alarm. The offer was as

threatening as it was attractive, and the more attractive, the more threatening. Dan squirmed in his seat and showed stifled annoyance. I looked over and saw that Newman saw it too, and, not knowing Dan, he was, of course, confused. Here he was bestowing a great favor and showing great faith in the man and getting resentment for it. I knew the battle going on inside Dan, and I sympathized. But then I remembered how he was with Alan Watts and started to fear something irrational, like the tirades I tolerated.

In response to Newman's sober, reasonable explanation of what could be expected, Dan blurted out defensively, "But I won't put my name on it."

But I didn't have to worry. Most of the time I had spent around Newman was in a classroom and it wasn't until that night that I noticed his immense charm and tact, his poise. Far from being the unworldly philosophy professor, this was a man with total control of the worldly social arts. He was taken aback a moment by Dan, but then he said with perfect equanimity, "Well, that shouldn't be a problem. But we don't know that there is a book . . . yet."

As we were leaving, I looked down and noticed that Newman hadn't touched his coke. Dan and I hadn't ordered anything.

I was relieved and excited, feeling that the book was launched. Dan was fretful for a few weeks, but in time he was seduced enough to start to look forward to it. But the book was never published, inspite of Newman's best efforts.

13

After the initial meeting, Newman and Dan met without me, and I just got occasional reports from Dan on the book. It was passed from admiring editor to admiring editor, never quite officially dying and never published. One of the editors told Dan, "We would have to make you the new Pascal or Kierkegaard." In other words, it was a marketing problem.

The failure of the book was the beginning of the end of our association.

Of course, he should have been grateful to me, but I think he, at least unconsciously, blamed me. I was the only available target anyway. He was also resentful of my refusal to acknowledge the pristine truth of his vision and become his disciple. Tensions came to a quiet finale one sweltering summer afternoon.

He no longer visited me. Whenever I saw him now, I visited him at home. I didn't mind this because it meant I could see him when I felt like it, and also because I liked his family.

He needed a lavish car for his job, but his house was a modest white-stucco place on a sycamore-lined street. I entered its delicious coolness, invited in by his wife who, typically, came to the door to meet me.

This was the first time I had stopped by in the day and I was a little unsure of myself, until I saw that she was genuinely glad to see me, and then I relaxed. She led me through the livingroom and diningroom to the familyroom where Dan sat in a recliner with a book nearly four inches thick. Their children, a girl of thirteen and a boy of eleven, were simply the most physically beautiful human beings I had ever seen. They were also intolerable brats. I saw them in the kitchen and they saw me and offered no sign of recognition. The greeting from Dan was hardly more animated.

"What's the book?" I asked, nodding toward it as I sat on the couch.

His latent testiness now became open, if subdued, hostility. He held the book closer and stared at me a moment, considering.

"A collection of symbols," he said, "visual symbols, like heraldry insignia."

He was obviously holding something back.

"Oh," I said.

There followed some idle chatter, weather talk, though with his wife that could be thoroughly delightful. She was delicacy incarnate. But as I listened to her, I realized she had a predisposition to like me because of what I represented to

Dan. I wondered if she sensed the strain between he and I. She offered iced lemonade then went to get it.

"What are you looking for in there?" I asked him, nodding at the book.

"Symbols."

"Oh. Find any good ones?"

He nodded, still staring at me with a vague, distant hostility.

"I finally found the one I've been looking for," he said.

"Really!?"

He nodded, now pressing the book to his stomach. His wife approached with three glasses on a tray. I was waiting for him to hand me the book.

When he didn't, I asked, "Can I see it?"

He turned his head slightly to one side, then the other, saying, "No."

I knew he was capable of petulance, but I was stunned.

Helen handed out the glasses. She asked me about a book of haiku she had lent me and conversation and my attention then drifted to other things.

But eventually my shock faded and I hardened and realized that I didn't really care about the symbol. Nothing new had been discussed in months. We had been coasting on habit. Dan was a dry well for me. I had all I was going to get from him. And when you get the message, you hang up the phone.

So, while sipping the icy lemonade, I looked at him realizing I would never see him again after today.

14

Even on that longest, most important day at my cottage, a year or so before, when I finally got to ask God a single hard-won question, even that day there were almost no new topics. I did finally slog through my torpor to a question

though, just seconds before Dan reentered from the last and culminating trance of the day.

I didn't like my question. I wasn't satisfied at all that it matched the opportunity. But I was desperate and it just popped out. The answer was the end of my quest. I would continue to read and argue and search, but more from habit and curiosity than burning need. That answer was the real beginning of my nihilism.

"Can what you learned from your experience," I asked him, "all this special knowledge, can it help us, does it have any practical value, does it do any good to know it?... Can it stop the pain?"

"No."

Humanity's Tail

Of course, when you ventured out of the Haight-Ashbury in the mid Sixties, you expected the threat of redneck violence. But it was another thing all together to stay in the Haight and still have to contend with it, to be victim of a home invasion. Even Haight Street itself wasn't always safe.

I was walking west on it one sunny afternoon late in the summer of '67, approaching Schrader Street, about a block from Golden Gate Park, when I was stopped by the sight of a redneck with a rifle.

Mid-twenties, crew-cut under a baseball cap and wobbly gut under a T shirt, he had just arrived at the curb on the south side and was apparently resuming an exchange of angry shouts with a freak across the street.

"Yeah?! How's *this* asshole?!" the redneck shouted shaking the rifle over his head.

There was a suspended second when the freak, and everyone watching, wondered how he would respond. Then he flipped the redneck off.

But before the redneck could react, he looked around and noticed the audience of dozens all around him. Then he started retreating south down Schrader toward Waller Street. I was transported with outrage and started following him. While he nervously scanned from one side to the other, I was close-reading

his face and ready to retreat. But then the fear steering his body fully emerged on his face and I felt bold enough to look around and saw across Schrader on the west side other freaks also advancing on the redneck, among them the one who flipped him off.

The redneck turned the corner and fast-walked west down Waller toward a tan Buick convertible parked across a driveway entrance. The engine was running and a trimmer redneck also in a baseball cap sat on the passenger side of the front seat. As the fat one reached the driver's door, he looked around for a cop one last time.

He then tossed the rifle on the back seat and opened the door and shouted at the freak who had flipped him off, "You... you... fuckin'... freak!!!"

"C'mon, les' get outta here," said the redneck on the passenger's side.

As they drove off, I searched my pockets for something to write down the license number and found nothing. I was about to ask a nearby freak for a pencil, when I saw a chick across the street writing it down.

I didn't see a cop the rest of the day and forgot about it. But even as early in the development of the Haight as the previous winter, of '66, before the global publicity of the summer of '67, I had a run-in with some rednecks that brought me much closer to serious injury or even death. At the same time it was, appropriate to its time and place, bizarre and unreal.

Late one night, I was walking up and down the hills of the Haight with a new friend, Greg, who I had met in a philosophy class at State. We were both high on acid and sharing insights and extolling discoveries and favorite books by favorite authors and finding nothing whatsoever to disagree about. A couple nights a week I would be in a similar conversation at a coffeehouse, though not on acid.

Tonight, however, we were under a clear, cold, winter night sky, and as we descended into a well-lit area in Buena Vista Park, where it slopes down to Haight Street, two straight teens came at us out of the dark, one on each side. On my side was a husky blond with a crowbar and a face so red and knotted with

rage that he seemed on the verge of bursting out a long-held breath. If the other assailant also had a weapon, I didn't notice.

But almost before the threat could register, a guy yelled up from Haight Street, "Hey!!! Knock that off!"

Then he crossed the street, leapt over the low retaining wall, and headed up the slope at a trot. The two assailants and Greg and I froze, watching the guy approach. He was medium height and muscular.

He went to the kid with the crowbar and grabbed it, "Gimme that! Whadya think you're doing? What is wrong with you?" He turned to Greg and I and asked in a low concerned tone, "You guys alright?"

We nodded dumbly.

Our rescuer turned and glared at the other assailant and then turned back to the crowbar wielder and shouted at both, "Go on, get outta here! You should be ashamed of yourselves. Why would you do something that stupid?"

The two assailants, confused and thoroughly deflated, turned around and left without a word.

"Dumb kids," the rescuer muttered and started down the slope back to Haight Street, crow bar in hand.

The weirdest part of this wasn't what the rescuer did but what he looked like. From his flawless greased pompadour to his black turtleneck to his gray slacks, his whole aspect was a composite of the heroes that I grew up watching on a black-and-white TV. There was *Route 66* with Buz and Todd, hipster knights errant roaming the legendary highway, and private detective *Peter Gunn*, the ultimate in urban cool played by a Cary Grant knock off. There were countless other private detectives, adventurers, soldiers-of-fortune, etc. whose stock-in-trade was the last second rescue.

When he reached Haight Street, our rescuer tossed the crowbar onto the sidewalk with a resounding clang, and then got into and drove off in (what else?) a black Corvette, as much a stock prop as the pompadour. If it wasn't for his skin tone, I couldn't have been sure he wasn't a black-and-white-TV hallucination. The only rational explanation I could imagine was that he was a straight who had modeled his appearance and

behavior on those very TV heroes, and maybe he had just been visiting hip friends or a hip chick. I knew immediately that I would have to tag this memory, "This really happened." But then, nothing that strange could be invented.

Others didn't have a last second rescuer. Real murders occurred on Haight Street. I witnessed one on a warm spring night in April '67, just before the Summer of Love. A redneck runaway chick shouted, "I'm tired of you niggers buggin' me!" as she drove a knife into the heart of a young black man.

At the same time, none of this was alien to me, having grown up with the threat of redneck violence in a Sierra mill town, where I was a freak, a strayed gene, an unexplainable fluke, and treated accordingly. So when I reached the Haight-Ashbury, I was choking with hatred for rednecks.

Although our California variety isn't a nigger-lyncher, it is an identifiable subspecies with its own unique brutishness. California rednecks were called "Pikers" in the latter nineteenth century. The name may have originated with poor migrants to California from Pike County in eastern Missouri, but it also was Australian slang for a useless lazy person, a loafer, a loser. There was a sizable Australian community in California during and after the Gold Rush.

According to a journalist of the time, Bayard Taylor, the Piker was "the Anglo-Saxon relapsed into semi-barbarism. . . . He takes naturally to whiskey . . . He has little respect for the rights of others; he distrusts men in 'store clothes' . . . Finally, he has an implacable dislike for trees." Other writers confirmed this, including Horace Greeley in *An Overland Journey*. Journalist Stephen Powers maintained that even Pikers who made a lot of money farming were "the most shiftless, thriftless men of the class found in the Union, except, perhaps, in Texas." There was concern that the low quality of the labor force in California would impede economic development.

Take some Piker descendants, stir-in some Depression Okies, add a few Mexicans and remnants of the Mi-Wok Indians, and you get my home town, dying before I was born, at the dead-end of a highway, where it didn't even get the slight rejuvenation

of drive-through tourism, so it was considered backward even by neighboring Piker towns. It was the backwater of a backwater.

And, even while I was on alert for redneck attacks, as much as I feared their violence, even more I feared their influence. Could I hate them this much but still be one of them? Was there a Piker lurking inside me? Was there some subtle subliminal influence, toxic seepage into my subconscious? Was I contaminated with the pollutant of redneckery? How could I not be infected?

The Beatles' Last Concert

There was rock 'n roll and there was the Beatles. Their last concert anywhere, ever, was in San Francisco on August 29, 1966, and later it was hard not to see some connection with the Counter Culture that would be bursting onto the world from the same location only six months later.

The concert was at Candlestick Park and the traffic on the freeway and on the frontage road into the ballpark was chaotic and tedious.

My roommate Mike and I were in my car, stopped dead on the approach to the parking lot, eagerness welling, frustration too, when suddenly Mike exclaimed, "Shit!"

I looked over at him and then looked where he was looking and exclaimed, "Shit!"

There was a car caravan with a Loomis armored car at the center and behind that a huge bus and behind that some cars, and at the head of the caravan was a cop station wagon, and they were tearing along the peripheral road on the far side of the parking lot. Behind the caravan's roostertail of dust, which was bent toward the Bay by ocean wind, two Volkswagen bugs were coming up fast.

A mob of a couple hundred kids also saw the caravan and ran screaming toward the right field entrance which was a sliding pink door that the caravan was also headed toward. But the rent-a-cops couldn't open the padlock so one of them waved the caravan to veer into the empty parking lot where it drove around in

circles chased by screaming kids a few of whom were able to leap onto the back of the armored car.

"It's just like ... *Hard Day's Night*," I said in an awed near-whisper.

"Yeah."

More rent-a-cops arrived at the pink door and were able finally to open it. The caravan drove toward it but slowly, with kids jumping off and on and rent-a-cops grabbing those they could. Then the caravan had to slow to a near stop because the doorway allowed only one car at a time. That gave rent-a-cops an opportunity to pry the last kids off the armored car.

Finally, the caravan was inside. The two Volkswagen bugs tried to follow but were blocked by rent-a-cops. Back on the frontage road approaching the parking lot, traffic started moving, and as Mike and I pulled away from the scene I saw a girl sobbing and shrieking, "I saw him! I saw him!" Her bellbottoms flapped in the wind.

Conservative Christians picketed the gates into the parking lot for some statement about Jesus by John Lennon that they willfully distorted.

As we passed through the gates, I asked, "Hear about them burning Beatle records?"

"Yeah ... This week records, last week crosses."

The Ku Klux Klan had led protests outside the Washington DC concert and there were assassination threats in Memphis where a firecracker exploded on stage and the Beatles thought they were being shot at. In Cleveland, twenty-five hundred fans broke through the rent-a-cops and forced the band to flee the stage. So, security at Candlestick was really tight, cops private and public everywhere, jamming the cop radar in Mike and I.

We had cheap tickets, $4.50 each, so we took our seats in the second section above third base. By then the shadow of the stadium from the setting sun was deep into the outfield. The stage was a little beyond second base, about five feet off the ground, with massive speakers on both sides of the drum platform. A wire fence all the way around the stage made it also a cage. Rent-a-cops ringed it also.

The wait was becoming painful, like holding-in piss. For the last couple of days, in the Haight-Ashbury pad I shared with Mike and two others, and at my part-time file clerk job, I had worn a silly grin all day because "The Beatles are in town!" Scanning the crowd as it filled the seats, I noticed a chick who reminded me of my sister and I remembered that it was through her I discovered the Beatles, three years before, when I was a junior in high school.

I thought the Beatles were O.K. I even bought their first single, *Please, Please Me*, before they were famous in the States. They sounded so odd without a bass singer that I thought they might be a one-hit novelty act. Then "Beatle-mania" hit, and they became idols of pubescent sexual frenzy to be sniffed at. My sister put their photographs on her bedroom wall.

Then my mother asked me one afternoon to drive my sister and two of her friends to see "that Beatle movie." It was a forty-five minute drive to the county's largest town and its only movie theater from the Sierra mill town I grew up in. At first, I decided to wait out the movie in the library and pocket the ticket money my mother gave me, but then when I met my sister and her friends after the first show, they begged me to let them stay for the next show. This pricked my curiosity so I went with them back into the theater.

Only fifteen minutes into the movie, I was shushing my sister and her friends and any others who squealed. I wanted to catch each word, each nuance of inflection and accent. That night I became a fan, that is, a fifth Beatle. I memorized all their lyrics, and whenever I heard them playing, I sat in for that song. Even the mistakes, the missed beat, the flat note, the wrong word, were savored.

And now, in the Haight-Ashbury, on grass and occasionally on acid, we microscopically analyzed favorite cuts and studied photographs on album covers and tried to squeeze around the myth and touch a person. We memorized the most minute expressions of their personalities: Ringo's metronomic oscillation of his torso and swaying of his head as he played; the level George held his guitar and the relaxed bounce of his knees in time to the music; the arch of Paul's left eyebrow; the sarcastic, puckish pulling in of John's lower lip and the way before the

microphone he spread his feet, leaned back and tilted his head as if peering through bi-focal lenses. Through their music and their personalities they became icons of that holiest of holies, "fun."

And if the Beatles could zing the old fogies (and the young fogies) all the better. The sneers of adults were praise. My parents dismissed the Beatles, which I took personally. Duke Ellington eventually ended the debate with the Solomonic declaration, "The Beatles have their area and they cover it well."

At first, the Beatles were, like the Counter Culture itself, the ephemeral fad that kept not ending. You didn't just listen to them; each album was a new era. They were reflecting it, not leading it, still, every time John changed his hair style it seemed another click in the turnstile for the entrance of a new age.

While waiting at the ballpark for the last concert to begin, I saw only two long hairs within fifty feet of us, though farther out there were more. Guys like Mike and I with hair as long or longer than the Beatles didn't have a name in the public imagination yet. With their long hair and pointed shoes, the Beatles had up-ended their asses at the bull of American virility. In the process, they split the ranks of rock n' roll. Now there was a sharp-edged hostility between guys who wore a Beatle cut, only a couple inches longer than normal, and those who didn't. Mike and I collided head-on with that hostility a couple months before, at the beginning of June, at "The Beach Boys Summer Spectacular" at the Cow Palace.

We didn't go for the Beach Boys but for the Lovin' Spoonful, who had second billing. The Spoonful was one of the American bands emerging after the first wave of the British invasion that followed the Beatles. The Spoonful had long hair and their music was easily the equal of the Beach Boys' so they were good stand-ins for the Beatles, the Rolling Stones, the Animals, etc., the new rock 'n roll.

The Cow Palace arena was the biggest building I had ever been in, airplane hangar-size, and we had seats almost in the last row of the balcony. The line-up seemed as vast as the venue. We sat through a succession of one-hit-wonders: the Leaves, Chad and Jeremy, Percy Sledge. Also, there was our own Jefferson Airplane, who were still only locally known and who we

saw regularly at the Fillmore Auditorium. The Byrds played but had technical problems with the mikes that threw off their set. The Brit band Sir Douglas Quintet got some of the audience singing the refrain from Dylan's current hit "Rainy Day Woman Nos. 12 & 35." Like pub mates, we sang together, "Every ... body ... must ... git ... stooooned!!"

Finally the Spoonful performed and they were exactly like on TV: Sebastion with his autoharp, Yanofsky's goofiness. They all moved well on stage and sounded exactly like, but richer than, the recordings of their hits, "Do You Believe in Magic?" "You Didn't Have to Be So Nice," "Summer in the City," and "Daydream." But their set seemed to end just after it began and then we were sitting there waiting for the Beach Boys. Neither Mike nor I had said anything about it but we each knew (How could anybody not know?!) the burning question was: would the Beach Boys be hip? Would they have made the change, turned the corner? To have the hair, they only had to let their surfer cuts grow out. Finally, they came on stage and they weren't. During the sustained cheers and applause, their striped shirts with buttoned-down collars, and their shaved faces and straight blond hair, straight off the album covers, became period costumes.

During "Surfin' U.S.A." Mike and I left. While we were brushing knees sidling toward the stairs, I looked around and was surprised to see others, dozens, here and there, all over the arena, also sidling toward stairs. Most had long hair of course. Then I noticed the expressions of those who were staying as they looked at us: confused, resentful, hostile, the glint of violence in some short-haired guys my age. I hardened as we descended the stairs.

"Jesus Christ!!" I said as the car approached the exit. "Republican rock!"

"The Bleached Boys ..."

"Yeah, that's right! ...Yeah ...That's, that's rock with absolutely no blues influence, no negro influence whatsoever ... It's disgusting ..."

"Yeah ..."

I suddenly realized what we had just done by walking out during the headliners' performance. We weren't leaving early to

beat the traffic or even to leave an event we had lost interest in. We were making a political statement... of some kind. While we were doing it, I wasn't sure what we were walking toward (other than the car) but I knew with painful certainty exactly what I was walking away from and hated it.

Though we were a tiny minority of the audience, we rated a mention the next day in the Chronicle column of Ralph J. Gleason, a prominent jazz critic who understood and now also championed the new rock. This was the biggest manifestation that either Mike or I had yet seen of the hip-straight divide. The first national media notice of that divide was still more than six months in the future at the Human Be-in.

Nevertheless, because I really liked the Beach Boys' music and wanted to see them perform, I felt a pang of regret as we passed through the gates of the Cow Palace parking lot. The next time the Spoonful were in town they were busted for grass and one of them ratted out the dealer to avoid deportation.

Even more than at the "The Beach Boys Summer Spectacular," the warm-up acts at the Beatles' last concert were perfunctory. The first group was completely unknown, the Remains, who did four numbers. They were followed by Bobby Heb who also did four numbers including his only hit "Sunny." Then the Cyrkle came on and did five numbers including their hit "Red Rubber Ball."

The Ronettes were the last of the warm-up acts, but they were special, three sexy Latina chicks with hair piled a foot high. I loved ""Be My Baby," "Do I Love You," and "Baby, I Love You," and Phil Spector's wall of sound behind them, and any other night I would have been ecstatic to see just them.

The Beatles' last concert ever was also the last concert of a fourteen city tour promoting *Revolver*, dubbed decades later the best rock album of all time in some polls. We were still savoring the previous album, *Rubber Soul,* when *Revolver* arrived with Harrison's sitar and *Eleanor Rigby*'s string quartet, deliberately discordant notes and electronic music.

Besides being an esthetic breakthrough, it answered the question: are they hip? We didn't know yet if they had smoked grass or taken acid. Then the climactic cut on *Revolver*,

"Tomorrow Never Knows," with lyrics from the Tibetan Book of the Dead, told us they had taken acid (which was still legal). The night we first listened to the album in the illegal basement apartment that Mike and I shared with our other roommates, Francine and Ralph, we decoded a message in a lyric that confirmed that the Beatles had smoked grass.

It was during "I'm Only Sleeping" that Mike and Francine suddenly exploded, simultaneously shouting "Oh!!!" and exchanging a quick awestruck glance and leaping to their feet. She was hooting and laughing but he had struck his head on the ceiling, hard. He was six six and the ceiling brushed my six two head. He winced and groaned and bent double rubbing his head.

Francine went over and took his head in both hands and tilted it toward the light and examined the bruise and then said, "Oh that's nothing."

Then she kissed the wound and he stood up and pressed his head against the ceiling. They locked glances, too long, and I caught the glint of a plea in his. She turned away and sat down in the threadbare stuffed recliner, her throne, the most comfortable piece of furniture in a pad partially furnished from the sidewalk.

Mike then bent over and lifted the needle from the record and sat down in a saggy stuffed chair and said to me, "You asked me how I knew the Beatles had smoked grass..."

"What happened... on the record?" I asked Mike. I was new to the Haight and ravenously curious.

"He said 'kief' instead of sleep," Francine said. "John sang 'Kief can hide all the world goin' by my window'."

"I wasn't sure when I heard it on the radio ..." Mike said to her.

We had already heard the album on AM car radio which made even our tinny, scratchy portable record player an improvement.

"So? What's that? What's 'kief'?" I asked Mike again.

Francine said, "It's Arabic for grass."

"In England a lot of the grass, almost all the hash, comes from Morocco," Mike added.

As a merchant seaman, he had spent a lot of time in England and could speak with authority.

"Oh ... Wow!" I said.

"What was that rock song you played for me when we were in high school?" she asked me. "A forty five with some dirty words ..."

We met in the grammar school band, where, though she was several years older, we became close and lasting friends. Now we were together in the Haight, members together of this colony of rejects, of winners disguised as losers.

"Oh yeah, that was 'Quarter to Three' by Gary U.S. Bonds," I said. Then I explained to Mike and Ralph, "At the beginning there's all this party noise and you can hear some guy in the background yelling, 'Open your legs baby... Here I come, baby... Get ready, here I come.' "

"Oh yeah ..." she said laughing at my impersonation of the record.

"I found another one though," I said. "In Jackie Wilson's 'Baby Workout.' A couple times he sings 'Work out ... work out ... *fuck* all night long.' "

Hidden in some blurred rock lyrics were contraband obscenities. Sometimes they required multiple careful listenings so that even if an adult listened to the song once, they wouldn't hear it, or believe their ears if they did.

" 'Good Golly Miss Molly, you sure like to ball!' " Francine sang impersonating Little Richard.

"Know what the lyrics to 'Please Please Me' are about?" Mike asked her.

She shook her head, smiling, sensing something shocking and lurid.

He explained slowly and carefully, "It's a cat complaining because he's goin' down on his ol' lady but she isn't goin' down on him..."

"Oh c'mon ..." Francine exclaimed.

"Listen to it! ..." I said. "On Chuck Berry's 'Rock 'n Roll Music,' John changes 'It's gotta back beat, you can't lose it' to 'It's gotta a *black* beat, you can't lose it.' "

"Let's hear 'Tomorrow Never Knows' again," Francine said.

"O.k. but then 'And Your Bird Can Sing,' " Mike said.

This was the first time I had gotten a sense of what Francine and Mike were like as a couple. He was right. They were great. But she had just dumped him for Ralph. Hence Mike's permanent bad mood. He was love gored. He bent over to put the needle on the record and my eyes went to the appropriately symbolic bandage on his right hand. During an argument with her, he had put a fist through a square section of the glass on the greenhouse door on the bathroom.

Francine said to me, "Oh yeah, hey, look at Dylan on *Bring It All Back Home*."

The album cover was on top of a heap of them on the coffee table and I picked it up.

Mike held the phonograph needle suspended, looking at her, and groaned, "Oh no."

Francine reached out and caught Mike's arm as he started again to lower the needle and she said to me, holding-in laughter, "Look at his lips ..."

"She thinks he's gay," Mike said.

"Well ..." she said to me. "Don't they look red?"

"Yeah ... sorta." I didn't know what to make of it and in my stoned blur (we had all smoked grass for the event of course) didn't particularly care.

Mention of someone being gay reminded me of Ralph sitting beside me on the couch. He was gay when Francine "got a hold of him" as she put it. He had a hapless, diffident quality that I liked, and I seemed to be the only one tonight who noticed he hadn't spoken in quite a while. He was glum, distracted, depressed even, and it was easy to guess why.

A few days before, a letter had arrived from Larry, who was Francine's husband, Ralph's best friend, and a recent draftee desperately trying to get out of the army. He had tried talking to army shrinks on acid and even cutting his wrists. Nothing worked. So in this most recent letter, he announced he was going to go AWOL just before his unit left for Vietnam and he was going to stop by the pad to pick up Francine on the way to Canada. A few weeks before that, while hitching back from visiting Larry at Fort Ord, Francine and Ralph spent a rainy night together in a motel

room and became lovers. After that, they frolicked and cavorted about the Haight like little kids. Then the Larry's letter arrived.

"Yellow Submarine" was just ending when there was a knock at the door. We all froze. It could be Larry ... or the landlord for overdue rent ... or a beat cop who smelled the grass ... From a jar-lid ashtray on the coffee table, Mike plucked a couple roaches and popped them into his mouth and then put the ashtray on the floor and pushed it under the couch. Meanwhile Francine had stood up and warily, slowly approached the door. In the silence that followed the fade out of "Yellow Submarine," I glanced at Ralph who was turned around toward the door watching Francine. She turned the knob, pulled the door toward her, and during the opening guitar riffs of "She Said She Said," Francine peered into the night.

It could have been Larry, the landlord, or a cop, but it was just Duffy, a couch nomad, looking for a place to crash.

That night I was safely out of reach of the army, and Larry's predicament, because of my student draft deferment. But when the Beatles' next album, *Sgt. Pepper's Lonely Hearts Club Band*, came out nine months later, at the beginning of the Summer of Love, I had already become fed up with the extortion payment of grades for the deferment and dropped out of school. I skydived without a parachute through that summer, with army or exile, Viet Nam or Canada inevitable.

Officially my college major was philosophy, in reality it was draft evasion, and when meeting any draft-eligible male, the first thing I said, sometimes while still shaking hands, was: "What are you doing about the draft?" I didn't know what I would do when my notice came. Part of me didn't believe it would. The draft was out there in a hazy-vague, irrelevant, so-called future. Welded to the moment, I wasn't capable of making plans more than a few days in advance. This was probably intensified by having grown up with civil defense drills for surprise nuclear attacks. Armageddon practice.

My opposition to the war caused shouting matches with my parents when I visited them and my sister, so my father, while driving me to the bus station the previous Christmas, asked me to "not come home... for awhile." We were in his pick-up. I was

surprised, then hurt, but said, "Yeah, sure," and turned to watch the pine forest flow by. I didn't need the explanation that followed. I dreaded the arguments as much as they did.

When *Sgt. Pepper* came out, I had just moved into a new apartment on Scott Street with a new roommate, Tim, and the two synchronicitous events, we agreed, deserved a party.

Tim and I both had fallen in love with, and been dumped in succession by, Ruth, and though he and I would become close friends, we had minor problems as roommates. What annoyed him most about me seemed to be my complaining about what annoyed me most about him: his habit of sleeping with the radio on all night. Late one night, on my way to bed, I razzed him and said his habit reminded me of kittens lulled to sleep by the ticking of a watch mistaken for their mother's heartbeat. He shrugged, bent to the radio dial and searched for a station. Usually it was classical FM.

I was lying in the dark of my room on my mattress on the floor listening to the stations shoot by: "...thumpff .... Johann .... ffwwuzz .... rrissugf .... completed by .... shhhik .... k-k-k-krang-yang-yang-yang."

"Hey, what was that?" I asked.

"I don't know," he said and went back to it.

Sure enough, it was an electric guitar. We had just discovered the first hip rock n' roll radio station, KMPX, in chrysalis on the farthest end of the dial in the after-midnight slot at a Chinese-language station.

That night, we joined the handful of people listening to Larry Miller. I knew there were few listeners because no one knew about the station when I mentioned it to friends, and quite a while after midnight, I had called with requests and was told I was the first to call. Once, I thought I caught a note of pleading in Miller's voice when he tried to start a conversation. Inspite of his scant audience, he was still a celebrity to me, so I felt uncomfortable and got off the phone. Maybe the best evidence that Larry Miller believed few were listening was the tape he played one night of a couple having sex.

His program was soon a hip household staple. Then the Chinese programs got bumped and the freaks took over round-

the-clock with deejays as unhurried as poured honey, as laid-back and lackadaisical in their ever-stoned blur as their AM counterparts were wired and frenzied, cramming sales pitches between shaved hits. KMPX played all the new groups with no other outlet. The previous winter even the Rolling Stones' single "Let's Spend the Night Together" couldn't get air play and for a while the only place to hear it was the jukebox at the Drogstore Café on Haight Street.

KMPX announced it would preview *Sgt. Pepper* the night before it went on sale, so that was the night Tim and I chose for our party. But when every day of that summer was a party, why take time out to plan and attend a "party"? (One exception was the capping party. A dealer invited friends over to stuff powdered LSD into capsules and they absorbed the acid through their skin and got very stoned. It was the hip equivalent of a barn raising.) But *Sgt. Pepper* wasn't just another new album and this wasn't going to be just another summer, so the occasion required something special.

Whether or not ours was a certifiable *party*, Tim and I invited everybody we knew and each got five or six to come. There were some of my friends from San Francisco State and my last job, part time file clerk at an insurance company. (I was now, with Tim, a successful bottom-feeding drug dealer.) Also, there was Cheryl, Ruth's best friend, and Cheryl's ol' man, Peter, a couple of chic wannabe junkies. Ruth was invited but, not surprisingly, didn't come. There were four neighbors who shared the three bedroom flat across the hall and who I didn't know well yet. There was a couple with backpacks Tim met on Haight Street an hour before who needed a place to crash.

Just before the party started, I tacked an American flag to the floor inside the front door. My middle finger at the government. The party guests had already walked over the flag, or were standing on it, when they noticed it. All were startled: some immediately leapt off, some recovered enough to saunter, *everyone* got off. I studied and savored reactions, especially that instant of realization: they had defiled the idol! Years of saluting it, singing to it, watching John Wayne die for it, congealed in their horror. I felt I knew a personal secret about each. It seemed to me

that Ol' Glory doormat was an almost scientific test for detecting latent straightness.

Straights supported a racist social structure. Mistook Vietnamese patriots reclaiming their homeland for agents of the international communist conspiracy. Worshiped a god killed in the Holocaust. Traded precious time for things. Were volunteer prisoners.

Yet it was the reaction of Tim, hip incarnate, that made me pull up the flag.

"I'm just afraid. . . if we get busted. . . ." he said in a conspiratorial hush, though we were alone in the kitchen, he boiling tea water, me pouring fruit juice for guests who had been arriving for twenty minutes.

"Look, if we get busted, we're screwed anyway," I said, then noticed the fear in his eyes. "When we hear 'em at the door we can just pull it up," I added in a conciliatory tone.

"Suppose we don't have a chance to pull it up?" he countered. "Or ... or they find it ... with footprints?"

"Think it's more provocative than Soviet propaganda posters in the livingroom and a poster of Ho Chi Minh in the can?" I asked, half-joking.

He considered my question with inappropriate seriousness, then replied, "Yes... It's just that it's. . . the flag. . . And even if we *can* pull it up, it'll still be covered with footprints . . . And you know they'll search the place . . ." He trailed off, tangled in paranoid thoughts.

There was more to his reaction than exaggerated caution. His confusion had a pathological edge. One thing that made him hip incarnate was his being a hero of the civil rights movement. He was driven out of Louisiana by threats from the Klan during "Freedom Summer" of 1964. Hence his oft-times paralyzing fear of cops. Another thing that made him hip incarnate was his being a recurring mental hospital patient, the ultimate imprimatur of hip.

So, heading back into the living room with a tray full of drinks, I said, "I'll think about it," but I knew I had lost.

Shoes and sandals and the crashers' backpacks were scattered about. The largest cluster of guests was by the view window and eventually I joined them. The Berkeley Hills were

phosphorescent with last sunlight, and sprinkled over them, here and there, was a piercing white glare from a window the size of a period. Were those us, the hip few, angled just-right to catch the light? I was pondering this, already stoned, when a circulating joint reached me. I took my toke and turned back to the room, handed off the joint, and evaluated the party.

I couldn't help fantasizing about the LSD orgies fantasized by the media. No one I knew had attended one. A recent article in *Playboy* described a plausible orgy in Berkeley. But if I had fantasized nudging our party into an orgy, I discovered as I faced it, that it needed to be nudged awake. There was a pall of self-consciousness on the room. Voices were low and people talked only to those they already knew. If we were all hanging out at a mutual friend's pad, everything would be fine, but this was a "party." Something should be happening that wasn't.

Then, in a nick of time, *Sergeant Pepper* was announced on KMPX. Conversation dwindled. The album started and we all froze, silent, listening. One of the crashers, the chick, eventually laid down on the floor. In twos and threes, we all followed her example until there was a carpet of silent rapt bodies, eyes closed, riding the funhouse-ride all the way to the mushroom-cloud-orgasm ending . . . .

It was over and there was street noise and then the mellow voice of the deejay. I opened my eyes, surprised by a darkness diluted only slightly by a candle flame with vibrato. I reached for the volume control and turned down the deejay. Others were still drifting. Some were on acid. I had wanted to stay as sober and lucid as possible. Slowly, gradually, the others stood and stretched and faced each other. As host, I felt compelled now to steer and make a critical appraisal, but when I actually focused on what we had just heard, all I could manage was a whispered, "Wow!"

Everyone else seemed as dazed and uncertain as me.
"What did you think?"
"I kinda liked it... Sorta."
"Yeah? ... I don't know..."
The rest of the summer we would study, analyze, decode the album.

Soon Peter and Cheryl stepped into their sandals and thanked Tim and I and mumbled about vague obligations elsewhere. That was when it started. While I was talking to somebody, somebody else was saying good night behind my back. And so it went, until the room eventually emptied. It wasn't that late so Tim went out with the crashers but I didn't feel like it and instead went to bed and read, then jerked off to orgy fantasies and fell asleep.

Nobody had to step around the flag as they left because I took it up right after Tim asked me to.

The Beatles of course felt the same about the Vietnam War as we did, and about ten months before that party, during that last tour, their attitude toward the war got them into almost as much trouble as John's comments about Jesus. At a press conference, George joined John in denouncing the war and Paul added they would elaborate back in England because they didn't feel free to do so in the States. Plus, they didn't hide the fact that they hung out with pacifist icon Joan Baez in their dressing room before the last concert.

And an hour and a half into that last concert, at about 9:30, the emcee, a popular deejay named Gene Nelson, stepped up to the microphone and asked the crowd, "Are you ready?"

"Yeeeeeeaaaaaaaah!!!!!!!!!!"

"Here they are!"

And there they were, only a quarter of a mile away, strolling out of a dugout, waving to the cheering ecstatic crowd and to the blinding volleys of flash bulbs. Mike and I, who were aloof and above it all, after all we were surrounded by the public, the boobs all that crass commercialism was aimed at, we leapt to our feet with everyone else, hearts in our throats. My God, IT'S THEM!!!

As John, Paul, George and Ringo ran out across the grass to the back of the stage, a roar went up and girls around us jumped onto their seats and waved and screamed and screamed and waved. Rolls of toilet paper arced through the air onto the field. The Beatles emerged onto the stage and did a quick tune-up, each chord answered by a surge of crowd roar, as was Paul when he tested a mike with "Hello." Then suddenly the probing

chords were cut off by rapid strumming and they tore into Chuck Berry's "Rock And Roll Music" which was then enveloped in crowd roar.

Wearing identical dark green suits with white shirts and no ties (George wore white socks) they sang flawless reproductions of recordings the audience knew like its own thoughts. They played for half an hour and performed 11 songs. The screaming, which was annoying but came in waves, and the wind and the crowd noise and the distance all smudged the sound. Still, most of the time you could hear the music. Each casual remark between songs was a candy lozenge sucked on for days afterwards.

After "Rock n Roll Music," they went right into "She's A Woman" and after that Paul went up to the mike and said, "Thank you! Thank you very much everybody, and hello, good evening. We'd like to carry on with a song, not surprisingly, by, er, written and sung by George. And this song was on our *Rubber Soul* LP. And the song is called 'If I Needed, er, Someone.' "

When that ended, it was John who stepped up to the mike and said, "Thank you everybody, thank you. We'd like to carry on now, er, carry on together, at will - one together and all for one - with another number that used to be a single record back in, er... a long time ago. And this one's about the naughty lady called 'Day Tripper' !"

During that one, a group of five boys climbed over a fence near the empty centerfield bleachers and sprinted toward the stage in a broken-field run through layers of rent-a-cops who eventually caught them all and hustled them into the stands. Of course, everyone rooted for the boys.

Then the Beatles did "Baby's In Black" and after that George went up to the mike and said, "Thank you! Thank you. We'd like to carry on with something that's very old indeed. And this one was recorded in about 1959, and it's called 'I Feel Fine.' "

After that, Paul sang "Yesterday" and then Ringo sang "I Wanna Be Your Man." That was when I noticed that John and Paul each had a camera and between songs were taking pictures of the crowd, the rest of the group, and themselves at arm's length.

"I Wanna Be Your Man" was followed by "Nowhere Man," and that was when another group of boys about the same size tried the same thing with the same results. As they played, John or Paul would turn and glance at a squirming knot of fan and rent-a-cops on the grass.

After "Nowhere Man," the Beatles hurriedly set up a camera on a speaker, and Ringo came down from the drum platform onto the main stage, and they stood with their backs to the audience and posed for a moment, and then Ringo rushed back to his drums and they did "Paperback Writer."

After that, Paul said, "Thank you very much everybody. Everybody … wonderful … We'd like to say that, erm, it's been wonderful being here, in this wonderful sea air. Sorry about the weather."

That was the first time I noticed it. The August heat of the Central Valley sucks off the ocean a chilling wind that scrapes over parts of San Francisco and the Peninsula, and tonight it was causing pennants at the top of the stadium to flap furiously. A couple times, there were even small dust devils in the infield. The weather might have explained why there were only twenty five thousand in a stadium for forty thousand. (That and unpopular statements about Jesus and the Vietnam War and an album that veered into psychedelia.)

"And we'd like to ask you to join in and, er, clap, sing, talk, do anything," Paul continued. "Anyway, the song is … 'Long Tall Sally' … Good night … One more time for just us there lads?!!"

At no time that night did it enter our heads what the cameras and the posing and that last comment could mean. Maybe because we were so dazzled by their presence … Only much later would we find out that, after more than 1400 live appearances, that was their last. They were fed up with the ordeal of what John called "the puppet show."

Then suddenly the concert was over and the three guitarists stood in a triangle in front of the drum platform and all four bowed in unison to the audience.

That was when a husky disheveled kid with terrible timing got onto the field near third base and made a determined run at the stage that required four rent-a-cops to stop. Meanwhile, far

below us, a couple dozen or so rows behind home plate, rent-a-cops were carrying down stairs a stretcher with a girl on it.

Just before leaving the stage, John teasingly played the opening bars of "In My Life" on the electric piano then ran off to join the rest of the group as they ran down stairs into the armored car, which then slowly crossed the outfield to the right field exit surrounded by nervous trotting rent-a-cops.

During the drive home, all the rock stations played the Beatles, which served as background music to the images Mike and I savored.

We had forgotten to bring binoculars, and when a boy of fourteen or so, in the next row up, wasn't using his, I asked if I could borrow them. It was during "Nowhere Man." I could see the boy was frightened and I should have said something to reassure him, but didn't. I was already used to people being intimidated by my appearance, and besides I was too anxious to look through the binoculars. I then kept them longer than the half minute or so that would have been good etiquette, much to the owner's fidgety consternation.

I adjusted the focus and the holes-through-space fell one behind the other. On what I now realized had been just four green specks, blurred but recognizable faces and wind slanted hair appeared. And there they were. It really was *them*. For a few stolen rushed moments, the music was made flesh.

If you enjoyed *San Fran '60s*, you might also enjoy the following other books written by M.W. Jacobs and published by Escallonia Press. *A History of the U.S. in 20 Movies: an All-Movie History Course* and *Choicest Rock Band Names as Tiny Poems* are also available on Amazon in both ebook and trade paperback editions. Also described below are his translations of the eminent Mexican modernist poets, Ramón López Velarde and José Gorostiza, both books jointly published by Berkeley and Floricanto Presses.

A History of the U.S. in 20 Movies: an All-Movie History Course
Volume One
the First Ten Movies

This is history made fun. This book will teach you history by explaining interesting movies, all of which are available on Netflix or Amazon or through other venues. This book will walk you through each movie using virtually every appropriate detail, providing historical context, explaining historical references, pointing out pertinent cinematic devices, and even occasionally tossing-in a tidbit of Hollywood history. Almost without noticing, you are going to absorb an accurate overview of the story of America. Like an introductory course, this book will help provide the indispensable foundation for more detailed knowledge in the future. Of course, this book can also be used piecemeal for brushing-up on a particular period in an entertaining way.

This is also a resource book with over 150 films referenced in addition to the core 20. The treaties, the dates, the statistics, etc. of American history are here in abundance, but they are presented unobtrusively, in a way that enhances the narrative. The teaching technique used is essentially that of PBS and the History Channel: reenactments intercut with expert talking heads, except here the movies are the reenactments and this book is the expert talking head.

There are many books about history as portrayed by Hollywood but nobody has come close to this. It could be the solution to the notorious lack of historical knowledge on the part of students and the general public.

"[Jacobs] has chosen his filmic texts well... employs the judgments of major academic historians... [his] historical judgments...are sound...." - **Film and History Journal,** Jerald Podair, Professor of History and American Studies at Lawrence University, Wisconsin

"Enthusiastic and detailed... passionate and knowledgeable... By going outside the mainstream... the book takes its historical analysis in intriguing and unexpected directions." - **Kirkus Review**

Table of Contents

Chapter One – **The New World**
Prehistory & Native Americans – European exploration & colonization of the Americas– Jamestown

Chapter Two – **The Crucible**
Early colonial period – Puritanism – Continuing conflict with Indians

Chapter Three – **John Adams**
Late colonial period & pre-Revolution – Politics of the Revolution – the Founders – Constitutional Convention – Early republic

Chapter Four – **The Crossing**
George Washington – Battles of the Revolution

Chapter Five – **Amistad**
Slavery – Abolitionism – John Quincy Adams – Andrew Jackson – Politics of Jackson Era

Chapter Six – **One Man's Hero**
The U.S.–Mexico War – Early immigration – the California Gold Rush

Chapter Seven – **Gettysburg**
Battles of the Civil War – Joshua Lawrence Chamberlain – Ulysses S Grant – William Tecumseh Sherman – Robert E. Lee

Chapter Eight – **Lincoln**
The president and the man – The politics of slavery – Reconstruction

Chapter Nine – **Little Big Man**
Westward migration – Plains Indian Wars – Old West - Robber Barons

Chapter Ten – **Matewan**
Organized labor – Later immigration – Spanish American War – World War I Homefront – Progressives – First Red Scare

M. W. Jacobs has the ultimate qualification for commenting on movies, one that nearly all "professional film critics" lack: he wrote, directed, produced, and edited a feature film (available on You Tube as "Twisted Tales from Edgar Allan Poe"). It was low budget and independently produced and made during the advent of the home video market in the early Eighties. In the late Eighties, he worked for George Lucas' special effects division, Industrial Light and Magic. Then he became a history teacher, and for twenty years, he searched for the most effective way to teach the subject that polls perennially rank as students' least favorite. This book is the result of that search.

Choicest Rock Band Names
as Tiny Poems

From thousands collected over decades throughout the Anglophone world, these are the choicest few hundred. A Darwinian welter of tens of thousands of rock bands desperate for attention has created some remarkable names, a tiny percentage of which qualify as "found poetry." Indeed this may be a form of anonymous folk poetry like graffiti, bumper stickers, advertising catch phrases, and especially idiom. The choicest rock band name may even be the culmination of literary historical trends and may be pointing the way to a new poetic form for the age of texting, tweeting, the six-word memoir, and haiku reviews. An essay in the book makes the case.

Two-word Band Names

Corner laughers

Cupid's alley

Lightning riders

Brain underfoot

Liquid Picasso

Reigning echoes

Guns debating

Define fiasco

Threshold dweller

Backwoods grin

Surreal Two-word Band Names

Cat spin

Colostomy pinata

Rutabaga paradox

Giddyup Einstein

The thes

Boxing Gandhis

Nonsense Two-Word Band Names

Flabbergasted hammerhandle

Pitbull bikiniwax

Whistle binkies

Starscream's blitzwing

Puns and Double Entendre
Two-Word Band Names

Mahatma candy

Piranha nongrata

Uncle Scam

Chop sueycide

Three-Word Band Names

Dying heart smile

End begins again

Reasons in amber

Murals in metaphors

Penis goes where

One star sky

Math hurt head

Intercourse by eye

Child left burning

Deaf to silence

Pick my nose

Surreal Three-Word Band Names

Pass the cat

Deputy hate angel

Sonic fuzz monkey

Smell the music

Icicle butt plug

Dead squirrel circus

One-Word Band Names

Pretaliation

McJesus

Idiocracy

Techstacy

Nawstalgia

Fognauts

Disasterpiece

Bubbabarian

Drunkenstein

Othercide

Siolence

Hipsy

Eargasm

Autocratisaurus

Powernoia

Blisster

Comfynumb

Bucoliciou

Prefamous

Corporuption

Nonsense One-Word Band Names

Scruffynurfherder

Schlafunkmotron

McRamahamasham

Tallulalunabella

Translations

Also, translated by M.W. Jacobs and published jointly by Berkeley and Floricanto Presses, are *Poems, Ramón López Velarde* (2014) and *Collected Poems of José Gorostiza* (2017). Both are available on Amazon and from the Floricanto website.

Ramón López Velarde wrote the Mexican national poem, *Suave Patria*. Nobel Laureate Pablo Neruda called him, "The essential and supreme poet of our extensive Americas... There is no more distilled poetry than his... [He] gave to the poetry of the Americas a flavor and a fragrance that will last forever." Compatriot and Nobel Laureate Octavio Paz said López Velarde is "the most admired and most carefully studied poet in Mexico... [He] left us a few poems ... so perfect that it is foolish to lament those that death prevented him from writing." Jorge Luis Borges called López Velarde "a wonder." Yet as López Velarde's Wikipedia entry correctly states: "Despite his importance, he remains a virtual unknown outside his own country." He is truly a forgotten modernist master.

José Gorostiza is another major 20th century master overlooked by Anglophones. Expressing the consensus of Spanish-language critics, *The Encyclopedia of Latin American Literature* (1997) says of Gorostiza's masterwork, *Muerte sin fin* (*Endless Death*) (1939), "It is impossible to overstate the importance of this poem in Mexican literature... among the finest in the Spanish language... takes its place alongside Eliot's *The Wasteland* (1922) or Valéry's *Le cimetière marin* (1920) as one of the pinnacles of sustained poetic achievement in the 20th century." In his essay on Gorostiza, Octavio Paz wrote that Gorostiza's poetry is "the most... concentrated of modern poetry in Spanish." (Hence, Gorostiza's unusually slender collected poems.) In his classic analysis of Mexican character and history, *The Labyrinth of Solitude* (1950), Paz wrote that *Muerte sin fin* "is perhaps the best evidence we have in Latin America of a truly modern consciousness."

Made in the USA
San Bernardino, CA
24 March 2017

G. Meyer Books specializes in autobiographical and fictional narratives that intersect with social, historical, and political issues, as well as books on contemporary social issues that vary from the norm and encourage questioning and debate. Inquiries regarding submissions may be sent to the G. Meyer Books website at http://www.gmeyerbooks.com.

 G.MEYERBOOKS